RAMA
REVEALED

Books by Arthur C. Clarke

NONFICTION

Ascent to Orbit: A Scientific
 Autobiography
Boy Beneath the Sea
The Challenge of the Sea
The Challenge of the Spaceship
The Coast of Coral
The Exploration of the Moon
The Exploration of Space
The First Five Fathoms
Going into Space
How the World Was One
Indian Ocean Adventure
Indian Ocean Treasure
Interplanetary Flight
The Making of a Moon
Profiles of the Future
The Promise of Space
The Reefs of Taprobane
Report on Planet Three
The Treasure of the Great Reef
The View from Serendip
Voice Across the Sea
Voices from the Sky
1984: Spring

WITH THE EDITORS OF *LIFE*

Man and Space

WITH THE ASTRONAUTS

First on the Moon

WITH ROBERT SILVERBERG

Into Space

WITH CHESLEY BONESTELL

Beyond Jupiter

WITH SIMON WELFARE AND JOHN FAIRLEY

Arthur C. Clarke's Mysterious World
Arthur C. Clarke's World of Strange
 Powers

FICTION

Across the Sea of Stars
Against the Fall of Night
Childhood's End
The City and the Stars
The Deep Range
Dolphin Island
Earthlight
Expedition to Earth
A Fall of Moondust
The Fountains of Paradise
From the Oceans, from the Stars
The Ghost from the Grand Banks
Glide Path
The Hammer of God
Imperial Earth
Islands in the Sky
The Lost Worlds of 2001
More Than One Universe
Prelude to Mars
Prelude to Space
Reach for Tomorrow
Rendezvous with Rama
The Sands of Mars
The Sentinel
Tales from the "White Hart"
2001: A Space Odyssey
2010: Odyssey Two
2061: Odyssey Three

WITH GENTRY LEE

Cradle
Rama II
The Garden of Rama
Rama Revealed

RAMA
REVEALED

ARTHUR C. CLARKE
AND
GENTRY LEE

BANTAM BOOKS
NEW YORK TORONTO LONDON SYDNEY AUCKLAND

RAMA REVEALED
A Bantam Spectra Book / March 1994

SPECTRA and the portrayal of a boxed "s" are trademarks of
Bantam Books, a division of Bantam Doubleday Dell Publishing
Group, Inc.

Library of Congress Cataloging-in-Publication Data

Clarke, Arthur Charles, 1917–
    Rama revealed / by Arthur C. Clarke and Gentry Lee.
    p.   cm.
    ISBN 0-553-09536-6 : $22.95
    I. Lee, Gentry. II. Title.
PR6005.L36R37   1994
823'.914—dc20   93-31459
                                                        CIP

Published simultaneously in the United States and Canada

Bantam Books are published by Bantam Books, a division of Bantam Doubleday
Dell Publishing Group, Inc. Its trademark, consisting of the words "Bantam
Books" and the portrayal of a rooster, is Registered in U.S. Patent and Trademark
Office and in other countries. Marca Registrada. Bantam Books, 1540 Broadway,
New York, New York 10036.

PRINTED IN THE UNITED STATES OF AMERICA

BVG   0 9 8 7 6 5 4 3 2 1

ACKNOWLEDGMENTS

We would like to thank Neal and Shelagh Ausman, as well as Gerry and Michelle Snyder, for representing the readers in making suggestions about topics that should be addressed in *Rama Revealed*. Gerry was also extremely helpful in discussions about the details of the octospider language.

Our Bantam editor Jennifer Hershey has been a source of strength and support throughout the development and writing of this novel, providing both unflagging encouragement and valuable recommendations about all aspects of the book. Thank you, Jennifer. We are also indebted to Richard Evans at Gollancz for several specific editorial remarks, including the suggestion of adding a prologue.

Lou Aronica and Russ Galen, our publisher and our agent, have helped us in countless ways during the five years since the Rama trilogy sequel was originally conceived. Their many contributions have allowed us to focus our energies on the actual writing of the novels.

Our final thanks go to our families, for their love and understanding throughout this time period. To Stacey Kiddoo Lee especially, we extend our heartfelt appreciation, not only for her willingness to manage a family of five small boys in the presence of difficult (and changing) constraints, but also for her insightful comments about Nicole and the other leading female characters of the trilogy.

RAMA
REVEALED

PROLOGUE

In one of the outlying spiral arms of the Milky Way Galaxy, an inconspicuous, solitary yellow star slowly orbits the galactic center thirty thousand light-years away. This stable star, the Sun, takes two hundred and twenty-five million years to complete one revolution in its galactic orbit. The last time the Sun was in its present position, giant reptiles of fearsome power had just begun to establish their dominion on the Earth, a small blue planet that is one of the satellites of the Sun.

Among the planets and other bodies in the family of the Sun, it is only on this Earth that any complex, enduring life has ever developed. Only on this special world did chemicals evolve into consciousness and then ask, as they began to understand the wonders and dimensions of the universe, if miracles similar to the ones that had produced them had indeed occurred elsewhere.

After all, these sentient Earthlings argued, there are a hundred billion stars in our galaxy alone. We are fairly certain that at least twenty percent of these stars have orbiting planets, and that a small but significant number of these planets have had, at some time in their history, atmospheric and thermal conditions conducive to the formation of amino acids and other organic chemicals that are the sine qua non for any biology we can reasonably hypothesize. At least once in history, here on Earth, these amino acids discovered self-replication, and the evolutionary miracle that eventually produced human beings was set into motion. How can we presume that this sequence occurred only that single time in all history? The heavier atoms necessary to create us have been forged in the stellar cataclysms exploding across this universe for billions of years. Is it likely that only here, in this one place, these atoms have concatenated into special molecules and evolved into an intelligent being capable of asking the question, "Are we alone?"

The humans on Earth began their search for cosmic companions first by building telescopes with which they could see their immediate planetary neighbors. Later, when their technology had developed to a higher level, sophisticated robotic spacecraft were sent to examine these other planets and to ascertain whether or not there were any signs of biology. These explorations proved that no intelligent life has ever existed on any other body in our solar system. If there is anyone out there, the human scientists concluded, any peer species with whom we might eventually communicate, they must be found beyond the void that separates our solar system from all the other stars.

At the end of the twentieth century in the human time system, the great antennae of the Earth began to search the sky for coherent signals, to determine if perhaps some other intelligence might be sending us a radio message. For over a hundred years the search continued, intensifying during the halcyon days of international science in the early twenty-first century, and then diminishing later, in the final decades of the century, after the fourth separate set of systematic listening techniques still failed to locate any alien signals.

In 2130, an unusual cylindrical object was observed approaching our solar system from the reaches of interstellar space. By that time, most thoughtful humans had concluded that life was scarce in the universe and that intelligence, if it existed anywhere except on Earth, was exceedingly rare. How else, the scientists contended, can we possibly explain the lack of positive results from all our careful extraterrestrial search efforts of the last century?

The Earth was therefore stunned when, upon closer inspection, the object entering our solar system in 2130 was identified unambiguously as an artifact of alien origin. Here was undeniable proof that advanced intelligence existed, or at least *had* existed at some prior epoch, in another part of the universe. When an ongoing space mission was diverted to rendezvous with the drab cylindrical behemoth, which turned out to have dimensions greater than the largest cities on Earth, the investigating cosmonauts found mystery after mystery. But they were unable to answer the most fundamental questions about the enigmatic alien spacecraft. The intruder from the stars provided no definitive clues about its origin or purpose.

That first group of human explorers not only cataloged the wonders of Rama (the name chosen for the gigantic cylindrical object before it was known to be an extraterrestrial artifact), but also explored and mapped its interior. After the exploration team left Rama and the alien spaceship dove around the Sun, departing from the solar system at hyperbolic velocity, scientists thoroughly analyzed all the data that had been gathered during the mission. Everyone acknowledged that the human visitors to Rama had never encountered the actual creators of the mysterious spacecraft. However, the careful postflight analysis did reveal one inescapable principle of Raman redundancy engineering. Every critical system and subsystem in the vehicle had two backups. The Ramans designed everything in threes. The scientists considered it very likely that two more similar spacecraft would soon follow.

The years immediately after the visit from Rama I in 2130 were full of expectation on the Earth. Scholars and politicians alike proclaimed that a new era in human history had begun. The International Space Agency (ISA), working with the Council of Governments (COG), developed careful procedures for handling the next visit from the Ramans. All telescopes were trained on the heavens, competing with each other for the acclaim that would come to the individual or observatory who first located the next Rama spacecraft. But there were no additional sightings.

In the second half of the 2130s an economic boom, fueled partially during its last stages by worldwide reactions to Rama, came to an abrupt halt. The world was plunged into the deepest depression in its history, known as the Great Chaos, which was accompanied by widespread anarchy and destitution. Virtually all scientific research activity was abandoned during this sorrowful era, and after several decades in which they were forced to address more mundane problems, people on the Earth had nearly forgotten the unexplained visitor from the stars.

In 2200 a second cylindrical intruder arrived in the solar system. The citizens of Earth dusted off the old procedures that had been developed after the first Rama had departed, and prepared to rendezvous with Rama II. A crew of twelve was chosen for the mission. Soon after the rendezvous, the dozen reported that the second Rama spacecraft was nearly identical to its predecessor. The humans encountered new mysteries and wonders, including some alien beings, but were still unable to answer questions about the origin and purpose of Rama.

Three strange deaths among the crew created great concern back on the Earth, where all aspects of the historic mission were followed on television. When the giant cylinder underwent a midcourse maneuver that placed it on a trajectory that would impact the Earth, this concern changed to alarm and fear. The leaders of the world reluctantly concluded that, in the absence of any other information, they had no choice except to assume that Rama II was hostile. They could not allow the alien spacecraft to impact the Earth, or to come close enough that it might deploy any advanced weapons it might possess. A decision was made to destroy Rama II while it was still a safe distance away.

The exploration crew was ordered home, but three of its members, two men and a woman, were still on board Rama II when the alien spaceship avoided a nuclear phalanx launched from the Earth. Rama maneuvered away from the hostile Earth and departed at high speed from the solar system, carrying both its intact secrets and the three human passengers.

It took thirteen years at relativistic velocities for Rama II to travel from the neighborhood of Earth to its destination, a huge engineering complex called the Node that was located in a distant orbit around the star Sirius. The three humans on board the giant cylinder added five children and grew into a family. As they investigated the marvels of their home in space, the family again encountered the extraterrestrial species they had met earlier. However, by the time they reached the Node, the humans had already convinced themselves that these other aliens were, like them, only passengers in Rama.

The human family remained at the Node for slightly more than a year. During this time the Rama spacecraft was refurbished and outfitted for its third and final journey to the solar system. The family learned from the Eagle, a nonbiological creation of the Nodal Intelligence, that the purpose of the Rama series of spacecraft was to acquire and catalog as much information as possible about spacefarers in the galaxy. The Eagle, who had the head, beak, and eyes of an eagle plus the body of a human, also informed them that the final Rama spacecraft, Rama III, would contain a carefully designed Earth habitat that could accommodate two thousand people.

A video was transmitted from the Node to the Earth announcing the imminent return of the third Rama spaceship. This video explained that an advanced extraterrestrial species wished to observe and study human activity over an extended period of time and requested that two thousand representative humans be sent to rendezvous with Rama III in orbit around Mars.

Rama III made the voyage from Sirius back to the solar system at a velocity more than half the speed of light. Inside the spacecraft, sleeping in special berths, were most of the human family who had been at the Node. In Mars orbit this family greeted the other humans from Earth and the pristine habitat inside Rama was quickly settled. The resultant colony, which was called New Eden, was completely enclosed and separated from the rest of the alien spacecraft by thick walls.

Almost immediately Rama III accelerated again to relativistic velocities, blasting out of the solar system in the direction of the yellow star Tau Ceti. Three years passed without any outside interference in human affairs. The citizens of New Eden became so involved with their everyday lives that they paid scant attention to the universe outside their settlement.

When a set of crises stressed the fledgling democracy in the paradise that had been created for the humans by the Ramans, an opportunistic tycoon seized power in the colony and began to ruthlessly suppress all opposition. One of the original Rama II explorers fled from New Eden at this time, eventually making contact with a symbiotic pair of alien species living in the adjacent enclosed habitat. His wife remained in the human colony and tried unsuccessfully to be a conscience for the community. She was imprisoned after a few months, convicted of treason, and eventually scheduled for execution.

As the environmental and living conditions inside New Eden continued to deteriorate, human troops invaded the adjacent living area in the Northern Hemicylinder of Rama and engaged in a war of annihilation against the symbiotic pair of alien species. Meanwhile, the mysterious Ramans, known only through the genius of their engineering creations, continued their detailed observation from afar, aware that it was only a matter of time until the humans came into contact with the advanced species inhabiting the region to the south of the Cylindrical Sea. . . .

ESCAPE

1

"Nicole."

At first the soft, mechanical voice seemed to be part of her dream. But when she heard her name repeated, slightly louder, Nicole awakened with a start.

A wave of intense fear swept through her. *They have come for me*, Nicole thought immediately. *It is morning. I am going to die in a few hours.*

She took a slow, deep breath and tried to quell her mounting panic. A few seconds later Nicole opened her eyes. It was completely dark in her cell. Puzzled, Nicole looked around for the person who had called her.

"We are here, on your cot, beside your right ear," the voice said very softly. "Richard sent us to help you escape . . . but we must move quickly."

For an instant Nicole thought that perhaps she was still dreaming. Then she heard a second voice, very similar to the first but nevertheless distinct. "Roll over on your right side and we will illuminate ourselves."

Nicole rolled over. Standing on the cot next to her head she saw two tiny figures, no more than eight or ten centimeters high, each in the shape of a woman. They were glowing momentarily from some internal light source. One had short hair and was dressed in the armor of a fifteenth century European knight. The second figure was wearing both a crown upon her head and the full, pleated dress of a medieval queen.

"I am Joan of Arc," the first figure said.

"And I am Eleanor of Aquitaine."

Nicole laughed nervously and stared in astonishment at the two figures. Several seconds later, when the robots' internal lights were extinguished, Nicole had finally composed herself enough to speak. "So Richard sent you to help me escape?" she said in a whisper. "Just how do you propose to do that?"

"We've already sabotaged the monitoring system," tiny Joan said proudly. "And reprogrammed a Garcia biot. . . . It should be here in a few minutes to let you out."

"We have a nominal escape plan, along with several contingencies," Eleanor added. "Richard has been working on it for months—ever since he finished making us."

Nicole laughed again. She was still absolutely stunned. "Really?" she said. "And may I ask just where my genius of a husband is at this moment?"

"Richard is in your old lair underneath New York," Joan replied. "He said to tell you that nothing has changed there. He is following our progress with a navigation beacon. . . . Incidentally, Richard sends his love. He hasn't forgotten—"

"Be still for a moment, please," Eleanor interrupted as Nicole automatically scratched at the tickling sensation behind her right ear. "I'm deploying your personal beacon right now, and it's very heavy for me."

Moments later Nicole touched the tiny instrument package next to her ear and shook her head. "And can he *hear* us also?" she asked.

"Richard decided we couldn't risk voice transmissions," Eleanor answered. "They could be too easily intercepted by Nakamura. . . . However, he will be monitoring our physical location."

"You may get up now," Joan said, "and put on your clothes. We want to be ready when the Garcia arrives."

Will wonders never cease? Nicole thought while she was washing her face in the dark in the primitive basin. For a few brief seconds Nicole imagined that the two robots might be part of a clever New Eden government plot and that she was going to be killed trying to escape. *Impossible,* she told herself a few moments later. *Even if one of Nakamura's minions could create robots like these, only Richard would know enough about me to make a Joan of Arc and an Eleanor of Aquitaine. . . . Anyway, what difference does it make if I'm killed while trying to escape? My electrocution is scheduled for eight o'clock this morning.*

There was the sound of a biot approaching outside her cell. Nicole tensed, still not completely convinced that her two tiny friends were indeed telling her the truth. "Sit back down on the cot," she heard Joan say behind her, "so Eleanor and I can climb into your pockets." Nicole felt the two robots scrambling up the front of her shirt. She smiled. *You are amazing, Richard,* she thought.

The Garcia biot was carrying a flashlight. It strode into Nicole's cell with an air of authority. "Come with me, Mrs. Wakefield," it said in a loud voice. "I have orders to move you to the preparations room."

Again Nicole was frightened. The biot certainly wasn't acting friendly. *What if . . .* But she had very little time to think. The Garcia led Nicole through the corridor outside her cell at a rapid pace. Twenty meters later, they passed both the regular set of biot guards and a human commanding officer, a young man Nicole had never seen before. "Wait," the man yelled from behind them just as Nicole and the Garcia were about to climb the stairs. Nicole froze.

"You forgot to sign the transfer papers," the man said, holding out a document to the Garcia.

"Certainly," the biot replied, entering its identification number on the papers with a flourish.

After less than a minute Nicole was outside the large house where she had been imprisoned for months. She took a deep breath of the fresh air and started to follow the Garcia down a path toward Central City.

"No," Nicole heard Eleanor call from her pocket. "We're not going with the biot. Go west. Toward that windmill with the light on top. And you must run. We must arrive at Max Puckett's before dawn."

Her prison was almost five kilometers from Max's farm. Nicole jogged down the small road at a steady pace, urged on periodically by one of the two robots, who were keeping careful track of the time. It was not long until dawn. Unlike on the Earth, where the transition from night to day was gradual, in New Eden dawn was a sudden, discontinuous event. One moment it would be dark and then, in the next instant, the artificial sun would ignite and begin its mini-arc across the ceiling of the colony habitat.

"Twelve more minutes until light," Joan said, as Nicole reached the bicycle path that led the final two hundred meters to the Puckett farmhouse. Nicole was nearly exhausted, but she kept running. Two separate times during her run across the farmland she had felt a dull ache in her chest. *I am definitely out of shape*, she thought, chastising herself for not having exercised regularly in her prison cell. *As well as sixty years old, more or less.*

The farmhouse was dark. Nicole stopped on the porch, catching her breath, and the door opened a few seconds later. "I have been waiting for you," Max said, his earnest expression underscoring the seriousness of the situation. He gave Nicole a quick hug. "Follow me," he said, moving quickly off toward the barn.

"There have been no police cars yet on the road," Max said when they were inside the barn. "They probably have not yet discovered that you're gone. But it's only a matter of minutes now."

The chickens were all kept on the far side of the barn. The hens had a separate enclosure, sealed off from the roosters and the rest of the building. When Max and Nicole entered the henhouse, there was a huge commotion. Animals scurried in all directions, clucking and squawking and beating their wings. The stench in the henhouse nearly overpowered Nicole.

Max smiled. "I guess I forget how bad chicken shit smells to everyone else," he said. "I've grown so used to it myself." He slapped Nicole lightly on the back. "Anyway, it's another level of protection for you, and I don't think you'll be able to smell the shit from your hideout."

Max walked over to a corner of the henhouse, chased several hens out of the way, and bent down on his knees. "When those weird little robots of Richard's first appeared," he said, pushing aside hay and chicken feed, "I couldn't decide where I should build your hideout. Then I thought about this place." Max pulled up a couple of boards to expose a rectangular hole in the floor of the barn. "I sure as hell hope I was right."

He motioned for Nicole to follow him and then crawled into the hole. They were both on their hands and knees in the dirt. The passageway, which ran parallel to the floor for a few meters and then turned downward at a steep angle, was extremely cramped. Nicole kept bumping up against Max in front of her and the dirt walls and ceiling all around her. The only light was the small flashlight that Max was carrying in his right hand. After fifteen meters the small tunnel opened into a dark room. Max stepped carefully down a rope ladder and then turned to help Nicole descend. A few seconds later they both walked into the center of the room, where Max reached up and switched on a solitary electric light.

"It's not a palace," he said as Nicole glanced around, "but I suspect it's a damn sight better than that prison of yours."

The room contained a bed, a chair, two shelves full of food, another shelf with electronic bookdiscs, a few clothes hanging in an open closet, basic toiletries, a large drum of water that must have barely fit through the passageway, and a deep, square latrine in the far corner.

"Did you do all this yourself?" Nicole asked.

"Yep," Max replied. "At night . . . during the last several weeks. I didn't dare ask anybody to help."

Nicole was touched. "How can I ever thank you?" she said.

"Don't get caught." Max grinned. "I don't want to die any more than you do. . . . Oh, by the way," he added, handing Nicole an electronic reader into which she could place the bookdiscs, "I hope the reading material is all right. Manuals on raising pigs and chickens are not the same as your father's novels, but I didn't want to attract too much attention by going to the bookstore."

Nicole crossed the room and kissed him on the cheek. "Max," she said lightly, "you are such a dear friend. I can't imagine how you—"

"It's dawn outside now," Joan of Arc interrupted from Nicole's pocket. "According to our timeline, we are behind schedule. Mr. Puckett, we must inspect our egress route before you leave us."

"Shit," said Max. "Here I go again, taking orders from a robot no longer than a cigarette." He lifted Joan and Eleanor out of Nicole's pockets and placed them on the top shelf behind a can of peas. "Do you see that little door?" he said. "There's a pipe on the other side. It comes out just beyond the pig trough. . . . Why don't you check it out?"

During the minute or two that the robots were gone, Max explained the situation to Nicole. "The police will be searching everywhere for you," he said. "Particularly here, since they know that I am a friend of the family. So I'm going to seal the entrance to your hideout. You should have everything you need to last for at least several weeks.

"The robots can come and go freely, unless they are eaten by the pigs," Max continued with a laugh. "They will be your only contact with the outside world. They'll let you know when it's time to move to the second phase of our escape plan."

"So I won't see you again?" Nicole asked.

"Not for at least a few weeks," Max answered. "It's too dangerous. . . . One more thing: if there are police on the premises, I will cut off your power. That will be your signal to stay especially quiet."

Eleanor of Aquitaine had returned and was standing on the shelf next to the can of peas. "Our egress route is excellent," she announced. "Joan has departed for a few days. She intends to leave the habitat and communicate with Richard."

"Now I must leave also," Max said to Nicole. He was silent for a few seconds. "But not before I tell you one thing, my lady friend. . . . As you probably know, I have been a fucking cynic all my life. There are not very many people who impress me. But *you* have convinced me that maybe some of us are superior to chickens and pigs." Max smiled. "Not many of us," he added quickly, "but at least some."

"Thank you, Max," Nicole said.

Max walked over to the ladder. He turned around and waved before he began his climb.

Nicole sat down in the chair and took a deep breath. From the sounds in the direction of the tunnel, she surmised correctly that Max was sealing the entrance to her hideout by placing the big bags of chicken feed directly over the hole.

So what happens now? Nicole asked herself. She realized that she had thought about very little except her approaching death during the five days since the conclusion of her trial. Without the fear of her imminent execution to structure her thought patterns, Nicole was able to let her mind drift freely.

She thought first of Richard, her husband and partner, from whom she had been separated now for almost two years. Nicole recalled vividly their last evening together, a horrible Walpurgisnacht of murder and destruction that had begun on a hopeful note with her daughter Ellie's marriage to Dr. Robert Turner. *Richard was certain that we, like Kenji and Pyotr, were also marked for death*, she remembered. *And he was probably right. Because he escaped, they made him the enemy and left me alone for a while.*

I thought you were dead, Richard, Nicole thought. *I should have had more faith. . . . But how in the world did you end up in New York again?*

As she sat in the only chair in the underground room, her heart ached for the company of her husband. A montage of memories paraded through her mind. She first saw herself again in the avian lair in Rama II, years and years earlier, temporarily a captive of the strange birdlike creatures whose language was jabbers and shrieks. It had been Richard who had found her there. He had risked his own life to return to New York to determine if Nicole was still alive. If Richard had not come, Nicole would have been marooned on the island of New York forever.

Richard and Nicole had become lovers during the time that they were struggling to figure out how to cross the Cylindrical Sea and return to their cosmonaut colleagues from the Newton spacecraft. Nicole was both surprised and amused by the strong stirrings inside her caused by her recollection of their early days of love. *We survived the nuclear missile attack together. We even survived my wrongheaded attempt to produce genetic variation in our offspring by sleeping with another man.*

Nicole winced at the memory of her own naïveté so many years before. *You forgave me, Richard, which could not have been easy for you. And then we grew even closer at the Node during our design sessions with the Eagle.*

What was the Eagle really? Nicole mused, shifting her train of thought. *And who or what created him?* In her mind was a vivid picture of the bizarre creature who had been their only contact while they had stayed at the Node during the refurbishing of the Rama spaceship. The alien being, who had had the face of an eagle and a body similar to a man's, had informed them that he was an advancement in artificial intelligence designed especially as a companion for humans. *His eyes were incredible, almost mystical*, Nicole remembered. *And they were as intense as Omeh's.*

Her great-grandfather Omeh had worn the green robe of the tribal shaman of the Senoufo when he had come to see Nicole in Rome two weeks before the launch of the Newton spacecraft. Nicole had met Omeh twice before, both times in her mother's native village in the Ivory Coast: once during the Poro ceremony when Nicole was seven, and then again three years later at her mother's funeral. During those brief encounters Omeh had started preparing Nicole for what the old shaman had assured her would be an extraordinary life. It had been Omeh who had insisted that Nicole was indeed the woman who the Senoufo chronicles had predicted would scatter their tribal seed "even to the stars."

Omeh, the Eagle, even Richard, Nicole thought. *Quite a group, to say the least.* The face of Henry, Prince of Wales, joined the other three men and Nicole remembered for a moment the powerful passion of their brief love affair in the days immediately after she had won her Olympic gold medal.

She recalled sharply the pain of rejection. *But without Henry,* she reminded herself, *there would not have been a Genevieve.*

While Nicole was remembering the love she had shared with her daughter on Earth, she glanced across the room at the shelf containing the electronic bookdiscs. Suddenly distracted, she crossed to the shelf and started reading titles. Sure enough, Max had left her some manuals on raising pigs and chickens. But that was not all. It looked as if he had given Nicole his entire private library.

Nicole smiled as she pulled out a book of fairy tales and inserted it into her reader. She flipped through the pages and stopped at the story of Sleeping Beauty. The phrase "and they lived happily ever after" summoned another vivid memory, this one of herself as a small child, maybe six or seven, sitting on her father's lap in their house in the Parisian suburb of Chilly-Mazarin.

I longed as a little girl to be a princess and live happily ever after, she thought. *There was no way I could have known then that my life would make even the fairy tales seem ordinary.*

Nicole replaced the bookdisc on the shelf and returned to her chair. *And now,* she thought, idly surveying the room, *when I thought this incredible life was over, I seem to have been given at least a few more days.*

She thought again of Richard and her intense longing to see him returned. *We have shared much, my Richard. I hope I can again feel your touch, hear your laughter, and see your face. But if not, I will try not to complain. My life has already seen its share of miracles.*

2

Eleanor Wakefield Turner arrived at the large auditorium in Central City at seven-thirty in the morning. Although the execution was not scheduled to take place until eight o'clock, there were already about thirty people in the front seats, some talking, most just sitting quietly. A television crew wandered around the electric chair on the stage. The execution was being broadcast live, but the policemen in the auditorium were nevertheless expecting a full house, for the government had encouraged the citizens of New Eden to witness personally the death of their former governor.

Ellie had argued with her husband the night before. "Spare yourself this pain, Ellie," Robert had said, when she had told him that she intended to attend the execution. "Seeing your mother one last time cannot be worth the horror of watching her die."

But Ellie had known something that Robert did not know. As she took her seat in the auditorium, Ellie tried to control the powerful feelings inside her. *There can be nothing on my face,* she told herself, *and nothing in my body language. Not the slightest hint. Nobody must suspect that I know anything about the escape.* Several pairs of eyes suddenly turned around to look at her. Ellie felt her heart skip before she realized that someone had recognized her and that it was completely natural for the curious to stare at her.

Ellie had first encountered her father's little robots Joan of Arc and Eleanor of Aquitaine only six weeks before, when she was outside of the main habitat, over in the quarantine village of Avalon helping her physician husband Robert take care of the patients who were doomed by the RV-41 retrovirus inside their bodies. Ellie had just finished a pleasant and encouraging late evening visit with her friend and former teacher Eponine. She had left Eponine's room and was walking along a dirt lane, expecting to see Robert at any moment. All of a sudden she had heard two strange voices calling her name. Ellie had searched the area around her before finally locating the pair of tiny figures on the roof of a nearby building.

After crossing the lane so that she could see and hear the robots better, the stunned Ellie had been informed by Joan and Eleanor that her father Richard was still alive. It had taken her a few moments to recover from the shock. Then Ellie had begun to question the robots. She had become quickly convinced that Joan and Eleanor were telling the truth; however, before Ellie had ascertained why her father had sent the robots to her, she had seen her husband approaching in the distance. The figures on the rooftop had then told her hurriedly that they would return soon. They had also cautioned Ellie not to tell anyone of their existence, not even Robert, at least not yet.

Ellie had been overjoyed that her father was still alive. It had been almost impossible for her to keep the news a secret, even though she was well aware of the political significance of her information. When, almost two weeks later, Ellie had been again confronted in Avalon by the little robots, she had been ready with a torrent of questions. However, on that occasion Joan and Eleanor had been programmed to discuss another subject—a possible forthcoming attempt to break Nicole out of prison. The robots told Ellie during this second meeting that Richard acknowledged such an escape would be a dangerous endeavor. "We would never attempt it," the robot Joan said, "unless your mother's execution were absolutely certain. But if we are not prepared ahead of time, there can be no possibility of a last-minute escape."

"What can I do to help?" Ellie had asked.

Joan and Eleanor had handed her a sheet of paper, on which there was a list of items including food, water, and clothing. Ellie had trembled when she recognized her father's handwriting.

"Cache these things at the following location," the robot Eleanor had said, handing Ellie a map. "No later than ten days from now." A moment later another colonist had come into sight and the two robots had vanished.

Enclosed inside the map had been a short note from her father. "Dearest Ellie," it had said, "I apologize for the brevity. I am safe and healthy, but deeply concerned about your mother. Please, please gather up these items and take them to the indicated spot in the Central Plain. If you cannot accomplish the task by yourself, please limit your support to a single person. And make certain that whoever you pick is as loyal and dedicated to Nicole as we are. I love you."

Ellie had quickly determined that she would need help. But whom should she select as an accomplice? Her husband Robert was a bad choice for two reasons. First, he had already shown that his dedication to his patients and the New Eden hospital was a higher priority in his mind than taking a political stand. Second, anyone caught helping Nicole escape would certainly be executed. If Ellie were to involve Robert in the escape plan, then their daughter Nicole might be left without both her parents.

What about Nai Watanabe? There was no question about her loyalty, but Nai was a single parent with twin four-year-old sons. It was not fair to ask her to take the chance. That left Eponine as the only reasonable choice. Any worries that Ellie might have had about her afflicted friend had been quickly dispelled. "Of course I'll help you," Eponine had replied immediately. "I have nothing to lose. According to your husband, this RV-41 is going to kill me in another year or two anyway."

Eponine and Ellie had clandestinely gathered the required items, one at a time, over a period of a week. They had wrapped them securely in a small sheet that was hidden in the corner of Eponine's normally cluttered room in Avalon. On the appointed day, Ellie had signed out of New Eden and walked across to Avalon, ostensibly to "monitor carefully" a full twelve hours of Eponine's biometry data. Actually, explaining to Robert why she wanted to spend the night with Eponine had been much more difficult than convincing the single human guard and the Garcia biot at the habitat exit of the legitimacy of her need for an overnight pass.

Just after midnight Ellie and Eponine had picked up their sheet and crept cautiously into the streets of Avalon. Being very careful to avoid the roving biots that Nakamura's police used to patrol the small outside village at night, the two women had sneaked through the outskirts of the town and into the Central Plain. They had then hiked for several kilometers and deposited the cache in the designated location. A Tiasso biot had confronted them outside Eponine's room upon their return and had asked what they were doing wandering around at such an absurd hour.

"This woman has RV-41," Ellie had said quickly, sensing the panic in her friend. "She is one of my husband's patients. She was in extreme pain and could not sleep, so we thought that an early morning walk might help. . . . Now, if you'll excuse us . . ."

The Tiasso had let them pass. Ellie and Eponine had been so frightened that neither of them had spoken for ten minutes.

Ellie had not seen the robots again. She had no idea whether or not an actual escape had been attempted. As the time for her mother's execution now drew near and the auditorium seats around her began to fill, Ellie's heart was pounding furiously. *What if nothing has happened?* she thought. *What if Mother is really going to die in twenty more minutes?*

Ellie glanced up at the stage. A two-meter stack of electronics, metallic gray, stood next to the large chair. The only other object on the stage was a digital clock that currently read 0742. Ellie stared at the chair. Hanging from the top was a hood that would fit over the victim's head. Ellie shuddered and fought against nausea. *How barbaric*, she thought. *How could any species that considers itself advanced tolerate this kind of gruesome spectacle?*

Her mind had just cleared away the execution images when there was a tap on her shoulder. Ellie turned around. A large, frowning policeman was leaning across the aisle in her direction. "Are you Eleanor Wakefield Turner?" he asked.

Ellie was so frightened she could barely respond. She nodded her head. "Will you come with me, please?" he said. "I need to ask you a couple of questions."

On shaky legs, Ellie edged past three people in her row and entered the aisle. *Something's gone wrong*, she thought. *The escape has been foiled. They've found the cache and somehow know that I'm involved.*

The policeman took her to a small conference room on the side of the auditorium. "I'm Captain Franz Bauer, Mrs. Turner," he said. "It is my job to dispose of your mother's body after she has been executed. We have, of course, arranged for the customary cremation with the undertaker. However . . ." At this point Captain Bauer paused, as if he were carefully selecting his words. ". . . in view of the past services that your mother has rendered for the colony, I thought perhaps that you, or some member of your family, might like to take care of the final procedures."

"Yes, of course, Captain Bauer," Ellie replied, weak with relief. "Certainly. Thank you very much," she added quickly.

"That will be all, Mrs. Turner," the policeman said. "You may now return to the auditorium."

Ellie stood up and discovered that she was still shaky. She put one hand on the table in the middle of the room. "Sir?" she said to Captain Bauer.

"Yes?" he replied.

"Would it be possible for me to see my mother alone, just for an instant, before . . . ?"

The policeman studied Ellie at length. "I don't think so," he said, "but I will ask on your behalf."

"Thank you very—"

Ellie was interrupted by the ring of the telephone. She delayed her departure from the conference room long enough to see the shocked expression on Captain Bauer's face. "Are you absolutely certain?" she heard him say as she left the room.

The big digital clock on the stage read 0836. "Come on, come on," the man behind Ellie grumbled. "Let's get on with it."

Ellie forced herself to stay calm. She glanced around at the restive crowd. Captain Bauer had informed everyone at five past eight that the "activities" would be delayed "a few minutes," but in the last half hour there had been no additional announcements. In the row in front of Ellie, a wild rumor was circulating that the extraterrestrials had rescued Nicole from her cell.

Some of the people had already started to leave when Governor Macmillan walked onto the stage. He looked harried and upset, but he broke quickly into his official open smile when he began addressing the crowd.

"Ladies and gentlemen," he said, "the execution of Nicole des Jardins Wakefield has been postponed. The government has discovered some small irregularities in the paperwork associated with her case—nothing really important, of course—but we felt these issues should be cleared up first, so that there can be no question of any impropriety. The execution will be rescheduled in the near future. All the citizens of New Eden will be informed of the details."

Ellie sat in her seat until the auditorium was nearly empty. She half expected to be detained by the police when she tried to leave, but nobody stopped her. Once outside, it was difficult for her not to scream with joy.

She suddenly noticed that several people were looking at her. *Uh-oh,* Ellie thought. *Am I giving myself away?* She met the other eyes with a polite smile. *Now, Ellie, comes your greatest challenge. You cannot under any circumstances behave as if you expected this.*

As usual, Robert, Ellie, and little Nicole stopped in Avalon to visit with Nai Watanabe and the twins after completing their weekly calls on the seventy-seven remaining RV-41 sufferers. It was just before dinner. Both Galileo and Kepler were playing in the dirt street in front of the ramshackle house. When the Turners arrived, the two little boys were involved in an argument.

"She is too," the four-year-old Galileo said heatedly.

"Is not," Kepler replied with much less passion.

Ellie bent down beside the twins. "Boys, boys," she said in a friendly voice. "What are you fighting about?"

"Oh, hi, Mrs. Turner," Kepler answered with an embarrassed smile. "It's really nothing. Galileo and I—"

"I say that Governor Wakefield is already dead," Galileo interrupted forcefully. "One of the boys at the center told me, and he should know. His daddy is a policeman."

For a moment Ellie was taken aback. Then she realized that the twins had not made the connection between Nicole and her. "Do you remember that Governor Wakefield is my mother, and little Nicole's grandmother?" Ellie said softly. "You and Kepler met her several times before she went to prison."

Galileo wrinkled his brow and then shook his head.

"I remember her . . . I think," Kepler said solemnly. "*Is* she dead, Mrs. Turner?" The ingenuous youngster then added after a brief pause.

"We don't know for certain, but we hope not," Ellie replied. She had almost slipped. It would have been so easy to tell these children. But it would only take one mistake. There was probably a biot within earshot.

As Ellie picked up Kepler and gave him a hug, she remembered her chance encounter with Max Puckett at the electronic supermarket three days earlier. In the middle of their ordinary conversation, Max had suddenly said, "Oh, by the way, Joan and Eleanor are fine and asked me to give you their regards."

Without thinking, Ellie had asked Max a leading question about the two little robots. He had ignored it completely. A few seconds later, just as Ellie was about to repeat her question, she noticed that the Garcia biot who was in charge of the market had moved over closer to them and was probably listening to their conversation.

"Hello, Ellie. Hello, Robert," Nai said now from the doorway of her house. She extended her arms and took Nicole from her father. "And how are you, my little beauty? I haven't seen you since your birthday party last week."

The adults went inside the house. After Nai checked to ensure that there were no spy biots in the area, she drew close to Robert and Ellie. "The police interrogated me again last night," she whispered to her friends. "I'm starting to believe there may be some truth in the rumor."

"*Which* rumor?" Ellie said. "There are so many."

"One of the women who works at our factory," Nai said, "has a brother in Nakamura's special service. He told her, one night after he had been drinking, that when the police showed up at Nicole's cell on the morning of the execution, the cell was empty. A Garcia biot had signed her out. They think it was the same Garcia that was reportedly destroyed in that explosion outside the munitions factory."

Ellie smiled, but her eyes said nothing in response to the intense, inquiring gaze from her friend. "The police have also questioned me, Nai," she said matter-of-factly. "Several different times. According to them, the questions are all designed to clear up what they call the 'irregularities' in Mother's case. Even Katie has had a visit from the police. She dropped by unexpectedly last week and remarked that the postponement of Mother's execution was certainly peculiar."

"My friend's brother," Nai said after a short silence, "says that Nakamura suspects a conspiracy."

"That's ridiculous," Robert scoffed. "There is no active opposition to the government anywhere in the colony."

Nai drew even closer to Ellie. "So what do you think is really happening?" she whispered. "Do you think your mother has actually escaped? Or did Nakamura change his mind and execute her in private to stop her from becoming a public martyr?"

Ellie looked first at her husband and then at her friend. "I have no idea," Ellie forced herself to answer. "I have, of course, considered all the possibilities you have mentioned. As well as a few others. But we have no way of knowing. . . . Even though I am certainly not what you would call a religious person, I have been praying in my own way that Mother is all right."

3

Nicole finished her dried apricots and crossed the room to drop the package in the wastebasket. It was nearly full. She tried to compress the waste with her foot, but the level barely changed.

My time is running out, she thought, her eyes mechanically scanning the food remaining on the shelf. *I can last maybe five more days. Then I must have some new supplies.*

Both Joan and Eleanor had been gone for forty-eight hours. During the first two weeks of Nicole's stay in the room underneath Max Puckett's barn, one of the two robots had been with her all the time. Talking with them had been almost like talking with her husband, Richard, at least originally, before Nicole had exhausted all the topics the little robots had stored in their memories.

These two robots are his greatest creations, Nicole said to herself, sitting down in the chair. *He must have spent months on them.* She remembered Richard's Shakespearean robots from the Newton days. *Joan and Eleanor are far more sophisticated than Prince Hal and Falstaff. Richard must have learned a lot from the engineering of the human biots in New Eden.*

Joan and Eleanor had kept Nicole informed about the major events occurring in the habitat. It was an easy task for them. Part of their programmed instruction was to observe and to report by radio to Richard during their periodic sorties outside of New Eden, so they passed the same information on to Nicole. She knew, for example, that Nakamura's special police had searched every building in the settlement, ostensibly looking for anyone hoarding critical resources, in the first two weeks after her escape. They had also come to the Puckett farm, of course, and for four hours Nicole had sat perfectly still in total darkness in her hideout. She had heard some noises above her, but whoever had conducted the search had not spent much time in the barn.

More recently, it had often been necessary for both Joan and Eleanor to be outside of the hideout at the same time. They told her that they were busy coordinating the next phase of her escape. Once, Nicole had asked the robots how they managed to pass so easily through the checkpoint at the entrance to New Eden. "It's really very simple," Joan had said. "Cargo trucks pass through the gate a dozen times a day, most carrying items to and from the troops and construction personnel over in the other habitat, some going out to Avalon. We're almost impossible to notice in any large load."

Joan and Eleanor had also brought Nicole up to date on all the colony history since she had been imprisoned. Nicole now knew that the humans had invaded the avian/sessile habitat and essentially routed its occupants. Richard had not wasted robot memory space or his own time by supplying Joan and Eleanor with too many of the details about the avians and sessiles; however, Nicole did know that Richard had managed to escape to New York with two avian eggs, four manna melons containing embryos of the bizarre sessile species, and a critical slice of an actual adult sessile. She also knew that the two avian hatchlings had been born a few months earlier and that Richard was being kept extremely busy tending to their needs.

It was difficult for Nicole to imagine her husband, Richard, playing both mother and father to a pair of aliens. She remembered that when their own children had been small, Richard had not shown much interest in their development, and he had often been insensitive to the children's emotional needs. Of course he had been marvelous at teaching them facts, especially abstract concepts from mathematics and science. But Nicole and Michael O'Toole had remarked to each other several times during their long voyage on Rama II that Richard did not seem to be capable of dealing with children on their own level.

His own childhood was so painful, Nicole thought, recalling her conversations with Richard about his abusive father. *He must have grown up with no capability to love or trust other people. All his friends were fantasies or robots he had created himself....* She paused for a moment in her thinking. *But during our years in New Eden he definitely changed.... I never had a chance to tell him how proud I was of him. That was why I wanted to leave the special letter....*

The solitary light in her room suddenly went out and Nicole was surrounded by darkness. She sat quite still in her chair and listened carefully for any sounds. Although Nicole knew that the police were again on the premises, she could hear nothing. As she became more frightened, Nicole realized how important Joan and Eleanor had become to her. During the first visit to the Puckett farm by the special police, both the little robots had been in the room to comfort her.

Time passed very slowly. Nicole could hear the beating of her heart. After what seemed like an eternity, she heard noises above her. It sounded as if there were many people in the barn. Nicole took a deep breath and tried to steady herself. Seconds later, she nearly jumped out of her skin when she heard a soft voice beside her reciting a poem.

> *Invade me now, my ruthless friend,*
> *And make me cower in the dark.*
> *Remind me that I'm all alone*
> *And draw upon my face your mark.*
> *How is it that you capture me,*
> *When all my thoughts deny your force?*
> *Is it the reptile in my brain*
> *That lets your terror run its course?*
>
> *Baseless Fear undoes us all*
> *Despite our quest for lofty goals.*
> *We would-be Galahads don't die,*
> *Fear just freezes all our souls.*
> *It keeps us mute when feeling love,*
> *Reminding us what we might lose.*
> *And if by chance we meet success,*
> *Fear tells us which safe route to choose.*

Nicole recognized eventually that the voice belonged to the robot Joan, and that she was reciting Benita Garcia's famous pair of stanzas about fear, written after Benita had been thoroughly politicized by the poverty and destitution of the Great Chaos. The friendly voice of the robot and the familiar lines of the poem temporarily mitigated Nicole's panic. For a while she listened more calmly despite the fact that the noises above her were growing in amplitude.

When Nicole heard the sound of the movement of the large bags of chicken feed stored above the entrance to her hideout, however, her fright was suddenly renewed. *This is it*, Nicole said to herself. *I am going to be captured.*

Nicole wondered briefly if the special police would kill her as soon as they found her. Then she heard loud metallic pounding at the end of the passage to her room and was unable to remain seated. As she rose, Nicole felt two sharp pains in her chest and her breathing became labored. *What's wrong with me?* she was thinking when Joan spoke up from beside her.

"After the first search," the robot said, "Max was afraid that he had not camouflaged your entrance well enough. One night while you were asleep he inserted into the top of the hole a full drainage system for the henhouse, with the discharge pipes running out above your hideout. That pounding you heard was someone beating on the pipes."

Nicole held her breath while a muffled conversation took place on the surface above her. After a minute, she again heard the movement of the bags of chicken feed. *Good old Max*, Nicole thought, relaxing somewhat. The pain in her chest subsided. After several more minutes the noises above her ceased altogether. Nicole heaved a sigh and sat down in the chair. But she did not fall asleep until the lights were on again.

The robot Eleanor had returned by the time Nicole awakened. She explained to Nicole that Max was going to start ripping out the drainage system in the next few hours and that Nicole was finally going to leave her hideout. Nicole was surprised when, after crawling through the tunnel, she encountered Eponine standing beside Max.

The two women embraced. *"Ça va bien? Je ne t'ai pas vue depuis si longtemps,"* Eponine said to Nicole.

"Mais mon amie, pourquoi es-tu ici? J'ai pensé que—"

"All right, you two," Max interrupted. "You'll have plenty of time later to become reacquainted. Right now we need to hurry. We're already behind schedule because I took too long to remove that damn drain. Ep, take Nicole inside and dress her. You can explain the plan while you're putting on your clothes. I need to shower and shave."

As the two women walked in the dark from the barn to Max's house, Eponine informed Nicole that everything was in place for her escape from the habitat. "During the last four days Max has hidden the diving gear piece by piece around the shore of Lake Shakespeare. He also has another full set stored in a warehouse in Beauvois, in case someone has removed your mask or air tanks from their hiding places. While you and I are at the party, Max will make sure that everything is all right."

"What party?" a confused Nicole asked.

Eponine laughed as they entered the house. "Of course," she said. "I forgot that you haven't been following the calendar. Tonight is Mardi Gras. There is a big party in Beauvois, and another over in Positano. Almost everyone will be out tonight. The government has been encouraging people to attend, probably to keep their minds off the other colony problems."

Nicole looked very strangely at her friend, and Eponine laughed again.

"Don't you understand? Our biggest difficulty was figuring out how to get you all the way across the colony to Lake Shakespeare without being seen. Everyone in New Eden knows your face. Even Richard agreed that this was our only reasonable opportunity. You'll be in costume, and wearing a mask—"

"Have you talked to Richard, then?" Nicole asked, starting to comprehend at least the outline of the plan.

"Not directly," replied Eponine. "But Max has communicated with him through the little robots. Richard was responsible for the drainage system idea that misled the police on their last visit to the farm. He was worried that you would be discovered."

The women entered the bedroom, where a magnificent white dress was spread out upon the bed. "You will attend the party as the queen of England," Eponine said. "I have been working on your dress nonstop all week. With this full mask and these long white gloves and leggings, none of your hair or skin will show. We shouldn't need to stay at the party for more than an hour or so, and you won't say much to anybody, but if anyone should ask, simply tell them that you're Ellie. She's staying home tonight with your granddaughter."

"Does Ellie know I have escaped?" Nicole asked a few seconds later. She was experiencing a strong yearning to see both her daughter and little Nicole, whom she had never even met.

"Probably," said Eponine. "At least she knew that an attempt was likely. It was Ellie who first involved *me* in your escape. Ellie and I cached your supplies out on the Central Plain."

"So you haven't seen her since I've been out of prison?"

"Oh, yes. But we haven't said anything. Right now Ellie must be very careful. Nakamura is watching her like a hawk."

"Is anyone else involved?" Nicole asked, holding up the dress to see how it would fit.

"No," answered Eponine. "Just Max, Ellie, and I. . . . And of course Richard and the little robots."

Nicole stood in front of the mirror for several seconds. *So here I am, finally the queen of England, at least for an hour or two.* She was certain that the idea for the specific costume had also come from Richard. *Nobody else could have made a choice so appropriate.* Nicole adjusted the crown upon her head. *With this white face,* she thought, *Henry might have even made me queen.*

Nicole was deep in a memory of many years earlier when Max and Eponine emerged from the bedroom. Nicole began to laugh immediately. Max was dressed in a scanty green outfit and was carrying a trident. He was Neptune, king of the sea, and Eponine was his sexy mermaid princess.

"You both look great!" Queen Nicole said, with a wink at Eponine. "Wow, Max," she added a second later in a teasing voice, "I had no idea you had such an imposing body."

"It's ridiculous," Max grumbled. "I have hair everywhere—all over my chest, down my back, in my ears, even—"

"Except it's a little thin up here," Eponine said, patting his head after removing his crown.

"Shit," said Max. "Now I know why I've never lived with a woman. . . . Come on, you two, let's get going. And by the way, the weather is wacky again tonight. You'll both need a shawl or a jacket during our ride in the buggy."

"The buggy?" Nicole said, glancing at Eponine.

Her friend smiled. "You'll see in a minute," Eponine said.

When the New Eden government had requisitioned all the trains to convert the lightweight extraterrestrial alloys into war planes and other weaponry, the colony of New Eden had been left without a comprehensive transportation system. Luckily most of the citizens had purchased bicycles, and a full set of bicycle paths had been developed during the first three years after the initial settlement. Otherwise, it would have been very difficult for people to move about in the colony.

By the time of Nicole's escape, the old train tracks had all been removed and roads had been laid where the tracks had once been. These roads were used by the electric cars (restricted to government leaders and key military personnel), the transport trucks (which also ran on stored electricity), and the creative and varied other transportation devices constructed by individual citizens of New Eden. Max's buggy was such a device. In front it was a bicycle. The back half, however, was a large pair of soft seats, almost a couch, resting on two wheels and a strong axle, much like the horse-drawn buggies three centuries earlier on the Earth.

King Neptune struggled with the pedals as the costumed trio eased onto the road toward Central City. "Shit," Max said as he strained to accelerate, "why did I ever agree to this absurd plan?"

Nicole and Eponine laughed in the seat behind him. "Because you're a wonderful man," Eponine said, "and you wanted us both to be comfortable. Besides, can you imagine a queen riding a bicycle for almost ten kilometers?"

The temperature was indeed on the cool side. Eponine spent a few minutes explaining to Nicole how the weather continued to grow more and more unstable. "There was a recent report on television," she said, "that the government intends to settle many of the colonists in the second habitat. Its environment is still unspoiled. Nobody has any confidence that we will ever fix the problems here in New Eden."

As they neared Central City, Nicole worried that Max was becoming chilled. She offered him the shawl Eponine had loaned her, which he eventually accepted. "You could have picked a warmer costume," Nicole said teasingly.

"Having Max be King Neptune was also Richard's idea," Eponine said. "That way, if he needs to carry any of your diving equipment tonight, he will look perfectly natural."

Nicole was surprisingly emotional as the buggy slowed in the growing traffic and wound its way through the colony's main buildings in Central City. She remembered a night, years before, when she had been the only human awake in New Eden. On that same night, after checking her family one last time, an apprehensive Nicole had climbed into her berth and prepared to sleep for the many-year trip back to the solar system.

An image of the Eagle, that strange manifestation of alien intelligence who had been their guide at the Node, appeared in her mind's eye. *Could you have predicted all this?* Nicole wondered, synthesizing quickly the entire colony history since that first rendezvous with the passengers from Earth onboard the Pinta. *And what do you think of us now?* Nicole grimly shook her head, acutely embarrassed by the behavior of her fellow humans.

"They never replaced it," Eponine was saying from the seat beside her. They had entered the main plaza.

"I'm sorry," Nicole said. "I'm afraid I was daydreaming."

"That wonderful monument your husband designed, the one that kept track of where Rama was in the galaxy. . . . Remember, it was destroyed the night the mob wanted to lynch Martinez. . . . Anyway, it was never replaced."

Again Nicole was deep in her memory. *Maybe that's what being old is,* she thought. *Too many memories always crowding out the present.* She recalled the unruly mob and the red-haired boy who hollered, "Kill the nigger bitch."

"What ever happened to Martinez?" Nicole asked softly, fearful of the answer.

"He was electrocuted soon after Nakamura and Macmillan took over the government. The trial dominated the news for several days."

They had passed through Central City and were continuing south toward Beauvois, the village where Nicole and Richard and their family had lived before Nakamura's coup. *It could have been so different,* she thought, looking at Mount Olympus towering over them on her left. *We could have had paradise here. If only we had tried harder. . . .*

It was a train of thought that Nicole had followed a hundred times since that terrible night, the same night that Richard had hurriedly departed from New Eden. Always there was the same profound sorrow in her heart, the same burning tears in her eyes.

We humans, she remembered saying once to the Eagle at the Node, *are capable of such dichotomous behavior. At times, when there is caring and compassion, we truly seem little lower than the angels. But more often, our greed and selfishness overwhelm our virtues and we become indistinguishable from the basest creatures from which we have evolved.*

4

Max had been gone from the party for almost two hours. Both Eponine and Nicole were becoming alarmed. As the two women tried to cross the crowded dance floor together, a pair of men dressed as Robin Hood and Friar Tuck stopped them.

"You are not Maid Marian," Robin Hood said to Eponine, "but Maid-Mer is nearly the same." He laughed heartily at his own joke, extended his arms, and began to dance with Eponine.

"May a lowly priest enjoy a dance with Her Majesty?" the other man said. Nicole smiled to herself. *What harm can there be in a single dance?* she thought. She slipped into Friar Tuck's arms and they began moving slowly around the floor.

Friar Tuck was a talkative fellow. After every several bars of the music, he would pull away from Nicole and ask a question. As planned, Nicole would indicate her response with a head movement or a gesture. Toward the end of the song, the priest in costume began to laugh. "Verily," he said, "I believe I am dancing with a mute. A graceful one, no doubt, but nevertheless a mute."

"I have a bad cold," Nicole said softly, trying to disguise her voice.

After she had spoken, Nicole detected a definite change in the friar's manner. Her concern increased when, after the dance was over, the man continued to hold her hands and to stare at her for several seconds.

"I've heard your voice somewhere before," he said seriously. "It's very distinctive. I wonder if we've met. I'm Wallace Michaelson, the senator from the western section of Beauvois."

Nicole vaguely remembered the man. She did not dare to say anything else. Fortunately, Eponine and Robin Hood returned to join Nicole and Friar Tuck before the silence had become dangerously long. Eponine sensed what had occurred and acted quickly. "The queen and I," she said, taking Nicole by the hand, "were on our way to the powder room when you Sherwood Forest outlaws ambushed us. If you will now excuse us, with thanks for the dance, we will continue toward our original destination."

As the women walked away, the two men dressed in green watched them carefully. Once inside the ladies' room, Eponine first opened all the stalls to ensure that she and Nicole were alone. "Something's happened," Eponine then whispered. "Probably Max had to go to the warehouse to replace your equipment."

"Friar Tuck is a senator from Beauvois," Nicole said. "He almost recognized my voice. I don't think I'm safe here."

"All right," said Eponine nervously after a moment's hesitation. "We will follow the alternate plan. We'll go out front and wait underneath the big tree."

Both women saw the small ceiling camera at the same time. It made just the slightest sound as it changed its orientation to follow them around the room. Nicole tried to remember every word that she and Eponine had said. *Was there anything that suggested who we were?* she wondered. Nicole was worried especially about Eponine, since her friend would continue to live in the colony after Nicole had either escaped or was captured.

When Nicole and Eponine returned to the ballroom, Robin Hood and his favorite priest gestured for the ladies to come toward them. In response Eponine motioned toward the front door, put her fingers to her lips to indicate that she was going outside to smoke, and then crossed the room with Nicole. Eponine glanced over her shoulder as she opened the outside door. "The green men are following us," she whispered to Nicole.

About twenty meters away from the entrance to the ballroom, which was in reality the gymnasium for Beauvois Middle School, there was a large elm tree that had been one of the few already-grown trees transported to Rama originally from the Earth. When Eponine and Queen Nicole reached the tree, Eponine reached into her purse, pulled out a cigarette, and lit it quickly. She blew the smoke away from Nicole. "I'm sorry," she whispered to her friend.

"I understand," Nicole had just finished saying when Robin Hood and Friar Tuck walked up beside them.

"Well, well," Robin Hood said, "so our mermaid princess is a smoker. Don't you know that you're taking years off your life?"

Eponine started to give her standard reply, to tell the man that RV-41 would kill her long before smoking would, but she decided that any conversation might encourage the men to stay. She just smiled wanly, inhaled deeply on her cigarette, and blew smoke above her head into the branches of the tree.

"Both the friar here and I were hoping that you ladies would join us for a drink," Robin Hood said, ignoring the fact that neither Eponine nor Nicole had responded to his earlier comment.

"Yes," added Friar Tuck, "we would like to know who you are." He stared at Nicole. "I'm certain we've met before, your voice is so familiar."

Nicole faked a cough and looked around. There were three policemen within a radius of fifty meters. *Not here*, she thought. *Not now. Not when I am so close.*

"The queen is not feeling well," Eponine said. "We may be leaving early. If not, we'll find you when we come back inside."

"I'm a doctor," Robin Hood interrupted, moving closer to Nicole. "Maybe I can help."

Nicole could feel the tension in her heart. Again her breath was short and labored. She coughed again and turned away from the two men.

"That's a terrible cough, Your Majesty," she heard a familiar voice say. "We'd better take you home."

Nicole glanced up at another man dressed in green. Max, a.k.a. King Neptune, was smiling broadly at her. Behind him Nicole could see the buggy parked no more than ten meters away. Nicole was joyful and relieved. She gave Max a huge hug and almost forgot the danger all around her. "Max," she said, before he put his finger to her lips.

"I know both you ladies are just delighted that King Neptune has finished his business for the evening," he then said with a flourish, "and can now squire you away to his castle, away from outlaws and other unsavory elements."

Max looked at the other two men, who were enjoying his performance even though he had foiled their plans for the evening. "Thank you, Robin. Thank you, Friar Tuck," Max said as he helped the ladies into the buggy seat. "Your kind attention to my friends is most appreciated."

Friar Tuck approached the buggy, obviously to ask one more question, but Max pedaled away. "It is a night of costumes and mystery," he said, waving at the man. "But we cannot tarry, for the sea is calling us."

"You were fantastic," Eponine said, giving Max another kiss.

Nicole nodded her head. "You may have missed your calling," she said. "Maybe you should have been an actor instead of a farmer."

"I played Marc Antony in our high school play in Arkansas," Max said, handing Nicole the diving mask for a final adjustment. "The pigs loved my rehearsals. . . . *Friends, Romans, Countrymen. Lend me your ears. I come to bury Caesar, not to praise him.*"

The three of them laughed. They were standing in a small clearing about five meters from the shore of Lake Shakespeare. The trees and tall underbrush concealed them from the nearby road and bicycle path. Max lifted up the air tank and helped Nicole adjust it on her back.

"Is everything ready, then?" he asked.

Nicole nodded.

"The robots will meet you at the cache," Max said. "They told me to remind you not to descend too rapidly. You have not done any diving in a long time."

Nicole stood in silence for several seconds. "I don't know how to thank you two," she said awkwardly. "Nothing I can think of to say seems adequate."

Eponine walked over to Nicole and gave her a hug. "Be safe, my friend," she said. "We love you very much."

"Me too," Max said a moment later, choking slightly as he embraced her. They both waved to Nicole as she backed into the lake.

Tears were running out of Nicole's eyes and collecting on the bottom of her mask. She waved one last time when the water was up to her waist.

The water was colder than Nicole had expected. She knew that the temperature variations in New Eden had been much greater since the colonists had taken over management of their own weather, but she had not considered that the changes in weather patterns would have altered the temperature of the lake.

Nicole changed the amount of air in her vest to slow her descent. *Don't hurry,* she counseled herself. *And stay relaxed. You have a long swim ahead of you.*

Joan and Eleanor had drilled Nicole repeatedly on the procedure she should follow to locate the long tunnel that ran under the habitat wall. She switched on her flashlight and studied the aquaculture farm off to her left. *Three hundred meters toward the center of the lake, directly perpendicular to the back wall of the salmon-feeding area,* she remembered. *Stay at a depth of twenty meters until you see the concrete platform below you.*

Nicole swam easily, but she was tiring quickly nevertheless. She found the concrete platform, descended another fifteen meters while carefully watching all her gauges, and eventually located one of the eight large pumping stations that were scattered on the bottom of the lake to keep the water continuously circulating. *Now, the tunnel entrance is supposed to be hidden just under one of these big motors.* Nicole did not find it easily. She kept swimming past it because of all the new growth around the pumping complex.

The tunnel was a four-meter-diameter circular pipe, completely full of water. It had been included as an emergency escape route in the original habitat design at the insistence of Richard, whose engineering background had taught him always to allow for unforeseen contingencies. From the entrance in Lake Shakespeare to the exit, out in the Central Plain beyond the walls of the habitat, was a swim of slightly over one kilometer. It had taken Nicole ten minutes longer than planned to find the entrance. She was already a very tired woman as she began her final swim.

During her two years in prison, Nicole's only exercise had been the walking, sit-ups, and push-ups that she had done at irregular intervals. Her aging muscles were no longer able to endure extreme fatigue without cramping. Three times during her swim through the tunnel, Nicole's leg muscles cramped. Each time she struggled, treading water, and forced herself to relax until the cramp completely dissipated. Her forward progress was very slow. Toward the end of her swim Nicole became frightened that she would run out of air before she reached the tunnel exit.

In the last hundred meters Nicole's body ached all over. Her arms did not want to push through the water and her legs had no strength left to kick. It was then that the ache began in her chest. The dull, disconcerting pain stayed with her even after her depth gauge indicated that the tunnel had turned slightly upward.

When she finally reached the end of the passage and stood up in a small underground room with only half a meter of water on the floor, Nicole almost collapsed. For several minutes she tried unsuccessfully to regain an equilibrium level in her breathing and pulse rate. Nicole did not even have enough strength left to lift off the metal exit cover above her head. Worried that she had pushed herself beyond safe physical limits, Nicole decided to remain in the tunnel and take a short nap.

She awakened two hours later when she heard a bizarre pitter-patter above her. Nicole stood directly under the cover and listened carefully. She could hear voices, but could not isolate what was being said. *What's going on?* she asked herself, her heart rate suddenly accelerating. *If I've been discovered by the police, why don't they just open the cover?*

Nicole moved quietly in the darkness over to her diving gear, which was sitting against the wall on the opposite side of the tunnel. Suddenly there was a sharp knock on the cover. "Are you down there, Nicole?" the robot Joan asked. "If so, identify yourself immediately. We have some warm clothes up here for you, but we are not strong enough to remove the cover."

"Yes, it's me," Nicole cried with relief. "I'll climb out as soon as I can."

In her wet suit Nicole became quickly chilled in the bracing outside air of Rama, where the temperature was only a few degrees above freezing. Her teeth chattered during the eighty-meter walk in the dark to where her food and dry clothing were cached.

When the trio reached the supplies, Joan and Eleanor instructed Nicole to put on the army uniform that Ellie and Eponine had left for her. When Nicole asked why, the robots explained that to reach New York, it was necessary for them to pass through the second habitat. "In case we are discovered," Eleanor said when she was safely sitting in Nicole's shirt pocket, "it will be easier to talk our way out of trouble if you are wearing a soldier's uniform."

Nicole put on the long underwear and the uniform. When she was no longer cold, she realized that she was extremely hungry. While she was eating the food Eponine had packed in the cache, Nicole placed all the other items that had been wrapped in the sheet into the backpack she had been carrying under her diving vest.

There was a problem entering the second habitat. Nicole and the two robots in her pocket had not encountered any humans at all in the Central Plain, but the entrance to what had once been the home of the avians and sessiles was guarded by a sentry. Eleanor had gone forward to scout and had reported the difficulty. The trio stopped three to four hundred meters away from the main traffic route between the two habitats.

"This must be a new security precaution, added since your escape," Joan said to Nicole. "We've never had any difficulties coming and going."

"Are there no other routes that lead to the inside?" Nicole asked.

"No," Eleanor answered. "The original probe site was here. It has since been considerably widened, of course, and a bridge was built across the moat so that the troops can move quickly. But there are no other entrances."

"And must we absolutely go through this habitat to reach Richard and New York?"

"Yes," Joan replied. "That huge gray barrier to the south, the one that forms the wall of the second habitat for many kilometers, prevents movement in and out of the Northern Hemicylinder of Rama. It's possible that we could fly over it, if we had an airplane that could reach an altitude of two kilometers, and a very clever pilot, but we don't. Besides, Richard is expecting us to come through the habitat."

They waited and waited in the dark and cold. Periodically one of the two robots would check the entrance, but there was always a sentry present. Nicole became tired and frustrated. "Look," she said at one point, "we can't stay here forever. There must be some other plan."

"We have no knowledge of any alternate or contingency plans in this situation," Eleanor said, reminding Nicole for once that they were only robots.

During a brief nap the exhausted Nicole dreamed that she was lying, naked, on the top of a very large and very flat ice cube. Avians were striking at her from the sky, and hundreds of little robots like Joan and Eleanor had surrounded her on the surface of the ice. They were chanting something in unison.

When Nicole awakened, she felt somewhat refreshed. She talked with the two robots and they worked out a new plan. The three of them decided not to move until there was a break in the traffic through the entrance to the second habitat. At that time, the robots would decoy the sentry so that Nicole could proceed inside. Joan and Eleanor instructed Nicole then to walk cautiously to the other side of the bridge and turn right along the shore of the moat. "Wait for us," Eleanor said, "in the small cove about three hundred meters from the bridge."

Twenty minutes later, Joan and Eleanor made a terrible commotion along the far wall, about fifty meters from the entrance. Nicole walked unmolested into the interior of the habitat when the sentry left his post to investigate the noise. On the inside, a long stairway wound back and forth, dropping the several hundred meters from the entrance altitude to the level of the wide moat that circumscribed the entire habitat. There were lights on the stairway at periodic intervals, and Nicole could see more lights on the bridge in front of her, but the overall illumination was quite sparse. Nicole tensed when she saw a pair of construction workers coming up the stairs in her direction. But they climbed right past her with only minimal acknowledgment. Nicole was thankful she was wearing the uniform.

As she waited beside the moat, Nicole stared toward the center of the alien habitat and tried to make out the fascinating features the little robots had described to her: the huge brown cylindrical structure, rising fifteen hundred meters straight up, that had once housed both the avian and sessile colonies; the great hooded ball that hung from the habitat ceiling and provided light; and the ring of mysterious white buildings, alongside a canal, that encircled the cylinder.

The hooded ball had not been illuminated for months, not since the first human incursion into the avian/sessile domain. The only lights that Nicole could see were small and widely scattered, obviously placed in the habitat by the human invaders. Thus all she could discern was a vague silhouette of the great cylinder, a shadow whose edges were very fuzzy. *It must have been glorious when Richard first entered,* Nicole thought, moved by the thought that she was in a location that had recently been the home of another sentient species. *So here also,* her mind continued, *we extend our hegemony, trampling underfoot all life-forms that are not as powerful as we.*

Eleanor and Joan took longer than expected to rejoin Nicole. The threesome then made slow progress along the side of the moat. One of the robots was always out front, scouting, making certain that contacts with other humans were avoided. Twice, in the part of the habitat that was very much like a jungle on Earth, Nicole waited quietly while a group of soldiers or workmen passed by on the road to their left. Both times she studied the new and interesting plants around her with fascination. Nicole even found a creature halfway between a leech and an earthworm trying to enter her right boot. Curious, she picked it up and put it in her pocket so that she could examine it later.

When Nicole and the two robots finally arrived at the specified spot for the rendezvous, it had been almost thirty-two hours since she had backed into Lake Shakespeare. They were on the far side of the second habitat, away from the entrance, where the normal density of human beings was at its lowest. A submarine surfaced within minutes after their arrival. The side of the submarine opened and Richard Wakefield, a gigantic smile upon his bearded face, rushed forward toward his beloved wife. Nicole's body shook with joy when she felt his arms around her.

5

Everything was so familiar. Except for Richard's clutter, accumulated during his months alone, and the conversion of the nursery into the bedroom of the two avian hatchlings, the lair underneath New York was exactly the same as it had been when Richard, Nicole, Michael O'Toole, and their children had departed from Rama years before.

Richard had parked the submarine at a natural harbor on the south side of the island, in a place he had called the Port.

"Where did you get the sub?" Nicole had asked him while they were walking together toward the lair.

"It was a gift," Richard had said. "Or at least I think it was. After the superchief of the avians showed me how to operate it, he or she disappeared, leaving the submarine here."

Walking in New York had been an eerie experience for Nicole. Even in the dark the skyscrapers reminded her vividly of the years that she had lived on this mysterious island in the middle of the Cylindrical Sea.

"How many years has it been since we left New York?" Nicole had asked as they entered their lair.

"I can't give you an accurate answer," Richard had answered with a shrug. "We've taken two long interstellar voyages at relativistic speeds. Unless we know our exact velocity profiles, we can't make the proper time corrections."

"The only changes made in the Rama spacecraft on each visit to the Node," Richard had said sometime later, while Nicole was still musing about the wonders of relativity, "are those necessary to accommodate the next mission. So nothing has changed in here. The black screen is still there in the White Room, as well as our old keyboard. The procedures for making requests from the Ramans, or whatever our hosts should be called, are still intact also."

"And what about the other lairs?" Nicole had asked. "Have you visited them also?"

"The avian lair is a tomb," Richard had replied. "I've been all through it several times. Once, I entered the octospider lair cautiously, but I went only as far as that cathedral room with the four tunnels leading away—"

Nicole had interrupted him, laughing. "The ones we called Eenie, Meenie, Mynie, and Moe."

"Yes," Richard had continued. "Anyway, I wasn't comfortable there. I had the feeling, although I could not identify anything specific, that the lair was still inhabited. And that the octos, or whatever might be living there, were watching my every step." This time it was his turn to laugh. "Believe it or not, I was also worried about what would happen to Tammy and Timmy if I didn't return for any reason."

Nicole's first introduction to Tammy and Timmy, the pair of avian hatchlings that Richard had raised from infancy, was priceless. Richard had built a half-door to the nursery and had closed it securely when he had left to meet Nicole inside the second habitat. Since the birdlike creatures couldn't yet fly, they had remained safely inside the nursery during Richard's absence. As soon as they heard his voice in the lair, however, the hatchlings began to shriek and jabber. They did not even stop squawking when Richard opened their door and cradled both of them in his arms.

"They're telling me," Richard shouted to Nicole above the frightful noise, "that I shouldn't have left them alone."

Nicole couldn't stop laughing as she watched the two hatchlings extend their long necks toward Richard's face. They interrupted their jabbers and shrieks only to rub the undersides of their beaks softly against Richard's bearded cheek. The avians were still small, about seventy centimeters tall when standing on their legs, but their necks were so long that they appeared to be much larger.

Nicole watched with admiration as her husband tended to his alien wards. He cleaned up their wastes, made certain that they had fresh food and water, and even checked the softness of their haylike beds in the corner of the nursery. *You have come a long, long way, Richard Wakefield,* Nicole thought, remembering his reluctance years earlier to deal with any of the more mundane duties associated with parenting. She was deeply touched by his obvious affection for the gangly hatchlings. *Is it possible,* Nicole asked herself, *that each of us has inside this kind of selfless love? And that we must somehow work through all the problems that both heredity and environment have created before we can find it?*

Richard had stored the four manna melons and the slice from the sessile in one corner of the White Room. He explained to Nicole that he hadn't noticed any changes in either the melons or the sessile material since he had arrived in New York. "Maybe the melons can rest dormant for a long time, like seeds," Nicole offered after listening to Richard's explanation of the complex life cycle of the sessile species.

"That's what I was thinking," Richard said. "Of course I have no idea at all under what conditions the melons might germinate. The species is so strange and so complicated, I wouldn't be surprised if the process is controlled somehow by that small piece of the sessile."

On their first evening together, Richard had difficulty getting the hatchlings to go to sleep. "They're afraid I'm going to leave them again," Richard explained when he returned to the White Room after the third time that Tammy's and Timmy's furious squawks had interrupted his dinner with Nicole. At length, Richard programmed Joan and Eleanor to amuse the avians. It was the only way he could keep his alien wards quiet so that he could have some time alone with Nicole.

They made love slowly and tenderly. Richard had admitted while he was undressing that he wasn't certain how well . . . But Nicole had informed him that his performance, or lack thereof, was of absolutely no consequence. She insisted that it would be a delight just to hold his body next to hers and that any actual sexual stimulation would be a marvelous bonus. They were, of course, compatible, as they had been since the first time they had slept together.

After their easy lovemaking, Richard and Nicole held hands and said nothing. Nicole fell asleep gloriously happy.

For the first time ever, there was no hurry in their lives. Every night they talked easily, sometimes even while they were making love. Richard told Nicole more about his childhood and adolescence than he ever had before. He included his most painful memories of his father's abuse, as well as the harrowing details of his disastrous first marriage to Sarah Tydings.

"I now realize that Sarah and Dad had something fundamental in common," Richard said late one evening. "They were both incapable of granting me the approval I so desperately sought—and somehow they both knew that I would continue to try to obtain that approval, even if it meant abandoning everything else in my life."

Nicole shared with Richard for the first time all the drama of her forty-eight-hour affair with the Prince of Wales right after she had won her Olympic gold medal. She even admitted to Richard that she had yearned to marry Henry and that she had been completely devastated when she had realized that the prince had excluded Nicole as a candidate to be the queen of England primarily because of her skin color. Richard was fascinated by the story that Nicole told. But never once did he seem even the least bit threatened or jealous.

He has become more mature, Nicole was thinking several nights later, while her husband was finishing his nightly task of tucking the hatchlings into bed. "Darling," Nicole said when Richard joined her in their bedroom in the lair, "there's something that I want to tell you. I have been waiting for the right time. . . ."

"Uh-oh." Richard feigned a frown. "This sounds serious. . . . I hope it won't take long, for I had some plans of my own for us this evening."

He crossed the room and started to kiss her. "Please, Richard, not now," she said, pushing him away gently. "This is very important to me."

Richard backed up a couple of steps. "When I thought I was going to be executed," Nicole said slowly, "I realized that all my personal affairs were in order, except for two. There were still things that I wanted to say, both to you and to Katie. I even asked the policeman who explained the execution procedure to me if he would give me pen and paper so that I could write two final letters."

Nicole paused a moment, as if she were searching for exactly the right words. "During those terrifying days, I couldn't remember, Richard," she continued, "if I had ever told you, explicitly, how glad I was that we had been husband and wife. . . . I also didn't want to die without . . ."

She paused a second time, glanced briefly around the room, and then looked directly into Richard's eyes again. "There was one more thing I wanted to accomplish with that last letter," Nicole said. "I believed at the time that it was necessary to make my life complete, so that I could depart from this world without any loose ends. . . . Richard, I wanted to apologize for my insensitivity back when you and Michael and I . . . I made a mistake then by going to Michael's bed too soon when I feared . . ." Nicole took a deep breath. "I should have had more faith," she said. "Not that I would for a minute remove either Patrick or Benjy from the world, but I realize now that I surrendered too quickly to my loneliness. I wish . . ."

Richard touched his finger to her lips. "No apology is necessary, Nicole," he said softly. "I know that you have loved me well."

They settled into an easy rhythm in their simple existence. In the mornings they would walk around New York, usually arm in arm, exploring anew every corner of the island domain they had called home once before. Because it was always dark, the city looked different now. Only their flashlight beams illuminated the enigmatic skyscrapers whose details were indelibly imprinted in their memories.

Often they walked along the ramparts of the city, looking out at the waters of the Cylindrical Sea. One morning they spent several hours standing in one place, the very spot where they had entrusted their lives to the three avians years and years before. Together they recalled both their fear and their excitement at the moment when the great bird creatures had lifted them off the ground to carry them across the sea.

Every day after lunch Nicole, who had always needed more sleep than her husband, would take a short nap. Richard would use the keyboard to order more food or supplies from the Ramans, or take the hatchlings topside for some exercise, or work on one of his myriad projects scattered around the lair. In the evening, after a leisurely dinner, they would lie together, side by side, and talk for hours before making love or just falling asleep. They talked about everything: the Eagle, the Ramans, the existence of God, the politics in New Eden, books of all kinds, and most of all, their children.

Although they could converse enthusiastically about Ellie, Patrick, Benjy, or even Simone, whom they had not seen for many years, it was difficult for Richard to talk about Katie for any length of time. He regularly castigated himself for not having been stricter with his favorite daughter during her childhood, and blamed her irresponsible behavior as an adult on his permissiveness. Nicole tried to console and reassure him, reminding Richard that their circumstances in Rama had been unusual and that, after all, nothing in his background had prepared him for the proper discipline required of a parent.

One afternoon when Nicole awakened from her nap, she could hear Richard mumbling to himself down the hall. Curious, she stood up quietly and walked down to the room that had once been Michael O'Toole's bedroom. Nicole stood at the door and watched Richard put the final touches on a large model that occupied most of the room.

"Voilà," he said, turning around to acknowledge that he had heard Nicole's footsteps. "It won't win any aesthetic awards," Richard said with a grin, motioning in the direction of the model, "but it's a reasonable representation of our part of the universe, and it certainly has provided me with plenty of food for thought."

A flat rectangular platform covered most of the floor. Thin vertical rods of varying heights had been inserted at twenty locations around the platform. At the top end of each rod was at least one colored sphere, representing a star.

The vertical rod in the center of the model, which had a yellow sphere attached to its top, rose about a meter and a half off the platform. "This, of course," Richard said to Nicole, "is our Sun. And here we are—or I should say Rama is—over in this quadrant, about one-fourth of the way between the Sun and our closest similar star, Tau Ceti. Sirius, where we were when we stayed at the Node, is back over there. . . ."

Nicole walked around in the model depicting the stellar neighborhood of the Sun. "There are twenty star systems within twelve and a half light-years of our home," Richard explained, "including six binary systems and one triplet group, our nearest neighbors, the Centauris, over here. Note that the Centauris are the only stars inside the five-light-year sphere."

Richard pointed at the three separate balls representing the Centauris. Each was a different size and color. The trio, attached to each other with tiny wires, were resting on top of the same vertical rod, just inside an open wire sphere centered at the sun and marked with a large number 5.

"During my many days of solitude down here," Richard continued, "I often found myself wondering why Rama is going in this particular direction. Do we have a specific destination? It would seem so, since our path has not varied since our initial acceleration. And if we are going to Tau Ceti, what will we find there? Another complex like the Node? Or will the *same* Node perhaps have moved during the intervening time?"

Richard stopped. Nicole had walked over to the edge of the model and was stretching her arms up to a pair of red stars at the end of a three-meter rod. "I assume you varied the length of these rods to demonstrate the full three-dimensional relationship of all these stars," she said.

"Yes. That particular binary group you are touching, incidentally, is called Struve 2398," Richard replied in his human catalog voice. "They have a very high declination and are slightly over ten light-years away from the Sun."

Seeing the slight grimace on Nicole's face, Richard laughed at himself and crossed the room to take her hand. "Come over here with me," he said, "and I will show you something really interesting."

They walked to the other side of the model and stood facing the Sun, halfway between the stars Sirius and Tau Ceti. "Wouldn't it be fantastic if our Node really *has* moved," Richard said excitedly, "and we will see it again, over here, on the opposite side of our solar system?"

Nicole laughed. "Of course," she said, "but we have absolutely no evidence—"

"But we do have brains, and imaginations," Richard interrupted. "And the Eagle *did* tell us that the entire Node was capable of moving. It just seems to me . . ." Richard stopped in midsentence and then changed the subject slightly. "Haven't you ever asked yourself," he said, "where our Rama spacecraft went, after we left the Node, during all those years that we were asleep? Suppose, for example, that the avians and the sessiles were picked up over here somewhere, around the Procyon binaries, perhaps, or maybe even over here, around Epsilon Eridani, which easily could have been on our trajectory. We know that there are planets around Eridani. At a significant fraction of the speed of light, Rama could have easily doubled back to the Sun—"

"Hold it, Richard," Nicole said. "You're way ahead of me on this subject. Why don't we start at the beginning?" She sat down on the platform in the interior of the model, next to a red ball elevated only a few centimeters by a very short rod, and crossed her legs. "If I understand your hypothesis, our current voyage will end at Tau Ceti?"

Richard nodded. "The trajectory is too perfect for it to be a coincidence. We will reach Tau Ceti in another fifteen years or so, and I believe our experiment will be concluded."

Nicole groaned. "I'm already old," she said. "By then, if I'm even still alive, I'll be as withered as a prune. . . . Just out of curiosity, what do you think will happen to us after our 'experiment is concluded,' as you put it?"

"That's where we need our imaginations. I suspect that we'll be unloaded from Rama, but what happens to us next is completely unknown. . . . I suppose our fate will be dependent in some way on what has been observed all this time."

"So you definitely agree with me that the Eagle and his buddies back at the Node have been watching us?"

"Absolutely. They have made such a huge investment in this project. I'm certain they're monitoring everything that's going on here in Rama. I must admit I'm surprised that they have left us completely to our own devices and have never interfered in our affairs, but that must be their method."

Nicole was silent for a few seconds. She played absentmindedly with the red ball beside her, which Richard informed her represented the star Epsilon Indi. "The judge in me," she said somberly, "fears what any reasonable extraterrestrial would conclude about us, based on our behavior in New Eden."

Richard shrugged. "We've been no worse in Rama than we have been for centuries on Earth. Besides, I can't accept that any truly advanced aliens would be making such subjective judgments. If this process of observing spacefarers has been going on for tens of thousands of years, as the Eagle suggested, then the Ramans must have developed quantitative metrics for assessing all aspects of the civilizations they encounter. They are almost certainly more interested in our exact natures, and what this means in some larger sense, than whether we are bad or good."

"I suppose you're right," Nicole said wistfully. "But it's depressing that we, as a species, behave so barbarically, even when we are fairly certain we're being observed." She paused and reflected. "So in your opinion our long interaction with the Ramans, beginning with that first spaceship over a hundred years ago, is almost over?"

"I think so," Richard replied. "Somewhere in the future, possibly when we reach Tau Ceti, our part of this experiment will be concluded. My guess is that after all the data on the creatures currently inside Rama are entered in the Great Galactic Data Base, Rama will be emptied. Who knows, maybe soon thereafter this great cylindrical spacecraft will appear in another planetary system where a different spacefarer is living, and another cycle will begin."

"And that brings us back to my earlier question, which you really did not answer. What will happen to us then?"

"Maybe we, or our offspring, will be sent on a slow journey back to the Earth. Or maybe we will be deemed expendable and terminated once all the data have been collected."

"Neither of those outcomes is very appealing," Nicole said. "And I must say that although I agree with you that we are heading for Tau Ceti, all the rest of your hypothesis strikes me as pure conjecture."

Richard grinned. "I have learned a lot from you, Nicole. Everything else in my hypothesis is intuitive. It *feels* right to me, based on everything I have learned about the Ramans."

"But wouldn't it be more straightforward to imagine that the Ramans simply have waystations scattered throughout the galaxy, and that the two nearest to us are at Sirius and Tau Ceti?"

"Yes," Richard replied, "but my gut feel is that it's unlikely. The Node was such an awesome engineering creation. If similar facilities exist every twenty or so light-years in the galaxy, there would be *billions* of them altogether. . . . And remember, the Eagle definitely said the Node could move."

Nicole acknowledged to herself that it was unlikely that a facility as astonishing as the Node had been duplicated billions of times in some great cosmic assembly process. Richard's hypothesis did make some sense. *But how sad*, Nicole thought briefly, *that our entry in the galactic data base will contain so much negative information.*

"So where do the avians, sessiles, and our old friends the octospiders fit into your scenario?" Nicole asked a minute later. "Are they just part of the same experiment, with us? And if so, are you suggesting that there is also a colony of octos onboard and that we just haven't met them yet?"

Richard nodded again. "That conclusion is inescapable. If the final phase of each experiment is observing a representative sample of the spacefarers under controlled conditions, it makes sense that the octos are here also." He laughed nervously. "There may even be some of our same friends from Rama II on the spacecraft with us at this very moment."

"What a lovely set of ideas to think about before sleeping," Nicole said with a smile. "If you're right, you and I have fifteen more years to spend on a spacecraft that's inhabited not only by humans who want to capture and kill us, but also by huge, possibly intelligent arachnids whose nature we do not understand."

"Remember," Richard said with a grin, "I could be wrong."

Nicole stood up and walked toward the door.

"Where are you going?" Richard asked.

"To my bed," Nicole replied with a laugh. "I think I'm developing a headache. I can only contemplate the infinite for a finite period of time."

6

The next morning when Nicole opened her eyes, Richard was standing over her holding two full backpacks. "We're going to explore and look for octospiders," he said excitedly, "behind the black screen. I've left enough food and water to last Tammy and Timmy for two days and I've programmed Joan and Eleanor to find us if there is an emergency."

Nicole watched her husband closely while she was eating her breakfast. His eyes were full of energy and life. *This is the Richard I remember the best*, Nicole said to herself happily.

"I've been back here twice," Richard said as soon as they had ducked under the raised screen. "But I've never reached the end of this first passageway."

The screen had closed behind them, leaving Richard and Nicole in the dark. "There's no problem with being trapped here on this side, is there?" Nicole asked while they both checked their flashlights.

"Not at all," Richard replied. "The screen will not raise or lower more often than once every minute or so. But if anyone or anything is still in this general area a minute from now, the screen will automatically lift again."

"Now, I should warn you before we start walking," he continued a few seconds later, "this is a *very* long passageway. I have followed it before, for at least a kilometer, and I have never found anything. Not even a turnoff. And there is absolutely no light. So the first part will be very boring—but it must eventually lead to something, for the biots bringing our supplies must be coming along this path."

Nicole took his hand in hers. "Just remember, Richard," she said easily. "We're not as young as we once were."

Richard shone his flashlight first on Nicole's hair, which was now completely gray, and then on his own gray beard. "We *are* a couple of old farts, aren't we?" he said gaily.

"Speak for yourself," Nicole rejoined, squeezing his hand.

The passageway was much longer than a kilometer. As Richard and Nicole trudged along, they talked mostly about his astonishing experiences in the second habitat. "I was absolutely terrified when the elevator door opened and I saw the myrmicats for the first time," Richard said.

He had already finished describing to Nicole his stay with the avians and had just reached the point in his chronology where he had descended to the bottom of the cylinder. "I was literally frozen with fear. They were only three or four meters away. Both of them were staring at me. The creamy fluid in their huge oval lower eyes was moving from side to side, and the pairs of eyes up on the stalks were bending around to see me from another point of view." Richard shuddered. "I will never forget that moment."

"Now, let me make certain I have the biology straight," Nicole said a few minutes later, as they approached what appeared to be a branching in the underground corridor. "The myrmicats develop in the manna melons, live fairly short but highly active lives, and then die inside a sessile, where their entire life experiences, you theorize, are somehow added to the neural net's base of knowledge. The life cycle completes when new manna melons grow in the interior of the sessiles. These fledgling creatures are then harvested at the appropriate time by the active myrmicat population."

Richard nodded. "That may not be exactly right," he said, "but it must be close."

"So what we're missing is only the necessary set of conditions for the manna melons to begin the germination process?"

"I was hoping you would help me with that puzzle," Richard said. "After all, Doctor, you are the only one of us with any formal biological training."

The corridor became a Y, each of the two continuations making a forty-five-degree angle with the long, straight passageway from their lair. "Which way, Cosmonaut des Jardins?" Richard asked with a smile, shining his flashlight in both directions. Neither of the two tunnels had a single distinguishing characteristic.

"Let's go to the left first," Nicole said a few seconds later after Richard had created an outline map in his portable computer. The left pathway started to change after only a few hundred meters. The corridor widened into a descending ramp that wound around an extremely thick pole and dropped at least a hundred meters deeper into the shell of Rama. As they climbed down, Richard and Nicole could see lights below them. At the bottom, they encountered a long, wide canal with broad, flat banks. To their left, they saw a pair of crab biots scuttling away from them on the opposite side of the canal, as well as a bridge in the distance, beyond the biots. To their right, a barge was moving down the canal, carrying a full load of diverse but unknown objects, gray and black and white in color, to some ultimate destination in the underground world.

Richard and Nicole surveyed the scene around them and then looked at each other. "We're back in wonderland, Alice," Richard said with a short laugh. "Why don't we have a snack while I enter all this real estate in my trusty computer?"

While they were eating, a centipede biot approached on their side of the canal, stopped briefly as if to study them, and then passed on by. It climbed the ramp Richard and Nicole had just descended. "Did you see any crab or centipede biots in the second habitat?" Nicole asked.

"No," said Richard.

"And we purposely designed them out of the plans for New Eden, didn't we?"

Richard laughed. "Indeed we did. You convinced both the Eagle and me that ordinary humans would not be able to deal easily with them."

"So does their presence here imply the existence of a third habitat?" Nicole asked.

"Possibly. After all, we have no idea what's now in the Southern Hemicylinder. We have not seen it since Rama was refurbished. But there's another explanation as well. Suppose the crabs, centipedes, and other Raman biots just go with the territory, if you know what I mean. Maybe they are functioning in all parts of Rama, on all voyages, unless specifically proscribed by a given spacefarer."

As Richard and Nicole finished lunch, another barge came into view on their left. Like its predecessor, it was loaded with stacks of white, black, and gray objects. "These are different from the first ones," Nicole remarked. "These piles remind me of the spare centipede biot parts that were stored in my pit."

"You could be right," Richard said, standing up. "Let's follow the canal and see where it leads us." He glanced around, first at the arched ceiling ten meters above their heads and then back at the ramp behind them. "Unless I have made an error in my computations, or the Cylindrical Sea is much deeper than I think, this canal runs from south to north under the sea itself."

"So following the barge will take us back under the Northern Hemicylinder?" Nicole asked.

"I believe so," Richard replied.

*   *   *

They followed the canal for more than two hours. Except for three spider biots, moving quickly as a team along the opposite bank, Richard and Nicole did not see anything else that was new. Two more barges passed them, carrying the same general kind of load downstream, and they intermittently encountered both centipede and crab biots without any interactions. They walked by one more bridge over the canal.

Richard and Nicole rested twice, drinking water or eating a snack while they talked. At the second rest stop Nicole suggested that perhaps they should turn back. Richard checked his watch. "Let's give it another hour," he said. "If my sense of position is correct, we should be under the Northern Hemicylinder already. Sooner or later we must find where the barges are taking all that stuff."

He was right. After another kilometer of hiking along the canal, Richard and Nicole saw a large pentagonal structure in the distance. As they drew closer, they could see that the canal flowed directly into the center of the pentagon. The building itself, which straddled the canal, was six meters tall. It had a flat roof, no windows, and a creamy white exterior. Each of its five sections or wings extended out twenty or thirty meters from the center of the structure.

The walkway along the canal ended in some stairs that rose to a perimeter lane that ran around the entire pentagon. There was a similar configuration on the other side of the canal; a centipede biot was at that moment using the perimeter lane as a bridge to change from one side of the canal to the other.

"Where do you suppose it's going?" Nicole asked as the two of them stood aside to permit the biot to trundle by.

"Maybe to New York," Richard answered. "On my long walks before the avians hatched I sometimes saw one of them in the distance."

They paused together outside the only door to the pentagon that was on the canal side of the building. "I guess we're going in?" Nicole said.

Richard nodded and pushed open the small door. Nicole bent down and entered the building. Surrounding them was a large room, well lit, perhaps a thousand cubic meters altogether, with a ceiling five meters above the floor. Their walkway was elevated above the floor by two or three meters, so Richard and Nicole could watch most of the activities taking place below them. Biot robot workers they had never seen before, each designed for a specialized task, were unloading the two barges in the room and separating the cargo according to some predefined plan. Many of the individual pieces from the stacks were loaded onto truck biots, which disappeared through one of the back doors once they were full.

After a few minutes of observation, Richard and Nicole continued along the walkway to where it intersected another path just above the center of the room. Richard stopped and made some notes in his computer. "I presume this layout is as simple as it looks," he said to Nicole. "We can go either left or right—each way we go into another wing of the pentagon."

Nicole chose the right walkway because the truck biots that she had thought were carrying parts for the centipede biot had gone in that direction. Her observations had been accurate. Soon after Richard and Nicole entered the second room, which was exactly the same size as the first, they realized that both a centipede and a crab biot were being manufactured on the floor below them. Richard and Nicole stopped to watch the process for several minutes.

"Absolutely fascinating," Richard said, finishing his computer diagram of the biot factory. "Are you ready to go?"

As Richard turned to face Nicole, she saw his eyes widen. "Don't look now," he said quietly a second later, "but we have company."

Nicole wheeled around and looked behind her. Across the room, forty meters behind them on the walkway, a pair of octospiders was slowly approaching them. Richard and Nicole had not heard their distinguishing sound, similar to dragging metallic brushes, because of the noise from the biot factory.

The octospiders stopped when they realized that the humans had noticed them. Nicole's heart was pumping furiously. She remembered clearly her last encounter with an octospider, when she had rescued Katie from the octo lair in Rama II. Then, as now, her overwhelming impulse had been to run.

She grabbed Richard's hand as they both stared at the aliens. "Let's go," Nicole said under her breath.

"I'm as scared as you are," he replied, "but let's not leave just yet. They aren't moving. I want to see what they are going to do."

Richard concentrated on the lead octospider and drew a careful picture in his mind. Its nearly spherical main body was charcoal gray, with a diameter of about a meter, and was featureless except for a vertical slit twenty or twenty-five centimeters wide that ran from the top to the bottom, where the body broke into the eight black and gold tentacles, each two meters long, that spread out across the floor. Inside the vertical slit were many unknown knobs and wrinkles—*Almost certainly sensors*, Richard thought—the largest of which was a big rectangular lens structure containing some kind of fluid.

As the two pairs of beings gazed at each other across the room, a broad band of bright purple coloring swept around the "head" of the lead octospider. This band originated on one of the parallel edges of the vertical slit. It moved around the head, disappearing into the opposite edge of the slit almost three hundred and sixty degrees later. It was followed in a few seconds by a complicated sequence containing some red bands, some green, and some that were apparently blank. This sequence made an identical journey around the head of the octospider.

"That's exactly what happened when that octospider confronted Katie and me," Nicole said nervously to Richard. "She said it was talking to us."

"But we have no way of knowing what it's saying," Richard replied. "Just because it can talk does not mean that it won't hurt us." As the lead octospider continued to talk in color, Richard suddenly remembered an episode from years earlier, during his odyssey in Rama II. At the time he had been lying on a table, surrounded by five or six octos, all with colored patterns on their heads. Richard recalled clearly the powerful terror that he had felt as he had watched some very small creatures, apparently under the control of the octospiders, crawl into his nose.

Richard's head began to throb with pain. "They weren't all that nice to me before," he said to Nicole. "When they—"

At that moment the far door to the room opened and four more octospiders entered. "That's enough," said Richard, feeling Nicole tense beside him. "I think it's time for us to make an exit."

Richard and Nicole walked quickly to the center of the room, where the walkway, as in the previous room, joined with the path leading to the outside of the building. They turned toward the outside but stopped after taking a few steps. Four more octospiders were coming through this door as well.

They didn't need to confer. Richard and Nicole spun around, returned to the main interior walkway, and bolted in the direction of the third wing of the pentagon. This time they raced on, without turning to the outside, until they were inside the fourth wing. It was completely dark in this section. They slowed as Richard pulled out his flashlight to examine their surroundings. There was sophisticated-looking equipment on the floor below them, but no activity of any kind.

"Should we try the outside again?" Richard asked as he was putting his flashlight back in his shirt pocket. Seeing her nod, Richard took Nicole's hand and they ran together toward the intersection, where they turned right and headed out of the pentagon altogether.

A few minutes later they were jogging down a dark corridor in completely unknown territory. Both of them were fatigued. Nicole was having difficulty breathing. "Richard," she said, "I need to rest. I can't keep running like this."

Richard and Nicole walked down the empty corridor for another fifty meters. They saw a door on their left. Richard cautiously opened the door, peered in, and scanned the room with his flashlight. "It must be a storage room of some kind," he said. "But it's currently empty."

Richard walked into the room, glanced through its back door into another empty chamber, and then returned for Nicole. They sat down with their backs against the wall. "When we return to our lair, darling," Nicole said a few seconds later, "I want you to help me check my heart. I have been having some strange pains lately."

"Are you all right now?" Richard asked, concern reflected in his voice.

"Yes," Nicole replied. She smiled in the dark and kissed her husband. "As well as can be expected after narrowly escaping from a gaggle of octospiders."

7

Nicole slept fitfully with her back against the wall and her head resting on Richard's shoulder. She had one nightmare after another, always waking with a start before dozing off again. In the last nightmare Nicole was on an island by the ocean with all her children. A huge tidal wave headed toward them on her dream screen. Nicole was frantic because her children were scattered all over the island. How could she possibly save all of them? She awakened with a shudder.

She nudged her husband in the dark. "Richard," Nicole said, "wake up. Something's not right."

At first Richard did not move. When Nicole touched him a second time, he slowly opened his eyes. "What's the matter?" he said at length.

"I have the feeling we're not safe here," she said. "I think we should go."

Richard switched on his flashlight and moved the beam slowly around the room. "There's nobody here," he said softly. "And I don't hear anything either. Don't you think we should rest some more?"

Nicole's fears increased as they sat in silence. "I'm still feeling a sense of danger, Richard," she said finally. "I know that you don't believe in anything you can't analyze, but I have learned to trust my premonitions."

"All right," Richard said unenthusiastically. He stood up and walked across the room, opening the back door, which led to a similar, adjacent area. He glanced inside. "Nothing here either," he said after several seconds. Richard next came back across the room and opened the door to the corridor they had used to escape from the pentagon. The moment the door was open, Nicole and he both heard the unmistakable sound of dragging brushes.

Nicole jumped to her feet. Richard closed the door without a sound and hurried over beside her. "Come on," he said in a whisper. "We have to find another way out of here."

They walked through the next room, then another and another. All were dark and empty. They lost their sense of direction as they raced through the unfamiliar territory. Eventually they came to a large double door at the far side of one of the many identical rooms. Richard told Nicole to stand back as he cautiously pushed open the door. "Holy shit!" he exclaimed as soon as he looked into the room. "What in the world is this?"

Nicole came up beside Richard and her eyes followed his flashlight beam as it fell on the bizarre contents of the adjoining chamber. The room was cluttered with large objects. The one closest to the door looked like a large amoeba on a skateboard, the next one like a gigantic ball of twine with two antennae sticking out of its center. There was no sound in the room and nothing moved. Richard lifted his beam higher and let it move quickly around the rest of the crowded room.

"Go back," Nicole said excitedly, catching a glimpse of something familiar. "Over there. A few meters to the left of the other door."

Seconds later the beam illuminated four humanlike figures, dressed in helmets and space suits, that were sitting against the far wall. "It's the human biots," Nicole said excitedly, "the ones we saw in Rama II out on the Central Plain."

"Norton and company?" Richard asked incredulously, a shiver of fear running down his spine.

"I bet it is," Nicole responded.

They entered the room slowly and tiptoed around the many objects as they made their way toward the figures in question. Both Richard and Nicole knelt down beside the four apparent humans. "This must be a biot dump," Nicole said, after they had verified that the face behind the transparent helmet was indeed a copy of the Commander Norton who led the first Rama expedition.

Richard stood up and shook his head. "Absolutely unbelievable," he said. "What are they doing here?" He let his flashlight beam wander around the room.

A second later Nicole screamed. No more than four meters away from her, an octospider was moving, or at least so it seemed in the peculiar light. Richard rushed to her side. The two of them quickly verified that what they were seeing was only an octospider biot, and then they both laughed for several minutes.

"Richard Wakefield," Nicole said when she could finally contain her nervous laughter, "may I go home now? I've had enough."

"I guess so," Richard said with a smile. "As long as we can find the way."

As they penetrated deeper and deeper into the maze of rooms and tunnels in the area around the pentagon, Nicole became convinced that they would never find their way out. Eventually Richard slowed the pace and started storing information in his portable computer. Afterward he was at least able to prevent their going in circles, but Richard never connected his growing map to any of the landmarks they had seen before they fled from the octospiders.

When both Richard and Nicole were starting to feel desperate, they chanced upon a small truck biot carrying an odd collection of small objects down a narrow corridor. Richard became more relaxed. "Those things look as if they have been custom-made to someone's specifications," he said to Nicole, "like the objects delivered to us in the White Room. If we go back in the direction from which the biot came, then maybe we will locate where all our objects are manufactured. From there, it should be easy to find the path to our lair."

It was a long hike. They were both worn out several hours later when their corridor widened into a huge factory area with a very high ceiling. At the center of the factory were twelve fat cylinders that looked like old-fashioned boilers on the Earth. Each was four or five meters high and a meter and a half wide. The boilers were arranged in four rows of three.

Conveyor belts, or at least the Rama equivalent, led into and out of each of the boilers, two of which were in operation at the moment. Richard was fascinated. "Look over there," he said, pointing at a vast warehouse floor covered with stacks of objects of all sizes and descriptions. "That must be all the raw material. A request arrives at the central computer, which is probably in that hut behind the boilers, where it is processed and allocated to one of these machines. Biots go out, gather up the proper items, and place them on the conveyor belts. Inside the boilers these raw materials are altered significantly, for what comes out is the object ordered by whatever intelligent species is using the keyboard or its equivalent to communicate with the Ramans."

Richard approached the closest active boiler. "But the real question," he said, overflowing with excitement, "is what *kind* of process takes place inside these boilers? Is it chemical? Is it perhaps nuclear, involving element transmutations? Or have the Ramans some other technology for manufacturing completely beyond our ken?"

He knocked several times very hard on the outside of the active boiler. "The walls are very thick," he announced. Richard then bent down where the conveyor belt entered the boiler and started to stick his hand inside. "Richard," Nicole yelled, "don't you think that's foolish?"

Richard glanced up at his wife and shrugged. As he bent down again to study the belt/boiler interface, a bizarre biot that looked like a camera box with legs scurried over from the back of the large room. It quickly wedged itself between Richard and the active conveyor belt and then expanded in size, forcing Richard away from the active process.

"Nice move," Richard said appreciatively. He turned to Nicole. "The system has excellent fault protection."

"Richard," Nicole now said, "if you don't mind, can we please return to our major task? Or have you forgotten that we do not know the way back to our lair?"

"Just a little while longer," Richard answered. "I want to see what comes out of the active boiler closest to us. Maybe by seeing the output, after having already seen the input, I can infer the kind of intervening process."

Nicole shook her head. "I had forgotten what a knowledge junkie you are. You're the only human I have ever met who would stop to study a new plant or animal while he was completely lost in a forest."

Nicole found another long passageway on the opposite side of the huge room. An hour later she finally convinced Richard to leave the fascinating alien factory. They had no way of knowing where this new passageway led, but it was their only hope. Again they walked and walked. Each time Nicole started to become tired or despondent, Richard would lift her spirits by extolling the wonder of everything they had seen since they had left their lair.

"This place is absolutely amazing, stupendous," he said at one point, barely able to contain himself. "I can't begin to assess what it all means. . . . Not only are humans not alone in this universe, we are not even near the top of the pyramid in terms of capability. . . ."

Richard's enthusiasm sustained them until finally, when they were both close to exhaustion, they saw ahead of them a branching in the corridor. Because of the angles, Richard felt certain that they had returned to the original Y no more than two kilometers from their lair. "Yippee," Richard yelled, picking up his pace. "Look"—he shouted over at Nicole, his flashlight pointed in front of him—"we're almost home."

Something Nicole heard at that moment made her stop dead in her tracks. "Richard," she cried, "turn off the light."

He spun quickly around, nearly falling, and switched off his flashlight. In the next few seconds there was no doubt. The sound of dragging brushes was growing louder.

"Run for it," yelled Nicole, bolting past her husband in a full sprint. Richard reached the intersection no more than fifteen seconds before the first of the octospiders. The aliens were coming up from the canal. As he was running away from them, Richard turned around and shone his flashlight behind him. In that brief instant he could see at least four colored patterns moving in the darkness.

They brought all the furniture they could find into the White Room and created a barrier across the bottom of the black screen. For several hours Richard and Nicole watched and waited, expecting that at any moment the screen would lift up and their lair would be invaded by the octospiders. But nothing happened. At length they left Joan and Eleanor in the White Room as sentries and spent the night in the nursery with Tammy and Timmy.

"Why didn't the octospiders follow us?" Richard said to Nicole early the next morning. "They almost certainly know the screen raises automatically. If they had come to the end of the corridor—"

"Maybe they didn't want to frighten us again," Nicole interrupted gently. Richard's brow furrowed and he gave Nicole a quizzical look. "We still have no hard evidence that the octospiders are hostile," Nicole continued, "despite your feelings that you were mistreated as their prisoner during your odyssey years ago. They did not harm Katie or me when they easily could have. And they did return you to us eventually."

"By that time I was in a deep coma," Richard replied. "And no good to them anymore as a test subject. Besides, how do you explain Takagishi? Or, for that matter, the attacks that were made on Prince Hal and Falstaff?"

"Each of those incidents has a plausible, nonhostile explanation. That's what is so confusing. Suppose Takagishi died of a heart attack. Suppose also that the octos preserved and stuffed his body to use as some sort of exhibit, for teaching other octospiders. We might do the same thing."

"I'm puzzled," Richard said after a moment's hesitation. "Here you are, defending the octospiders. But you ran away from them yesterday even faster than I did."

"Yes," Nicole answered contemplatively. "I admit that I was terrified. My animal instinct was to assume hostility and flee. Today I'm disappointed in myself. We humans are supposed to use our brains to overcome instinctive reactions. . . . Especially you and I. After everything we have seen in Rama and at the Node, we should be completely immune from xenophobia."

Richard smiled and nodded. "So are you suggesting now that maybe the octospiders were just trying to establish some kind of peaceful contact?"

"Perhaps," Nicole answered. "I don't know what they want. But I *do* know that I have never seen them do anything unambiguously hostile."

Richard stared distractedly at the walls for a few seconds and then rubbed his forehead. "I wish I could remember more of the details about my time with them. I still have these blinding headaches when I try to concentrate on that period of my life—only while I was inside the sessile were my memories of the octos not accompanied by pain."

"Your odyssey was long ago," Nicole said. "Maybe the octospiders also are capable of learning and have adopted a different attitude toward us now."

Richard stood up. "All right," he said. "You have convinced me. The next time we see an octospider, we won't run away." He laughed. "At least not immediately."

Another month passed. Richard and Nicole did not go behind the black screen again and they did not have any more encounters with the octospiders. They passed the days tending to the hatchlings (who were learning to fly) and enjoying each other. During much of their conversation they talked about their children and reminisced about the past.

"I guess we are now old," Nicole said one morning as she and Richard were walking through one of the three central plazas of New York.

"How can you say that?" Richard replied with a mischievous grin. "Just because we spend most of our time talking about what happened long ago, and our everyday bathroom functions occupy more of our attention and energy than sex, does that mean we're old?"

Nicole laughed. "Is it as bad as that?" she said.

"Not quite," Richard said in a kidding tone. "I still love you like a schoolboy. But every now and then that love is pushed aside by aches and pains that I never had before. . . . Which reminds me, wasn't I supposed to help you examine your heart?"

"Yes." Nicole nodded. "But there's really nothing you can do. The only instruments I brought with me in my medicine kit when I escaped were the stethoscope and the sphygmomanometer. I have used them both several times to examine myself. . . . I haven't been able to find anything unusual except an occasional leaky valve, and my shortness of breath has not recurred." She smiled. "It was probably all the excitement . . . and age."

"If our son-in-law the cardiologist were here," Richard said, "then he could give you a complete examination."

They walked together in silence for several minutes. "You miss the children a lot, don't you?" Richard said.

"Yes," Nicole replied with a sigh. "But I try not to think about them too much. I am happy to be alive and here with you—it's certainly much better than those last months in prison. And I have many wonderful memories of the children. . . ."

"God grant me the wisdom to accept the things I cannot change," Richard quoted. "It is one of your best qualities, Nicole. . . . I have always been envious of your equanimity."

A few moments later Richard stopped abruptly and turned to face Nicole. "I love you very much," he said, embracing her vigorously.

"What is this all about?" Nicole asked, puzzled by his sudden show of emotion.

Richard's eyes had a faraway look. "During the last week," he said excitedly, "a wild and crazy plan has been developing in my brain. I have known from the outset that it was dangerous, and probably insane, but like all my projects it has taken hold of me. Twice I have even gotten out of our bed in the middle of the night to work on the details. I have wanted to tell you about it before now, but I needed to convince myself that it was indeed possible."

"I have no idea at all what you are talking about," Nicole said impatiently.

"The children," Richard said with a flourish. "I have a plan for them to escape, to join us here in New York. I have even begun to reprogram Joan and Eleanor."

Nicole stared at her husband, her emotions struggling with her reason. He started to explain his escape plan. "Wait a minute, Richard," Nicole interrupted after several seconds. "There's an important question we must answer first. What makes you think the children would even *want* to escape? They are not under indictment in New Eden, or in prison. Granted, Nakamura is a tyrant and life in the colony is difficult and depressing, but as far as I know, the children are as free as any of the other citizens. And if they were to try to join us and fail, their lives would be in danger. Besides, our existence here, although fine for us, would hardly be considered a paradise for them."

"I know . . . I know," Richard replied, "and perhaps I have been carried away by my desire to see them. But what do we risk by sending Joan and Eleanor to talk to them? Patrick and Ellie are adults and can make up their own minds."

"And what about Benjy and Katie?" Nicole asked.

A frown creased Richard's face. "Obviously Benjy could not come by himself, so his participation depends on whether or not any of the others decide to help him. As for Katie, she is so unstable and unpredictable . . . she might conceivably even decide to tell Nakamura. I think we have no choice except to leave her out."

"A parent never gives up hope," Nicole said softly, as much to herself as to Richard. "By the way," she added, "does your scheme also include Max and Eponine? They are virtually members of the family."

"Max is really the perfect choice to coordinate the escape from inside the colony," Richard said, growing excited again. "He did a fantastic job hiding you and then getting you to Lake Shakespeare without being detected. Patrick and Ellie will need someone mature and levelheaded to guide them through all the details. In my plan, Joan and Eleanor approach Max first. Not only is he already familiar with the robots, but also he will give his honest assessment as to whether or not the plan can work. If he tells us through the robots that the whole idea is preposterous, then we'll drop it."

Nicole tried to imagine the joy she would feel at the moment of embracing any of her children again. It was impossible. "All right, Richard," she said, finally smiling. "I admit that I'm interested. Let's talk about it. But we must promise ourselves that we won't do anything unless we are certain that we are not going to endanger the children."

8

Max Puckett and Ellie Turner excused themselves from Eponine, Robert, and little Nicole shortly after dinner and walked outside at Max's farmhouse in New Eden. As soon as they were out of earshot, Max began telling Ellie about his recent visits from the little robots. Ellie could not believe what she was hearing. "Surely you're mistaken," she said in a loud voice to Max. "They can't be suggesting that we just leave—"

Max put a finger to his lips as they walked the final few meters to the barn. "You can talk to them yourself," he said in a whisper. "But according to these little characters, there is plenty of room for all of us in that lair you lived in the first few years after you were born."

It was dark inside the barn. Before Max switched on the light, Ellie had already glimpsed the tiny glowing robots beside her on one of the windowsills. "Hello again, Ellie," said little Joan, still dressed in her armor. "Your mother and father are both fine and send their greetings."

"We have come to see you tonight," the robot Eleanor added, "because Max thought it was necessary for you to hear for yourself what we have to say. Richard and Nicole are inviting you and your friends to join them in your old lair in New York, where your parents are living a Spartan but peaceful existence."

"Everything about your lair," Joan now said, "is the same as it was when you were a small child. Food, clothing, and other objects are still supplied by the Ramans after requests are made by using the keyboard in the White Room. Unlimited supplies of fresh water are available at the cistern near the bottom of the entry staircase."

Ellie listened, fascinated, while Joan reminded her of the living conditions under the island city on the southern side of the second habitat. Ellie tried to recall the lair from her memory, but the picture that came to her mind was surprisingly vague. What she could remember clearly from that period of her life were the last few days in Rama, including the spectacular rings of color emanating from the Big Horn and drifting slowly toward the north of the giant cylinder. But her memory of the inside of the lair was foggy. *Why can't I remember at least the nursery more clearly?* she wondered. *Because too much has happened since? And made deeper impressions in my memory?*

A montage of images from her early childhood streamed through Ellie's mental vision. Some of the pictures were indeed from Rama, but far more of them were from the family apartment at the Node. The indelible features of the Eagle, a godlike figure to the child Ellie, seemed to preside over the montage.

Eleanor of Aquitaine had asked Ellie something, but the young woman had not been paying attention. "I'm sorry, Eleanor," Ellie said, "please repeat your question. I'm afraid I was temporarily lost in my childhood."

"Your mother asked about Benjy. Is he still in the ward out in Avalon?"

"Yes," Ellie replied. "And doing as well as can be expected. His best friend in the whole world is now Nai Watanabe. When the war ended, she volunteered to work with those who had been assigned, for one reason or another, to the Avalon Ward. She spends time with Benjy almost every day and has helped him immensely. Her twins Kepler and Galileo love to play with him—Benjy is essentially just a big child himself—although Galileo is sometimes unkind and causes Nai considerable heartache."

"As I told you," Max said, turning the conversation back to their primary business, "Nicole and Richard have left it up to our discretion to decide who should be involved if we do attempt a mass exodus. Will Benjy follow directions?"

"I think so," Ellie said. "As long as he trusts the person giving them. But there is no way we could tell him about the escape ahead of time. We couldn't possibly expect him not to say something about it. Secrecy and guile are not part of Benjy's personality. He will be overjoyed, but—"

"Mr. Puckett," Joan of Arc interrupted, "what should I tell Richard and Nicole?"

"Shit, Joanie," Max replied, "have a little patience. Better still, come back again in a week, after Ellie, Eponine, and I have had more time to talk this thing through, and I'll give you a tentative answer. And tell Richard I find the whole damn thing intriguing, even if it is certifiably insane."

Max placed the two robots on the floor of the barn and they scampered away. When Max and Ellie were back outside in the fresh air, Max pulled a cigarette out of his pocket. "I assume that it doesn't offend you *too* much if I smoke out here?" he said with a grin.

Ellie smiled. "You don't want to tell Robert, do you, Max?" she then said quietly a moment later, as Max blew smoke rings into the night air.

Max shook his head. "Not yet," he replied. "Maybe not until the last moment." He put his arm around Ellie. "Young lady, I like your doctor husband, I really do, but sometimes I think his attitudes and priorities are a little strange. I can't say for certain that he wouldn't tell someone."

"Do you think, Max," Ellie said, "that maybe Robert has made a private vow of some kind never to act against authority again? And that he is afraid?"

"Shit, Ellie, I'm no psychologist. I don't think either of us can possibly understand what killing two people in cold blood did to him. But I can say that there is a finite chance that he would not keep our secret—to avoid a painful personal decision, if nothing else." Max inhaled deeply on his cigarette and stared at his young friend.

"You don't think he'll come, do you, Max? Not even if I want him to."

Again Max shook his head. "I don't know, Ellie. It will depend on how much he needs you and little Nicole. Robert has made room for the two of you in his life, but he still hides his feelings behind continuous work."

"What about you, Max?" Ellie now asked. "What do you *really* think of this whole scheme?"

"Eponine and I are both ready to go, to have ourselves a little ad-ven-toor," Max said with a grin. "It's just a matter of time before I get into serious trouble with Nakamura anyway."

"And Patrick?"

"He'll love the idea. But I'm worried that he might say something to Katie. They have a special relationship—"

Max stopped in midsentence when he saw that Robert, who was carrying his tired daughter, had come out onto the front porch.

"Oh, there you are, Ellie," Robert said. "I thought that maybe you and Max were lost in the barn. Nicole is tired and I have a very early morning at the hospital."

"Of course, darling," Ellie replied. "Max and I were just sharing memories of my mother and father."

It must look like a perfectly normal day, Ellie thought as she showed her identification card to the Garcia biot in the atrium of the Beauvois supermarket. *I must do everything exactly as if this were an ordinary Thursday.*

"Mrs. Turner," the Garcia said a few seconds later, handing her a list printed out of the computer against the wall behind the biot, "here is your ration allocation for the week. We are out of broccoli and tomatoes again, so we have included two extra measures of rice. You may now proceed to the line to pick up your groceries."

Little Nicole walked beside her as Ellie entered the main part of the supermarket. On the other side of a mesh screen, where in the early days of the colony the citizens of New Eden had done their own shopping, five or six Tiasso and Lincoln biots, all from the 300 series completely reprogrammed by the Nakamura government, were moving up and down the aisles filling the orders. Most of the shelves were empty. Even though the war had been over for some time, the unstable weather in New Eden, as well as the dislike of most of the farmers for Nakamura's heavy-handed ways, had kept food production at a minimum level. The government had found it necessary, therefore, to supervise the allocation of food. Only the governmental favorites had more than the bare essentials to eat.

There were half a dozen people in the queue in front of Ellie and her almost-two-year-old daughter. Ellie shopped with the same people every Thursday afternoon. Most of them turned around when Ellie and Nicole entered the line.

"There's that darling little girl," a pleasant woman with gray hair said. "How are you today, Nicole?" she asked.

Nicole didn't answer. She just backed up a couple of steps and fastened herself tightly to one of her mother's legs. "Nicole's still in her shy stage," Ellie said. "She only talks to people she knows."

A Lincoln biot brought out two small boxes of food and handed them to the father and adolescent son at the head of the supermarket line. "We won't be using a cart today," the father said to the Lincoln. "Please make a note of that on our record. Two weeks ago, when we also hand-carried our groceries, nobody noted that we didn't take a cart and we were awakened in the middle of the night by a Garcia demanding that we return our cart to the store."

There must be no trivial mistakes, Ellie said to herself. *No carts not returned, nothing that anyone could suspect before morning.* As she waited in the line, Ellie reviewed again the details of the escape plan that she and Patrick had discussed with Max and Eponine the previous day. A Thursday had been chosen because that was the day that Robert made his regular visits to the RV-41 sufferers in Avalon. Max and Eponine had applied for, and received, a pass to visit Nai Watanabe for dinner. They would look after Kepler and Galileo while Nai went to the ward for Benjy. Everything was in order. There was only one major uncertainty left.

Ellie had rehearsed her speech to Robert a hundred times. *His initial reaction will be negative*, she thought. *He will say it's too dangerous, that I am jeopardizing Nicole's security. And he'll be angry because I didn't tell him earlier.*

In her mind she had already answered all his objections and had carefully described the life they would have in New York in a positive light. But Ellie was still extremely nervous. She had not been able to convince herself that Robert would agree to come. And she had no idea what he would do if she declared that she and little Nicole were prepared to leave without him.

As her groceries were placed in the small shopping cart that she would return to the supermarket after unpacking everything at her home, Ellie squeezed her daughter's hand. *I must have courage*, she thought.

"How in the world do you *expect* me to react?" Robert Turner said. "I come home from an exceptionally busy day at the hospital, my mind on the hundred things that I must do tomorrow, and you tell me over dinner that you want us to leave New Eden forever? And to go *tonight*? Ellie, dear Ellie, this whole thing is absurd. Even if it could work, I would need time to sort out everything. . . . I have projects—"

"I know it's sudden, Robert," Ellie said, growing fearful that she had underestimated the difficulty of her task, "but I couldn't have told you any earlier. It would have been too dangerous. What if you had slipped and said something to Ed Stafford or another member of your staff, and one of the biots had overheard?"

"But I can't just leave without saying anything to anybody." Robert shook his head vigorously. "Do you have any idea how many *years* of work would be wasted?"

"Couldn't you write down what needs to be done on each project?" Ellie suggested. "And maybe summarize what's already been accomplished?"

"Not in one night," Robert replied emphatically. "No, Ellie, it's really out of the question. We can't go. The long-term health of the colony may depend on the results of my research. Besides, even if I accept that your parents are living comfortably in that bizarre place you described, wherever it is, it certainly does not sound like a good place to raise a child. And you haven't even mentioned the possible danger to all of us. Our leaving will be viewed as treason. We could both be executed if we were caught. What would happen to Nicole then? . . . "

Ellie listened to Robert's objections for another minute and then realized that the time had come for her declaration. Summoning all her courage, she walked around the table and took both her husband's hands. "I have been thinking about this for almost three weeks, Robert. You must understand how difficult this decision is for me. . . . I love you with all my heart, but if we must, Nicole and I will go without you. I know that there is a lot of uncertainty in leaving, but life here in New Eden is definitely not healthy for any of us."

"No, no, *no*," Robert said immediately, freeing himself from Ellie and starting to pace wildly around the room. "I don't believe *any* of this. It's all a bad dream." He paused and looked across the room at Ellie. "You cannot take Nicole with you," he said with passion. "Do you hear me? I forbid you to take our daughter."

"*Robert*," Ellie interrupted him with a shout. Tears were now streaming down her cheeks. "Look at me . . . I am your wife, the mother of your daughter. I love you. I beg you to *listen* to what I am saying."

Nicole had come running into the room and was now crying beside her mother. Ellie composed herself before continuing. "I don't believe that you are the only one in this family who is allowed to make decisions. I have that right as well. I can respect your desire not to go, but I am Nicole's mother. If you and I are to be separated, then I believe that it would be better for Nicole to come with me."

Ellie stopped. Robert's face was contorted in anger. He took a step toward her and, for the first time in her life, Ellie feared that Robert was going to hit her.

"What would be better for *me*," Robert shouted, with his right hand raised in a fist, "would be for you to forget this foolishness."

Ellie backed up slightly. Nicole continued to cry. Robert struggled to control himself. "I swore," he said, his voice quavering with emotion, "that nobody and nothing would ever cause me to hurt like that again."

Tears burst from his eyes. "*Goddammit*," he said, smashing his fist down on a nearby table. Without saying anything else, Robert sat down in the chair and buried his face in his hands.

Ellie consoled Nicole and said nothing for several seconds. "I know how painful it was for you to lose your first family," she said at length. "But Robert, this is an entirely different situation. Nobody is going to harm Nicole and me."

She walked over and put her arms around him. "I'm not saying this is an easy decision, Robert," Ellie said. "But I'm convinced it's the right thing for Nicole and me."

Robert returned Ellie's hug, but without much enthusiasm. "I will not keep you and Nicole from going," he said resignedly several seconds later.

"But I don't know what I am going to do. I would like to think about all this over the next several hours, while we're out in Avalon."

"All right, dear," Ellie replied, "but please don't forget that Nicole and I need you even more than your patients do. You are our only husband and father."

9

Nicole could not contain her excitement. As she put the finishing touches on the decorations in the nursery, she imagined what the room would be like when the human children were sharing it with the two avians. Timmy, who was now almost as tall as Nicole, clambered over beside her to inspect her handiwork. He uttered a few jabbers of appreciation.

"Just think, Timmy," Nicole said, knowing that the avian could not understand her exact words but could interpret the timbre of her voice, "when Richard and I return, we will be bringing you three new roommates."

"Are you ready, Nicole?" she heard Richard yell at that moment. "It's almost time for us to leave."

"Yes, darling," she answered. "I'm here in the nursery. Why don't you come and take a look?"

Richard stuck his head in the door and gave the new decorations a perfunctory inspection. "Great, just great," he said. "Now we need to move. This operation requires precise timing."

As they walked together to the Port, Richard informed Nicole that there had been no more reports from the Northern Hemicylinder. The lack of news could indicate that Joan and Eleanor were too involved with the escape, he said, or too close to a possible enemy, or even that the implementation of the escape plan was in trouble. Nicole could not remember seeing Richard so nervous before. She tried to calm him.

"We still don't know if Robert is coming?" Nicole asked a few minutes later as they approached the submarine.

"No. Nor anything at all about how he reacted when Ellie told him the plan. They did show up together in Avalon, as scheduled, but they were busy with his patients. Joan and Eleanor did not have a chance to talk to Ellie after they helped Nai pick up Benjy at the ward."

Richard had checked out the submarine at least twice the day before. Nevertheless, he issued a sigh of relief when the operating system engaged and the craft slid into the water. When they were submerged in the waters of the Cylindrical Sea, both Richard and Nicole were quiet. Each of them was anticipating the emotional reunion that would take place in less than an hour.

Images of all six of her children filed slowly into Nicole's mind. She saw Genevieve, her first child, born on the Earth after her union with Prince Henry. Next in line was serene Simone, whom Nicole had left at the Node with a husband almost sixty years her senior. The two oldest girls were followed in the mental procession by the four children still living in Rama, her wayward daughter Katie, her precious Ellie, and her two sons by Michael O'Toole, Patrick and the mentally handicapped Benjy. *They are all so different*, Nicole thought. *Each a miracle in his or her own way.*

I do not believe in universal truths, Nicole mused as the submarine drew closer to the tunnel under the wall of what was once the avian/sessile habitat, *but there cannot be many humans who have lived through the singular experience of parenting without being irrevocably changed by the process. We all wonder, as our children grow into adults, what we have done, or not done, that has contributed to, or detracted from, the happiness of these special beings we have brought into existence.*

The excitement inside Nicole was overwhelming. Richard checked his watch and began to maneuver the submarine into position for the rendezvous. When their ship broke through the surface of the water, they could see eight figures standing on the shore at the appointed location. When the water stopped running down the window, Nicole recognized Ellie, her husband Robert, Eponine, Nai holding Benjy's hand, and the three small children, including her granddaughter and namesake, whom Nicole had never seen before. Nicole's eyes brimmed with tears. She pounded on the window, knowing that it was senseless, and that none of the people on the shore could possibly hear or see her.

Richard and Nicole heard the gunshots as soon as they opened the door. A worried Robert Turner glanced behind him and then lifted little Nicole quickly off the ground. Ellie and Eponine each picked up one of the Watanabe twins. Galileo struggled against Eponine and received a reprimand from his mother Nai, who was trying to guide Benjy into the submarine.

Another round of gunfire, much closer, occurred just as the boarding party was crossing into the ship. There was no time for embraces. "Max said to leave as soon as we were all on board," Ellie said hurriedly to her parents. "He and Patrick are holding off the platoon that was sent to capture us."

Richard was preparing to close the door when two armed figures, one clutching at his side, burst from the nearby bushes. "Get ready to go," Patrick yelled, shouldering and firing his rifle twice. "They are right behind us."

Max stumbled, but Patrick half carried his wounded friend the final fifty meters to the submarine. Three of the colony soldiers fired upon the ship as it submerged in the moat. For a brief moment, none of the people on board the submarine said anything. Then the tiny compartment exploded in a cacophony of sound. Everyone was shouting and weeping. Both Nicole and Robert bent down over Max, who was sitting with his back against a wall.

"Are you seriously hurt?" Nicole asked.

"Hell, no," Max replied with passion. "There's just a solitary bullet in my gut somewhere. It takes much more firepower than that to kill a son of a bitch like me."

When Nicole stood up and turned around, Benjy was right behind her. "Mama," he said, his arms outstretched and his big body trembling with joy. Nicole and Benjy exchanged a long and powerful embrace in the center of the compartment. Benjy's sobs of happiness reflected the sentiment of every person on the ship.

While they were on board the submarine, the newcomers essentially suspended between two alien worlds, most of the conversation was personal. Nicole spent some private moments with each of her children and held her granddaughter for the first time. Little Nicole did not know what to make of this woman with the gray hair who wanted to hug and kiss her. "This is your grandmother," Ellie said, trying to persuade the child to return Nicole's affection. "She is my mother, Nikki, and she has the same name that you have."

Nicole knew enough about children to understand that it would take some time for the girl to accept her. At first there was some confusion about their common name, and every time someone said "Nicole," both the grandmother and the little girl would turn around. But after Ellie and Robert both started using "Nikki" for the child, the rest of the group quickly followed suit.

Before the submarine even reached New York, Benjy was showing his mother that his reading had significantly improved. Nai had been an excellent teacher. Benjy had brought two books in his backpack, one a collection of the tales of Hans Christian Andersen written three centuries earlier. Benjy's favorite story was "The Ugly Duckling," which he read in its entirety as both his delighted mother and his teacher sat beside him.

There was a wonderful, ingenuous excitement in his voice when the spurned duckling turned into a beautiful swan.

"I am very proud of you, darling," Nicole said when Benjy was finished reading. "And I thank you, Nai," she said to her friend, "from the bottom of my heart."

"It's been a lot of fun working with Benjy," the Thai woman replied. "I had forgotten what a thrill it was to teach an interested and appreciative pupil."

Robert Turner cleaned Max Puckett's wound and removed the bullet. His procedure was closely monitored by the five-year-old Watanabe twins, both of whom were fascinated by the inside of Max's body. The aggressive Galileo was always pushing for the better view; Nai had to adjudicate two brotherly disputes in favor of Kepler.

Dr. Turner confirmed Max's statement that the wound was not serious and prescribed a short period of convalescence.

"I guess I'll just have to take it easy," Max said, winking at Eponine. "Which is what I was planning to do anyway. I don't think there will be too many pigs or chickens in this alien city of skyscrapers. And I don't know a goddamn thing about *bi-ots*."

Nicole had a brief conversation with Eponine, just before the submarine arrived at the Port, in which she thanked Ellie's erstwhile teacher profusely for everything she and Max had done for the family. Eponine accepted the thanks graciously and told Nicole that Patrick had been "absolutely fantastic" in helping them with all aspects of the escape. "He has grown into a superb young man," Eponine said.

"How is your health, then?" Nicole asked Eponine delicately a few moments later.

The Frenchwoman shrugged. "The good doctor says the RV-41 virus is still there, poised and waiting for an opportunity to overwhelm my immune system. Whenever that happens, I should have between six months and a year more to live."

Patrick informed Richard that Joan and Eleanor had tried to decoy the Nakamura platoon by making a lot of noise, as they had been programmed to do, and had almost certainly been captured and destroyed.

"I'm sorry about Joan and Eleanor," Nicole said to Richard during a rare private moment on board the submarine. "I know how much your little robots mean to you."

"They served their purpose," Richard replied. He forced a smile. "After all, wasn't it you who told me once they're not the same as people?"

Nicole reached up and kissed her husband.

None of the new escapees had ever been in New York as an adult. Nicole's three children had all been born on the island and had lived there in their early childhood, but a child has a much different sense of place than an adult. Even Ellie, Patrick, and Benjy were awestruck when they first stepped on the shore and saw the tall, thin silhouettes reaching toward the Rama sky in the near darkness.

Max Puckett was uncharacteristically speechless. He stood beside Eponine, holding her hand, and gawked at the thin, towering spires rising over two hundred meters above the island. "This is too damn much for an Arkansas farm boy," he said at length, shaking his head. Max and Eponine walked at the end of the procession that was winding its way toward the lair which Richard and Nicole had converted into a multifamily apartment for all of them to share.

"Who built all this?" Robert Turner asked Richard as the troupe paused briefly in front of a giant polyhedron. Robert was growing increasingly apprehensive. He had been reluctant to come with Ellie and Nikki in the first place, and he was now rapidly becoming convinced that he had indeed made a big mistake.

"Probably the engineers at the Node," Richard answered. "Although we can't know for certain. We humans have added new construction in our habitat. It's possible that whoever, or whatever, lived here long ago might have built a few or even all of these amazing buildings."

"Where are they now?" Robert asked next, more than a little frightened at the prospect of encountering beings with the technological expertise necessary to create such impressive edifices.

"We have no way of knowing. According to the Eagle, this Rama spacecraft has been making voyages to discover spacefaring species for thousands of years. Somewhere in our part of the galaxy is another spacefarer who would have been comfortable in an environment like this. What that creature was, or is, and why it wanted to live in and among these incredible skyscrapers is a riddle we will probably never answer."

"What about the avians and the octospiders, Uncle Richard?" Patrick asked. "Are they still living here in New York?"

"I have not seen any avians on the island since I arrived, except of course for the hatchlings that we are raising. But there are still octospiders around. Your mother and I encountered some of them when we were exploring behind the black screen."

At that moment a centipede biot approached the procession from a side alley. Richard shone his flashlight in its direction. Robert Turner momentarily froze with fear, but he followed Richard's instructions and moved out of the way as the biot trundled by.

"Skyscrapers built by ghosts, octospiders, centipede biots," Robert grumbled. "What a lovely place!"

"In my opinion it's a hell of a lot better than living under that tyrant Nakamura," Richard said. "At least here we're free and can make our own decisions."

"Wakefield," Max Puckett shouted from the back of the line. "What would happen if we didn't move out of the way of one of those centipede biots?"

"I don't know for sure, Max," Richard replied. "But it would probably go over or around you just as if you were an inanimate object."

It was Nicole's turn to be the tour guide when they arrived at the lair. She personally showed each person his or her quarters. There was one room for Max and Eponine, another for Ellie and Robert, and a room divided by a partition for Patrick and Nai. The large nursery had been subdivided to provide space and privacy for Benjy, the three children, and the two avians. Richard and Nicole had also decided to use the small area adjacent to their bedroom as a common dining room for the entire group.

While the adults unpacked the meager belongings they had loaded into backpacks, the children had their first experience with Tammy and Timmy. The avians did not know what to make of the little humans, especially Galileo, who insisted on pulling or tweaking anything he could touch. After about an hour of such treatment, Timmy scratched Galileo lightly with one of his talons as a warning, and the boy raised an incredible din.

"I just don't understand it," Richard said to Nai in apology. "The avians are really very gentle creatures."

"I *do* understand," Nai replied. "Galileo was almost certainly up to some mischief." She sighed. "It's amazing, you know. You raise two children exactly the same way, and they turn out so differently. Kepler is so good he's almost an angel—I can hardly teach him to defend himself. And Galileo pays almost no attention to anything I tell him."

When everyone had finished unpacking, Nicole completed the tour, including the two bathrooms, the corridors, the suspension tanks where the family had stayed during the period of high acceleration between the Earth and the Node, and finally the White Room, with the black screen and keyboard, which was also Richard and Nicole's bedroom. Richard demonstrated how the black screen worked by requesting, and receiving about an hour later, some new and simple toys for the children. He also gave Robert and Max each a copy of a short command dictionary that would allow them to use the keyboard.

The children were all asleep soon after dinner. The adults gathered in the White Room. Max asked questions about the octospiders. In the course of describing their adventures behind the black screen, Nicole mentioned her heart irregularities. Robert insisted on examining her right away.

Ellie helped Robert with the examination. Robert had brought as much practical medical equipment as he could fit in his backpack, including all the miniaturized instruments and monitors necessary to do a full electrocardiogram, or EKG. The results were not good, but not as bad as Nicole had privately feared. Before bedtime Robert informed the rest of the family that the years had definitely taken their toll on Nicole's heart, but that he didn't think she would require surgery in the immediate future. Robert advised Nicole to take it easy, even though he knew that his mother-in-law would probably ignore his prescription.

When everyone was asleep, Richard and Nicole moved the furniture to make room for their mats. They lay side by side, holding hands. "Are you happy?" Richard asked.

"Yes," Nicole answered, "very. It's really wonderful to have all the children here." She leaned over and gave Richard a kiss. "I am also exhausted, husband of mine, but I'm not about to go to sleep without first thanking you for arranging all of this."

"They're my children too, you know," he said.

"Yes, darling," Nicole said, lying down on her back again. "But I know that you would never have done all this if it weren't for me. You would have been content to stay here with the hatchlings, all your gadgets, and the extraterrestrial mysteries."

"Maybe," Richard said. "But I also am delighted to have everyone in our lair. . . . By the way, did you have a chance to talk to Patrick about Katie?"

"Only briefly," Nicole replied. She sighed. "I could tell from his eyes that he is still very worried about her."

"Aren't we all?" Richard said softly. They lay in silence for a couple of minutes before Richard propped himself up on an elbow. "I want you to know," he said, "that I think our granddaughter is absolutely precious."

"So do I," Nicole replied with a laugh, "but there's not a chance that we could be considered unbiased on the subject."

"Hey, does having Nikki with us mean that I can no longer call *you* Nikki, not even at special moments?"

Nicole turned her head to look at Richard. He was grinning. She had seen that particular expression on his face many times before. "Go to sleep," Nicole said with another short laugh. "I'm too emotionally exhausted for anything else tonight."

In the beginning time passed very quickly. There was so much to do, so much fascinating territory to explore. Even though it was perpetually dark in the mysterious city above them, the family made regular excursions into New York. Virtually every place on the island had a special story that Richard or Nicole could tell. "It was here," Nicole said one afternoon, shining her flashlight at the huge lattice that hung suspended between two skyscrapers like a spider web, "that I rescued the trapped avian, who subsequently invited me into its lair."

"Down there," she said on another occasion, when they were in the large barn with its peculiar pits and spheres, "I was trapped for many days and thought I was going to die."

The extended family developed a set of rules to keep the children from getting into trouble. The rules were not needed for little Nikki, who hardly ever wandered far from her mother and doting grandfather, but the boys Kepler and Galileo were difficult to constrain. The Watanabe twins seemed to possess infinite energy. Once they were found bouncing on the hammocks in the suspension tanks, as if the hammocks were trampolines. Another time Galileo and Kepler "borrowed" the family flashlights and went topside, without adult supervision, to explore New York. It was ten nervous hours before the boys were located in the maze of alleys and streets on the far side of the island.

The avians practiced flying almost every day. The children delighted in accompanying their birdlike friends to the plazas, where there was more room for Tammy and Timmy to display their developing skills. Richard always took Nikki to watch the avians fly. In fact, he took his granddaughter with him everywhere he went. From time to time Nikki would walk, but mostly Richard carried her in a comfortable papooselike contraption that he affixed to his back. The unlikely pair were inseparable. Richard became Nikki's main teacher as well. Very early he announced to everyone that his granddaughter was a mathematical genius.

At night he would regale Nicole with Nikki's latest exploits. "Do you know what she did today?" he would say, usually when he and Nicole were alone in bed.

"No, dear," was Nicole's standard reply; she knew very well that neither she nor Richard would sleep until he told her.

"I asked her how many black balls she would have if she already had three and I gave her two more." Here there was a dramatic pause. "And do you know what she answered?" Another dramatic pause. "*Five!* She said five. And this little girl just had her second birthday last week."

Nicole was thrilled by Richard's interest in Nikki. For both the little girl and the aging man, it was a perfect match. As a parent, Richard had never been able to overcome both his own repressed emotional problems and his acute sense of responsibility, so this was the first time in his life that he had experienced the joy of truly innocent love. Nikki's father, Robert, on the other hand, was a great doctor, but he was not a very warm person and he did not fully appreciate the purposeless time periods that parents must spend with their children.

Patrick and Nicole had several long talks about Katie, all of which left Nicole feeling extremely depressed. Patrick did not hide from his mother the fact that Katie was deeply involved in all of Nakamura's machinations, that she drank often and too much, and that she had been sexually promiscuous. He did not tell Nicole that Katie was managing Nakamura's prostitution business, or that he suspected his sister had become a drug addict.

10

Their near perfect existence in New York continued until early one morning, when Richard and Nikki were topside together along the northern ramparts of the island. Actually it was the little girl who first saw the silhouettes of the ships in the dim Raman light. She pointed out across the dark water. "Look, Boobah," she said, "Nikki sees something."

Richard's weakened eyes could not detect anything in the darkness, and his flashlight beam did not travel far enough to reach whatever it was that Nikki was seeing. Richard pulled out the powerful binoculars that he always carried with him and confirmed that there were indeed two vessels in the middle of the Cylindrical Sea. Richard placed Nikki in the carrier on his back and hurried home to the lair.

The rest of the family was just waking up and had difficulty initially understanding why Richard was so alarmed. "But who else could it be in a boat?" he said. "Especially on the northern side. It has to be an exploration party sent by Nakamura."

A family council was held over breakfast. Everyone agreed that they were facing a serious crisis. When Patrick confessed that he had seen Katie on the day of the escape, primarily because he had wanted to tell his sister good-bye, and that he had made a few unusual comments which had caused Katie to start asking questions, Nicole and the others became silent.

"I didn't say anything specific," Patrick said apologetically, "but it was still a dumb thing to do. Katie is very smart. After we all disappeared, she must have put all the pieces together."

"But what do we do now?" Robert Turner voiced everyone's apprehension. "Katie knows New York very well—she was almost a teenager when she left here—and she can lead Nakamura's men directly to this lair. We'll be sitting ducks for them down here."

"Is there any other place we can go?" Max asked.

"Not really," Richard replied. "The old avian lair is empty, but I don't know how we would feed ourselves down there. The octospider lair was also vacant when I visited it several months ago, but I haven't been inside their domain again since Nicole arrived in New York. We must assume, of course, based on what happened when Nicole and I went exploring, that our friends with the black and gold tentacles are still around. Even if they aren't living in their old lair anymore, we would still have the same problem of obtaining food if we were to move over there."

"What about the area behind the screen, Uncle Richard?" Patrick asked. "You said that's where our food is manufactured. Maybe we could find a couple of rooms there."

"I'm not very optimistic," Richard said after a short pause, "but your suggestion is probably our only reasonable option at this point."

The family decided that Richard, Max, and Patrick would reconnoiter the region behind the black screen, both to find out exactly where the human food was being produced and to determine if another suitable living area existed. Robert, Benjy, the women, and the children would stay in the lair. Their assignment was to start developing the procedures for a rapid evacuation of their living quarters, in case such action ever became necessary.

Before going, Richard finished testing a new radio system that he had designed in his spare time. It was strong enough that the explorers and the rest of the family would be able to remain in radio contact during the entire time that they were separated. The existence of the radio link made it easier for Richard and Nicole to convince Max Puckett to leave his rifle in the lair.

The three men had no difficulty following the map in Richard's computer and reaching the boiler room that Richard and Nicole had visited on their previous exploration. Max and Patrick both stared in wonder at the twelve huge boilers, the vast area of neatly arranged raw materials, and the many varieties of biots scurrying about. The factory was active. In fact, every single one of the boilers was involved in some kind of manufacturing process.

"All right," Richard said into his radio to Nicole back in the lair. "We're here and we're ready. Place the dinner order and we'll see what happens."

Less than a minute later one of the boilers closest to the three men terminated whatever it was doing. Meanwhile, not far from the hut behind the boilers, three biots that looked like boxcars with hands moved out into the arrays of raw material, quickly picking up small quantities of many different items. These three biots next converged on the inactive boiler system near Richard, Max, and Patrick, where they emptied their containers onto the conveyor belt entering the boiler. Immediately the men heard the boiler surge into active operation. A long, skinny biot, resembling three crickets tied together in a row, each with a bowl-shaped carapace, crawled up on the conveyor belt system when the short manufacturing process was almost finished. Moments later, the boiler stopped again and the processed material came out on the conveyor belt. The segmented cricket biot deployed a scoop from its rear end, placed all the human food upon its backs, and scampered quickly away.

"Well, I'll be goddamned," Max said, watching the cricket biot disappear down the corridor behind the hut. Before any of the men could say anything else, another set of boxcars with hands loaded the conveyor belts with thick, long rods, and in less than a minute the boiler that had made their food was operating for another purpose.

"What a fantastic system," Richard exclaimed. "It must have a complex interrupt process, with food orders at the top of the priority queue. I can't believe—"

"Hold on just a damn minute," Max interrupted, "and repeat what you just said in normal English."

"We have automatic translation subroutines back at the lair—I designed them originally when we were here years ago," Richard said excitedly. "When Nicole entered chicken, potatoes, and spinach into her own computer, a listing of keyboard commands which represent the complex chemicals in those particular foods was printed on her output buffer. After I signaled that we were ready, she typed that string of commands on the keyboard. They were immediately received here and what we saw was the response. At the time, all the processing systems were active; however, the Raman equivalent of a computer here in this factory recognized that the incoming request was for food, and made it the highest priority."

"Are you saying, Uncle Richard," Patrick said, "that the controlling computer here shut down that operating boiler so that it could make our food?"

"Yes, indeed," said Richard.

Max had moved some distance away and was staring at the other boilers in the huge factory. Richard and Patrick walked over beside him.

"When I was a little boy, about eight or nine," Max said, "my father and I went on our first overnight camping trip, up in the Ozarks several hours from our farm. It was a magnificent night and the sky was full of stars. I remember lying on my back on my sleeping bag and staring at all those tiny twinkling lights in the sky. That night I had a big, big thought for an

Arkansas farm boy. I wondered how many alien children, out there somewhere in the universe, were looking up at the stars at exactly that moment and realizing, for the first time, how very small their tiny domain was in the overall scheme of the cosmos."

Max turned around and smiled at his two friends. "That's one of the reasons I remained a farmer," he said with a laugh. "With my chickens and pigs, I was always important. I brought them their food. It was a major event when ole Max showed up at their pen. . . ."

He paused for a moment. Neither Richard nor Patrick said anything. "I think that deep down I always wanted to be an astronomer," Max continued, "to see if I could understand the mysteries of the universe. But every time I thought about billions of years and trillions of kilometers, I became depressed. I couldn't stand the feeling of complete and total insignificance that came over me. It was as if a voice inside my head was saying, over and over, 'Puckett, you aren't shit. You are absolutely zero.'"

"But *knowing* that insignificance, especially being able to measure it, makes us humans very special," Richard said quietly.

"Now we're talking philosophy," Max replied, "and I'm completely out of my element. I'm comfortable with farm animals, tequila, and even wild midwestern thunderstorms. All this," Max said, waving his arms at the boilers and the factory, "scares the shit out of me. If I had known, when I signed up for that Martian colony, that I would meet machines that are smarter than people—"

"Richard, Richard," they all heard Nicole's anxious voice on the radio. "We have an emergency. Ellie has just returned from the northern shore. Four large boats are about to land. Ellie says she's positive she spotted a police uniform on one of the men. Also, she has reported some kind of large rainbow in the south. Can you get back here in a few minutes?"

"No we can't," Richard answered. "We're still down in the room with the boilers. We must be at least three and a half kilometers away. Did Ellie say how many people might be on each boat?"

"I would guess about ten or twelve, Dad," Ellie replied. "I didn't stay around to count them. But the boats were not the only unusual thing I saw while I was topside. During my run back to the lair, the southern sky lit up with wild bursts of color that eventually became a giant rainbow. It's near where you told us the Big Horn should be."

Ten seconds later Richard shouted into the radio. "Listen to me, Nicole, Ellie, all of you. Evacuate our lair immediately. Take the children, the hatchlings, the melons, the sessile material, the two rifles, all the food, and as many personal belongings as you can comfortably carry. Leave *our* stuff alone—we have enough on our backs to survive in an emergency. Go directly to the octospider lair and wait for us in that large room that was a photo gallery years ago. Nakamura's troops will come to our lair first. When they don't find us, if Katie's with them, they may go to the octospider lair as well, but I don't believe they will go into the tunnels there."

"What about you and Max and Patrick?" Nicole asked.

"We'll come back as fast as we can. If there is nobody— By the way, Nicole, leave a transmitter, with the volume on high, in the White Room, and another in the nursery. That way we'll know if anybody is in our lair. . . . Anyway, as I was saying, if our home has not been invaded, we'll join you right away. If Nakamura's men are occupying our living quarters, we'll try to find another entrance to the octospider lair from down here. There must be one."

"All right," Nicole interrupted. "We must get started with the packing. I'll leave the receiver on in case you need us."

"So you think we'll be safest in the octospider lair?" Max said after Richard had switched off his transmitter.

"It's a choice," Richard said with a wan smile. "There are too many unknowns here behind the screen. And we know for certain we won't be safe if Nakamura's police and troops find us. The octospiders may not even be living in their lair anymore. Besides, as Nicole has said many times, we have no unambiguous evidence that the octos are hostile."

The men moved as quickly as they could. At one point they halted briefly while Patrick transferred some of the weight off Richard's pack into his own. Both Richard and Max were sweating profusely by the time they reached the Y in the corridor.

"We must stop for a minute," Max said to Patrick, who was out in front of his two older companions. "Your Uncle Richard needs a rest."

Patrick pulled a water bottle from his pack and passed it around. Richard drank eagerly from the bottle, wiped his brow with a handkerchief, and after a minute's rest began jogging again toward the lair.

About five hundred meters away from the small platform behind the black screen, Richard's receiver began picking up indistinct noises from the inside of the lair. "Maybe someone in the family forgot something important," Richard said, slowing down to listen, "and came back to retrieve it."

A short time later the three men heard a voice they could not identify. They stopped and waited. "It looks as if some kind of animal has been living back here," the voice said. "Why don't you come take a look?"

"Damn," said a second voice. "They have definitely been here recently. I wonder how long ago they left."

"Captain Bauer," someone shouted. "What do you want me to do with all this electronic gear?"

"Leave it for now," the second voice answered. "The rest of the troops should be down in a few minutes. We'll decide what to do then."

Richard, Max, and Patrick sat quietly in the dark tunnel. For about a minute they didn't hear anything on the receiver. Apparently none of the members of the search party was in the White Room or the nursery during that time. Then the three men heard Franz Bauer's voice again.

"What's that, Morgan?" Bauer said. "I can barely hear you. . . . There's some kind of racket. . . . What? Fireworks? Colors? . . . What in the world are you talking about? All right. All right. We'll come up immediately."

For another fifteen seconds the receiver was quiet. "Ah, here you are, Pfeiffer," they then heard Captain Bauer say plainly. "Round up the other men and let's go back upstairs. Morgan says there's an amazing fireworks demonstration in the southern sky. Most of the troops were already spooked by the skyscrapers and the dark. I'm going up to calm everyone's nerves."

"This is our chance," Richard whispered, rising to his feet. "They will certainly be out of the lair for a few minutes." He started to run and then stopped himself. "We may need to separate. Do both of you remember how to find the octospider lair?"

Max shook his head. "I've never been over—"

"Here," Richard said, handing Max his portable computer. "Enter an *M* and a *P* for an overview of New York. The octospider lair is marked with a red circle. If you touch *L*, followed by another *L*, a map of the inside of their lair will be displayed. Now let's go, while we still have some time."

Richard, Max, and Patrick encountered no troops inside their lair. A pair of guards were stationed, however, a few meters away from the exit to New York. Fortunately, the guards were so transfixed by the fireworks in the Rama sky above their heads that they didn't hear the three men slipping up the stairs behind them. For safety, the threesome split up, each taking a different route to the octospider lair.

Richard and Patrick arrived at their destination within a minute of each other, but Max was delayed. As luck would have it, the route he had chosen led through one of the plazas where five or six of the colony troops had gathered for a better view of the fireworks. Max raced down an alley and huddled against one of the buildings. He pulled out the computer and studied the map on the monitor, trying to figure out an alternate path to the octospider lair.

Meanwhile, the spectacular fireworks show continued overhead. Max glanced up and was dazzled as a great blue ball exploded, throwing hundreds of rays of blue light in all directions. For almost a minute, Max watched the hypnotic display. It was grander than anything he had ever seen on Earth.

When Max finally reached the octospider lair, he descended the ramp quickly and entered the cathedral room from which the four tunnels led into the other parts of the lair. Max entered two *L*s on the computer and the map of the octospider domain appeared on the tiny monitor. Max was so engrossed in the map that at first he did not hear the sound of dragging mechanical brushes accompanied by a soft, high-pitched whine.

He did not look up until the sound became quite loud. When Max finally raised his head, the large octospider was standing no more than five meters away from him. The sight of the creature sent powerful shivers down Max's spine. He stood quite still and fought against his desire to flee. The creamy liquid in the octospider's single lens moved from side to side, but the alien did not advance any closer to Max.

Out of one of the parallel indentations on both sides of the lens came a burst of purple color, which circumnavigated the octospider's spherical head, followed by bands of other colors, all of which disappeared into the second of the two parallel slits. When the same color pattern repeated, Max, whose heart was pounding so fiercely he could feel it in his jaw, shook his head and said, "I don't understand." The octospider hesitated for a moment and then lifted two of its tentacles off the ground, clearly pointing in the direction of one of the four tunnels. As if to underscore its point, the octo shuffled in that general direction and then repeated the gesture.

Max stood up and walked slowly toward the indicated tunnel, being careful not to come too close to the octospider. When he reached the entrance, another series of color splashes raced around the head of the alien. "Thank you very much," Max said politely as he turned and walked into the passageway.

He didn't even stop to look at his map until he was three or four hundred meters into the tunnel. As Max walked along, the lights always came on automatically in front of him and were extinguished in the tunnel segments through which he had already passed. When he did finally examine the map carefully, Max discovered that he was not far from the designated room.

A few minutes later Max entered the chamber where the rest of the family was gathered. He had a big grin on his face. "You'll never guess who I just met," Max said only moments before Eponine greeted him with an embrace.

Soon after Max finished entertaining everyone with the story of his encounter with the octospider, Richard and Patrick cautiously backtracked to the cathedral room, stopping every hundred meters or so and listening carefully for the telltale sounds of the aliens. They heard nothing. Nor did they hear or see anything that indicated the forces dispatched from New Eden were in the vicinity. After about an hour, Richard and Patrick returned to the rest of the group and joined in the discussion of what they should do next.

The extended family had enough food for five days, maybe six if each portion was carefully rationed. Water was available at the cistern near the cathedral room. Everyone quickly agreed that the search party from New Eden, at least this first one, would probably not stay in New York too long. There was a short debate about whether or not Katie might have told

Captain Bauer and his men the location of the octospider lair. On one critical point there was no argument: The next day or two was the most likely time period for them to be discovered by the other humans. As a result, except for physical necessities, none of the family left the large room in which they were staying for the next thirty-six hours.

At the end of that time the whole group, especially the hatchlings and the twins, had a bad case of cabin fever. Richard and Nai took Tammy, Timmy, Benjy, and the small children out into the passageway, trying unsuccessfully to keep them quiet, and led them away from the cathedral room, toward the vertical corridor with the protruding spikes that descended deeper into the octospider lair. Richard, who had Nikki on his back most of the time, warned Nai and the twins several times about the dangers of the area they were approaching. Even so, very soon after the tunnel widened and they arrived at the vertical corridor, the impetuous Galileo climbed into the barrel-shaped hole before his mother could stop him. He quickly became frozen with fright. Richard had to rescue the boy from his precarious perch on two spikes just a short distance below the level of the walkway that encircled the top of the huge abyss. The young avians, delighted to be able to fly again, soared freely around the area and twice dropped several meters into the dark chasm, but they never went deep enough to trigger the next lower bank of lights.

Before returning to the rest of the family, Richard took Benjy with him for a quick inspection of what Richard and Nicole had always called the octospider museum. This large room, located several hundred meters from the vertical corridor, was still completely empty. Several hours later, following Richard's suggestion, half of the extended family moved into the museum to give everyone more living space.

On the third day of their stay in the octospider lair, Richard and Max decided that someone should try to discover if the colony troops were still in New York. Patrick was the logical choice to be the family scout. Richard's and Max's instructions to Patrick were straightforward—he was to proceed cautiously to the cathedral room and then up the ramp into New York. From there, using his flashlight and portable computer as little as possible, he should cross to the northern shore of the island and see if the boats were still there. Whatever the result of his investigation, he should return directly to the lair and give them a full report.

"There is one other thing to remember," Richard said, "that is extremely important. If at any time you hear either an octospider or a soldier, you are to turn around immediately and come back to us. But with this one added proviso: Under no circumstances should any human see you descend into this lair. You cannot do anything that will endanger the rest of us."

Max insisted that Patrick should take one of the two rifles. Richard and Nicole did not argue. After receiving best wishes from everybody,

Patrick set out on his scouting mission. He had only walked five hundred meters down the tunnel, however, when he heard a noise in front of him. He stopped to listen, but could not identify what he was hearing. After another hundred meters some of the sounds began to resolve themselves. Patrick definitely heard the sound of dragging brushes several times. There was some clanging as well, as if metal objects were hitting against each other, or against a wall. He listened for several minutes and then, remembering his instructions, he returned to his family and friends.

After a long discussion Patrick was sent out again. He was told this time to approach as close to the octospiders as he dared and to watch them quietly for as long as he could. Again he heard the dragging brush sound as he drew close to the cathedral room. But when Patrick actually reached the large chamber at the bottom of the ramp, there were no octospiders around. Where had they gone? he wondered. Patrick's first impulse was to turn around and go back in the direction from which he had come. However, since he had not encountered any actual octospiders yet, he decided that he might as well go up the ramp, out into New York, and carry out the remainder of his earlier assignment.

Patrick was shocked to discover, about a minute later, that the exit from the octospider lair had been sealed tight with a thick combination of metal rods and a cementlike material. He could barely see through the cover, and it was certainly sufficiently heavy that all the humans together would not be able to budge it. *The octospiders have done this*, he thought immediately, *but why have they trapped us here?*

Before returning to give his report, Patrick inspected the cathedral room and found that one of the four egress tunnels had also been sealed with what appeared to be a thick door or gate. *That must have been the tunnel that led to the canal*, he thought. Patrick remained in the area for another ten minutes, listening for the sounds of the octospiders, but heard nothing more.

11

"So the octospiders have never done anything hostile?" Max was saying angrily. "Then what the hell do you call this? We're fucking trapped." He shook his head vigorously. "I thought it was stupid to come here in the first place."

"Please, Max," Eponine said. "Let's not argue. Fighting among ourselves is not going to help."

All the adults except Nai and Benjy had trekked the one kilometer down the passageway to the cathedral room to examine what the octospiders had done. The humans were indeed sealed inside the lair. Two of the three open tunnels leading out of the chamber went to the vertical corridor and the third, they quickly discovered, led to a large, empty storeroom from which there was no exit.

"Well, we'd better think of something fast," Max said. "We have only four days worth of food and absolutely no idea where to get any more."

"I'm sorry, Max," Nicole said, "but I still think Richard's initial decision was correct. If we had stayed in our lair, we would have been captured and taken back to New Eden, where we almost certainly would have been executed."

"Maybe," Max interrupted. "And maybe not. At least in that case the children would have been spared. And I don't think either Benjy or the doctor would have been killed."

"This is all academic," Richard said, "and doesn't deal with our main problem, which is, what do we do now?"

"All right, genius," Max said with a sting in his voice. "This has been your show so far. What do you suggest?"

Again Eponine interceded. "You're being unfair, Max. It's not Richard's fault we're in this predicament. And as I said before, it doesn't help."

"Okay, okay," Max said. He walked toward the passage that led to the storeroom. "I'm going in this tunnel to calm down and to smoke a cigarette." He glanced back at Eponine. "Do you want to share? We have exactly twenty-nine left after we smoke this one."

Eponine smiled faintly at Nicole and Ellie. "He's still pissed off at me for not taking all our cigarettes when we evacuated the lair," she said quietly. "Don't worry. Max has a bad temper, but he gets over it fast. We'll be back in a few minutes."

"What *is* your plan, darling?" Nicole said to Richard a few seconds after Max and Eponine had left.

"We don't have much choice," Richard said grimly. "A bare minimum number of adults should stay with Benjy, the children, and the avians, while the rest of us explore this lair as quickly as possible. I have a hard time believing that the octospiders really intend for us to starve to death."

"Excuse me, Richard," Robert Turner now said, speaking for the first time since Patrick had reported that the exit to New York was sealed, "but aren't you again assuming that the octospiders are friendly? Suppose they're not, or more likely in my opinion, suppose our survival is insignificant to them one way or the other, and that they simply sealed off this lair to protect themselves from all the humans who have recently appeared. . . ."

Robert stopped, apparently having lost his train of thought. "What I was trying to say," he continued a few seconds later, "is that the children, including your granddaughter, are in considerable jeopardy—psychological as well as physical, I might add—in our current situation, and I would be against any plan that left them unprotected and vulnerable—"

"You're right, Robert," Richard interrupted. "Several adults, including at least one man, must stay with Benjy and the children. In fact, Nai must have her hands full right this minute. Why don't you, Patrick, and Ellie return to the children now? Nicole and I will wait for Max and Eponine and join you shortly."

Richard and Nicole were alone after the others departed. "Ellie says that Robert is angry most of the time now," Nicole said quietly, "but he doesn't know how to express his anger constructively. He told her he thinks the whole enterprise has been a mistake from the beginning, and he spends hours brooding about it. Ellie says she's even worried about his stability."

Richard shook his head. "Maybe it was a mistake," he said. "Maybe you and I should have lived the rest of our life here alone. I just thought—"

At that moment Max and Eponine came back into the chamber. "I want to apologize," Max said, extending his hand, "to both of you. I guess I let my fear and frustration get the best of me."

"Thank you, Max," Nicole answered. "But an apology really isn't necessary. It would be ridiculous to assume that this many people could go through an experience like this without any disagreements."

Everyone was together in the museum. "Let's review the plan one more time," Richard said. "The five of us will climb down the spikes and explore the area around the subway platform. We will thoroughly investigate every tunnel we can find. Then, if we have not found any means of escape and the large subway is indeed there waiting, Max, Eponine, Nicole, and I will go on board. At that point Patrick will climb back up and rejoin you here in the museum."

"Don't you think having all four of you on the subway is reckless?" Robert asked. "Why not just two of you at first? . . . What if the subway leaves and never comes back?"

"Time is our enemy, Robert," Richard answered. "If we weren't running so low on food, then we could follow a more conservative plan. In that case maybe only two of us would enter the subway. But what if the subway leads to more than one place? Since we have already decided that for safety we will explore only in pairs, it could take us a long time to find the escape route with just a single couple doing the searching."

There was a protracted silence in the room until Timmy began to jabber at his sister. Nikki wandered over and began to stroke the avian's velvet underside. "I don't pretend that I have all the answers," Richard said. "Nor do I underestimate the seriousness of our situation. But if there is a way out of here—and both Nicole and I believe that there must be—then the sooner we find it, the better."

"Assuming that all four of you do take the subway," Patrick now asked, "how long do we wait for you here in the museum?"

"That's a difficult question," Richard replied. "You have enough food for four more days, and the plentiful water at the cistern should keep you alive for some period after that. . . . I don't know, Patrick. I guess you should stay here for at least two or three days. After that, you have to make your own decision. If it is at all possible, one or more of us will return."

Benjy had been following the conversation with rapt attention. He obviously understood more or less what was happening, for he began to cry softly. Nicole went over to comfort him. "Don't worry, son," she said. "Everything is going to be all right."

The child-man looked up at his mother. "I hope so, Mom-ma," he said, "but I'm scared."

Galileo Watanabe suddenly jumped up and ran across the room to where the two rifles were leaning against the wall. "If one of those octospider things comes in here," he said, touching the closest rifle for a few seconds before Max lifted it free of the boy's grasp, "then I'll shoot it. *Bang! Bang!*"

His shouts caused the avians to shriek and little Nikki to cry. After Ellie wiped away her daughter's tears, Max and Patrick shouldered the rifles and all five of the explorers said their good-byes. Ellie walked out into the tunnel with them. "I didn't want to say this in front of the children," she said, "but what *should* we do if we see an octospider while you're gone?"

"Try not to panic," Richard answered.

"And don't do anything aggressive," Nicole added.

"Grab Nikki and run like hell," Max said with a wink.

Nothing unusual happened while they climbed down the spikes. Just as they had years earlier, the lights at the next lower level always turned on when anyone descending approached an unlit area. All five of the explorers were on the subway platform in less than an hour. "Now we'll find out if those mysterious vehicles are still operating," Richard said.

In the center of the circular platform there was a smaller hole, also round and with metal spikes protruding from its sides, that descended deeper into the darkness. On opposite ends of the platform, ninety degrees away to the left and right from where the five of them were standing, two dark tunnels were cut into the rock and metal. One of the tunnels was large, five or six meters from top to bottom, while the opposite tunnel was almost exactly an order of magnitude smaller. When Richard approached to within twenty degrees of the large tunnel, it suddenly became illuminated and its interior could be clearly seen. The tunnel looked like a large sewer pipe back on Earth.

The rest of the exploration party hurried over beside Richard as soon as the first whooshing sound was heard coming from the tunnel. Less than a minute later a subway sped around a distant corner and headed rapidly toward them, stopping with its front end a meter or so shy of where the spiked corridor continued to descend.

The inside of the subway was also illuminated. There were no seats, but there were vertical rods from the ceiling to the floor, scattered in the car in seemingly random fashion. The door slid open about fifteen seconds after the subway arrived. On the opposite side of the platform an identical vehicle, exactly one-tenth as large, pulled up and stopped no more than five seconds later.

Even though Max, Patrick, and Eponine had all heard stories about the two ghost subways many times, actually seeing the vehicles left all three of them full of apprehension. "Are you really serious, my friend?" Max said to Richard after the two men quickly examined the outside of the larger subway. "Do you really intend to *board* that damn thing if we find no other way out?"

Richard nodded.

"But it could go *any*where," Max said. "We don't have the foggiest fucking idea what it is, or who built it, or what the hell it's doing here. And once we're on board, we're completely helpless."

"That's right," Richard said. He smiled wanly. "Max, you have an excellent grasp of our situation."

Max shook his head. "Well, we'd better find something down in this damn hole, because I don't know if Eponine and I—"

"All right," Patrick said, approaching the other two men. "I guess it's time for the next phase of this operation. Come on, Max, are you ready for some more spike climbing?"

Richard did not have any of his clever robots to place in the smaller subway. He did, however, have in his possession a miniature camera with a crude mobility system that he hoped would weigh enough to activate the smaller subway. "Under any circumstances," he told the others, "the small tunnel does not provide a possible exit for us. I just want to determine for myself if anything significant has changed during these years. Besides, there does not seem to be any reason, at least not yet, for more than two of us to descend any farther."

While Max and Patrick were climbing slowly down the additional spikes and Richard was absorbed with a final checkout of his mobile camera, Nicole and Eponine strolled around the platform. "How's it going, farmer?" Eponine said to Max on the radio.

"Fine so far," he replied. "But we're only about ten meters below you. These spikes are not as close together as the ones above, so we're being more cautious."

"Your relationship with Max must have really blossomed while I was in prison," Nicole commented a few moments later.

"Yes, it did," Eponine replied easily. "Quite frankly, it surprised me. I didn't think a man was capable of having a serious affair with someone who . . . you know . . . but I underestimated Max. He is really an unusual person. Underneath that brusque, macho exterior . . ."

Eponine stopped. Nicole was smiling broadly. "I don't think Max really fools anybody—at least not those who know him. The tough, foul-mouthed Max is an act, developed for some reason, probably self-protection, back on that farm in Arkansas."

The two women were silent for several seconds. "But I don't think I have ever given him full credit either," Nicole added. "It is a tribute to him that he adores you so completely even though you two have never been able to really—"

"Oh, Nicole," Eponine said, suddenly emotional. "Don't think I haven't wanted to, haven't dreamed about it. And Dr. Turner has told us many times that the odds are very small that Max would contract RV-41 if we used protection. But 'very small' is not good enough for me. What if somehow, some way, I passed to Max this horrible scourge that is killing me? How could I ever forgive myself for condemning the man I love to death?"

Tears filled Eponine's eyes. "We are intimate, of course," she said. "In our own safe way. . . . And Max has never once complained. But I can tell from his eyes that he misses—"

"All right, now," they heard Max say on the radio. "We can see the bottom. It looks like a normal floor, maybe five more meters below us. There are two tunnels leading away, one the size of the smaller tunnel up at your level, and another that is really tiny. We're going on down for a closer inspection."

The time had come for the explorers to enter the subway. Richard's mobile camera had not found anything substantively new and there was definitely no exit the humans could use on the only level below them in the lair. Richard and Patrick finished a private conversation in which they reviewed, in detail, what the young man was going to do when he returned to the others. Then they rejoined Max, Nicole, and Eponine, and the five of them walked slowly around the platform to the waiting subway.

Eponine had butterflies in her stomach. She remembered a similar feeling, when she was fourteen, just before her first one-woman art exhibit opened at her orphanage in Limoges. She took a deep breath.

"I don't mind saying it," Eponine said. "I'm scared."

"Shit," said Max, "that's an understatement. . . . Say, Richard, how do we know this thing is not going to hurtle over that cliff you told us about, with us inside?"

Richard smiled but didn't reply. They reached the side of the subway. "All right," he said, "since we don't know exactly how this thing is activated, we want to be very careful. We will all enter more or less simultaneously. That will preclude the possibility that the doors will close and the subway will take off when we are not all yet on board."

Nobody said anything for almost a minute. They lined up four abreast, Max and Eponine on the side closest to the tunnel. "Now I'm going to count," Richard said. "When I say three, we'll all step on together."

"May I close my eyes?" Max asked with a grin. "That made it easier for me on roller coasters when I was a little boy."

"If you like," Nicole answered.

They stepped into the subway and each of them grabbed a vertical rod. Nothing happened. Patrick stood staring at them on the other side of the open door. "Maybe it's waiting for Patrick," Richard said quietly.

"I don't know," Max mumbled, "but if this fucking train doesn't move in a few seconds, I'm going to jump off."

The door closed slowly only moments after Max's comment. There was time for two breaths each before the subway lurched into motion, accelerating rapidly into the illuminated tunnel.

Patrick waved and followed the subway with his eyes until it disappeared around the first corner. Then he put his rifle on his shoulder and began climbing up the spikes. *Please come back quickly,* he was thinking, *before the uncertainty becomes too much for all of us.*

He returned to their living level in less than fifteen minutes. After taking a short drink from his water bottle, he hurried down the tunnel to the museum. While he was walking, he was thinking about what he was going to say to everybody.

Patrick did not even notice that the room was dark when he crossed the threshold. When he entered, however, and the lights came on, he was momentarily disoriented. *I'm not in the right place,* he thought first. *I have taken the wrong tunnel. But no,* his jumbled mind now said, as he glanced quickly around the room, *this must be the room after all. I see a couple of feathers over there in the corner, and one of Nikki's funny diapers. . . .*

With each passing second his heart beat faster. *Where are they?* Patrick said to himself, his eyes now darting frantically around the room for a second time. *What could have happened to them?* The longer he stared at the empty walls, carefully recalling all the conversation before he had departed, the more Patrick realized that his sister and friends could not possibly have left of their own volition. Unless there was a note! Patrick spent two minutes searching every nook in the room. There were no messages. *So someone, or something, must have forced them to leave,* he thought.

Patrick tried to think rationally, but it was impossible. His mind kept jumping back and forth between what he ought to do and terrible pictures of what might have happened to the others. At length he concluded that perhaps they had all moved back to the original room, the one his mother and Richard called the photo gallery, maybe because the lights in the museum were malfunctioning or for some other equally trivial reason. Buoyed by this thought, Patrick dashed out into the tunnel.

He reached the photo gallery three minutes later. It was also empty. Patrick sat down against the wall. There were only two directions his companions could have taken. Since Patrick had not seen anyone on his climb, the others must have gone toward the cathedral room and the sealed exit. As he walked down the long corridor, his hand tight around the rifle, Patrick convinced himself that the Nakamura troops had *not* left the island and that they had somehow broken into the lair and captured everybody else.

Just before he entered the cathedral room, Patrick heard Nikki crying. *"Mom-my, Mom-my,"* she screamed, and then let out a mournful wail. Patrick charged into the large room, not seeing anybody, and then turned up the ramp in the direction of his niece's cry.

On the landing beneath the still-sealed exit was a chaotic scene. In addition to Nikki's continued wailing, Robert Turner was walking around in a daze, his arms outstretched and his eyes upward, repeating over and over,

"No, God, no." Benjy was quietly sobbing in a corner while Nai was trying, without much success, to comfort her twin sons.

When Nai saw Patrick, she jumped up and ran toward him. "Oh, Patrick," she said, tears running from her eyes, "Ellie has been kidnapped by the octospiders."

12

It was several hours before Patrick put together a coherent story about what had happened after his exploration party had left the museum room. Nai was still near shock from the experience, Robert could not talk for more than a minute without breaking into tears, and the children and Benjy frequently interrupted, often without making any sense. At first all Patrick knew for certain was that the octospiders had come and not only had kidnapped Ellie, but also had taken away the avians, the manna melons, and the sessile material. Eventually, however, after repeated questioning, Patrick thought he understood most of the details of what had occurred.

Apparently about an hour after the five explorers had departed, which would have been during the time that Richard, Patrick, and the others were down on the subway platform, the humans who had remained in the museum room heard the dragging brush sound outside the door. When Ellie went out to investigate, she saw octospiders approaching from both directions. She returned to the room with her news and tried to calm Benjy and the children.

When the first octospider appeared in the doorway, all the humans moved as far away as they could, making space for the nine or ten octos who came inside. At first the creatures stood together in a group, their heads bright with the moving, colored messages that they used to communicate. After a few minutes, one of the octospiders came slightly forward, pointed directly at Ellie by lifting one of its black and gold tentacles off the floor, and then went through a long sequence of colors that was quickly repeated.

Ellie guessed (according to Nai—Robert, on the other hand, insisted that somehow Ellie *knew* what the octospider was saying) that the aliens were asking for the manna melons and the sessile material. She retrieved them from the corner and handed them to the lead octospider. It took the objects in three of its tentacles ("A sight to behold," Robert exclaimed, "the way they use those trunklike things and the cilia underneath") and passed them to its subordinates.

Ellie and the others thought that the octospiders would then leave, but they were sadly mistaken. The lead octo continued to face Ellie and flash his colored messages. Another pair of octospiders started moving slowly in the direction of Tammy and Timmy. "No," Ellie said. "No, you can't."

But it was too late. The pair of octospiders wrapped many arms each around the hatchlings and then, oblivious of the jabbers and shrieks, carried the two avians away. Galileo Watanabe raced out and attacked the octospider that had three of its tentacles wrapped around Timmy. The octo simply used a fourth tentacle to lift the boy off the ground and hand him to one of its colleagues. Galileo was passed among them until he was put down, unhurt, in the far corner of the room. The intruders allowed Nai to rush over to comfort her son.

By this time three or four octospiders, the avians, the melons, and the sessile material had all disappeared out into the hallway. There were still six of the aliens in the room. For about ten minutes they talked among themselves. All during this time, according to Robert ("I wasn't paying close attention," Nai said. "I was too frightened and too concerned about my children"), Ellie was watching the colored messages the octospiders were exchanging. At one point Ellie brought Nikki over to Robert and put their daughter in his arms. "I think I understand a little of what they're saying," Ellie said (again, according to Robert), her face absolutely white. "They intend to take me as well."

Again the lead octospider moved toward them and started speaking in color, seemingly focusing on Ellie. Exactly what happened during the next ten minutes was a subject of considerable argument between Nai and Robert, with Benjy siding mostly with Nai. In Nai's version of the story, Ellie tried to protect everyone else in the room, to make some kind of bargain with the octospiders. With repeated hand gestures as well as speech, Ellie told the aliens that she would go with them, provided that the octospiders guaranteed that all the other humans in the room would be allowed to leave the lair safely.

"Ellie was explicit," Nai insisted. "She explained that we were trapped and did not have enough food. Unfortunately, they grabbed her before she was certain that they understood the bargain."

"You're naive, Nai," Robert said, his eyes wild with confusion and pain. "You don't understand how really sinister those creatures are. They hypnotized Ellie. Yes, they did. During the early part of their visit, when she was watching their colors so carefully. I'm telling you, she was not herself. All that malarkey about guaranteeing everyone safe passage was a subterfuge. She *wanted* to go with them. They altered her personality right there on the spot with those crazy colored patterns. And nobody saw it but me."

Patrick discounted Robert's account considerably because Ellie's husband was so distraught. Nai, however, agreed with Robert on two final points: Ellie did not struggle or protest after the first octospider enwrapped her, and before she disappeared from the room, she calmly recited to them a long list of minutiae about caring for Nikki.

"How can anyone in her right mind," Robert said, "after having been seized by an alien, calmly rattle off what blankets her daughter hugs while she is sleeping, when Nikki last had a bowel movement, and other such things? She was obviously hypnotized, or drugged, or something."

The tale of how everyone happened to be on the landing beneath the sealed exit was relatively straightforward. After the octospiders left with Ellie, Benjy ran out into the corridor, screaming and yelling and vainly attacking the rear guard of the octos. Robert joined him and the two of them followed Ellie and the alien contingent all the way to the cathedral room. The gate was open to the fourth tunnel. One octospider held Benjy and Robert off with four long tentacles while the others departed. The final octospider then locked the gate behind itself.

The subway ride was exhilarating for Max. It reminded him of a trip he had made to a large amusement park outside of Little Rock when he was ten years old. The train was suspended above what looked like a metal tape and touched nothing as it sped through the tunnel. Richard conjectured that it was powered in some way by magnetism.

The subway stopped after about two minutes and the door quickly opened. The four explorers looked out at a plain platform, creamy white in color, behind which was an archway about three meters high. "I guess, according to Plan A," Max said, "Eponine and I should exit here."

"Yes," said Richard. "Of course, if the subway doesn't move again, then Nicole and I will join you shortly."

Max took Eponine's hand and stepped gingerly down on the platform. As soon as they were clear of the subway, the door closed. Several seconds later the train sped away.

"Well, isn't this romantic?" Max said after he and Eponine had waved good-bye to Richard and Nicole. "Here we are, just the two of us, finally all alone." He put his arms around Eponine and kissed her. "I just want you to know, Frenchie, that I love you. I have no idea where in the fuck we are, but wherever it is, I'm glad to be here with you."

Eponine laughed. "I had a girlfriend at the orphanage whose fantasy was to be all alone on a desert island with a famous French actor named

Marcel du Bois, who had a mammoth chest and arms like tree trunks. I wonder how she would have felt in this place." She looked around. "I guess we're supposed to go under the archway."

Max shrugged. "Unless a white rabbit comes along that we can follow into some kind of a hole."

On the other side of the archway was a large rectangular room with blue walls. The room was absolutely empty and there was only one exit, through an open doorway into a narrow, illuminated corridor that ran parallel to the subway tunnel. All the walls in this corridor, which continued in both directions for as far as Max and Eponine could see, were the same blue color as in the room behind the archway.

"Which way do we go?" Max asked.

"In this direction I can see what looks like two doors leading away from the subway," Eponine said, pointing to her right.

"And there are two more this way as well," Max said, looking left. "Why don't we walk to the first doorway, look into it, and then decide on a strategy?"

Arm in arm they walked fifty meters down the blue corridor. What they saw when they came to the next doorway dismayed them. Another identical blue corridor, with occasional doorways along its length, stretched in front of them for many meters.

"Shit," said Max. "We are about to enter some kind of a maze. We damn sure don't want to get lost."

"So what do you think we should do?" Eponine asked.

"I think . . ." Max said, hesitating, "I think we should smoke a cigarette and talk this over."

Eponine laughed. "I couldn't agree with you more," she said.

They proceeded very carefully. Each time they turned into another blue corridor, Max made marks with Eponine's lipstick on the wall, indicating the entire path back to the room behind the archway. He also insisted that Eponine, who was more adroit with a computer than he was, keep duplicate records on her portable—"In case something comes along that removes my marks," Max said.

In the beginning their adventure was fun, and the first two times they backtracked to the archway, just to prove they could do it, Max and Eponine felt a certain sense of accomplishment. But after an hour or so, when every turn kept producing another identical blue scene, their excitement began to wane. At length Max and Eponine stopped, sat down on the floor, and shared another cigarette.

"Now, why would any intelligent creature," Max said, blowing smoke rings into the air, "create a place like this? Either we are unwittingly undergoing a test of some kind—"

"Or there's something here that they don't want anybody to find easily," Eponine finished. She took the cigarette from Max and inhaled deeply. "Now, if that's the case," she continued, "then there must be some simple code that defines the location of the special place or thing, a code like one of those ancient combination locks, second right, fourth left, and—"

"Straight on until morning," Max interrupted with a grin. He kissed Eponine briefly and then stood up. "So what we should do is *assume* we're looking for something special and organize our search logically."

When Eponine was on her feet, she looked at Max with a furrowed brow. "Just exactly what did that last statement of yours mean?"

"I'm not certain," Max replied with a laugh, "but it sure as hell *sounded* intelligent."

Max and Eponine had been walking up and down blue corridors for almost four hours when they decided it was time to eat. They had just started their lunch of Raman food when off to their left, at a full intersection of corridors, they saw something pass. Max jumped to his feet and ran to the intersection. He arrived not more than a few seconds before a tiny vehicle, maybe ten centimeters high, made a right turn into the next nearby hallway. Max scrambled forward and was barely able to see the vehicle disappear under a small archway, cut into the wall of another blue corridor, about twenty meters away.

"Come here," he yelled at Eponine. "I've found something."

Eponine was quickly beside him. The top of the small archway in the wall was only about twenty-five centimeters above the floor, so both of them had to drop down on their knees, and then bend over some more, to see where the vehicle had gone. What they saw first was fifty or sixty tiny creatures, about the size of ants, climbing out of the buslike vehicle and then scattering in all directions.

"What the hell is this?" Max exclaimed.

"Look, Max," Eponine said excitedly. "Look carefully. . . . Those little creatures are octospiders. . . . You see. . . . They look just like the one you described to me."

"Well, I'll be damned," Max said. "You're right. They must be baby octospiders."

"I don't think so," Eponine replied. "The way they're going into those little hives, or houses, or whatever. Look, there's a canal of some kind, and a boat—"

"The camera," Max shouted. "Go back and get the camera. There's an entire miniature city here."

Max and Eponine had taken off their backpacks and other gear, including Eponine's camera, when they had sat down on the floor to eat. Eponine jumped up and raced back for the camera. Max continued to be fascinated by the complex miniature world he saw on the other side of the archway. A minute later he heard a faint scream and a cold shiver of fear coursed through him.

Max immediately cursed himself for having left his rifle back where they had been eating. He jumped up and ran in the direction of Eponine's scream. When Max turned the last corner, he stopped sharply. Five octospiders were in front of him in the corridor. One had enwrapped Eponine with three of its tentacles, another had seized Max's rifle. A third octospider was holding Eponine's backpack, into which all her personal items had been neatly placed.

The look on her face was sheer terror. "Help me, Max . . . please," Eponine entreated.

Max stepped forward but was blocked by two of the octospiders. One of them sent a stream of colored bands around its head. "I don't understand what the fuck you're telling me," Max shouted in frustration. "But you must let her go."

Like a football halfback, Max darted past the first two octospiders and had almost reached Eponine when he felt tentacles coiling around him, pinning his arms to his chest. Struggle was useless. The creature was unbelievably strong.

Three of the octospiders, including the one who had captured Eponine, began to move down the blue corridor away from him. "Max . . . Max," the terrified Eponine cried. He could do nothing. After another minute Max could no longer hear Eponine's cries.

Max was enwrapped for about ten more minutes before he felt the powerful muscles that were holding him relax. "So what happens now?" Max said when he was free. "What are you bastards going to do next?"

One of the octos pointed toward his pack, which was still leaning against the wall where Max had left it. He slumped down beside it and pulled out some food and water. The octospiders talked to each other in color while Max, who understood very well that he was being guarded, ate a few bites of his food.

These corridors are too narrow, he thought, thinking about trying to escape. *And those goddamn things are too big, especially with their long tentacles.*

The two octospiders did not move from their post for hours. At length Max fell asleep on the floor between them.

When he woke up, Max was alone. He walked cautiously to the first corner and looked both ways down the blue corridor. He saw nothing. After spending a minute studying the lipstick marks on the wall and adding a few scribbles describing the location of the city of the tiny octospiders, Max returned to the room behind the subway platform.

He had no clear idea of what he should do next. Max spent several minutes wandering the blue corridors and yelling Eponine's name periodically, but his effort was wasted. He eventually decided to sit on the platform and wait for the subway. After more than an hour, Max was almost ready to return to the miniature octospider city when he heard the whoosh of the approaching subway. It was coming from the direction opposite the spiked vertical corridors.

As the subway drew near, he saw Richard and Nicole through the windows. "Max!" They yelled simultaneously, even before the door opened.

Both Richard and Nicole were wildly excited. "We have found it," Richard exclaimed as he jumped down onto the platform. "A large room, with a dome maybe forty meters high, in rainbow colors. It's on the other side of the Cylindrical Sea—the subway goes right through the sea in a transparent tunnel. . . ." He paused as the subway whooshed away.

"It has bathrooms and beds and running water," Nicole added rapidly.

"And fresh food, believe it or not. Some weird kinds of fruits and vegetables, but they're really great for all—"

"Where's Eponine?" Nicole said suddenly, interrupting Richard in the middle of his sentence.

"She's gone," Max replied tersely.

"Gone?" said Richard. "But how? Where?"

"Your nonhostile friends have kidnapped her," Max said dryly.

"Whaaat?" said Richard.

Max told the story slowly and accurately, without omitting anything important. Both Richard and Nicole listened attentively until he was finished. "They outsmarted us," Richard commented at the end, shaking his head.

"Not *us*," Max said in frustration. "They outsmarted *me*. They lulled Ep and me into believing we were solving some kind of puzzle in that maze of blue corridors. . . . Shit. Just shit."

"Don't be too hard on yourself," Nicole said quietly, touching Max on the shoulder. "You had no way of knowing."

"But what colossal stupidity," Max said, raising his voice. "I bring along a rifle for protection, and where is that rifle when our eight-legged monster friends show up? Leaning against the fucking wall."

"We were initially in a similar place," Richard said, "except all our corridors were red instead of blue. Nicole and I explored for about an hour and then returned to the platform. The subway picked us up again in ten minutes and then took us through the Cylindrical Sea."

"Have you looked any for Eponine?" Nicole asked.

Max nodded. "Sort of. I wandered around and shouted her name a few times."

"Maybe we should give it another try," Nicole suggested.

The three friends returned to the world of the blue corridors. When they came to the first intersection, Max explained his lipstick marks on the wall to Richard and Nicole. "I guess we should split up," Max said. "That would probably be a more efficient way to search for her. Why don't we meet at the room behind the archway in, say, half an hour?"

At the second corner Max, who was now by himself, found no lipstick map. Puzzled, he tried to remember if he could possibly have failed to make a map at every turn. Or maybe he never even came this way. While he was deep in thought, he felt a hand on his shoulder and nearly jumped out of his skin.

"Whoa," said Richard, seeing his friend's face. "It's only me. Didn't you hear me calling your name?"

"No," said Max, shaking his head.

"I was only two corridors away. There must be fantastic acoustic attenuation in this place. Anyway, neither Nicole nor I found one of your maps when we made our second turn. So we weren't certain—"

"*Shit*," said Max emphatically. "Those clever bastards have cleaned the walls. Don't you see? They have planned this entire affair from the beginning, and we have done exactly what they expected."

"But Max," Richard said, "there's no way they could have accurately predicted *everything* we were going to do. *We* didn't even know our strategy completely. So how could they?"

"I can't explain it," Max said. "But I feel it. Those creatures deliberately waited until Eponine and I were eating before they let us see that vehicle. They *knew* we would give chase and that they would have a chance to seize Eponine. And somehow they were watching us all the time."

Even Max agreed that it was useless to search any longer for Eponine in the maze of blue corridors. "She's almost certainly not here anymore," he said dejectedly.

While the trio waited on the platform for the subway, Richard and Nicole told Max more details about the large room with the rainbow dome on the southern side of the Cylindrical Sea. "Okay," said Max when they were finished, "one connection is clear, even to this Arkansas farm boy. The rainbow in the dome is obviously connected with the rainbow in the sky that distracted Nakamura's troops. So the rainbow people, whoever they are, don't want us to get captured. And they don't want us to starve to death. They're probably the ones who built the subway—or at least that makes some sense to me. But what is the relationship between the rainbow people and the octospiders?"

"Before you told me about Eponine's kidnapping," Richard replied, "I was virtually certain they were one and the same. Now I don't know. It's difficult to interpret what you experienced as anything other than a hostile act."

Max laughed. "Richard, you have such a way with words. Why do you keep giving those ugly bastards the benefit of the doubt? I would have expected it from Nicole, but those octospiders once kept you prisoner for months, sent little creatures up your nose, and probably even tampered with your brain."

"We don't know that for sure," Richard said quietly, for what felt like the hundredth time.

"All right," said Max. "But I think you're discounting a lot of evidence—"

Max stopped when he heard the familiar whoosh. The subway arrived, heading in the direction of the octospider lair. "Now why is it," Max said with a trace of sarcasm just before they stepped into the train, "that this subway always happens to be going in the right direction?"

Patrick had managed eventually to talk Robert and Nai into returning to the museum room. It had not been easy. Both the adults and the children had been severely traumatized by the octospider attack. Robert could not sleep at all, and the twins were plagued by dreams from which they would awaken screaming. By the time Richard, Nicole, and Max showed up, the remaining food was almost gone and Patrick had already started formulating contingency plans.

It was a subdued reunion. Both the kidnappings were discussed at length, leaving all the adults, even Nicole, acutely depressed. There was very little excitement about the rainbow dome in the south. But there was no question about what they should do. Richard summarized their situation succinctly. "At least there's food under the dome," he said.

They packed all their belongings in silence. Patrick and Max carried the children down the spiked vertical corridor. The subway appeared soon after everyone was on the platform. It did not stop at either of the two intermediate stations, just as Max had wryly predicted, but instead hurtled on into the transparent tunnel through the Cylindrical Sea. The strange and wonderful sea creatures on the other sides of the tunnel wall, almost certainly all biots, fascinated the children and reminded Richard of his voyage to New York years earlier, when he had come to look for Nicole.

The large chamber under the dome at the other end of the subway line was indeed staggering. Although Benjy and the children were more interested initially in the variety of fresh new food that was spread out along a long table on one side of the room, the adults all wandered around in amazement, not only staring at the brilliant colors of the rainbow far above their heads, but also examining all the alcoves off the back of the platform, where bathrooms and individual sleeping suites were located.

Max marched off the dimensions of the main floor. It was roughly fifty meters wide, and forty meters from the subway platform to the alcove entrances. A few minutes later Patrick came over to talk to Max, who was now standing beside the slot cut into the platform for the subway. Everyone else was discussing the allocation of the sleeping suites.

"I'm sorry about Eponine," Patrick said, putting his hand on his friend's shoulder.

Max shrugged. "In a way it's worse that Ellie is gone. I don't know if Robert or Nikki will ever recover completely."

The two men stood side by side and stared at the long, dark, empty tunnel. "You know, Patrick," Max said grimly, "I wish I could convince the farmer in me that our troubles are over and that the rainbow people are going to take care of us."

Kepler came running up with a long vegetable that looked like a green carrot. "Mr. Puckett," he said, "you must try this. It's the best."

Max accepted the little boy's gift and placed the vegetable in his mouth. He took a bite. "This *is* good, Kepler," he said, tousling the boy's hair. "Thank you very much."

Kepler raced back to the others. Max chewed the vegetable slowly. "I always took excellent care of my pigs and chickens," he said to Patrick. "They had good food and great living conditions." Max gestured with his right hand toward the dome and the table laden with food. "But I also removed the animals, a few at a time, when I was ready to slaughter them or sell them at the market."

THE RAINBOW
CONNECTION

1

Nicole was lying on her back, awake again in the middle of the night. In the dim light of their bedroom she could see Richard sleeping soundlessly beside her. At length she rose quietly and crossed the room, exiting into the large main chamber of their temporary home.

The intelligence that controlled the illumination made it easy for the humans to sleep, always sharply reducing the light shining through the rainbow dome for roughly eight hours in each twenty-four-hour period. During these "night" intervals, the main chamber underneath the dome was only softly lit, and the individual bedrooms cut into the walls, which had no lights of their own, were dark enough for restful sleep.

For several consecutive nights Nicole had slept fitfully, awakening often from disquieting dreams that she could not quite remember. This particular night, as she struggled unsuccessfully to recapture the images that had disturbed her rest, Nicole walked slowly around the perimeter of the large circular room in which her family and friends spent most of their time. On the far side of the chamber, near the empty subway platform, she stopped and stared into the dark tunnel that led through the Cylindrical Sea.

What is really going on here? Nicole wondered. *What power or intelligence is providing for us now?*

It had been four weeks since the small human contingent had first reached this magnificent cavern constructed underneath the Southern Hemicylinder of Rama. The new living quarters had obviously been designed, at considerable effort, specifically for them. The bedrooms and the bathrooms in the alcoves were indistinguishable from those in New Eden. The first subway to return after they had arrived at the dome had brought more food and water, plus couches, chairs, and tables to furnish their living areas. The humans had even been supplied with dishes, glasses, and eating utensils. Who, or what, knew enough about everyday human activity to provide such detailed implements?

It is obviously someone who has observed us very carefully, Nicole was thinking. Her mind conjured up an image of the Eagle and she realized that she was engaging in wishful thinking. *But who else could it be? Only the Ramans and the Nodal Intelligence have enough information . . .*

Her thoughts were broken by a sound behind her. Nicole turned and saw Max Puckett approaching from across the chamber. "You can't sleep either?" he said as he drew near.

Nicole shook her head. "These last few nights I've been having bad dreams."

"I keep worrying about Eponine," Max said. "I can still see the terror in her eyes as she was dragged away." He turned away in silence and faced the subway tunnel.

And what about you, Ellie? Nicole wondered, feeling a sharp pang of anxiety. *Are you safe with the octospiders? Or is Max correct about them? Are Richard and I deluding ourselves by believing the octos do not intend to harm us?*

"I can't just sit here any longer," Max said quietly to Nicole. "I must do something to help Eponine. Or at least to convince myself I'm trying."

"But what can you do, Max?" Nicole asked after a short pause.

"Our only contact with the outside world is that damn subway," Max said. "The next time it comes to bring us food and water, which should be either tonight or tomorrow, I intend to climb on board and stay there. When it leaves, I will ride until it stops. Then I will try to find an octospider and have myself captured."

Nicole recognized the desperation in her friend's face. "You're grasping at straws, Max," she said softly. "You will not find an octospider unless they are willing. Besides, we need you."

"Shit, Nicole, I'm not needed here." Max had raised his voice. "And there's absolutely nothing to *do,* except talk to each other and play with the children. At least in your lair there was always the option of taking a walk in the dark of New York. Meanwhile, Eponine and Ellie may be dead, or wishing they were. It's time we *did* something."

As he was talking, they both saw lights flicker in the distant reaches of the subway tunnel. "Here it comes again," Max said. "I'll help you unload after I finish packing my things." He ran off in the direction of his bedroom.

Nicole stayed to watch the approaching subway. As always, lights came on in front of the train as it rushed through the tunnel. A few minutes later the subway pulled into its slot, an incision in the circular floor of the room, and stopped abruptly. After the doors opened, Nicole went over to examine the inside of the car.

In addition to four large jugs of water, the subway contained the usual collection of fresh produce that the humans had learned to eat and enjoy, plus a large squeeze tube of a sticky substance that tasted like a mixture of oranges and honey. *But where is all this food grown?* Nicole asked herself for the hundredth time as she began unloading the food. She recalled the many family discussions of the subject. The consensus conclusion was always that there must be large farms somewhere in the Southern Hemicylinder.

About *who* was feeding them there was less agreement. Richard was certain that they were being fed by the octospiders themselves, primarily because all their supplies passed through territory he considered to be octospider domain. It was hard to argue with his logic. Max agreed that what they were eating was indeed being supplied by the octospiders. However, he attributed sinister motives to all octospider actions. If they were being fed by the octospiders, he asserted, then it was not for humanitarian purposes.

Why would *the octospiders be our benefactors?* Nicole wondered. *I agree with Max that feeding us is inconsistent with kidnapping Eponine and Ellie. Isn't it just possible that some other species is involved? One that has chosen to intercede on our behalf?* Despite Richard's gentle ridicule in the privacy of their own bedroom, a part of Nicole clung stubbornly to the hope that there were indeed some "rainbow people," higher in the development hierarchy than the octospiders, who were somehow interested in the preservation of the vulnerable humans and were ordering the octospiders to feed them.

The contents of the subway always included a surprise. At the back of the car this time were six balls of various sizes, each a different bright color.

"Look, Max," Nicole said. He had returned with his pack and was helping her unload. "They have even sent balls for the children to play with."

"Wonderful," Max said sarcastically. "Now we can all listen to the children argue about which ball belongs to whom."

When they had finished emptying the subway, Max climbed into the car and sat down on the floor. "How long will you wait?" Nicole asked.

"As long as it takes," Max said grimly.

"Did you discuss what you're doing with anyone else?" Nicole inquired.

"Hell, no," Max replied vehemently. "Why should I? We're not operating a democracy here." Max leaned forward in his sitting position. "Sorry, Nicole, but I'm just generally pissed off right now. Eponine has been gone for a month, I've run out of cigarettes, and I'm easily annoyed." He forced a smile. "Clyde and Winona used to tell me, when I was acting like this, that I had a burr up my ass."

"It's all right, Max," Nicole said. She hugged him briefly before leaving. "I just hope you'll be safe, wherever you go."

The subway did not depart. Max stubbornly refused to leave the train, not even to go to the bathroom. His friends brought Max food, water, and the necessary materials for him to keep the train clean. By the end of the third day, the food supply was dwindling rapidly.

"Someone must talk to Max soon," Robert said to the other adults after the children were asleep. "It's clear that the subway is not going to move as long as he is on board."

"I plan to discuss the situation with him in the morning," Nicole said.

"But we're running out of food *now*," Robert protested. "And we don't know how long it takes."

"We can ration what we have left," Richard interrupted, "and make it last at least two more days. Look, Robert, we're all tense and tired. It will be better to talk to Max after a good night's sleep."

"What do we do if Max does not willingly leave the subway?" Richard asked Nicole when they were alone.

"I don't know," Nicole said. "Patrick asked me the same question this afternoon. He's afraid of what will happen if we try to force Max out of the train. Patrick says that Max is very tired and very angry."

When Nicole finally fell asleep, she was exhausted. Again her dreams were troubled. In her first dream, the villa at Beauvois was on fire and she could not find Genevieve. Then the dream venue changed abruptly and Nicole was again seven years old in the Ivory Coast, participating in the Poro ceremony. She was swimming half naked in the little pond in the center of the oasis. On the banks of the pond the lioness was on the prowl, searching for the human girl who had disturbed her cub. Nicole submerged to avoid the sharp eyes of the lioness. When she came up for a breath, the lioness was gone, but three octospiders were now patrolling the pond.

"Mother, mother," Nicole heard Ellie's voice say.

As she was treading water, Nicole's eyes raced around the perimeter of the pond. "We're all right, Mother," Ellie's voice distinctly said. "Don't worry about us."

But where was Ellie in the scene? Dreaming, Nicole saw a human silhouette in the woods behind the three octospiders and called out, "Ellie, is that you, Ellie?"

The dark figure said "Yes" in Ellie's voice and then walked out to where he could be seen in the moonlight. Nicole recognized the bright white teeth immediately. "Omeh," she shouted, a wave of terror running down her spine. "Omeh—"

Nicole was awakened by a persistent nudging. Richard was sitting beside her in the bed. "Are you all right, darling?" he said. "You were shouting Ellie's name . . . and then Omeh."

"I had another one of my vivid dreams," Nicole said, rising and putting on her clothes. "I was told that Eponine and Ellie are safe, wherever they are."

Nicole finished dressing. "Where are you going at this hour?" Richard asked.

"To talk to Max," Nicole replied.

She hurried out of their bedroom and into the main chamber underneath the dome. For some reason, Nicole glanced up at the ceiling just when she entered the chamber. She saw something she had never noticed. There appeared to be a landing or platform cut several meters beneath the dome. Nicole wondered why she had never seen it before.

Max was sleeping in a ball in the corner of the subway. Nicole entered very quietly. A few seconds before she touched him, Max murmured Eponine's name twice. Then his head jerked. "Yes, dear," he said quite distinctly.

"Max," Nicole whispered in his ear. "Wake up, Max."

When Max awakened, he looked as if he had seen a ghost. "I've had the most amazing dream, Max," Nicole said. "I now know that Ellie and Eponine are all right. . . . I've come to ask you to leave the subway, so it can bring us more food. I know how much you want to do something—"

Nicole stopped. Max had risen to his feet and was preparing to descend from the subway. He still had a completely bewildered expression on his face. "Let's go," he said.

"Just like that?" Nicole said, astonished that she had encountered so little resistance.

"Yes," said Max, stepping down from the train. Only a few moments after Nicole had also left the subway, the doors closed and the vehicle accelerated swiftly away from them.

"When you woke me up," Max said as Nicole and he watched the subway disappear, "I was in the middle of a dream. I was talking to Eponine. The instant before I heard your voice she told me you were going to bring me an important message."

Max shuddered, then laughed and started walking toward the alcoves. "Of course I don't believe in any of that ESP shit, but it certainly was a remarkable coincidence."

The subway returned before it was dark again. This time there were two cars on the train. The front car was bright and open and full of food and water as it had always been before. The second car was totally dark. Its doors did not open and its windows were covered.

"Well, well," Max said, walking to the edge of the subway slot and trying unsuccessfully to open the second car, "what have we here?"

After the food and water had been unloaded from the front car, the subway did not depart as usual. The humans waited, but the mysterious second car refused to yield its secrets. At length Nicole and her friends decided to proceed with dinner. The conversation during the meal was subdued and full of wary speculation about their intruder.

When little Kepler innocently suggested that perhaps Eponine and Ellie might be inside the dark car, Nicole told the story again of finding Richard in a coma after his long sojourn with the octospiders. A sense of foreboding spread among the humans.

"We should keep a watch throughout the night," Max suggested after dinner, "so that there can be no possibility of any kind of devious trick while we're asleep. I'll take the first four-hour shift."

Patrick and Richard also volunteered to help with the watch. Before going to bed, the whole family, including Benjy and the children, marched to the edge of the platform and stared at the subway. "What could be inside, Mama?" Benjy asked.

"I don't know, darling," Nicole answered, hugging her son. "I really have no idea at all."

An hour before the lights in the dome brightened the next morning, Richard and Nicole were awakened by Patrick and Max. "Come," Max said to them excitedly, "you've got to see this."

In the center of the main chamber were four large black segmented creatures that were antlike in shape and structure. To each of their three body segments were attached both a pair of legs and another pair of prehensile appendages that were, as the humans watched, busily stacking material in piles. The creatures were a wonder to behold. Each of the long, snakelike "arms" had the versatility of an elephant's trunk, with one additional capability. When any particular arm was not being used, either to lift something or to balance a weight being carried by its opposite member, that arm would withdraw into its "case" in the side of the being, where it would remain tightly coiled until needed again. Thus, when the alien beings were not performing any task, their arms were out of sight and did not impede their movement.

The stunned humans continued to watch with rapt attention as the bizarre creatures, almost two meters long and a meter tall, quickly emptied the contents of the dark subway car, briefly surveyed their stacks, and then departed with the train. As soon as the aliens had disappeared, Max, Patrick, Richard, and Nicole walked over to examine the piles. There were objects of all shapes and sizes in the stacks, but the dominant single part was a long flat piece that resembled a conventional stairstep.

"If I had to guess," Richard said, picking up a small item that was shaped like a fountain pen, "I would say that this stuff is between cement and steel in bearing strength."

"But what is it for, Uncle Richard?" Patrick asked.

"They are going to build something, I would assume."

"And *who* are *they*?" Max said.

Richard shrugged and shook his head. "These creatures that just left struck me as advanced domestic animals, capable of complicated sequential tasks but not real thinking."

"So they are not Mama's rainbow people?" Patrick said.

"Certainly not," Nicole answered with a wan smile.

The rest of the humans, including the children, were thoroughly briefed about the new creatures during breakfast. All the adults agreed that if the aliens returned, as expected, there should be no interference with whatever task they were doing, unless it was determined that the creatures' activities constituted some kind of serious threat.

When the subway pulled into its slot three hours later, two of the new beings clambered out of the front car and hurried into the center of the main chamber. Each was carrying a small pot, into which it dipped one of its arms frequently as it made bright red markings on the floor. Eventually these red lines circumscribed a region containing the subway platform, all the material that had been placed in stacks, and about half the area of the room.

Moments later, another dozen of the huge animals with the trunklike appendages poured forth from the two subway cars, several carrying on their backs large and heavy curvilinear structures. They were followed by two octospiders with unusually bright colors streaming around their spherical heads. The two octospiders sauntered into the center of the chamber, where they inspected the piles of material and then ordered the antlike creatures to begin some kind of construction task.

"So the plot thickens," Max said to Patrick as the two men watched together from a distance. "It is indeed our octospider friends who are in control here, but just what in the world are they doing?"

"Who knows?" Patrick replied, mesmerized by what he was seeing.

"Look, Nicole," Richard said a few minutes later, "over by that large stack. That ant thing is definitely reading the octospider's colors."

"So what do we do now?" Nicole said in a low voice.

"I guess we just watch and wait," Richard answered.

All the construction activity took place inside the red lines that had been painted on the floor. Several hours later, after another subway load of the large curvilinear components was delivered and unloaded, the overall shape of what was being built became clear. On one side of the room a vertical cylinder, four meters in diameter, was being erected. Its top segment was eventually positioned even with the bottom of the dome. Inside the cylinder, the stairsteps were placed so that they wound up and around the center of the structure.

The work continued unabated for thirty-six hours. The octospider architects supervised the giant ants with the versatile arms. The only significant break in the activity came when Kepler and Galileo, who tired of watching the alien construction after several hours, inadvertently allowed a ball to bounce across the red paint and into one of the antlike creatures. All work halted instantly and an octospider hurried over, both to retrieve the ball and seemingly to reassure the worker. With an adroit motion of two of its tentacles, the octospider threw the ball back to the children and the work resumed.

Everyone except Max and Nicole was asleep when the aliens finished their staircase, picked up their residual materials, and departed in the subway. Max walked over to the cylinder and stuck his head inside. "Pretty impressive," he said coyly, "but what is it for?"

"Come on, Max," Nicole replied, "be serious. It's obvious that we are supposed to climb the stairs."

"Shit, Nicole," Max said. "I know that. But *why*? Why do those octospiders want us to climb out of here? You know, they've manipulated us since the moment we entered their lair. They have kidnapped Eponine and Ellie, moved us into the Southern Hemicylinder, and refused to let me go back to New York. What would happen if we decided not to go along with their plan?"

Nicole stared at her friend. "Max, would it be all right with you if we postponed this conversation until we're all together in the morning? I'm very tired."

"Certainly," Max said. "But tell that husband of yours I think we should do something completely unpredictable, like maybe even walking back through the tunnel to the octospider lair. I have an uneasy feeling about where all this is leading us."

"We don't know all the answers, Max," Nicole answered wearily, "but I really don't see where we have much choice except to comply with their wishes as long as the octospiders control our food and water supply. Maybe in this situation we must simply have some faith."

"Faith?" said Max. "That's just another word for not thinking." He walked back over to the cylinder. "And this amazing staircase could be taking us to hell as easily as heaven."

2

In the morning the subway returned with new food and water. After it had departed and everyone had inspected the enclosed cylindrical structure, Max argued that the time had come for the humans to show that they were "tired of being pushed around" by the octospiders. Max suggested that he, and anyone who wanted to go with him, should take the single remaining rifle and trek back through the tunnel under the Cylindrical Sea.

"But what exactly are you trying to accomplish?" Richard asked.

"I want them to capture me and take me to where they are holding Eponine and Ellie. Then I will know for certain they are all right. Nicole's dreams are really not sufficient."

"But Max," Richard countered, "your plan is not logical. Think about it. Even assuming that you are not run over by the subway while you're in the tunnel, how are you going to explain what you want to the octospiders?"

"I was hoping for some help from you, Richard," Max said. "I remember how you and Nicole communicated with the avians. Maybe you could use your computer skills to make a graphics picture of Eponine for me. Then I could show it to the octospiders, using my monitor."

Nicole sensed the entreaty in Max's voice. She touched Richard's hand. "Why not?" she said. "Someone could explore where the staircase leads while you create computer pictures of Eponine and Ellie for Max."

"I would like to go with Max," Robert Turner said suddenly. "If there's any chance at all of finding Ellie, then I want to take it. Nikki will be all right as long as she is here with her grandparents."

Although Richard and Nicole were both concerned about what they were hearing, they chose not to express their anxieties in front of everyone else. Patrick was asked to climb the staircase and do some minimal exploring while Richard was performing his computer graphics wizardry. Max and Robert went to their bedrooms to prepare for their trek. Meanwhile, Nicole and Nai were left alone with Benjy and the children in the main chamber.

"You think it's a mistake for Max and Robert to go back, don't you, Nicole?" Nai's question was asked, as always, in the gentle tone that characterized her personality.

"Yes," said Nicole. "But I'm not certain that *my* thoughts are relevant in this situation. Both men feel bereft and frustrated. It is important to them that some action be taken that is aimed at reuniting them with their partners. . . . Even if the action doesn't make a lot of logical sense."

"What do you think will happen to them?" Nai asked.

"I don't know," Nicole replied. "But I don't think Max and Robert will find Eponine and Ellie. In my opinion, each woman was kidnapped for a specific reason. Although I have no idea what those reasons were, I believe the octospiders will not harm Eponine and Ellie and will eventually return them both to us."

"You are very trusting," Nai said.

"Not really," said Nicole. "My experiences with the octospiders lead me to believe that we are dealing with a species with a highly developed sense of morality. I admit that the kidnappings do not *seem* to be in concert with that picture—and I don't fault either Max or Robert for coming to their own, very different conclusions about the octospiders—but I would bet that we will, in the long run, understand even the purpose of the kidnappings."

"In the meantime," Nai said, "we face a difficult situation. If Max and Robert both leave and never return . . ."

"I know," said Nicole, "but there's nothing we can really do about it. They have decided, Max especially, that they must make some kind of statement now. It's a little old-fashioned—macho, even—but understandable. The rest of us must accommodate their needs, even if in our opinion their actions seem capricious."

Patrick returned in less than an hour. He reported that the staircase ended on a landing that narrowed into a hallway behind the dome. That hallway eventually led to another, smaller staircase which climbed another ten meters and came out inside an igloo-shaped hut about fifty meters south of the cliff overlooking the Cylindrical Sea.

"And what was it like, outside in Rama?" Richard asked.

"The same as in the north," Patrick answered. "Cold—about five degrees Celsius, I would estimate—and dark, with only traces of background light. The igloo hut is warm and well lighted. There are beds and a single bathroom, certainly designed for us, but altogether not much living space."

"Are there no other corridors or passages?" Max asked.

"No," said Patrick, shaking his head.

"Uncle Richard has made great pictures of Ellie and Eponine," Benjy said to his brother at this juncture. "You should see them."

Max pushed two buttons on his portable computer and an excellent rendition of Eponine's face appeared. "Richard didn't have her eyes right the first time," Max said, "but I straightened him out. Ellie was a much easier picture for him."

"So are you all ready to go, then?" Patrick asked Max.

"Just about. We're going to wait until morning so that the light from this room will illuminate more of the tunnel."

"How long do you think it will take to reach the other side?"

"An hour or so at a brisk pace," Max said. "I hope Robert can push himself that hard."

"And what will you do if you hear a subway coming?" Patrick said.

"There's not much we can do," Max replied with a shrug. "We've already surveyed the tunnel and there's very little clearance. Your Uncle Richard says we must rely on the subway's 'fault protection system.'"

There was an argument at dinner about the rifle. Both Richard and Nicole were strongly opposed to Max's taking the rifle, not because they particularly wanted the weapon to stay with the rest of the family, but rather because they feared an "incident" that might ultimately affect everyone. Richard was not very tactful with his remarks and angered Max.

"So, Mr. Expert," Max replied at one point, "would you mind telling me just how you *know* that my rifle will be 'useless' in finding Eponine."

"Max," Richard said stridently, "the octospiders must—"

"Let me, please, dear," Nicole interceded. "Max," she said in a softer tone, "I cannot imagine a scenario in which the rifle is a valuable asset for you on this trip. If you need it in any way to deal with the octospiders, then they must be hostile, and the fates of both Eponine and Ellie would have been decided long ago. We just don't want—"

"What if we encounter some other hostile creatures, nonoctospiders," Max said stubbornly, "and we must protect ourselves? Or what if I need to use the rifle to signal Robert in some way? I can think of many situations. . . ."

The group was unable to resolve the issue. Richard was still frustrated when Nicole and he were undressing for bed. "Can't Max understand," Richard said, "that the real reason he wants to have a gun is to give himself a feeling of security? And a false feeling at that? What if he does something hotheaded and the octospiders withdraw our food and water?"

"We can't worry about that now, Richard," Nicole said. "At this stage

I don't think there's anything we can do except ask Max to be careful and remind him that he is our representative. No amount of talking is going to change his mind."

"Then maybe we should call for a vote about whether or not he should take the rifle," Richard said. "And show Max that everyone is opposed to what he is doing."

"My instinct tells me," Nicole replied quickly, "that any kind of vote would be absolutely the wrong way to handle Max. He already senses what everyone is feeling. A coordinated censure would alienate Max and could make an 'incident' more likely to occur. No, darling, in this case we must just hope that nothing untoward happens."

Richard was quiet for almost a minute. "I guess you're right," he said finally.

"We will wait here together for forty-eight hours," Richard was saying to Max and Robert. "After that time some of us may begin moving our things up to the igloo."

"All right," said Max, tightening the straps on his backpack. He grinned. "And don't worry. I won't shoot one of your octospider friends unless it's absolutely necessary." He turned to Robert. "Well, *mi amigo*, are you ready for an adventure?"

Robert did not look comfortable wearing his backpack. He bent down awkwardly and picked up his daughter. "Daddy will only be gone a short while, Nikki," he said. "Nonni and Boobah will both be staying here with you."

Just before the two men departed, Galileo came running across the chamber with a small pack on his back. "I'm going too," he shouted. "I want to fight the octospiders."

Everyone laughed while Nai explained to Galileo why he couldn't go with Max and Robert. Patrick softened the little boy's disappointment by telling him that he could be the first one up the staircase when the family moved to the igloo.

The two men marched quickly into the tunnel. For the first few hundred meters they walked in silence, entertained by the fascinating sea creatures on the other side of the transparent plastic or glass. Twice Max had to slow down to wait for Robert, who was in poor physical shape. The two men did not encounter any subways. After slightly more than an hour, their flashlight beams illuminated the first station on the other side of the Cylindrical Sea. When Max and Robert were within fifty meters of the station platform, all the lights switched on and they could see where they were going.

"Richard and Nicole visited this place," Max said. "Behind the archway there is a kind of atrium, and then a maze of red corridors."

"What will we do here?" Robert asked. He was out of his element and completely content to follow Max's lead.

"I haven't decided exactly," Max said. "I guess we'll explore awhile and hope we find some octospiders."

Much to Max's surprise, beyond the station platform, in the middle of the atrium floor, was a large blue painted circle, out of which ran a thick blue line that turned right at the beginning of the maze of red corridors. "Richard and Nicole never mentioned a blue line," Max said to Robert.

"It's obviously an idiot-proof set of directions," Robert said. He laughed nervously. "Following the thick blue line is as easy as following the yellow brick road."

They walked into the first corridor. The blue line in the center of the floor stretched a hundred meters in front of them and then turned left at a distant intersection.

"You think we should follow the line, don't you?" Max said to Robert.

"Why not?" Robert answered, taking a few steps along the corridor.

"It's *too* obvious," said Max, as much to himself as to his companion. He clutched his rifle and followed Robert. "Say"—he spoke again after they made their first left turn—"you don't think this line was put here specifically for us, do you?"

"No," Robert replied, stopping for a moment. "How could anyone have known we were coming?"

"That's just what I asked myself," Max mumbled.

Max and Robert walked on in silence, making three more turns following the blue line before coming to an archway that rose a meter and a half above the floor. They bent down and entered a large room with dark red ceilings and walls. The thick blue line ended in a large blue circle that was in the middle of the room.

Less than a second after they were both standing in the blue circle, the lights in the room went out. A crude, silent motion picture, whose image was about one meter square, immediately appeared on the wall directly in front of Max and Robert. In the center of the image were Eponine and Ellie, both dressed in strange, smocklike yellow outfits. They were talking to each other and to some unknown person or thing who was off to the right, but of course Max and Robert could not hear anything they were saying. A few moments later, the two women moved a few meters to their right, past an octospider, and appeared beside a strange fat animal, vaguely resembling a cow, that had a flat white underbelly. Ellie held a snakelike pen against the white surface, squeezed it multiple times, and wrote the following message: *Don't worry. We're fine.* Both women smiled and the image abruptly terminated one second later.

As Max and Robert stood in the room thunderstruck, the ninety-second motion picture repeated twice in its entirety. By the time of the second repetition, the men had managed to collect themselves enough that they were able to pay careful attention to the details. Lights flooded the red room again when the movie was finished.

"Jesus Christ," Max said, shaking his head.

Robert was joyful. "She's alive!" he exclaimed. "Ellie is still alive."

"If we can believe what we've seen," Max said.

"Come on, Max," Robert said several seconds later. "What possible reason could the octospiders have for making a film like that to deceive us? Wouldn't it be much easier for them to do nothing?"

"I don't know," Max replied. "But you answer a question for me. How did they know that the two of us, coming here together at this time, were worried about Ellie and Eponine? There are only two possible explanations. Either they have been watching everything we have been doing and saying since we entered their lair, or someone—"

"—from our group has been providing information to the octospiders. Max, surely you don't think for an instant that either Richard or Nicole—"

"No, of course not," Max interrupted. "But I'm having a damn hard time understanding how we could have been observed so carefully. We have not seen any suggestion of eavesdropping devices. Unless some pretty sophisticated transmitters are planted *on* us, or *in* us, none of this makes any sense."

"But how could they have done that without our knowledge?"

"Beats the shit out of me," Max replied, bending down to walk through the archway. He stood up in the red corridor on the opposite side of the arch. "Now, unless I miss my guess, that damn subway will be waiting for us when we arrive at the station and we'll be expected to return peacefully to the others. Everything is just too nice and neat."

Max was correct. The subway was parked with its door open when Robert and he turned into the atrium from the maze of red corridors. Max stopped. He had a wild gleam in his eyes.

"I'm not going to board the damn train," he said in a low voice.

"What are you going to do?" asked Robert, a little frightened.

"I'm going to go back into the maze," Max said.

He clutched his rifle, spun around, and raced back into the corridor. Max turned away from the blue line and ran about fifty meters before the first octospider appeared in front of him. It was quickly joined by several more octos, which spread across the corridor from one side to the other. They began to move toward Max.

Max stopped, looked at the advancing octospiders, and then glanced behind him. At the far end of the corridor another group of octospiders was moving in his direction.

"Wait just a damn minute," Max shouted. "I have something to say. You guys must understand at least part of our language or you could never have figured out that we were coming here. . . . I'm not satisfied. I want *proof* that Eponine is alive."

The octospiders, their heads rippling with color, were almost upon him. A wave of fear swept through Max and he fired the rifle in the air as a warning. No more than two seconds later he felt a sharp sting in the back of his neck. Max collapsed immediately on the floor.

Robert, whose indecision had kept him standing in the station, raced across the platform at the sound of the gunfire. When he arrived in the red corridor, he saw two octospiders lifting Max off the floor. Robert stood aside as the extraterrestrials carried Max into the subway and gently deposited him in the corner of the car. The octospiders then gestured at the open subway door and Robert climbed inside. Less than ten minutes later the two men had returned to the chamber underneath the rainbow dome.

3

M ax did not awaken for ten hours. During that time both Robert and Nicole examined him thoroughly and found no evidence of any wound or injury. Meanwhile, Robert repeatedly told the story of their adventure, except of course what happened during the critical minute when Max was by himself in the red corridor.

Most of the questions from the family were about what Robert and Max had seen in the motion picture. Were there any indications of stress in Ellie or Eponine, suggesting that perhaps they might have been coerced into making the film? Did they appear to have lost any weight? Did they look rested?

"I believe we now know much more about the nature of our hosts," Richard said near the end of the family's second and more lengthy discussion of Robert's story. "First and foremost, it is clear that the octospiders, or whatever species is in charge here, both observe us regularly and are able to understand our conversations. There is no other possible explanation for the fact that the film showed to Max and Robert featured Ellie and Eponine.

"Second, their technological level, at least where motion pictures are concerned, is either several hundred years behind ours, or, if Robert is right when he insists that there could not have been a projecting device either in the room or behind the wall, they are so far advanced that their technology appears like magic to us. Third—"

"But Uncle Richard," Patrick interrupted. "Why didn't the motion picture have sound? Wouldn't it have been much easier for Eponine and Ellie just to *say* they were all right? Isn't it more likely that the octospiders are deaf than it is that their technology has not developed beyond silent movies?"

"What an interesting idea, Patrick," Richard replied. "That's something we have never even considered. And of course they don't need to hear to communicate."

"Creatures that have spent most of their evolutionary lives deep in the ocean are often deaf," Nicole offered. "Their primary sensory needs for survival are at other wavelengths, and with only a limited number of cells available for both the sensors and their processing, the ability to hear simply never develops."

"I worked with the hearing impaired in Thailand," Nai added, "and I was fascinated by the fact that being unable to hear is not a significant drawback in an advanced culture. The sign language of the deaf has extraordinary range and is quite complex. Humans on Earth no longer need to hear to hunt or to escape animals that might prey on them. The octospider language of colors is more than adequate for communication."

"Hold on just a minute," Robert said. "Aren't we overlooking some pretty strong evidence that the octospiders *can* hear? How could they have known that Max and I were going out to find Ellie and Eponine if they didn't overhear our conversation?"

There was silence for several seconds. "They might have had the two women translate what was being said," Richard suggested.

"But that would require two unlikely events," Patrick said. "First, if the octospiders are deaf, why would they have sophisticated miniaturized equipment available that would record sounds at all? Second, having Eponine and Ellie translate what we said for the octospiders implies a level of communication interaction that could hardly have developed in a month's time. . . . No, in my opinion, the octos probably determined the purpose of Max and Robert's trip on the basis of visual evidence—the portraits of the two women on the portable computer monitors."

"Bravo," shouted Richard. "That's excellent thinking."

"Are you guys going to yak about this shit all night long?" Max said as he walked into the middle of the group.

Everyone jumped up. "Are you all right?" Nicole asked.

"Sure," said Max. "I even feel well rested."

"Tell us what happened," Robert interrupted. "I heard your rifle fire, but by the time I came around the corner, a pair of octospiders was already carrying your body."

"I don't know myself," Max said. "Just before I passed out I felt a stinging hot pain in the back of my neck. . . . That was it. One of the octos behind me must have hit me with their equivalent of a tranquilizing dart."

Max rubbed the back of his neck. Nicole came over to inspect. "I cannot even find a small hole now," she said. "They must use very thin darts."

Max glanced at Robert. "I don't suppose you retrieved the rifle."

"I'm sorry, Max," Robert said. "I never even thought about it until after we were on the train."

Max looked at his friends. "Well, guys, I want you to know my rebellion is over. I'm convinced we cannot fight these creatures. So we might as well try to follow their plan."

Nicole put a hand on her friend's shoulder. "This is the new Max Puckett," she said with a smile.

"I may be stubborn," Max replied with a smile of his own, "but I don't believe I'm stupid."

"I don't think we're all supposed to move into Patrick's igloo," Max said the next morning after another subway had come and replenished their food and water.

"Why do you say that?" Richard asked. "Look at the evidence. The igloo was definitely designed for human habitation. Why else would they have built the staircase?"

"It just doesn't make sense," Max replied. "Especially for the children. There's not enough room to live for any period of time. I think the igloo is some kind of waystation—a cabin in the woods, if you like."

Nicole tried to imagine the ten of them living in the cramped quarters that Patrick had described. "I can see your point, Max," she said, "but what do you suggest?"

"Why don't a few of us return to the igloo and look around carefully? Patrick's quick reconnoiter may have missed something. Anyway, whatever we're supposed to do should be obvious. It wouldn't be like the octospiders, or whatever is guiding us, to leave us in uncertainty."

Richard, Max, and Patrick were selected for the scouting mission. Their departure was delayed, however, so that Patrick could keep his promise to Galileo. Patrick followed the five-year-old up the long, winding staircase and down the hallway to the bottom of the second stairs. The boy was too exhausted to climb any more. In fact, when they were coming down from the dome, the little boy's legs gave out and Patrick had to carry Galileo the final twelve meters of the descent.

"Can you make it up a second time?" Richard asked Patrick.

"I believe so," said Patrick, adjusting his pack.

"At least now he won't be waiting for us old farts all the time," Max said with a grin.

The three men stopped to admire the view from the landing at the top of the cylindrical stairs. "Sometimes," Max said, as he took a long look at the magnificent colors of the rainbow strips in the dome only a few meters above him, "I think that everything that has happened to me since I boarded the Pinta is a dream. How do pigs, chickens, and even Arkansas fit into this picture? It's just too much."

"It must be difficult," Patrick said while they were walking along the hallway, "to reconcile all this with your normal life on Earth. But consider my situation. I was born on an extraterrestrial spacecraft headed for an artificial world located near the star Sirius. I have spent more than half my life asleep. I have no idea what normal means."

"Shit, Patrick," Max said, putting his arm around the young man, "if I were you I would be as crazy as a bedbug."

Later, when they were climbing the second stairs, Max stopped and turned to Richard below him. "I hope you realize, Wakefield," he said in a warm tone, "that I'm just an ornery bastard and didn't mean anything personal during our arguments the last few days."

Richard smiled. "I understand, Max. I also know that I'm as arrogant as you are ornery. I will accept your oblique apology if you will accept mine."

Max feigned indignation. "That wasn't a damn apology," he said, walking up to the next step.

The igloo hut was just as Patrick had described it. The three men pulled on their jackets and prepared to go outside. Richard, who was the first one out the door, saw the other igloo before Max and Patrick had even taken their first breath of the bracing Rama air.

"That other igloo wasn't there, Uncle Richard," Patrick insisted. "I walked completely around the area."

The second igloo, which was almost exactly one-tenth the size of the larger hut, was about thirty meters farther away from the cliff bordering the Cylindrical Sea. It was glowing in the Rama dark. As the men started walking toward it, the door of the smaller igloo opened and two tiny human figures came out. The figures were about twenty centimeters high and were illuminated from the inside.

"What the hell . . . ?" Max exclaimed.

"Look," said Patrick excitedly, "it's Mother and Uncle Richard!"

The two figures turned south in the darkness, away from the cliff and the sea. Richard, Max, and Patrick scrambled up beside them for a better view. The figures were dressed in exactly the same clothes that Richard and Nicole had worn the previous day. The attention to detail was extraordinary. The hair, faces, skin coloring, even the shape and color of Richard's beard, were a perfect match for the Wakefields. The figures were also wearing backpacks.

Max stooped down to pick up the figure of Nicole but received an electrical jolt when he touched it. The figure turned in Max's direction and shook her head emphatically. The men followed the pair for another hundred meters and then stopped.

"There's not much doubt about what we're supposed to do next," Richard said.

"Nope," said Max. "It looks as if you and Nicole are being summoned."

The next afternoon Richard and Nicole packed several days worth of food and water into their packs and said good-bye to their extended family. Nikki had slept between them the night before and was especially tearful when her grandparents departed.

It was quite a climb up the staircase. "I should have taken the stairs more slowly," Nicole said, breathing hard as she and Richard stood on the landing beneath the dome and waved one final time to everybody. Nicole could feel her heart beating arrhythmically in her chest. She waited patiently for the palpitations to subside.

Richard was also out of breath. "We're not as young as we were those many years ago in New York," he said after a short silence. He smiled and put his arms around Nicole. "Are you ready to continue our adventure?" he asked.

Nicole nodded. They walked slowly, hand in hand, down the long hallway. When they reached the second stairs, Nicole turned to Richard. "Darling," she said with sudden intensity, "isn't it great to be alone again, just the two of us, even if it's only for a few hours? I love all the others, but it's a pain being so damn responsible all the time."

Richard laughed easily. "It's a role you chose, Nicole," he said, "not one that was forced on you."

He leaned down to kiss her on the cheek. Nicole turned her face toward him and kissed him strongly on the lips.

"Were you suggesting with that kiss," Richard asked immediately with a wide grin, "that we should spend tonight in the igloo and begin our journey tomorrow?"

"I think that you have been reading my mind, Mr. Wakefield," Nicole said with a coquettish smile. "Actually, I was thinking how much fun it would be to imagine tonight that we were young lovers again." She laughed. "At least our imaginations should still work all right."

When they were three hundred meters south of the two igloos, Richard and Nicole could no longer see anything except whatever they illuminated with their flashlights. Although the floor beneath them, mostly dirt with an occasional collection of small rocks, was generally smooth, from time to time one or both of them would stumble when not paying careful attention.

"This may be a very long and tiring walk in the dark," Nicole said when they stopped for some water.

"And cold too," Richard said, taking a drink. "Are you warm enough?"

"As long as we're moving," Nicole said. She stretched out her arms and adjusted her backpack.

It was almost an hour before they saw a light in the sky to the south. The light was moving toward them and was growing larger.

"What do you think it is?" Nicole asked.

"Maybe the Blue Fairy?" Richard replied. "'When you wish upon a star, makes no difference who you are. . . .'"

Nicole laughed. "You're impossible," she said.

"After last night," Richard said as the light continued to move in their direction, "I feel like a boy again."

Nicole chuckled and shook her head. They held hands in silence while the ball of light continued to grow in size. A minute later it stopped twenty to thirty meters in front of them and about twenty meters above their heads. Richard and Nicole switched off their flashlights, for they could now see the terrain around them for a distance of more than a hundred meters.

Richard shaded his eyes and tried to determine the source of the illumination, but the light was too bright. He could not look directly at it. "Whatever it is," Nicole said after they were walking again, "it appears to know where we're supposed to go."

Two hours later, Richard and Nicole encountered a path heading to the southwest, with fields of growing plants on either side of the path. When they stopped for lunch, they wandered into the fields and discovered that one of their staple foods under the dome, a vegetable with a taste similar to a green bean but with the physical appearance of a yellow squash, was the principal crop being grown. These vegetables were interspersed with rows of a short, bright red plant that they had never seen before. Richard pulled one of the red plants out of the ground and dropped it immediately when the green, leathery sphere that had been beneath the surface began to writhe at the bottom of its red stalk. When it hit the ground, the creature scooted the few centimeters back to its original hole and buried its green sphere again in the same place.

Richard laughed. "I guess I'll think twice before I do something like that again."

"Look over there," Nicole said a moment later. "Isn't that one of the animals that built the staircase?"

They moved down the path and then back into the field itself for a better view. Coming toward them was indeed one of the large, antlike creatures with the six long arms. It was harvesting the vegetables with amazing efficiency, handling the three rows on either side of where its main body was located. Each arm, or trunk, was stripping the vegetables in a single row and stacking them in piles that were between the rows and about two meters apart. It was an astonishing sight, the six arms all operating simultaneously on different tasks, and at different distances from its main body.

When the creature reached the path, its arms quickly recoiled. It then moved six rows down the line and entered the field going in the opposite direction. The field was being harvested from south to north, so when Richard and Nicole started walking again, they passed through the part of the field that the giant ant thing had already finished. There they saw swift rodentlike creatures picking up the scattered piles and scampering away with them to the west.

Richard and Nicole came to several intersections while they were walking along the path among the fields, and each time the hovering light indicated which route they should take. The fields extended for many kilometers. They came upon several different crops, but Richard and Nicole, who were becoming hungry and weary, no longer stopped to examine each new vegetable.

At length they reached a flat open area covered with soft dirt. The light above them circled three times and then hovered over the center of the area. "I'm guessing that this is where we're supposed to spend the night," Richard said.

"Gladly," said Nicole, accepting Richard's help in removing her backpack. "I don't think I'll have any trouble sleeping, even on this hard ground."

They ate dinner and found a comfortable spot where they could sleep nestled together. When Richard and Nicole were both in the twilight zone between waking and sleeping, the light above them began to dim a little and then drop in altitude.

"Look," Richard whispered, "it's going to land."

Nicole opened her eyes and watched as the light, continuing to dim, made a graceful arc and landed on the opposite side of the open area. It was still glowing slightly even after it was already on the ground. Although Richard and Nicole could not see the creature very well, they could tell that it was long and skinny and had wings more than twice as large as its body.

"It's a giant firefly," Richard exclaimed when they could no longer see its outline.

4

"Biology for lights, biology for farm and construction equipment—do you have the impression that our octospider friends, or perhaps whatever is above them in some amazing symbiotic hierarchy, are the great biologists of the galaxy?"

"I don't know, Richard," Nicole said as she finished her breakfast. "But it certainly looks as if their technological evolution has followed a markedly different path than ours."

They had both watched with wonder as the giant firefly, upon hearing their first movements after sleeping, had ignited itself and taken its accustomed hovering position above them. A few minutes later, a second, similar creature had approached them from the south. The two lights now combined to provide local illumination that was equivalent to daylight in New Eden.

Richard and Nicole had both slept well and were quite refreshed. Their two guides led them along paths through several more kilometers of fields, including one that was characterized by grasses over three meters tall. One hundred meters after making a sharp left turn in the tall grasses, Richard and Nicole found themselves at the edge of a vast array of shallow water tanks that stretched in front of them as far as they could see.

They walked to the left for several minutes until they came to what Richard properly identified as the northeast corner of the array. The system consisted of a series of long, narrow, rectangular tanks that were metallic gray in color. Each of the individual tanks in the array was about twenty meters wide and as much as several hundred meters long. The tanks were as tall as Nicole's waist and were three-quarters filled with a liquid that appeared to be water. At each tank corner was a thick, bright-red cylinder, twice as high as the tank, that was topped with a white sphere.

Richard and Nicole walked beside the long edge of the array for several minutes, peering inside each individual tank and examining the thick cylindrical poles marking where adjacent tanks shared common sides. They saw nothing in the tanks except the water. "So is this some kind of purification plant?" Nicole asked.

"I doubt it," Richard answered. They stopped at the western edge. "Look at that mass of small, detailed parts affixed to the inside wall of this tank, just in front of the cylinder. I would guess that those are complicated electronic components of some kind. There would be no need for all that in a simple water purification system."

Nicole looked askance at her husband. "Come on, Richard, that's quite a leap of faith. How can you possibly claim to know the function of a bunch of three-dimensional squiggles on the inside of an alien water tank?"

"I said I was guessing," Richard responded with a laugh. "I was only trying to make the point that it looks too complex to be a place to purify water."

The guide lights above them were urging them to the south. The second bank of narrow tanks also contained nothing but water; however, when they reached the third set of rectangular tanks and cylindrical poles, Richard and Nicole discovered that the water was full of tiny fuzzy balls of many colors. Richard rolled up his sleeve and stuck his hand into the water, pulling out several hundred of the objects.

"Those are eggs," Nicole said firmly. "I know that fact with the same certainty that you knew those little gadgets on the insides of the tank wall were electronic components."

Richard laughed again. "Look," he said, putting his mound of little objects in front of Nicole's eyes, "there are really only five different kinds, if you study them closely."

"Five different kinds of *what*?" Nicole asked. Richard shook his head and shrugged as he replaced the eggs in the tank.

The egglike things filled the entire length of the third set of tanks. By the time Richard and Nicole were approaching the fourth row of cylinders and another set of tanks, which were several more hundred meters to the south, both of them were growing tired. "If we don't see anything new here," she said, "how about lunch?"

"You're on," he answered.

But they could discern something new already when they were still fifty meters away from the fourth row of tanks. A square robot vehicle, perhaps thirty centimeters in length and width and another ten centimeters high, was moving swiftly back and forth between the cylindrical poles. "I *knew* those were tracks for some kind of vehicle," Nicole said, kidding Richard.

Richard was too fascinated to respond. In addition to the scurrying robot, which made a full cycle across the array from east to west every three minutes or so, there were several more wonders to observe. Each of the individual tanks here was further subdivided into two long pieces by a mesh fence parallel to the walls that was only slightly higher than the water level. On one side of the mesh was an absolute swarm of tiny swimming creatures in five different colors. On the other side, gleaming circles, resembling sand dollars, were scattered the complete length of the tank. The fence was positioned so that three-fourths of the tank volume was available to the gleaming circles, giving them far more room to maneuver than the densely packed swimmers.

Richard and Nicole bent over to study the activity. The sand dollars were moving in all directions. Because the water was teeming with so many creatures and so much activity, it took several minutes for Richard and Nicole to perceive the common pattern. At irregular intervals each of the sand dollars would propel itself over to the mesh fence using the whiplike cilia underneath its flat body and then, while anchored to the fence, would use another pair of cilia to capture a tiny swimmer and pull it through one of the holes in the mesh. While the sand dollar was against the fence, its light would dim. If it stayed long enough and caught several of the swimmers to eat, then its gleam would fade altogether.

"Watch what happens now when it leaves the fence," Richard said to Nicole, pointing out one specific sand dollar just underneath them. "As it swims along with its companions, its light will be slowly replenished."

Richard hurried back to the nearest cylindrical pole and bent down on his knees on the ground. He dug into the soil with one of the tools from his pack. "There's much more to this system underground," he said excitedly. "I bet this entire array is part of a gigantic power generator."

He took three large, measured steps to the south, noted his position carefully, and leaned over the tank to count the sand dollars in the region between the cylindrical pole and him. It was a difficult count because of the constant motion of the gleaming circles.

"Roughly three hundred of them in three meters of tank length, making approximately twenty-five thousand per complete tank, or two hundred thousand in a complete row," Richard said.

"Are you assuming, then," Nicole asked, "that these cylindrical poles are some sort of storage system? Like batteries?"

"Probably," said Richard. "What a fabulous idea! Find a living creature that generates electricity internally. Force it to give up its accumulated charge in order to eat. What could be better?"

"And that robot vehicle, moving back and forth between the poles, what is its purpose?"

"I would guess it's a monitor of some kind," Richard replied.

Richard and Nicole ate their lunch and then finished their inspection of the putative power plant. Altogether there were eight columns and eight rows in the array, for a total of sixty-four tanks. Only twenty were active at the time. "Plenty of excess capacity," Richard commented. "Their engineers clearly understand the concepts of growth and margin."

The giant fireflies now headed due east, along what appeared to be some kind of major highway. Twice Richard and Nicole encountered small herds of the large antlike creatures going in the opposite direction, but there were no interactions. "Are those creatures intelligent enough to operate without supervision?" Nicole asked Richard. "Or are we just not being allowed to see whatever beings give them instructions?"

"That's an interesting question," Richard said. "Remember how quickly the octospider came over to the ant thing when it was struck by the ball? Perhaps they have some limited intelligence, but cannot function well in new or unknown environments."

"Like some people we have known," Nicole said with a laugh.

Their long march to the east ended when their two guiding lights hovered over a large dirt field just off the road. The field was empty except for what looked at a distance like forty football goalposts covered with ivy, arranged in five rows of eight posts each.

"Will you check the guidebook, please?" Richard said. "It's easier to understand what we're seeing if we read about it first."

Nicole smiled. "We really are being given some kind of tour, aren't we? Why do you suppose our hosts want us to see all this?"

Richard was silent for a moment. "I'm fairly certain that it's the octospiders who are the lords of all this territory," he said finally, "or at least they are the dominant species in a complicated hierarchy. Whoever it was that picked us personally for this tour must believe that informing us about their capabilities will make future interactions easier."

"But if it really is the octospiders," Nicole said, "why didn't they simply kidnap all of us as they did Ellie and Eponine?"

"I don't know," Richard replied. "Maybe their sense of morality is far more complicated than we have imagined."

Both of the giant fireflies were dancing in the air over the collection of ivy-covered goalposts. "I think our tour guides are becoming impatient," Nicole said.

If Richard and Nicole had not been so fatigued from their two days of arduous hiking, and if they had not already seen so many fabulous sights in this alien world that existed in the Southern Hemicylinder of Rama, they would have been both captivated and overwhelmed by the complex symbiosis they discovered in the next several hours.

What was all over the goalposts was not ivy at all. What appeared to be individual leaves from a distance were in reality little cone-shaped nests, made of thousands of tiny creatures that resembled aphids. The creatures were glued together to form the nest by the sweet, sticky, honeylike substance the humans had enjoyed eating under the dome. The alien aphids manufactured large quantities of the substance as part of their normal activity.

During the time that Richard and Nicole were watching, convoys of snout-nosed beetles, who lived in mounds several meters high surrounding the entire enclave, burst from their homes every forty minutes or so and crawled all over the posts, harvesting the excess goo from the nests. The beetle creatures, which were about ten centimeters long when empty, swelled to three or four times their normal size before completing their harvest cycle and regurgitating the contents of their swollen bodies in sunken vats at the base of the posts.

Richard and Nicole did not talk much while they were watching the activity. The overall biological system displayed in front of them was both intricate and wonderful—another example of the astonishing advancements in symbiosis that had been made by their hosts. "I bet," said a weary Richard as he and Nicole prepared to sleep not far from one of the beetle mounds, "that if we wait long enough, some beast of burden will show up to lift the vats of this honey, or whatever it is, out of the ground and then carry them to another site."

As they were lying side by side on the dirt, they observed the two fireflies landing in the distance. Then it was suddenly dark. "I don't believe all this just happened," Nicole said. "Not on another planet. Not anywhere. Natural evolution simply does not result in the kind of interspecies harmony we have witnessed the last two days."

"What are you suggesting?" Richard asked. "That all these creatures were somehow designed, like machines, to perform their functions?"

"It is the only explanation I can accept," Nicole said. "The octospiders, or somebody, must have reached the level of advancement where they can manipulate the genes to produce a plant or animal that does exactly what they want. *Why* do those beetle things deposit the honey substance in the vats? What is their biological payoff for that action?"

"They must be compensated in some way that we have not yet discovered," Richard said.

"Of course," Nicole said. "And behind that compensation is some incredible biological systems architect or engineer who is tuning all the interrelationships, not only so that each species is happy, however we choose to define that word, but also so that the architects themselves reap some profit—namely, food in the form of excess honey. Now, do you believe that kind of optimization could possibly take place without some sophisticated genetic engineering involved?"

Richard was silent for almost a minute. "Imagine," he finally said slowly, "a master biological engineer sitting at a keyboard, designing a living organism to meet certain system specifications. It is a mind-boggling concept."

Once more the beetles swarmed out of their mounds, barely missing the sleeping humans as they rushed for the goalposts and their harvesting task. Nicole watched the beetles until they disappeared in the dark. Then she yawned and curled up on her side. *We humans have entered a new era,* she thought before she fell asleep. *In the future all history will be noted as* BC, *before contact, and* AC, *after contact. For from that first moment when we knew unambiguously that simple chemicals had risen to consciousness and intelligence somewhere else in the vastness of our universe, the past history of our species became only an isolated paradigm, one small and relatively insignificant fragment in the infinite tapestry that depicts the astonishing variety of sentient life.*

After breakfast the next morning Richard and Nicole had a brief discussion about their dwindling food supply and then decided to take some of the honey substance from one of the vats. "I guess if we're not supposed to do this," Nicole said, glancing around while she was filling a small container, "then some alien policeman will come along and stop us."

Their guide lights moved directly south at first, leading Richard and Nicole toward a thick forest of very tall trees that extended as far as they could see in the east-west direction. The fireflies turned to the right and moved parallel to the edge of the trees. The forest on their left was dark and foreboding. From time to time Richard and Nicole heard strange, loud sounds coming from its interior.

Once Richard stopped and walked over to where the thick growth began. Between the trees were many smaller plants, with large leaves in green, red, and brown, as well as several different kinds of vine that laced together the middle and upper branches of the trees. Richard jumped back when he heard a sharp howl that sounded as if it were only a few meters away. His eyes searched the forest, but he could not find the source of the howl.

"There's something weird about this forest," he said, turning back to Nicole. "It feels out of place, as if it doesn't belong here."

For over an hour the fireflies continued in a westerly direction. The bizarre sounds became more frequent as Richard and Nicole trudged slowly along in silence. Nicole agreed with Richard about the forest. Its undisciplined growth, especially when compared to the order of the fields on her right, was both surprising and disquieting.

They took a brief rest in the middle of the morning. Richard calculated that they had already walked more than five kilometers since waking. Nicole asked for some of the fresh honey that was in Richard's backpack.

"My feet hurt," she said, after eating and then taking a long drink of water. "And my legs never stopped aching last night. I hope we reach wherever we're going before too much longer."

"I'm tired too," Richard said. "But we're not doing badly for a couple in their early sixties."

"I feel older than that right now," Nicole said. She stood up and stretched. "You know, our hearts must be almost ninety. They may not have done much work all those years we were asleep, but they had to keep pumping nevertheless."

As they were talking, a strange little spherical animal with a solitary eye, white fuzzy hair, and a dozen spindly legs darted out of the nearby forest and snatched the container of honey. The creature and the food were gone in an instant.

"What was that?" Nicole asked, startled.

"Something with a sweet tooth," Richard said. He stared off into the forest, where the animal had disappeared. "That is definitely another world over there."

Half an hour later, the pair of fireflies moved off to the left and hovered over a path leading into the forest. The path was five meters wide and was lined on both sides by dense growth. Nicole's intuition told her not to follow the fireflies, but she said nothing. Her apprehension increased when, after Richard and she had taken a couple of steps into the forest, noises erupted from the trees all around them. They stopped, held hands, and listened.

"It sounds like birds, monkeys, and frogs," Richard said.

"They must be signaling our presence," Nicole said. She turned around and looked behind her. "Are you sure we're doing the right thing?"

Richard pointed at the lights in front of them. "We've been following those big bugs for two and a half days. It doesn't make much sense to lose faith in them now."

They started walking down the path again. The caws, howls, and croaking sounds accompanied them. From time to time the kind of foliage on both sides of them would change a little, but it always remained dense and dark.

"There must be a group of alien gardeners," Richard said at one point, "who work the area around this path several times a week. Look how perfectly trimmed all the bushes and trees are. They don't protrude one iota into the air space above our heads."

"Richard," Nicole said a little later, "if the sounds we are hearing are coming from alien animals, why don't we ever see one? Not a single creature has ever come out on the path." She bent down and examined the dirt at her feet. "And there is no visible evidence here of any life, not now and not ever. Not even an ant."

"We must be walking on a magical path," Richard said with a grin. "Perhaps it leads to a gingerbread house and a wicked old witch. . . . Let us sing, Gretel, and perhaps we will feel better."

The path, which had been absolutely straight for the first kilometer or so, began to meander. Because of its wandering, the sounds of the forest creatures surrounded Richard and Nicole. Richard sang popular songs from his adolescent years in England. Nicole joined him some of the time, when she knew the song, but mostly she spent her energy trying to contain her growing anxiety. She told herself not to think about what an easy target they would be for any large alien animal that might be lurking in the forest.

Richard suddenly stopped. He pulled two deep breaths of air through his nose into his lungs. "Do you smell that?" he asked Nicole.

She sniffed the air. "Yes," she said, "I do. It's a little like gardenias."

"Only much much better," Richard said. "It's positively divine."

Ahead of them, the path turned abruptly to the right. At the turn there was a large bush beside the path that was covered with huge yellow flowers, the first flowers they had seen since they entered the forest. Each individual flower was the size of a basketball. As Richard and Nicole drew nearer to the bush, the enticing smell intensified.

Richard could not restrain himself. Before Nicole could say anything, he stepped the few meters off the path, stuck his face in one of the huge flowers, and inhaled deeply. The smell was magnificent. Meanwhile, one of the two fireflies flew back in their direction and began zigging and zagging in the sky over their heads.

"I don't think our guides approved of your sortie," Nicole said.

"Probably not," Richard replied, returning to the path. "But it was worth it."

As they continued to walk, more flowers, of all shapes, sizes, and colors, surrounded them on both sides. Neither of them had ever seen such a profusion of color. At the same time, the sounds they had been hearing abated. A little later, when Richard and Nicole were in the middle of the flower region, the noises disappeared altogether.

The path narrowed to a couple of meters, barely wide enough for them to walk side by side and not brush the plants on which the flowers were growing. Richard left the trail several times to inspect and smell one of the amazing flowers. Each excursion caused the fireflies to swoop back in their direction. Despite Richard's enthusiasm for his trips into the forest, Nicole heeded the guides and remained on the path.

Richard was about eight meters off to the left, trying to obtain a closer look at a gigantic flower that looked like an Oriental carpet, when he disappeared suddenly from view. "Ouch," Nicole heard him yell as he fell to the ground.

"Are you all right?" she said immediately.

"Yes," he said. "I just tripped over some vines and fell into a bunch of thorns. The bush surrounding me has red leaves as well as tiny, bizarre flowers that look like bullets. They smell like cinnamon, incidentally."

"Do you need any help?" Nicole asked.

"Nope. I'll just climb out of here in a jiffy."

Nicole glanced up and noticed that one of the two fireflies was racing off in the distance. *Now, what's that all about?* she was wondering when she heard Richard again.

"I may need some help after all," he said. "I seem to be stuck."

Nicole took a cautious step off the path. The remaining firefly went crazy, zooming down almost into her face. Nicole was temporarily blinded.

"Don't come over here, Nicole," Richard said abruptly a few seconds later. "Unless I am losing my mind, I believe this plant is preparing to eat me."

"*What?*" Nicole said, now frightened. "Are you serious?" She waited impatiently for her eyes to recover from the overdose of light.

"Yes, I am," Richard said. "Get back on the path. This bizarre bush has wrapped yellow tendrils around my arms and legs . . . some crawling bugs are already drinking the blood caused by the thorns . . . and there is an opening in the bush, toward which I am slowly being pulled, that looks like a distant cousin of some of the more unpleasant mouths I have seen in zoos. I can even see some teeth."

Nicole could hear the panic in Richard's voice. She took another step in his direction, but again the firefly blinded her.

"I can't see anything," she yelled. "Richard, are you still there?"

"Yes," he answered. "But I don't know for how much longer."

They heard the sound of animals moving quickly through the forest, along with a high-pitched whine. Suddenly three octospiders appeared, brandishing peculiar long, skinny weapons. The octos fired a liquid spray at the carnivorous bush and within seconds the bush released Richard. The aggressive plant immediately hid its mouth again behind its many branches.

Richard stumbled over and hugged Nicole. They both yelled "Thank you" as the trio of octospiders vanished into the forest as swiftly as they had appeared. Neither Richard nor Nicole noticed that the two fireflies were again hovering over their heads.

Nicole examined Richard carefully but found nothing except cuts and scratches. "I think I'll stay on the path awhile," he said, smiling wanly.

"That's probably not a bad idea," Nicole replied.

They talked about what had happened as they continued to walk through the forest. Richard was still shaken. "The branches close to my left shoulder pulled apart," he said, "and there was this hole, initially about the size of a baseball. But as the wave action of the tendrils carried me in that direction, the hole grew larger." He shuddered. "That's when I saw the little teeth, ringing the circumference. I had just started thinking about how it would feel to be eaten when our friends the octospiders arrived."

"So what's going on here?" Nicole said a little later. They had left the flower region and were again surrounded by trees and jungle growth and intermittent animal noises.

"Damned if I know," Richard replied.

The forest ended abruptly just as Richard and Nicole were becoming unbearably hungry. They stepped out upon an empty plain. In front of them, perhaps two kilometers away, a great green dome filled their view.

"Now what is—"

"It's the Emerald City, darling," Richard said. "Certainly you recognize it from the old movie. And inside is the Wizard of Oz, ready to grant all our wishes."

Nicole smiled and kissed her husband. "The wizard was a fake, you know," she said. "He didn't really have any power."

"That's open to some question," Richard said with a grin.

While they were talking, the two lights that had been guiding them sped away toward the green dome, leaving Richard and Nicole in near darkness. They pulled their flashlights out of their packs. "Something tells me we're near the end of our hike," Richard said, striding across the ground in the direction of the Emerald City.

They could see the gates through their binoculars from a distance of more than a kilometer. Both Richard and Nicole were becoming quite excited. "Do you think that's the home city of the octospiders?" Nicole asked.

"Yes, indeed," Richard said. "It must be quite a place. The top of that green dome is at least three hundred meters above the ground. I would guess that the area underneath exceeds ten square kilometers."

"Richard," Nicole asked when they were only about six hundred meters away, "what is our plan? Are we just going to walk up and knock on the gate?"

"Why not?" Richard answered, his pace quickening.

When they were two hundred meters from the gate, it opened and three figures emerged. Richard and Nicole heard a yell as one of the figures began moving rapidly toward them. Richard stopped and used his binoculars again. "It's Ellie," he shouted. "And Eponine.... They're with an octospider."

Nicole had already dropped her pack and was jogging across the plain. She grabbed her beloved daughter in her arms and lifted her off the ground with the strength of her embrace. "Oh, Ellie, Ellie," she said, the tears cascading down her cheeks.

5

"This is our friend Archie. He has been a big help to us while we have been staying here. Archie, meet my mother and father."

The octospider responded with a sequence that began with a brilliant crimson and was followed by a teal green, a lavender, two different yellows (one a saffron and the other a lemon, tending toward chartreuse), and a final purple. The band of colors ran completely around the octospider's spherical head and then disappeared back into the left side of the slit formed by the two long, parallel indentations in the middle of its face.

"Archie says it's a pleasure to meet you, especially after hearing so much about you," Ellie said.

"You can read their colors?" Nicole asked, quite shocked.

"Ellie's great," said Eponine. "She's picked up their language very quickly."

"But how do you speak to them?" Nicole asked.

"Their eyesight is incredibly keen," Ellie replied, "and they are remarkably intelligent. Archie and a dozen others have already learned to read lips. But we can talk about all that later, Mother. First tell me about Nikki and Robert. Are they all right?"

"Your daughter grows more adorable every day, and she misses you terribly. But I'm afraid Robert has never completely recovered. He still blames himself for not having protected you better."

The octospider Archie politely followed the personal conversation for several minutes before tapping Ellie on the shoulder and then reminding her that her parents were probably tired and cold.

"Thanks, Archie," Ellie said. "Okay, here's the plan. The two of you are to come inside the city for at least tonight and tomorrow—a kind of hotel suite has been set up just inside the gate for the four of us—and the day after tomorrow, or whenever you are properly rested, we will all return to the others. Archie will go with us."

"Why didn't the three of you simply come to where we were in the first place?" Richard said after a brief silence.

"I asked the same question, Dad . . . and never did receive what I considered a satisfactory answer."

The bands of color on Archie's head interrupted what Ellie was saying. "All right," she said to the octospider before turning back to her parents. "Archie says the octos wanted you two especially to have a clear idea of what they are all about—anyway, we can discuss all this after we settle in our suite."

The great gates of the Emerald City were thrown open when the four humans and their octospider companion were about ten meters away. Richard and Nicole were unprepared for the overwhelming variety of strange sights that greeted their eyes as they entered the city. Directly in front of them was a broad avenue, with continuous low structures on either side, leading to a tall, pink and blue, pyramid-shaped building several hundred meters in the distance.

Richard and Nicole were virtually in a trance when they took their initial steps into the octospider city. Neither of them would ever forget that incredible first moment. They were surrounded by a kaleidoscope of color. Every element of the city, including the streets, the buildings, the unexplained decorations that lined the avenue, the plants in the garden (if that's indeed what they were), and the wide range of animal creatures that seemed to be scurrying in all directions, was emblazoned with bright colors. A group of four large worms, or snakes, resembling wriggling candy canes except much more profusely colored, were coiled just inside the gate on the ground to Richard and Nicole's left. They had their heads lifted high, apparently straining to get a view of the alien visitors. Bright red and yellow animals with eight legs and lobsterlike claws were carrying thick green rods across an intersection fifty meters in front of Richard and Nicole.

Of course there were dozens, maybe hundreds of octospiders, all of whom had come to the gate area to catch a glimpse of the two newest humans to visit their city. They were sitting in groups in front of the buildings, standing beside the avenue, even walking on the rooftops. And they were all talking simultaneously in their bright bands of color, accenting the static decorations of the street scene with dynamic bursts of various hues.

Nicole looked around, glancing only for a moment at each of the bizarre creatures staring at her. Then she leaned her head back and gazed at the green dome far above her head. Some kind of thin, flexible ribbing could be seen in isolated spots, but it was mostly covered over by a thick green canopy.

"The ceiling is all growing vines and other plants, along with the insectlike animals that harvest the useful fruits and flowers," she heard Ellie say beside her. "It is a complete living ecosystem that has the additional advantage of being an excellent covering for the city, sealing out the Raman cold and atmosphere. After the gates are closed, you'll see how comfortable the temperatures are normally inside the city."

Scattered around under the dome were about twenty very bright sources of light, considerably larger than the individual fireflies that had guided Richard and Nicole through the octospider domain. Nicole tried to study one of the lights, but quickly gave up because it was too bright for her eyes. The illumination seemed to be provided by clusters of the same fireflies that had led them to the Emerald City.

Was it fatigue or excitement or a combination of both that caused Nicole to lose her equilibrium? Whatever the reason, while she was gazing at the green dome above her, Nicole began to feel as if she were spinning around. She stumbled and reached out a hand for Richard. The burst of adrenaline that accompanied her dizziness and sudden fear caused her heart rate to surge.

"What is it, Mother?" Ellie said, alarmed at her mother's pallor.

"Nothing," said Nicole, breathing slowly and deliberately. "It's nothing. . . . I was just dizzy for a moment."

Nicole glanced down at the ground to steady herself. The street was paved with brightly colored squares that looked like ceramics. Sitting on the street no more than fifty centimeters in front of her were three of the strangest creatures that Nicole had ever seen. They were about the size of basketballs. Their hemispherical tops were royal blue undulating material that resembled, in some ways, both human brains and the part of a jellyfish that floats on top of the water. In the center of this constantly moving mass was a dark, round hole, out of which were poking two long, thin antennae, perhaps twenty centimeters long, with ganglia or knots roughly two or three centimeters apart. When Nicole involuntarily recoiled, stepping back because she felt instinctively threatened by these bizarre animals, their antennae spun around and the trio scampered quickly to the side of the avenue.

Nicole glanced quickly around her. Bands of color were streaming around the heads of all the octospiders she could see. Nicole *knew* that they were dissecting her latest reaction. She suddenly felt naked, lost, and completely overwhelmed. From somewhere deep inside her came an ancient and powerful signal of distress. Nicole was afraid that she was about to scream.

"Ellie," she said quietly, "I think I've had enough for today. . . . Can we go inside soon?"

Ellie took her mother by the arm and guided her toward a doorway in the second structure to the right of the avenue. "The octos have been working day and night to convert these quarters. I hope they are satisfactory."

Nicole continued to stare fixedly at the octospider street scene, but what she was seeing was no longer penetrating deep into her cognitive mind. *This is a dream,* she thought, as a group of thin green creatures that looked like bowling balls on stilts walked through her field of view. *There cannot really be a place like this anywhere.*

"I too was feeling a little overwrought," Richard was saying. "We had that scare in the forest. And we have walked a long way in three days, especially for old folks. It's not surprising that your mother became disoriented—that scene outside was weird."

"Before he left," Ellie said, "Archie apologized in three different ways. He tried to explain that they had permitted free access to the gate area, thinking that you and Mother would be fascinated. He hadn't thought about the fact that it might be a little too much."

Nicole sat up slowly in her bed. "Don't worry, Ellie," she said. "I haven't really become that fragile. I guess I just wasn't prepared, especially after so much exercise and emotion."

"So would you like to rest some more, Mother, or would you prefer to have something to eat?"

"I'm fine, really," Nicole reiterated. "Let's go on with whatever you have planned. By the way, Eponine," she said, turning to the Frenchwoman, who had said very little since their initial greetings outside the city, "I must apologize for our rudeness. Richard and I have been so busy talking with Ellie and seeing everything . . . I forgot to tell you that Max sends his love. He made me promise that if I saw you, I would tell you that he misses you terribly."

"Thanks, Nicole," Eponine replied. "I have thought of Max and the rest of you every day since the octospiders brought us here."

"Have you been learning the octospider language too, like Ellie?" Nicole asked.

"No," Eponine answered slowly, "I've been doing something altogether different." She glanced around for Ellie, who had stepped out momentarily, presumably to arrange dinner. "In fact," Eponine continued, "I had hardly seen Ellie for two weeks until we started making plans for your arrival."

There was a strange silence for several seconds. "Have you and Ellie been prisoners here?" Richard then asked in a low voice. "And have you figured out why they kidnapped you?"

"No, not exactly," Eponine replied. She stood up in the small room. "Ellie," she shouted, "are you out there? Your father is asking questions. . . ."

"Just a minute," they all heard Ellie yell. A few moments later she returned to the room with the octospider Archie behind her. Ellie read the look on her father's face. "Archie is all right," Ellie said. "And we agreed that when we told you everything, he could be here . . . to explain and clarify and maybe answer questions that we can't."

The octospider sat down among the humans and there was another temporary silence. "Why do I have the feeling that this entire scene has been rehearsed?" Richard asked at length.

A worried Nicole leaned forward and took her daughter's hand. "There's not any bad news, is there, Ellie? You did tell us that you would be coming back with us."

"No, Mother," Ellie said. "There are just a few things that Eponine and I want to tell you. . . . Ep, why don't you go first?"

Bands of color were streaming around Archie's head as the octospider, who had obviously been following the conversation closely, changed his position to be more directly opposite Eponine. Ellie watched the bands carefully.

"What is he—or *it*—saying?" Nicole asked. She was still stunned by her daughter's proficiency with the alien language.

"'It' would be strictly proper, I guess," Ellie said with a short laugh. "At least that's what Archie told me when I explained pronouns. But Ep and I have been using 'he' and 'him' when we refer to both Archie and Dr. Blue. . . . Anyway, Archie wants us to inform you that both Eponine and I have been cared for very well, that we have not suffered in any way, and that we were only kidnapped by the octospiders because they had not been able to figure out how to establish a nonhostile and communicative interaction with us—"

"Kidnapping is not exactly the proper way to begin," Richard interrupted.

"I have explained all that to Archie and the others, Daddy," Ellie continued, "which is why he wants me to set the record straight now. They *have* treated us magnificently, and I have seen no indication that their species is even capable of hostile acts."

"All right," Richard said, "your mother and I understand the gist of this preamble."

They were delayed momentarily by some comments in color from Archie. After Ellie explained to the octospider the meanings of "gist" and "preamble," she looked across at her parents. "Their intelligence is really staggering," Ellie said. "Archie has never asked me the meaning of any word more than once."

"When I arrived here," Eponine began, "Ellie was just beginning to understand the octospider language. At first everything was terribly confusing. But after a few days Ellie and I understood why the octospiders had kidnapped me."

"We talked about it an entire evening," Ellie interjected. "We were both flabbergasted. We couldn't figure out how they could possibly have known."

"Known *what*?" Richard said. "I'm sorry, ladies, but I'm having trouble following."

"They knew that I had RV-41," Eponine said. "And both Archie and Dr. Blue—he's another octospider, a physician—we call him Dr. Blue because when he's talking his cobalt blue band spills way outside the normal boundaries—"

"Wait a minute," Nicole said now, shaking her head vigorously. "Let me get this straight. You're telling us the octospiders *knew* that Eponine had the RV-41 virus. How can that be possible?"

Archie went through a long color sequence that Ellie asked him to repeat. "He says that they have been monitoring all our activities very closely ever since we left New Eden. The octos deduced from our actions, he says, that Eponine had an incurable disease of some kind."

Richard began to pace. "That is one of the most amazing statements that I have ever heard," he said with passion. He turned toward the wall, temporarily lost in his thoughts. Archie reminded Ellie that he could not understand anything unless Richard was facing him. At length Richard spun around. "How could they *possibly* . . . Look, Ellie, aren't the octospiders deaf?"

When Ellie nodded affirmatively, Richard and Nicole learned their first little bit of the octospider language. Archie flashed a broad crimson band—indicating the following sentence would be declarative—followed by a magnificent aquamarine.

"Well, if they're deaf," Richard exclaimed, "how in the world could they have figured out that you had RV-41, unless they are masters of mind reading, or have a record of every . . . No, even then it's not possible."

He sat back down. There was another period of silence.

"Should I continue?" Eponine asked eventually. Richard nodded.

"As I was saying, Dr. Blue and Archie explained to Ellie and me that they were really very advanced in biology and medicine . . . and if we would try to cooperate with them, they would see if perhaps they had techniques that could cure me—assuming, of course, that I would be willing to submit to all the procedures."

"When we asked them *why* they wanted to cure Eponine," Ellie said, "Dr. Blue told us that the octospiders were trying to make a grand gesture of friendship, something that would pave the way for harmonious interactions between our two species."

Richard and Nicole were both absolutely astounded by what they were hearing. They looked at each other in disbelief as Ellie continued.

"Because I was still a beginner at the language," Ellie said, "it was very difficult to communicate what we knew about RV-41. Eventually, after many long, intense language sessions, we were able to tell the octospiders what we knew."

"Both Ellie and I tried to remember everything Robert had ever said about the disease. All along, Dr. Blue, Archie, and a couple of the other octospiders were around us. They never took a single note that we could see. But we never, ever told them the same information twice."

"In fact," Ellie added, "whenever we inadvertently repeated ourselves, they reminded us that we had told them *that* before."

"About three weeks ago," Eponine continued, "the octospiders informed us that their information-gathering process was over and that they were now ready to subject me to some tests. They explained that the tests might be painful at times and were extraordinary by human standards."

"Most of the tests," Ellie said, "involved inserting living creatures, some microscopic and some that Eponine could actually see, into her body—either by injection—"

"Or by allowing the creatures to enter through my, uh, I guess the best word would be orifices."

Archie interrupted here and asked for the meanings of "inadvertently" and "orifices." While Ellie was explaining, Nicole leaned over to Richard. "Sound familiar?" she asked.

Richard nodded. "But I never had any kind of interaction, at least not that I can remember. . . . I was isolated."

"I have experienced some weird feelings in my life," Eponine was saying, "but nothing quite like I felt the day five or six tiny worms, no bigger than a pin, crawled into the lower part of my body." She shivered. "I told myself that if I survived the days of having my insides invaded, I would never again complain about any physical discomfort."

"Did you believe that the octospiders were going to be able to cure you?" Nicole asked.

"Not at first," Eponine replied. "But as the days passed, I began to think that it was possible. I certainly could see that they possessed medical capabilities altogether different from ours. And I had the feeling they were making progress.

"Then one day, after the testing was over, Ellie showed up in my room—throughout this time I was kept somewhere else in the city, probably in their equivalent of a hospital—and told me that the octospiders had isolated the RV-41 virus and understood how it operated on its host, namely, me. They had Ellie tell me then that they were going to insert a 'biological agent' into my system which would seek out the RV-41 virus and destroy it completely. The agent would not be able to reduce the damage already done by the virus, which they assured me through Ellie was not that severe, but it would absolutely cleanse my system of RV-41."

"I was told to explain to Eponine also," Ellie said, "that there could be some side effects from the agent. They didn't know exactly what to expect, for of course they had never used the agent in humans before, but their 'models' predicted nausea and possibly headaches."

"They were correct about the nausea," Eponine said. "I threw up every three or four hours for a couple of days. At the end of that time, Dr. Blue, Archie, Ellie, and the other octospiders all gathered beside my bed to tell me that I was cured."

"Whaaat?" said Richard, jumping to his feet again.

"Oh, Eponine," Nicole said immediately, "I'm so happy for you." She stood up and hugged her friend.

"And you *believe* this?" Richard said to Nicole. "You believe that the octospider doctors, who can't possibly yet understand very well how the human body works, could accomplish in several days what your brilliant son-in-law and his staff at the hospital could not do in four years?"

"Why not, Richard?" Nicole said. "If it had been done by the Eagle at the Node, you would have accepted it immediately. Why can't the octospiders be much more advanced than we are in biology? Look at everything we saw."

"All right," said Richard. He shook his head a few times and then turned to Eponine. "I'm sorry," he said, "but it's just difficult for me to . . . Congratulations. I too am delighted." He embraced Eponine awkwardly.

While they had been talking, someone had noiselessly stacked fresh vegetables and water just outside their door. Nicole saw the materials for their feast when she went to use the bathroom.

"That must have been an astonishing experience," she said to Eponine when she returned to where everyone else was sitting.

"That's an understatement," Eponine said. She smiled. "Even though I feel in my heart that I'm cured, I can't wait to have it confirmed by you and Dr. Turner."

Both Richard and Nicole were bone tired after their large dinner. Ellie told her parents that there was more to talk about, but that she could wait until after Richard and Nicole had slept.

"I wish I could remember more about my period with the octospiders before we reached the Node," Richard said, when he and Nicole were lying together on the large bed their hosts had provided. "Then maybe I would understand better what I feel about the story that Ellie and Eponine told."

"Do you still doubt that she's cured?" Nicole asked.

"I don't know," Richard said. "But I will admit that I am rather puzzled by the difference in behavior between these octospiders and the ones who examined and tested me years before. I cannot believe that the octos in Rama II would *ever* have rescued me from a voracious plant."

"Maybe octospiders are capable of widely varying behavior. That's certainly true for human beings. In fact, it's true for all higher-order mammals on Earth. Why should you expect all octospiders to be the same?"

"I know you're going to say that I'm being xenophobic," Richard said, "but it's difficult for me to accept these 'new' octospiders. They seem too good to be true. As a biologist, what do you think is their payoff, to use your word, for being nice to us?"

"It's a legitimate question, darling," Nicole replied, "and I don't know the answer. The idealist in me, however, wants to believe that we have encountered a species that behaves, most of the time, in a moral fashion because doing good is its own reward."

Richard laughed. "I should have known you'd say something like that. It's consistent with your comments about Sisyphus during that discussion we had in New Eden long ago."

6

"You would find their language fascinating, Daddy," Ellie was saying when Nicole finally awakened after sleeping for eleven hours. Richard and Ellie were already eating breakfast. "It's extremely mathematical. They use sixty-four colors altogether, but only fifty-one are what we would call alphabetical. The other thirteen are clarifiers—they are used to specify tenses, or as counters, or even to identify comparatives and superlatives. Their language is really quite elegant."

"I can't imagine how a language can be elegant—your mother is the linguist in the family," Richard said. "I managed to learn to read German, but my speaking skills were atrocious."

"Good morning, everybody," Nicole said, stretching in her bed. "What's for breakfast?"

"Some new and different vegetables," Ellie replied. "Or maybe they are fruits, for there's really no equivalence in our world. Almost everything the octospiders eat is what we would probably call a plant, deriving its energy from light. Worms are about the only thing the octospiders eat regularly that does not get its primary energy from photons."

"So all the plants in the fields that we passed are powered by a kind of photosynthesis?"

"Something similar," Ellie replied, "if I understood properly what Archie told me. Very little is wasted in the octospider society. Those creatures that you and Daddy call 'giant fireflies' hover over each field for precisely scheduled periods of time each week or month. And all the water is managed as carefully as the photons."

"Where's Eponine?" Nicole asked while she surveyed the food laid out on the table in the middle of the room.

"She's off packing her things," Ellie said. "Besides, she thought that she really shouldn't participate in this morning's conversation."

"Are we going to be shocked again, like last night?" Nicole asked lightly.

"Perhaps," Ellie said slowly. "I really don't know how you are going to react. . . . Do you want to finish your breakfast before we start, or should I tell Archie we're ready?"

"You mean the octospider is going to be part of the conversation and Eponine is not?" Richard asked.

"It was her choice," Ellie said. "Besides, Archie, at least in his capacity as a representative of the octospiders, is far more involved in the subject matter than Eponine."

Richard and Nicole looked at each other. "Do you have any idea at all what this is about?" Richard said.

Nicole shook her head. "But we might as well begin," she said.

Archie spread out his tentacles on the floor so that his head was about the same height as those of the sitting humans. Ellie then informed her parents, and everyone laughed, that this time Archie would provide the "preamble." Ellie translated, at times hesitantly, as Archie began with an apology to Richard for the way Richard had been treated by Archie's "cousins" years previously. Archie explained that *those* octospiders, the ones the humans had encountered in Rama prior to arriving at the Node, were from a separate, splinter colony, only remotely related to the octospiders that were currently on board Rama. Archie emphasized that it was not until Rama came into their sphere of influence for the third time that the octospiders, as a species, concluded that the great cylindrical spacecraft were important.

A few of the survivors of that *other* octospider colony—a "vastly inferior group," according to Archie (this was one of the places where Ellie asked him to repeat what he was saying)—were still passengers on Rama when the spacecraft was intercepted, early in its trajectory, by the current octospider colony that had been specifically selected to represent their species. The splinter group survivors were removed from Rama, but all their records were preserved. Archie and the others in his colony learned the details of what had happened to Richard at that time and they now wished to make amends for that treatment.

"So all this preamble, in addition to being fascinating," said Richard, "is an elaborate apology to me?"

Ellie nodded and Archie flashed the broad crimson followed by the brilliant aquamarine.

"May I ask a question before we continue?" Nicole said. She turned toward the octospider. "I assume, from what you told us, that you and your colony boarded Rama during the period that we were all asleep. Did you know we were there?"

Archie answered that the octospiders had presumed the humans were living inside the far northern habitat in Rama, but had not known for certain until the external seal of the human habitat was first broken. By that time, according to Archie, the octospider colony had already been in place for twelve human years.

"Archie insisted that he make this apology himself," Ellie said, glancing at her father and then waiting for him to respond.

"Okay, I accept, I guess," Richard replied. "Although I have no idea what the proper protocol should be. . . . "

Archie asked Ellie to define "protocol." Nicole laughed. "Richard," she said, "sometimes you are so stiff."

"Anyway," Ellie said again, "in the interest of time, I will tell you everything else myself. According to Archie, the records from the splinter colony show that they conducted a number of experiments on you, most of which are outlawed in those octospider colonies Archie refers to as 'highly developed.' One experiment, Daddy, as you have often suggested, involved inserting into your brain a series of specialized microbes to void all your memory of the time period you stayed with the octospiders. I have reported to Archie and the others that the memory experiment was mostly but not completely successful.

"The most complex experiment they conducted on your body was an attempt to alter your sperm. The splinter colony of octospiders knew no more about where Rama was going than our family did. They thought that perhaps the humans and octospiders on board would be coexisting for centuries, maybe even eons, and the octospiders determined that it was absolutely essential for the two species to communicate.

"What they attempted to do was to change the chromosomes in your sperm so that your offspring would have both expanded language capability and greater visual resolution of colors. In short, they tried to engineer me genetically—for I was the only child born to you and Mother after your long odyssey—so that I would be able to communicate with them without undue difficulty. To accomplish this, they introduced a set of special creatures into your body."

Ellie stopped. Both Richard and Nicole were staring at her as if they were in shock.

"So you are some kind of hybrid?" Richard asked finally.

"Maybe a little," said Ellie, laughing to defuse the tension. "If I understand correctly, only a few thousand of the three billion kilobases that define my genome have been altered. . . . And speaking of that, Archie and the octospiders would like to revalidate, for their scientific research, that I am indeed the result of an altered sperm. They would like blood and other cell samples from both of you, so that they can conclude unequivocally that I could not have come from a 'normal' union of the two of you. Then they would know for certain that my facility with their language was indeed 'engineered' and not just incredible good luck."

"What difference does it make at this point?" Richard asked. "I would think that all that matters is that you can communicate."

"I'm surprised at you, Father—you who have always been such a knowledge junkie. The octospider society places information at the top of the value scale. They are already virtually certain, as a result of the tests they have performed on me plus the records kept by the splinter group, that I am indeed the result of an altered sperm. Looking at both your genomes in detail, however, would allow them to confirm it."

"All right," said Nicole after only a brief hesitation. "I'm willing." She walked over and hugged Ellie. "Whatever caused you to be, you are my daughter and I love you with all my heart." Nicole glanced back at Richard. "And I'm certain your father will agree as soon as he has had time to think about it."

Nicole smiled at Archie. The octospider flashed the broad crimson, followed by a more narrow cobalt blue and a bright yellow. The sentence meant "Thank you" in the octospider language.

The next morning Nicole wished that she had asked a few more questions before volunteering to help the octospiders with their scientific research. Just after breakfast, their constant alien companion Archie was joined by two other octospiders in the humans' small suite. One of the newcomers, introduced by Ellie as "Dr. Blue—a most distinguished medical scholar," explained what was going to occur. Richard's procedure would be simple and straightforward. Essentially, the octos only wanted enough data on Richard to corroborate the historical record of his visit to the splinter colony years before.

As for Nicole, since the octospider data base contained no physiological information on her, and the octos had already learned from their detailed examination of Ellie that the way in which human genetic characteristics are expressed is dominated by the mother's contribution to the offspring, a much more elaborate procedure would be required. Dr. Blue proposed to perform a complex series of tests on Nicole, the most important of which involved data gathering inside her body by a dozen tiny, coiled creatures that were about two centimeters long and the width of a pin. Nicole recoiled with horror when the octospider doctor held up an equivalent of a plastic bag and Nicole first saw the writhing, slimy creatures that were going to be inside her.

"But I thought all you needed was my genetic code," Nicole said, "and that's contained in each and every cell. It shouldn't be necessary—"

Bright colors circled Dr. Blue's head as the octospider interrupted before Nicole had a chance to finish her protest. "Our techniques of extracting your genome information," Dr. Blue said through Ellie, "are not yet very advanced. Our methods work best if we have many cells, chosen from several different organs and biological subsystems."

The doctor then politely thanked Nicole again for her cooperation, finishing with the sequence of cobalt blue and bright yellow bands she had already learned to interpret. The blue part of the "Thank you" spilled down the side of Dr. Blue's head, producing a beautiful visual effect that momentarily distracted the linguist in Nicole. *So keeping those color bands regular must be a learned behavior,* she thought. *And our doctor has a kind of speech impediment.*

Nicole's attention was forcibly returned to the pending procedure a few moments later when Dr. Blue explained that the coiled creatures would burrow through her skin into her body and then remain inside her for half an hour. *Yuch,* thought Nicole immediately, *they remind me of leeches.*

One was placed on her forearm. Nicole raised her arm up in front of her face and watched the tiny animal screw its way through her skin. Nicole felt nothing while the creature was invading her, but when it had disappeared she shuddered involuntarily.

Nicole was asked to lie down on her back. Dr. Blue then showed her two small eight-legged creatures, one red and one blue, each the size of a fruit fly. "You may feel some discomfort soon," Dr. Blue said to Nicole through Ellie, "as the coilers reach your internal organs. These little guys can be used for anesthesia if you would like some relief from the pain."

Less than a minute later Nicole experienced a sharp stabbing sensation in her chest. Nicole's first thought was that something was cutting into one of the chambers of her heart. When Dr. Blue saw Nicole's face wrenched in pain, he placed the two anesthetic bugs on Nicole's neck. In only seconds Nicole was suspended in a peculiar state between waking and dreaming. She could still hear Ellie's voice, continuing to explain what was happening, but she could not feel anything occurring inside her body.

Nicole found her gaze fixed on the front of the head of Dr. Blue, who was supervising the entire procedure. Much to her astonishment, Nicole thought that she was beginning to recognize emotional expressions in the subtle surface wrinkles of the octospider's face. She remembered once as a child being certain that she had seen her pet dog smile. *There's so much to seeing,* her floating mind thought, *so much more than we ever use.*

She felt astonishingly peaceful. Nicole closed her eyes briefly and when she opened them again she was a ten-year-old girl, weeping beside her father as her mother's bier was consumed by flames in a burial ceremony befitting the Senoufo queen. The old man, her great-grandfather Omeh, dressed in a frightening mask to scare off any demons that might try to accompany Nicole's mother to the afterlife, came over beside her and took her hand. "It is as the chronicles prophesied, Ronata," he said, using Nicole's Senoufo name, "our blood has been scattered to the stars."

The variegated mask of the shaman disappeared into another set of colors, these in bands streaking around Dr. Blue's head. Again Nicole heard Ellie's voice. *My daughter is a hybrid*, she thought to herself without emotion. *I have given birth to something that is more than human. A new kind of evolution has begun.*

Her mind drifted again and she was a great bird/plane flying high in the dark above the savannas of the Ivory Coast. Nicole had left the Earth, turned her back on the Sun, and blasted like a rocket toward the blackness and void beyond the solar system. In her mind's eye she could clearly see Omeh's face. "Ronata," he called into the night sky in the Ivory Coast, "do not forget. You are the chosen one."

And could he really have known, Nicole thought, still in the twilight zone between waking and sleeping, *all those years ago, in Africa, on Earth? And if so, how? Or is there still another dimension to seeing that we have only just begun to understand?*

Richard and Nicole were sitting together in the near darkness. They were temporarily alone. Ellie and Eponine were out with Archie, making all the arrangements for the departure the next morning.

"You've been very quiet all day," Richard said.

"Yes, I have," Nicole answered. "I have felt strange, almost drugged, ever since that last procedure this morning. . . . My memory is unusually active. I've been thinking about my parents. And Omeh. And visions I had years ago."

"Were you surprised at the results of the tests?" Richard asked after a short silence.

"Not really. I guess so much has happened to us. . . . And you know, Richard, I can still remember when Ellie was conceived. You were not really yourself again yet."

"I talked to Ellie and Archie quite a bit this afternoon while you were napping. The changes the octospiders induced in Ellie are permanent, like mutations. Nikki probably has some of the same characteristics—it depends on the exact genetic mixture. Of course hers will be diluted by another generation. . . ."

Richard didn't finish his thought. He yawned, and then reached over for Nicole's hand. They sat quietly together for several minutes before Nicole broke the silence.

"Richard, do you remember my telling you about the Senoufo chronicles? About the woman from the tribe, the daughter of a queen, who was prophesied to carry the Senoufo blood 'even unto the stars'?"

"Vaguely," Richard answered. "We haven't spoken about it for a long time."

"Omeh was certain that I was the woman in the chronicles . . . 'the woman without companion,' he called her. Do you believe there is any possible way that we can have knowledge of the future?"

Richard laughed. "Everything in nature follows certain laws. Those laws can be expressed as differential equations in time. If we know precisely the initial conditions of the system at any given epoch, and the exact equations representing the laws of nature, then theoretically we can predict all outcomes. We can't, of course, because our knowledge is always imperfect, and the rules of chaos limit the applicability of our estimation techniques."

"Suppose," Nicole said, propping herself up on an elbow, "there were individuals or even groups who did not know mathematics, but could somehow *see* or *feel* both the laws and the initial conditions you mentioned. Couldn't they perhaps intuitively solve at least part of the equations and predict the future using insight that we cannot model or quantify?"

"It's possible," said Richard. "But remember, extraordinary claims require—"

"—extraordinary evidence. I know," said Nicole. She paused for a moment. "I wonder what destiny is, then. Is it something we humans make up after the fact? Or is it real? And if destiny really exists as a concept, how can it be explained by the laws of physics?"

"I'm not following you, darling," Richard said.

"It's confusing even to me," Nicole said. "Am I who I am because, as Omeh insisted when I was a little girl, it was always my destiny to travel in space? Or am I the person I am because of all the choices I have personally made and the skills I have consciously developed?"

Richard laughed again. "Now you're very close to one of the fundamental philosophical conundrums, the debate between God's omniscience and man's free will."

"I didn't mean to be," said Nicole reflectively. "I just can't shake the notion that nothing that has happened in my absolutely incredible life would have been a surprise to Omeh."

7

Their departure breakfast was a feast. The octospiders provided more than a dozen different fruits and vegetables, as well as a hot, thick cereal made, according to Archie and Ellie, from the very tall grasses just north of the power plant. While they were eating, Richard asked the octospider what had happened to the avian hatchlings Tammy and Timmy, as well as the manna melons and the sessile material. He was not satisfied with the translated, somewhat vague response that all the other species were fine.

"Look, Archie," Richard said in his characteristic brusque manner. He was now comfortable enough with his alien host that he no longer felt it necessary to be overly polite. "I have far more than a casual interest in those creatures. I rescued them and raised them from birth by myself. I would like to see them, even if only briefly. . . . Under any circumstances, I think I deserve a more definitive answer to my question."

Archie stood up, ambled out the door of the suite, and returned in a few minutes. "We have arranged for you to see the avians for yourself later on today during our journey back to your friends," he said. "As for the other species, two of the eggs have just completed germination and are in the infant myrmicat stage. Their development is being closely monitored on the other side of our domain and it is not possible for you to visit them."

Richard's face brightened. "Two of them germinated! How did you accomplish that?"

"Eggs of the sessile species must be placed in a thermally controlled liquid for a month of your time before the embryonic development process will even begin," Ellie interpreted Archie's colors very slowly. "The temperature must be maintained within an extremely small range, less than a degree by your measures, at the same value that is optimal for the myrmicat manifestation of the species. Otherwise the growth and development process does not occur."

Richard was on his feet. "So that's the secret," he said, nearly shouting. "Dammit, I should have figured it out. I certainly had plenty of clues, both from the conditions inside their habitat and those murals they showed me." He began to pace around the room. "But how did the octospiders know?" he said, with his back to Archie.

Archie replied quickly after Ellie's translation. "We had information from the other octospider colony. Their records explained the entire metamorphosis of the sessiles."

It seemed too simple to Richard. He suspected that maybe their alien colleague was not telling him the whole truth. Richard was ready to ask some more questions when Dr. Blue came into the suite, followed by three other octospiders, two of whom were carrying a large hexagonal object wrapped in a paperlike material.

"What's this?" Richard asked.

"This is our official farewell party," Ellie answered. "Together with a present from the residents of the city."

One of the new octos asked Ellie if all the humans could gather outside on the avenue for the departure ceremony. The humans picked up their belongings and walked through the hallway out into the brighter lights. Nicole was surprised by what she saw. Except for the octospiders who filed out of their suite behind them, the avenue was deserted. Even the colors of the gardens seemed more muted, as if they had somehow been temporarily brightened by all the surrounding activity two days earlier when Richard and Nicole had arrived.

"Where is everyone?" Nicole asked Ellie.

"It's very quiet on purpose," her daughter replied. "The octos didn't want to overwhelm you again."

The five octospiders arranged themselves in a line in the middle of the avenue, with the pyramid-shaped building directly behind them. The two octos on the right side balanced the hexagonal package between them. It was larger than they were. The four humans were lined up opposite the octospiders, just in front of the gates to the city. The octospider in the center, whom Ellie introduced as the "Chief Optimizer" (based on Archie's description of the duties of the octospider leader), then stepped forward to speak.

The Chief Optimizer expressed its gratitude to Richard, Nicole, Ellie, and Eponine, including a personal note with each thank-you, and said that it hoped this brief interaction would be the "first of many" that would lead to more understanding between the two species. The octospider then indicated that Archie was going to return with the humans, not only so that the interaction could be continued and expanded, but also to demonstrate to the other humans that a mutual trust between the two species now existed.

During a brief pause Archie shuffled forward into the zone between the two lines and Ellie symbolically welcomed him to their traveling party. The two octos on the right then unveiled the present, which was a magnificent detailed painting of the sight that Richard and Nicole had seen at the moment of their entrance into the Emerald City. The painting was so lifelike that Nicole was momentarily stunned. A few moments later the humans all moved closer to the painting to study its details. All the weird creatures were in the picture, including the three royal blue undulators, whose two long, upright, knobby antennae thrust upward from a teeming body mass reminded Nicole how disoriented she had been the previous day.

As she examined the painting and wondered how it could have been created, Nicole recalled the near swoon that had accompanied her actual viewing of the scene. *Was I having a premonition of danger then?* she mused. *Or was it something else?* She glanced away from the painting and watched the octospiders talking among themselves. *Perhaps it was an epiphany,* she thought, *an instant burst of recognition of something way beyond my understanding. Some force or power never before experienced by any human being.* A chill ran down her back as the gates of the Emerald City began to open.

Richard was always concerned about naming things. After less than a minute of inspection of the creatures they were going to ride, he called them "ostrichsaurs."

"That's not very imaginative, darling," Nicole chided him.

"Maybe not," he said, "but it is a perfect description. They are just like a giant ostrich with the face and neck of one of those herbivorous dinosaurs."

The creature had four birdlike legs, a soft, feathery main body with an indented bowl in the middle where four humans could easily sit, and a long neck that could be extended three meters in any direction. Since the legs were about two meters long, the neck could reach the surrounding ground without difficulty.

The two ostrichsaurs were surprisingly swift. Archie, Ellie, and Eponine rode on one of the creatures, on whose side the large hexagonal painting had been tied with a kind of twine. Nicole and Richard were by themselves on the other ostrichsaur. There were no reins or other obvious means of controlling the creatures; however, before the group departed from the Emerald City, Archie spent almost ten minutes "talking" to the ostrichsaurs.

"He's explaining the entire route," Ellie said. "And also outlining what to do in case of an accident."

"What kind of an accident?" Richard asked, but Ellie simply shrugged in reply.

At first both Richard and Nicole hung on to the "feathers" that surrounded the bowl in which they were sitting, but after a few minutes they relaxed. The ride was very smooth, with very little jostling up and down. "Now, do you suppose," Richard said after the Emerald City faded from view, "these animals naturally evolved this way, with this near perfect bowl in the middle of their backs? Or did the octospider genetic engineers somehow breed them for transportation?"

"There's no doubt in my mind at all," Nicole replied. "I believe that most of the living things we have encountered, certainly including those dark, wriggling coiled things that crawled through my skin, have been designed for a specific function by the octospiders. How could it be otherwise?"

"But you can't believe these animals were designed from scratch," Richard said. "That would suggest an incredible technology, far beyond anything we can even imagine."

"I don't know, darling," Nicole said. "Maybe the octospiders have traveled to many different planetary systems, in each place finding life-forms that could be slightly altered to fit into their grand symbiotic schemes. But I can't accept for a minute the idea that this harmonious biology just happened by natural evolution."

The two ostrichsaurs and their five riders were guided by three of the giant fireflies. After a couple of hours, the group approached a vast lake stretching to the south and west. Both the ostrichsaurs squatted on the ground so that Archie and the four humans could descend.

"We're going to have lunch and a drink of water here," Archie said to the others. He handed Ellie a container filled with food and then led the two ostrichsaurs over to the lake. Nicole and Eponine walked off in the direction of some blue plants growing at the edge of the water, leaving Richard and Ellie by themselves.

"Your proficiency in their language is very impressive, to say the least," Richard said in between bites of food.

Ellie laughed. "I'm afraid I'm not as good as you think. The octos purposely keep their sentences very simple for me. And they speak slowly, with broad bands. But I am improving. . . . You realize, don't you, that they are not using their *true* language when speaking to us? It's just a derivative form."

"What do you mean?" Richard asked.

"I explained it to Mother back at the Emerald City. I guess she didn't have a chance to tell you." Ellie swallowed before continuing. "Their *true* language has sixty-four color symbols, just as I mentioned, but eleven of them are not accessible to us. Eight lie in the infrared part of the spectrum, and another three in the ultraviolet. So we can only distinguish clearly fifty-three of their symbols. This was quite a problem in the beginning. Luckily, five of the eleven outside symbols are clarifiers. Anyway, for our benefit they have developed what amounts to a new dialect of their language, using only the color wavelengths that we can see. Archie says that this new dialect is already being taught in some of their advanced classes."

"Amazing," Richard said. "You mean they have *adjusted* their language to accommodate our physical limitations?"

"Not exactly, Father. They still use their true language when talking to each other. That's why I cannot always understand what they are saying. However, this new dialect has been developed, and is now being expanded, just to make communications with us as easy as possible."

Richard finished his lunch. He was about to ask Ellie another question about the octospider language when he heard Nicole yell. "Richard," she shouted from fifty meters away, "look over there, in the air, toward the forest."

Richard craned his neck and shaded his eyes. In the distance he could see two birds flying toward them. For some reason his recognition was delayed until he heard the familiar shrieking sound. Then he jumped up and ran in the direction of the avians. Tammy and Timmy, now full-grown, swooped down out of the sky and landed beside him. Richard was ecstatic. His wards jabbered incessantly and pressed their velvet underbellies against him for a rub.

They looked perfectly healthy. There was not a trace of sadness in their huge expressive eyes. A few minutes later Timmy suddenly stepped away, shrieked something in a very loud voice, and became airborne. Within a few minutes the avian returned with a companion, a female with an orange velvet covering unlike any Richard had ever seen. Richard was a little confused, but he did realize that Timmy was trying to introduce him to his mate.

The remainder of the reunion with the avians lasted only ten or fifteen minutes. Archie insisted, after he first explained that the vast lake system supplied almost half of the fresh water in the octospider domain, that the entourage needed to continue on its journey. Richard and Nicole were already in the bowl on the back of their ostrichsaur when the three avians departed. Tammy hovered over them for a good-bye jabber, obviously disturbing the creature on which they were riding. At length she followed her brother and his mate in their flight toward the forest.

Richard was strangely quiet as their mounts also headed north in the direction of the forest. "They really mean a lot to you, don't they?" Nicole said.

"Absolutely," her husband replied. "I was all alone except for the hatchlings for a long time. Timmy and Tammy depended on me for their survival. . . . Committing myself to rescuing them was probably the first selfless act of my life. It opened up new dimensions of both anxiety and happiness for me."

Nicole reached over and took Richard's hand. "Your emotional life has had an odyssey of its own," she said softly, "every bit as diverse as the physical journey you have experienced."

Richard kissed her. "I still have a few demons that are not yet exorcised," he said. "Maybe, with your help, in another ten years I'll be a decent human being."

"You don't give yourself enough credit," Nicole said.

"My *brain* I give plenty of credit," Richard said with a grin, changing the tone of the conversation. "And do you know what it is thinking right now? Where did that avian with the orange underbelly come from?"

Nicole looked puzzled. "From the second habitat," she replied. "You yourself told us that there must have been a population of almost a thousand before Nakamura's troops invaded. The octospiders must have rescued a few also."

"But I lived there for months," Richard protested. "And I never ever saw an avian with an orange underbelly. Not one. I would have remembered."

"What are you suggesting?"

"Nothing. Your explanation is definitely consistent with Occam's Razor. But I'm starting to wonder if maybe our octospider buddies have some secrets they have not yet discussed with us."

They reached the large igloo hut not far from the Cylindrical Sea after several more hours. The tiny glowing igloo that had been beside it was gone. Archie and the four humans dismounted. The octospider and Richard untied the hexagonal painting and stored it against the side of the igloo. Then Archie led the ostrichsaurs aside and gave them directions for their homeward trek.

"Can't they stay a little while?" Nicole asked. "The children would be absolutely delighted with them."

"Unfortunately, no," Archie replied. "We have only a few and they are very much in demand."

Although Eponine, Ellie, Richard, and Nicole were all tired from their journey, they were still extremely excited about the forthcoming reunion. Before leaving the igloo hut, first Eponine and then Ellie used the mirror and freshened their faces. "Please, all of you," Eponine said, "I ask one favor. Don't say anything about my cure to anybody until I have had a chance to tell Max in private. I want it to be my surprise."

"I hope Nikki still recognizes me," Ellie said nervously as they descended the first staircase and entered the corridor that led to the landing. When the group walked out onto the landing and gazed at the circular floor below them, the twins Kepler and Galileo were playing a game of tag, with little Nikki watching them and laughing. Nai and Max were unloading food from a subway that had apparently recently arrived. Eponine could not restrain herself. "Max," she shouted, "Max!"

Max reacted as if he had been shot. He dropped the food he was carrying and turned toward the landing. He saw Eponine waving at him and broke like a thoroughbred for the cylindrical staircase. It could not have been more than two minutes before he emerged onto the landing and threw his arms around Eponine.

"Oh, Frenchie," he said, lifting her half a meter off the ground and hugging her fiercely, "how I have missed you!"

8

Archie could do all kinds of tricks with the colored balls. The octospider could catch two balls at once and then throw them in distinctly different directions. Archie could even juggle all six of the balls simultaneously, using four tentacles, for he needed only the other four tentacles on the ground to maintain his balance. The children loved for him to swing all three of them at the same time. Archie never seemed to tire of playing with the smaller humans.

In the beginning, of course, the children had been afraid of their alien visitor. Little Nikki, despite Ellie's repeated assurances that Archie was friendly, was especially wary because of her memory of the terror of her mother's kidnapping. Benjy was the first to accept Archie as a playmate. The Watanabe twins were not coordinated enough to play complicated games, so Benjy was delighted to discover that Archie would gladly join him for an active game of catch or Benjy's version of dodgeball.

Max and Robert were both disturbed by Archie's presence. Within an hour after the arrival of the four humans and the octospider, in fact, Max had confronted Richard and Nicole in their bedroom. "Eponine tells me," Max had said angrily, "that the damn octospider is going to *live* with us here. Have you all lost your minds?"

"Think of Archie as an ambassador, Max," Nicole had said. "The octos want to establish regular communications with us."

"But these same octospiders kidnapped your daughter and my

girlfriend and held them against their will for over a month. Are you telling me that we are to *ignore* their actions altogether?"

"There were extenuating reasons for the kidnappings," Nicole had replied, exchanging a brief glance with Richard. "And the women were treated very well. Why don't you talk to Eponine about it?"

"Eponine has nothing but praise for the octospiders," Max had said. "It's almost as if she has been brainwashed. I thought you two would be more reasonable."

Even after Eponine had informed Max that the octospiders had cured her of RV-41, he was still skeptical. "If it's true," he had said, "then it's the most wonderful news I've received since those little robots showed up at the farm and confirmed that Nicole had safely reached New York. But I am having a very hard time seeing those eight-legged monsters as our benefactors. I want Doc Turner to examine you very carefully. If he tells me you're cured, then I'll believe it."

Robert Turner was overtly hostile to Archie from the beginning. Nothing Nicole or even Ellie could say could neutralize the anger that he still felt over Ellie's forcible kidnapping. His professional pride was also severely wounded by the apparent ease with which Eponine had been purportedly cured.

"You're expecting too much, Ellie, as always," Robert said on the second night they were together. "You come in here, all full of glowing reports about these aliens who snatched you away from Nikki and me, and you expect me to embrace them immediately. That's not fair. I need time to understand and to synthesize everything you're telling me. Don't you realize that both Nikki and I were traumatized by your kidnapping? I can't change my opinion overnight."

Ellie's revelation about the genetic changes made in her father's sperm also disturbed Robert, even though it did explain why his wife's genome had defied classification in the tests his colleague Ed Stafford had conducted back in New Eden.

"How can you be so calm about discovering that you're a hybrid?" he said to Ellie. "Don't you understand what it means? When the octospiders altered your DNA to improve your visual resolution and to make learning their language easier, they tampered with a robust genetic code that has evolved naturally over millions of years. Who knows what disease suscep-tibilities, infirmities, or even negative changes in fertility may show up in you or subsequent generations? The octos may have unwittingly doomed all our grandchildren."

Ellie was not able to mollify her husband. When Nicole began working with Robert to ascertain whether Eponine had indeed been cured of RV-41, she noticed that Robert bristled every time Nicole made a favorable statement about Archie or the octospiders.

"We must give Robert more time," Nicole counseled her daughter a week after their return. "He still feels that the octospiders violated him, not only by kidnapping you, but also by contaminating the genes of his daughter."

"Mother, there is another problem as well. I almost feel that Robert is *jealous* in some peculiar way. He thinks that I spend too much time with Archie. He doesn't seem to accept the fact that Archie cannot communicate with anyone else unless I am there to interpret."

"As I said, we must be patient. Eventually Robert will accept the situation."

But in private Nicole had her doubts. Robert was determined to find some remnant of the RV-41 virus in Eponine and, when test after test with his relatively unsophisticated portable equipment showed no evidence of the pathogen in her system, he continued to request additional procedures. In Nicole's professional opinion, there was nothing to be gained from more testing. Although there existed a very small probability that the virus had eluded them and did still dwell somewhere in Eponine, Nicole felt that it was virtually certain that Eponine had been cured.

The two doctors clashed the day after Ellie had confided to her mother that Robert was jealous of Archie. When Nicole suggested that they terminate the tests on Eponine and pronounce her healthy, she was shocked to hear her son-in-law say that he proposed to open up Eponine's chest cavity and take a direct sample from the tissues around her heart.

"But Robert," Nicole said, "have you ever had a case where so many other tests have been virus-negative but the pathogen was still locally active in the cardiac region?"

"Only when death was imminent and the heart had already deteriorated," he admitted. "But that doesn't preclude that the same situation could occur earlier in the cycle of the disease."

Nicole was staggered. She did not argue with Robert, for she could tell from the rigid set of his muscles that he had already decided on his next course of action. But Nicole knew full well that open-heart surgery of any kind was risky, even when performed by skilled hands. She also realized that if Robert didn't come to his senses, she would be forced to oppose him on Eponine's behalf.

Max asked to talk to Nicole privately very soon after Robert recommended that the heart surgery be performed. "Eponine is frightened," Max confided, "and I am too. She came back from the Emerald City more full of life than I have ever seen her. Robert originally told me that the tests would be over in a couple of days. They have dragged on for almost two weeks and now he says he wants to take a tissue sample from her heart."

"I know," said Nicole grimly. "He told me last night he was going to recommend the open-heart procedure."

"Help me, please," Max said. "I want to make certain that I

understand the facts properly. You and Robert have examined her blood many times, as well as several other bodily tissues that sometimes show minute quantities of the virus, and all the specimens have been unambiguously negative?"

"That's correct," Nicole said.

"Isn't it true also that every other time that Eponine has been examined, ever since she was first diagnosed as RV-41-positive years ago, her blood samples have indicated the presence of the virus?"

"Yes," Nicole replied.

"Then why does Robert want to operate? Does he simply not want to believe that she is cured? Or is he just being extra careful?"

"I cannot answer for him," Nicole said.

She looked searchingly at her friend and knew both what his next question would be and how she would answer it.

"If you were the doctor in charge, Nicole," Max asked, "would you operate on Eponine?"

"No, I would not," Nicole replied carefully. "I believe that it is almost certain that Eponine was indeed cured by the octospiders and that the risk of the operation cannot be justified."

Max smiled and kissed his friend on the forehead. "Thank you," he said.

Robert was outraged. He reminded everyone that he had dedicated more than four years of his life to studying this particular disease, as well as trying to find a cure, and that he certainly knew more about RV-41 than all of them put together. How could they possibly trust an alien cure more than his surgical talent? How could his own mother-in-law, whose knowledge of RV-41 was limited to what he himself had taught her, have dared to offer an opinion different from his? He could not be placated by any of the group, not even by Ellie, whom he eventually banished from his presence after several unpleasant exchanges.

For two days Robert refused to come out of his room. He didn't even reply when his daughter Nikki wished him "Sweet dreams, Daddy" before her naps and bedtime. His family and friends were deeply troubled by Robert's torment, but could not figure out how to ease his pain. The question of Robert's mental stability came up in several discussions. Everyone agreed that Robert had seemed out of place ever since the escape from New Eden and that his behavior had become even more erratic and unpredictable after Ellie's kidnapping.

Ellie confided to her mother that Robert had been "peculiar" with her since their recent reunion. "He has not approached me even once, as a woman," she said sorrowfully. "It has been as if he felt I was contaminated by my experience. He keeps saying weird things like, 'Ellie, did you *want* to be kidnapped?'"

"I feel sorry for him," Nicole replied. "He is carrying such a heavy emotional burden, going all the way back to Texas. This has all been simply too much. We should have—"

"But what can we do for him now?" Ellie interrupted.

"I don't know, darling," Nicole said. "I just don't know."

Ellie tried to pass the difficult time helping Benjy with octospider language lessons. Her half brother was absolutely fascinated by everything about the aliens, including the hexagonal octospider painting that had been brought back from the Emerald City. Benjy stared at the picture several times a day and never missed an opportunity to ask questions about the amazing creatures depicted in the painting. Through Ellie, Archie always patiently answered whatever Benjy asked.

Benjy had decided, soon after he began playing regularly with Archie, that he wanted to learn to recognize at least a few phrases in the octospider lexicon. Benjy knew that Archie was able to read lips and he wanted to show the octospider that even a "slow human," if properly motivated, could pick up enough understanding of the octospider language for a simple conversation.

Ellie and Archie started Benjy with the fundamentals. He learned the octospider colors for "yes," "no," "please," and "thank you" without any difficulty. The numbers were fairly easy as well, because both the cardinals and the ordinals were essentially combination sequences of two basic colors, blood red and malachite green, that were used in a binary fashion and marked in the flow of the sentence by a salmon clarifier. What gave Benjy the most trouble was comprehending that the individual colors by themselves did not have any meaning. A burnt sienna band, for example, represented the verb "to understand" if followed by a mauve and then a clarifier; however, if the burnt sienna/mauve combination was followed by a vermilion, the three-band symbol meant "flowering plant."

Nor were the individual colors members of an alphabet in the strictest sense. Sometimes the width of the colors, when compared with others in the longer sequence defining a single word, completely changed the meaning. The burnt sienna/mauve combination only meant "to under-stand" if the two bands were of approximately equal width. The word defined by a narrow burnt sienna followed by a mauve of roughly double the width was "capacity."

Benjy struggled with the language, doing all the required repetitions, with an uncommon zeal. His ardor for learning warmed Ellie's heart at a time when she was deeply concerned about how the crisis with Robert would be resolved.

At the beginning of the third day of Robert's self-imposed exile in his room, the subway pulled into its slot, as expected, with their semiweekly supply of food and water. Only this time there were two new octospiders on board. They disembarked and had a detailed conversation with Archie. The family gathered together, expecting some unusual news.

"Human troops are again in New York," Archie reported, "and they are in the process of breaking the seal to our lair. It's just a matter of time until they discover the subway tunnels."

"So what should we do now?" Nicole asked.

"We would like you to come and live with us in the Emerald City," Archie said. "My colleagues anticipated this possibility and have already finished the design of a special section in the city just for you. It could be ready in a few more days."

"And what if we don't want to go?" Max asked.

Archie conferred briefly with the other two octospiders. "Then you can stay here and wait for the troops," he said. "We will provide as much food as we can, but we will begin dismantling the subway as soon as we have evacuated all our associates on the northern side of the Cylindrical Sea."

Archie continued speaking, but Ellie stopped translating. She asked the octospider to repeat his next few sentences several times before turning, a little pale, to her friends and family.

"Unfortunately," she translated, "we octospiders must be concerned for our own welfare. Therefore, any of you who decide not to come with us will have your short-term memories blocked and will not be able to recall in detail any events from the last several weeks."

Max whistled. "So much for friendship and communication," he said. "When push comes to shove, all of the species use power."

He walked over to Eponine and took her hand. She looked at him quizzically as Max pulled her over in front of Nicole. "Will you marry us, please?" he said.

Nicole was flustered. "Right now?" she asked.

"Right this very goddamn minute," Max answered. "I love this woman beside me and I want to have an orgy of a honeymoon with her up in that igloo hut before all hell breaks loose."

"But I'm not qualified—" Nicole protested.

"You're the best available," Max interrupted. "Come on, at least do a good approximation." The speechless bride was beaming.

"Do you, Max Puckett, take this woman, Eponine," Nicole said hesitantly, "to be your wife?"

"I *do* and should have done months ago," Max replied.

"And do you, Eponine, take this man, Max Puckett, to be your husband?"

"Oh, yes, Nicole, with pleasure."

Max pulled Eponine toward him and kissed her passionately. "Now, *Ar-chi-bald*," he said as he and Eponine headed for the staircase, "in case you're wondering, Frenchie and I intend to go with you to that Emerald

City she talks so much about. But we'll be gone for the next twenty-four hours or so, maybe longer if Eponine's energy holds out, and we do not want to be disturbed."

Max and Eponine walked briskly over to the cylindrical staircase and disappeared. Ellie had almost finished explaining to Archie what was going on with Max and Eponine when the newlyweds emerged on the landing and waved. Everyone laughed as Max pulled Eponine back toward the corridor.

Ellie sat by herself against the wall in the dim light. *It's now or never,* she thought. *I have to try one more time.*

She recalled the angry scene several hours earlier. "Of course you want to go with your friend Archie the octospider," Robert had said bitterly. "And you expect to take Nikki with you."

"Everyone else is going to accept the invitation," Ellie had replied, not even attempting to hide her tears. "Please come with us, Robert. They are a very gentle, very moral species."

"They have brainwashed all of you," Robert had said. "Somehow they have seduced you into believing that they are even better than your own kind." Robert had then looked at Ellie with disgust. "Your own kind," he had repeated. "What a joke. Why, I guess you're as much an octospider as you are a human."

"That's not true, darling," Ellie had said. "I've told you several times that only very small changes were made. I'm as human as you are."

"Why, why, *why?*" Robert had suddenly shouted. "Why did I let you talk me into coming to New York in the first place? I should have stayed behind, where I was surrounded by things I understood."

Despite her pleas, Robert had been adamant. He was not going to the Emerald City. He had even seemed strangely pleased that his short-term memory would be blocked by the octospiders. "Perhaps," he had said, laughing harshly, "I will have no memory at all of your return. I will not recall that my wife and daughter are both hybrids and that my closest friends have no respect for my professional abilities. Yes," he had continued, "I will be able to forget this nightmare of the last few weeks and remember only that you were stolen away from me, as my first wife was, while I still loved you desperately."

Robert had stalked around the room in anger. Ellie had tried to soothe and comfort him. "No, *no*," he had shouted, recoiling from her touch. "It's too late. There is too much pain. I can't stand any more."

In the early hours of the evening Ellie had sought counsel from her mother. Nicole had not been able to provide Ellie with any relief. Nicole had agreed that Ellie should not give up, but had cautioned her daughter that nothing in Robert's behavior suggested that he might change his mind.

At Nicole's suggestion, Ellie approached Archie and asked a favor of the octospider. If Robert insisted on not going with them, Ellie entreated, would it be possible for Archie, or one of the other octospiders, to take Robert back to the lair, where he would be found quickly by the other humans? Archie had reluctantly agreed.

I love you, Robert, Ellie said to herself as she finally stood up. *And Nikki does too. We want you to come with us, for you are my husband and her father.* Ellie took a deep breath and entered her bedroom.

Even Richard had tears in his eyes as a mumbling Robert Turner, after exchanging a final hug with his wife and daughter, walked off haltingly behind Archie toward the subway only twenty meters away. Nikki was crying softly, but the girl couldn't have realized fully what was occurring. She was still too young.

Robert turned, waved slightly, and entered the train. In a few seconds it accelerated into the tunnel. Less than a minute later the somber mood was broken by cries of joy from the landing above them.

"All right, down there," Max shouted, "you'd better be ready for a big party."

Nicole looked up under the dome, and even at that distance, in the dim light, she could see the radiant smiles of the newlyweds. *And so it is,* she thought, her heart still heavy from her daughter's loss. *Sorrow and joy. Joy and sorrow. Wherever there are humans. On Earth. In new worlds beyond the stars. Now and forever.*

THE EMERALD CITY

1

The small driverless transport stopped at a circular plaza from which streets extended in five directions. A dark woman with gray hair and her octospider companion descended together from the car, leaving it empty. As the octospider and the human walked slowly away from the plaza, the transport departed with its interior lights now extinguished.

A solitary giant firefly preceded Nicole and Dr. Blue as they continued their conversation in the near darkness. Nicole was careful to exaggerate each word so that her alien friend would have no difficulty reading her lips. Dr. Blue replied in broad swaths of color, using simple sentences that he knew Nicole understood.

When they reached the first of four cream-white, single-story dwellings at the end of the cul-de-sac, the octospider lifted one of his tentacles from the street and shook hands with Nicole. "Good night," she replied with a wan smile. "It was quite a day. . . . Thank you for everything."

After Dr. Blue went inside his house, Nicole walked over to the decorative fountain forming an island in the center of the street and drank from one of the four spigots jetting forth a continuous stream of water at waist level. Some of the water that touched Nicole's face fell back into the basin, causing a flurry of activity in the shallow pool. Even in the dim light Nicole could see the swimming creatures darting to and fro. *The cleaners are everywhere*, she thought, *especially when we're around. The water that touched my face will be purified in seconds.*

She turned and approached the largest of the three remaining dwellings in the cul-de-sac. When Nicole crossed the threshold of her house, the outside firefly flew quickly down the street to the plaza. In the atrium, Nicole tapped the wall lightly one time, and in a few seconds a smaller firefly, barely glowing, appeared in the hallway in front of her. She stopped in one of the family's two bathrooms and then paused at the doorway of Benjy's room. He was snoring loudly. Nicole watched her son sleep for almost a full minute and then continued down the hallway to the master bedroom she shared with her husband.

Richard was also asleep. He did not respond to Nicole's soft greeting. She took off her shoes and left the bedroom. When she reached the study, Nicole tapped on the wall twice more and the illumination increased. The study was cluttered with Richard's electronic components, which he had had the octospiders gather for him over a period of several months. Nicole laughed to herself as she picked her way through the mess to her desk. *He always has a project*, she thought. *At least the translator will be very useful.*

Nicole sat in the chair at her desk and opened the middle drawer. She pulled out her portable computer, for which the octospiders had finally provided acceptable new power and storage subsystems. After calling up her journal from the menu, Nicole began typing on the keyboard, intermittently glancing at the small monitor to read what she was writing.

Day 221

I have arrived at home very late and, as I expected, everyone is asleep. I was tempted to take off my clothes and snuggle into bed beside Richard, but this day has been so extraordinary that I feel compelled to write while my thoughts and feelings are still fresh in my mind.

I had breakfast, as always, with our entire human clan here about one hour after dawn. Nai talked about what the children were going to do in school before their long nap, Eponine reported that both her heartburn and morning sickness had abated, and Richard complained that the "biological wizards" (our octospider hosts, of course) were mediocre electrical engineers. I tried to participate in the conversation, but my growing anticipation and anxiety about this morning's meetings with the octospider doctors kept occupying my thoughts.

My stomach was full of butterflies when I arrived at the conference room in the pyramid just after breakfast. Dr. Blue and his medical colleagues were prompt, and the octos launched immediately into a lengthy discussion of what they had learned from Benjy's tests. Medical jargon is hard enough to understand in one's own native language—it was nearly impossible for me at times to follow what they were saying with their colors. Often I had to ask them to repeat.

It did not take long for their answer to be apparent. Yes, the octospiders could definitely see, by comparison, where Benjy's genome was different from everyone else's. Yes, they agreed that the specific string of genes on chromosome 14 was almost certainly the source of Whittingham's syndrome. But no, they were sorry, they didn't see any way—not even using something I interpreted as a gene transplant—that they could cure his problem. It was too complex, the octospiders said, involving too many amino acid chains, they had not had enough experience with human beings, there were too many chances that something might go terribly wrong. . . .

I cried when I understood what they were telling me. Had I expected otherwise? Had I thought that somehow the same miraculous medical capability that had freed Eponine from the curse of the RV-41 virus might be successful in curing Benjy's birth defect? I realized, in my despair, that I had indeed been hoping for a miracle, even though my brain recognized very clearly the significant difference between a congenital ailment and an acquired virus. Dr. Blue tried his best to console me. I let my mother's tears flow there, in front of the octospiders, knowing that I would need my strength when I returned home to tell the others.

Nai and Eponine both knew the results as soon as they saw my face. Nai adores Benjy and never stops praising his determination to learn in spite of the obstacles. Benjy *is* amazing. He spends hours and hours in his room, working laboriously through all his lessons, struggling for days to grasp a concept in fractions or decimals that a gifted nine-year-old might learn in half an hour. Only last week Benjy beamed with pride when he showed me he could find the least common denominator to add the fractions 1/4, 1/5, and 1/6.

Nai has been his main teacher. Eponine has been Benjy's pal. Ep probably felt worse than anybody this morning. She had been certain, because the octospiders had healed her so quickly, that Benjy's problem as well would succumb to their medical magic. It was not to be. Eponine sobbed so hard and so long this morning that I became concerned about the welfare of her baby. She patted her swollen belly and told me not to worry. Ep laughed and said, through her tears, that her reaction was probably mostly due to her overactive hormones.

All three of the men were clearly upset, but they didn't show much emotion. Patrick left the room quickly without saying anything. Max expressed his disappointment with an unusually colorful set of four-letter words. Richard just grimaced and shook his head.

We had all agreed, before the examination began, not to say anything to Benjy about the actual purpose of all the tests the octospiders were conducting. Could he have known? Might he have surmised what was going on? Perhaps. But this morning, when I told him that the octospiders had concluded that he was a healthy young man, I saw nothing in Benjy's eyes that even hinted he was aware of what had taken place. After I hugged him hard, fighting against another set of tears threatening to destroy my facade, I returned to my room and allowed the sorrow of my son's handicap to overcome me one more time.

I'm certain that Richard and Dr. Blue conspired together to keep my mind busy the rest of the day. I had not been in my room for more than twenty minutes when there was a soft knock on the door. Richard explained that Dr. Blue was in the atrium and that two other octospider scientists were waiting for me in the conference room. Had I forgotten that a detailed presentation on the octospider digestive system had been scheduled for me today?

The discussion with the octospiders turned out to be so fascinating that I was indeed able temporarily to forget that my son's handicap was beyond their medical magic. Dr. Blue's colleagues showed me complex anatomical drawings of octospider insides, identifying all the major organs of their digestive sequence. The drawings were made on some kind of parchment or hide and were spread out across the large table. The octospiders explained to me, in their wonderful language of colors, absolutely everything that happens to food inside their body.

The most unusual feature of the octospider digestive process is the two large sacs, or buffers, at both ends of the system. Everything they eat goes directly into an intake buffer, where it can sit for as long as thirty days. The octospider's body itself, based on the activity level of the individual, automatically determines the rate at which the food in the bottom of the sac is accessed, broken down chemically, and distributed to the cells for energy.

At the other end is a waste buffer, into which is discharged all the material that cannot be converted into useful energy by the octospider's body. Every healthy octospider, I learned, has a small animal permanently living in this buffer. They showed me one of the tiny, centipedelike creatures that begins life as a minuscule egg deposited by its predecessor inside the host octospider. The "waster" is essentially omnivorous. It consumes ninety-nine percent of the waste deposited in the buffer during the two human months that it takes to grow to maturity. When the waster reaches adulthood, it deposits a pair of new eggs, only one of which will germinate, and then leaves forever the octospider in which it has been living.

The intake buffer is located just behind and below the mouth. The octospiders eat very rarely; however, they absolutely gorge themselves when they do have meals. We had a long discussion about their eating habits. Two of the facts that Dr. Blue told me were extremely surprising—first, that an empty octo intake buffer leads to *immediate* death, in less than a minute, and second, that a baby octospider must be *taught* to monitor the status of its food supply. Imagine! It does not know instinctively when it is hungry! When Dr. Blue saw the astonishment on my face, he laughed—a jumbled-up sequence of short color bursts—and then hastened to assure me that unexpected starvation is not a leading cause of death among the octospiders.

After my three-hour nap (I still cannot make it through the long octospider day without some sleep—of our group only Richard is capable of forgoing the nap on a regular basis), Dr. Blue informed me that, because of my keen interest in their digestive process, the octospiders had decided to show me a couple of other unusual characteristics of their biology.

I boarded a transport with the three octos, passed through one of the two gates out of our zone, and crossed the Emerald City. I suspect that this field trip was also planned to mitigate my disappointment about Benjy. Dr. Blue reminded me while we were traveling (it was hard for me to pay close attention to what he was saying—once we were outside our zone, there were all kinds of fascinating creatures beside our car and along the street, including many of the same species that I saw briefly during my first few moments in the Emerald City) that the octospiders were a polymorphic genus and that there were six separate adult manifestations of the particular octo species that had colonized our Rama spacecraft. "Remember," he told me in color, "that one of the possible parameter variations is size."

There is no way that I could have been prepared for what I saw about twenty minutes later. We descended from the transport outside a large warehouse. At each end of the windowless building were two mammoth, drooling octospiders, with heads at least ten meters in diameter, bodies that looked like small blimps, and long tentacles that were slate-gray instead of the usual black and gold. Dr. Blue informed me that this particular morph had one, and only one, function: to serve as a food repository for the colony.

"Each 'replete' [my translation of Dr. Blue's colors] can store up to several hundred full buffers worth of food for a regular adult octospi-der," Dr. Blue said. "Since our individual intake buffers hold thirty days worth of normal sustenance, forty-five on a reduced-energy diet, you can see what a vast storehouse a dozen of these repletes represent."

As I watched, five octospiders approached one of their huge brothers and said something in color. Within seconds the creature leaned forward, bent its head down almost to the ground, and ejected a thick slurry from the enlarged mouth just below its milky lens. The five normal-sized octos gathered around the mound of slurry and fed themselves with their tentacles.

"We practice this several times every day, with every replete," Dr. Blue said. "These morphs must have practice, for they are not very smart. You might have noticed that none of them spoke in color. They do not have any language transmission capability, and their mobility is extremely limited. Their genomes have been designed so that they can efficiently store food, preserve it for long periods of time, and regurgitate it to feed the colony upon request."

I was still thinking about the huge repletes when our transport arrived at what I was told was an octospider school. I commented, while we were crossing the grounds, that the large facility seemed deserted. One of the other doctors said something about the colony not having had a "recent replenishment," if I interpreted the colors correctly, but I never received a clear explanation of just what was meant by his remark.

At one end of the school facility, we entered a small building that had no furnishings. Inside were two adult octospiders and about twenty juveniles, maybe one-half the size of their larger companions. From the activity it was obvious that a repetitive drill of some kind was under way. I could not, however, follow the conversation between the juveniles and their teachers, both because the octospiders were using their full alphabet, including the ultraviolet and the infrared, and because the juvenile "talk" did not flow in the neat, regular bands that I have learned to read.

Dr. Blue explained that we were witnessing part of a "measuring class," where the juveniles were being trained to perform assessments of their own health, including estimating the magnitude of food contained in their intake buffers. After Dr. Blue told me that "measuring" was an integral part of the early learning curriculum for their juveniles, I inquired about the irregularity of the juvenile colors. Dr. Blue informed me that these particular octos were very young, not much past "first color," and were barely able to communicate distinct ideas.

After we returned to the conference room, I was asked a set of questions about human digestive systems. The questions were extremely sophisticated (we went through the Krebs citric acid cycle step by step, for example, and discussed other elements of human biochemistry that I could barely remember), and I was struck again by how much more the octospiders know about us than we know about them. As always, it was never necessary for me to repeat an answer.

What a day! It began with the pain of discovering that the octospiders were not going to be able to help Benjy. Later on I was reminded of how resilient the human psyche is when I was actually lifted out of my despondency by the stimulation of learning more about the octospiders. I remain astonished by the range of emotions we humans possess—and how very quickly we can change and adapt.

Eponine and I were talking last night about our life here in the Emerald City and how our unusual living conditions will affect the attitudes of the child she is carrying. At one point Ep shook her head and smiled. "You know what's so amazing?" she said. "Here we are, an isolated human contingent living in an alien domain inside a gargantuan spacecraft hurtling toward an unknown destination. . . . Yet our days here are full of laughter, elation, sadness, and disappointment, just as they would be if we were still back on Earth."

"This may look like a waffle," Max said, "and it may feel like a waffle when you first put it in your mouth, but it damn sure doesn't *taste* like a waffle."

"Put more syrup on it," Eponine said, laughing. "And pass the plate over here."

Max handed the waffles across the table to his wife. "Shit, Frenchie," he said, "these last few weeks you've been eating everything in sight. If I didn't know better, I would think that you and that unborn child of ours both had one of those 'intake buffers' Nicole was telling us about."

"It would be handy, though," Richard said distractedly. "You could load up on food and not have to stop work just because your stomach was calling."

"This cereal is the best yet," little Kepler said from the other end of the table. "I bet even Hercules would like it—"

"Speaking of whom," Max interrupted in a lower voice, glancing from one end of the table to the other, "what is his, or *its*, purpose? That damn octospider shows up every morning two hours after dawn and just hangs around. If the children are having school with Nai, he sits in the back of the room—"

"He plays with us, Uncle Max," Galileo shouted. "Hercules is really a lot of fun. He does everything we ask. Yesterday he let me use the back of his head as a punching bag."

"According to Archie," Nicole said between bites, "Hercules is the official observer. The octospiders are curious about everything. They want to know all about us, even the most mundane details."

"That's great," Max replied, "but we have a slight problem. When you and Ellie and Richard are gone, nobody here can understand what Hercules is saying. Oh, sure, Nai knows a few simple phrases, but nothing that's involved. Yesterday, for example, while everyone else was taking the long nap, that damned Hercules followed me into the crapper. Now, I don't know about you, but it's hard for me to do my business even with Eponine within earshot. With an alien staring at me from a few meters away, my sphincter was absolutely paralyzed."

"Why didn't you tell Hercules to go away?" Patrick said, laughing.

"I did," Max answered. "But he just stared at me with fluid running around in his lens and kept repeating the same color pattern that was totally unintelligible to me."

"Can you remember the pattern?" Ellie said. "Maybe I can tell you what Hercules was saying."

"Hell, no, I can't remember it," Max replied. "Besides, it doesn't make any difference now—I'm not sitting here trying to shit."

The Watanabe twins broke into howls of laughter and Eponine frowned at her husband. Benjy, who had said very little during breakfast, asked to be excused.

"Are you all right, dear?" Nicole asked.

Benjy nodded and left the dining room in the direction of his bedroom.

"Does he know anything?" Nai said quietly.

Nicole shook her head quickly and turned to her granddaughter. "Are you finished with your breakfast, Nikki?"

"Yes, Nonni," the little girl replied. She excused herself and moments later was joined by Kepler and Galileo.

"I think that Benjy knows more than any of us give him credit for," Max said as soon as the children were gone.

"You could be right," Nicole said softly. "But yesterday when I talked to him, I saw no indication that he—" Nicole stopped in midsentence and turned to Eponine. "By the way," she said, "how are *you* feeling this morning?"

"Great," Eponine replied. "The baby was very active before dawn. He kicked hard for almost an hour—I could even watch his feet moving around on my tummy. I tried to get Max to feel one of his kicks, but he was too squeamish."

"Now, why do you call that baby 'he,' Frenchie, when you know damn well that I want a little girl who looks just like you."

"I don't believe you for a moment, Max Puckett," Eponine interrupted. "You only *say* you want a girl so that you won't be disappointed. Nothing would please you more than a boy you can raise to be your buddy. Besides, as you know, it's customary in English to use the pronoun 'he' when the sex is not known or specified."

"Which brings me to another question for our octospider *ex-perts*," Max said after taking a sip of quasi-coffee. He glanced first at Ellie and then at Nicole. "Do either of you know what sex, if any, our octospider friends might be?" He laughed. "I certainly haven't seen anything on their naked bodies that gives me a clue."

Ellie shook her head. "I don't really know, Max. Archie did tell me that Jamie is not his child, and not Dr. Blue's either, at least not in the strictest biological sense."

"So Jamie must be adopted," Max said. "But is Archie the man and Dr.

Blue the woman? Or vice versa? Or are our next-door neighbors a gay couple raising a child?"

"Maybe the octospiders don't have what we call sex," Patrick said.

"Then where do *new* octospiders come from?" Max asked. "They certainly don't just materialize out of thin air."

"The octospiders are so advanced biologically," Richard said, "they may have a reproduction process that would seem like magic to us."

"I have asked Dr. Blue about their reproduction several times," Nicole said. "He says it's a complicated subject, especially since the octospiders are polymorphic, and that they'll explain it to me after I understand the other aspects of their biology."

"Now, if I were an octospider," Max said with a grin, "I would want to be one of those fat slobs Nicole saw yesterday. Wouldn't it be great if your only function in life was to eat and eat, storing food for all your brethren? What an existence! I knew a pig farmer's son back in Arkansas who was like a *re-plete*. Only he kept all the food for himself. Wouldn't even share it with the pigs. I think he weighed almost three hundred kilograms when he died at the age of thirty."

Eponine finished her waffle. "Fat jokes in the presence of pregnant women show a lack of sensitivity," she said, feigning indignation.

"Oh, shit, Ep," Max replied, "you know that none of that crap applies anymore. We're zoo animals here in the Emerald City, and we're stuck with each other. Humans only worry about what they look like if they're worried about being compared with someone else."

Nai excused herself from the table. "I have a few more preparations to complete for today's school lessons," she said. "Nikki will be starting on consonant sounds—she has already breezed through the alphabet drills."

"Like mother, like daughter," Max said. After Patrick left the dining room, leaving only the two couples and Ellie at the table, Max leaned forward with a mischievous smile on his face. "Are my eyes deceiving me," he said, "or is young Patrick spending a lot more time with Nai than he did when we first arrived?"

"I think you're right, Max," Ellie said. "I have noticed the same thing. He told me he feels useful helping Nai with Benjy and the children. After all, you and Eponine are engrossed with each other and the baby that is coming, my time is completely occupied between Nikki and the octospiders, Mother and Father are always busy—"

"You're missing the point, young lady," Max said. "I'm wondering if we have another *cup-el* forming in our midst."

"Patrick and Nai?" Richard asked, as if the idea had just occurred to him for the first time.

"Yes, dear," Nicole said. She laughed. "Richard belongs to that category of genius with very selective observational skills. No detail from one of his projects, no matter how small, goes unnoticed. Yet he misses obvious changes in people's behavior. I remember once in New Eden when Katie started wearing low-cut dresses—"

Nicole stopped herself. It was still difficult for her to talk about Katie without becoming emotional.

"Kepler and Galileo have both noticed that Patrick is around every day," Eponine said. "Nai says that Galileo has become quite jealous."

"And what does Nai say about Patrick's attention?" Nicole asked. "Is she happy with it?"

"You know Nai," Eponine replied. "Always gracious, always thinking of others. I think she's concerned about how any possible relationship between Patrick and her might affect the twins."

All eyes turned toward the visitor who appeared in the doorway. "Well, well. Good morning, Hercules," Max said, standing up from his chair. "What a pleasant surprise! What can we do for you this morning?"

The octospider stepped into the dining room as the colors streamed around his head. "He says that he has come to help Richard with his automatic translator," Ellie said. "Especially the parts outside our visible spectrum."

2

Nicole was dreaming. She was also dancing to an African rhythm around a campfire in an Ivory Coast grove. Omeh was leading the dance. He was dressed in the green robe he had been wearing when he had come to visit her in Rome a few days before the launch of the Newton. All of her human friends in the Emerald City, plus their four closest octospider acquaintances, were also dancing in the circle around the campfire. Kepler and Galileo were fighting. Ellie and Nikki were holding hands. Hercules the octospider was dressed in a bright purple African costume. Eponine was very pregnant and heavy on her feet. Nicole heard her name being called from outside the circle. Was it Katie? Her heart raced as she strained to recognize the voice.

"Nicole," Eponine said beside her bed. "I'm having contractions."

Nicole sat up and shook the dream from her head. "How often?" she asked automatically.

"They're irregular," Eponine replied. "I'll have a couple about five minutes apart, and then nothing for half an hour."

"Most likely they're Braxton Hicks contractions," Nicole said to her friend after she put on her robe. "You're still five weeks short of full term."

"What's a Braxton Hicks contraction?" Eponine asked.

"Fake labor, essentially. It's as if your body is practicing. Come lie down on the couch, and I'll take a look."

Max was waiting in the living room with Eponine after Nicole finished washing her hands. "Is she going to have the baby?" he asked.

"Someday," Nicole said, smiling at the nervous father. "But probably not now." She began putting slight pressure on Eponine's midsection, trying to locate the baby. "Tell me when the next contraction begins," she said.

Meanwhile, Max paced fitfully around the room. "I would absolutely kill for a cigarette right now," he mumbled.

When Eponine had another contraction, Nicole noticed that there was some slight pressure on the undilated cervix. She was worried because she wasn't absolutely certain where the baby was. "I'm sorry, Ep," Nicole said after another contraction six minutes later. "I *think* this is all Braxton Hicks, but I could be wrong. I've never dealt with a pregnancy at this stage before without some kind of monitoring equipment to help me."

"Some women *do* have babies this early, don't they?" Eponine asked.

"Yes. But it's rare. Only about one percent of first-time mothers deliver more than four weeks before their due date. And it's almost always due to some kind of complication. Or heredity. Do you know by any chance if you or any of your siblings were premature?"

Eponine shook her head. "I never knew anything at all about my natural family," she said.

Nicole told Eponine to dress and return to her home. "Keep a record of your contractions. What is especially important is the interval between them. If they start occurring regularly, every four minutes or so without significant gaps, then come and get me again."

"Might there be a problem?" Max whispered to Nicole while Eponine was dressing.

"Unlikely, Max, but there is always that possibility."

"What do you think about asking our friends the biological wizards for some help?" Max asked. "Please forgive me if I am offending you, it's just—"

"I'm ahead of you, Max," Nicole said. "I had already decided to consult with Dr. Blue in the morning."

Max was nervous long before Dr. Blue started to open what Max called the "bug jar." "Hold on, Doc," Max said, gently putting his hands on the tentacle holding the jar. "Would you mind explaining to me just what you're doing before you let those creatures out?"

Eponine was lying down on the sofa in the Puckett living room. She was naked, but mostly covered by a pair of sheets provided by the octospiders. Nicole had been holding Eponine's hand during most of the several minutes that the three octospiders had been setting up the portable laboratory. Now Nicole walked over beside Max so that she could translate what Dr. Blue was saying.

"Dr. Blue is not an expert in this field," Nicole interpreted. "He says that one of the other two octospiders will have to explain the details of the process."

After a short conversation among the three octospiders, Dr. Blue moved aside and another alien stood directly in front of Nicole and Max. Dr. Blue then informed Nicole that this particular octo, whom he called the "image engineer," had only recently started learning the simpler octospider dialect used to communicate with humans. "He might be a little difficult to understand," Dr. Blue told her.

"The tiny beings in the jar," Nicole said several seconds later as the colors began streaming around the engineer's head, "are called . . . image quadroids, I guess would be a satisfactory translation. Anyway, they are living miniature cameras that will crawl inside Eponine and take pictures of the baby. Each quadroid has the capability of . . . several million photographic picture elements that can be allocated to as many as five hundred and twelve images per octospider nillet. They can even create a moving picture if you choose."

She hesitated and turned to Max. "I'm simplifying all this, if that's all right. It's highly technical, and all in their octal mathematics. The engineer was explaining there at the end all the different ways in which the user can specify pictures—Richard would have absolutely loved it."

"Remind me again how long a nillet is?" Max said.

"About twenty-eight seconds," Nicole replied. "Richard named all the time terms. The nillet is the shortest unit in octospider time: Eight nillets in a feng, eight fengs in a woden, eight wodens in a tert, and eight terts in an octospider day. Richard calculates their day at thirty-two hours, fourteen minutes, and a little more than six seconds."

"I'm glad somebody understands all this," Max said quietly.

Nicole faced the image engineer again and the conversation continued. "Each image quadroid," she translated slowly, "enters the specified target area, takes its pictures, and then returns to the image processor— that's the gray box over against the wall—where it 'dumps' its images, receives its reward, and returns to the queue."

"What?" said Max. "What kind of reward?"

"Later, Max," Nicole said. She was struggling to understand a sentence that she had already asked the octospider to repeat. Nicole was silent for a few seconds before she shook her head and turned to Dr. Blue. "I'm sorry," she said, "but I still don't understand that last sentence."

The two octospiders had a rapid exchange in their natural dialect and then the image engineer faced Nicole again. "Okay," she said at length, "I think I've got it now. . . . Max, the gray box is some kind of a programmable data manager, both storing the data in living cells and preparing the outputs from the quadroids for projection on the wall, or wherever we want to see the image, according to the protocol selected—"

"I have an idea," Max interrupted. "This is all way beyond me. If you're satisfied that this contraption is not going to hurt Ep in any way, why don't we get on with it?"

Dr. Blue understood what Max said. At a signal from Nicole, he and the other octospiders walked outside the Puckett home and retrieved what looked like a covered drawer from the parked transport. "In this container," Dr. Blue said to Nicole, "are a group of twenty or thirty of the smallest members of our species, morphs whose primary function is to communicate directly with the quadroids and the other tiny creatures that make this system work. The morphs will actually manage the procedure."

"Well, I'll be goddamned," said Max when the drawer opened and the tiny octospiders, only a couple of centimeters tall, scampered into the middle of the room. "Those . . ." Max stammered excitedly, "are what Eponine and I saw back in the blue maze, in the lair on the other side of the Cylindrical Sea."

"The midget morphs," Dr. Blue explained, "take our directions and then organize the entire process. It is they who will actually program the gray box. Now all we need to start is a few specifications on what kind of images you want and where you want to see them."

The large colored picture on the wall in the Puckett living room showed a perfectly formed, handsome boy fetus filling almost all of his mother's womb. Max and Eponine had been celebrating for an hour, ever since they had first been able to distinguish that their unborn child was indeed a boy. As the afternoon had progressed and Nicole had learned better how to specify what she wanted to see, the quality of the pictures had improved markedly. Now, the twice-life-size image on the wall was stunning for its clarity.

"Can I watch him kick one more time?" Eponine asked.

The image engineer said something to the lead midget morph and in less than a nillet there was a replay of young master Puckett kicking upward against his mother's tummy.

"Look at the strength of those legs," Max exclaimed. He was more relaxed now. After he had recovered from the shock of the initial images, Max had become concerned about all the "paraphre-nalia" surrounding his son in the womb. Nicole had calmed the first-time father by identifying the umbilical cord and the placenta and then assuring Max that everything was normal.

"So I'm not going to deliver my son anytime soon?" Eponine asked when the replay of the movie was over.

"No," Nicole answered. "My guess is you have five or six more weeks. Often first babies are a little late. You may still have some of those intermittent contractions between now and the birth, but don't worry about them."

Nicole thanked Dr. Blue profusely, as did Max and Eponine. Then the octospiders gathered up all the components, both biological and nonbiological, of their portable laboratory. When the octos had departed, Nicole crossed the room and took Eponine's hand. "*Es-tu heureuse?*" she asked her friend.

"*Absolument*," Eponine replied. "And relieved as well. I thought that something had gone wrong."

"No," Nicole said. "It was just a simple false alarm."

Max crossed the room and gave Eponine a hug. He was beaming. Nicole withdrew slightly and watched the tender scene between her friends. She started to leave the house. "Wait a minute," said Max. "Don't you want to know what we're going to name him?"

"Of course," Nicole replied.

"Marius Clyde Puckett," Max said proudly.

"Marius," Eponine added, "because he was the waif Eponine's dream lover in *Les Miserables*—I longed for a Marius during my long and lonely nights at the orphanage. And Clyde, after Max's brother back in Arkansas."

"It's an excellent name," Nicole said, smiling to herself as she turned to leave. "An excellent name," she repeated.

Richard could not contain his excitement when he came home later that afternoon. "I have just spent two absolutely fascinating hours over in the conference room with Archie and the other octospiders," he said to Nicole in his loudest voice. "They showed me the entire apparatus they used with you and Eponine earlier today. Amazing. What incredible genius! No, wizardry is a better term—I've said it from the beginning, the damn octospiders are biological wizards.

"Just imagine. They have living creatures that are cameras, another set of microscopic bugs that read the images and carefully store each individual pixel, a special genetic warping of themselves that controls the process, and a limited amount of electronics, where necessary, to perform the mundane data management tasks. How many thousands of years did it take for all this to occur? Who engineered it in the first place? It is absolutely mind-boggling!"

Nicole smiled at her husband. "Did you see Marius? What did you think?"

"I saw all the pictures from this afternoon," Richard continued to shout. "Do you know how the midget morphs communicate with the image quadroids? They use a special wavelength range in the far ultraviolet part of the spectrum. That's right. Archie told me those little bugs and the midget octospiders actually have a common language. And that's not all. Some of the morphs know as many as *eight* different microspecies languages. Even Archie himself can communicate with forty other species, fifteen using their basic octospider colors and the rest in a range of languages that includes signs, chemicals, and other parts of the electromagnetic spectrum."

Richard stood still for a moment in the middle of the room. "This is incredible, Nicole, simply incredible."

He was about to launch into another monologue when Nicole asked him how the regular octos and the midget morphs communicated. "I never saw any color patterns on the heads of the morphs today," she said.

"All their conversation is in the ultraviolet," Richard said, starting to pace again. Suddenly he turned and pointed at the center of his forehead. "Nicole," he said, "that lens thing in the middle of their slit is a veritable telescope, able to receive information at practically any wavelength. It's staggering. Somehow they have organized all these life-forms into a grand symbiotic system of complexity far beyond anything we could ever conceive of."

Richard sat down on the couch next to Nicole. "Look," he said, showing his arms to her, "I *still* have goose bumps. I am in absolute awe of these creatures. . . . Jesus, it's a good thing they aren't hostile."

Nicole looked at her husband with a furrowed brow. "Why do you say that?"

"They could command an army of *billions*, maybe even *trillions*. I bet they even talk to their *plants*! You saw how quickly they scared off that thing in the forest. Imagine what it would be like if your enemy could control all the bacteria, even the *viruses*, and make them do their bidding. What a frightening concept!"

Nicole laughed. "Don't you think you're getting carried away? Just because they have genetically engineered a set of living cameras, it does not follow—"

"I know," said Richard, jumping up from the couch. "But I can't help thinking about the logical extension of what we have seen here today. Nicole, Archie admitted to me that the *sole* purpose of the midget morphs is to be able to deal with the world of the tiny. The midgets can *see* things as small as a micrometer—that's one-*thousandth* of a millimeter. Now extend that idea another several orders of magnitude. Imagine a species whose morphs span four or five relationships similar to the one between the normal octos and the midgets. Communication with bacteria might not be impossible after all."

"Richard," Nicole said at this juncture, "don't you have anything at all to say about the fact that Max and Eponine are going to have a son? And that the boy looks perfectly healthy?"

Richard stood silent for a few seconds. "It *is* wonderful," he said a little sheepishly. "I guess I should go next door and congratulate them."

"You can probably wait until after dinner," Nicole said, glancing at one of the special watches Richard had made for them. The watch kept human time in an octospider frame of reference.

"Patrick, Ellie, Nikki, and Benjy have been over at Max and Eponine's for the last hour," Nicole continued, "ever since Dr. Blue stopped by with some parchment photographs of little Marius in the womb." She smiled. "As you would say, they should be home in about a feng."

3

Nicole finished brushing her teeth and gazed at her reflection in the mirror. *Galileo was right,* she thought. *I am an old woman.*

She began rubbing her face with her fingers, methodically massaging the wrinkles that seemed to be everywhere. She heard Benjy and the twins playing outside and then both Nai and Patrick calling them to school. *I was not always old,* she said to herself. *There was a time when I too went to school.*

Nicole closed her eyes, attempting to remember what she had looked like as a young girl. She was unable to conjure up a clear picture of herself as a child. Too many other pictures from the intervening years blurred and distorted Nicole's image of herself as a schoolgirl.

At length she reopened her eyes and stared at the image in the mirror. In her mind she painted out all the bags and wrinkles on her face. She changed the color of her hair and eyebrows from gray to a deep black. Finally she managed to see herself as a beautiful woman of twenty-one. Nicole felt a brief but intense yearning for those days of her youth. *For we were young, and we knew that we would never die,* she remembered.

Richard stuck his head around the corner. "Ellie and I will be working with Hercules in the study," he said. "Why don't you join us?"

"In a few minutes," Nicole answered. While she touched up her hair, Nicole reflected on the daily patterns of the human clan in the Emerald City. They usually all gathered for breakfast in the Wakefields' dining room. School ended before lunch. Then everyone except Richard napped, their accommodation to the eight-hour-longer day. Most afternoons Nicole and Ellie and Richard were with the octospiders, learning more about their hosts or sharing experiences from the planet Earth. The other four adults spent almost all their time with Benjy and the children in their enclave at the end of the cul-de-sac.

And where does all this take us? Nicole suddenly wondered. *For how many years will we be the guests of the octospiders? And what will happen if and when Rama reaches its destination?*

They were all questions for which Nicole had no answers. Even Richard had apparently stopped worrying about what was going on outside the Emerald City. He was completely absorbed by the octospiders and his translator project. Now he only asked Archie for celestial navigation data every two months or so. Each time Richard would report to the others, without editorial comment, that Rama was still headed in the general direction of the star Tau Ceti.

Like little Marius, Nicole thought, *we are content here in our womb. As long as the outside world does not force itself upon us, we do not ask the overwhelming questions.*

Nicole left the bathroom and walked down the hall to the study. Richard was sitting on the floor between Hercules and Ellie. "The easy part is tracking the color pattern and having the sequence stored in the processor," he was saying. "The hardest part of the translation is automatically converting that pattern into a recognizable English sentence."

Richard faced Hercules and spoke very slowly. "Because your language is so mathematical, with every color having an acceptable angstrom range defined a priori, all the sensor has to do is identify the stream of colors and the widths of the bands. The entire information content has then been captured. Because the rules are so precise, it's not even difficult to code a simple fault protection algorithm, for use with juveniles or careless speakers, in case any single color errs to the left or the right in the spectrum.

"Changing what an octospider has said into our language, however, is a much more complex process. The dictionary for the translation is straightforward enough. Each word and the appropriate clarifiers can be readily identified. But it's damn near impossible to make the next step, into sentences, without some human intervention."

"That's because the octospider language is fundamentally different from ours," Ellie commented. "Everything is specified and quantified, to minimize the possibility of misunderstanding. There is no subtlety or nuance. Look how they use the pronouns 'we,' 'they,' and 'you.' The pronouns are always marked with numerical clarifiers, including ranges when there are uncertainties. An octospider never says 'a few wodens' or 'several nillets'—always a number, or a numerical range, is used to specify the length of time more precisely."

"From our point of view," Hercules said in color, "there are two aspects to human language that are extremely difficult. One is the lack of precise specification, which leads to a massive vocabulary. The other is your use of indirectness to communicate. I still have trouble understanding Max because often what he says is not literally what he means."

"I don't know how to do this in your computer," Nicole now said to Richard, "but somehow all the quantitative information contained in each octospider statement must be reflected by the translation. Almost every verb or adjective they use has a connected numerical clarifier. How, for example, did Ellie just translate 'extremely difficult' and 'massive vocabulary'? What Hercules said, in octospider, was 'difficult,' with the number five used to clarify it, and 'big vocabulary,' with the number six as a clarifier for 'big.' All comparative clarifiers address the question of the strength of the adjective. Since their base number system is octal, the range for the comparatives is between one and seven. If Hercules had used a seven to clarify the word 'difficult,' Ellie would have translated the phrase as 'impossibly difficult.' If he had used a two as a clarifier in the same phrase, she might have said 'slightly difficult.'"

"Mistakes in the strengths of the adjectives, although important," Richard said as he fiddled absentmindedly with a small processor, "almost never lead to misunderstandings. Failure to interpret properly the *verb* clarifiers, however, is another issue altogether . . . as I have learned recently from my preliminary tests. Take the simple octospider verb 'to go,' which means, as you know, to move unaided, without a transport. The maroon-purple-lemon yellow strip, each color the same width, covers several dozen words in English, everything from 'walk' to 'stroll,' 'saunter,' 'run,' and even 'sprint.'"

"That's the same point I was just making," Ellie said. "There is no translation without full interpretation of the clarifiers. For that particular verb, the octos use a double clarifier to address the issue of 'how fast.' In a sense, there are sixty-three different speeds at which they 'go.' To make matters even more complex, they may use a range clarifier as well, so their statement 'Let's go' is subject to many, many possible translations."

Richard grimaced and shook his head.

"What's the matter, Father?" Ellie asked.

"I'm just disappointed," he answered. "I had hoped to have a simplified version of the translator completed by now. But I made the assumption that the gist of what was being said could be determined without tracking *all* the clarifiers. To include all those short color strips will both increase the storage required and significantly slow down the translation. I may have trouble ever designing a translator that works in real time."

"So what?" Hercules asked. "Why are you so concerned about this translator? Ellie and Nicole already understand our language very well."

"Not really," Nicole said. "Ellie is the only one of us who is *truly* fluent with your colors. I am still learning daily."

"Although I originally began this project both as a challenge and as a means to force myself to become familiar with your language," Richard replied to Hercules, "Nicole and I were talking last week about how important the translator has become. She says, and I agree with her, that our human clan here in the Emerald City is dividing into two groups. Ellie, Nicole, and I have made our life more interesting because of our increasing interactions with your species. The rest of the humans, including the children, remain essentially isolated. Eventually, if the others don't have some way of communicating with you, they will become dissatisfied and/or unhappy. A good automatic translator is the key that will open up their lives here."

The map was wrinkled and torn in a few places. Patrick helped Nai unroll it slowly and tack it to the wall of her dining room, which doubled as the schoolroom for the children.

"Nikki, do you remember what this is?" Nai asked.

"Of course, Ms. Watanabe," the little girl replied. "It's our map of the Earth."

"Benjy, can you show us where your parents and grandparents were born?"

"Not again," Galileo muttered audibly to Kepler. "He'll never get it right. He's too dumb."

"*Galileo Watanabe.*" The response was swift. "Go to your room and sit on your bed for fifteen minutes."

"That's all right, Nai," Benjy said as he walked up to the map. "I'm used to it by now."

Galileo, almost seven years old by human accounting, stopped at the door to see if his sentence would be reprieved. "What are you waiting for?" his mother scolded. "I said for you to go to your room."

Benjy stood quietly in front of the map for about twenty seconds. "My mother," he said at length, "was born here in France." He backed away from the map briefly and located the United States on the opposite side of the Atlantic Ocean. "My father," Benjy said, "was born here in Boston, in America."

Benjy started to sit down. "What about your grandparents?" Nai prompted. "Where were they born?"

"My mother's mother, my grandmother," Benjy said slowly, "was born in Africa." He stared at the map for several seconds. "But I do not remember where that is."

"I know, Mrs. Watanabe," said little Nikki immediately. "May I show Benjy?"

Benjy turned and looked at the pretty girl with the jet-black hair. He smiled. "You can tell me, Nikki."

The girl rose from her chair and crossed the room. She placed her finger on the western section of Africa. "Nonni's mother was born here," she said proudly, "in this green country. It's called the Ivory Coast."

"That's very good, Nikki," Nai said.

"I'm sorry, Nai," Benjy now said. "I've been working so hard on fractions I haven't had any time for geography." His eyes followed his three-year-old niece back to her seat. When he turned to face Nai again, Benjy's cheeks were wet with tears. "Nai," he said, "I don't feel like school today. . . . I think I'll go back to my own house."

"Okay, Benjy," Nai said softly. Benjy moved toward the door. Patrick started to come over to his brother, but Nai waved him away.

The schoolroom was uncomfortably quiet for almost a minute. "Is it my turn now?" Kepler finally asked.

Nai nodded and the boy walked up to the map. "My mother was born here, in Thailand, in the town of Lamphun. That's where her father was also born. My grandmother on my mother's side was also born in Thailand, but in another city called Chiang Saen. Here it is, next to the Chinese border."

Kepler took one step to the east and pointed at Japan. "My father, Kenji Watanabe, and both his parents were born in the Japanese city of Kyoto."

The boy backed away from the map. He seemed to be struggling to say something. "What is it, Kepler?" Nai asked.

"Mother," the small boy said after an agonizing silence, "was Daddy a bad man?"

"Whaat?" said Nai, completely stunned. She bent down to her son's level and looked him straight in the eyes. "Your father was a wonderful human being. He was intelligent, sensitive, loving, humorous—an absolute prince of a person. He . . ."

Nai had to stop herself. She could feel her own emotions ready to erupt. She stood up, gazed at the ceiling for a brief moment, and regained her composure. "Kepler," she then said, "why are you asking such a question? You adored your father. How could you have possibly—"

"Uncle Max told us that Mr. Nakamura came from Japan. We know that he is a bad man. Galileo says that since Daddy came from the same place—"

"*Galileo,*" Nai's voice thundered, scaring all the children. "Come here immediately."

The boy scampered into the room and gave his mother a puzzled look.

"What have you been saying to your brother about your father?"

"What do you mean?" Galileo said, trying to look innocent.

"You told me that Daddy may have been a bad man, since he came from Japan like Mr. Nakamura."

"Well, I don't remember Daddy very clearly. All I said was that maybe—"

It took all of Nai's self-control to keep her from slapping Galileo. She grabbed the boy by both of his shoulders. "Young man," she said, "if I *ever* hear you say one word against your father again . . ."

Nai could not finish her sentence. She did not know what to threaten, or even what to say next. She suddenly felt completely overwhelmed by everything in her life.

"Sit down, please," she said at length to her twin sons, "and listen very carefully." Nai took a deep breath. "This map on the wall," she said, pointing, "shows all the countries on the planet Earth. In every nation there are all kinds of people, some good, some bad, most a complex mixture of good and bad. No country has only good people, or bad people. Your father grew up in Japan. So did Mr. Nakamura. I agree with Uncle Max that Mr. Nakamura is a very evil man. But the fact that he is bad has nothing to do with his being Japanese. Your father, Mr. Kenji Watanabe, who was also Japanese, was as good a man as ever lived. I'm sorry that you cannot remember him and never really knew what he was like. . . ."

Nai paused for a moment. "I will never forget your father," she said in a softer voice, almost to herself. "I can still see him returning to our home in New Eden in the late afternoon. The two of you always shouted together, 'Hi Daddy, Hi Daddy,' as he entered the house. He would kiss me, lift both of you in his arms, and take you out to the swing set in the backyard. Always, no matter how trying his day had been, he was patient and caring. . . ."

Her voice trailed off. Tears flooded Nai's eyes and she felt her body beginning to tremble. She turned her back and faced the map. "Class dismissed for today," she said.

Patrick stood beside Nai as the two of them watched the twins and Nikki playing with a big blue ball in the cul-de-sac. It was half an hour later. "I'm sorry, Patrick," Nai said. "I didn't expect to become . . ."

"You have nothing to be sorry for," the young man replied.

"Yes, I do," Nai said. "Years ago I promised myself that I would never show such feelings in front of Kepler and Galileo. They can't possibly understand."

"They've forgotten it already," Patrick said after a brief silence. "Look at them. They're totally engrossed in their game."

At that moment the twins were having one of their typical arguments. As usual, Galileo was trying to gain an advantage for himself in a game that did not have rigorous rules. Nikki stood beside the boys, following every word of their dispute.

"Boys, boys," Nai called out. "Stop it. If you can't play without arguing, then you'll have to come inside."

A few seconds later the blue ball was bouncing down the street toward the plaza and all three children were running gleefully after it. "Would you like something to drink?" Nai asked Patrick.

"Yes, I would. . . . Do you have any more of that light green melon juice that Hercules brought last week? It was really tasty."

"Yes," answered Nai, bending down to the small cabinet in which they kept cool drinks. "By the way, where is Hercules? I haven't seen him for several days."

Patrick laughed. "Uncle Richard has recruited him to work full-time on the translator. Ellie and Archie are even there with them every afternoon." He thanked Nai for the glass of juice.

Nai took a sip of her own drink and walked back into the living room. "I know you wanted to comfort Benjy this morning," she said. "I only stopped you because I know your brother so well. He is very proud. He does not want anyone's pity."

"I understood," Patrick said.

"Benjy realized this morning, at some level, that even little Nikki—whom he still thinks of as a baby—will quickly surpass him in school. The discovery shocked him, and reminded him again of his own limitations."

Nai was standing in front of the map of Earth, which was still affixed to the wall. "Nothing on this map means anything significant to you, does it?" she said.

"Not really," Patrick replied. "I have seen many photographs and movies, of course, and when I was about the twins' age my father used to tell me about Boston, and the color of the leaves in New England during the autumn, and the trip he took to Ireland with *his* father. But my memories are of other places. The lair in New York is quite vivid, as well as the astonishing year we spent at the Node." He was silent for a moment. "And the Eagle! What a creature! I remember him even more clearly than my father."

"So do you consider yourself to be an Earthling?" Nai asked.

"That's an interesting question," Patrick replied. He finished his drink. "You know, I've never really thought about it. . . .Certainly I consider myself to be a human. But an Earthling? I guess not."

Nai reached out and touched the map. "My hometown of Lamphun, if it were larger, would have appeared here, just south of Chiang Mai. Sometimes it doesn't seem possible to me that I actually lived there as a child."

Nai's fingers ran over the outline of Thailand as she stood quietly beside Patrick. "The other night," she said at length, "Galileo threw a cup of water on my head while I was bathing the boys, and I suddenly had an incredibly vivid memory of the three days I spent in Chiang Mai with my cousins when I was fourteen years old. It was the time of the Songkran Festival in April, and everyone in the city was celebrating the Thai New Year. There were parades and speeches—the usual stuff about how all the

Chakri kings since the first Rama had prepared the Thai people for their important role in the world—but what I remember most clearly was riding around the city at night in the back of an electric pickup with my cousin Oni and her friends. Everywhere we went we threw a bucket of water on somebody—and they threw one on us. We laughed and laughed."

"Why was everyone throwing water?" Patrick asked.

"I've forgotten now," Nai said with a shrug. "It had something to do with the ceremony. But the experience itself, the shared laughter, and even what it felt like to have my clothes absolutely soaked, and suddenly to be hit by another burst of water—all that I can recall in detail."

They were again silent as Nai reached up to take the map off the wall. "So I guess Kepler and Galileo will not consider themselves to be Earthlings either," she mused. She rolled up the map very carefully. "Maybe even studying the geography and history of the Earth is a waste of time."

"I don't think so," Patrick said. "What else are the children going to study? And besides, all of us need to understand where we came from."

Three young faces peered into the living room from the atrium. "Is it lunchtime yet?" asked Galileo.

"Almost," Nai replied. "Go wash up first . . . *one at a time*," she said, as the young feet pounded down the hallway.

Nai turned around abruptly and caught Patrick staring at her in an unusual way. She smiled. "I'm glad you spend the mornings with us," she said.

Nai extended both her arms and took Patrick's hands in hers. "You have been a big help to me with Benjy and the children these last two months," she said, her eyes meeting his. "And it would be foolish of me not to acknowledge that I have not felt nearly as lonely since you began coming over here every morning."

Patrick made an awkward step toward Nai, but she held his hands firmly in place. "Not yet," she said gently. "It's still too early."

4

Less than a minute after the great firefly clusters in the Emerald City dome announced that another day had begun, little Nikki was in her grandparents' room. "It's light, Nonni," she said. "They'll be coming for us soon."

Nicole rolled over and gave her granddaughter a hug. "We still have a couple of hours, Nikki," she said to the excited girl. "Boobah is still sleeping. . . . Why don't you go back to your room and play with your toys while we take a shower?"

When the disappointed girl finally left, Richard was sitting up, rubbing his eyes. "Nikki has talked about nothing but this day for the last week," Nicole said to him. "She is always in Benjy's room, looking at the painting. Nikki and the twins have even given names to all those bizarre animals."

Nicole reached unconsciously for the hairbrush beside the bed. "Why is it that small children have such difficulty understanding the concept of time? Even though Ellie has made her a calendar and has been counting off the days one by one, Nikki has asked me every morning if 'today's the day.'"

"She's just excited. Everybody is," Richard said, rising from the bed. "I hope that we're not all disappointed."

"How could we be?" Nicole replied. "Dr. Blue says that we will see sights even more amazing than those you and I saw when we entered the city for the first time."

"I guess the whole menagerie will be out in force," Richard said. "By the way, do you understand what the octospiders are celebrating?"

"Sort of. . . . I guess the closest equivalent holiday I know about would be the American Thanksgiving. The octos call this 'Bounty Day.' They set aside a day to celebrate the quality of their life. . . . At least that's the way Dr. Blue explained it to me."

Richard started to go to the shower but stuck his head back in the room. "Do you think they invited us to participate today because you told them about our family discussion at breakfast two weeks ago?"

"You mean when Patrick and Max said they wished they could return to New Eden?"

Richard nodded.

"Yes, I do," Nicole answered. "I think the octospiders had convinced themselves that we were all completely content here. Having us attend their celebration is part of their attempt to integrate us more into their society."

"I wish I had all the damn translators finished," Richard said. "As it is, I only have two . . . and they're not completely checked out. Should I give the second one to Max?"

"That would be a good idea," Nicole said, crowding her husband in the doorway.

"What are you doing?" Richard said.

"I'm joining you in the shower," Nicole answered with a laugh, "unless, of course, you're too old to have company."

Jamie came over from next door to tell them that the transport was ready. He was the youngest of their three octospider neighbors (Hercules lived by himself just on the other side of the plaza), and the humans had had the least contact with him. Jamie's "guardians," Archie and Dr. Blue, explained that Jamie was very much involved with his studies and was approaching a major milestone in his life. Although at first glance Jamie looked almost exactly like the three adult octospiders the clan saw regularly, he was a little smaller than the older octos and the gold stripes in his tentacles were slightly brighter.

The humans had briefly been in a quandary about what to wear for the octospider celebration, but they had soon realized that their clothing was of absolutely no significance. None of the alien species in the Emerald City wore any coverings, a fact that the octospiders had often commented upon. When Richard had once suggested, only partly in jest, that perhaps the humans too should dispense with clothing while they were in the Emerald City—"When in Rome . . ." he had said—the group had quickly understood how fundamental clothing was to human psychological comfort. "I could not be naked, even among you, my closest friends, without being extremely self-conscious," Eponine had said, summarizing all their feelings.

The motley contingent of eleven humans and their four octospider colleagues traipsed down the street to the plaza. The very pregnant Eponine was at the back of the group, walking slowly and keeping one hand on her stomach. The women had all chosen to dress up a little—Nai was even wearing her colorful Thai silk dress with the blue and green flowers—but the men and children, except for Max (who had on the outrageous Hawaiian shirt he saved for special occasions), were in the T-shirts and jeans that had been their regular costume since the first day they had arrived at the Emerald City.

At least all their clothes were clean. In the beginning, finding a way to do the laundry had been an acute problem for the humans. However, once they had explained their difficulty to Archie, it was only a few days before he introduced them to the dromos, insect-sized beings that automatically cleaned their clothes.

The group boarded the transport at the plaza. Just before the gate marking the end of their zone, the transport stopped and two octospiders they had never seen before climbed into the car. Richard practiced using his translator during the ensuing conversation between Dr. Blue and the newcomers. Ellie read her father's monitor over his shoulder and congratulated him on the accuracy of the translation. The fidelity of the translation was fairly good, but the speed, at least at the normal octospider conversation rate, was much too slow. One sentence would be translated while three were "spoken," causing Richard to reset the system regularly. He couldn't, of course, glean much from a conversation in which he missed two out of three sentences.

Once on the other side of the gate, the view from the transport was a mosaic of strange shapes and bright colors. Nikki's eyes stayed open at their widest levels as she, Benjy, and the twins, with much shouting, identified most of the animals from the octospider painting. The broad streets were full of traffic. There were not only many transports, which moved in both directions on rails like a city trolley, but also pedestrians of all species and sizes, creatures riding wheeled vehicles like unicycles and bicycles, and an occasional mixed group of beings on an ostrichsaur.

Max, who had never once been outside the human zone since his arrival, punctuated his observations with "shits," "damns," and some of the other words Eponine had requested that he remove from his vocabulary before the birth of their child. Max did not start to worry about Eponine's safety until, at the first transport stop after the gate, some strange new creatures crowded onto their car. Four of the newcomers headed immediately in Eponine's direction to examine the special seat the octospiders had installed in the transport because of her advanced pregnancy. Max stood protectively beside her, holding on to one of the vertical rails that were scattered throughout the ten-meter length of the car.

A pair of the new passengers were what the children called "striped crabs," eight-legged red-and-yellow creatures about Nikki's size, with round bodies covered with a hard shell and fearsome-looking claws. Both of them began immediately rubbing their antennae against one of Eponine's bare legs below her dress. They were only being curious, but the combination of the peculiar sensation and the bizarre appearance of the aliens caused Eponine to recoil from fright. Archie, who was standing on the other side of Eponine, reached down quickly with a tentacle and pushed the aliens gently away. One of the striped crabs then reared up on its back four legs, its claws snapping the air in front of Eponine's face, and apparently said something threatening with its rapidly vibrating antennae. An instant later Archie extended two tentacles, lifted the hostile striped crab off the floor of the transport, and deposited the creature on the street outside.

The scene dramatically altered the mood of all the humans. As Ellie translated Archie's explanation of what had occurred for Max and Eponine, the Watanabe twins huddled up close to Nai, and Nikki stretched out her arms for her grandfather to pick her up.

"That species is not very intelligent," Archie told his human friends, "and we have had difficulty engineering out its aggressive tendencies. The particular creature that I threw off the bus has been a troublemaker before. The optimizer responsible for the species had already marked it—you may have noticed—with the two small green dots at the rear of the carapace. This latest transgression will certainly result in termination."

When Ellie finished with the translation, the humans methodically inspected the other aliens on the transport, checking for any more green dots. Relieved that all the other creatures on board were safe, the adults relaxed a little.

"What did that thing say?" Richard asked Archie as the transport approached another stop.

"It was a standard threat response," Archie replied, "typical of animals with constrained intelligence capability. Its antenna patterns conveyed a crude message, with very little real information content."

"Shit," said Max.

The transport continued down the avenue for eight or ten more nillets, stopping twice to receive additional passengers, including half a dozen octospiders and about twenty other creatures representing five different species. Four of the royal blue animals, the ones with the hemispherical tops that looked like they contained undulating brains, squatted right opposite Richard, who was still holding Nikki. Their collective assortment of eight knotted antennae extended upward toward Nikki's feet and became intertwined, as if they were communicating. When the human girl moved her feet slightly, the antennae were quickly retracted back into the strange mass that formed the bulk of the bodies of the alien creatures.

By this time it was very crowded in the transport. An animal the humans had never seen before, which Max later described accurately as a Polish sausage with a long nose and six short legs, raised itself up on one of the vertical bars and grabbed Nai's small purse with its two front paws. Jamie interceded before any damage was done to either the purse or Nai, but a few seconds later Galileo kicked the sausage hard, causing it to lose its grip on the bar. The boy explained that he had thought the sausage was preparing for another grab at the purse. The creature backed away into another section of the transport, its solitary eye fixed warily on Galileo.

"You'd better be careful," Max said with a grin, tousling the boy's hair. "Or the octos will place two green dots on your behind."

The avenue was lined with one- and two-story buildings, almost all painted with geometric patterns in brilliant colors. Garlands and wreaths of brightly colored flowers and leaves festooned the doorways and the roofs. On one long wall, which Hercules told Nai was the back of the main hospital, a huge rectangular mural, four meters high and twenty meters long, depicted the octospider physicians ministering to their own injured, as well as helping many of the other creatures that lived in the Emerald City.

The transport slowed slightly and began to ascend a ramp. The ramp led to a bridge hundreds of meters long that spanned a wide river or canal that contained boats, frolicking octospiders, and other unknown marine creatures. Archie explained that they were entering the heart of the Emerald City, where all the main ceremonies took place and the "most important" optimizers lived and worked. "Over there," he said, pointing at an octagonal building about thirty meters tall, "is our library and information center."

In response to Richard's question, Archie said that the canal, or moat, completely encircled the "administrative center." "Except on special occasions like today, or for some official purpose approved by the optimizers," Archie said, "only octospiders are allowed access to this area."

The transport parked in a large, flat plain beside an oval structure that looked like a stadium, or perhaps an outdoor auditorium. Nai told Patrick, after they descended from the car, that she had felt more claustrophobic during the last part of the ride than at any time since she had been on the Kyoto subway at rush hour during her trip to meet Kenji's family.

"At least in Japan," Patrick said with a brief shudder, "you were surrounded by other human beings. . . . Here it was so weird. I felt as if I were being scrutinized by all of them. I had to close my eyes or I would have gone crazy."

As they disembarked and began moving toward the stadium, the humans walked in a group, surrounded by their four octospider friends and the other two octos who had boarded the transport before it had left the human zone. These six octospiders protected Nicole and the others from the teeming hordes of living creatures swarming in all directions. Eponine started feeling faint, as much from the combination of sights and smells as from the walking, so Archie stopped their procession about every fifty meters. Eventually they entered one of the gates and the octospiders led the humans to their assigned section.

There was only one seat in the section that had been reserved for the humans. In fact, Eponine may have had the only seat in the stadium. Looking around the upper deck of the arena with Richard's binoculars, Max and Patrick saw many beings leaning against, or holding on to, the sturdy vertical poles scattered throughout the terraced bleachers, but nowhere else could they find any seats.

Benjy was intrigued by the cloth bags that Archie and a few of the other octospiders were carrying. The off-white bags, all of which were identical, were about the size of a woman's purse. They hung at what might be called octospider hip level, attached over the head with a simple strap. Never before had any of the humans seen an octo with an accessory. Benjy had noticed the bags immediately and had asked Archie about them while they had been standing together at the plaza. Benjy had assumed that Archie had not understood his question at that time, and Benjy had in fact forgotten it himself until they reached the stadium and he saw the other similar bags.

Archie was uncharacteristically vague in his explanation of the purpose of the bag. Nicole had to ask the octospider to repeat his colors before she told Benjy what had been said. "Archie says it's equipment he might need to protect us in an emergency."

"What kind of equipment?" Benjy asked, but Archie had already moved several meters away and was talking with an octospider in an adjacent section.

The humans were separated from the other species both by two strips of taut metal rope around the tops and bottoms of the vertical poles on the outside of their enclave, and by their octospider protectors (or "guards," as Max called them), who stationed themselves in the empty area between the different species. Beside the humans on the right was a group of several hundred of the aliens with the six flexible arms, the same creatures who had built the staircase under the rainbow dome. On the left and below the human clan, on the other side of a large empty area, were as many as a thousand brown, chunky, iguanalike animals with long, tapered tails and protruding teeth. The iguanas were the size of domestic cats.

What was immediately obvious was that the entire stadium was rigidly segregated. Each species was sitting with its own kind. What's more, except for the "guards," there were no octospiders on the upper deck. All fifteen thousand of the octos (Richard's estimate) who were present as spectators were sitting in the lower deck.

"There are several reasons for the segregation," Archie explained, with Ellie translating for everyone else. "First, what the Chief Optimizer says is going to be broadcast in thirty or forty languages simultaneously. If you look carefully, you'll see that each special section has an apparatus—here's yours, for example, what Richard calls a speaker—that presents what's being said in the language of that species. We have been working with the Chief Optimizer's text for days, preparing the proper translations. Since all the octos, including the various morphs, can understand our standard language of color, they're all down on the lower deck, where there is no special translation equipment.

"Let me show you what I'm talking about. Look over there." Archie extended a tentacle. "Do you see that group of striped crabs? See the two large vertical wires on that table at the front of their section? When the Chief Optimizer starts to speak, those wires will activate and present what is being said in their antenna language."

Far below them, over the top of what would have been a sunken field in an Earth stadium, a vast cover with colored stripes was suspended from stanchions attached to the bottom sections of the lower deck.

"Can you read what it says?" Ellie asked her father.

"What?" said Richard, still stunned by the magnitude of the spectacle.

"There's a message on the cover," Ellie said, pointing downward. "Read the colors."

"So there is." Richard read very slowly. "Bounty means food, water, energy, information, balance, and . . . What's the last word?"

"I would translate it as 'diversity,'" Ellie said.

"What does the message mean?" Eponine asked.

"I guess we're going to find out."

A few minutes later, after Archie had told the humans that another reason for the species segregation was to confirm the octospiders' census statistics, the field cover was rolled up on two long, thick poles by two pairs of giant black animals. The pairs started on opposite sides of the middle of the arena and then moved toward the ends of the stadium, wrapping the cover around their poles to unveil the entire field.

Simultaneously, an additional cluster of fireflies descended from far above the stadium so that all the spectators could clearly see not only the abundance of fruits, vegetables, and grains stacked in hundreds of piles on both ends of the field, but also the two collections of diverse beings that were in separate regions on the floor of the arena, on either side of its middle. The first group of aliens was walking around in a large circle on a normal dirt surface. They were attached to each other by some kind of rope. Next to them was a large pool of water, in which another thirty or forty species, also connected to each other, were swimming in a second large circle.

In the absolute center of the field was a raised platform, empty except for some scattered black boxes, with ramps descending in the direction of the two adjacent regions. As everyone watched, four octospiders broke from the circle in the swimming pool and climbed the ramp onto the platform. Another four octospiders left the group walking on the dirt surface and joined their colleagues. One of these eight octos then stood up on a box in the middle of the platform and began to speak in color.

"We have gathered here today..." The voice from the speaker startled the humans. Little Nikki began to cry. At first it was extremely difficult for them to understand what they were hearing, for each syllable was stressed exactly the same and, although carefully pronounced, the sounds were not quite right, as if they were made by someone who had never heard a human speak. Richard was flabbergasted. He immediately abandoned his attempt to use his own real-time translator and bent down to study the octospider device.

Ellie borrowed Richard's binoculars so that she could follow the colors more readily. Even though she had to guess at some of the words because of the strip pieces outside her visible range, it was easier for her to watch than to concentrate fully on what was coming out of the octospider audio equipment.

Eventually the adults tuned their ears somewhat to the cadence and pronunciation of the alien voice and caught most of what was being said. The octospider Chief Optimizer indicated that all was well in their bountiful realm and that the continued success of their complex and diverse society was reflected in the variety of foods found on the field. "None of this bounty," the speaker said, "could have been produced without strong interspecies cooperation."

Later in his brief message the Chief Optimizer handed out kudos for exceptional performance. Several specific species were singled out—for example, production of the honeylike substance had apparently been outstanding, for a dozen hovering fireflies spotlighted the snout-nosed beetle section for a few moments. About three fengs into the speech, the humans grew tired of the strain of listening to the strange voice and stopped following the speech altogether. The group was therefore surprised when the fireflies appeared over their heads and they were introduced to the alien multitudes. Thousands of strange eyes were aimed in their direction for half a nillet.

"What did he say about us?" Max asked Ellie, who had continued to translate the colors. Max had been talking to Eponine during the most recent part of the Chief Optimizer's speech.

"Just that we were new in the domain and that they were still learning about our capabilities. Then there were some numbers that must have been some way of describing us. I didn't understand that part."

After another two species were briefly introduced, the Chief Optimizer started summarizing the main points of his speech. "*Mommy, Mommy.*" Nikki's terrified scream suddenly overpowered the alien voice. Somehow, while the adult humans were absorbed with the speech and the spectacle surrounding them, Nikki had climbed over the lower barrier around their section and entered the open space separating them from the iguana creatures. The octospider Hercules, who had been patrolling that area, had apparently not noticed her either, for he was unaware that one of the iguanas had stuck its head in the gap between the two metal ropes around its section and grabbed Nikki's dress with its sharp teeth.

The terror in the child's voice momentarily paralyzed everyone but Benjy. He acted instantly, leaping over the barrier, rushing to Nikki's aid, and smashing the iguana creature in the head with all his strength. The startled alien let go of Nikki's dress. Pandemonium ensued. Nikki raced back to her mother's arms, but before Hercules and Archie could reach Benjy, the enraged alien had forced itself through the gap and jumped upon Benjy's back. He screamed from the intense pain of the iguana's teeth in his shoulder and began to flail about, trying to shake the creature off. A few seconds later the creature dropped to the ground, completely unconscious. Two green spots were clearly visible where the creature's tail joined the rest of its body.

The entire incident had occurred in less than a minute. The speech had not been interrupted. Except in the immediate surrounding sections, there had been no notice of the event. But Nikki was hopelessly frightened, Benjy was seriously injured, and Eponine had started having a contraction. Below them, the angry iguanas were straining against their metal ropes, disregarding the threats of the ten octospiders who had now moved into the space between the two species.

Archie told the humans that it was time for them to leave. There was no argument. Archie escorted them out of the stadium in a hurry, with Ellie carrying her sobbing daughter and Nicole frantically rubbing antiseptic taken from her medical bag into Benjy's wound.

Richard rose up on his elbows when Nicole came into the bedroom. "Is he all right?" Richard asked.

"I believe so," Nicole said with a heavy sigh. "I'm still worried that there may be poisonous chemicals in that creature's saliva. Dr. Blue has been very helpful. He has explained to me that the iguanas have no toxic venom, but he agrees we must watch out for some kind of allergic reaction in Benjy. The next day or two will tell us whether or not we have a problem."

"And the pain? Has it subsided?"

"Benjy refuses to complain. I think that he is actually quite proud of himself—as well he should be—and doesn't want to say anything that would detract from his moment as the hero of the family."

"What about Eponine?" Richard said after a brief silence. "Is she still having contractions?"

"No, they've stopped temporarily. But if she delivers in the next day or so, Marius will not be the first baby whose birth was induced by adrenaline."

Nicole started to undress. "Ellie's taking it the hardest. She says that she is a terrible mother and that she will never forgive herself for not keeping a closer eye on Nikki. A few minutes ago she even sounded like Max and Patrick. She was wondering aloud if maybe we should all go back to New Eden and take our chances with Nakamura. 'For the children's sake,' she said."

Nicole finished undressing and climbed into bed. She kissed Richard lightly and put her hands behind her head. "Richard," she said, "there is a very serious issue here. Do you think the octospiders would even *permit* us to return to New Eden?"

"No," he said after a pause. "At least not all of us."

"I'm afraid I agree with you," Nicole said. "But I don't want to say so to the others. Maybe I should bring the question up with Archie again."

"He'll try to evade it, as he did the first time."

They lay together holding hands for several minutes. "What are you thinking about, darling?" Nicole asked when she noticed that Richard's eyes were still open.

"Today," he said. "Everything that happened today. I'm going back over it in my mind, scene by incredible scene. Now that I'm old and my memory isn't as good as it once was, I try to use refresh techniques."

Nicole laughed. "You're impossible," she said. "But I love you anyway."

5

Max was agitated. "I, for one, do not want to stay in this place one minute longer than necessary. I no longer trust them. Look, Richard, you know damn well I'm right. Did you see how fast Archie took that tube thing out of his bag when the alien iguana jumped on Benjy's back? And he didn't hesitate a second to use it. *Pffft* was all I heard, and presto, that lizard was either dead or paralyzed. He would have done the same thing to one of us if we had misbehaved."

"Max, I think you're overreacting," Richard said.

"Am I? And is it another overreaction that the entire scene yesterday reinforced in my mind just how powerless we are?"

"Max," Nicole interrupted, "don't you think this is a discussion that we should have at another time, when we're not so emotional?"

"No," Max replied emphatically. "I do not. I want to have it *now*, this morning. That's why I asked Nai to feed the children breakfast in her house."

"But surely you're not suggesting that we should leave at this moment, when Eponine is due any minute," Nicole said.

"Of course not," Max said. "But I think we should get our butts out of here as soon as she is able to travel. Jesus, Nicole, what kind of life can we have here anyway? Nikki and the twins are now scared shitless. I bet they won't be willing to leave our zone again for weeks, maybe not ever. And that doesn't even address the bigger question of why the octospiders have brought us here in the first place. Did you see all those creatures in that stadium yesterday? Didn't you get the impression that *all* of them work for the octospiders in one way or another? Isn't it likely that we too will soon be occupying some niche in their system?"

Ellie spoke for the first time since the conversation started. "I have always trusted the octospiders," she said. "I still do. I do not believe they have some kind of diabolical plot to integrate us into their overall scheme in a way that is unacceptable to us. But I did learn something yesterday, or I should say I relearned something. As a mother, it is my responsibility to provide for my daughter an environment in which she can flourish and have a chance to be happy. I no longer think that's possible here in the Emerald City."

Nicole looked at Ellie with surprise. "So you would like to leave too?" she said.

"Yes, Mother."

Nicole glanced around the table. She could tell from Eponine's and Patrick's expressions that they agreed with Max and Ellie. "Does anyone know how Nai feels about this subject?" she inquired.

Patrick blushed slightly when Max and Eponine looked at him, as if he were expected to answer. "We talked about it last night," he said at length. "Nai has been convinced, for some time, that the children have too narrow a life isolated here in our own zone. But she is also worried, especially after what happened yesterday, that there are significant dangers to the children if we try to live freely in the octospider society."

"I guess that settles it," Nicole said with a shrug. "I will talk to Archie about our leaving at the first opportunity."

Nai was a good storyteller. The children loved the school days when she would dispense with the planned activities and simply tell them stories instead. She had been telling the children both Greek and Chinese myths, in fact, the first day that Hercules had appeared to observe them. The children had given the octospider his name after he had helped Nai move the furniture in the room into a different configuration.

Most of the stories that Nai told had a hero. Since even Nikki still had some memory of the human biots in New Eden, the children were more interested in stories about Albert Einstein, Abraham Lincoln, and Benita Garcia than they were in historic or mythical characters with whom they had had no personal involvement.

On the morning after Bounty Day, Nai explained how, during the last phases of the Great Chaos, Benita Garcia used her considerable fame to help the millions of poor people in Mexico. Nikki, who had inherited the compassion of her mother and grandmother, was moved by the story of Benita's courageous defiance of the Mexican oligarchy and the American multinational corporations. The little girl proclaimed that Benita Garcia was her hero.

"Heroine," the always precise Kepler corrected. "And what about you, Mother?" the boy said a few seconds later. "Did you have a hero or heroine when you were a little girl?"

Despite the fact that she was in an alien city on an extraterrestrial spacecraft at an unbelievable distance away from her home town of Lamphun in Thailand, for an extraordinary fifteen or twenty seconds Nai's memory transported her back to her childhood, and she saw herself clearly, in a simple cotton dress, walking barefoot into the Buddhist temple to pay homage to Queen Chamatevi. Nai could also see the monks in their saffron robes, and she believed that for a moment she could even smell the joss in the *viharn* in front of the temple's principal Buddha.

"Yes," she said, quite moved by the power of her flashback, "I did have a heroine . . . Queen Chamatevi of the Haripunchai."

"Who was she, Mrs. Watanabe?" Nikki said. "Was she like Benita Garcia?"

"Not exactly," Nai began. "Chamatevi was a beautiful young woman who lived in the Mons kingdom in the south of Indochina over a thousand years ago. Her family was rich and closely connected to the king of the Mons. But Chamatevi, who was exceedingly well educated for a woman of that time, longed to do something different and unusual. Once upon a time, when Chamatevi was nineteen or twenty years old, a soothsayer visited—"

"What's a soothsayer, Mother?" Kepler asked.

Nai smiled. "Someone who predicts the future, or at least tries to," she answered.

"Anyway, this soothsayer told the king that there was an ancient legend saying that a beautiful young Mons woman of noble birth would go north through the jungles to the valley of the Haripunchai and unite all the warring tribes of the region. This young woman, the soothsayer continued, would create a kingdom whose splendor would equal the Mons', and she would be known in many lands for her outstanding leadership. The soothsayer told this story during a feast at the court, and Chamatevi was listening. When the story was completed, the young woman came forward to the king of the Mons and told him that *she* must be the woman in the legend.

"Despite her father's opposition, Chamatevi accepted the king's offer of money and provisions and elephants, even though there was only enough food to last the five months of trekking through the jungle to the land of the Haripunchai. She knew that if the tribes of the north did not accept her as their queen, she would be forced to sell herself as a slave. But never for a moment was Chamatevi afraid.

"Of course the legend was fulfilled, the valley tribes embraced her as their queen, and she reigned for many years in what is known in Thai history as the Golden Age of the Haripunchai. When Chamatevi was very old, she carefully divided her kingdom into two equal parts, which she gave to her twin sons. She then retired to a Buddhist monastery to thank God for His love and protection. Chamatevi remained alert and healthy until she died at the age of ninety-nine."

For reasons she did not completely understand, Nai felt herself becoming very emotional while she was telling the story. When she was finished, Nai could still see, in her mind's eye, the wall panels in the temple in Lamphun that illustrated Chamatevi's story. Nai had been so engrossed in her story that she had not even noticed that Patrick, Nicole, and Archie had all come into the schoolroom and were sitting on the floor behind the children.

"We have many similar stories," Archie said a few minutes later, with Nicole translating, "which we also tell to our juveniles. Most of them are very, very old. Are they true? It doesn't really matter to an octospider. The stories entertain, they instruct, and they inspire."

"I'm sure the children would love to hear one of your stories," Nai said to Archie. "In fact, all of us would."

Archie did not say anything for almost a nillet. His lens fluid was very active, moving back and forth, as if he were carefully studying the human beings staring at him. At length the colored strips began to roll out of his slit and circumnavigate his gray head. "A long, long time ago," he began, "on a faraway world blessed with bounteous resources and beauty beyond description, all the octospiders lived in a vast ocean. On the land there were many creatures, one of which, the . . ."

"I'm sorry," Nicole said both to Archie and the others, "I don't know how to translate the next color pattern."

Archie used several new sentences to try to define the word in other terms. "Those that have gone before . . ." Nicole said to herself. "Oh, well, it's probably not essential for the story that every word be exactly correct. I'll simply call them the Precursors.

"On the land portions of this beautiful planet," Nicole continued for Archie, "were many creatures, of whom by far the most intelligent were the Precursors. They had built vehicles that could fly into the air, they had explored all the neighboring planets and stars, they had even learned how to create life from simple chemicals, where there had been no life before. They had changed the nature of the land and of the oceans with their incredible knowledge.

"It happened that the Precursors determined that the octospider species had enormous untapped potential, capabilities that had never been expressed during their many, many years of aquatic existence, and they began to show the octospiders how to develop and use their latent abilities. As the years passed, the octospider species, thanks to the Precursors, became the second most intelligent on the planet and evolved a very complicated and close relationship with the Precursors.

"During this time the Precursors helped the octospiders learn to live outside the water by taking oxygen directly from the air of the beautiful planet. Entire colonies of octos began to spend their whole lives on land. One day, after a major meeting between the chief optimizers of the Precursors and the octospiders, it was announced that *all* octospiders would become land creatures and give up their colonies in the oceans.

"Down at great depths in the sea was one small colony of octospiders, no more than a thousand altogether, that was managed by a local optimizer who did not think the chief optimizers of the two species had come to a correct decision. This local optimizer resisted the announcement and, although he and his colony were ostracized by the others and did not share in the bounty offered by the Precursors, he and many generations that followed him continued to live their isolated, uncomplicated life on the bottom of the ocean.

"It happened that a great calamity struck the planet, and it became impossible to survive on the land. Many millions of creatures died and only those octospiders who could live comfortably in the water survived the thousands of years that the planet was laid waste.

"When eventually the planet recovered and a few of the ocean octospiders ventured out on land, they found none of their kindred—and none of the Precursors either. That local optimizer who had lived thousands of years before had been visionary. Without his action, every single octospider might have perished. And that's why, even today, smart octospiders retain their capability to live either on land or in water."

Nicole had recognized, early in the story, that Archie was sharing with them something altogether different from anything he had ever told them before. Was it because of their conversation that morning, when she had told Archie that they wanted to return to New Eden soon after the Puckett child was born? She wasn't certain. But she did know that the legend Archie had related told them things about the octospiders that the humans could never have figured out in any other way.

"That was truly marvelous," Nicole said, touching Archie lightly. "I don't know if the children enjoyed it—"

"I thought it was neat," Kepler said. "I didn't know you guys could breathe water."

"Just like an unborn baby," Nai was saying, when an excited Max Puckett raced through the door.

"Come quickly, Nicole," Max said. "The contractions are only four minutes apart."

As Nicole rose, she turned to Archie. "Please tell Dr. Blue to bring the image engineer and the quadroid system. And hurry!"

It was amazing to watch a birth from the outside and inside simultaneously. Nicole was giving directions to both Eponine and the octospider image engineer through Dr. Blue. "*Breathe*—you must breathe through your contractions," she would shout at Eponine. "Move them closer, lower in the birth canal, with a little more light," she would say to Dr. Blue.

Richard was absolutely fascinated. He stood out of the way, over to one side of the bedroom, his eyes darting back and forth from the pictures on the wall to the two octospiders and their equipment. What was being shown in the images was delayed an entire contraction from what was happening on the bed. At the end of each contraction, Dr. Blue would hand Nicole a small round patch, which Nicole would stick on the inside of Eponine's upper thigh. Within seconds the tiny quadroids that had been inside Eponine for the last contraction would race to the patch, and the new ones would then scramble up the birth canal. After a twenty- or thirty-second delay for data processing, another set of pictures would appear on the wall.

Max was driving everybody crazy. When he heard Eponine scream or moan, as she occasionally did near the peak of each contraction, he would rush over to her side and grab her hand. "She's in terrible pain," he would say to Nicole. "You must do something to help her."

Between contractions, when at Nicole's suggestion Eponine would stand up beside the bed to let the artificial gravity help with the birthing process, Max was even worse. The image of his unborn son wedged tightly in the birth canal, struggling with discomfort from the pressure of the previous contraction, would send him into a tirade. "Oh, my God, look, look," Max said after a particularly severe contraction. "His head is *squashed*. Oh, fuck. There's not enough room. He's not going to make it."

Nicole made a couple of major decisions a few minutes before Marius Clyde Puckett entered the universe. First, she concluded that the baby boy was not going to be born without some help. It would be necessary, she decided, for her to perform an episiotomy to mitigate the pain and tearing of the actual birth. Nicole also concluded that Max should be removed from the bedroom before he became hysterical and/or did something that might interfere with the birthing process.

Ellie sterilized the scalpel at Nicole's request. Max looked at the scalpel with wild eyes. "What are you going to do with *that?*" he asked Nicole.

"Max," Nicole said calmly as Eponine felt the advent of another contraction, "I love you dearly, but I want you to leave the room. Please. What I am about to do will make it easier for Marius to be born, but it won't look pretty."

Max didn't move. Patrick, who was standing in the doorway, put a hand on his friend's shoulder as Eponine began to moan again. The baby's head was clearly pressing against the vaginal opening. Nicole began to cut. Eponine screamed in pain. "No," a frantic Max cried at the first sight of blood. "*No* . . . Oh, shit . . . oh, shit."

"*Now* . . . leave *now*," Nicole yelled imperiously as she concluded the episiotomy. Ellie was swabbing up the blood as fast as she could. Patrick turned Max around, gave him a hug, and led him into the living room.

Nicole checked the picture on the wall as soon as it was available. Little Marius was in perfect position. *What a fantastic technology,* she thought fleetingly. *It would change birthing altogether.*

She had no more time to reflect. Another contraction was beginning. Nicole reached up and took Eponine's hand. "This could be it," she said. "I want you to push with all your might. All the way through the whole contraction." Nicole told Dr. Blue that no more images would be needed.

"Push," Nicole and Ellie yelled together.

The baby crowned. They could see swatches of light brown hair.

"Again," Nicole said. "Push again."

"I *can't,*" Eponine wailed.

"Yes, you can. . . . *Push.*"

Eponine arched her back, took a deep breath, and moments later baby Marius squirted into Nicole's hands. Ellie was ready with the scissors to cut the umbilical cord. The boy cried naturally, without needing to be incited. Max rushed into the room.

"Your son has arrived," Nicole said. She finished wiping off the excess fluid, tied off the umbilical, and handed the baby to the proud father.

"Oh my . . . oh my . . . What do I do now?" said the flustered but beaming Max, who was holding the child as if Marius were as fragile as glass and as precious as diamonds.

"You could kiss him," Nicole said with a smile. "That would be a good start."

Max lowered his head and kissed Marius very gently. "And you might bring him over to meet his mother," Eponine said.

Tears of joy were streaming down the new mother's cheeks when she looked at her baby boy close up for the first time. Nicole helped Max lay the child across Eponine's chest. "Oh, Frenchie," Max then said, squeezing Eponine's hand, "how I love you . . . how very much I love you."

Marius, who had been crying steadily since moments after his birth, quieted down in his new position on his mother's chest. Eponine reached down with the hand that Max was not holding and tenderly caressed her new son. Suddenly Max's eyes exploded with tears. "Thank you, honey," he said to Eponine. "Thank you, Nicole. Thanks, Ellie."

Max thanked everybody in the room multiple times, including the two octospiders. For the next five minutes Max was also a veritable hugging machine. Not even the octospiders escaped from his grateful embraces.

6

Nicole knocked lightly on the door and then stuck her head into the room. "Excuse me," she said. "Is anybody awake?"

Eponine and Max both stirred, but no eyes opened to greet Nicole. Little Marius was nestled between his parents, sleeping contentedly. At length Max mumbled, "What time is it?"

"Fifteen minutes *after* the scheduled time for our examination of Marius," Nicole said. "Dr. Blue will be back in a little while."

Max groaned and nudged Eponine. "Come on in," he said to Nicole. Max looked terrible. His eyes were red and puffy and both of them had double bags underneath. "Why do babies not sleep for more than two hours at a time?" he asked with a yawn.

Nicole stood in the doorway. "Some do, Max. But every baby is different. Just after they're born, they usually follow the same routine they were comfortable with in the womb."

"What are you complaining about anyway?" Eponine said, struggling to sit up. "All you have to do is listen to some cries, change a diaper occasionally, and go back to sleep. I have to stay awake while he nurses. Have you ever tried to fall asleep while a little munchkin is sucking on your nipples?"

"What's this?" said Nicole, laughing. "Have our new parents lost their neophyte aura in only four days?"

"Not really," said Eponine, forcing a smile as she put on her clothes. "But Jesus, I am so tired!"

"That's normal," Nicole said. "Your body has been through a trauma. You need rest. As I told you and Max the day after Marius was born when you insisted that we have a party, the only way you'll get enough sleep in the first two weeks is if you adapt *your* schedule to conform with *his*."

"I believe you," Max said. He stumbled out the door with his clothes and headed for the bathroom.

Eponine glanced at the light blue rectangular pad that Nicole had just taken out of her bag. "Is that one of the new diapers?" she said.

"Yes," Nicole answered. "The octospider engineers have made some more improvements. By the way, their offer about the special waster is still open. They don't have anything yet for Marius's urine, but they calculate that with the waster he would only poop—"

"Max is completely against the idea," Eponine interrupted. "He says that his little boy is not going to be an experiment for the octospiders."

"I wouldn't exactly call it an experiment," Nicole said. "The special waster species they have designed is only a slight modification from the ones that have been cleaning our toilets for six months now. And think of the trouble you would avoid—"

"No," Eponine said firmly. "But thank the octospiders anyway."

When Max returned, he was dressed for the day, although still unshaven. "I wanted to tell you, Max," Nicole said, "before Dr. Blue comes back, that I did finally have a long conversation with Archie about our leaving New Eden. When I explained to Archie that we *all* wanted to go, and tried to give him some of the reasons why, he told me it was not in his power to approve our leaving."

"What does that mean?" Max asked.

"Archie said it was an issue for the Chief Optimizer."

"Ah-ha! So I must have been right all along," Max said. "We really *are* prisoners here, and not guests."

"No, not if I understood correctly what Archie said. He told me that it 'can be arranged, if necessary,' but only the Chief Optimizer understands 'all the factors' well enough to make an informed decision."

"More goddamn octospider gobbledygook," Max grumbled.

"I don't think so," Nicole replied. "I was actually encouraged. But Archie said we will not be able to schedule a meeting with the Chief Optimizer until after the Matriculation is over. That's the process that has been taking all of Jamie's time. Apparently it only happens every two years or so and involves the whole colony."

"How long does this Matriculation thing last?" Max asked.

"Only another week. Richard, Ellie, and I have been invited to participate in some facet of the process tonight. It sounds intriguing."

"Marius and I won't be able to leave for several weeks anyway," Eponine said to Max. "So waiting a week is certainly no problem."

At that moment Dr. Blue knocked on the door. The octospider

entered the bedroom with the specialized equipment that was going to be used in the examination of Marius. Max looked askance at a pair of plastic bags containing writhing creatures that looked like black pasta.

"What are those damn things?" Max asked with a scowl.

Nicole finished laying out her own instruments on the table beside the bed. "Max," she said with a smile, "why don't you go next door for the next fifteen minutes or so?"

Max's brow furrowed. "What are you going to do to my little boy? Boil him in oil?"

"No." Nicole laughed. "But from time to time it may sound as if that's what we're doing."

Ellie picked up Nikki and gave her a hug. The little girl momentarily stopped crying. "Mommy is going out with Nonni and Boobah and Archie and Dr. Blue," she said. "We'll be back after your bedtime. You'll be fine here with Mrs. Watanabe, Benjy, and the twins."

"I don't *want* to stay here," Nikki said in her most unpleasant voice. "I want to go with Mommy." She kissed Ellie on the cheek. The little girl's face was expectant.

When Ellie put the child back down on the floor a few seconds later, Nikki's beautiful face scrunched up and she began to wail. "I don't *want* to," she screamed as her mother walked out the door.

Ellie shook her head as the five of them strolled toward the plaza. "I wish I knew what to do for her," Ellie said. "Ever since that incident in the stadium, she has been clinging to me."

"It could be just a normal phase," Nicole said. "Children change very rapidly at her age. And Nikki's no longer the center of attention, now that Marius is here."

"I think the problem's deeper than that," Ellie said several seconds later. She turned to Nicole. "I'm sorry, Mother, but I believe Nikki's insecurity has more to do with Robert than with Marius."

"But Robert has been gone for over a year," Richard said.

"I don't think that matters," Ellie replied. "At some level Nikki must still remember what it was like to have two parents. To her it probably seems like first I abandoned her, then Robert. No wonder she is insecure."

Nicole touched her daughter gently. "But Ellie, if you're right, why is she just *now* reacting so strongly?"

"I can't say for certain," Ellie said. "Maybe the encounter with the iguana thing reminded her how vulnerable she was . . . and how much she misses the protection of her father."

They heard Nikki's loud wail behind them. "Whatever is bothering her," Ellie said with a sigh, "I hope she outgrows it soon. When she cries like that, I feel as if a hot knife were cutting into my stomach."

There was no transport at the plaza. Archie and Dr. Blue kept on walking, heading for the pyramid, where the octospiders and the humans usually held their conferences. "This is a very special evening," Dr. Blue explained, "and there are many things that we must tell you before we leave your zone."

"Where is Jamie?" Nicole asked as they were entering the building. "I thought originally he was going with us. And while I'm at it, what ever happened to Hercules? We haven't seen him since Bounty Day."

While they walked together up the ramp to the second floor of the pyramid, Dr. Blue informed them that Jamie was with his fellow matriculating octospiders that evening and that Hercules had been "reassigned."

"Goodness," said Richard jokingly, "Hercules didn't even say good-bye."

The octospiders, who still hadn't learned to recognize human humor very well, apologized for Hercules' lack of manners. They then mentioned that there would no longer be an octospider among the humans as a daily observer.

"Was Hercules fired for some reason?" Richard asked, still in a lighter vein. The two octospiders ignored the question altogether.

They entered the same conference room where Nicole had learned about the digestive process of the octospiders. Several large sheets of the parchment or hide on which the octos made their drawings and diagrams were over in the corner facing the wall. Dr. Blue asked Richard, Nicole, and Ellie to sit down.

"What you are going to see later tonight," Archie then said, "has never been witnessed by a nonoctospider since our colony was formed here in Rama. We are taking you with us in an attempt to increase the quality of communication between our two species. It is imperative that you understand, before we leave this room and head for the Alternate Domain, not only what you are going to see, but also how you are expected to behave."

"Under no circumstances," Dr. Blue added, "are you to disturb the proceedings or try to interact with anyone or anything along the way, either coming or going. You are to follow our instructions at all times. If you cannot or do not want to accept these conditions, then you must tell us now and we will not take you with us."

The three humans looked at each other with alarm. "You know us well," Nicole said at length. "I trust that we're not going to be asked to do something that is inconsistent with our values and principles. We could not—"

"That's not our concern," Archie interrupted. "We are simply asking you to be passive observers, no matter what you see or experience. If you become confused or frightened and for some reason cannot locate one of us, sit down, wherever you are, with your hands at your sides, and wait for us to come."

There was a brief pause. "I cannot stress too much," Archie continued, "how important your behavior is this evening. Most of the other optimizers objected when I requested that you be allowed to attend. Dr. Blue and I have personally vouched for your ability not to do anything untoward."

"Are our *lives* in danger?" Richard asked.

"Probably not," Archie replied. "But they *could* be. And if tonight were to turn into some kind of a fiasco because of something that one of you did, I'm not certain . . ." In a very unusual action for an octospider, Archie did not finish his sentence.

"Are you telling us," Nicole now said, "that our request to return to New Eden is somehow tied up in all this?"

"Our mutual relationship," Archie said, "has reached a cusp. By sharing a critical portion of our Matriculation process with you, we are attempting to attain a new level of understanding. In that sense, the answer to your question is yes."

They spent almost half a tert, two human hours, in the conference room. Archie began by explaining what the entire Matriculation activity was all about. Jamie and his compatriots, the octospider told them, had finished their adolescence and were about to make the transition to adulthood. As juveniles, their lives had been mostly controlled, and they had not been allowed to make any decisions of great significance. At the end of the Matriculation, Jamie and the other young octos would make a single monumental decision, one that would fundamentally alter the rest of their lives. It was the purpose of the Matriculation, and even much of the final year prior to the transition, to provide the adolescent octospiders with information that would help them make that important decision.

"Tonight," Archie said, "the juveniles will all be taken, as a group, over to the Alternate Domain to see a . . ."

Neither Ellie nor Nicole could figure out at first how to translate into English what the young octospiders were going to see. Eventually, after some discussion between them and several sentences of clarification from Dr. Blue and Archie, the women decided that the best interpretation for what Archie had said in color was "morality play."

For the next several minutes the conversation digressed as Dr. Blue and Archie explained, in response to questions from the humans, that the Alternate Domain was a specific section of the octospider realm that was not under the dome. "South of the Emerald City," Archie said, "there is another settlement with a decidedly different life-style from ours. About two thousand octospiders live in the Alternate Domain at the present time, along with another three thousand or four thousand other creatures representing a dozen different species. Their lives are chaotic and unstructured. The alternate octospiders have no dome over their heads to protect them, no assigned tasks, no planned entertainment, no access to the information in the library, no roads or homes except those they collectively build for themselves, and a life expectancy about one-tenth that of the average octospider in the Emerald City."

Ellie thought about how the Avalon area had been created by Nakamura to deal with the problems that the colonists in New Eden wanted to forget. She thought that perhaps the Alternate Domain was a similar settlement. "Why," she asked, "have so many of your kindred— over ten percent, if my math is accurate—been forced to live outside the dome?"

"No normal octospider has been forced to live in the Alternate Domain," Dr. Blue said. "They are living there because of a personal choice."

"But *why?*" all three humans said, almost in unison.

Dr. Blue went over to the corner and retrieved a few of the charts. The two octospiders used the diagrams extensively during the long discussion that followed. First they explained that hundreds of generations earlier their biologists had correctly identified the connection between sexuality in their species and many other behavioral characteristics, including personal ambition, aggression, territoriality, and aging, to name the most important. This discovery had been made during a period of octospider history when the transition to Optimization was first occurring. But despite the supposedly universal acceptance of a theoretically better structure for octospider society, the transition was severely impeded by regular outbreaks of warfare, tribal dissension, and other mayhem. The octo biologists at the time speculated that only a sexless society, or one in which only a small fraction of the population was sexual, would be able to abide by the principles of Optimization, in which the desires of the individual were subordinated to the welfare of the colony as a whole.

A seemingly endless succession of conflicts convinced all of the forward-looking octospiders of the period that Optimization was only a foolish dream unless some method or technique could be found to combat the individualism that inevitably blocked acceptance of the new order. But what could be done? It was several more generations before a brilliant discovery was made. Research found that special chemicals in a sugarcane-like product called barrican actually slowed down sexual maturation in the octospiders. Within several hundred years the octo genetic engineers had succeeded in designing and producing a variation of this barrican which, if ingested regularly, stopped the advent of sexual maturity altogether.

Test cases and test colonies succeeded beyond the wildest dreams of both the biologists and the progressive political scientists. Sexually immature octos were more responsive to the group concepts of Optimization. In addition, aging was also somehow retarded in those octos who ate barrican. Aging, the octospider scientists then learned very quickly, was tied to the same internal clock mechanism as puberty, and in fact the enzymes causing the cells not to replenish properly in older octospiders did not even activate until a specified time period *after* sexual maturity.

Octospider society underwent rapid changes, Archie and Dr. Blue both asserted, after these colossal discoveries. Optimization took a firm hold everywhere. Octospider social scientists began to envision a society in which the individual octos would be nearly immortal, dying only from accidents or the sudden failure of a major and critical organ. Sexless octospiders populated all the colonies and, as the biologists had predicted, personal ambition and aggression became almost nonexistent.

"All this history took place many generations ago," Archie said, "and is primarily background information to help you understand what the Matriculation is all about. Without going into the complex intervening history, Dr. Blue will summarize where we are today in our particular colony."

"Every octospider that you have encountered so far," Dr. Blue said, "except for the midget morphs and the repletes, both of whom are permanently sexless, is a creature whose sexual maturity has been retarded by the barrican. Many years ago, before a rogue biologist showed how a different kind of sexuality could be genetically engineered into our species, only an octospider queen could produce offspring.

"Among the normal adult octospider population there were two sexes, but the only significant differentiation between them was that one of the two had the ability, if mature, to fertilize a queen. Sexual adults copulated for pleasure, but because there was no issue from this contact, the distinctions between the sexes were blurred. In fact, long-term bonding in the colony was more frequent among members of the same sex, because of similar feelings and common points of view.

"Now the situation is vastly more complicated. In our octospider species, thanks to the genetic engineering genius of our predecessors, an adult female octo is capable of producing, as the result of a sexual union with a mature male octospider, a single, infertile juvenile of limited life expectancy and somewhat reduced capability. You have not yet seen one of these morphs because all of them live, by decree, in the Alternate Domain."

Dr. Blue paused and Archie continued. "Right after Matriculation, each juvenile citizen of our colony decides whether he or she wishes to become sexually mature. If the answer is no, then the octo places his or her sexuality in trust with the optimizers and the colony as a whole. That's what Dr. Blue, who is a female, and I each did long ago. Under octospider law, it is only immediately after Matriculation that an individual can make his or her own sexual choice without any consequences. The optimizers are not lenient toward those who decide to undergo a sexual metamorphosis, without explicit colony permission, after their careers have been carefully structured and planned."

Again Dr. Blue spoke. "As we have presented it tonight, it might seem unlikely that a juvenile octospider would ever make the decision for early sexual maturity. However, in the interest of fairness we should point out that there are compelling reasons, at least in the minds of *some* young octospiders, for choosing to become alternates. First and foremost, a female octo knows that her chances of ever bearing offspring are significantly diminished if she chooses to remain nonsexual after Matriculation. Our history suggests that only in an emergency will a large number of these females ever be called upon to produce juvenile octospiders. In general, the reduced capability and infertility of this kind of offspring makes them less desirable, from the point of view of the colony as a whole, unless of course more octos are needed to support the infrastructure of the society.

"Some of the young octospiders don't like the regimentation and predictability of our life in the Emerald City and want an existence in which they can make all their own decisions. Others fear that the optimizers will place them in an improper career. All of those choosing early sexuality see the Alternate Domain as a free and exciting place, full of glamor and adventure. They discount what they are giving up . . . and in their momentary exuberance, the quality of their life is more important than its likely duration. . . ."

Throughout the long conversation, Richard, Nicole, and Ellie asked many questions. As the evening progressed, all three of the humans started feeling overwhelmed. There was just too much information to digest in a single discussion.

"Wait a minute," Richard said abruptly when Archie indicated it was past time for them to leave. "I'm sorry . . . there's something fundamental about this that I still don't understand. Why is this choice permitted at all? Why do the optimizers not simply decree that all the octospiders will always eat the barrican and remain sexless until the colony has a requirement for reproduction?"

"That's a very good question," Archie replied, "with a complex answer. Let me oversimplify, in the interests of time, by saying that our species believes in permitting some free choice. Also, as you will see tonight, there are some functions for which the alternates are uniquely suited and from which the whole colony derives benefits."

7

After leaving their zone, the transport followed a different route
from the one that had taken the humans to the stadium on Bounty Day.
This time it stayed on dimly lit streets on the periphery of the city. The
party encountered none of the busy, colorful scenes that they had seen in
their previous excursion. After several fengs the transport approached a
large closed gate very much like the one through which they had initially
entered the Emerald City.

Two octospiders came over and peered in the car. Archie said
something to them in color, and one of the octospiders returned to what
must have been their equivalent of a guardhouse. In the distance Richard
could see colors flashing on a flat wall. "She's checking with the authori-
ties," Dr. Blue told the humans. "We're outside our expected arrival
interval, so our exit code is no longer valid."

During a wait of several more nillets, the other octospider entered the
transport and inspected it thoroughly. None of the humans had ever
experienced such stringent security precautions in the Emerald City, not
even at the stadium. Ellie's discomfort was heightened when the octospider
security officer, without saying anything to her, opened up her purse to see
its contents. Eventually the inspector returned Ellie's purse and disembarked. The gate swung open, the transport moved out from under the
green dome, and then it parked in the dark less than a minute later.

The transport was surrounded in the parking lot by thirty or forty other
vehicles. "This area," Dr. Blue explained as they descended from the car

and a pair of fireflies joined them, "is called the Arts District. It and the zoo, which is not too far from here, are the only two sections of the Alternate Domain visited with any regularity by the octospiders who live in the Emerald City. The optimizers do not approve many visitation requests to the alternate living areas that are farther south—in fact, for most octospiders, the only comprehensive view of the Alternate Domain that they ever have is the tour during the last week of Matriculation."

The air was much colder than it had been in the Emerald City. Archie and Dr. Blue both started walking faster than the humans had ever seen an octospider move before. "We must hurry," Archie turned and said, "or we will be late." The human trio ran to keep up with the fast pace.

As they neared an illuminated area about three hundred meters from their transport, Archie and Dr. Blue moved to either end of the line of humans so that they were walking five abreast. "We're entering Artisan's Square," Dr. Blue said, "which is where the alternates offer their artistic works for transfer."

"What do you mean, 'transfer'?" Nicole asked.

"The artists need credits for food and other essentials. They offer their works of art to an Emerald City resident who has credits to spare," Dr. Blue replied.

As much as Nicole might have wanted to pursue the conversation, she was immediately sidetracked by the dazzling array of unusual objects, makeshift stalls, octospiders, and other animals that greeted her eyes in Artisan's Square. The square, a large plaza seventy or eighty meters on a side, was directly across a broad avenue from the theater that was their destination. Archie and Dr. Blue, at the ends of their line, each extended a single tentacle along the collective backs of the humans so that the five of them moved as one across the bustling square.

The group was confronted by several octospiders holding out objects to transfer. Richard, Nicole, and Ellie quickly confirmed what Archie had told them during the long meeting, namely that the alternates did not conform to the official language specification used by the octospiders in the Emerald City. There were no neat color bands sweeping around the heads of these octospiders, only sloppy sequences of colored blotches of widely variable heights. One of the hawkers who accosted them was small, obviously a juvenile, and he or she, after being waved away by Archie, gave Ellie a sudden fright by wrapping a tentacle around Ellie's arm for a few fractions of a second. Archie seized the offender with three of his own tentacles and hurled him roughly out of the way, in the direction of one of the octospiders with a cloth bag over its shoulder. Dr. Blue explained that the bag identified the octo as a policeman.

Nicole was walking so fast, and there was so much around her to see, that she found herself holding her breath. Although she had no idea what to make of many of the objects being offered for transfer in the square, she could recognize and appreciate the occasional painting, or piece of sculpture, or those tiny representations, in wood or some similar medium, of all the different animals who lived in the Emerald City. In one section of the square there were displays of colored patterns pressed upon the parchment material—Dr. Blue explained later, when they were inside the theater, that the particular art form represented by the patterns was a combination, as he understood the human terms, of both poetry and calligraphy.

Just before they crossed the street, Nicole caught sight, on a wall twenty meters away on her left, of a large mural that was astonishingly beautiful. The colors were bold and eye-catching, the composition the work of an artist who understood both structure and optical appeal. The technical skill was also extremely impressive, but it was the emotions rendered in the bodies and faces of the octospiders and other creatures in the mural that fascinated Nicole.

"*The Triumph of Optimization*," Nicole mumbled to herself as she craned her neck to read the title in colors across the upper portion of the mural. The painting had a spacecraft against a star background in one section, an ocean teeming with living things in another, and both a jungle and a desert in opposite corners. The central image, however, was a giant octospider, carrying a stave and standing on a pile of thirty disparate animals, who were squirming in the dust underneath its tentacles. Nicole's heart nearly jumped out of her body when she saw that one of the trampled beings was a young human woman with brown skin, piercing eyes, and short curly hair.

"Look," she yelled suddenly to the others, "over there—at that mural."

At that moment some kind of small animal was making itself a nuisance around their feet. It succeeded in distracting everyone's attention. The two octospiders dealt with the animal and pulled the line again toward the theater. As she moved into the street, Nicole glanced back at the mural to make certain that she had not imagined the presence of a young woman in the picture. From the added distance the face of the woman and her features were vague, but Nicole was nevertheless convinced that she had definitely seen a human being in the artwork. *But how is that possible?* Nicole was asking herself as they entered the theater.

Preoccupied with her discovery, Nicole listened with only half an ear to Richard's discussion with Archie about how he intended to use his translator during the play. She didn't even look when, after they took their standing positions in the fifth row above a theater-in-the-round, Dr. Blue pointed out with one of his tentacles the sector to the left of them containing Jamie and the other matriculating octospiders. *I must have made a mistake*, Nicole thought. She was seized by a powerful impulse to run back to the square and verify what she had seen. Then she remembered what Archie had told them about the importance of carefully following instructions on this particular evening. *I know I saw a woman in that painting,* Nicole told herself as three large fireflies flew down and hovered over the stage in the center of the theater. *But if I did, what does it mean?*

There were no intermissions in the play, which lasted slightly more than an hour. The action was continuous, with one or more of the octospider actors occupying the lit stage at all times. No props were used and no costumes. At the beginning of the play the seven main "characters" came forward and briefly introduced themselves—two matriculating octos, one of either sex, a pair of adoptive parents for each, and one alternate male whose bright and beautiful colors spread all the way to the end of his tentacles when he spoke.

The first several minutes of the actual play established that the two matriculating juveniles had been best friends for years and that, despite the good and sound advice of their assigned parents, they had selected early sexual maturity together. "My desire," the young female octospider said in her first monologue, "is to produce a baby from a union with my cherished companion." Or at least that's how Richard translated what she said. He was gleeful at the performance of his much-improved translator and, after remembering that the octospiders were deaf, he talked intermittently throughout the performance.

The four octo parents came together in the center of the stage and expressed anxiety about what would happen when the "powerful new emotions" that accompanied the sexual transformation were first encountered by their adopted children. They did, however, try to be fair, and all four of the adults admitted that their own choices not to become sexually mature after Matriculation meant that they could not give advice based on any actual experience.

In the middle of the play the two young octospiders were isolated at opposite corners of the stage, and the audience concluded from the pyrotechnics of the fireflies, plus a few brief statements from the octospider actors, that each of them had stopped eating the barrican and was alone in some kind of Transition Domain.

When later the two transformed octospiders walked across the stage and met in the center, the color patterns in their conversation had already altered. It was a powerful effect, however it was achieved by the actors, because not only were the individual colors brighter than they had been before the transition, but also the rigid, nearly perfect strips that had characterized the early conversations between the two juveniles were already marked with some different and interesting individual designs. Around them on the stage at this point were half a dozen other octospiders—all alternates, judging from their language—and a couple of Polish sausage animals chasing anything they could find. The pair were now clearly in the Alternate Domain.

Enter from the darkness off the stage the alternate male introduced at the beginning of the play. The octospider actor first made a brilliant display of horizontal and vertical patterns moving in both directions and then created advanced wave action, geometric structures, and even fireworkslike explosions of color starting at random locations around his head. The newcomer's Technicolor display mesmerized the young female octo and won her away from the best friend of her childhood. Soon after, the interloper with the amazing colors, who had obviously parented the baby octo being carried in the frontal pouch of the female, left her sitting forlorn and alone in the corner of the stage, sending out pulse after unstructured pulse of meaningless colors.

At this point in the play the male octospider who had matriculated in the earlier scenes stormed into the light, saw his true love in despair with her baby, and jumped off into the darkness surrounding the stage. Moments later he returned with the alternate who had corrupted his girlfriend, and the two male octos engaged in a horrible but fascinating fight in the middle of the stage. Their heads a riot of expletive color, they beat, twisted, choked, and battled each other for an entire feng. The younger male octo eventually won the fight, for the alternate lay motionless on the stage when the action was over. The sadness expressed in the closing remarks of the hero and the heroine made certain that the moral of the play was very clear. When the play was finished, Richard glanced at Nicole and Ellie and commented, with an irreverent grin, "This is one of those downer plays, like *Othello*, where everyone dies in the end."

Under the supervision of the octospider ushers, all with bags, the matriculating youngsters left the theater first, followed next by Archie, Dr. Blue, and their human companions. The orderly procession stopped just outside a few minutes later and formed a crowded ring around three other octospiders who were in the middle of the avenue. Richard, Nicole, and Ellie felt the presence of their friends' powerful tentacles across their backs as they moved into position to see what was taking place. Two of the octospiders in the center of the street were holding staves and wearing bags, while the third octo, who was crouching between them, was transmitting the color message, in broad and unstructured bands, "Please, help me."

"This octospider," one of the policemen said in crisp, measured strips, "has consistently failed to earn her credits since coming to the Alternate Domain after her Matriculation four cycles ago. Last cycle she was warned that she had become an unacceptable drain upon our common resources, and recently, two days before Bounty Day, she was told to report for termination. Since that time she has been hiding among friends in the Alternate Domain."

The crouching octospider suddenly bolted and leaped into the audience near where the humans were standing. The crowd sagged back from the impact and Ellie, who was nearest the point where the escape attempt occurred, was knocked to the ground in the melee that ensued. In less than a nillet the police, with help from Archie and several of the matriculating juveniles, again had the fugitive under control.

"Failure to report for a scheduled termination is one of the worst crimes an octospider can commit," the policeman then said. "It is punishable by immediate termination upon apprehension." One of the policemen pulled several wriggling, wormlike creatures from its shoulder bag. The outlaw octo struggled hard the first time the two policemen tried to force the wormlike creatures into her mouth. However, after each of the policemen hit the renegade twice with a stave, the doomed octospider collapsed between her captors. Ellie, who had regained her footing by this time, was unable to suppress a scream of terror as the creatures entered the octo's mouth, and she began to regurgitate. Death came quickly.

None of the humans said a word as they walked arm in arm with Archie and Dr. Blue across the square and into the parking area where their transport was waiting. Nicole was so stunned by what she had witnessed that she did not even remember to look for the painting that she thought had included a human face.

In the middle of the night Nicole, who had not been able to sleep, heard a noise in the living room. She rose from her bed quietly and slipped into a robe. Ellie was sitting on the couch in the dark. Nicole sat down beside her daughter and took her hand.

"I couldn't sleep, Mother," Ellie said. "I have been going over everything in my mind and it doesn't make any sense. I feel as if I have been betrayed."

"I know, Ellie," Nicole said. "I feel the same way."

"I thought I *knew* the octospiders," Ellie said. "I trusted them. In many ways I thought they were superior to *us*, but after what I saw tonight . . ."

"None of us is comfortable with killing," Nicole said. "Even Richard was horrified at first. But after we were in bed, he told me that he was certain the street scene was carefully staged for the benefit of the matriculators. He also said that we should be careful not to jump to too many conclusions or let ourselves react emotionally to one isolated incident."

"I have never before watched an intelligent being murdered before my very eyes. And what was her crime? Failure to report for termination?"

"We cannot judge them as we would judge human beings. The octospiders are an entirely different species, with a completely separate social organization, one that may be even more complex than ours. We are only beginning to understand them. Have you already forgotten that they cured Eponine of RV-41? And allowed us to use their technology when we were worried about Marius's birth?"

"No, I haven't," Ellie replied. She was silent for several seconds. "You know, Mother, I'm feeling as frustrated now as I did often in New Eden, when I kept wondering how human beings, who are capable of so much that is good, could possibly tolerate a tyrant like Nakamura. Now it looks as if the octospiders can be just as bad in their own way. There is so much inconsistency everywhere."

Nicole tried to console her daughter with a hug. In her mind's eye Nicole again saw a highlight montage of the night's incredible activities, including the fleeting glimpse in which she believed she had seen an unknown human woman in an octospider mural. *And what was that about, old woman?* she asked herself. *Was it really there, that face, or did your tired and imaginative brain create it to confuse you?*

8

Max finished shaving and washed the rest of the approximation of shaving cream off his face. Moments later he pulled the plug and the water disappeared from the stone basin. After wiping his face thoroughly with a small towel, Max turned to Eponine, who was sitting on the bed behind him nursing Marius.

"Well, Frenchie," he said with a laugh, "I must admit I'm damn nervous. I've never met a Chief Optimizer before." He walked over beside her. "Once, when I was in Little Rock for a farmers' convention, I sat next to the governor of Arkansas during a banquet. I was a little nervous then too."

Eponine smiled. "It's hard for me to imagine you being nervous," she said.

Max stood silently for several seconds, watching his wife and infant son. The baby made soft cooing sounds as he ate. "You really enjoy this nursing business, don't you?"

Eponine nodded. "It's a pleasure unlike any I have ever experienced. The sense of . . . I don't know the exact word—maybe 'communion' would be close—is indescribable."

Max shook his head. "Ours is an amazing existence, isn't it? Last night, when I was changing Marius, I thought of how similar we probably were to millions of other human couples, doting on our first child . . . yet just outside that door is an alien city run by a species . . ." He did not finish his thought.

"Ellie has been different since last week," Eponine said. "She's lost her spark and talks about Robert more."

"She was horrified by the execution," Max commented. "I wonder if women are naturally more sensitive to violence. I remember after Clyde and Winona got married, when he brought her back to the farm, the first time she watched us slaughter a couple of pigs, her face became white as a ghost. She didn't say anything, but she never came to watch again."

"Ellie won't talk much about that night," Eponine said, switching Marius over to the other breast. "And that's not like her at all."

"Richard asked Archie about the incident yesterday, when he requested the components to build translators for the rest of us. According to Richard, the damn octo was real foxy and did not give many straight answers. Archie would not even confirm what Dr. Blue told Nicole about their basic termination policy."

"It's pretty scary, isn't it?" she said. Ellie grimaced before continuing. "Nicole insisted that she made Dr. Blue repeat the policy to her several times, and she even tried several different versions in English, in Dr. Blue's presence, to make certain that she had understood it correctly."

"It's simple enough," Max said with a forced grin, "even for a farmer. 'Any adult octospider whose total contribution to the colony over a defined period of time is not at least equal in worth to the resources necessary to sustain that individual will be entered onto the termination list. If the negative account is not corrected in a prescribed amount of time, the octospider will then be terminated.'"

"According to Dr. Blue," Eponine said after a short silence, "it's the optimizers who interpret the policies. They are the ones who decide what everything is worth."

"I know," Max said, reaching down and caressing his baby son's back, "and I think that's one of the reasons Nicole and Richard are anxious about today. Nobody has said anything explicit, but we have been using a lot of resources for a long time—and it's pretty damn hard to see what we've been contributing."

"Are you ready, Max?" Nicole stuck her head in the door. "Everyone else is out here by the fountain."

Max bent down to kiss Eponine. "Will you and Patrick be able to handle Benjy and the children?" he asked.

"Certainly," Eponine replied. "Benjy's no effort, and Patrick has been spending so much time with the children that he's become a child care specialist."

"I love you, Frenchie," Max said, waving good-bye.

There were five chairs for them outside the Chief Optimizer's operating area. Even when Nicole explained the word "office" to Archie and Dr. Blue a second time, their two octospider colleagues still insisted that "operating area" was a better translation into English for the place where the Chief Optimizer worked.

"The Chief Optimizer is sometimes a little late," Archie said apologetically. "Unexpected events in the colony can force her to deviate from the planned schedule."

"There must be something really unusual going on," Richard said to Max. "Punctuality is one of the hallmarks of the octospider species."

The five humans waited silently for their meeting, each engrossed in his or her own thoughts. Nai's heart was pounding rapidly. She was both apprehensive and excited. She remembered having had a similar feeling as a schoolgirl when she was waiting for her audience with the king of Thailand's daughter, the Princess Suri, after Nai had won a top prize in a nationwide academic competition.

A few minutes later an octospider bade them enter the next room, where they were informed they would be joined in a moment by the Chief Optimizer and a few of her advisers. The new room had transparent windows. They could see activity all around them. Where they were sitting reminded Richard of a control area for a nuclear power plant, or perhaps for a manned space flight. Octospider computers and visual monitors were everywhere, as were octospider technicians. Richard asked a question about something happening in a distant area, but before Archie could answer, three octospiders entered the room.

All five humans rose in a reflex action. Archie introduced the Chief Optimizer, the Deputy Chief Optimizer for the Emerald City, and the Optimizer Security Chief. The three octos each extended a tentacle to the humans and handshakes were exchanged. Archie motioned for the humans to sit down and the Chief Optimizer began speaking immediately.

"We are aware," she said, "that you have requested, through our representative, that you be allowed to return to New Eden to rejoin the other members of your species in Rama. We were not completely surprised by this request because our historical data indicate that most intelligent species with strong emotions, after a period of time living in an alien community, develop a sense of disconnection and yearn to return to a more familiar world. What we would like to do this morning is provide some additional information to you that could influence your request that we permit you to return to New Eden."

Archie asked all the humans to follow the Chief Optimizer. The group passed through a room similar to the two in which they had been sitting and then entered a rectangular area with a dozen wall screens spread around the sides at octospider eye level.

"We have been monitoring closely the developments in your habitat," the Chief Optimizer said when they were all together, "ever since long before your escape. This morning we want to share with you some of the events that we have recently observed."

An instant later all the wall screens switched on. Each contained a motion picture segment from the daily life among the humans remaining in New Eden. The quality of the videos was not perfect and no segment was continuous for longer than a few nillets, but there was no mistaking what was being presented on the screens.

For several seconds the humans were all speechless. They stood transfixed, glued to the images on the wall. On one of the screens Nakamura, dressed as a Japanese shogun, was making a speech to a large crowd in the square in Central City. He was holding up a large hand-drawn picture of an octospider. Although the videos were silent, it was apparent from his gestures and the pictures of the crowd that Nakamura was exhorting everyone to action against the octospiders.

"Well, I'll be goddamned," Max said, his eyes moving from one screen to another.

"Look over here," Nicole said. "It's El Mercado in San Miguel."

In the poorest of the four villages of New Eden, a dozen white and yellow toughs with karate bands around their heads were beating up four black and brown youths in full view of a pair of New Eden policemen and a sorrowful crowd of perhaps twenty villagers. Tiasso and Lincoln biots picked up the broken, bloodied bodies after the beatings and placed them in a large tricycle carriage.

On another screen a segment showed a well-dressed crowd, mostly white and Oriental, arriving for a party or a festival in Nakamura's Vegas. Bright lights beckoned them to the casino, over which a huge sign proclaimed CITIZEN APPRECIATION DAY and announced that every partygoer would receive a dozen free lottery tickets to celebrate the occasion. Two large posters of Nakamura, chest shots showing him smiling and wearing a white shirt and tie, flanked the sign.

A monitor on the wall behind the Chief Optimizer showed the interior of the Central City jail. A new felon, a female with a multicolored hairdo, was being placed in a cell that already contained two other convicts. It appeared as if the newcomer were complaining about the crowded conditions, but the policeman just pushed her into the cell and laughed. When the policeman returned to his desk, the video revealed two photographs on the wall behind him, one of Richard and the other of Nicole, under both of which the word REWARD was written in large block letters.

The octospiders waited patiently as the humans' eyes moved from screen to screen. "*How* in the world?" Richard kept asking, shaking his head. Then the screens went suddenly blank.

"We have put together a total of forty-eight segments to show you today," the Chief Optimizer said, "all taken from observations made the last eight days in New Eden. The optimizer you call Archie will have a catalog of the segments, which have been classified according to location, time, and event description. You may spend as much time here as you like, looking at the segments, talking among yourselves, and asking questions of the two octospiders who accompanied you here. I, unfortunately, have other tasks to perform. If, at the end of your viewing, you wish to communicate with me again, I will make myself available."

The Chief Optimizer then departed, followed by her two assistants. Nicole sat down in one of the chairs. She looked pale and weak. Ellie walked over beside her.

"Are you all right, Mother?" Ellie asked.

"I think so," Nicole replied. "Right after the videos began to play, I felt a sharp pain in my chest—probably from the surprise and excitement—but it has subsided now."

"Do you want to go home and rest?" Richard asked.

"Are you kidding?" said Nicole with her characteristic smile. "I wouldn't miss seeing this show even if there was a chance that I would drop dead in the middle."

They watched the silent movies for almost three hours. It was clear from the videos both that there was no longer any individual freedom in New Eden and that most of the colonists were struggling to sustain even a meager existence. Nakamura had consolidated his hold on the colony and crushed all the opposition. But the colony he ruled was peopled mostly by gloomy and unhappy citizens.

At first all the humans watched the same segment together, but after three or four had been played, Richard suggested that it was terribly inefficient for them to watch the segments one at a time. "Spoken like a true optimizer," said Max, who nevertheless agreed with Richard.

There was one segment in which Katie briefly appeared. It was a late-night scene from Vegas. The street prostitutes were plying their trade outside one of the clubs. Katie approached one of the women, had a brief conversation about some unknown subject, and then disappeared from view. Richard and Nicole couldn't help but notice that Katie looked terribly thin, even gaunt. They asked Archie to rerun the segment several times.

Another sequence was entirely devoted to the hospital in Central City. No words were needed for the viewers to understand that there were shortages of critical medicines, not enough staff members, and problems with equipment falling into disrepair. One particularly poignant scene showed a young woman of Mediterranean extraction, possibly Greek, dying after a painful breech childbirth. Her delivery room was lit with candles while the monitoring equipment that might have identified her difficulties and saved her life lay inexplicably unpowered beside the bed.

Robert Turner was everywhere in the hospital segment. The first time Ellie saw him walking through the halls, she burst into tears. She sobbed throughout the segment and then immediately requested a replay. Only when she was watching for a third time did she make any comment. "He looks haggard," she said, "and overworked. He has never learned to take care of himself."

When they were all emotionally exhausted and nobody requested the replay of another segment, Archie asked the humans if they wished to visit again with the Chief Optimizer. "Not now," Nicole said, reflecting everyone's opinion. "We haven't had time to digest what we've seen."

Nai asked if perhaps they could take some of the segments back to their homes in the Emerald City. "I would like to see them again," she said, "at a more leisurely pace. And it would be great if we could show them to Patrick and Eponine." Archie replied that he was sorry, but the segments could only be viewed in one of the octospider communication centers.

On the ride back to their zone, Richard showed Archie how well his real-time translator was working. Richard had just finished his final tests the day prior to the meeting with the Chief Optimizer. The translator could translate either the octospiders' natural dialect or the language specifically tailored to the visual spectrum of the humans. Archie acknowledged that he was impressed.

"By the way," Richard added in a louder voice, so that all his compatriots could hear him, "I guess there's not much chance that you'd tell us *how* you managed to obtain all those video segments from New Eden, is there?"

Archie did not hesitate to answer. "Flying image quadroids," he said. "More advanced genus. Much smaller."

Nicole translated for Max and Nai. "Fuck me," Max muttered under his breath. He rose and walked to the opposite end of the transport, shaking his head vigorously.

"I have never seen Max so solemn or so tense," Richard said to Nicole.

"Nor have I," she answered. They were taking an exercise walk an hour after having finished dinner with their family and friends. A lone firefly kept pace above Richard and Nicole as they repeated multiple times the walk from the end of their cul-de-sac to the plaza at the other end of the street.

"Do you think Max will change his mind about leaving?" Richard asked as they circled the fountain again.

"I don't know," Nicole replied. "I think he's still in shock, in a way. He detests the fact that the octospiders are able to watch everything we do. That's why he insists that he and his family will return to New Eden, even if everyone else stays here."

"Have you had a chance to talk with Eponine alone?"

"The day before yesterday she brought Marius over just after naptime. While I was putting some medication on his diaper rash, she asked me if I had mentioned to Archie that they wanted to leave. She seemed frightened."

They marched briskly into the plaza. Without stopping, Richard pulled out a small cloth and wiped the sweat from his brow. "Everything has changed," he said, as much to himself as to Nicole.

"I'm certain it's all part of the octospider plan," Nicole replied. "They didn't show us those videos only to demonstrate that all is not well in New Eden. They *knew* how we would react after we had had time to assess the real significance of what we had seen."

The pair walked silently back in the direction of their temporary home. On the next swing around the fountain, Richard said, "So do they observe everything we do, including even this conversation?"

"Of course," Nicole replied. "That was the primary message the octospiders transmitted to us by allowing us to see the videos. We can have no secrets. Escape is out of the question. We are completely in their power. I may be the only one, but I still do not believe that they intend to harm us. And they might even allow us to return to New Eden. . . . Eventually."

"It will never happen," Richard said. "Then they would have wasted a lot of resources for no measurable return, a decidedly nonoptimal situation. No, I'm certain the octospiders are still trying to figure out our proper placement in their overall system."

Richard and Nicole walked at top speed on their final lap. They finished at the fountain and both of them drank some water. "How do you feel?" Richard asked.

"Fine," Nicole answered. "No pains, no shortness of breath. When Dr. Blue examined me yesterday, she found no new pathology. My heart is just old and weak. I should expect intermittent problems."

"I wonder what niche we'll occupy in the octospider world," Richard said a few moments later when they were washing their faces.

Nicole glanced at her husband. "Aren't you the one," she said, "who laughed at me some months ago for making inferences about their motives? How can you be so certain now that you understand what the octospiders are trying to accomplish?"

"I'm not." Richard grinned. "But it's natural to assume that a superior species would at least be logical."

Richard woke Nicole up in the middle of the night. "I'm sorry to bother you, darling, but I have a problem."

"What is it?" Nicole asked, sitting up in bed.

"It's embarrassing," Richard said. "That's why I haven't mentioned it earlier. . . . It started right after Bounty Day. I thought it would go away, but this last week the pain has become unbearable."

"Come on, Richard," Nicole said, a little irritated at having her sleep disturbed, "get to the point. What pain are you talking about?"

"Every time I urinate, I have this burning sensation. . . ."

Nicole tried to stifle a yawn while she was thinking. "And have you been urinating more frequently?" she asked.

"Yes . . . how did you know?"

"Achilles should have been held by his prostate when he was dipped in the River Styx," she said. "It is certainly the weakest structure in the male anatomy. Roll over on your stomach and let me examine you."

"*Now?*" said Richard.

"If you can wake me from a deep sleep because of your pain," Nicole said with a laugh, "then the least you can do is grit your teeth while I try to verify my instant diagnosis."

Dr. Blue and Nicole were sitting together in the octospider's house. On one of the walls four quadroid frames were projected. "The image on the far left," Dr. Blue said, "shows the growth as it looked that first morning, ten days ago, when you asked me to confirm your diagnosis. The second frame is a much magnified picture of a pair of cells taken from the tumor. The cell abnormalities—what you call cancer—are marked with the blue stain."

Nicole smiled wanly. "I'm having a little difficulty reorienting my thinking," she said. "You never use the colors for 'disease' when you describe Richard's problem—only the word which in your language I define as 'abnormality.' "

"To us," Dr. Blue responded, "a disease is a malfunction caused by an outside agent, such as a bacterium or a hostile virus. An irregularity in the cell chemistry leading to the manufacture of improper cells is a completely different kind of problem. In our medicine the treatment regimens are completely different for the two cases. This cancer in your husband is more closely related to aging, generically, than it is to a disease like your pneumonia or gastroenteritis."

Dr. Blue extended a tentacle toward the third picture. "This image," she said, "shows the tumor three days ago, after the special chemicals carried by our microbiological agents had been carefully dispersed at the site of the abnormality. The growth has already begun to shrink because the production of the malignant cells has stopped. In the final image, taken this morning, Richard's prostate again looks normal. By this time all the original cancer cells have died, and no new ones have been produced."

"So will he be all right now?" Nicole asked.

"Probably," Dr. Blue answered. "We can't be absolutely certain because we still do not have as much data as we would like on the life cycle of your cells. There are a few unique characteristics about your cells—as there always are in species who have undergone an evolution distinct from any of our previously examined beings—that might permit a recurrence of the abnormality. However, based on our experience with many other living creatures, I would have to say that the development of another prostate tumor is unlikely."

Nicole thanked her octospider colleague. "This has been incredible," she said. "How wonderful it would be if your medical knowledge could somehow be transported back to Earth."

The images vanished from the wall. "There would be many social problems created as well," Dr. Blue said, "assuming that I have properly understood our discussions of your home planet. If individual members of your species did not die from diseases or cell abnormalities, life expectancy would increase markedly. Our species went through a similar upheaval after our Golden Age of Biology, when octospider life spans doubled in just a few generations. It wasn't until optimization became firmly implanted as our governing structure that any kind of societal equilibrium was reached. We have plenty of evidence that without sound termination and replenishment policies, a colony of nearly immortal beings undergoes chaos in a relatively short period of time."

Nicole's interest was piqued. "I can appreciate what you're saying, at least intellectually," she said. "If everyone lives forever, or nearly so, and the resources are finite, the population will soon overwhelm the available food and living space. But I must admit, especially as an old person, that even the idea of a 'termination policy' frightens me."

"In our early history," Dr. Blue said, "our society was structured much like yours, with almost all of the decision-making power resting with the older members of the species. It was easier to restrict replenishment, therefore, after life expectancy dramatically increased, than it was to deal with the difficult issue of planned terminations. After a comparatively brief period of time, however, the aging society began to stagnate. As Archie or any good optimizer would explain, the 'ossification' coefficient of our colonies became so large that eventually *all* new ideas were rejected. These geriatric colonies collapsed, basically because they were not able to deal with the changing conditions of the universe around them."

"So that's where optimization comes in?"

"Yes," said Dr. Blue. "If every individual embraces the precept that the welfare of the overall colony should be awarded the highest weight in the master objective function, then it quickly becomes clear that planned terminations are a critical element of the optimal solution. Archie would be able to show you quantitatively how disastrous it is, from the point of view of the colony as a whole, to spend huge amounts of collective resource on those citizens whose integrated remaining contribution is comparatively low. The colony benefits most by investing in those members who have a long, healthy lifetime still available and therefore a high probability of repaying the investment."

Nicole repeated back to Dr. Blue some of the octospider's key sentences, just to make certain that she had understood properly. Then she was silent for two or three nillets. "I suppose," Nicole said eventually, "that even though your aging is delayed both by postponing sexual maturity and by your amazing medical capability, at some point preserving the life of an old octospider becomes prohibitively expensive, by some measure."

"Exactly," Dr. Blue replied. "We can extend the life of an individual almost forever. However, there are three major factors that make extra life extension decidedly nonoptimal for the colony. First, as you mentioned, the cost of the effort to extend life increases dramatically as each biological subsystem, or organ, begins to operate at less than peak efficiency. Second, as an individual octospider's time becomes more and more consumed with the process of simply staying alive, the amount of energy that he or she might have to contribute to the colony's welfare lessens considerably. Third, and the sociological optimizers proved this controversial point many years ago—although for some number of years after mental quickness and learning ability start to drop, accumulated wisdom more than compensates—in terms of value to the colony, for the diminished brain-power, there comes a time in the life of every octospider when the sheer weight of his or her past experience makes any additional learning extremely difficult. Even in a healthy octospider this phase of life, called the Onset of Limited Flexibility by our optimizers, signals a reduced ability to contribute to the colony."

"So the optimizers determine when it is termination time?"

"Yes," said Dr. Blue, "but I don't know exactly how they do it. There is a probationary period first, during which time the individual octospider is entered on the termination list and given time to improve his or her net balance. This balance, if I have understood Archie's explanation, is calculated for each octospider by comparing its contributions made with the resources necessary to sustain that particular individual. If the balance does not improve, then termination is scheduled."

"And how do those selected for termination react?" Nicole asked, involuntarily shuddering as she remembered facing her own execution.

"In different ways," Dr. Blue replied. "Some, especially those who have been unhealthy, accept that they are not going to be able to redress the unsatisfactory balance and plan for their deaths in an organized fashion. Others ask for optimizer counseling and request new assignments that have a higher probability of allowing them to meet their contribution quotas. . . . That's what Hercules did just before your arrival."

Nicole was momentarily speechless. A chill ran down her back. "Are you going to tell me what happened to Hercules?" she said, finally summoning her courage.

"He was severely reprimanded for not providing proper protection for Nikki on Bounty Day," Dr. Blue said. "Hercules was then reassigned and informed by the Termination Optimizer that there was virtually no way he could recover from the high negative assessment of his recent work. Hercules requested early and immediate termination."

Nicole gasped. In her mind's eye she saw the friendly octospider standing in the cul-de-sac, juggling many balls to the delight of the children. She tried to tell herself that she should be rejoicing because Richard's prostate cancer had been cured, and should not be concerned about the death of a relatively meaningless octospider. But the image of Hercules continued to haunt her. *They are an altogether different species,* she told herself. *Do not judge them by human standards.*

As she was about to leave Dr. Blue's house, Nicole suddenly had an overpowering desire to know more about Katie. She remembered that one recent night, after an especially vivid dream involving Katie, she had awakened and wondered if perhaps the octospider records might allow her to see more of Katie's life in New Eden.

"Dr. Blue," Nicole said as she was standing in the door, "I would like to ask a favor. I don't know whether to ask you or Archie. I don't even know if what I'm asking is possible."

The octospider asked her what the favor was.

"As you know," Nicole said, "I have another daughter who is still living in New Eden. I saw her very briefly in one of the videos the Chief Optimizer showed us last month. . . . I would like very much to know what is happening in her life."

9

During a conversation the next day, Archie told Nicole that her request to see videos of Katie could not be granted. Nevertheless, Nicole persisted, taking advantage of every opportunity when she was alone with Archie or Dr. Blue to reiterate her request. Because neither of the octospiders ever indicated that images from Katie's life in New Eden did not exist in their files, Nicole was certain that the video data were available. Viewing these data became an obsession with her.

"Dr. Blue and I talked today about Jamie," Nicole said late one night after she and Richard were in bed. "He has decided to enter optimizer training."

"That's good," said Richard sleepily.

"I told Dr. Blue that she was lucky, as a parent, to be able to participate in the events in her child's life. I then expressed again our concern about knowing so little about what's happened to Katie. . . . Richard," Nicole said in a slightly louder voice, "Dr. Blue did *not* say today that I would be unable to see the videos of Katie. Do you think that signals a change in their attitude? Am I wearing down their resistance?"

Richard did not respond at first. After some prompting, he sat up in bed. "Can't we go to sleep just this one night without another discussion of Katie and the damn octospider videos? Jesus, Nicole, you've talked about nothing else for over two weeks. You're losing your balance—"

"I am *not*," Nicole interrupted defensively. "I'm simply concerned about what has happened to our daughter. I'm certain that the octospiders have many many segments they could put together to show us. Don't *you* want to know?"

"Of course I do," Richard said, sighing heavily. "But we've had this same conversation several times already. What is to be gained from having it again at this hour?"

"I *told* you," Nicole said. "I sensed a change in their attitude today. Dr. Blue didn't—"

"I heard you," Richard interrupted crossly, "and I don't think it means anything. Dr. Blue is probably as tired of discussing the subject as I am." Richard shook his head. "Look, Nicole, our little group is coming apart at the seams. We desperately need some wisdom and sanity from you. Max grumbles every day about the octospiders' invasion of his privacy, Ellie is downright lugubrious except during the rare moments when Nikki causes her to smile, and now, in the middle of everything, Patrick has announced that he and Nai want to get married. But you are so obsessed with Katie and the videos that you aren't even able to give advice to anybody else."

Nicole gave Richard a harsh glance and lay down on her back. She didn't reply to his last comment.

"Please don't be sullen, Nicole," Richard said about a minute later. "I'm only asking you to be as objective about your own behavior as you usually are about the actions of others."

"I'm not being sullen," Nicole replied, "and I'm not ignoring everyone else. Anyway, why must I always be the one who is responsible for the happiness of our little family? Why can't somebody else play the role of group mother occasionally?"

"Because nobody else is you," Richard said. "You have always been everyone's best friend."

"Well, now I'm tired," Nicole said. "And I have a problem of my own, an 'obsession,' according to you. . . . By the way, Richard, I'm disappointed in your apparent lack of interest. I always thought Katie was your favorite."

"That's unfair, Nicole," Richard said quickly. "Nothing would please me more than to know that Katie was all right. But I do have other things on my mind."

Neither of them said anything for about a minute. "Tell me something, dear," Richard said then in a softer tone. "Why has Katie become so important all of a sudden? What has changed? I don't remember your being so incredibly concerned about Katie before."

"I have asked myself the same question," Nicole said. "And I don't have a straightforward answer. I do know that Katie has been in my dreams a lot lately, since even before we saw her in the video, and that I have been having an intense desire to talk with her. Also, my first thought after Dr. Blue told me about Hercules' death was that I *had* to see Katie again before I died. I don't really know why, and I don't know either what I want to say to her, but the relationship still seems terribly incomplete to me."

Again there was a long silence in the bedroom. "I'm sorry that I was a little insensitive just now," Richard said.

Nicole reached over and caressed her husband. "I accept your apology," she said, kissing him on the cheek.

Nicole was surprised to see Archie so early in the morning. Patrick, Nai, Benjy, and the children had just left to go next door to the schoolroom. The rest of the adults had still not finished breakfast when the octospider appeared in the Wakefield dining room.

Max was rude. "Sorry, Archie," he said, "but we don't allow visitors—at least not those we can see—before our morning coffee, or whatever this shit is that we drink with breakfast each day."

Nicole rose from the table as the octospider turned to leave. "Don't pay any attention to Max," she said. "He is in a permanent bad mood."

Max now jumped up from his chair, holding one of the mostly empty packages in which there was a little cereal remaining. He swooped the container through the air, first in one direction, then in another, before sealing it tight and handing the package to Archie. "Have a few *quad-roids*," Max said in a loud voice. "Or did they move too quickly for me?"

Archie did not reply. The rest of the humans felt awkward and embarrassed. Max returned to his place at the table beside Eponine and Marius. "Shit, Archie," he said, facing the octospider, "I guess pretty soon you'll be marking me with a pair of those green dots. Or will you just terminate me instead?"

"*Max,*" Richard shouted. "You're out of line. At least think of your wife and son."

"That's all I've been thinking about, friend," he said, "for almost a month now. And you know what, Richard? This Arkansas farm boy cannot figure out *anything* he can do to change . . ." His voice trailed off. Suddenly Max slammed his fist against one of the chairs. "*Goddamm it!*" he yelled. "I feel so useless."

Marius began to cry. Eponine scooted away from the table with the baby and Ellie went to help her. Nicole took Archie with her into the atrium, leaving Richard and Max alone. Richard leaned across the table. "I think I know what you're feeling, Max," he said gently, "and I empathize with you. But we don't improve our situation any by insulting the octospiders."

"What difference does it make?" Max said, looking up at Richard. "We are prisoners here, that's obvious. I have allowed my son to be born into a world where he will always be a prisoner. What kind of a father does that make me?"

While Richard was trying to soothe Max, Nicole was receiving from Archie the message that she had been seeking for weeks. "We have obtained permission," the octospider said, "for you to use the data library today. We have compiled videos featuring your daughter Katie from our historical files."

Nicole made Archie repeat his colors to make certain that she had not misunderstood.

Archie and Nicole did not converse as the transport carried them, without stopping, across the Emerald City to the tall building that housed the octospider library. Nor did Nicole pay much attention to the street scenes outside the transport. She was completely immersed in her own emotions and her thoughts of Katie. In her mind's eye she recalled, one after another, key moments from her life when Katie was a child. In the longest memory segment, Nicole relived both the terror and the joy of her descent into the octospider lair years earlier to find her missing four-year-old daughter. *You've always been missing, Katie,* Nicole thought. *In one way or another. I have never been able to keep you safe.*

Nicole could feel her heart pounding furiously when Archie finally led her into a room that was empty except for a chair, a large desk, and a wall screen. Archie indicated that Nicole should sit down in the chair. "Before I show you how to use the equipment," the octospider said, "there are two things that I want to tell you. First, I want to respond officially, as the optimizer for your group, to the request by some of you to rejoin the others of your species in New Eden."

Archie paused. Nicole collected herself. It was difficult for her to put Katie temporarily out of her mind, but she knew she had to concentrate completely on what Archie was about to tell her. The others in the group would expect a verbatim report.

"I'm afraid," Archie continued a few moments later, "that it is not possible for any of you to leave in the near future. I am not at liberty to tell you anything more than that the issue was considered by the Chief Optimizer herself, in a major staff meeting, and that your request was denied for security reasons."

Nicole was stunned. She had not expected this news, certainly not at this time. She had told everyone that she thought they would be allowed—

"So Max is right," she said, fighting the tears that were threatening to flow. "We are your prisoners."

"You must interpret the decision for yourself," Archie said. "But I will tell you that insofar as I understand your language, I think the term 'prisoner,' which Max has often used lately, is not correct."

"Then give me a *better* word, and some more explanation," Nicole said angrily, rising from her chair. "You know what the others will say."

"I cannot," Archie replied. "I have transmitted our entire message."

Nicole paced around the room, her emotions swinging wildly from rage to depression. She knew how Max would react. Everyone would be angry. Even Richard and Patrick would remind her that she had been wrong. *But* why *won't they explain?* she thought. *It's not like them.* Nicole felt a slight pain in her heart and slumped into her chair.

"And what's the second thing you want to tell me?" Nicole said at length.

"I have personally worked with the data engineers," Archie said, "to prepare the video files you are about to access. From what I know about human beings, and you specifically, I think that if you see this material, it will cause you extreme distress. I would like to ask you to consider not looking at the files at all."

Archie had chosen carefully what he had said, doubtless because he understood how important the videos were to Nicole. His message was clear. *What I am about to see will cause me grief,* she thought. *But what choice do I have? "Between nothing and grief,"* she remembered, *"I will choose grief."*

After Nicole thanked Archie for his concern and informed the octospider that she wanted to see the videos anyway, Archie pushed the chair in which she was sitting over in front of the desk and showed her how to control the data access. The time code had been translated by the octospiders into human numbers, in terms of days before the present, and there were four speeds at which the images could be shown, covering four octal orders of magnitude, from one-eighth real time to sixty-four times normal speed.

"The data on Katie are nearly complete," Archie said, "for about the last six months of your time. It is our normal data management process to filter and compress older data, based on its importance. The extended files on Katie show most of the key events for the past two years, but are fairly scarce before that."

Nicole reached out for the controls. As she dialed up the most recent data entry and saw Katie's face appear on the screen, she felt Archie tapping on her shoulder. "You may use this facility the rest of today," the octospider said to her when she turned around, "but that is all. Since the amount of data available is enormous, I suggest you use the high speeds to locate events of interest."

Nicole took a deep breath and turned back around to the screen.

She felt as if she could not cry anymore. Her eyes were nearly swollen shut from the constant stream of tears. Nicole had watched Katie inject herself with the drug kokomo at least half a dozen times already, but as she saw her daughter tie the rubber cord around her upper arm and plunge the needle into a bulging vein again, a new set of burning tears found their way into Nicole's eyes.

What she had seen in almost ten hours was so much worse than her most horrible imaginings that Nicole was utterly destroyed. Despite the fact that there was no sound with any of the pictures, it had been easy for Nicole to understand what Katie's life was all about. First, her daughter was a hopeless drug addict. At least four times a day—more if life was not going well for her—Katie retreated to her fancy apartment, either by herself or with friends, and used the elegant drug paraphernalia that she kept in a large locked box in her dressing room.

Katie was charming immediately after the drug rush. She was friendly, funny, and full of both energy and apparent self-confidence. But if the drugs wore off while she was still partying, Katie was quickly transformed into a screaming, hostile bitch who ended many evenings alone with her needle in her apartment.

Katie's official job was the management of the Vegas prostitutes. In that position Katie was also responsible for recruiting new talent. At first Nicole's broken heart was unwilling to acknowledge what her eyes were telling her. But one long, sordid sequence, which began with Katie befriending a lovely but poor teenage Hispanic in San Miguel and ended with the girl, now magnificently dressed and bejeweled, becoming a temporary concubine for one of Nakamura's *zaibatsu* chiefs a few days later, forced Nicole to admit to herself that her daughter had absolutely no morals or scruples.

After Nicole had been watching the videos for many hours, Archie entered the room and offered her something to eat. Nicole declined. She knew that in her agitated state there was no way she could have retained any food in her stomach.

Why did Nicole keep watching for so long? Why didn't she just switch off the controls and leave the room? Later she would ask herself the same questions. Nicole concluded, when she thought about it later, that after the first few hours of watching she began, at least subconsciously, to search for the existence of some signs of hope in Katie's life. It was not in her nature to accept without argument that her daughter was fundamentally corrupt. Nicole longed desperately to see something in the videos that would suggest to her that Katie's future might be different.

Nicole eventually found two elements in Katie's unhappy life that Nicole somehow convinced herself were signs that her daughter might someday break out of her self-destructive pattern. During Katie's terrible bouts of depression, which occurred most often when her supply of drugs was low, Katie would often fly into a frenzy, smashing everything she could find in her apartment. Except for her framed photographs of Richard and Patrick. Toward the end of these frenetic tantrums, when her energy was exhausted, Katie would always take those two pictures off her dresser and lay them gently on her bed. She would then lie beside the photographs and sob for twenty to thirty minutes. To Nicole, this recurrent behavior indicated that Katie still retained some love for her family.

The other hopeful element, in Nicole's mind, was Franz Bauer, the police captain who was Katie's regular consort. Nicole did not pretend to understand their bizarre relationship—one night the pair would have a terrible, obscene fight, and the next Franz would read Katie the poems of Rainer Maria Rilke as a prelude to several hours of endless, energetic sex—but she thought she could tell from the videos both that Franz loved Katie in his own strange way and that he did not approve of her drug addiction. During one of their fights, in fact, Franz picked up Katie's drug supply and threatened to flush it down the toilet. Katie went completely berserk and attacked Franz wildly with a hairbrush.

Hour after hour, Nicole continued to watch in an attempt to comprehend her daughter's tragic life. As the long day progressed and Nicole scanned through the earlier videos, some as early as the first days of Katie's drug addiction, Nicole discovered that Katie had even had a sordid affair with Nakamura himself and that the New Eden tyrant had regularly provided Katie with drugs during the time they were sexual partners.

By this time Nicole was numb. She was also so emotionally drained that she did not have the strength to move. When Nicole finally switched off the controls, she put her head down on the desk, cried for a few more minutes, and then fell asleep. Archie woke her four hours later and told her it was time to return home.

It was dark. The transport had been parked at the plaza for ten minutes, but Nicole had still not disembarked. Archie was standing beside her.

"There is no way that I can tell Richard about what I have seen today," she said, glancing up at the octospider. "He will be absolutely destroyed."

"I understand," Archie said sympathetically. "Now you see why I suggested that you not watch the videos."

"You were right," Nicole said, slowly releasing her grasp on the vertical bar and resignedly extending one leg out of the car, "but it's too late now. I can't erase the horrible pictures that are in my mind."

"You told me earlier," Archie said as soon as they were outside the transport, "that it was obvious from the videos that Patrick had known something about the life Katie was leading before his escape. He elected not to tell you and Richard the worst details. Is it a violation of your personal principles to do something similar?"

"Thanks, Archie," Nicole said, patting the octospider on the shoulder and almost smiling, "for reading my mind. You're beginning to know us too well."

"We have a difficult time with truth in our society also," Archie commented. "One of our fundamental guidelines for new optimizers is to tell the truth at all times. It is acceptable to withhold information, the policy says, but not to pass falsehoods. The youngest optimizers are very zealous about telling the truth, without regard for the consequences. Sometimes truth and compassion are not compatible."

"I agree with you, my wise alien friend," Nicole said with a heavy sigh.

"And now, after what I can definitely say was one of the worst days of my life, I face not one, but two very difficult tasks. I must tell Max that he will not be able to leave the Emerald City, and I must inform my husband, Richard, that his favorite daughter is a dope addict and a manager of whores. I hope that somewhere in this old and exhausted human is the strength necessary to handle those two duties properly."

10

Richard was asleep when Nicole arrived at home. She was thankful that she did not need to explain anything right away. Nicole slipped into her nightgown and climbed gently into bed. But she could not fall asleep. Her mind kept jumping back and forth between the horrible images she had seen during the day and thoughts about what she was going to tell Richard and the others.

In her twilight state Nicole suddenly saw herself sitting in the bleachers in Rouen beside her father, in the square where Joan of Arc had been burned to death eight hundred years earlier. Nicole was a teenager again, as she had been when her father had actually taken her to Rouen to see the conclusion of the Joan of Arc pageant. The oxcart carrying Joan was coming into the square and the people were shouting.

"Daddy," the teenage Nicole said, yelling to be heard above the din, "what can I do to help Katie?"

Her father had not heard the question. His attention was completely focused on the Maid of Orleans, or rather the French girl who was playing Joan. Nicole watched as the girl, who had the same clear and piercing eyes attributed to Joan, was tied to the stake. The girl began to pray softly as one of the bishops read her death sentence.

"What about Katie?" Nicole said again. There was no response. The audience around her in the bleachers gasped as the piles of wood surrounding Joan were set on fire. Nicole stood up with the crowd as the flames spread quickly around the base of the huge wooden stake. She could clearly hear the prayers of St. Joan, invoking the blessing of Jesus.

The flames moved closer to the girl. Nicole looked at the face of the teenager who had changed history and a cold shudder ran down her back. "*Katie*," she screamed. "*No! No!*"

Nicole tried desperately to find some way out of the bleachers, but she was blocked on all sides. There was no way she could save her burning daughter. "*Katie! Katie!*" Nicole screamed again, flailing wildly at the people around her.

She felt arms around her chest. It took a few seconds for Nicole to realize that she had been dreaming. Richard was staring at her with alarm. Before Nicole could speak, Ellie walked into the bedroom in her robe.

"Are you all right, Mother?" she asked. "I was up checking on Nikki and I heard you scream Katie's name."

Nicole glanced first at Robert, then at Ellie. She closed her eyes. She could still see Katie's anguished face, contorted in pain, just above the flames. Nicole opened her eyes again and looked at her husband and daughter. "Katie is very unhappy," she said, and then she burst into tears.

Nicole could not be consoled. Each time she would start to tell Richard and Ellie the details about what she had seen, she would start crying again. "I feel so frustrated, so helpless," Nicole said when she could finally control herself. "Katie is in dire straits and there is absolutely nothing any of us can do to help her."

Summarizing Katie's life without omitting anything except some of the more kinky sexual escapades, Nicole abandoned her tentative plan to soften her report. Both Richard and Ellie were stunned and saddened by the news.

"I don't know how you managed to sit there and watch for all those hours," Richard said at one point. "I would have been out of there in a few minutes."

"Katie's so lost, so utterly lost," said Ellie, shaking her head. A few minutes later little Nikki wandered into the bedroom looking for her mother. Ellie embraced Nicole and took Nikki back to their room.

"I'm sorry I was so distraught, Richard," Nicole said a few minutes later, just before they went back to sleep.

"It's understandable," Richard said. "The day must have been absolutely horrible."

Nicole wiped her eyes for the umpteenth time. "I can only remember one other time in my life when I cried like this," she said, managing a tiny smile. "Back when I was fifteen. My father told me one day that he was thinking about proposing to this Englishwoman he was dating. I didn't like her—she was a cold and distant woman—but I didn't think it was proper for me to say anything negative to my father. Anyway, I was devastated. I picked up my pet mallard Dunois and raced down to our pond at Beauvois.

I rowed out into the middle of the pond, brought the oars into the boat, and cried for several hours."

They lay in silence for a few minutes. "Oh, Jesus," Nicole suddenly said, "I almost forgot. Archie also told me today that none of us would be permitted to return to New Eden. He said it was a security issue. Max will be furious."

"Don't worry about it now," Richard said softly. "Try to get some sleep. We'll talk about it in the morning."

Nicole snuggled into Richard's arms and fell asleep.

"For *see-cur-i-tee* reasons?" Max yelled. "Now, just what the fuck does that mean?"

Patrick and Nai both rose from the breakfast table. "Just leave your food," Nai said, motioning for the children to follow her. "We can have some fruit and cereal in the schoolroom."

Both Kepler and Galileo were reluctant to leave. They sensed that something important was going to be discussed. Only when Patrick came around the table toward them did they push back their chairs and rise.

Benjy was allowed to remain after he promised Nicole he would not repeat any of the conversation to the children. Eponine left the table to nurse the waking Marius in one of the corners of the room.

"I don't know what it means," Nicole said to Max after the children had departed. "Archie would not elaborate."

"Well, this is just *god-damn* wonderful," Max said. "We can't leave, but those slimy friends of yours won't even tell us why. Why didn't you demand to see the Chief Optimizer right there on the spot? Don't you think they *owe* us some kind of explanation?"

"Yes, I do," Nicole replied. "And perhaps we should all ask for another audience with the Chief Optimizer. I'm sorry, Max, but I didn't handle the situation very well. I was prepared to watch the videos of Katie and, quite frankly, Archie's pronouncement caught me off guard."

"Shit, Nicole," Max said, "I don't blame you personally. Anyway, since Ep, Marius, and I are the only ones who still want to return to New Eden, it's *our* job to appeal this decision. I doubt if the Chief Optimizer has ever seen a two-month-old baby human in the flesh."

The rest of the breakfast conversation was mostly about Katie and what Nicole had seen the day before in the videos. The family explained the gist of Katie's unhappy life without too many specifics.

When Patrick returned, he reported that the children were already busy with their lessons. "Nai and I have been talking about a lot of things," he said, addressing everyone at the table. "First, Max, we would like to ask you to be a little more careful in front of the children with your negative comments about the octospiders. They are now quite fearful when Archie or Dr. Blue are around, and their reactions must be based on what they have overheard in our conversations."

Max bridled and started to reply. "Please, Max," Patrick added quickly, "you know that I'm your friend. Let's not argue about it. Just think about what I've said and remember that we may all be staying here with the octospiders for a long time.

"Second," he continued, "Nai and I both feel, especially in view of what we learned this morning, that the children should be learning the octospider language. We want them to start as soon as possible. We think we need Ellie or Mother, plus an octospider or two . . . not just to teach, but also to familiarize the children again with their alien hosts. Hercules has been gone for a couple of months now. Mother, will you talk to Archie about this, please?"

Nicole nodded and Patrick excused himself, saying that he needed to return to the classroom. "Patrick has become a good teacher," Benjy volunteered. "He is very patient with me and the children."

Nicole smiled to herself and looked across the breakfast table at her daughter. *Considering everything,* she thought, *our children have turned out fine. I should be thankful for Patrick, Ellie, and Benjy. And not worry myself sick about Katie.*

In one of the corners of her bedroom, Nai Watanabe finished her meditation and said the Buddhist morning prayers that had been part of her daily routine since she was a small child in Thailand. She crossed into the living room, heading for the other bedroom to wake the twins, and found, much to her surprise, that Patrick was asleep on the couch. He was still dressed and her electronic reader was lying on his stomach.

She shook him gently. "Wake up, Patrick," she said. "It's morning. . . . You've slept the whole night here."

Patrick awakened quickly and apologized to Nai. As he was leaving, he told Nai that he had several issues to discuss with her—about Buddhism, of course—but he guessed that they could wait until a more convenient time. Nai smiled and kissed him lightly on the cheek before telling him that she and the boys would be over for breakfast in half an hour.

He is so young and earnest, Nai said to herself as she watched him walk away. *And I do enjoy his company. But can anyone ever replace Kenji as my husband?*

Nai recalled the previous night. After the twins had fallen asleep, Patrick and she had had a long and serious talk. Patrick had pressed for an early marriage. She had replied that she would not be hurried, that she would agree to a specific date only when she felt entirely comfortable with the idea. Patrick had then awkwardly inquired about the possibility of what he called "more physical involvement" while they were waiting. Nai had reminded Patrick that she had told him from the beginning that there would be nothing but kisses until their wedding. To assuage his feelings, Nai had reassured Patrick that she found him very attractive physically and was definitely looking forward to lovemaking after they were married, but for all the reasons they had discussed a dozen times, Nai insisted that their "physical involvement" remain constrained for the time being.

Most of the rest of the evening the pair had talked about either the twins or Buddhism. Nai had expressed concern that their marriage might have a bad impact on Galileo, especially since the boy often cast himself in the role of his mother's protector. Patrick told Nai that he did not believe that his frequent clashes with Galileo had anything to do with jealousy. "The boy just resents all authority," Patrick had said, "and resists discipline. Kepler, on the other hand . . ."

How many times in the past seven years, Nai thought, *has someone started a comment with the phrase "Kepler, on the other hand"?* She remembered when Kenji was still alive and the boys were just starting to walk. Galileo was constantly falling down and running into things. Kepler, *on the other hand,* was careful and precise in his steps. He almost never fell.

The giant fireflies had still not brought dawn to the Emerald City. Nai continued to let her mind roam freely, as she often did after a peaceful meditation. She noted to herself that she had been making a lot of comparisons recently between Kenji and Patrick. *That's unfair of me,* she told herself. *I cannot marry Patrick until that process has completely stopped.*

Again she thought of the previous night. Nai smiled when she recalled their ardent discussion about the life of Buddha. *Patrick still has a child's naïveté, a pure idealism,* Nai said to herself. *It's one of the things about him I love the most.*

"I admire both Buddha's basic philosophy and his approach," Patrick had said. "I really do. But I have a few problems. How can you worship a man, for example, who leaves his wife and son and goes off to be a beggar? What about his responsibility to his family?"

"You're taking Buddha's action out of its historical context," Nai had replied. "First, twenty-seven hundred years ago, in northern India, being a wandering mendicant was an acceptable way of life. There were some in every village, many in the towns. When a man wanted to seek 'the truth,' his normal first step was to disavow all material comforts. Besides, you have forgotten that Buddha came from a very wealthy family. There was never any question about whether or not his wife and child would have food, shelter, clothing, or any other essential . . . "

They had talked for two hours or so, and then kissed for a while before Nai had gone alone to her bedroom. Patrick had already returned to his reading about Buddhism by the time Nai had whispered good night from her doorway.

How difficult it is, Nai mused as the firefly dawn burst upon the octospider city, *to explain the relevance of Buddhism to someone who has never seen the Earth. Yet even here, in this strange alien world among the stars, desire still causes suffering and human beings still search for spiritual peace.*

11

Richard bounced out of bed with more than his usual enthusiasm and began jabbering at Nicole. "Wish me luck," he said as he dressed. "Archie said that we'll be gone all day."

Nicole, who always woke up very slowly and intensely disliked frenetic activity of any kind in the early morning hours, rolled over and tried to enjoy the last few moments of her rest. She opened one eye slightly, saw that it was still dark, and closed it again.

"I haven't been this excited since I made those two final breakthroughs on the translator," Richard said. "I know that the octospiders are serious about putting me to work. They're just trying to find the right task for me."

Richard left the bedroom for several minutes. From the noises in the kitchen, the half-asleep Nicole could tell that Richard was preparing breakfast for himself. He returned eating one of the large pink fruits that had become his favorite. He stood beside the bed, chewing noisily.

Nicole opened her eyes slowly and looked at her husband. "I assume," she said with a sigh, "that you are waiting for me to say something."

"Yes," he said. "It would be nice if we could exchange a few pleasantries before I leave. After all, this could be the most important day for me since we arrived in the Emerald City."

"You're certain," Nicole said, "that Archie intends to find a job for you?"

"Absolutely," Richard replied. "That's the whole purpose of today. He is going to show me some of their more complex engineering systems and try to ascertain where my talents can best be used. At least that's what he told me yesterday afternoon."

"But why are you leaving so early?" Nicole asked.

"Because there's so much to see, I guess. Anyway, give me a kiss. He'll be here in a few minutes."

Nicole kissed Richard dutifully and closed her eyes again.

The Embryo Bank was a large rectangular building located far to the south of the Emerald City, very close to where the Central Plain ended. Less than a kilometer from where the bank had been built, a set of three staircases, each with tens of thousands of individual steps, ascended the south polar bowl. Above the Embryo Bank, in the near darkness of Rama, loomed the imposing, buttressed structures of the Big Horn and its six sharply pointed acolytes, each larger than any single engineering construction on the planet Earth.

Richard and Archie had mounted an ostrichsaur on the outskirts of the Emerald City. Together with an escort and a trio of fireflies, they had passed through the Alternate Domain in only a matter of minutes. Out in the southern reaches of the octospider realm there were very few buildings. Despite the occasional fields of grain, most of the territory through which they traveled on their southerly trek reminded Richard, even in the dim light, of the Northern Hemicylinder in Rama II, before the two habitats had been built.

Richard and his octospider friend entered the Embryo Bank through a pair of extra-thick doors that took them directly into a large conference room. There Richard was introduced to several other octospiders, who were obviously expecting his visit. Richard used his translator and the octos read his lips, although he had to speak slowly and distinctly because they were not nearly as skilled in the human language as Archie.

After some brief formalities, one of the octospiders led the pair to a series of control panels housing the equivalent of keyboards made from octo color strips. "We have almost ten million embryos stored here," the lead octospider said in her introduction, "representing over a hundred thousand distinct species and three times that many hybrids. Their natural life spans range in duration from half a tert to several million days, or about ten thousand of your human years. Their adult sizes range from a fraction of a nanometer to behemoths nearly as large as this building. Each embryo is stored in what are believed to be near-optimal conditions for its preservation. In fact, however, only about a thousand distinct environments, combinations of temperature, pressure, and ambient chemicals, are needed to span the range of required conditions.

"This building also houses an immense data management and monitoring system. This system automatically tracks the conditions in each of the distinct environments and monitors the early development of the several thousand embryos that are always in active germination. The system has some automatic fault detection and correction, a dual-parameter warning structure, and also drives the displays which can exhibit status and/or catalog information, both on the walls here or in any of the research areas on the upper floors."

Richard's brain went into overdrive as he began to understand more clearly the purpose of the Embryo Bank. *What a fantastic concept,* he thought. *The octospiders store here all the seeds of other plant and animal species that might ever be needed for any purpose.*

". . . Testing is continuous," the lead octospider was saying, "both to ensure the integrity of the storage and preservation systems and to provide specimens for the genetic engineering activities. At any given time approximately two hundred octospider biologists are actively engaged in genetic experiments here. The goal of these many experiments is to produce altered life-forms that will improve the efficiency of our society—"

"Can you show me an example," Richard interrupted, "of such a genetic experiment?"

"Certainly," the octospider replied. She shuffled over to the control panel and used three of her tentacles to press a sequence of colored buttons. "I believe you are familiar with one of our primary methods of power generation," she said, as a video appeared on the wall. "The basic principle is quite simple, as you know. The circular marine creatures generate and store electric charge in their bodies. We capture this charge along a wire mesh, against which the animals must press to reach their food supply. Although this system is quite satisfactory, our engineers have pointed out that it could be improved substantially if the behavior of the creature could be altered somewhat.

"Look at this fast-motion close-up of half a dozen of the marine creatures that generate the power. Notice that during this brief motion picture each of the animals will go through three or four charge-discharge cycles. What feature of these cycles would be of primary interest to a system engineer?"

Richard watched the video carefully. *The sand dollars are dim after their discharge,* he thought, *but regain their full glow in a comparatively short period of time.*

"Assuming that the glow is a measure of the stored charge," Richard said, suddenly wondering if he was undergoing some kind of a test, "the system could be made more efficient by increasing the feeding frequency."

"Exactly," the lead octospider responded. Archie flashed a quick message to the host octo that was completed before Richard had even had a chance to aim the telescope on his translator. Meanwhile, a different picture appeared on the wall. "Here are three genetic variants of the circular marine creature that are currently under test and evaluation. The leading replacement candidate is the one on the left. This prototype eats roughly twice as frequently as the component currently being used; however, the prototype has a metabolic imbalance that increases significantly its susceptibility to communicable diseases. All factors are being weighed in the current evaluation."

Richard was taken from one demonstration to another. Archie accompanied him at all times, but at each venue a different set of octospider specialists joined them for the prepared minilecture and the group discussion that always followed. One of the presentations was focused on the relationships between the Embryo Bank, the large zoo that occupied considerable territory in the Alternate Domain, and the barrier forest that formed a complete annulus around Rama, slightly less than a kilometer north of the Emerald City. "All living species in our realm," the presenter said, "are either in active symbiosis, temporary observation in an isolated domain—in the zoo, the forest, or, in your specific case, in the Emerald City itself—or undergoing experimentation here at the Embryo Bank."

After a long walk down many corridors, Richard and Archie attended a meeting of half a dozen octospiders evaluating a recommendation to replace an entire symbiotic chain of four different species. The chain was responsible for the production of a gelatin that cured a specific octospider lens malady. Richard listened with fascination as the test parameters of the proposed new symbiosis—resources consumed, reproduction rates, octospider interactions required, fault coefficients, and behavior predictability—were compared with the existing system. The outcome of the meeting was that in one of the three manufacturing "zones," the new symbiosis would be installed for several hundred operational days, after which time the decision would again be reviewed.

In the middle of the workday Archie and Richard were scheduled to be alone for half a tert. At Richard's request, they packed their lunches and drinks, remounted the ostrichsaur, commandeered a pair of fireflies, and wandered out into the cold and dark of the Central Plain. When he eventually dismounted, Richard walked around with his arms outstretched and gazed up into the vastness of Rama.

"Who among you," Richard asked Archie, "worries about, or even tries to figure out, the significance of all this?" He waved his arms in a circular motion.

The octospider replied that he didn't understand the question. "Yes, you did, you sly thing," Richard said, smiling. "Except that this time period was obviously set aside by your optimizers for a different kind of conversation between us. What I want to discuss, Archie, is not in which specific engineering department in your Embryo Bank I would like to work so that I can make my 'contribution' that will justify the 'resources' necessary to sustain me . . . what I want to talk to you about is what is *really* going on here? Why are we—humans, sessiles, avians, and you with all your menagerie—on this huge, mysterious spacecraft bound for the star we humans call Tau Ceti?"

Archie did not respond for almost thirty seconds. "Members of our genus were told while they were at the Node, just as you were, that some higher intelligence is cataloging life-forms in the galaxy, with a special emphasis on spacefarers. We assembled a typical colony, as requested, and established it inside this Rama vehicle so that the required detailed observations of our species could take place."

"So you octospiders don't know anything more about *who* or *what* is behind this grand scheme than we humans do?"

"No," Archie replied. "In fact, we probably know less. None of the octospiders who spent time at the Node is still part of our colony. As I told you, that octospider contingent on Rama II was a different, inferior species. The only firsthand information about the Node that exists on board this spacecraft comes from you, your family, and whatever compressed data may reside inside that small volume of sessile material we are still keeping in our zoo."

"And that's it?" Richard said. "None of you asks any more questions?"

"We are trained as juveniles," Archie answered, "not to waste time on issues for which we are unable to obtain any significant data."

Richard was momentarily silent. "How do you know so much about the avians and the sessiles?" he then asked abruptly.

"I'm sorry, Richard," Archie said after a brief pause, "but I cannot talk with you about that subject now. My assignment for this lunch period, as you surmised, is to ascertain whether or not you would be pleased to accept an engineering assignment in the Embryo Bank and, if so, which of the many areas you have seen today seems most interesting to you."

"It's a hell of a commute," Richard said, laughing. "Yes, Archie," he then added, "everything is fascinating, especially what I call the encyclopedia department. I think I would like to work there—that way I could expand my meager knowledge of biology. But why are you asking me this question now? Aren't we going to have more 'demonstrations' after lunch?"

"Yes," Archie said. "But this afternoon's schedule has been included primarily for completeness. Almost half of the Embryo Bank is devoted to microbiology. Management of that activity is more complex and involves communication with the midget morphs. It is difficult for us to imagine your working in any of those departments."

Underneath the primary microbiological laboratory was a basement that could only be entered with special credentials. When Archie mentioned that large quantities of flying image quadroids were produced in that Embryo Bank basement, Richard virtually begged to observe the process. His official tour was halted and Richard stood idly around for several fengs while Archie obtained permission for them to visit the quadroid "nursery."

Two other octospiders guided them down a sequence of long ramps to the subterranean area. "The nursery has been purposely built far below ground level," Archie told Richard, "for extra isolation and protection. We have three other similar facilities scattered around our domain."

Holy shit, Richard said to himself when he and his three octospider companions walked out on a platform overlooking a large rectangular floor. His recognition was instant. Several meters below them, about a hundred midget morphs were scattered around the facility, performing unknown functions. Hanging down from the ceiling were eight rectangular lattices, each about five meters long and two meters wide, that were symmetrically placed around the room. Directly underneath each of the lattices was a large oval object with a hardened exterior. These eight objects resembled huge nuts and were surrounded by thick viney growths or webbing.

"I have seen a similar layout before, many years ago," Richard said excitedly. "Underneath New York. It was just before my first personal encounter with one of your cousins. Nicole and I were both scared out of our wits."

"I think I read something about that incident," Archie replied. "Prior to our bringing Ellie and Eponine to the Emerald City, I studied all the old files on your species. Some of the data were compressed, so there were not many specifics—"

"I remember that incident as if it were yesterday," Richard interrupted. "I had placed a couple of miniature robots on a small subway and they had disappeared into a tunnel. They came into an area like this one and, after climbing through some of that webbing, were chased and captured by one of your cousins."

"Doubtless the robots had stumbled into a quadroid nursery. Those octos acted to protect it. It's really very simple." Archie signaled their guide engineer that it was time for his explanation.

"The quadroid queens spend their gestation periods in special compartments that are just off the main floor," the octo engineer said. "Each queen lays thousands of eggs. When several million eggs have been laid, they are collected together and placed in one of those oval containers. The inside of the containers is maintained at a very high temperature, which markedly reduces the development time of the quadroids. The thick webbing around the containers absorbs the excess heat so that the working conditions are acceptable for the midget morphs who oversee the nursery. . . ."

Richard was partially listening, but his real focus was on a moment many years earlier. *Now it is all clear,* he said to himself. *And that tiny subway was for the midget morphs.*

". . . monitoring probes inside the containers identify exactly when the quadroids are ready to swarm. The lattices above are soaked with the proper chemical agents a few fengs prior to the automatic opening of the ovals. The new queens fly first, attracted to the lattice elements. The frenzied hordes of males follow, making visible black clouds despite their minuscule size. The quadroids are harvested from the lattice and go immediately into mass training."

"Very elegant," Richard said. "But I have a simple question. *Why* do the quadroids take all those pictures for you?"

"The short answer," Archie replied, "is that they have been genetically engineered over thousands of years to be receptive to our direction. We—or rather our midget morph specialists—speak the chemical language the quadroids use to communicate with each other. If they do what is asked of them, the quadroids are given food. If they perform satisfactorily over a long period of time, they are allowed the pleasures of sex."

"Out of a given litter, or swarm, what percentage of the quadroids follow your directions?"

"The failure rate for first picture is about ten percent," the octospider engineer answered. "Once the pattern has been established and the reward cycle reinforced, the failure rate drops dramatically."

"Pretty damn impressive," Richard said appreciatively. "Maybe there's more to this biology stuff than I ever considered."

On the ride back to the Emerald City, Richard and Archie discussed the comparative strengths and weaknesses of biological and nonbiological engineering systems. It was mostly an esoteric, philosophical conversation with few definitive conclusions. They did agree, however, that the encyclopedia function, which was primarily the storage, manipulation, and presentation of vast amounts of information, was more optimally handled by nonbiological systems.

As they drew near to the domed city, the green glow was suddenly extinguished. Night had come again to the center of the octospider domain. Soon thereafter, an additional pair of fireflies appeared to give their ostrichsaur extra light.

It had been a long day and Richard was tired. When they entered the outskirts of the Alternate Domain, Richard thought he saw something flying in the darkness off to his right. "What has happened to Tammy and Timmy?" he asked.

"They have both mated," Archie replied, "and have several offspring. Their young hatchlings are cared for in the zoo."

"Could I see them?" Richard said. "You told me once, a few months ago, that someday it might be possible."

"I guess so," Archie replied after a short silence. "Even though the zoo is a restricted zone, the avian compound is very close to the entrance."

When they reached the first large structure of the Alternate Domain, Archie dismounted and went inside the building. When he returned, the octospider said something to the ostrichsaur. "We are only cleared for a brief visit," Archie said as their mount turned off the main path and began to thread its way through the smaller lanes of the community.

Richard was introduced to the zookeeper, who drove them in a cart to a compound only about a hundred meters inside the zoo entrance. Both Tammy and Timmy were present. They recognized Richard immediately, and their jabbers and shrieks of pleasure filled the darkened skies. Tammy and Timmy introduced Richard to a new group of avian hatchlings in the compound. The juveniles were very shy around Richard, and would not let him touch them. However, Tammy and Timmy still loved to have their soft underbellies stroked by the man who had raised them from infancy. Richard felt powerful emotions as he recalled the days when he had been their sole protector in the lair underneath New York.

He said good-bye to his wards and boarded the cart with Archie and the zookeeper. Halfway back to the zoo entrance he heard a sound that jolted him into alertness and made his skin crawl with goose bumps. He sat perfectly still and concentrated. The sound repeated just before the silent cart came to a stop.

"I could not possibly be mistaken," Richard insisted to Nicole. "I heard it twice. There is no other sound like the cry of a human child."

"I'm not doubting you, Richard," Nicole said. "I'm just trying to exclude logically all other possible sources for the sound you heard. Juvenile avians do have a particular shriek that can sound a little like a baby crying ... and you were, after all, in a zoo. It could have been another animal."

"No," said Richard. "I know what I heard. I have lived with enough children and heard enough cries in my life."

Nicole smiled. "Now the shoe is on the other foot, isn't it, darling? Do you remember your response when I told you I had seen a woman's face in that mural the night we went to see the octospider play? You scoffed at me and told me that I was 'absurd,' if I remember correctly."

"So what's the explanation? Did the octospiders somehow kidnap some other humans from Avalon? And the incident was never reported? But how could they have—"

"Did you say anything to Archie?" Nicole asked.

"No. I was too stunned. At first I was amazed that neither he nor the zookeeper made any comment, and then I remembered that the octospiders are deaf."

They were both silent for several seconds. "You weren't supposed to hear that cry, Richard," Nicole then said. "Our nearly perfect hosts have made a nonoptimal slipup."

Richard laughed. "Of course, they are recording this conversation. By tomorrow *they* will know that *we* know."

"Let's not say anything just yet to the others," Nicole said. "Maybe the octos will decide to share their secret with us. By the way, when do you start to work?"

"Whenever I want," Richard replied. "I told Archie I had a few tasks of my own to finish first."

"Sounds as if you had a fascinating day," Nicole said. "Everything was mostly quiet around here. Except for one thing. Patrick and Nai have set a date for their wedding. Three weeks from tomorrow."

"What?" Richard said. "Why didn't you tell me earlier?"

Nicole laughed. "I didn't have a chance. You came in here talking nonstop about cries in the zoo, and avians, and quadroids, and the Embryo Bank. . . . I knew from experience that my news would have to wait until you wound down."

"Well, mother of the groom," Richard said a few seconds later, "how do you feel?"

"Considering everything," Nicole said, "I'm very pleased. You know how I feel about Nai. It just strikes me as a strange time and place to start a marriage."

12

They were sitting in the Wakefield living room waiting for the appearance of the bride. Patrick was nervously wringing his hands. "Be patient, young man," Max said, crossing the room and putting his arm around Patrick. "She'll be here. A woman wants to look her finest on her wedding day."

"I didn't look *my* finest," Eponine said. "In fact, I don't even remember what I was wearing on my wedding day."

"I remember it well, Frenchie," Max said with a grin, "especially up in the igloo. As I recall, most of the time you were wearing your birthday suit."

Everyone laughed. Nicole entered the room. "She'll be here in a few more minutes. Ellie is helping Nai with the final arrangement of her dress." She glanced around. "Where are Archie and Dr. Blue?" she asked.

"They went to their house for a minute," Ellie said. "They have a special present for the bride."

"I don't like having those octospiders around," Galileo said in a nasty voice. "They give me the creeps."

"Starting next week, Galileo," Ellie said gently, "there will be an octospider with you in school nearly all the time. She'll help you learn their language."

"I don't want to learn their language," the boy said defiantly.

Max walked over next to Richard. "So how is the work going, amigo? We haven't seen much of you these last two weeks."

"It's completely absorbing, Max," Richard said enthusiastically. "I'm working on an encyclopedia project, helping them design a new set of software to display all the critical information about the hundreds of thousands of species in the Embryo Bank. The octospiders accumulate such an enormous wealth of data in their testing, yet they are surprisingly limited in their knowledge of how to manage it efficiently. Just yesterday, I began working with some recent test data on a set of microbiological agents that are classified, in the octospider taxonomy, by the range of plants and animals for which they are lethal—"

Richard stopped as Archie and Dr. Blue entered together carrying a box about a meter tall that was wrapped with their parchment. The octospiders set their present down in a corner and stood at the side of the room. Ellie arrived a moment later, humming Mendelssohn's wedding march. Nai followed her.

Patrick's bride was wearing her Thai silk dress. It was adorned by the brilliant yellow and black flowers that the octospiders had given to Ellie. She had pinned them to the dress at strategic locations. Patrick rose to stand beside Nai in front of his mother. The couple held hands.

Nicole had been asked to perform the ceremony, and to keep it as simple as possible. As she prepared to begin her brief statement, Nicole's mind was suddenly flooded by memories of other wedding days in her life. She saw Max and Eponine, Michael O'Toole and her daughter Simone, Robert and Ellie. . . . Nicole shuddered involuntarily as the memory of the sound of gunshots intruded into her mind. *Once again*, Nicole thought, forcing herself to return to the present, *we have gathered here together.*

She could barely speak. Nicole was overwhelmed by her feelings. *This is my last wedding*, she realized, almost thinking out loud. *There will not be another.*

A tear ran down her left cheek. "Are you all right, Nicole?" the always sensitive bride asked quietly. Nicole nodded and smiled.

"Friends," Nicole said, "we have joined together today to witness and celebrate the wedding of Patrick Ryan O'Toole and Nai Buatong Watanabe. Let us form a circle around them, locking arms to show our love and support for their marriage."

Nicole gestured to the two octospiders as the circle was forming and they too put their tentacles around the humans beside them.

"Do you, Patrick," Nicole said, her voice cracking, "take this woman, Nai, to love and cherish as your wife and partner in life?"

"I do," said Patrick.

"And do you, Nai," Nicole continued, "take this man, Patrick, to love and cherish as your husband and partner in life?"

"I do," said Nai.

"Then I announce that you are husband and wife." Patrick and Nai embraced, and everyone shouted. The newlyweds shared their first married hug with Nicole.

"Did you ever talk to Patrick about sex?" Nicole asked Richard after the party was over and the crowd had dispersed.

"No," said Richard. "Max volunteered. But it shouldn't be necessary. After all, Nai has been married before. . . . Goodness, you were certainly emotional tonight. What was that all about?"

Nicole smiled. "I was thinking about other weddings, Richard. Simone and Michael's, Ellie and Robert's . . ."

"That's one I would like to forget," Richard said. "For many reasons."

"I thought, during the ceremony, that I was crying because this was probably the last wedding I would ever attend. But later, during the party, I thought of something else. Has it ever bothered you, Richard, that we have never had an official ceremony?"

"No," Richard said, shaking his head. "I had a ceremony with Sarah, and that was enough."

"But *you* have had a wedding, Richard. I never have. I have given birth to children from three different fathers, but I have never once been a bride."

Richard was silent for several seconds. "And you think that's why you were crying?"

"Maybe," Nicole said. "I don't know for certain."

Nicole walked around while Richard was in deep thought. "Wasn't that a magnificent statue of Buddha the octospiders gave to Nai?" she said. "The artistry was superb. I really thought both Archie and Dr. Blue were enjoying themselves. I wonder why Jamie came to get them so early—"

"Would you like to have a wedding ceremony?" Richard asked suddenly.

"At our age?" Nicole laughed. "We're already grandparents."

"Still, if it would make you happy . . ."

"Are you proposing to me, Richard Wakefield?"

"I guess so," he said. "I wouldn't want you to be unhappy because you've never been a bride."

Nicole crossed the room and kissed her husband. "It might be fun," she said. "But let's not plan anything until Patrick and Nai are settled. I wouldn't want to steal their limelight."

Richard and Nicole walked toward the bedroom with their arms around each other. They were startled to find their passage blocked by Archie and Dr. Blue.

"You must come with us right away," Archie said. "This is an emergency."

"*Now?*" Nicole replied. "At this hour?"

"Yes," said Dr. Blue. "Only the two of you. The Chief Optimizer is waiting. She'll explain everything."

Nicole felt her heart rate surge as the adrenaline poured into her system. "Do I need a coat?" she said. "Will we be leaving the city?"

For some reason, Nicole's first thought had been that the summons was related to the child's cry that Richard had heard after his first visit to the Embryo Bank. Was the child sick? Perhaps dying? Then why weren't they going directly to the zoo, which was outside the dome, in the Alternate Domain?

The Chief Optimizer and her staff were indeed waiting. Two chairs were in the room. As soon as Richard and Nicole were seated, the octospider leader started speaking in color.

"We have a major crisis under way," she said, "one that could unfortunately lead to war between our two species." She waved a tentacle and video images began to appear on the wall. "Early today, two helicopters began ferrying human troops from the island of New York to the northern-most section of our domain, right next to the Cylindrical Sea. Our quadroid data indicate not only that your species is preparing to launch an assault against us, but also that your leader Nakamura has convinced the human populace that we are your enemy. He has obtained the support of the senate for the war effort and, in a comparatively short period of time, has created an arsenal that could inflict substantial damage on our colony."

The Chief Optimizer stopped while Richard and Nicole watched video snapshots showing bombs, bazookas, and machine guns being manufactured in New Eden.

"Investigative forays have been carried out during the last four days by small groups of humans on the ground and the pair of helicopters in the air. These reconnaissance missions have penetrated as far south as the barrier forest and have covered the entire cylindrical range of our territory. Almost thirty percent of our food, power, and water supply is contained in the region that the humans have reconnoitered.

"There has been no combat, for we have offered no resistance to the exploration activities. We have, however, placed signs in key places, using what we know of your language, informing the human troops that the entire Southern Hemicylinder is the realm of another advanced, but peaceful, species, and requesting that the humans return to their own region. Our signs have been ignored.

"Two days ago a troublesome incident occurred. While we were harvesting grain from one of our large fields, there was a helicopter overflight. The vehicle made a nearby landing and dispatched four soldiers. Without any provocation, these humans executed the three animals doing the harvesting—the same six-armed creatures the two of you saw on your initial tour of our domain—and set fire to the grain field. Since that incident, the content of our signs has changed, and we have made it clear that any other similar behavior will be considered an act of war.

"Nevertheless, it is apparent from actions earlier today that our warnings have not been heeded and that your species is planning to start a conflict it cannot possibly win. I was today considering announcing a declaration of war, an extremely grave event in an octospider colony, with ramifications at every level of our society. Before I took the irreversible action, however, I consulted with those other optimizers whose opinions I most respected.

"The majority of my staff favored the war declaration, seeing no way of convincing your fellow humans that a conflict with us would be a disaster for them. The octospider you call Archie, however, made a proposal to my staff that we think has some small probability of working. Even though our statistical analysts say war is still the most likely outcome, our principles demand that we do everything possible to avoid war. Since Archie's proposal requires your involvement and cooperation, we have called you here tonight."

The Chief Optimizer stopped speaking in colors and shuffled to the side of the room. Richard and Nicole glanced at each other. "Did your translator follow all that?" she asked.

"Most of it," Richard replied. "I certainly understand the gist of the situation. Do *you* have any questions? Or should we suggest they proceed with Archie's proposal?"

When Nicole didn't say anything Archie moved to the center of the room. "I have volunteered," their octospider friend said, "to negotiate personally with the human leaders in an attempt to stop this conflict before it escalates into full-scale war. To accomplish this, however, I must obviously have some help. If I suddenly appear in the camp of the human soldiers, they will kill me. Even if they do not, they will have no way of understanding what I am telling them. So some human who understands our language must accompany me to translate my colors or there's no way that a meaningful dialogue can be started."

After Richard and Nicole told the Chief Optimizer that they had no disagreement with the basic concept proposed by Archie, the two humans and their octospider colleague were left alone to discuss the details. Archie's idea was straightforward. Nicole and he would approach the camp near the Cylindrical Sea together and would request a meeting with Nakamura and the other human leaders. At that meeting Archie and Nicole would explain that the octospiders were a peace-loving species who had no territorial claims on the north side of the Cylindrical Sea. Archie would request that the humans withdraw from their camp and cease their overflights. If necessary, as a token of the goodwill of the octospiders, Archie would offer to supply quantities of food and water to help the humans through their current difficulties. A permanent relationship between the two species would be established and a treaty drafted to codify the agreement.

"Jesus," Richard said after he finished translating Archie's comments. "And I thought Nicole was an idealist!"

Archie did not understand Richard's remark. Nicole patiently explained to the octospider that the leaders of New Eden were not likely to be as reasonable as Archie was assuming. "It is entirely possible," Nicole said, to stress the danger of what Archie was proposing, "that they will kill us *both* before we are ever allowed to say anything."

Archie kept insisting that what he was proposing was bound to be accepted eventually because it was clearly in the best interests of the humans living in New Eden.

"Look, Archie," Richard responded in frustration, "what you said is just not correct. There are many human beings, including Nakamura, who do not give a shit what is good for the colony. In fact, the common welfare is not even a factor in the subconscious objective function, to use your terms, that governs their behavior. All they care about is themselves. Every decision is weighed in terms of whether or not it will increase their own personal power or influence. In our history, leaders have often destroyed their own countries or colonies in attempts to retain their power."

The octospider was stubborn. "What you are describing just cannot be true in an advanced species," Archie insisted. "The fundamental laws of evolution clearly indicate that those species whose primary value is the welfare of the group will outlast those in which the individual is supreme. Are you suggesting that human beings are an aberration of some kind, a freak of nature violating a fundamental—"

Nicole interrupted. "This is all very interesting, you two," she said, "but we have some more pressing business. We must design a plan of action that has no pitfalls. . . . Richard, if you don't like Archie's plan, what do you suggest?"

Richard reflected for several seconds before speaking. "I believe that Nakamura has committed New Eden to this action against the octospiders for many reasons, one of which is to preclude criticism of the domestic failures by his government. I do not think he will be dissuaded from his course unless the citizens are overwhelmingly against the war, and, I'm sorry to say, I don't think *that* will happen unless the colonists are convinced the war will be a disaster."

"So you think threats are necessary?" Nicole said.

"As a minimum. What would be perfect would be a demonstration of military might by the octospiders," Richard said.

"I'm afraid that's impossible," Archie commented, "at least under the current circumstances."

"Why?" Richard asked. "The Chief Optimizer spoke with confidence about winning any war that might occur. If you were to attack and utterly destroy that camp—"

"Now it is *you* who do not understand *us*," Archie said. "Because war, or any conflict that can result in deliberate deaths, is such a nonoptimal way of resolving disputes, our colony has very strict regulations governing concerted hostile actions. Controls are built into our society to make war absolutely the solution of the last resort. We have no standing army and no stockpile of weapons, for example. And there are other restraints as well. All optimizers participating in a decision to declare war, as well as all octospiders engaging in an armed conflict, are immediately terminated after the war."

"Whaaat?" said Richard, not believing his translator. "That's not possible."

"Yes, it is," Archie said. "As you can imagine, these factors significantly deter our participation in nondefensive hostilities. The Chief Optimizer knows that she signed her own death warrant two weeks ago when she authorized the beginning of war preparations. All eighty of the octospiders now living and working in the War Domain will be terminated when this war is either concluded or the threat of war has officially passed. . . . I myself, since I was part of the discussions today, will be placed on the termination lists if war is declared."

Richard and Nicole were speechless. "The only possible justification for war to an octospider," Archie continued, "is an unambiguous threat to the very survival of the colony. Once that threat is identified and acknowledged, our species undergoes a metamorphosis and prosecutes the war, without mercy, until either the threat is obliterated or our colony has been destroyed. Generations ago, some very wise optimizers realized that those individual octospiders who were engaged in killing, and the design of killing, were so psychologically altered by their experiences that they became a significant detriment to the operation of a peaceful colony. That's why the termination codicils were enacted."

Richard and Nicole were still silent even after Archie had finished talking. At length Richard started to ask Archie to leave the room so that he could speak privately to his wife, but he quickly remembered the ubiquitous quadroids. "Nicole, darling," he said finally, "I don't think Archie's plan is quite right for several reasons. For one thing, I should be going with him instead of you—"

When Nicole started to interrupt, Richard gestured with his hands for her to remain quiet. "Now hear me out," he said. "Throughout our marriage, especially since we left the Node, you have always been the one out front, giving of your time and energy for the benefit of the family or the colony. Now it's my turn. In this particular instance, I believe that I am also better suited to the proposed task. I can more easily scare our fellow humans by conjuring up images of doomsday blows delivered by the octospiders."

"But you don't speak their language well," Nicole protested. "Without your translator—"

"I've thought about that," Richard said. "And I think that Ellie and Nikki should go with Archie and me. First, with a child among us, the probability that we will be killed by the advance force is significantly reduced. Second, Ellie is completely fluent in the octospider language and can back me up if my translator is either not available or inadequate. Third, and this may be the most important reason, the only crime that Nakamura and his minions can possibly be attributing to the octospiders is Ellie's kidnapping. If she shows up, healthy and praising the alien enemy, then the war effort will be undermined."

Nicole frowned. "I don't like the idea of Nikki going along. It's much too dangerous. I would never forgive myself if something happened to that child."

"Nor would I," Richard said. "But I don't think Ellie will go without her. . . . Nicole, there are no *good* plans. We will be forced to choose the least unsatisfactory option."

During a brief pause in the conversation Archie spoke in color. "Richard's points are all excellent," the octospider said to Nicole. "And there is one additional reason why it might be better for you to remain here in the Emerald City—the rest of the humans who stay behind will need your leadership in the difficult days ahead."

Nicole's mind was racing. She had not been prepared for Richard to volunteer to go. "Are you telling me, Archie," she said, "that you *endorse* Richard's suggestions, including taking Ellie and Nikki with you?"

"Yes," the octospider replied.

"But Richard," Nicole then said, turning to her husband, "you know how you hate what you call political crap. Are you certain you have thought this through?"

Richard nodded. Nicole shrugged. "All right, then," she said. "We'll talk to Ellie. If she agrees, we have a plan."

The Chief Optimizer thought that the amended proposal had some chance of success, but felt compelled to remind everyone that, based on the detailed octospider analysis of the likely outcome, there was still a high probability that both Archie and Richard would be killed, and a nonzero chance that Ellie and Nikki would not survive as well. Nicole's heart skipped a beat when she translated the octospider leader's reminder. The Chief Optimizer was not telling her anything that Nicole did not already know; however, Nicole had been so involved in the planning and discussions that she had not yet confronted any of the likely outcomes of their decisions.

Nicole said very little while the principals all agreed upon a baseline timetable. When she heard Richard say that Archie and he, with or without

Ellie and Nikki, would leave the Emerald City one tert after dawn the next day, Nicole shuddered. *Tomorrow,* flashed quickly through her mind. *Tomorrow our lives will change again.*

She remained quiet on the transport ride back to their zone. While Richard and Archie talked about many different subjects, Nicole tried to wrestle with the growing fear inside her. An inner voice, one that she had not heard for years, was telling her that she would never see Richard again after tomorrow. *Is this perhaps some peculiar reaction on my part?* she asked herself critically. *Am I having trouble letting Richard be the hero?*

The strength of the premonition grew, despite Nicole's attempts to combat it. She remembered a terrible night many, many years earlier, when she had been in her bedroom in the little house in Chilly-Mazarin. Nicole had awakened screaming from a violent and vivid nightmare. "Mommy is dead," the ten-year-old girl had cried.

Her father had tried to console her and had explained that her mother was just away on a trip visiting her family in the Ivory Coast. The telegram announcing her mother's death had arrived at the house seven hours later.

"If you don't have any weapons stockpiled and no trained soldiers," Richard was now saying, "how in the world can you prepare for a war fast enough to defend yourself?"

"I cannot tell you that," Archie replied. "But believe me, I know for a fact that a conflict at this time between our two species could result in the total annihilation of the human civilization in Rama."

Nicole could not calm her tormented soul. No matter how many times she told herself she was overreacting, the premonitory fear did not diminish. She reached over and took Richard's hand. He wrapped his fingers through hers and continued his conversation with Archie.

Nicole gazed intently at him. *I am proud of you, Richard,* she thought, *but I am also scared. And I am not yet ready to say good-bye.*

It was very late when Nicole went to bed. She had awakened Ellie gently, without disturbing Nikki and the Watanabe twins, who were sleeping in the Wakefield house so that Patrick and Nai could have their wedding night alone. Ellie, of course, had had many questions. Richard and Nicole had explained the plan, including everything important they had learned from Archie and the Chief Optimizer earlier in the evening. Ellie had been fearful, but had finally agreed that Nikki and she would accompany Richard and Archie the next day.

Nicole could not fall into a deep sleep. After tossing and turning for an hour, she began a sequence of short, chaotic dreams. In her final dream Nicole was again seven years old back in the Ivory Coast, in the middle of her Poro ceremony. She was half naked out in the water, with the lioness prowling around the perimeter of the pond. Little Nicole took a deep breath and dove under the water. When she surfaced, Richard was standing on the shore where the lioness had been. It was a young Richard smiling at her initially, but as Nicole watched, he aged rapidly and became the same Richard who was beside her that moment in the bed. She heard Omeh's voice in her ear. "Look carefully, Ronata," the voice said. "And remember. . . ."

Nicole woke up. Richard was sleeping peacefully. She sat up in the bed and tapped on the wall one time. A solitary firefly appeared in the doorway, shining some light into the bedroom. Nicole stared at her husband. She looked at his hair and beard, gray from age, and remembered them when they had been black. She recalled fondly his ardor and humor during their courtship in New York. Nicole grimaced, took a deep breath, and kissed her index finger. She placed the finger on Richard's lips. He did not stir. Nicole sat quietly for several more minutes, studying every feature of her husband's face. Soft tears flowed down her cheeks and dropped from her chin onto the sheets. "I love you, Richard," she said.

WAR IN RAMA

1

REPORT #319

Time of Transmission: 156 307 872 574.2009
Time Since First-Stage Alert: 111.9766
References: Node 23-419
                  Spacecraft 947
                  Spacefarers 47 249 (A & B)
                          32 806
                           2 666

   During the last interval the structure and order in the spacefaring
communities inside the spacecraft have continued to disintegrate. Despite
the warnings of the octospiders (Spacefarers #2 666) and their laudable
attempts to avoid a broad conflict with the humans (#32 806), it is now even
more likely that a disastrous war between the two species, which could
leave only a few survivors, may take place in the next several intervals. The
situation therefore meets all the prerequisite conditions for a Stage 2
intercession.
   Prior intercessionary activity has been declared a failure, primarily
because the more aggressive of the two species, the humans, are fundamentally insensitive to the entire range of subtle intercessionary techniques. Only a few of the humans have responded to the many attempts to
alter their hostile behavior, and those who did react were unable to stop the

genocide of the avians and sessiles (#47 249, A & B) perpetrated by their rulers.

The humans are organized in the rigid, hierarchical manner often observed in prespacefaring species. They continue to be dominated by a leadership whose focus is the retention of personal power. The welfare of the human community and even its survival are subordinated in the implicit objective function of the current human leaders to the continuation of a political system which gives them absolute authority. There is consequently little likelihood that the threatened expanded conflict between the humans and the octospiders can be avoided by any logical appeals.

A small cadre of humans, including almost all of the family that lived at the Node for over a year, remains in residence in the main octospider city. Their interaction with their hosts has demonstrated that it is possible for the two species to live together in harmony. Recently a mixed delegation of those humans and one octospider have decided to make a concerted effort to prevent a full-scale interspecies war by contacting the leaders of the human colony directly. However, the probability that this delegation will be successful is very low.

Thus far the octospiders have taken no overt hostile action. Nevertheless, they have begun the process of preparing for a war against the humans. Although they will fight only if they determine that the survival of their community is in jeopardy, the advanced biological capabilities of the octospiders makes the outcome of such a war a foregone conclusion.

What is not certain is how the humans will react once the conflict escalates and they suffer heavy losses. It is possible that the war might terminate quickly and, in time, the two surviving communities might again reach a near equilibrium status. Based on the available observational data on the humans, however, there is a nontrivial probability that this species will continue the battle until most or all of them perish. Such an outcome would destroy all the vestiges of at least one of the two spacefaring societies remaining in the spacecraft. To preclude such a disadvantageous result for the project, consideration of a Stage 2 intercession is recommended.

2

Nicole was awakened by the sound of the three children playing in the living room. As she was slipping on her robe, Ellie came to the door of the bedroom and asked if she had seen Nikki's favorite doll. "I think it's under her bed," Nicole replied.

Ellie returned to her packing. Nicole could hear Richard in the bathroom. *It won't be long now,* she was thinking when her granddaughter suddenly appeared in the doorway. "Mommy and I are leaving, Nonni," the little girl said with a smile. "We're going to see Daddy."

Nicole opened her arms and the little girl ran over for a hug. "I know, darling," Nicole said. She held the girl tightly in her arms and then began to stroke her hair. "I will miss you, Nikki," she said.

A few seconds later the Watanabe twins both bounded into the room. "I'm hungry, Mrs. Wakefield," Galileo said.

"Me too," Kepler added.

Nicole reluctantly released her granddaughter and started walking across the bedroom. "All right, boys," she said. "I'll have your breakfast in a few minutes."

When the three children were almost finished eating, Max, Eponine, and Marius arrived at the door. "Guess what, Uncle Max," Nikki said before Nicole had even had a chance to greet the Pucketts. "I'm going to see my daddy."

The four hours flew by quickly. Richard and Nicole explained everything twice, first to Max and Eponine and then to the newlyweds, both of whom were still radiant from the pleasures of their wedding night. As the time neared for the departure of Richard, Ellie, and Nikki, the excitement and energy that had characterized the morning conversation began to wane. Butterflies started fluttering in Nicole's stomach.

Max was the first to say good-bye. "Come over here, Princess," he said to Nikki, "and give your Uncle Max a kiss." The girl obediently followed directions. Max then stood up and crossed the room to where Ellie was talking with her mother. "Take care of that little girl, Ellie," he said, embracing her, "and don't let the bastards get away with anything." Max shook hands with Richard and then called the Watanabe twins to join him outside.

The mood in the room was swiftly altered. Despite her promise to herself that she would remain calm, Nicole felt a surge of panic as she suddenly realized that she had only a few minutes to complete her farewells. Patrick, Nai, Benjy, and Eponine had followed Max's cue and were hugging the departing trio.

Nicole tried to embrace Nikki again, but the little girl scurried away, running outside to play with the twins. Ellie finished saying good-bye to Eponine and turned to Nicole. "I will miss you, Mother," she said brightly. "I love you very much."

Nicole struggled to maintain her emotional equilibrium. "I couldn't have asked for a better daughter," she said. While the two women hugged, Nicole spoke softly in her daughter's ear. "Be careful," she said. "There's a lot at stake."

Ellie pulled away and looked in her mother's eyes. She took a deep breath. "I know, Mother," she said somberly, "and it frightens me. I hope I don't disappoint—"

"You won't," Nicole said lightly, patting her daughter's shoulders. "Just remember what the cricket said in *Pinocchio*."

Ellie smiled. "And always let your conscience be your guide."

"Archie's here!" Nicole heard Nikki shout. She looked around for her husband. *Where's Richard?* she thought in a fright. *I haven't said good-bye.* Ellie passed by her quickly, headed for the door carrying two packs on her back.

Nicole could hardly breathe. She heard Patrick say, "Where's Uncle Richard?" and a voice from the study reply, "I'm back here."

She ran down the hall to the study. Richard was sitting on the floor amid electronic components and his own open backpack. Nicole stood in the doorway for a second, catching her breath.

Richard heard her behind him and turned around. "Oh, hi, darling," he said nonchalantly. "I'm still trying to figure out how many backup components I should take for my translators."

"Archie's here," Nicole said quietly.

Richard glanced at his watch. "I guess it's time to go," he said. He picked up a handful of electronic parts and stuffed them into his backpack. Then he stood up and walked toward Nicole.

"Uncle Richard," Patrick yelled.

"I'm coming," Richard shouted. "Just a minute."

Nicole began to tremble the moment Richard put his arms around her. "Hey," he said, "it's all right. . . . We've been apart before."

The fear inside Nicole had become so strong that she could not speak. She tried desperately to be brave, but it was impossible. She knew that this was the last time she would ever touch her husband.

She put one hand behind Richard's head and pulled away slightly so that she could kiss him. Nicole wanted to stop time, to make this one moment last an eternity. Her eyes took a photograph of Richard's face, and she kissed him gently on the lips.

"I love you, Nicole," he said.

For an instant she didn't think she was going to be able to reply. "I love you too," she finally managed to say.

He hoisted his backpack and gave a little wave. Nicole stood in the doorway and watched him walk toward the door. *Remember,* she heard Omeh's voice say inside her head.

Nikki could hardly believe her good fortune. There in front of her, barely outside the gates of the Emerald City, an ostrichsaur was waiting for them, just as Archie had said. She moved about impatiently as her mother zipped her coat. "Can I feed it, Mother?" she said. "Can I? Can I?"

Even with the ostrichsaur sitting on the ground, Richard had to help Nikki mount the animal. "Thank you, Boobah," the girl said when she was comfortably nestled in the bowl.

"The timing has been worked out very carefully," Archie told Richard and Ellie while they were moving along the path through the forest. "We will arrive at the camp when all the troops are starting breakfast. That way everyone will see us."

"How will we know precisely when to appear?" Richard asked.

"Some of the quadroids are being managed from the far northern fields. Soon after the first soldiers are awake and are moving around outside their tents, your avian friend Timmy, carrying a written announcement of our imminent arrival, will fly over their heads in the dark. Our message will indicate that we will be preceded by the fireflies and that we will be waving a white flag, as you suggested."

Nikki noticed some strange eyes looking out at them from the dark of the forest. "Isn't this fun?" she said to her mother. Ellie did not respond.

Archie stopped the ostrichsaur about a kilometer south of the human camp. The lanterns and other lights outside the distant tents in front of them looked like stars twinkling in the night. "Timmy should be dropping our message just about now," Archie said.

They had been moving cautiously in the dark for several hours, not wanting to use the fireflies because of the possibility that they might be noticed too early. Nikki was sleeping peacefully, her head in her mother's lap. Both Richard and Ellie were tense. "What are we going to do," Richard had inquired before they stopped, "if the troops fire on us before we can say anything?"

"We'll turn around and retreat as fast as we can," Archie had replied.

"And what happens if they come after us with the helicopters and the searchlights?" Ellie had asked.

"At full speed it will take the ostrichsaur almost four wodens to reach the forest," Archie had said.

Timmy returned to the group and reported, in a brief jabber and color conversation with Archie, that he had accomplished his mission. Richard and Timmy then said farewell to each other. The avian's large eyes expressed an emotion Richard had not seen before as Richard rubbed his underbelly. A few moments later, as Timmy flew away in the direction of the Emerald City, a pair of fireflies ignited beside the path and then headed in the direction of the human camp. Richard led the procession, clutching the white flag in his right hand. The ostrichsaur followed about fifty meters behind carrying Ellie, Archie, and the sleeping child.

Richard could see the soldiers with his binoculars when their party was about four hundred meters away. The troops were standing around, looking in their general direction. Richard counted twenty-six of them altogether, including three with rifles poised and another pair scanning the darkness with binoculars.

As planned, Ellie, Nikki, and Archie dismounted when they were about two hundred meters from the camp. The ostrichsaur was sent back while the four of them walked toward the human soldiers. Nikki, who had not been ready to awaken, complained at first but became quiet when she sensed the importance of her mother's request to remain silent.

Archie walked between the two adult humans. Nikki was holding her mother's hand and scampering to keep up with the pace. "Hello, there," Richard shouted when he thought he was within earshot. "This is Richard Wakefield. We come in peace." He waved the white flag vigorously. "I am with my daughter Ellie, my granddaughter Nikki, and an octospider representative."

They must have been an amazing sight for the soldiers, none of whom had ever seen an octospider before. With the fireflies hovering over the heads of the troops, Richard and his party emerged from the Raman dark.

One of the soldiers stepped forward. "I am Captain Enrico Pioggi," he said, "the commanding officer of this camp. I accept your surrender on behalf of the armed forces of New Eden."

                         *   *   *

Because the announcement of their impending arrival had been
delivered to the camp less than half an hour earlier, the New Eden chain of
command had not had time to formulate a plan of what to do with the
prisoners. As soon as he had confirmed that a party of a man, a woman, a
child, and an alien octospider were indeed approaching his camp, Captain
Pioggi had again radioed the front headquarters in New York and requested
instructions on how to proceed. The colonel in charge of the campaign told
him to "secure the prisoners" and "stand by for further orders."

Richard had anticipated that none of the officers would be willing to
take any definitive action until Nakamura himself had been consulted. He
had told Archie, during their long ride on the ostrichsaur, that it would be
important to use whatever time they might have with the soldiers in the
camp to start rebutting the propaganda that the New Eden government was
spreading.

"This creature," Richard said in a loud voice after the prisoners had
been searched and the curious troops were milling around them, "is what
we call an octospider. All octospiders are very intelligent—in some ways
more intelligent than we are—and about fifteen thousand of them live in
the Southern Hemicylinder, which extends from here to the base of the
south polar bowl. My family and I have been living in their realm for over
a year—of our own choice, I might add—and we have found the
octospiders to be moral and peace-loving. My daughter Ellie and I have
come forward with this octospider representative, whom we call Archie, to
try to find some way of stopping a military confrontation between our two
species."

"Aren't you Dr. Robert Turner's wife?" said one of the troops to Ellie.
"The one who was kidnapped by the octospiders?"

"Yes, I am," Ellie said in a clear voice. "Except that I wasn't
kidnapped in the truest sense of the word. The octospiders wanted to
establish communications with us and had been unable to do so. I was
taken because they believed that I had the capacity to learn their
language."

"That thing *talks*?" another soldier said with disbelief.

Until that moment Archie, as planned, had been silent. The troops all
stared dumbfounded as colors began pouring out of the right side of his slit
and circumnavigating his head. "Archie says greetings," Ellie translated.
"He asks each of you to understand that neither he nor any member of his
species wishes you any harm. Archie also wants me to inform you that he
can read lips and will be happy to answer any questions you might have."

"Is this for real?" a soldier said.

Meanwhile, a frustrated Captain Pioggi was standing off to the side,
providing an eyewitness account by radio to the colonel in New York. "Yes,
sir," he was saying, "colors on its head . . . all different colors, sir, red, blue,

yellow . . . like rectangles, moving rectangles, they go around its head, and then more of them follow. . . . What's that, sir? . . . The woman, the doctor's wife, sir. . . . She apparently knows what the colors mean. . . . No, sir, there aren't any colored letters, just the colored strips. . . .

"Right now, sir, the alien is talking to the soldiers. . . . No, sir, they are not using colors. . . . According to the woman, sir, the octospider can read lips . . . like a hearing impaired person, sir . . . same technique I guess. . . . Anyway, it then answers in color and the doctor's wife translates. . . .

"No weapons of any kind, sir. . . . Plenty of toys, clothes, weird-looking objects prisoner Wakefield says are electronic components. . . . Toys, sir, I said toys . . . the little girl had a lot of toys in her backpack. . . . No, we don't have a scanner up here. . . . Right, sir. . . . Do you have any idea how long we might be waiting, sir?"

By the time Captain Pioggi finally received orders to send the prisoners to New York in one of the helicopters, Archie had thoroughly impressed all the soldiers at the camp. The octospider had begun the demonstration of his prodigious mental abilities by multiplying five- and six-place numbers in his head.

"Now, how do we know that the octospider thing is really coming up with the right answer?" one of the younger soldiers had asked. "All it does is show a string of colors."

"My man," Richard had replied with a laugh, "didn't you just verify on the lieutenant's calculator that the number my daughter gave was correct? Do you think *she* computed the product in *her* head?"

"Oh, yeah," the youth said. "I see what you mean."

What really overwhelmed the soldiers was Archie's phenomenal memory. At Richard's urging, one of the troops listed a sequence of several hundred numbers on a sheet of paper and then read the sequence to Archie, a single number at a time. The octospider repeated them back through Ellie, without any errors. Some of the soldiers thought that there had been a trick involved, that maybe Richard was flashing coded signals to Archie. However, when Archie duplicated his feat under carefully controlled conditions, all the doubters were convinced.

The atmosphere in the camp was relaxed and amiable by the time the orders were received to transport the prisoners to New York. The first part of their plan had succeeded beyond their wildest imaginings. Nevertheless, Richard was nervous as they climbed on board the helicopter to cross a portion of the Cylindrical Sea.

They only stayed in New York for about an hour. Armed guards met the prisoners at the helicopter pad in the western plaza, confiscated their backpacks over Richard's and Nikki's loud protests, and marched them to the Port. Richard carried Nikki in his arms. He barely had time to admire his favorite skyscrapers looming overhead in the dark.

The yacht that carried them across the northern half of the Cylindrical Sea was similar to the pleasure boats that Nakamura and his cronies used on Lake Shakespeare. At no time during the crossing did any of the guards speak to them. "Boobah," Nikki whispered to Richard after several of her questions had gone unheeded, "don't these men know how to talk?" She giggled.

A rover was waiting for them on a dock that had been recently constructed to support the new activities in New York and the Southern Hemicylinder. At considerable effort and expense, the humans had cut an opening through the southern barrier wall in an area adjacent to the avian/sessile habitat and had built a large docking facility.

Richard wondered at first why he and his companions had not been flown directly back to New Eden in the helicopter. After a few quick mental calculations, however, he correctly concluded that because of the enormous height of the barrier wall, which extended well up into the region where the artificial gravity caused by the spinning Rama spacecraft began to drop substantially, as well as the probable lack of skilled pilots, there was an upper limit placed on the altitude at which the hastily built helicopters were allowed to fly. *That means,* Richard was thinking as he boarded the rover, *that the humans must move all their equipment and personnel either through this dock or by means of the moat and tunnel underneath the second habitat.*

Their rover was driven by a Garcia biot. In front and behind them were two other rovers, both with armed humans. They sped across the darkness to the Central Plain. Richard sat in the front seat beside the driver, with Archie, Ellie, and Nikki in the back. Richard had turned around in his seat and was reminding Archie of the five kinds of biots in New Eden when the Garcia interrupted him. "The prisoner Wakefield is to face forward and remain silent," the biot said.

"Isn't that just a little bit ridiculous?" Richard said lightly.

The Garcia pulled its right arm off the steering wheel and struck Richard hard in the face with the back of its hand. "Face forward and remain silent," the biot repeated, as Richard recoiled from the force of the slap.

Nikki started crying after the sudden display of violence. Ellie tried both to quiet and to comfort her. "I don't like the driver, Mommy," the little girl said. "I really don't."

It was night inside New Eden after they were ushered through the checkpoint at the entrance to the habitat. Archie and the three humans were placed into an open electric car driven by another Garcia biot. Richard noticed immediately that it was almost as cold in New Eden as it had been in Rama. The car bounced down the road, which was in an acute state of disrepair, and turned north at what had once been the train station for the village of Positano. Fifteen or twenty people were huddled around campfires on the concrete areas surrounding the old station, and another three or four were stretched out and sleeping underneath cardboard boxes and old clothing.

"What are those people doing, Mommy?" Nikki asked. Ellie did not answer because the Garcia turned around quickly with a hostile stare.

The neon lights of Vegas could already be seen in front of them when the car took a sharp left turn onto a residential lane in a wooded section that had once been part of Sherwood Forest. The car came to an abrupt halt in front of a large, rambling ranch house. Two Oriental men, armed with both pistols and daggers, approached the car. They gestured for the passengers to climb out of the car and then dismissed the biot. "Come with us," said one of the men.

Archie and his human companions entered the house and were taken down a long flight of stairs into a basement with no windows. "There is food and water on the table," the second man said. He turned and started to climb the stairs.

"Wait a minute," Richard said. "Our backpacks . . . we need to have our backpacks."

"They will be returned," the man said impatiently, "as soon as all the contents have been carefully checked."

"And when do we see Nakamura?" Richard inquired.

The man shrugged. His face was expressionless. He walked quickly up the stairs.

3

The days passed very slowly. Richard, Ellie, and Nikki were without a time reference at first, but they soon learned that octospiders have a wonderfully precise inner clock that is calibrated and enhanced during their juvenile education. After they converted Archie to using human time measurements (Richard used his oft-quoted "When in Rome . . ." to convince Archie to abandon, at least temporarily, his terts, wodens, fengs, and nillets), they discovered, by sneaking glances at their guard's digital watch when he brought food and water, that Archie's internal timing accuracy was better than ten seconds out of every twenty-four hours.

Nikki amused herself by constantly asking Archie the time. As a result, after repeated observation, Richard and even Nikki learned how to read Archie's colors for time references and small numbers. In fact, as the days passed, the regular conversation in the basement significantly improved Richard's overall comprehension of the octospider language. Although his skill in understanding the color strips was still not as advanced as Ellie's, after a week Richard could comfortably converse with Archie without needing Ellie as an interpreter.

The humans slept on futons on the floor. Archie curled up behind them for the few hours each night that he slept. One or the other of the two Oriental men replenished their supplies once each day. Richard never failed to remind the guards that they were still waiting for their backpacks and for their audience with Nakamura.

After eight days the daily sponge baths in the washbasin adjoining the basement toilet were no longer satisfactory. Richard asked if they could have access to a shower and some soap. Several hours later a large laundry tub was carried down the stairs. Each of the humans bathed, although Nikki was at first surprisingly reluctant to be naked in front of Archie. Richard and Ellie felt enough better after bathing that they managed to share some optimism. "There's no way he can keep our existence a secret forever," Richard said. "Too many of the troops saw us . . . and it would not be possible for them not to say anything, no matter what Nakamura ordered."

"I'm certain they will come for us soon," Ellie added brightly.

By the end of their second week of imprisonment, however, their temporary optimism had waned. Richard and Ellie were beginning to lose hope. It didn't help that Nikki had become a complete brat, announcing regularly that she was bored and complaining about not having anything to do. Archie began to tell Nikki stories to keep her occupied. His octospider "legends" (he had a long discussion with Ellie about the exact meaning of the word before he finally accepted the term) delighted the little girl.

It helped that Ellie's translations rang with the resonant phrases the girl already associated with bedtime fairy tales. "Once upon a time, back in the days of the Precursors . . ." Archie would begin a story, and Nikki would squeal with anticipation.

"What did the Precursors look like, Archie?" the little girl asked after one such story.

"The legends never say," Archie replied. "So I guess you can create whatever picture of them you want in your imagination."

"Is that story true?" Nikki asked Archie on another occasion. "Would the octospiders *really* never have left their own planet if the Precursors had not taken them into space first?"

"So the legends indicate," Archie replied. "They say that almost everything we knew until about fifty thousand years ago was taught to us originally by the Precursors."

One night, after Nikki was asleep, Richard and Ellie asked Archie about the origin of the legends. "They have been around for tens of thousands of your years," the octospider said. "The earliest documented records from our genus contain many of the stories I have shared with you these last few days. There are several different opinions about how factual the legends are. Dr. Blue believes that they are basically accurate and probably the work of some master storyteller—an alternate, of course— whose genius was not recognized in his or her lifetime.

"If the legends can be believed," Archie said in answer to another of Richard's questions, "many, many years ago we octospiders were simple seafaring creatures whose natural evolution had produced only minimal intelligence and awareness. It was the Precursors who discovered our potential by mapping our genetic structure, and they who altered us over many generations into what we had become when the Great Calamity occurred."

"What exactly happened to the Precursors?" Ellie asked.

"There are many stories, some contradictory. Most or all of the Precursors living on the primary planet we shared with them were probably killed in the Calamity. Some of the legends suggest that their remote colonial outposts around nearby stars survived for several hundred years, but ultimately succumbed as well. One legend says that the Precursors continued to thrive in other, more favorable star systems and became the dominant form of intelligence in the galaxy. We do not know. All that is known for certain is that the land portion of our primary planet was uninhabitable for many, many years and that when the octospider civilization again ventured out of the water, none of the Precursors were alive."

The group of four in the basement developed their own diurnal rhythm as the days stretched into weeks. Each morning, before Nikki and Ellie awakened, Archie and Richard would talk about a wide range of topics of mutual interest. By this time, Archie's lip-reading was nearly flawless, and Richard's comprehension of the octospider colors was good enough that the octospider was only rarely asked to repeat what he had said.

Many of the conversations were about science. Archie was especially fascinated by the history of science in the human species. He wanted to know what discoveries were made when, what prompted the key investigations or experiments in the first place, and what inaccurate or competing models explaining the phenomena were discarded as a result of each new understanding.

"So it was actually war that accelerated the development of both aeronautics and nuclear physics in your species," Archie said one morning. "What an amazing concept! . . . You cannot possibly appreciate," the octospider added a few seconds later, "how staggering it is for me to experience, even vicariously, your incremental process of learning about nature. Our history is totally different. In the beginning our species was completely ignorant. Shortly thereafter a new kind of octospider was created, one that could not only think, but also observe the world and understand what it was seeing. Our mentors and creators, the Precursors, already had explanations for everything. Our task as a species was quite simple. We learned what we could from our teachers. Naturally, we did not have any concept of the trial and error that is involved in science. For that matter, we had no idea at all of how any component in a culture evolves. The brilliant engineering of the Precursors allowed us to skip hundreds of millions of years of evolution.

"Needless to say, we were woefully unprepared for taking care of ourselves after the Great Calamity occurred. According to the more historical of our legends, our primary intellectual activity for the next several hundred years was to accumulate and understand as much of the Precursor information as we could find and/or remember. In the meantime, with our benefactors no longer around to provide ethical guidelines, we regressed sociologically. We entered a long, long period in which it was questionable whether or not the new, intelligent octospiders created by the Precursors would indeed survive."

Richard was overwhelmed by the idea of what he called a "derivative technological species." "I had never imagined," he told Archie one morning with his usual excitement of discovery, "that there might exist a spacefaring species that had *never* worked out on its own the laws of gravity and had *never* derived, in a long sequence of experiments, the essentials of physics, such as the characteristics of the electromagnetic spectrum. It is a mind-boggling thought. But now that I understand what you are telling me, it seems quite natural. If species A, who are advanced spacefarers, encounters species B, intelligent but somewhere lower on the technological ladder, it is perfectly logical to assume that, after contact, species B would skip the rungs between."

"Our case, of course," Archie explained, "was even more unusual. The paradigm that you are describing is indeed quite natural and has happened, according to both our history and the legends, with great frequency. More spacefarers are derivative, to use your word, than naturally evolved. Take the avians and the sessiles, for example. Their symbiosis, which developed without any outside interference, had already existed in a star system not far from our home planet for thousands of years when they were first visited on an exploratory mission by the Precursors. The avians and sessiles would almost certainly never have developed a spacefaring capability of their own. However, after meeting the Precursors and seeing their first spacecraft, they asked for and received the technology necessary to achieve space-flight.

"Our situation is generically different, and definitely much more derivative. If our legends are true, the Precursors were already spacefarers when we octospiders were still totally insentient. At that epoch we were not even capable of conceiving of the idea of a planet, much less of the space surrounding it. Our fate was decided by the advanced beings with whom we shared our world. The Precursors recognized the potential in our genetic structure. Using their engineering skills, they improved us, gave us minds, shared their information with us, and created an advanced culture where none would probably have ever existed."

A deep bonding developed between Richard and Archie as a result of the regular early morning conversations. Unencumbered by any distractions, the two were able to share their fundamental love for knowledge. Each expanded the understanding of the other, thereby enriching their mutual appreciation for the wonders of the universe.

Nikki almost always woke up before Ellie. Soon after the girl had finished her breakfast, the group entered the second segment of their daily schedule. Although Nikki occasionally played games with Archie, she spent most of what might be called her morning in informal classes. She had three teachers. With Ellie, Nikki read a little, and did elementary addition and subtraction. She talked to her grandfather about science and nature, and had lessons with Archie on morals and ethics. She also learned the octospider alphabet and a few simple phrases. Nikki was very quick with the language of color, a fact that the others attributed both to her altered genes and to her natural intelligence.

"Our juveniles spend a significant amount of their schooling time discussing and interpreting case studies that raise critical moral problems," Archie told Richard and Ellie one morning during a discussion of education. "Real-life situations are chosen as examples—although the actual facts may be slightly altered to sharpen the issues—and the young octospiders are asked to assess the acceptability of various possible responses. They do this in open discussion."

"Is this to expose the juveniles at an early age to the concept of optimization?" Richard asked.

"Not really," Archie replied. "What we are trying to do is to prepare the young for the real task of living, which involves regular interaction with others, with many behavioral choices. Each juvenile is strongly encouraged to use the case studies to develop his or her own value system. Our species believes that knowledge does not exist in a vacuum. Only when knowledge is an integral part of a way of living does it achieve any real significance."

Archie's case studies presented Nikki with simple but elegant ethical problems. The basic issues of lying, fairness, prejudice, and selfishness were all covered in the first eight lessons. The girl's responses to the situations often drew upon examples from her own life.

"Galileo will always say or do whatever he thinks will allow him to have his own way," Nikki remarked during one lesson. "To him, what *he* wants is more important than anything else. Kepler is different. He never makes me cry."

Nikki napped in the afternoon. While she was sleeping, Richard, Ellie, and Archie often exchanged comments and insights that highlighted the similarities and differences between the two species. "If I have understood correctly," Ellie said one day after a lively conversation about how intelligent, sensitive beings should handle members of their community who exhibit antisocial behavior, "your society is much less tolerant than ours. There is clearly a 'preferred way of living' that is advanced by your communities. Those octospiders who do not embrace that preferred model are not only ostracized early, but also denied participation in many of life's more rewarding activities and 'terminated' after a shorter than normal life span."

"In our society," Archie said in reply, "what is acceptable is always clear—there is no confusion, as there is in yours. Thus *our* individuals make their choices with full knowledge of the consequences. Incidentally, the Alternate Domain is *not* like one of your prisons. It is a place where octospiders, and other species as well, can live without the regimentation and optimization necessary for the continued development and survival of the colony. Some of the alternates live to be very old and are quite happy.

"Your society, at least what I have observed of it, seems not to understand the fundamental inconsistency between individual freedom and the common welfare. The two must be carefully balanced. No group can survive, let alone thrive, unless what is good for the overall community is more important than individual freedom. Take, for example, resource allocation. How can anyone with any intelligence possibly justify, in terms of the overall community, the accumulation and hoarding of enormous material assets by a few individuals when others do not even have food, clothing, and other essentials?"

In the basement Archie was not as reticent and evasive as he had sometimes been in the Emerald City. He spoke openly about all aspects of his civilization, as if the common mission he was undertaking with his human colleagues had somehow freed him from all constraints. Was Archie consciously sending a message to the other humans who were almost certainly monitoring the conversation? Perhaps. But how much of the conversation could Nakamura's men have understood, since they knew nothing of the language of color? No, it was more likely that Archie, better than any of the humans, realized that his death was imminent and wanted his final days to be as meaningful and stimulating as possible.

One night before Richard and Ellie went to sleep, Archie said that he had something "personal" to tell them. "I do not want to alarm you," the octospider said, "but I have consumed almost all of the supply of barrican that is in my intake buffer. If we stay here much longer and my barrican runs out, as you know I will begin to undergo sexual maturity. According to our files, I will become more aggressive and possessive at that time."

"Don't worry about it," Richard said with a laugh. "I have dealt with teenagers before. Certainly I can handle an octospider who no longer has a perfect temperament."

One morning the guard bringing their food and water told Ellie to prepare herself and the girl to leave. "When?" Ellie said.

"Ten minutes," the guard replied.

"Where are we going?" Ellie inquired.

The guard said nothing and disappeared up the stairway.

While Ellie was doing her best to freshen herself and Nikki, she reviewed with Richard and Archie what she would say if she was able to meet with Nakamura or any of the other colony leaders.

"Don't forget," her father stressed in a rapid whisper over in one corner of the room, "although it is all right to say that the octospiders are a peace-loving species, we will not be able to stop any war unless we convince Nakamura that he cannot possibly win an armed conflict. The point must be made that their technology has advanced far beyond ours."

"But what if they ask for specifics?"

"You wouldn't be expected to know any details. Tell them that I can supply all the specifics."

Ellie and Nikki were taken by electric car to the colony hospital in Central City. They were whisked through the emergency entrance and into a small, sterile office with two chairs, a couch or bed used for examinations, and some complex electronic equipment. Ellie and Nikki sat alone for ten minutes before Dr. Robert Turner walked into the room.

He looked very old. "Hi, Nikki," he said, smiling and squatting down with his arms outstretched. "Come give your daddy a hug."

The girl hesitated for a moment and then ran across the room to her father. Robert picked her up and swung her around in his arms. "It's so good to see you, Nikki," he said.

Ellie stood up and waited. After several seconds Robert put his daughter back down on the floor and looked at his wife. "How are you, Ellie?" he asked.

"Fine," Ellie replied, suddenly feeling awkward. "How are *you*, Robert?"

"About the same," he said.

They met in the middle of the room and embraced. Ellie tried to kiss him tenderly, but their lips merely brushed before Robert turned away. She could sense the tension in his body.

"What is it, Robert?" Ellie said softly. "What's wrong?"

"I've just been working too hard, as usual," he replied. He moved over beside the examination bed. "Would you take off your clothes and lie down here, please, Ellie? I want to make certain you're all right."

"Right this minute?" an incredulous Ellie asked. "Before we even talk about what has happened to us during the months that we've been apart?"

"I'm sorry, Ellie," Robert said with a trace of a smile. "I'm very busy tonight. The hospital is terribly understaffed. I talked them into releasing you by promising—"

Ellie had walked around the bed and was standing very close to her husband. She reached down and took his hand. "Robert," she said gently, "I am your wife. I love you. We have not seen each other for over a year. Surely you can take a minute . . ."

Tears formed in Robert's eyes. "What is it, Robert? Tell me." Ellie had a sudden fright. *He's married someone else*, she thought in panic.

"What has happened to *you*, Ellie?" he said suddenly in a loud voice. "How could you possibly tell those soldiers that you were not kidnapped, and that the octospiders were not hostile? You have made me a laughingstock. Every single citizen in New Eden has heard me on television describing that terrible moment that you were abducted. . . . My memories are so horribly clear."

Ellie backed up at first when Robert began his outburst. As she stood there listening, still holding his hand, his anguish was obvious. "I made those comments, Robert, because I was, and am, trying to do whatever I can to stop any conflict between the octospiders and us. I am sorry if my remarks caused you pain."

"The octospiders have brainwashed you, Ellie," Robert said bitterly. "I knew it as soon as Nakamura's men showed me the reports. Somehow they have tampered with your mind so that you are no longer in touch with reality."

Nikki had started whimpering when Robert had first raised his voice. She did not understand what the disagreement between her parents was about, but she could tell that everything was not all right. She began to cry and to cling to her mother's leg.

"It's all right, Nikki," Ellie said soothingly. "Your father and I are just talking."

When Ellie glanced up, Robert had taken a transparent skullcap out of a drawer and was holding it in his hand. "So you're going to give me an EEG," she said nervously, "to make certain that I haven't become one of them?"

"It's not funny, Ellie," Robert replied. "My EEGs have all been weird since I returned to New Eden. I can't explain it, nor can the neurologist on my staff. He says he has never seen such radical changes in an individual's brain activity, except in the case of severe injury."

"Robert," Ellie said, taking his hand again. "The octospiders planted a microbiological block in your memory when you departed. To protect themselves. That could be part of the explanation for your peculiar brain waves."

Robert looked at Ellie for a long time without speaking. "They kidnapped you," he said. "They tampered with my brain. Who knows what they may have done to our daughter? How can you possibly defend them?"

Ellie submitted to the EEG and the results showed neither irregularities nor major differences from the routine brain testing that she had undergone during the early days of the colony. Robert seemed genuinely relieved. He then told Ellie that Nakamura and the government were prepared to drop all charges against her and would let her return home with Nikki—under house arrest temporarily, of course—if she would provide information about the octospiders. Ellie thought about the request for a few minutes and then agreed.

Robert smiled and gave her a brisk hug. "Good," he said. "You'll start tomorrow. I'll tell them right away."

Richard had warned Ellie during the ride on the ostrichsaur that Nakamura might try to use her in some way, most likely to justify his continued prosecution of the war. Ellie knew that by agreeing ostensibly to help the New Eden government she was committing herself to a very dangerous course.

Nikki was unfamiliar with her old bedroom at first, but after an hour or so of playing with some of her toys, she seemed quite content. She came into the bathroom, where Ellie was taking a bath, and stood next to the tub. "When will Daddy be home?" she asked her mother.

"He'll be late, darling," Ellie replied. "After you've gone to bed."

"I like my room, Mommy," Nikki said. "It's much better than that old basement."

"I'm glad," Ellie replied. The little girl smiled and left the bathroom. Ellie took a deep breath. *It would have served no purpose*, she rationalized, *if I had refused and we had been returned to confinement.*

4

Katie had not finished with her makeup when she heard the buzzer sound. She took a drag on the cigarette burning in the ashtray beside her and pushed the TALK button. "Who is it?" she said.

"It's me," came the reply.

"What are you doing here in the middle of the day?"

"I have some important news," Captain Franz Bauer said. "Buzz me up."

Katie inhaled deeply on the cigarette and stubbed it out. She stood up and looked at herself in the full-length mirror. She adjusted her hair slightly just before the knock on her door.

"This had better be important, Franz," Katie said, letting him into the room, "or your ass is mud. You know I have a disciplinary meeting with two of the girls in a few minutes and I hate to be late."

Franz grinned. "You caught them skimming again? Jesus, Katie, I'd hate for you to be my boss."

Katie looked at Franz impatiently. "Well?" she said. "What was too important for the telephone?"

Franz had begun to walk around the living room. The room was tastefully decorated, with a black and white sofa and loveseat, two matching chairs, and several interesting objets d'art on both the end tables and the coffee table. "There's not any chance that your apartment is bugged, is there?"

"You tell *me*, Mr. Police Captain," Katie said. "Now, really, Franz," she added, glancing at her watch, "I don't have—"

"There is a reliable report," Franz said, "that your father is in New Eden at this very moment."

"*Whaat?*" said Katie. "How is that possible?" She was stunned. She sat down on the couch and reached for another cigarette from the coffee table.

"A lieutenant of mine is close friends with one of your father's guards. He was told that Richard and one of those octospider creatures are being held in the basement of a private residence not far from here."

Katie crossed the room and picked up the telephone. "Darla," she said, "tell Lauren and Atsuko that the meeting today is off. Something has come up. Reschedule for two o'clock tomorrow afternoon. . . . Oh, that's right, I forgot. Dammit. . . . All right, make it eleven in the morning. No, eleven-*thirty*. I don't want to wake up too early."

Katie returned to the couch and picked up her cigarette. She took a huge drag and blew smoke rings into the air over her head. "I want to know everything that you have heard about my father."

Franz informed Katie that, according to his sources, her father, her sister Ellie, her niece, and an octospider had suddenly appeared, carrying a white flag, at the troop encampment on the southern edge of the Cylindrical Sea about two months ago. They had been quite relaxed and had even joked with the soldiers, Franz said. Her father and sister had told the troops that they had come forward with an octospider representative to see if an armed conflict between the two species could be avoided through negotiation. Nakamura had ordered that the entire affair be kept secret and had taken them.

Katie was pacing around the room. "My father is not only alive," she said excitedly, "he is *here*, in New Eden. Have I ever told you, Franz," she said, "that my father is absolutely the smartest human being who ever lived?"

"About a dozen times," Franz said. He laughed. "I can't imagine how anyone could be smarter than you."

Katie waved her hand. "He makes me look like an absolute idiot. He was always such a dear. I could get away with *any*thing." She stopped her pacing and inhaled on her cigarette. Her eyes sparkled as she exhaled the smoke. "Franz," she said. "I *must* see him. I absolutely must."

"That's impossible, Katie," he said. "Nobody is even supposed to know that he's here. I could be fired, or worse, if anyone ever found out that I told you."

"I'm pleading with you, Franz," Katie said, crossing the room and grabbing him by the shoulders. "You know how I hate asking anyone for favors . . . but this is very important to me."

Franz was delighted that for once, Katie was requesting something from *him*. Nevertheless, he told her the truth. "Katie," he said, "you still don't understand. There is an armed guard around the house at all times. The entire basement is bugged with audio and video monitors. There is just no way."

"There's *always* a way," Katie said emphatically, "if something is important enough." She reached inside his shirt and began tweaking his right nipple. "You *do* love me, don't you, Franz?" She kissed him, a full open-mouthed kiss, with her tongue darting teasingly across his. Katie pulled away slightly, continuing to play with his nipple.

"Of course I love you, Katie," Franz said, already very much aroused. "But I'm not crazy."

Katie marched off into her bedroom and returned less than a minute later with two stacks of bills. "I am going to see my father, Franz," she said, throwing the money on the coffee table. "And you are going to help me. You can bribe anyone you want with this money."

Franz was impressed. The money was more than adequate. "And what are you going to do for me?" he said almost jokingly.

"What am I going to do for *you*?" Katie said. "What am I going to do for you?" Katie took him by the hand and led him to the bedroom. "Now, Captain Bauer," she said in an accented voice, "you just take off all your clothes and lie here on your back. You'll see what I am going to do for you."

Katie's apartment had a dressing room adjacent to her bedroom. She walked into the smaller room and closed the door. With a key she unlocked a large decorated box on the top of the counter and pulled out one of the full syringes she had prepared earlier in the day. Katie lifted her dress and tied a tight tourniquet around her upper thigh with a piece of small black tubing. She waited momentarily until she could clearly identify a blood vessel in the mass of bruises on her thigh, and then she deftly inserted the syringe. After pressing all the fluid into her bloodstream, Katie waited a few seconds for the fantastic rush and then removed the tourniquet.

"What am I supposed to do while I'm waiting?"

"Rilke is in my electronic reader, darling," she said, "both in German and English. I'll only be a few more minutes."

Katie was flying. She started humming a dance tune while she threw the syringe away and returned the tourniquet to the box. She took off all her clothes, stopping twice to admire her body in the mirror, and put them in a pile upon the vanity stool. Then she opened a large drawer in the vanity and pulled out a blindfold.

She paraded into the bedroom. Franz's eyes feasted admiringly upon her lithe body. "Look carefully," Katie said, "'cause this is all you're going to see this afternoon."

Katie draped her naked body casually across his and kissed him intermittently while she attached the blindfold. She made certain that the blindfold was snug and then jumped down from the bed. "What happens now?" Franz asked.

"You'll just have to wait and see," Katie said teasingly as she rummaged through a large drawer at the bottom of her dresser. The drawer contained a smorgasbord of sexual paraphernalia, including electronic aids of all kinds, lotions, ropes and other bondage equipment, masks, and assorted models of genitalia. Katie selected a small bottle of lotion, a vial of white powder, and some beads strung along a piece of thin cord.

Still humming and laughing to herself, Katie rejoined Franz on the bed and began to run her fingers over his chest. She kissed him provocatively with her body pressed against his and then sat up. After pouring the lotion on her hands and rubbing them together vigorously, Katie spread his legs, crawled onto his stomach with her back toward Franz's face, and began to apply the lotion to his most sensitive parts.

"Ummm," Franz murmured as the warm lotion began to take effect. "That's wonderful."

Katie dusted his genitalia with the white powder and then mounted him very slowly. Franz was in ecstasy. Katie rocked back and forth in an easy rhythm for a few minutes. When she could tell that Franz was nearing a climax, she halted her motion temporarily and reached under him to insert the beads. She rocked two or three more times and then halted again.

"Don't stop now," Franz shouted.

"Repeat after me," Katie said with a chuckle, moving slowly back and forth one more time. "I promise—"

"Anything," Franz yelled, "just don't stop again."

"I promise," she continued, "that Katie Wakefield will see her father sometime in the next few days."

Franz repeated the promise and Katie rewarded him. When she pulled the cord just after he started his climax, Franz screamed at the top of his lungs like an animal in the forest.

Ellie did not like her two interrogators. They were both dry, humorless individuals who treated her with complete disdain. "This isn't going to work, gentlemen," she said in an exasperated tone at one point during the first day of questioning, "if you insist on asking the same questions over and over. I understood that I was being asked to supply some information about the octospiders. Thus far the questions, which you are now repeating, have all been about my mother and my father."

"Mrs. Turner," the first man said, "the government is trying to gather all possible information about this case. Your mother and father have both been fugitives for many—"

"Look," Ellie interrupted, "I have already told you that I know nothing whatsoever about how, when, or even why either of my parents left New Eden. Nor do I have any knowledge of whether they were helped to escape, in any way, by the octospiders. Now, unless you are prepared to change the line of questioning—"

"It is not you, young lady," the second man said, his eyes flashing, "who decides what are appropriate questions in this inquiry. Perhaps you do not understand the seriousness of your situation. You will be granted freedom from prosecution—on a very serious charge, I might add—*only* if you cooperate totally with us."

"Just what is the charge against me?" Ellie asked. "I'm curious. I have never been a criminal before."

"You can be charged with first-degree treason," the first man said. "Deliberately aiding and abetting the enemy during a period of declared hostilities."

"That's absurd," Ellie replied, frightened nevertheless. "I have no idea what you're talking about."

"Do you deny that during the period of time that you were staying with the aliens you freely gave them information about New Eden that could be useful during a war?"

"Of course I did," Ellie said, laughing nervously. "I told them as much as I could about our colony. And they reciprocated. The octospiders shared all the same information with us."

Both men scribbled furiously on their pads. *How did they get like this?* Ellie wondered. *How can a laughing, curious child be transformed into such a grim and hostile adult?*

"Look, gentlemen," Ellie said when the next question was asked, "this is not going well for me. I would like to declare a recess and organize my thoughts. Maybe I'll even make a few notes before we reconvene. I had envisioned an altogether different process, something much more relaxed."

The two men agreed to the break. Ellie walked down the hallway to where a government sitter was staying with Nikki. "You can go now, Mrs. Adams," Ellie said. "We're taking time off for lunch."

Nikki could read the worried look on Ellie's face. "Are those men being mean to you, Mommy?" she asked.

At length Ellie smiled. "You could say that, Nikki," she said. "You certainly could say that."

Richard completed the last of his walking laps around the basement and headed for the washbasin in the corner of the room. He stopped first at the table for a quick drink of water. Archie remained motionless on the floor behind Richard's mattress. "Good morning," Richard said as he wiped his sweat with a washcloth. "Are you ready for some breakfast?"

"I'm not hungry," the octospider replied in color.

"You have to eat *some*thing," Richard said cheerfully. "I agree with you that the food is terrible, but you can't survive on water alone."

Archie did not move or say anything. For the last several days, ever since the supply of his stored barrican had been exhausted, the octospider had not been very good company. Richard had been unable to engage Archie in their usual stimulating conversation and had become concerned about the octospider's health. Richard put some grain in a bowl, sprinkled water on it, and carried it over to his friend. "Here," he said gently, "try to eat a little."

Archie lifted a pair of tentacles and took the bowl. As he began to eat, a bright orange burst came out of his slit and moved halfway down one of his other tentacles before fading away.

"What was that?" Richard asked.

"An emotional expression," Archie answered, his response accompanied by more irregular color bursts.

Richard smiled. "Okay," he said, "but what kind of emotion?"

After a long pause, Archie's colored strips were more regimented. "I guess you would call it depression," the octospider said.

"Is that what happens when the barrican is gone?" Richard asked.

Archie did not reply. At length Richard returned to the table and prepared himself a big bowl of grain. Then he came back and sat beside Archie on the floor. "You might as well talk about it," Richard said softly. "We have nothing else to do."

From the motion in Archie's lens Richard could tell that the octo was studying him carefully. Richard took several spoonfuls of his breakfast before Archie began to speak.

"In our society," Archie said, "the young males and females who are undergoing sexual maturation are taken away from their everyday lives and placed in a highly appropriate environment with individuals who have been through the process before. They are encouraged to describe what they are feeling and are reassured that the new and complex emotions they are experiencing are completely normal. Now I understand why such a program of intense attention is necessary."

Archie paused for a moment and Richard smiled sympathetically. "These last few days," the octospider continued, "for the first time since I was a very young juvenile, my emotions have not accepted the domination of my mind. During optimizer training we learned how important it was, whenever a decision was to be made, to sift carefully through all the available evidence and remove all prejudice that might be due to personal emotional responses. With the intensity of the feelings I am having presently, it would be quite impossible to relegate them to a low priority."

Richard laughed. "Please don't misunderstand me, Archie—I'm not laughing *at* you—but you just described, in a typical octospider phrase, what most humans feel *all* the time. Very few of us *ever* achieve the control of our 'personal emotional responses' that we would like. This may be the first time that you have ever been able to really understand us, if you know what I mean."

"It's terrible," Archie said. "I am feeling both an acute sense of loss—I miss Dr. Blue and Jamie—and powerful anger toward Nakamura for holding us prisoner. I fear that my outrage will cause me to take some action that is nonoptimal."

"But the emotions you are describing are not usually connected, at least in humans, with sexuality," Richard said. "Does the barrican also act as some kind of tranquilizer, subduing all feelings?"

Archie finished his breakfast before responding. "You and I are very different creatures and, as I have mentioned before, it is dangerous to project from one species to another. I remember our initial discussions about humans at the optimizers' meeting just after you had breached the integrity of your habitat. In the middle of the meeting, the Chief Optimizer stressed that we must not look at your species in *our* terms. We must observe carefully, she said, obtain data, and correlate it consistently, without coloring the data with our own experience.

"I suppose this all amounts to a disclaimer, in some sense, of what I am about to tell you. Nevertheless, it is my personal opinion, based on my observations of humans, that sexual desire is the driving force behind *all* the strong emotions in your species. We octospiders undergo a step discontinuity at sexual maturation. We change from being completely sexless to sexual in a very short period of time. In humans the process is much slower and more subtle. Sexual hormones are present in varying quantities from early in your fetal development. I contend, and have told the Chief Optimizer this, that it is possible that *all* your uncontrollable emotions can be traced to these sexual hormones. A human without *any* sexuality might be capable of the same optimized thought as an octospider."

"What an interesting idea!" Richard said excitedly, standing up and beginning to pace. "So are you suggesting that even such things as a child's unwillingness to share a toy, for example, might be linked in some way to our sexuality?"

"Perhaps," Archie replied. "Maybe Galileo is practicing the possessiveness of his adult sexuality when he refuses to share one of his toys with Kepler. Certainly the human child's devotion to the parent of the opposite sex is a precursor of adult attitudes."

Archie stopped, for Richard had turned his back and had increased his pacing. "I'm sorry," he said, returning a few moments later and again sitting on the floor beside the octospider. "Something occurred to me just now, something I thought about briefly earlier this morning when we were talking about controlling our emotions. Do you remember an earlier conversation in which you dismissed the concept of a personal God as an 'evolutionary aberration' necessary for all developing species as a temporary bridge during transition from the first awareness phase to the Information

Era? Have the recent changes in you altered in any way your attitude about God?"

A broad burst of multicolored strips, which Richard recognized as laughter, spilled over most of the octospider's upper body. "You humans," Archie said, "are absolutely preoccupied with this notion of God. Even those like you, Richard, who profess not to believe, still spend an inordinate amount of time thinking about or discussing the subject. As I explained to you months ago, we octospiders value information foremost, as we were taught by the Precursors. There is no verifiable information available about any God, especially not one who is involved in any way with the daily affairs of the universe—"

"You didn't exactly understand my question," Richard interrupted, "or maybe I didn't phrase it precisely enough. What I want to know is, in your new, more emotional state, can you understand why other intelligent beings might create a personal God as a device to give them comfort and also to explain all those things that they cannot comprehend?"

Archie laughed again with bursts of color. "You're very clever, Richard," the octospider said. "You want me to confirm what *you* think, namely that God also is an emotional concept, born out of a yearning not unlike sexual desire. Therefore God too is derived from sexual hormones. I cannot go that far. I do not have enough information. But I can say, based on the turmoil inside *me* these last few days, that I now understand this word 'yearning' which was meaningless to me before."

Archie seemed like his old self this morning. Richard smiled. He was pleased. Their exchanges had been like this daily before Archie's buffer had become empty of barrican. "It would be great, wouldn't it," Richard said suddenly, "if we could still talk with all our friends back in the Emerald City?"

Archie knew what Richard was suggesting. The two of them had been careful never to mention the quadroids or even to hint that the octospiders had an intelligence-gathering system. They did not want to alert Nakamura and their guards. Now, as Richard watched silently, bands of color streamed around Archie's head. Although the octospider was no longer using the derivative language that had been developed for communication with the humans, Richard was able to understand the gist of the transmission.

After formally greeting the Chief Optimizer and apologizing for the lack of success of their mission, Archie sent two personal messages, a short one to Jamie and a longer one to Dr. Blue. During the transmission to his life partner Dr. Blue, variegated bursts of color broke out of the measured pattern of Archie's message. Richard, who had grown to know his basement companion well in their two months together, was both fascinated and touched by this beautiful display of uninhibited emotion.

When Archie was finished, Richard came over and put a hand on the octospider's back. "Do you feel better now?" he asked.

"In some ways," Archie replied. "But I also feel worse at the same time. I am more aware now than I was before that I may never see Dr. Blue or Jamie again."

"Sometimes I imagine what I would say to Nicole," Richard interrupted, "if I could talk to her on the telephone." He spoke his words very correctly, exaggerating the movements of his mouth. "I miss you very much, Nicole," he said, "and I love you with all my heart."

Richard did not have very vivid dreams. Therefore, external sounds were not likely to be incorporated into an ongoing dream. When he heard what he thought was a shuffling of feet above him in the middle of the night, he awakened quickly.

Archie was sleeping. Richard looked around and realized that the night light in the toilet area was extinguished. Alarmed, he awakened his octospider companion.

"What is it?" Archie asked in color.

"I heard something unusual upstairs," Richard whispered.

There was a sound of the door to the basement stairs opening slowly. Richard heard a soft footstep, then another, on the top of the stairs. He strained his eyes, but Richard could see nothing in the near darkness.

"It's a woman and a policeman," Archie said, his lens picking up the infrared heat of the intruders. "They have stopped for the moment on the third step."

We're going to be killed, Richard thought. A powerful fear swept through him and he drew closer to Archie. He heard the slow closing of the basement door and then the footsteps descending the stairs.

"Where are they now?" he whispered.

"At the bottom," Archie said. "They are coming. I think the woman is—"

"Dad." Richard heard a voice from his past. "Where are you, Dad?"

"Holy shit! It's Katie," Richard said. "Over here," he added, too loud, trying to contain his excitement.

A very small flashlight beam wandered around the wall behind his mattress and eventually landed on his bearded face. A few seconds later Katie tripped over Archie and literally fell into her father's arms.

She kissed and hugged him, tears running down her cheeks. Richard was so startled by the entire event that he was at first unable to respond to any of Katie's questions. "Yes . . . yes, I'm fine," he said eventually. "I can't believe it's you. . . . Katie, oh, Katie. . . . Oh, yes, that gray mass over there, the one you kicked a moment ago, is my friend and fellow prisoner, Archie the octospider."

Several seconds later Richard exchanged a firm handshake in the dark with a man Katie introduced only as her "friend." "We don't have much time," Katie said hurriedly after several minutes of conversation about the family. "We've short-circuited the power systems in this entire residential area, and they should be repaired before too much longer."

"Are we going to escape, then?" Richard asked.

"No," Katie said. "They would certainly catch and kill you. . . . I just wanted to see you. When I heard the rumor that you were being held somewhere in New Eden . . . Oh, Daddy, how I have missed you! I love you so very much."

Richard put his arms around his daughter and held her as she cried. She felt so thin and fragile in his arms. "I love you too, Katie," Richard said. "Here," he added, pulling away slightly, "shine the light on your face. . . . Let me see your beautiful eyes."

"No, Daddy," Katie said, burying herself again in his embrace. "I look old and used. . . . I want you to remember me as I was. I have lived a hard—"

"It's unlikely that they will be keeping you here much longer, Mr. Wakefield," the male voice in the dark interrupted. "Almost everyone in the colony has heard the story of your appearance at the soldiers' camp."

"Are you all right, Daddy?" Katie said after a short silence. "Are they feeding you properly?"

"I'm fine, Katie . . . but what have *you* been doing? Are you happy?"

"I've had another promotion," she said rapidly. "And my new apartment is beautiful. You should see it. . . . And I have a friend who cares about me."

"I'm so glad," Richard said as Franz reminded Katie that they needed to be going. "You were always the smartest of the children. . . . You deserve some happiness."

Katie suddenly began sobbing and lowered her head against her father's chest. "Daddy, oh, Daddy," she said through her tears, "please hold me."

Richard put his arms around his daughter. "What is it, Katie?" he said softly.

"I don't want to lie to you," Katie said. "I work for Nakamura, managing prostitutes. And I'm a drug addict . . . a complete and total drug addict."

Katie cried for a long time. Richard held her tightly and patted her on the back. "But I *do* love *you*, Daddy," Katie said when she finally raised her head. "I always have, and I always will. . . . I'm terribly sorry that I have disappointed you."

"Katie, we must be leaving now," Franz said firmly. "If the power is restored while we are still in the house, we'll be in deep shit."

Katie kissed her father hurriedly on the lips and stroked his beard affectionately with her fingers one final time. "Take care of yourself, Daddy," she said. "And don't give up hope."

The flashlight beam was a thin finger of light preceding the visiting pair as they quickly crossed the room to the bottom of the stairs. "Good-bye, Daddy," Katie said.

"I love you too, Katie," Richard said as he heard the sound of his daughter's feet running up the stairs.

5

The octospider on the table was unconscious. Nicole handed Dr. Blue the small plastic container that the alien physician had requested and watched as the tiny creatures were dumped onto the greenish black fluid that covered the open wound. In less than a minute the fluid was gone and her octospider colleague deftly sewed up the incision using the forward five centimeters of three of her tentacles.

"That's the last one for today," Dr. Blue said in color. "As always, Nicole, we thank you for your help."

The two of them walked together out of the operating area into an adjacent room. Nicole had not yet accustomed herself to the cleaning process. She took a deep breath before removing her protective gown and placing her arms in a large bowl filled with dozens of silverfishlike animals. Nicole fought against her personal revulsion as the slimy things clambered all over her arms and hands.

"I know this part is not pleasant for you," Dr. Blue said, "but we really have no choice now that the forward water supply has been contaminated by the bombing. And we can't take a chance that anything here might be toxic for you."

"Is everything destroyed north of the forest?" Nicole asked while Dr. Blue finished cleaning herself up.

"Almost," the octospider replied. "And it looks as if the human engineers have now finished their modifications to the helicopters. The

Chief Optimizer fears that they will make their first flights over the forest in another week or two."

"And there have been no replies to the messages you have sent?"

"None at all. We know that Nakamura has read them . . . but the humans captured and killed the last messenger near the power plant—despite the fact that our octospider was carrying a white flag."

Nicole sighed. She remembered something Max had said the night before when she had expressed bewilderment that Nakamura was ignoring all the messages. "Of course he is," Max had shouted angrily. "That man understands nothing but force. All those stupid messages say is that the octos want peace and will be forced to defend themselves if the humans don't desist. The threats that follow are meaningless. What is Nakamura to think when his troops and helicopters move around unimpeded, destroying everything in sight? Hasn't the Chief Optimizer learned anything about humans? The octospiders must engage Nakamura's army in some kind of battle."

"That's not their way," Nicole had replied. "They do not involve themselves in skirmishes or limited wars. They only fight when their survival is threatened. The messages have spelled this all out very carefully and have repeatedly urged Nakamura to talk to Richard and Archie."

In the hospital, Dr. Blue was flashing colors at Nicole. She shook her head and returned to the present. "Are you going to wait today for Benjy?" the octospider asked. "Or will you go directly over to the administrative center?"

Nicole checked her watch. "I think I'll go now. It usually takes me a couple of hours to digest all the quadroid data from the day before. So much is happening. Please tell Benjy to tell the others that I'll be home for dinner."

She walked out of the hospital a few minutes later and headed for the administrative center. Even though it was daytime, the streets of the Emerald City were nearly deserted. Nicole passed three octospiders, all hurrying on the other side of the road, and a pair of crab biots, who looked strangely out of place. Dr. Blue had told Nicole that the crab biots had been recruited for Emerald City garbage duty.

The city has changed so much since the decree, Nicole thought. *Most of the older octos are now over in the war domain. And we never saw a single biot here until a month ago, after most of the support creatures had supposedly been moved to another location. Max thinks many of them might have been terminated because of the shortages. Max always thinks the worst of the octospiders.*

Often after work Nicole would accompany Benjy to the transport stop. Her son was also helping the shorthanded staff at the hospital. As Benjy had become more aware of what was occurring in the Emerald City, it had grown increasingly difficult for Nicole to hide the seriousness of their situation.

"Why are our people fighting against the octospiders?" Benjy had asked the previous week. "Don't they know that the octos don't want to hurt anybody?"

"The colonists in New Eden don't understand the octospiders," Nicole had replied. "And they won't let Archie and Uncle Richard explain anything."

"Then they're stupider than I am," Benjy had said gruffly.

Dr. Blue and the other members of the octospider hospital staff who had not been reassigned because of the war were all very impressed with Benjy. In the beginning, when he had volunteered to help, the octospiders had had reservations about what he could do with his limited capabilities. Once a simple task had been explained to him by Nicole, however, and he had repeated it back to her, Benjy never made a mistake. With his strong, youthful body, he was especially helpful performing heavy labor, a valuable attribute now that so many of the larger creatures were no longer around.

While Nicole was walking toward the administrative center, she found herself thinking about both Benjy and Katie. In her mind's eye Nicole glanced back and forth between pictures of the two children. *As parents*, she said to herself, *we often spend too much time focusing on intellectual potential instead of more substantive qualities. What matters most is not how much intellect the child has, but rather what he or she decides to do with it. Benjy has succeeded beyond our wildest imaginings, primarily because of who he is inside. As for Katie, never, in my worst nightmares . . .*

Nicole broke her train of thought as she entered the building. An octospider guard waved at her and she smiled. When she reached her usual viewing room, Nicole was surprised to find the Chief Optimizer waiting for her. "I wanted to take this opportunity," the head octospider said, "both to thank you for the contribution you are making in this difficult period and to reassure you that all your family and friends here in the Emerald City will be cared for as if they were members of our species, no matter what happens in the next few weeks."

The Chief Optimizer started to leave the room. "The situation is deteriorating, then?" Nicole asked.

"Yes," the octospider replied. "As soon as the humans fly over the forest, we will be forced to retaliate."

When the Chief Optimizer was gone, Nicole sat down in front of her console to scan through the quadroid data from the day before. She was not allowed access to all the information from New Eden, but she was permitted to call up the images of the daily activities of all the members of her family. Nicole could see each day what was happening in the basement with Richard and Archie, how Ellie and Nikki were adjusting to being back in New Eden, and what was occurring in Katie's world.

As time passed, Nicole watched Katie less and less. It was simply too painful for her. Observing her granddaughter Nikki, by contrast, was pure delight. Nicole especially enjoyed watching Nikki on those afternoons when the little girl went to the Beauvois playground to play with the other children of the village. Although the images were soundless, Nicole could almost hear the squeals of mirthful delight as Nikki and the others tumbled over one another in pursuit of an elusive soccer ball.

Nicole's heart ached for Ellie. Despite her daughter's heroic efforts, Ellie was not having any luck resuscitating her marriage. Robert had remained withdrawn in his workaholic pattern, using the demands of the hospital to keep him from facing all emotions, including his own. He was a dutiful but restrained parent with Nikki, only rarely showing any true delight. He did not make love with Ellie and would not talk about it, except to say that he was "not ready" when she tearfully brought up the subject three weeks after they had been reunited.

She always saved Richard for last. Although Nicole never really shook the premonition that she would not touch her husband again, she did not let that feeling detract from the daily pleasure she experienced sharing his life in the basement in New Eden. She especially enjoyed his conversations with Archie, even though it was often difficult for her to read his lips. Their discussions reminded Nicole of earlier days, after her escape from prison and New Eden, when Richard and she would talk and talk about everything. Watching Richard always left Nicole feeling uplifted and much more able to deal with her own loneliness.

The reunion between Richard and Katie caught her by surprise. She had not been following Katie's life closely enough to know that her daughter and Franz had successfully designed a plan to secure a short visit with Richard. Because the quadroid images covered the infrared portion of the spectrum as well as the visible, Nicole actually had a better view of the reunion than the participants. She was deeply moved by Katie's action, and even more by Katie's sudden admission (which Nicole watched over and over, in super slow motion, to make certain she was properly reading Katie's lips) that she was a drug addict. *The first step to overcoming a problem*, Nicole remembered from somewhere, *is to admit to someone you love that the problem exists*.

There were happy tears in Nicole's eyes as she rode the nearly empty transport back to the human enclave in the Emerald City. Despite the fact that the bizarre world around her was deteriorating into chaos, for once Nicole was optimistic about Katie.

Patrick and the twins were outside when Nicole stepped off the transport at the end of the street. As she drew closer, she could tell that Patrick was trying to adjudicate one of the boys' innumerable disputes.

"He *always* cheats," Kepler was saying. "I told him that I wasn't going to play with him anymore and he hit me."

"That's a lie," Galileo replied. "I hit him because he made a face at me. Kepler's a sore loser. If he can't win, he thinks it's all right to quit."

Patrick separated the two boys and sent them, as punishment, to sit against opposite corners of the house. He then greeted his mother with a kiss and a hug.

"I have some big news," Nicole said, smiling at her son. "Richard had a surprise visitor today—Katie!"

Of course Patrick wanted to know all the details of the visit between his sister and Richard. Nicole summarized what she had seen, admitting that she was encouraged by Katie's confession of her drug habit. "Don't read too much into her action," Patrick admonished. "The Katie I knew would rather die than be without her precious kokomo."

Patrick had turned around and was almost ready to tell the twins that they could resume playing, when a pair of rockets raced skyward, bursting into bright red balls of light just underneath the dome. Moments later the city was plunged into darkness. "Come on, boys," Patrick said. "We must go inside."

"That's the third time today," Patrick commented to Nicole as they followed Kepler and Galileo into the house.

"Dr. Blue said they extinguish the city lights the moment any helicopter rises to within twenty meters of the top of the forest canopy. Under no circumstances do the octospiders want to risk showing the location of the Emerald City."

"Do you think Archie and Uncle Richard will ever have a chance to meet with Nakamura?" Patrick asked.

"I doubt it," Nicole replied. "If he were going to see them, it should have happened before now."

Eponine and Nai greeted Nicole and embraced her. The three women talked briefly about the blackout. Eponine was holding little Marius on her hip. The boy was a fat, happy baby with a major drooling habit. She wiped off his face with a cloth so that Nicole could kiss him.

"Ah-ha," she heard Max say behind her, "the Queen of Frowns is now kissing the Prince of Drools."

Nicole turned around and gave Max a hug. "What's this Queen of Frowns bit?" she said lightly.

Max handed her a glass containing some clear liquid. "Here, Nicole, I want you to drink this. It's not tequila, but it's the best substitute the octospiders could make from my description. We're all hoping that maybe you'll find your sense of humor before you finish the drink."

"Come on, Max," Eponine said. "Don't make Nicole think that we're all somehow involved. This was *your* idea, after all. The only thing that Patrick, Nai, and I did was agree with you that she had been very serious lately."

"Now, my lady," Max said to Nicole, raising his glass and clinking it against hers, "I want to propose a toast. To all of us, who have absolutely no control over our future. May we love each other and share laughter until the end, whenever and however it might come."

Nicole had not seen Max drunk since before she went to prison. At his insistence she took a small drink. Her throat and esophagus burned and her eyes watered. The drink contained a lot of alcohol.

"Before dinner tonight," Max now said, opening his arms in a dramatic flourish, "we are going to tell farm jokes. This will provide us some much-needed comic relief. You, Nicole des Jardins Wakefield, as our leader by example if not by election, will have the floor first."

Nicole managed a smile. "But I don't know any farm jokes," she protested.

Eponine was relieved to see that Nicole was not offended by Max's behavior. "That's all right, Nicole," Eponine said, "none of us do. Max knows enough farm jokes for all of us."

"Once upon a time," Max began a few moments later, "there was a farmer from Oklahoma who had a fat wife named Whistle. She was called Whistle because, at the climax of her lovemaking, she would close her eyes, screw up her mouth, and make a long whistling sound."

Max belched. The twins giggled. Nicole worried that maybe it was not appropriate for the children to hear Max's story, but Nai was sitting behind her boys, laughing with them. *Relax*, Nicole told herself. *You really have become the Queen of Frowns.*

"Now, one night," Max continued, "this farmer and Whistle had a big brouhaha—that's a fight, to you, boys—and she went to bed early and fuming. The farmer sat by himself at the table, drinking some fine tequila. As the evening progressed, he became sorry that he had been such an ornery son of a bitch and began to apologize in a loud voice.

"Meanwhile, ole Whistle, who was now angry all over again because the farmer had awakened her, knew that when he finished drinking, her husband was going to enter the bedroom and try to seal his apology with some wild lovemaking. While the farmer emptied the bottle of tequila, Whistle slipped out of the house, went over to the pigpen, and carried the youngest and smallest of the sows back into their bedroom.

"When the drunken farmer staggered into the dark bedroom later that night, singing one of his favorite hymns, Whistle was watching from the corner and the sow was in the bed. The farmer took all his clothes off and jumped under the sheets. He grabbed the sow by the ears and kissed her on the lips. The sow squealed and the farmer pulled back. 'Whistle, my love,' he said, 'did you forget to brush your teeth tonight?'

"His wife bolted from the corner and began beating the farmer on the head with a broom."

Everyone was laughing. Max was so amused by his own joke that he could not sit upright. When he finished laughing, he took another drink of the octospider alcohol.

"My brother Clyde," Max said, "knew more farm jokes than anyone I ever met. He courted Winona with them, or so he claimed. Clyde used to tell me that a 'laughing woman already has one hand on her panties.' When we would go duck hunting with the guys, we'd never shoot a single goddamn duck. Clyde would start telling stories, and we'd be laughing and drinking. After a while we'd forget why we got up at five ayem to go and sit in the cold."

Max stopped talking and there was a momentary quiet in the room. "Damn," he said after the brief silence. "For a while there I was imagining I was back in Arkansas." He stood up. "I don't even know now which way Arkansas is from here, or how many billions of kilometers away it is." Max shook his head. "Sometimes, when I'm dreaming and it's real lifelike, I think the dream is reality. I believe I'm back in Arkansas. Then when I wake up I am lost, and I think for a few seconds that this life we're living here in the Emerald City is the dream."

"The same thing happens to me," Nai said. "Two nights ago I dreamed I was doing my morning meditation in the *hawng pra* in my family home in Lamphun. As I was reciting my mantra, Patrick awakened me. He told me that I was talking in my sleep. For a few seconds, however, I didn't know who he was. It was frightening."

"All right," Max said after a protracted silence. He turned to Nicole. "I guess we're ready for the news of the day. What do you have to tell us?"

"The quadroid videos today were very peculiar," a smiling Nicole replied. "For the first few minutes, I was certain I had entered the wrong data base. Image after image showed a pig, or a chicken, or a drunken Oklahoma farm boy trying to court a sweet young thing. In the last series of pictures a farmer was trying to drink tequila, eat fried chicken, and make love with his sweetheart all at the same time—which reminds me, that chicken sure looked good. Is anyone else hungry?"

6

"I think they were somewhat reassured by what the Chief Optimizer told me," Nicole said to Dr. Blue. "Max, of course, had his doubts. He doesn't believe taking care of us will be a very high priority if the situation really becomes desperate."

"That's very unlikely," the octospider replied. "Any further escalation of hostilities will be met by a massive retaliation. Many octospiders have been working on our war plans for almost two months."

"Have I understood correctly, then," Nicole asked, "that every individual member of your species who has been involved in the design and prosecution of this war will be terminated when it is over?"

"Yes," Dr. Blue replied, "although they will not all die immediately. They will be notified that they have been placed on the termination list. The new Chief Optimizer will define the exact schedule for the terminations, depending on the needs of the colony and the pace of replenishment."

Nicole and her octospider colleague were sharing lunch at the hospital. They had spent the morning trying unsuccessfully to save the lives of two of the six-armed utility creatures who had been blasted by human troops while they were working in one of the few remaining grain fields on the north side of the forest.

During their lunch, a centipede biot trundled by in the hall beside them. Dr. Blue noticed that Nicole followed the biot with her eyes for several seconds. "When we first came inside Rama," the octospider said, "before we had developed our full cadre of support animals, we used the available biots for routine tasks, like maintenance. Now we need their help again."

"But how do you give them instructions?" Nicole asked. "We were never able to communicate with them at all."

"Their programming is done in firmware, at the time of their manufacture. What we did in the early days, using a kind of keyboard analogous to the one you had in your lair, was ask the Ramans to alter the programming for our specific uses. That's what all the biots are here for . . . to be turned into useful servants by the passengers on board."

Well, Richard, Nicole thought, *that's at least one concept we missed altogether. In fact, I don't think the idea ever even occurred to us.*

"We wanted our settlement here in Rama to be indistinguishable from any of our other colonies," Dr. Blue continued, "so as soon as we no longer needed the biots, we requested that they be removed from our domain in Rama."

"And since then you have had no direct contact at all with the Ramans?"

"Not much," Dr. Blue replied. "But we have maintained the capability to communicate with the high-technology factories underneath the surface, primarily so that we can request the manufacture of certain raw materials that we do not have in our warehouses."

A door opened from the corridor and an octospider entered. It talked rapidly with Dr. Blue in their language, using very narrow color bands. Nicole recognized the words "permission" and "this afternoon," but very little else.

After the visitor had departed, Dr. Blue told Nicole that she had a surprise for her. "Today one of our queens is going to have her egg rush. Her attendants are estimating it will take place in half a tert. The Chief Optimizer has approved my request for you to observe. To my knowledge, you are the only alien—except for the Precursors, of course—who has ever had the privilege of witnessing an egg rush. I think you will find it very interesting."

During the transport ride to the Queen's Domain, which was in a part of the Emerald City that Nicole had never visited before, Dr. Blue reminded Nicole of some of the more unusual aspects of octospider reproduction. "In normal times, each of the three queens in our colony is fertilized once every three to five years, and only a small fraction of the fertilized eggs is permitted to grow to maturity. Because of the war preparations, however, the Chief Optimizer recently declared a Replenishment Event. All three of our queens are now producing a full set of eggs. They have been fertilized by the new warrior males, those octospiders selected for the war effort who have recently passed through sexual transition. This activity is very important, for it ensures, at least symbolically, that each of these octospiders will have continued genetic involvement in the colony. Remember, they know, as soon as they are designated as warriors, that their termination time is not too far away."

Whenever I think that we have a lot in common with the octospiders, Nicole was thinking, *I see something so bizarre that I am reminded how very different we are. But, as Richard would say, how could it be otherwise? They are the product of a process totally alien to us.*

"Don't be alarmed at the size of the queen," Dr. Blue continued, "and please, under no circumstances should you express anything but delight at what you see. When I first suggested that you attend the egg rush, one of the Chief Optimizer's staff members objected, saying that there was no way you could fully appreciate what you were seeing. Some of the other staff members were worried that you might display discomfort or even disgust and thereby detract from the experience for the other octospiders in attendance."

Nicole assured Dr. Blue that she would do nothing untoward during the ceremony. She was indeed flattered that she had been included in the activity, and was feeling considerable excitement when the transport deposited them outside the thick walls of the Queen's Domain.

The building Nicole entered with Dr. Blue was dome-shaped and built of blocks of white rock. It was about ten meters tall inside and covered a ground area of roughly thirty-five hundred square meters. There was a large map just inside the door in the atrium area, and a written message in color identifying where the egg rush would take place. Nicole followed Dr. Blue and several other octospiders up a pair of ramps and then down a long corridor. At the end of the hallway they turned right and entered a balcony area that overlooked a rectangular floor fifteen meters long and five or six meters wide.

Dr. Blue took Nicole to the front row, where a railing a meter high protected the audience from falling onto the floor four meters below. Behind them the five elevated rows filled up quickly. Across the way, there was another, similar viewing area that would hold about sixty octospiders.

Looking down, Nicole could see a pool of water resembling a canal that ran the length of the floor and then disappeared under an arch on the right. There were narrow walkways on either side of the pool. On the opposite side, however, the walkway expanded into a broad platform three meters or so before it encountered the rock wall that formed the entire left side of the large room. This wall, painted with many different colors and designs, contained a hundred or so protruding silver rods or spikes, each standing out a meter from where it was embedded in the wall. Nicole noticed immediately the similarity between the wall and the vertical corridor, shaped like a barrel, that she and her friends had descended inside the octospider lair beneath New York.

Less than ten minutes after the two balcony areas were filled, the

Chief Optimizer shuffled through a doorway on the lower level, stood on the walkway beside the pool, and made a short speech. Dr. Blue helped Nicole translate as the Chief Optimizer reminded the onlookers that although the exact timing of an egg rush was never known, it was likely the queen would be ready to enter the room in several more fengs. After making a few comments about the critical importance of replenishment in the continuity of the colony, the Chief Optimizer made her exit.

After what seemed like a long wait, the great doors at the left end of the far walkway opened and the massive queen lumbered in. She was huge, at least six meters tall, with a gigantic swollen body above her eight long tentacles. She stopped on the platform and said something to the audience. Bright colors spilled in profusion all over her body, creating a vivid spectacle. Nicole could not understand what the queen was saying because she could not follow the exact sequence of colors pouring out of the slit.

The queen slowly turned toward the wall, extended her tentacles, and began the laborious process of pulling herself up onto the spikes. Throughout the climb, disordered bursts of color decorated her body. Nicole assumed these were emotional expressions of some kind, perhaps pain and fatigue. Looking around her, Nicole noticed that the octospiders in the audience were all silent, their heads dark and devoid of color.

When the queen had finally positioned herself in the center of the wall, she wrapped all eight tentacles around the spikes and exposed her cream-colored underbelly. While she had been working in the hospital, Nicole had become quite familiar with octospider anatomy, but she had never imagined that the soft tissue underneath their bellies could be distended so much. As Nicole watched, the queen began rocking slightly, moving forward and backward, gently bouncing off the rock wall with each motion. The emotional color display continued. The colors reached their peak intensity when a geyser of greenish black fluid spewed forth from the queen's underside, followed immediately by an immense outpouring of white objects of different sizes contained in a thick, viscous fluid.

Nicole was stupefied. Below her, a dozen or so octospiders on either side of the pool were hurriedly brushing into the water the eggs and fluid that had landed on the walkways. Another eight octos were pouring the unknown contents of huge containers into the pool. The water was now teeming with octospider blood, eggs, and the high-viscosity fluid that was ejected along with the eggs. In less than a minute the entire slurry in the pool moved under the arch to the right.

The queen had not yet changed position. Once the pool below them was clear running water again, all lenses turned to watch the queen. Nicole was staggered by how much the octospider had already shrunk. She estimated that the queen must have lost half her body weight in the fraction of a second it took the egg mass and accompanying fluids to pour forth from her body. The queen was bleeding still, and two normal-sized octospiders had climbed up the wall to minister to her. At this point Dr. Blue tapped Nicole on the shoulder, indicating it was time to leave.

Sitting by herself in one of the small rooms in the octospider hospital, Nicole played the egg rush scene over and over in her mind. She had not expected that the event would affect her so emotionally. Nicole had only half watched while Dr. Blue explained to her, after they had returned to the hospital, that the containers emptied into the slurry were full of tiny animals that would seek out and kill specific embryos. In that way the octospiders controlled, he said, the exact composition of the next genera-tion, including the number of queens, repletes, midget morphs, and all the other variations.

The mother in Nicole was struggling to understand what it would feel like to be an octospider queen during an egg rush. In some undefinable way, Nicole felt deeply connected to that mammoth creature that had crawled up onto the spikes. During the instant of the egg rush, Nicole's loins had contracted, and she had recalled both the pain and the exhilara-tion of her own six births. *What is there about the birth process,* she wondered briefly, *that unites all creatures who have ever experienced it?*

Nicole was overwhelmed by a desire to communicate with the queen octospider, to know what that other intelligent mother had been thinking and feeling just prior to and during the egg rush. Had the queen, amid the pain and wonder of the moment, felt an epiphanic serenity, a vision of her own offspring and their offspring continuing into the unforeseen future, the miraculous cycle of life? Had there been a deep and ineffable peace in the seconds just after the rush, a peace unlike any the creature had ever known at any time other than immediately after birth?

Nicole knew that the imaginary conversation she was having with the queen could never take place. Again she closed her eyes, attempting to reconstruct the exact bursts of color she had seen on the queen's body immediately before and after the event. Had those surges of color told the other octospiders what the queen was feeling? Were they somehow able, Nicole wondered, with their rich language of color, to communicate complex feelings like ecstasy better than humans, with their limited language of words?

There were no answers. Nicole realized that there were tasks waiting for her outside the room, in the octospider hospital, but she was not ready for her solitude to end. She did not want the strong emotions she was feeling to be diminished by the demands of everyday life.

Nicole had also begun to experience a profound loneliness. She did not at first connect her loneliness directly to the egg rush. Nicole was, however, quite aware that she was having a strong desire to talk to a close friend, preferably Richard. She wanted to share with someone what she had seen and felt in the Queen's Domain. In her isolation Nicole suddenly remembered a few lines from a relevant poem by Benita Garcia. She opened her portable computer and, after a short search, found the entire poem.

> *In moments of deep doubt or intense pain,*
> *When I am overpowered by my life,*
> *I search around me everywhere I can*
> *For kindred souls who know what I know not,*
> *For those who have the strength to mitigate*
> *What makes me tremble, weep, and often brood.*
> *They tell me that I cannot live my way*
> *Where all my feelings rule my conscious mind.*
> *I must control myself before the act,*
> *Or else accept what I have long endured,*
> *The brutal days of feeling lost and blind.*
>
> *There have been times, not many but a few,*
> *When someone has possessed the soothing balm,*
> *Providing surcease for my angst or pain.*
> *But age has taught me now one simple rule.*
> *Inside myself I must the screams contain,*
> *Whatever devils must be wrestled there,*
> *The lessons learned will not be lost again.*
> *We walk alone upon our final trip.*
> *No hand can help us on that day of death.*
> *It's best we learn, while time is still our friend,*
> *To trust ourselves, and save our precious breath.*

Nicole read the words several times. Then, realizing that she was completely exhausted, she put her head down on the only table in the room and fell asleep.

Dr. Blue tapped gently on Nicole's shoulder with one of her tentacles. Nicole stirred and opened her eyes. "You've been asleep for almost two hours," the octospider said. "They have been expecting you over at the administrative center."

"What's going on?" Nicole asked, rubbing her eyes. "Why is anyone waiting for me?"

"Nakamura has made a major speech in New Eden. The Chief Optimizer wants to discuss it with you."

Nicole jumped up quickly and then reached out to touch the desk. In a few seconds her dizziness was gone. "Thank you again, Dr. Blue, for everything," she said. "I'll be on my way in another minute."

7

"I really don't think Nikki should be allowed to watch the speech," Robert said. "It will certainly scare her."

"What Nakamura says will affect her life as much as it will ours," Ellie replied. "If she wants to watch, I think we should let her. After all, Robert, she has *lived* with the octospiders."

"But she can't possibly understand what any of this really means," Robert argued. "She's not even four years old yet."

The issue remained unresolved until a few minutes before the New Eden dictator was scheduled to appear on television. At that time Nikki approached her mother in the living room. "I'm not going to watch," the little girl said with astonishing insight, "because I don't want you and Daddy to fight."

One of the rooms in Nakamura's palace had been converted into a television studio. It was from this studio that the tyrant usually addressed the citizens of New Eden. His last speech had been three months earlier, when he had announced that troops were going to be deployed in the Southern Hemicylinder to confront the "alien menace." Although the government-controlled newspapers and television had regularly been featuring news items from the front, many of them fabricating the "intense resistance" being offered by the octospiders, this would be Nakamura's first public comment on the progress and direction of the war in the south.

For the address, Nakamura had ordered his tailors to make him a new shogun's outfit, complete with ornamented sword and dagger. He was appearing in Japanese martial dress, he told his aides, to stress his role as the "lead warrior and protector" of the colonists. On the day of the broadcast Nakamura's attendants helped him put on a pair of heavy, constraining girdles so that he would project the "powerful and menacing" look of the warrior.

Mr. Nakamura spoke standing up, staring directly at the camera. His scowl never changed during his entire speech.

"We have all sacrificed in recent months," he began, "to support our valiant soldiers doing battle south of the Cylindrical Sea with a heinous and ruthless alien enemy. Our intelligence now informs us that these octospiders, who were described to you in detail by Dr. Robert Turner after his brave escape, are planning a major attack against New Eden in the very near future. At this critical moment in our history, we must redouble our resolve and stand united against the alien aggressor.

"Our generals at the front have recommended that we penetrate beyond the barrier forest protecting most of the octospider domain and interdict their supplies and war materiel before they can launch their attack. Our engineers, working night and day for the survival of the colony, have made modifications to our helicopter fleet that will permit this interdiction to take place. We will strike in the near future. We will convince the aliens that they cannot attack us with impunity.

"Meanwhile, our warriors have finished securing the entire area of Rama between the Cylindrical Sea and the barrier forest. During the fierce battles, we have destroyed many hundreds of the enemy, as well as water and power facilities. Our casualties have been modest, primarily because of our superb battle plans and the heroism of our troops. But we must not become overconfident. On the contrary, we have every reason to believe that we have not yet even engaged the elite Death Corps that Dr. Turner heard mentioned while he was being held captive. It is this Death Corps, we are certain, that will be in the alien vanguard if we do not move quickly to preclude an attack on New Eden. Remember, time is our enemy. We must strike now and totally demolish their war-making capability.

"There is one other brief item I would like to report tonight. Recently the traitor Richard Wakefield and an octospider companion surrendered to our troops in the south. They say that they are representing the alien military command and have come forward to talk about peace. I suspect a trick here, a Trojan horse of some kind, but it is my duty as your leader to conduct a hearing into this matter in the next few days. Rest assured that I will not negotiate away our security. I will report the outcome of this hearing very soon after it is completed."

"But Robert," Ellie said, "you know that much of what he is saying is a *lie*. There is no Death Corps, and the octospiders have not offered any resistance. How can you say nothing? How can you let him attribute statements to you that you never made?"

"It's all politics, Ellie," Robert replied. "Everybody knows that. Nobody really believes—"

"But that's even worse. Don't you see what is happening?"

Robert started to leave the house. "Where are you going now?" Ellie asked.

"Back to the hospital," Robert replied. "I have rounds to make."

Ellie couldn't believe it. She stood there for a few seconds, staring at her husband. Then she erupted. "*That's* your response," she shouted. "Business as usual. A lunatic announces a plan that will most likely result in all of us being killed, and for you it's business as usual. . . . Robert, who are you? Don't you care about anything?"

Robert moved toward her angrily. "Don't start again with that 'holier than thou' attitude," he said. "You are not always right, Ellie, and you do not know for certain that we'll all be killed. Maybe Nakamura's plan will work."

"You're kidding yourself, Robert. You turn the other way and tell yourself that as long as your little world is not affected, maybe it's okay. You're wrong, Robert. Dead wrong. And if you won't do anything about it, then I *will*."

"And what will you do?" Robert said, his voice rising. "Tell the world that your husband is a *liar*? Try to convince everyone that those slimy octospiders are peaceful? No one will believe you, Ellie. And I'll tell you one more thing: The minute you open your mouth, you'll be arrested and tried for treason. They'll kill you, Ellie, just like they're going to kill your father. Is that what you want? Never to see your daughter again?"

Ellie recognized the mixture of pain and anger in Robert's eyes. *I don't know him,* flashed through her mind, followed by *How can this be the same man who has spent thousands of hours caring for dying patients? It doesn't make any sense.*

Ellie chose not to say anything more. "I'm going now," Robert said at length. "I'll be home around midnight."

She walked to the back of the house and opened Nikki's door. Luckily the girl had slept through the argument. Ellie was deeply depressed when she returned to the living room. She wished more than ever that she had stayed in Emerald City. But she hadn't, so what was she going to do now? *It would be so easy if I didn't have Nikki to think about,* Ellie said to herself. She shook her head slowly, back and forth, and finally allowed herself to shed the tears she had been restraining.

"So how do I look?" Katie said, pirouetting in front of Franz.

"Beautiful, ravishing," he replied. "Better than I have ever seen you look."

She was wearing a simple black dress, custom-fitted to her thin body. The dress had a defining white stripe running down both sides. It was cut low in the front, highlighting her necklace of diamonds and gold, but was not so low that it would be considered improper.

Katie glanced at her watch. "Good," she said. "For once I'm early." She crossed the room to the table and lit a cigarette.

Franz's uniform was newly pressed and his shoes perfectly shined. "Then I guess we have time," he said, following Katie to the couch, "for my surprise." He handed her a small velvet box.

"What's this?" Katie asked.

"Open it," Franz said.

Inside was a diamond ring, a solitaire. "Katie," Franz said awkwardly, "will you marry me?"

Katie glanced at Franz and then looked away. She inhaled slowly on her cigarette and blew the smoke into the air above her. "I'm flattered, Franz," she said, standing up and kissing him on the cheek, "I really am . . . but it just wouldn't work." She closed the box and handed him back the ring.

"Why not?" Franz asked. "Don't you love me?"

"Yes, I do . . . I guess . . . if I'm capable of such an emotion. But Franz, we've been through this before. I'm just not the kind of woman you should marry."

"Why can't you let *me* decide that, Katie?" Franz said. "How do you know what 'kind of woman' I need?"

"Look, Franz," Katie said, showing some agitation, "I'd rather not talk about this now. As I said, I'm very flattered . . . but I'm already nervous about this hearing for my father and you know I don't deal well with too much shit at once."

"You'll always have some reason for not wanting to talk about it," Franz said angrily. "If you love me, I think I deserve more of an explanation. And now."

Katie's eyes flashed. "You want an explanation *now*, Captain Bauer? All right, I'll give you one. Follow me, if you please." Katie led him into her dressing room. "Now stand there, Franz, and watch very closely."

Katie reached into her dresser. She pulled out a syringe and a piece of black tubing. She placed her right leg on the vanity stool and hiked her dress up above the bruises on her thigh. Franz instinctively turned his head away.

"No," Katie said, reaching out with one hand and turning his head back to face her. "You cannot look away, Franz. You must see me as I am."

She pulled down her panty hose and tied the tube in place. Katie glanced up to make certain Franz was still watching. There was pain in her eyes. "Don't you see, Franz?" she said. "I cannot marry you because I'm already married . . . to this magic drug that never disappoints me. Don't you understand? There's no way that you could ever compete with kokomo."

Katie plunged the syringe into a vein and waited several seconds for the rush. "You might be fine for a few weeks, or even months," Katie said now, speaking more rapidly, "but sooner or later you'd come up short. And I would replace you in my heart with old reliable again."

She wiped off the two drops of blood with a tissue and placed the syringe in the sink. Franz looked distraught. "Cheer up," Katie said, patting him lightly on the cheek. "You haven't lost your bed partner. I'll still be here for whatever kinky things we can dream up together."

Franz turned away and placed the velvet box back in one of the pockets of his uniform. Katie walked over to the table and took one final drag from the cigarette that had been left burning in the ashtray. "Now, Captain Bauer," Katie said, "we have a hearing to attend."

The hearing was held in the ballroom on the main floor of Nakamura's palace. About sixty chairs had been set up in four rows along the walls for "special guests." Nakamura himself, wearing the same Japanese costume in which he had appeared on television two days earlier, sat in a large, embroidered chair above a raised platform at one end of the room. Two bodyguards, also in samurai dress, were beside him. The ballroom was completely decorated in a sixteenth century Japanese motif, adding to the image Nakamura was trying to create of himself as the all-powerful shogun of New Eden.

Richard and Archie, who had only been told the hearing was going to occur four hours before they left the basement, were brought in by three policemen and instructed to sit on small pillows on the floor twenty meters in front of Nakamura. Katie noticed that her father looked tired and very old. She resisted an impulse to run out and talk to him.

A functionary announced that the hearing was now under way and reminded all the spectators that they were to say nothing and interfere in no way with the proceedings. As soon as the announcement was completed, Nakamura stood up and swaggered down the two broad steps connecting his chair to the raised platform.

"This hearing has been convened by the New Eden government," he said gruffly, walking back and forth, "to determine if the alien enemy representative is prepared, on behalf of his species, to accept the unconditional surrender that we demand as a necessary prerequisite for ceasing the hostilities between us. If ex-citizen Wakefield, who is able to communicate with the alien, has been able to convince the alien of the wisdom of accepting our demands, including relinquishing all weapons of war and preparing for our occupation and administration of all alien lands, then we are prepared to be merciful. As a reward for his services in ending this terrible conflict, we would be willing to commute Mr. Wakefield's execution sentence to life imprisonment.

"If, however"—Nakamura now raised his voice—"this convicted traitor and his alien accomplice surrendered to our victorious troops as part of some treacherous plot to undermine our collective will to punish the aliens for their aggressive attacks against us, then we will use these two as examples to send an unambiguous message to our enemy. We want the alien leaders to know that the citizens of New Eden stand steadfast against their expansionist aims."

Up until this moment Nakamura had been addressing the entire audience. Now he turned to face the two prisoners isolated in the middle of the ballroom floor. "Mr. Wakefield," he said, "does the alien beside you have the authority to speak for his species?"

Richard stood up. "To the best of my knowledge, yes," he answered.

"And is the alien then prepared to ratify the document of unconditional surrender that you have been shown?"

"We only received the document a few hours ago and have not yet had time to talk about all its contents. I have explained the most important parts to Archie, but I don't yet know."

"They are stalling," Nakamura thundered, addressing the audience and waving a piece of paper in the air. "This single sheet contains all the terms of the surrender." He turned again to face Richard and Archie. "The question requires only a simple answer," Nakamura said. "Is it yes or no?"

Color bands rolled around Archie's head and there was a murmur in the audience. Richard watched Archie, whispered a question to his octospider colleague, and then interpreted Archie's response. He looked at Nakamura. "The octospider wants to know," Richard said, "exactly what happens if the document is ratified. What are the events that take place then, and in what order? None of this is spelled out in the agreement."

Nakamura paused briefly. "First, all the alien soldiers must come forward with their weapons and surrender to our troops now in the south. Second, the alien government, or whatever is its equivalent, must turn over to us a complete inventory of everything that exists in their domain. Third, they must announce to all members of their species that we are going to occupy their colony and that all aliens are to cooperate in every way with our soldiers and citizens."

Richard and Archie had another brief conversation. "What will happen to all the octospiders and the other animals who support this society?" Richard asked.

"They will be permitted to resume their normal lives, with some constraints, of course. Our laws and our citizens will be put in place as the acting government of the occupied lands."

"And will you, then," Richard said, "write an amendment or an appendix to this surrender document, guaranteeing the lives and safety of the octospiders, as well as the other animals, providing they do not violate any of the laws promulgated in the occupied territory?"

Nakamura's eyes narrowed. "Except for those individual aliens who are found to have been responsible for the aggressive war that has been launched against us, I will personally guarantee the safety of those octospiders who obey the laws of occupation. But these are details. They do not need to be written in the surrender document."

This time Richard and Archie engaged in a long discussion. From the side of the room, Katie watched her father's face closely. She thought in the beginning that he was disagreeing with the octospider, but later in the conversation Richard seemed subdued, almost resigned. It looked as if her father were memorizing something.

The long pause in the proceedings was irritating Nakamura. The special guests were starting to whisper among themselves. Finally Nakamura spoke again. "All right," he said. "That's enough time. What is your answer?"

Colors were still streaking around Archie's head. At length, the patterns stopped and Richard took a step forward toward Nakamura. Richard hesitated a moment before speaking.

"The octospiders want peace," he said slowly, "and would like to find a way to end this conflict. If they were not a moral species, they might agree to ratify this surrender document just to buy some time. But the octospiders are not like that. My alien friend, whose name is Archie, would not make an agreement for his species unless he was certain both that the treaty was proper for his colony and that his fellow octospiders would honor it."

Richard paused. "We do not need a speech," Nakamura said impatiently, "just answer the question."

"The octospiders," Richard said in a louder voice, "sent Archie and me to negotiate an honorable peace, *not* to surrender unconditionally. If New Eden is not willing to negotiate and to make an agreement that respects the integrity of the octospider domain, then they have no choice. *Please,*" Richard now shouted, looking back and forth at the guests on both sides of the room, "understand that you cannot win if the octospiders *really* fight. So far they have put up no resistance at all. You must convince your leaders to enter into *balanced* discussions—"

"*Seize the prisoners,*" Nakamura ordered.

"—or you will all perish. The octospiders are much more advanced than we are. Believe me. I know. I have been living with them for more than—"

One of the policemen struck Richard on the back of the head and he fell to the floor, bleeding. Katie jumped up, but Franz restrained her with both arms. Richard was holding the side of his head as Archie and he were ushered out of the room.

                              *   *   *

Richard and Archie were in a small jail cell at the police station in Hakone, not far from Nakamura's palace. "Is your head all right?" Archie asked in color.

"I think so," Richard answered, "although it is still swelling."

"They'll kill us now, won't they?" Archie asked.

"Probably," Richard said grimly.

"Thanks for trying," Archie said after a short silence.

Richard shrugged. "I didn't do much good. Anyway, it's you who should be thanked. If you hadn't volunteered, you would still be safe and sound in the Emerald City."

Richard walked over to the washbasin in the corner to clean the cloth he was holding against his head wound. "Didn't you tell me that most humans believe in life after death?" Archie asked after Richard had rejoined him in the front of the cell.

"Yes," Richard replied. "Some people believe we're reincarnated and return to live again, as another human or even as some other animal. Many others believe that if a good life has been lived, there is a reward, an eternal life in a beautiful, stressless place called heaven."

"And you, Richard," Archie's colors interrupted. "What do you personally believe?"

Richard smiled and thought for several seconds before answering. "I've always believed that whatever there was in us that was unique and defined our special, individual personality disappeared at the moment of death. Oh, sure, our chemicals may be recycled into other living creatures, but there is no real continuity, not in terms of what some humans call the soul."

He laughed. "Right now, however, when my logical mind says I could not possibly have much more time to live, a voice inside is begging me to embrace one of those fairy tales about the afterlife. It would be easy, I admit. But such a last-minute conversion would be inconsistent with the way I have lived all these years."

Richard walked slowly over to the front of their cell. He put his hands on the bars and stared down the corridor for several seconds without saying anything. "And what do octospiders think happens after death?" he asked softly, turning around to face his cellmate.

"The Precursors taught us that each life is a finite interval, with a beginning and an end. Any individual creature, although a miracle, is not that important in the overall scheme of things. What matters, the Precursors said, is continuity and renewal. In their view each of us is immortal, not because anything related to a specific individual lives forever, but because each life becomes a critical link, either culturally or genetically or both, in the never-ending chain of life. When the Precursors engineered us out of our ignorance, they taught us not to fear death, but to go willingly in support of the renewal that would follow."

"So you experience no sorrow and no fear as your death approaches?"

"Ideally," Archie replied. "That is the accepted way in our society to face death. It is far easier, however, if an individual is surrounded, at the time of termination, by friends and others who represent the renewal that his death will enable."

Richard walked over and put his arm around Archie. "You and I have only each other, my friend," he said. "Plus the knowledge that we have tried, together, to stop a war that will probably end up killing thousands. There can't be many causes—"

He stopped when he heard the door to the cellblock open. The local police captain, along with one of his men, stood to the side as four biots—two Garcias and two Lincolns—all wearing gloves, came down the hallway to their cell. None of the biots spoke. One of the Garcias opened the door and all four biots crowded into the cell with Richard and Archie. The captain closed the cellblock door. Moments later the lights went out, there was the sound of a scuffle for several seconds, Richard screamed, and a body fell against the bars of the cell. Then it was quiet.

"Now, Franz," Katie said as they opened the door to the police station, "don't be afraid to pull rank. He's just a local captain. He's not going to tell you that you can't see the prisoners."

They walked inside only a second or two after the cellblock door closed behind the biots. "Captain Miyazawa," Franz said in his most official tone, "I am Captain Franz Bauer from headquarters. I have come to visit the prisoners."

"I have strict orders from the highest authority, Captain Bauer," the policeman replied, "not to allow *anyone* into that cellblock."

The room was suddenly plunged into darkness. "What's going on?" Franz said.

"We must have blown a fuse," Captain Miyazawa replied. "Westermark, go outside and check the circuit breakers."

Franz and Katie heard a scream. After what seemed to be an eternity, they heard the cellblock door open and the sound of footsteps. Three biots disappeared out the front door of the station as the lights flickered on again.

Katie ran to the door. "Look, Franz," she yelled. "Blood—they have blood on their clothes." She spun around, frantic. "We must see my father."

Katie outran the three police officers down the corridor. "Oh, God," she screamed as she neared the cell and saw her father lying on the floor against the bars. There was blood everywhere. "He's dead, Franz," Katie wailed. "Daddy's dead!"

8

Nicole had watched the video twice before. Despite her swollen eyes and utter emotional exhaustion, she asked if she could see it one more time. Beside her Dr. Blue handed her a cup of water. "Are you certain?" the octospider asked.

She nodded. "Please start at the hearing," Nicole requested. "Normal speed until the biots enter the cellblock. Then slow it down to one-eighth."

Richard never wanted to be a hero, Nicole was thinking as the video replayed the scene at the hearing. *That wasn't his style. He only went with Archie so that it wouldn't be necessary for me.* She winced when the guard struck Richard and he tumbled to the floor. *The plan was hopeless from the beginning,* she told herself as the New Eden policemen led Richard and Archie out of Nakamura's palace. *The octospiders all knew it. I knew it. Why didn't I speak up after my premonition?*

Nicole asked Dr. Blue to fast-forward the video to the final minutes. *At least they had each other at the end,* she thought as Richard and Archie were sharing their final conversation. *And Archie tried to protect him.* The four biots appeared on the screen and the video slowed. Nicole saw surprise change to fear in Richard's eyes as the biots entered the cell.

When the lights were extinguished, the picture quality changed. The infrared images taken by the quadroids were more like photo negatives, highlighting the heat levels in each frame. The biots looked eerie. Their eyes bulged out of their heads in the infrared pictures.

The instant the cell was dark, one of the Garcias grabbed Richard by the throat. The other three took off their gloves, exposing sharp, pointed fingers and knife-edged hands. Four of Archie's powerful tentacles enwrapped the Garcia trying to strangle Richard. As the Garcia's frame crumbled and the biot collapsed in a heap on the floor of the cell, the other three biots attacked Archie furiously. Richard tried to help in the battle. A Lincoln caught Archie's neck with a savage blow from its hand and nearly decapitated the octospider. Richard screamed as he was drenched by Archie's internal body fluid. With Archie out of the fight, the remaining biots devastated Richard, puncturing his body over and over with jabs from their fingers. He fell against the front of the cell and slipped down onto the floor. His blood and Archie's, which were different colors in the infrared image, ran together and formed a pool on the floor of the cell.

The video continued, but Nicole was no longer seeing anything. Now, for the first time, she understood that her husband, Richard, the only really close friend she had ever had in her adult life, was actually dead. On the screen Franz led the sobbing Katie down the corridor and then the monitor went blank. Nicole did not move. She sat perfectly still, staring forward where the images had been just seconds before. There were no tears in her eyes, her body was not trembling, she seemed completely in control. Yet she could not move.

A low level of light came on in the viewing room. Dr. Blue was still sitting beside her. "I don't think," Nicole said slowly, surprised that her voice sounded so far away, "that I realized the first two times . . . I mean, I must have been in shock . . . maybe I still am." She couldn't continue. Nicole was having trouble breathing.

"You need a drink of water and some rest," Dr. Blue said.

Richard has been killed. Richard is dead. "Yes, please," Nicole said faintly. *I will never see him again. I will never talk to him again.* "Cold water, if you have any." *I saw him die. Once. Twice. Three times. Richard is dead.*

There was another octospider in the viewing room. They were talking, but Nicole could not follow their colors. *Richard is gone forever. I am alone.* Dr. Blue held the water up to Nicole's lips, but she could not drink. *Richard has been killed.* There was nothing but blackness.

Someone was holding her hand. It was a warm, pleasant hand, gently caressing hers. She opened her eyes.

"Hello, Mother," Patrick said softly. "Are you feeling any better?"

Nicole closed her eyes again. *Where am I?* she thought. Then she remembered. *Richard is dead. I must have fainted.*

"Ummm," she said.

"Would you like some water?" Patrick asked.

"Yes, please," she whispered. Her voice sounded strange.

Nicole tried to sit up and drink the water. She could not make it.

"Take it easy," Patrick said. "There's no hurry."

Her mind began to work. *I must tell them that Richard and Archie are dead. The helicopters are coming. We must be very careful and protect the children.* "Richard," she managed to say.

"We know, Mother," Patrick replied.

How do they know? Nicole thought. *I'm the only one left here who can read colors.*

"The octospiders went to a lot of trouble to write everything down. It wasn't perfect English, but we certainly understood what they were telling us. They told us about the war too."

Good, Nicole thought. *They know. I can sleep.* From somewhere in her head there was still an echo. *Richard is dead.*

"From time to time I can hear the bombs, but as far as I can tell none of them yet has hit the dome." It was Max's voice. "Maybe they haven't figured out where the city is."

"It would be completely dark from the outside," Patrick said. "They have thickened the canopy and there are no lights on the streets."

"The bombs must be hitting the Alternate Domain. There would be no way the octos could hide its existence," Max said.

"What are the octospiders doing?" Patrick asked. "Do we even know if they're counterattacking?"

"Not for certain," Max replied, "but I can't believe they're still sitting around doing nothing."

Nicole heard soft footsteps in the hallway. "The boys are really developing a bad case of cabin fever," Nai said. "Do you think it would be all right if I let them play outside? The all-clear flares were half an hour ago."

"I don't see why not," Patrick said. "But tell them to come in if they see a flare or hear any bombs."

"I'll be out there with them," Nai said.

"What's my wife doing?" Max asked.

"Reading with Benjy," Nai replied. "Marius is asleep."

"Why don't you ask her to come over for a few minutes?"

Nicole rolled over on her other side. She thought about trying to sit up, but she felt so tired. She began daydreaming, remembering her childhood. *What does it take to be a princess?* little Nicole asked her father. *Either a king for a father, or a prince for a husband,* he answered. He smiled and kissed her. *Then I'm already a princess,* she told him. *For you're a king to me. . . .*

"How is Nicole?" Eponine asked.

"She stirred again this morning," Patrick replied. "Dr. Blue's note said that she may be able to sit up tonight or tomorrow. It also said they have verified that the attack was not severe, that the heart was not permanently damaged, and that she is responding well to the treatment."

"Can I see her now?" Benjy asked.

"No, Benjy, not yet," said Eponine, "she's still resting."

"The octospiders have really been great, haven't they?" Patrick said. "Even in the middle of this war, they have taken time to write us such complete messages."

"They've even made a believer out of me," Max said. "And I never thought that was possible."

So I had a heart attack, Nicole thought. *I didn't just collapse because Richard* . . . she could not complete the sentence at first. *Because he is gone.*

She drifted in the twilight zone between waking and sleeping until she heard a familiar voice calling her name. *Is that you, Richard?* Nicole said excitedly. *Yes, Nicole*, he answered. *Where are you? I want to see you*, she said, and his face appeared in a cloud in the middle of her dream screen. *You look great*, she said, *are you all right? Yes*, Richard answered, *but I must talk to you.*

What is it, darling? Nicole asked. *You must go on without me*, he said. *You must set an example for the others.* His face began to alter as the shapes of the clouds changed. *Of course*, Nicole said, *but where are you going?* She could not see him anymore. *Good-bye*, his voice said. *Good-bye, Richard*, Nicole answered.

When she woke up the next time, her mind was clear. Nicole sat up in bed and looked around her. It was dark, but she could tell she was in her own room in the house in Emerald City.

Nicole could hear no sounds. She assumed it was night. She pushed off the covers and swung her legs over the edge of the bed. *So far, so good*, she thought. Nicole eased herself off the bed and stood up very slowly. Her legs were wobbly.

There was a glass of juice on the end table beside the bed. Nicole took two cautious steps, holding on to the bed with her right hand, and picked up the glass. The juice was delicious. Pleased with herself, Nicole started toward the closet to find some clothes. She became woozy after a few steps, however, and headed back toward the bed.

"Mother," she heard Patrick say, "is that you?" She could see his silhouette in the doorway.

"Yes, Patrick," she answered.

"Here," he said, "why don't we have some light?" He knocked on the wall and a firefly flew into the middle of the room. "Goodness," he said, "what are you doing up?"

"I can't stay in bed forever," Nicole answered.

"But you should take it easy at first," Patrick said, coming over beside her and helping her the rest of the way to bed.

She grabbed his arm. "Listen to me, son," Nicole said. "I have no intention of being an invalid, nor do I want to be treated like one. I expect to be my old self in a few days, a week at the most."

"Yes, Mother," Patrick said with a concerned smile.

*   *   *

Dr. Blue was delighted with her recovery. After four more days Nicole walked, albeit slowly, and, with a little help from Benjy, all the way to the transport stop and back to the house.

"Don't push yourself too hard," Dr. Blue told Nicole during an evening examination. "You're doing great, but I worry."

When the octospider was finished and was preparing to leave the room, Max entered and announced that two more octospiders were waiting at the front door. Dr. Blue hurried out, returning a few minutes later with the Chief Optimizer and one of the members of her staff.

The Chief Optimizer first apologized, both for coming unexpectedly and for not waiting until Nicole had completely recovered. "However," the octospider leader then said, "we are now in an emergency situation and we felt that we needed to communicate with you immediately."

Nicole felt her pulse rate rise and tried to calm herself. "What has happened?" she said.

"You have probably noticed that there have been no bombings for the last several days," the Chief Optimizer said. "The humans temporarily stopped the helicopter attacks while they were evaluating our ultimatum. Five days ago we took the same written message to each of three troop encampments. The message said that we could no longer tolerate the bombings and that we would use our superior technology to launch a decisive attack if the hostilities were not ceased immediately. As an illustration of our technological capabilities, we included in the message a nillet-by-nillet chronology of everything both Nakamura and Macmillan had done during two workdays last week.

"The human leaders were frantic. They suspected that we had somehow bribed some high official of the government and now knew all of their war plans as well. Macmillan recommended accepting our cease-fire and withdrawing from our territory. Nakamura was furious. He banished Macmillan from his presence and reorganized his command structure. Privately, he admitted to his security chief that any retreat would ruin his position in the colony.

"The day before yesterday someone suggested to Nakamura that perhaps your daughter Ellie might have some knowledge of how we had obtained our information. She was taken to the palace and interrogated by Nakamura himself. At first slightly cooperative, Ellie acknowledged that in certain fields we were more advanced than the humans. She also said that she believed it was entirely within our capabilities to obtain information about events in New Eden without using any spies or other conventional means of gathering intelligence.

"Because she was so forthright, Nakamura became convinced that Ellie knew more than she was telling. He asked her questions for hours, about many subjects, including our military capabilities and the geography of our domain. Ellie astutely avoided giving away any critical information—she never mentioned the Emerald City, for example—and repeatedly answered that she had never seen any weapons or even any soldiers. Nakamura did not believe her. At length he had her thrown in prison and beaten. Since then Ellie has remained defiantly silent, despite additional rough treatment."

The Chief Optimizer paused. Nicole had paled during his description of Ellie's mistreatment. The octospider leader turned to Dr. Blue. "Should I continue?" she said.

Max and Patrick were standing in the doorway. They could not, of course, understand what the Chief Optimizer was saying, but they could see the pallor on Nicole's face. Patrick walked into the room. "My mother has been quite ill . . ." he said.

"It's all right," Nicole said, waving him away. She took a deep breath. "Please go on," she said to the Chief Optimizer.

"Nakamura," the Chief Optimizer continued, "has now convinced himself and his main lieutenants that our threat is a bluff. He believes that even though our technology is very advanced in some areas, we possess no military capabilities. In his last staff meeting, only a few terts ago, he agreed to a plan to bomb us into submission, using all available firepower. The first of the massive raids will come in the morning.

"We have therefore reluctantly concluded that we must now fight back. Failure to act could put the survival of our colony in jeopardy. Before coming to see you, I authorized the implementation of War Plan Number Forty-one, one of our intermediate-strength responses. This plan does not result in the total annihilation of all the colonists in New Eden, but should be devastating enough to bring the war to a quick end. Our analysts estimate that between twenty and thirty percent of the humans will die."

The Chief Optimizer stopped when she saw the pained expression on Nicole's face. Nicole asked for something to drink. "Are we allowed to know any more details about your attack?" Nicole said slowly after she finished drinking the glass of water.

"We have chosen a microbiological agent, chemically much like an enzyme, that interferes with cell reproduction in your species. Young, healthy humans below the age of forty or so have sufficiently strong natural defenses that they will withstand the onslaught of the agent. Older or unhealthy humans will succumb quickly. Their cells will not be able to reproduce properly and their bodies will simply stop functioning. We have used blood, skin, and other cells taken from all of you here in the Emerald City to verify our theoretical predictions. We are quite certain that the young will be unharmed."

"Our species regards biological warfare as immoral," Nicole said after a brief pause.

"We are aware," the Chief Optimizer said, "that within your system of values, some kinds of warfare are more acceptable than others. To us, all war is unacceptable. We fight only if we absolutely must. We can't imagine it makes any difference to the dead being if it has been killed by a gun, a bomb, a nuclear weapon, or a biological agent. Besides, we must fight back with whatever weapons we possess."

There was a long silence. Nicole sighed and shook her head. "I guess," she said at length, "I should be thankful that you have told us what is happening in this stupid war, even though the specter of so many deaths is very frightening. I wish there could have been some other outcome."

The three octospiders prepared to leave the room. Max and Patrick were asking Nicole questions before the visitors had even departed from the house. "Hold it," Nicole said wearily. "Call the others in here first. I only want to explain what the octospiders told me a single time."

Nicole could not sleep. No matter how hard she tried, she could not stop thinking about the people who were going to die in New Eden. Faces—older faces, mostly, faces of people that Nicole had known and worked with during her active days in the colony—swam in and out of her mind.

And what about Katie and Ellie? Nicole thought. *What if the octospiders have made a mistake?* She pictured Ellie as she had last seen her, in her house with her husband and her daughter. Nicole recalled the arguments that she had witnessed between Ellie and Robert. His tired, worn visage remained fixed in her mental image. *And Robert,* she thought. *Oh, my God. He's older, and doesn't take care of himself at all.*

Nicole squirmed in her bed, frustrated by her inability to do anything. Finally she decided to sit up in the darkness. *I wonder if it's too late,* Nicole asked herself. Again she thought of Robert. *I don't agree with him. I'm not even certain he's a good husband for Ellie. But he is still Nikki's father.*

A plan had begun to develop in her mind. Nicole gingerly slid out of bed and walked across to the closet. She put on some clothes and tiptoed into the hall. She did not want to wake Patrick or Nai, who had been sleeping in Ellie's room since her heart attack. *They would just make me go back to bed.*

Outside, in the Emerald City, it was almost as dark as it had been inside the house. Nicole stood at the doorway, hoping that her eyes would adjust enough that she could find the house next door. Eventually she could make out some shadows. She stepped off the porch, heading to the right.

Her progress was slow. She would take half a dozen steps and then stop to look around. It took her several minutes to reach the atrium of Dr. Blue's house.

When she entered the octospider's sleeping quarters, Nicole tapped lightly on the wall. A firefly dimly illuminated a pair of octospiders in a single heap. Dr. Blue and Jamie were sleeping with their bodies pressed together and their tentacles tangled in a confusing pattern. Nicole walked over and touched Dr. Blue on the top of the head. There was no response. She tapped a little harder the second time and Dr. Blue's lens material began to move around.

"What are you doing here?" Dr. Blue said in color a few seconds later.

"I need your help," Nicole answered. "It's important."

The octospider moved very slowly, trying to untangle her tentacles without disturbing Jamie. She was unsuccessful; the young octospider awakened anyway. Dr. Blue told Jamie to go back to sleep and shuffled into the atrium with Nicole.

"You should be in bed," Dr. Blue said.

"I know," Nicole replied. "But this is an emergency. I need to talk to the Chief Optimizer, and I would like for you to go with me."

"At this time of night?"

"I don't know how much time we have," Nicole said. "I must see the Chief Optimizer before those biological agents start killing people in New Eden. I'm worried about Katie, and all of Ellie's family as well."

"Nikki and Ellie will not be harmed. Katie should be young enough too, if I understood—"

"But Katie's system is screwed up by all the drugs," Nicole interrupted the colors. "Her body probably acts as if it's old . . . and Robert is all worn-out from working all the time."

"I'm not certain I understand what you are telling me," said Dr. Blue. "Why is it that you want to see the Chief Optimizer?"

"To plead for special treatment for Katie and Robert, assuming of course that Ellie and Nikki are all right. There must be some way, with your biological magic, that they can be singled out and spared. That's why I want you to come with me—to support my case."

The octospider didn't say anything for several seconds. "All right, Nicole," she said finally, "I will go with you. Even though I think you should be resting in bed. . . . And I doubt if there's anything that can be done."

"Thank you very much," Nicole said, forgetting herself for a moment and hugging Dr. Blue.

"You must promise me one thing," Dr. Blue said as they walked together out the front door. "You must not push yourself too hard tonight. Tell me if you are feeling weak."

"I'll even lean on you as we walk," Nicole said with a smile.

They moved slowly into the street, the unlikely pair. Two of Dr. Blue's tentacles were supporting Nicole at all times. Nevertheless, the day's activities and emotions had taken a toll on Nicole's meager energy supply. She was feeling fatigue before they reached the transport stop.

She stopped to rest. The distant sounds she had been hearing, but not noticing, became more prominent. "Bombs," Nicole said to Dr. Blue. "A lot of them."

"We were told to expect helicopter raids," the octospider said. "But I wonder why there were no flares."

Suddenly part of the domed canopy over their heads exploded in a great fireball. Moments later Nicole heard a deafening sound. She held tightly to Dr. Blue and stared at the inferno above her. In the flames she thought she could see the remnants of a helicopter. Burning pieces of the dome were falling from the sky, some landing no more than a kilometer away.

Nicole could not catch her breath. Dr. Blue could see the strain on her face. "I'll never make it," Nicole said. She clutched the octospider with all the strength she had remaining. "You must go see the Chief Optimizer without me," she said. "As my friend. Ask her—no, *beg* her to do something for Katie and Robert. Tell her it's a personal favor. . . . For me."

"I'll do what I can," Dr. Blue replied. "But first we must take you back."

"*Mother,*" Nicole heard Patrick yell behind her. He was running down the street toward them. When he reached them, Dr. Blue boarded the transport. Nicole looked up at the dome just as a helicopter blade, wrapped in burning foliage, fell out of the sky and crashed in the distance.

9

Katie dropped the syringe in the sink and looked at herself in the mirror. "There," she said out loud, "that's much better. I'm not trembling anymore." She was wearing the same dress she had worn to her father's hearing. Katie had made that decision also the week before, when she had told Franz what she was planning to do.

She turned around, watching her reflection critically. *What is that swelling on my forearm?* she wondered. Katie had not noticed it before. On her right arm, halfway between her elbow and her wrist, there was a lump the size of a golf ball. She rubbed it. The swelling felt tender when she pressed it, but it neither hurt nor itched unless she touched it directly.

Katie shrugged and walked into her living room. The papers she had prepared were lying on the coffee table. She smoked a cigarette while she organized the document. Then she placed the papers in a large envelope.

The phone call from Nakamura's office had come that morning. The sweet female voice had told Katie that Nakamura could see her at five o'clock in the afternoon. When she had put down the phone, Katie had hardly been able to contain herself. She had almost given up hope that she would be able to see him at all. Three days earlier, when she had called to make an appointment "to talk about their mutual business," Nakamura's receptionist had told her that he was extremely busy with the war effort and was not scheduling unrelated meetings.

Katie checked her watch again. It was fifteen minutes until five. To walk from her apartment to the palace would take ten minutes. She picked up the envelope and opened the door to her apartment.

The wait was destroying her self-confidence. It was already six o'clock and Katie had not even been admitted yet to the inner sanctum, the Japanese part of the palace where Nakamura worked and lived. Twice she had gone to the rest room, both times inquiring on her way back to her seat if the wait would be much longer. The girl at the desk next to the door had twice responded with a vague, unknowing gesture.

Katie was struggling with herself. The kokomo was starting to wear off, and she was having doubts. While smoking a cigarette in the rest room, she had tried to forget her anxieties by thinking about Franz. She remembered the last time that they had made love. His eyes had been heavy with sadness when he had departed. *He does love me*, Katie thought, *in his own way*.

The Japanese girl was standing at the door. "You may go in now," she said. Katie crossed back through the waiting room and entered the main part of the palace. She took off her shoes, placed them on a shelf, and walked on the tatami in her stocking feet. An escort, a policewoman named Marge, greeted her and instructed Katie to follow her. Clutching her envelope of papers in her hand, Katie walked behind the policewoman for ten or fifteen meters until a screen opened on their right. "Please go in," Marge said.

Another policewoman, Oriental but not Japanese, was waiting in the room. She was wearing a gun in a holster on her hip. "Security around Nakamura-san is especially tight right now," Marge explained. "Please take off all your clothes and jewelry."

"All my clothes?" Katie asked. "Even my panties?"

"Everything," the other woman said.

Her clothes were all folded neatly and placed in a basket marked with her name. The jewelry went into a special box. While Katie was naked, Marge checked her everywhere, including her private parts. She even inspected the inside of Katie's mouth, holding her tongue depressed for almost thirty seconds. Katie was then handed a blue and white *yukata* and a pair of Japanese slippers. "You may now go with Bangorn to the last waiting room," Marge said.

Katie picked up her envelope and started to leave. The Oriental policewoman stopped her. "*Every*thing stays here," she said.

"But this is a business meeting," Katie protested. "What I want to discuss with Mr. Nakamura is in this envelope."

The two women opened the envelope and took out the papers. They held each individual paper up to the light and then passed them, one at a time, through some kind of screening machine. Finally they replaced the papers in the envelope and the woman named Bangorn motioned for Katie to follow her.

The final waiting room was another fifteen meters down the hall. Again Katie had to sit and wait. She could feel herself starting to shake. *It isn't going to work*, she said to herself. *What a fool I am!*

As she sat, Katie began to yearn desperately for some kokomo. She could not recall ever wanting anything so much. Fearful that she was going to start crying, she asked Bangorn if she could go again to the rest room. The policewoman accompanied her. At least Katie was able to wash her face.

When the two of them returned, Nakamura himself was standing in the waiting room. Katie thought her heart was going to jump out of her chest. Nakamura was wearing a yellow and black kimono covered with bright flowers. "Hello, Katie," he said with a leering smile. "I have not seen you for a long time."

"Hello, Toshio-san," she replied, her voice breaking.

Katie followed him into his office and sat down, cross-legged, at a low table. Nakamura was opposite her. Bangorn stayed in the room, standing unobtrusively over in a corner. *Oh, no*, Katie said to herself when the policewoman did not leave. *What do I do now?*

"I thought," Katie said to Nakamura a moment later, trying to sound normal, "that a report on our business was long overdue." She pulled the papers out of the envelope. "Despite the poor economy, we have managed to increase our profits by ten percent. In this summary sheet," she said, handing a page to Nakamura, "you can see that although the Vegas revenues are down, the local take, where the prices are cheaper, is up substantially. Even in San Miguel—"

He glanced at the paper quickly and then put it down on the table. "You don't need to show me any data," Nakamura said. "Everyone knows what a superb businesswoman you are." He reached over to his left and retrieved a large black-lacquer box. "Your performance has been outstanding," he said. "If times were not so tough, you would definitely merit a large raise. As it is, I would like to offer you this gift as a token of my appreciation."

Nakamura pushed the box across the table to Katie. "Thank you," she said, admiring the mountains and snow inlaid on its top. It was indeed beautiful.

"Open it," he said, reaching for one of the wrapped candies in the bowl on the table.

Katie opened the box. It was full of kokomo. A genuine smile of delight crossed her face. "Thank you, Toshio-san," she said. "You are most generous."

"You may sample it," he said, now grinning. "You won't insult me."

Katie put a small amount of the powder on her tongue. It was top quality. Without hesitation, she pinched a chunk of powder out of the box and held it against her left nostril with her little finger. Closing off the right nostril, Katie inhaled deeply. She took slow, deep breaths while the rush took effect. Then she laughed. "Whewee," Katie said uninhibitedly. "That's great stuff!"

"I thought you would like it," Nakamura said. He idly tossed his candy wrapper in the small wastebasket next to the table. *It will be in there somewhere,* Katie remembered Franz telling her. *In some inconspicuous spot. Look in the wastebaskets. Look behind the curtains.*

The New Eden dictator was smiling at her from across the table. "Was there anything else?" he asked.

Katie took a deep breath as she smiled. "Only this," she said. She stretched forward, put her elbows on the table, and kissed him on the lips. She felt the policewoman's rough hands on her shoulders moments later. "That's a small token of my thanks for the kokomo."

She had not misjudged him. The lust in his eyes was unmistakable. Nakamura waved Bangorn away. "You may leave us," he said to the policewoman as he rose from his sitting position. "Come over here, Katie. Give me a real kiss."

Katie checked the small wastebasket as she danced around the table. There was nothing except candy wrappers in it. *Of course,* she thought. *That would be too obvious. Now I must make this good.* She teased Nakamura first with one kiss and then with another. Her tongue tickled his lips and tongue. Then she pulled away quickly, still laughing. Nakamura started to follow her.

"No," she said, backing up toward the door. "Not yet . . . we're just getting started."

Nakamura stood still and grinned. "I had forgotten how talented you are," he said. "Those girls are lucky to have you as a mentor."

"It takes an exceptional man to bring out the best in me," Katie said, locking and bolting the door. Her eyes roamed quickly around the office and landed on another small wastebasket, over in the far corner. *That would be the perfect place,* she said to herself excitedly.

"Are you just going to stand there, Toshio," Katie said now, "or are you going to get me a drink?"

"Of course," Nakamura said, moving toward the hand-carved liquor cabinet under the solitary window. "Straight whiskey, wasn't it?"

"Your memory is phenomenal," Katie said.

"I remember you very well," Nakamura said as he prepared two drinks. "How could I ever forget all those games—especially the princess and the slave, that was my favorite. . . . We had such fun there for a while."

Until you insisted on bringing in others. And even more disgusting things, Katie thought. *You made it clear that I was not enough by myself.* "Boy," she barked suddenly in an imperious tone, "I am thirsty. Where is my drink?"

A quick frown crossed Nakamura's face before he broke into a wide smile. "Yes, Your Highness," he said, bringing her a drink with his head held low. He bowed. "Is there anything else, Your Highness?" he said obsequiously.

"Yes," Katie responded, taking the drink with her left hand and reaching aggressively under Nakamura's kimono with her right. She watched him close his eyes. Katie kissed him hard while continuing to arouse him.

She pulled away abruptly. While he was watching her, Katie slowly took off her *yukata*. Nakamura advanced. Katie stuck out her arms. "Now, boy," she ordered, "turn down those lights and lie over there on the mat, on your back, next to the table."

Nakamura dutifully complied. Katie walked over to where he was lying. "Now," she said in a gentler tone, "you do remember what your princess needs, don't you? Slowly, very slowly, without any hurry." She reached down and fondled him. "I do believe that Musashi is almost ready."

Katie kissed Nakamura, caressing his face and neck with her fingers. "Now close your eyes," she whispered in his ear, "and count to ten, very slowly."

"*Ichi, ni, san . . .*" he said breathlessly.

With astonishing celerity, Katie swept across the room to the other wastebasket. She pushed aside some papers and found the gun.

"*. . . shi, go, ryoku . . .*"

Her heart pounding furiously, Katie picked up the gun, turned around, and headed back toward Nakamura.

"*. . . shichi, hachi, kyu . . .*"

"This is for what you did to my father," Katie said, sticking the barrel of the gun against his forehead. She pulled the trigger just as the astonished Nakamura opened his eyes.

"And this is for what you did to me," she said, firing three bullets into his genitals in rapid succession.

The guards broke down the door in seconds. But she was too quick. "And this, Katie Wakefield," she said in a loud voice, sticking the gun in her mouth, "is for what you did to yourself."

Ellie awakened when she heard the keys rustling in the lock on her cell. She rubbed her eyes. "Is that you, Robert?" she asked.

"Yes, Ellie," he said. He came into the cell just as she stood up. Robert put his arms around Ellie and hugged her fiercely. "I'm so glad to see you," he said. "I came as soon as Herbert told me the guards had abandoned the station."

Robert kissed his puzzled wife. "I'm terribly sorry, Ellie," he said. "I was very, very wrong."

It took Ellie a few seconds to gather her bearings. "They *abandoned* the station?" she said. "Why, Robert? What's going on?"

"Complete and total chaos," he said heavily. He looked utterly defeated.

"What do you mean, Robert?" Ellie said, suddenly afraid. "Nikki's all right, isn't she?"

"She's fine, Ellie. But people are dying in droves. And we don't know why. Ed Stafford collapsed an hour ago and was dead before I could even examine him. It's some kind of monstrous plague."

The octospiders, Ellie thought immediately. *They have finally fought back.* She held her husband against her while he wept. After several seconds he pulled away and spoke. "I'm sorry, Ellie. There has been so much turmoil. Are you all right?"

"I'm okay, Robert. No one has questioned or tortured me for several days. But where's Nikki?"

"She's with Brian Walsh at our house. You remember Brian, Patrick's computer friend? He's been helping me take care of Nikki since you've been gone. Poor guy, he found both his parents dead the day before yesterday when he woke up."

Ellie walked out of the police station with Robert. He was talking continuously, rambling from subject to subject, but Ellie was able to comprehend a few things from his almost incoherent chatter. According to Robert, there had been over three hundred unexplained deaths in New Eden in just the last two days. And the end was nowhere in sight. "It's strange," he muttered. "Only one child has died. Most of the victims have been old."

In front of the Beauvois police station, a desperate woman in her mid-thirties recognized and then grabbed Robert. "You must come with me, Doctor, immediately," the woman yelled in a shrill voice. "My husband is unconscious. He was sitting there with me eating lunch and he began to complain of a headache. When I came back from the kitchen, he was lying on the floor. I'm afraid he's dead."

"You see," Robert said, turning to Ellie.

"Go with her," Ellie said, "and then to the hospital if you must. I'll go home and take care of Nikki. We'll be waiting for you." She leaned over and kissed him. Ellie started to say something to Robert about the octospiders but decided against it.

"Mommy, Mommy," Nikki yelled. She ran down the hall and jumped into Ellie's arms. "I've missed you, Mommy."

"And I have missed you, my angel," Ellie said. "What have you been doing?"

"I've been playing with Brian," Nikki answered. "He's a very nice man. He reads to me and teaches me all about numbers."

Brian Walsh, who was in his early twenties, came around the corner holding a children's book. "Hello, Mrs. Turner," he said. "I don't know if you remember me . . ."

"Of course I do, Brian. And I'm just Ellie. I really do want to thank you for helping with Nikki."

"I'm glad to do it, Ellie. She's a great kid. She's kept my mind off a lot of painful thoughts—"

"Robert told me about your parents," Ellie interrupted. "I'm terribly sorry."

Brian shook his head. "It was so weird. They were both perfectly fine the night before, when they went to bed." Tears came into his eyes. "They looked so peaceful. . . ."

He turned away and pulled out a handkerchief to wipe his eyes. "Several of my friends say this plague, or whatever it is, was caused by the octospiders. Do you think that maybe—"

"Possibly," Ellie said. "We may have pushed them too far."

"Are we *all* going to die?" Brian asked.

"I don't know," Ellie answered. "I really don't."

They stood in awkward silence for several seconds. "Well, at least your sister got rid of Nakamura," Brian said suddenly.

Ellie was certain she had not heard the sentence correctly. "What are you talking about, Brian?" she asked.

"You didn't hear about it? Four days ago Katie assassinated Nakamura . . . and then killed herself."

Ellie was stunned. She stared at Brian in utter disbelief. "Daddy told me about Aunt Katie yesterday," Nikki said to her mother. "He said he wanted to be the one to tell me."

Ellie could not say anything. Her head was spinning. She managed to say good-bye to Brian and to thank him again. Then she sat down on the couch. Nikki crawled up beside her mother and put her head on Ellie's lap. They sat together quietly for a long time.

"And how has your father been while I've been gone?" Ellie finally asked.

"Mostly fine," the little girl replied. "Except for the lump."

"What lump?" Ellie said.

"On his shoulder," Nikki said. "As big as my fist. I saw it there when he was shaving, three days ago. He said it must be a spider bite or something."

10

"Benjy and I are leaving for the hospital," Nicole announced. The others were still finishing their breakfast. "Sit down, Nicole, please," said Eponine. "At least finish your coffee."

"Thanks anyway," she replied. "But I promised Dr. Blue we would come in early today. There were a lot of casualties in yesterday's raid."

"But you've been working very hard, Mother," Patrick said. "And not sleeping nearly enough."

"It helps to stay busy," Nicole said. "That way I don't have any time to think."

"Let's go, Mama," Benjy said, coming into the room and handing Nicole her coat. While he was standing beside his mother, Benjy smiled and waved at the twins, who had been uncharacteristically quiet. Galileo made a bizarre face and both Benjy and Kepler laughed.

"She hasn't yet allowed herself to grieve over Katie's death," Nai said softly a minute later, as soon as Nicole had left. "That worries me. Sooner or later . . ."

"She's afraid, Nai," Eponine said. "Maybe of another heart attack. Maybe even for her sanity. Nicole is still in denial."

"There you go, Frenchie, with that damn psychology again," Max said. "Don't worry about Nicole. She's stronger than any of us. She'll weep for Katie when she's ready."

"Mother hasn't been to the viewing room since her heart attack. When Dr. Blue told her about the assassination and Katie's suicide, I felt certain

Mother would want to see some of the videos . . . to see Katie one last time . . . or at least to see how Ellie was doing."

"Best goddamn thing your sister ever did, Patrick," Max commented, "killing that bastard. Whatever else anybody could say about her, she had courage."

"Katie had a lot of outstanding qualities," Patrick said sadly. "She was brilliant, she could be charming . . . she just had that other side."

There was a brief silence around the breakfast table. Eponine was about to say something when there was a glow of light at the front door. "Uh-oh," she said, standing up. "I'm going to move Marius next door. The raids are starting again."

Nai turned to Galileo and Kepler. "Finish up quickly, boys. We're going back into that special house Uncle Max made for us."

Galileo screwed up his face. "Not again," he complained.

Nicole and Benjy had barely reached the hospital when the first bombs started falling through the tattered dome. The heavy raids had been occurring daily. More than half of the Emerald City ceiling was now gone. Bombs had fallen on almost every section of the city.

Dr. Blue greeted them and immediately sent Benjy down to the receiving area. "It's terrible," the octospider physician said to Nicole. "Over two hundred dead from yesterday alone."

"What is happening in New Eden?" Nicole asked. "I would have thought that by now—"

"The micro-agents are working somewhat slower than predicted," Dr. Blue replied. "But they are finally having an impact. The Chief Optimizer says the raids should cease in another day or two, at the most. She and her staff are drawing up plans for the next phase."

"Surely the colonists will not continue the war," Nicole said, forcing herself not to think too much about what was occurring in New Eden, "especially not with Nakamura dead."

"We feel we must be prepared for any contingency," Dr. Blue said. "But I certainly hope you're right."

As they were moving down the corridor together, they were approached by another octospider doctor, the one that Benjy had named Penny because of the round mark, resembling a New Eden coin, just to the right of her slit. Penny described to Dr. Blue the terrible scenes she had witnessed earlier that morning out in the Alternate Domain. Nicole was able to understand most of what Penny said, not only because the octospider repeated herself several times, but also because Penny used very simple sentences in their language of color.

Penny informed Dr. Blue that medical personnel and supplies were desperately needed immediately to help with the wounded in the Alternate

Domain. Dr. Blue tried to explain to Penny that there were not even enough staff members available to handle all the patients in the hospital.

"I could go with Penny for a few hours this morning," Nicole suggested, "if that would be any help."

Dr. Blue glanced at her human friend. "Are you certain you feel up to it, Nicole?" the octospider asked. "I understand it's pretty gruesome out there."

"I have been getting stronger every day," Nicole replied. "And I want to be where I'm most needed."

Dr. Blue told Penny that Nicole would be able to assist her in the Alternate Domain for a maximum of a tert, as long as Penny accepted the responsibility for escorting Nicole back to the hospital. Penny agreed and thanked Nicole for volunteering to help.

Soon after they boarded the transport, Penny explained to Nicole what was happening in the Alternate Domain. "The wounded are taken to any building that is still undamaged, where they are examined, treated with emergency medicines if necessary, and scheduled for transportation to the hospital. The situation has been getting worse each day. Many of the alternates have already given up hope."

The rest of the transport ride was equally depressing. In the light from the few scattered fireflies, Nicole could see destruction everywhere. To open the south gate, the guards had to push aside two dozen alternates, a few of them wounded, who were clamoring to enter the city. After the transport passed the gate, the devastation around them increased. The theater where Nicole and her friends had attended the morality play was in shambles. More than half of the structures near the Arts District had been flattened. Nicole started feeling sick. Suddenly a bomb exploded on top of the transport.

Nicole was thrown out of the car onto the street. Dazed, she struggled slowly to her feet. The transport had been severed into two twisted pieces. Penny and the other octospider doctor were buried in the debris. Nicole attempted for several minutes to reach Penny, but eventually realized it was hopeless. Another bomb exploded nearby. Nicole grabbed her small medical bag, which had been thrown into the street beside her, and staggered down a side lane in search of a shelter.

A solitary octospider was lying motionless in the middle of the lane. Nicole bent down and pulled her flashlight from her bag. There was no activity in the octospider's lens. She rolled the octo over on its side and immediately saw the wound in the back of its head. A large mass of white corrugated material had oozed out of the wound onto the street. Nicole shuddered and almost gagged. She glanced around her quickly for something to cover the dead octospider. A bomb hit a building not more than two hundred meters away. Nicole stood up and walked on.

She found a small shed on the right side of the lane, but it was already occupied by five or six of the little Polish sausage animals. They chased her away, one of them snapping at her heels for twenty or twenty-five meters. At length the animal was gone and Nicole stopped to catch her breath. She spent a few minutes examining herself and discovered, much to her amazement, that she had no significant injuries, only a few isolated bruises.

There was a hiatus in the bombing. The Alternate Domain was eerily quiet. In front of Nicole, about a hundred meters down the street, a firefly was hovering over a building that appeared to be undamaged. Nicole saw a pair of octospiders, one of whom was obviously wounded, enter the building. *That must be one of the temporary hospitals,* she said to herself. She started to walk in that direction.

A few seconds later, Nicole heard a peculiar sound, barely above the threshold of her hearing. At first the sound did not register in her mind, but the second time she heard the cry, Nicole stopped abruptly in the street. A chill ran down her spine. *That was a baby's cry,* she thought, standing completely still. She heard nothing for several seconds. *Could I have imagined it?* Nicole asked herself.

Nicole strained her eyes and looked in the semidarkness to her right, in what she perceived had been the direction of the cry. She could make out a wire fence, lying mostly on its side, about forty meters down a crossing lane. She glanced again at the nearby building, knowing the octospiders needed her inside. The cry resounded in the night, clearer this time, rising and falling in amplitude like the typical wail of a desperate human baby.

She walked hurriedly over to the toppled fence. A broken sign in color was lying on the ground in front of it. Nicole knelt down and picked up a piece of the sign. When she recognized the octospider colors for "zoo," her heart rate surged. *Richard heard the cry when he was at the zoo,* she remembered.

There was an explosion about a kilometer away to her left, and then another, much closer. The helicopters had returned for another sortie. The baby's wail became continuous. Nicole tried to keep moving in the direction of the cry, but her progress was slow. It was difficult to isolate the wail amid the noise from the explosions.

A bomb burst in front of her less than a hundred meters away. In the silence that followed, Nicole heard nothing. *Oh, no,* her heart cried out, *not now. Not when I am this close.* There was another explosion in the distance, followed by another period of quiet. *It might be some other kind of animal,* she remembered telling Richard. *Somewhere in the universe there may be a creature that sounds like a human baby.*

Her thoughts were interrupted by the return of the piercing wail. Nicole moved as fast as she dared. *No,* she kept saying to herself, her mother's heart torn apart by the desperate cry, *it's unmistakable. There cannot be any other sound like that.* A battered fence ran along the right side of the narrow lane. She crossed through it. In the shadows ahead of her Nicole saw some movement.

The crying baby was sitting on the ground next to the lifeless form of an adult human, presumably its mother. The woman was lying facedown on the dirt. Blood covered the lower half of the adult's body. After quickly determining that the woman was indeed dead, Nicole reached down gingerly and picked up the dark-haired child. Astonished by the action, the baby fought against her and split the night with a powerful bawl. Nicole put the child against her shoulder and patted it lightly on the back. "There, there," she said as the baby continued to shriek, "everything is going to be all right."

In the dim light Nicole could see that the child's bizarre clothes, which were little more than two layers of heavy sacks with holes cut in appropriate places, were smeared with blood. Despite the baby's protests and thrashing, Nicole gave the child a quick examination. Except for a flesh wound in the leg and the filth that covered her entire body, the little girl appeared to be all right. Nicole estimated that she was about a year old.

Ever so gently, Nicole laid the girl down on a small fresh cloth taken from the medical bag. While Nicole was cleaning up the child, she felt the girl jerk and recoil each time a bomb exploded in the vicinity. Nicole tried to soothe her by singing Brahms's Lullaby. Once during the time that Nicole was dressing the leg wound, the girl stopped crying temporarily and stared at Nicole with her huge, surprisingly blue eyes. She offered no protest even when Nicole took a damp cleansing pad and began to wipe the dirt off her skin. A little later, however, when Nicole was cleaning underneath the girl's shirts of sackcloth and found, to her astonishment, a small rope necklace against the baby's tiny chest, the child started howling again.

Nicole gathered the crying baby in her arms and stood up. *She is undoubtedly hungry,* Nicole thought, looking around the area for some kind of hut or shelter. *There must be some food nearby.* Under a deep overhanging rock about fifteen meters away, which had clearly been an enclosed area before the bombing raids began, Nicole found a large pan of water, some small objects of unknown purpose, a sleeping pad, and several more of the sacks out of which the clothing of both the woman and the child were made. But there was no food. Nicole tried unsuccessfully to get the girl to drink from the pan. Then she had another idea.

Returning to the body of the dead mother, Nicole determined that there was still some good milk left in her breasts. The woman had obviously died recently. Nicole lifted the mother's torso and slid in behind her on the ground. Supporting the mother's body against her own, Nicole held the baby girl against her mother's breasts and watched her suck.

The child ate hungrily. In the middle of the feeding, a bomb blast illuminated the dead woman's features. It was the same face Nicole had seen in the octospider painting in Artist's Square. *So I did not imagine it,* Nicole thought.

The baby girl fell asleep when she was finished nursing. Nicole wrapped her in one of the extra sacks and placed her softly on the ground. Nicole now examined the dead mother thoroughly for the first time. Based on the gaping wounds in the woman's lower midsection and right thigh, Nicole surmised that two large pieces of a single bomb had torn through her and that she had subsequently bled to death. While she was inspecting the thigh wound, Nicole felt a strange bulge in the woman's right buttock. Curious, she lifted the woman's body slightly off the ground and ran her fingers over and around the bulge. It felt as if some hard object had been implanted underneath the skin.

Nicole retrieved her medical bag and then, with her small scissors, made an incision just to one side of the bulge. She pulled out an object that appeared to be silver in the dim light. It was the size and shape of a small cigar, twelve to fifteen centimeters in length, and about two centimeters in diameter. A puzzled Nicole twirled the object around in her right hand and tried to imagine what it could be. It was incredibly smooth, with no discernible breaks anywhere. *Probably this is some kind of identifier for the zoo,* she was thinking when a bomb exploded nearby, waking the sleeping girl.

Over in the direction of the Emerald City, bombs were falling with increasing intensity. While Nicole comforted the child, she thought about what she should do next. A large fireball raced toward the sky as one of the falling bombs caused an even larger explosion on the ground. In the temporary light, Nicole could see that she and the child were on the top of a small hill, very close to the edge of the developed part of the Alternate Domain. The Central Plain began no more than a hundred meters to the west.

Nicole stood up with the girl on her shoulder. She was near exhaustion. "We're going out there, away from the bombs," she said out loud to the baby, motioning in the direction of the Central Plain. Nicole tossed the cylindrical object in her medical bag and grabbed a pair of the clean sacks. *These may be useful in the cold,* Nicole thought, throwing the heavy sacks over her shoulders.

It took an hour for her to trudge with the baby and the sacks to a spot in the Central Plain that Nicole thought was far enough away from the bombs. She lay down on her back, the child cradled on her chest, and wrapped the sacks around both of them. Nicole was asleep in seconds.

Nicole was awakened by the movement of the girl. She had been having a conversation with Katie in her dream, but Nicole could not recall what they had been saying to each other. She sat up and changed the baby, using a clean cloth from her medical bag. The child stared at Nicole curiously with her wide blue eyes. "Good morning, little girl, whoever you are," Nicole said brightly. The child smiled for the first time.

It was no longer completely dark. Firefly clusters illuminated the

Emerald City in the distance, and the gaping holes in the dome allowed the light to shine on the surrounding area of Rama. *The war must have ended,* Nicole thought, seeing the light, *or at least the raids have been suspended.*

"Well, my newest friend," Nicole said, standing up and stretching after placing the baby carefully on one of the clean sacks, "let's see what adventures are in store for us today."

The girl quickly crawled off the sack into the dirt of the Central Plain. Nicole picked her up and replaced her in the middle of the sack. Again she crawled toward the dirt. "Whoa, there, little one," Nicole said with a laugh, picking the girl up a second time.

It was difficult for Nicole to gather up their belongings while she was holding the child in her arms. Eventually she succeeded and began walking slowly toward civilization. They were about three hundred meters from the closest buildings of the Alternate Domain. During her walk, Nicole decided that she would go first to the hospital to find Dr. Blue. Assuming that she had correctly concluded that the war was over or at least had been temporarily halted, Nicole planned to spend the morning finding out everything she could about the child. *Who were her parents,* Nicole formed the questions in her mind, *and how long ago were they kidnapped from New Eden?* She was angry with the octospiders. *Why didn't you tell me there were other human beings in the Emerald City?* Nicole intended to ask the Chief Optimizer. *And how can you defend the way you treated this child and her mother?*

The girl, who was wide awake, would not sit still in Nicole's arms. Nicole became uncomfortable. She decided to stop for a rest. While the child was playing in the dirt, Nicole stared at the destruction in front of her, both in the Alternate Domain and, in the distance, in the part of the Emerald City that she could see. Nicole suddenly felt very sad. *What is it all for?* she asked herself. An image of Katie entered her mind, but Nicole pushed it aside, choosing instead to sit down in the dirt and entertain the child. Five minutes later they heard the whistle.

The sound was coming from the sky, from Rama itself. Nicole jumped to her feet, her pulse immediately skyrocketing. She felt a slight pain in her chest, but nothing could diminish her excitement. "Look," she shouted to the baby girl, "look over there, in the south!"

In the distant southern bowl, streamers of colored light were playing around the tip of the Big Horn, the massive spire that thrust upward along the spin axis of the cylindrical spacecraft. The streamers coalesced and formed a red ring near the tip of the spire. A few moments later this huge red ring sailed slowly north along the axis of Rama. Around the Big Horn, more colors danced until they formed into a second ring, orange in color, which eventually followed the red ring, also in a northerly direction in the sky of Rama.

The whistle continued. It was not a harsh or shrill whistle. To Nicole it almost sounded musical. "Something's going to happen," Nicole said exultantly to the girl, "something good!"

The little girl had no idea what was occurring, but she laughed heartily when the woman picked her up and tossed her skyward. And for her the rings were definitely eye-catching. Now a yellow and a green ring were both crossing the black sky of Rama, and the red one in the front of the procession had just reached the Cylindrical Sea.

Again Nicole tossed the child a foot or two in the air. This time the girl's necklace escaped from under her shirts and nearly flew off her head. Nicole caught the girl and gave her a hug. "I had almost forgotten about your necklace," Nicole said. "Now that we have some decent light, may I take a look at it?"

The girl giggled as Nicole pulled the rope necklace over her head. At the bottom of the necklace, carved on a round piece of wood about four centimeters in diameter, was the outline of a man with arms upraised, surrounded on all sides by what appeared to be a fire. Nicole had seen a similar wood carving many years before, on Michael O'Toole's desk in his room inside the Newton. *Saint Michael of Siena*, Nicole said to herself, turning the carving over.

On the back the word MARIA was carefully printed in lowercase letters. "That must be your name," Nicole said to the girl. "Maria . . . Maria." There was no indication of recognition. The child started to frown just before Nicole laughed and tossed her into the air one more time.

A few minutes later Nicole put the squirming child down again. Maria immediately crawled into the dirt. Nicole kept one eye on Maria and one eye on the colored rings in the Rama sky. All eight rings could now be seen, the blue, brown, pink, and purple over the Southern Hemicylinder and the first four in the line in the sky above the north. As the red ring vanished in the northern bowl, another red ring formed at the tip of the Big Horn.

Just like all those years ago, Nicole thought. But her mind was not really focused on the rings yet. She was searching her memory, trying to remember every missing person report that had ever been filed in New Eden. There had been a handful of boating accidents on Lake Shakespeare, she recalled, and every now and then one of the patients in the mental hospital at Avalon had disappeared. *But how could a couple vanish like that? And where was Maria's father?* There were many questions that Nicole wanted to ask the octospiders.

The dazzling rings continued to float above her head. Nicole remembered that day long ago when Katie, as a girl of ten or eleven, had been so thrilled by the huge rings in the sky that she had screamed with joy. *She was always my most uninhibited child,* Nicole thought, unable to stop herself. *Her laugh was so complete, so genuine. . . . Katie had so much potential.*

With great effort Nicole forced herself to concentrate on Maria. The child was sitting down, merrily eating the dirt from the Central Plain. "No, Maria," Nicole said, gently touching the child's hands. "That's dirty."

The girl screwed up her beautiful face and began to cry. *Like Katie*, Nicole thought immediately. *She couldn't stand for me to tell her no.* Memories of Katie now flooded into her mind. Nicole saw her daughter first as a baby, then as a precocious early adolescent at the Node, and finally as a young woman in New Eden. The deep heartache that accompanied the images of her lost daughter completely overwhelmed Nicole. Tears ran down her cheeks and her body began to shake with sobs. "Oh, Katie," Nicole yelled out loud. *"Why? Why? Why?"*

She buried her face in her hands. Maria had stopped crying and was looking at Nicole with a quizzical look.

"It's all right, Nicole," a voice behind her said. "It will all be over soon."

Nicole thought her mind was playing tricks. She turned around slowly. The Eagle was approaching with outstretched arms.

The third red ring had reached the northern bowl and there were no more colored lights around the Big Horn. "So will all the lights come on when the rings are finished?" Nicole asked the Eagle.

"What a good memory," he said. "You might be right."

Nicole was again holding Maria in her arms. She kissed the child gently on the cheek and Maria smiled. "Thank you for the girl," Nicole said. "She is wonderful . . . and I understand what you're telling me."

The Eagle faced Nicole. "What are you talking about?" he said. "We didn't have anything to do with the child."

Nicole searched the alien's mystical blue eyes with her own. She had never seen a pair of eyes that had such a wide range of expression. But Nicole had had no recent practice reading what the Eagle was saying with his eyes. Was he teasing her about Maria? Or was he serious? Surely it wasn't just chance that she discovered the child so soon after Katie killed herself.

You're being too rigid in your thinking, Nicole recalled Richard saying to her at the Node. *Just because the Eagle is not biological like you and me does not mean that he's not alive. He's a robot, all right, but he's much smarter than we are. . . . And much more subtle.*

"So have you been hiding in Rama all this time?" Nicole asked several seconds later.

"No," the Eagle replied. He did not elaborate.

Nicole smiled. "You've already told me that we haven't reached the Node or an equivalent place, and I'm certain that you didn't just drop by for a social visit. Are you going to tell me why you *are* here?"

"This is a Stage Two intercession," the Eagle said. "We have decided to interrupt the observation process."

"Okay," Nicole said, placing Maria back down on the ground, "I understand the concept. But what exactly will happen now?"

"Everyone will go to sleep," the Eagle said.

"And after they awaken . . . ?" Nicole asked.

"All I can tell you is that everyone will go to sleep."

Nicole stepped away in the direction of the Emerald City and raised her arms to the sky. Only three colored rings remained now, and they were all far away, over above the Northern Hemicylinder. "Just out of curiosity— I'm not complaining, you understand . . ." Nicole said with a trace of sarcasm. She paused and turned around to face the Eagle. "Why didn't you intercede a long time ago? *Before* all this occurred? *Before* there were so many deaths?"

The Eagle didn't answer immediately. "You can't have it both ways, Nicole," he said at length. "You can't have both free will and a benevolent higher power who protects you from yourself."

"Excuse me," Nicole said with a puzzled look on her face. "Did I mistakenly ask a religious question?"

"Not really," the Eagle replied. "What you must understand is that our objective is to develop a complete catalog on all the spacefarers in this region of the Galaxy. We are not judgmental. We are scientists. We do not care if it is your natural predilection to destroy yourself. We *do* care, however, if the likely future return from *our* project no longer justifies the significant resources we have assigned."

"Huh?" said Nicole. "Are you telling me that you're not interceding to stop the bloodshed, but for some other reason?"

"Yes," said the Eagle. "However, I'm going to change the subject because our time is extremely limited. The lights will be coming on in two more minutes. You will be asleep a minute after that. If you have anything you wish to communicate to the girl child—"

"Are we going to *die*?" Nicole said, suddenly frightened.

"Not immediately," said the Eagle. "But I cannot guarantee that everyone will live through the sleeping period."

Nicole dropped down in the dirt beside the girl. Maria had another clod in her mouth and wet dirt lined her lips. Nicole wiped her face off very gently and offered the child a drink of water from a cup. To Nicole's surprise, Maria sipped at the water, spilling it down her chin.

Nicole smiled and Maria giggled. Nicole stuck her finger under the girl's chin and tickled her. Maria's giggles erupted into laughter, the pure, uninhibited, magical laughter of the small child. The sound was incredibly beautiful. Nicole's eyes filled with tears.

Suddenly all of Rama was filled with light. It was an awesome spectacle. The Big Horn and its six surrounding acolytes, attached by massive flying buttresses, dominated the sky above them. "Forty-five seconds?" Nicole said to the Eagle.

The alien birdman nodded. Nicole reached over and picked up the girl. "I know that nothing that has happened to you recently makes any sense, Maria," Nicole said, holding the child in her lap, "but I want you to know that you have already been terribly important in my life and I love you very much."

There was a look of astonishing wisdom in the little girl's eyes. She leaned forward and put her head on Nicole's shoulder. For a few seconds Nicole did not know what to do. Then she began patting Maria on the back. And singing softly. "Lay thee down . . . Now and Rest . . . May thy slumber be Blessed . . ."

RETURN TO THE NODE

1

The dreams came before the light. They were disconnected dreams, random images sometimes expanding into short, unified sets without apparent purpose or direction. Colors and geometric patterns were the earliest dreams she remembered. Nicole could not recall when they had started. At some point she had thought for the first time, *I am Nicole. I must still be alive*, but that had been long ago. Since then she had seen, in her mind's eye, entire scenes, including the faces of other people. Some she had recognized. *That's Omeh*, she had said to herself. *That's my father.* She had felt sadness as she had awakened more each time. Richard had been in her last several dreams. And Katie. *They're both dead*, Nicole had remembered. *They died before I went to sleep.*

When she opened her eyes, she could still see nothing. The darkness was complete. Slowly Nicole became more aware of her surroundings. She dropped her hands beside her and felt the soft texture of the foam with her fingers. She turned over on her side with very little effort. *I must be weightless*, Nicole thought, her mind beginning to function after years of being dormant. *But where am I?* she asked herself before falling asleep again.

The next time she awakened, Nicole could see a solitary light source at the other end of the closed container in which she was lying. She wiggled her feet free of the white foam and held them up in front of the light. They were both covered with clear slippers. She stretched out to see if she could touch the light source with her toes, but it was too far away.

Nicole put her hands in front of her eyes. The light was so dim that she could not see any details, only a dark outline that silhouetted all the fingers. There was not enough room in the container for her to sit up, but she could manage to reach the top with one hand, if she propped herself up with the other. Nicole pressed her fingers against the soft foam. Behind the foam was a hard surface, wood or possibly even metal.

The slight activity wore her out. She was breathing rapidly and her heart rate had increased. Her mind became more alert. Nicole remembered clearly the last moments before she had gone to sleep in Rama. *The Eagle came,* she thought, *just after I found that baby girl in the Alternate Domain. So where am I now? And how long have I slept?*

She heard a gentle knocking on the container and lay back down in the foam. *Someone has come. My questions will be answered soon.* The lid of the container was slowly raised. Nicole shielded her eyes from the light. She saw the Eagle's face and heard his voice.

The two of them were sitting together in a large room. Everything was white. The walls, the ceiling, the small round table in front of them, even the chairs, the cup, the bowl, and the spoon were white. Nicole took another sip of the warm soup. It tasted like chicken broth. Over to her left the white container in which she had been lying rested against the wall. There were no other objects in the room.

"... About sixteen years altogether—traveler's time, of course," the Eagle was saying. *Traveler's time,* Nicole thought. *That's the same term that Richard used.* "... We did not retard your aging nearly as efficiently as before. Our preparations were somewhat hurried."

Despite the weightlessness, it seemed to Nicole that every physical act was a monumental effort. Her muscles had been inactive for too long. The Eagle had helped her shuffle the few steps between the container and the table. Her hands had trembled some while she had drunk the water and eaten the soup.

"So am I about eighty?" she now asked the Eagle in a halting voice, one that she barely recognized.

"More or less," the alien replied. "It would be impossible to give you a meaningful age."

Nicole stared across the table at her companion. The Eagle looked just the same as always. The powder-blue eyes on either side of his protruding gray beak had lost none of their mystical intensity. The feathers on the top of his head were still pure white, contrasting sharply with the dark gray feathers of his face, neck, and back. The four fingers on each hand, creamy white and featherless, were as smooth as a child's.

Nicole studied her own hands for the first time. They were wrinkled and discolored from age spots. She turned them over and from somewhere in her memory she heard a laugh. *Phthisic,* Richard was saying. *Isn't that a great word? It means more withered than 'withered.' ... I wonder if I'll ever have a chance to use it. . . .* The memory faded. *My hands are phthisic,* Nicole thought.

"Don't you ever age?" she asked the Eagle.

"No," he replied. "At least not in the sense that you use the word. I am regularly maintained and subsystems that are exhibiting performance degradation are replaced."

"So you never die either?"

He hesitated for a moment. "That's not completely accurate," the Eagle said. "Like all members of my group, I was created for a specific purpose. If there is no longer a need for me to exist and I cannot be readily programmed to accomplish some new, necessary function, then I will be unpowered."

Nicole started to laugh but caught herself. "I'm sorry," she said, "I know it's not funny . . . but your choice of words struck me as peculiar. 'Unpowered' is such a—"

"It's also the correct word," the Eagle said. "Inside me are several tiny power sources, as well as a sophisticated power distribution system. All the power elements are essentially modular and therefore transferable from one of us to another. If I am no longer needed, the elements can be removed and used in another being."

"Like an organ transplant," Nicole said, finishing her water.

"Somewhat," the Eagle replied. "Which brings me to another issue. . . . During your long sleep, your heart actually stopped beating twice, the second time just after we arrived here in the Tau Ceti system. We have managed to keep you alive with drugs and mechanical stimulation, but your heart is now extremely weak. If you want to have an active life for any appreciable additional period, you will need to consider replacing your heart."

"Is that why you left me in there"—Nicole pointed at the container—"for so long?" she asked.

"Partially," said the Eagle. He had already explained to Nicole that most of the others from Rama had awakened much earlier, some as long as a year ago, and that they were living in crowded conditions in another venue not very far away. "But we were also concerned about how comfortable you might be over in the converted starfish. We refurbished that spacecraft in a hurry, so there are not many amenities. We were also concerned because you are by far our oldest human survivor."

That's right, Nicole said to herself. *The octospider attack wiped out everyone over forty or so. I am the only old person left.*

The Eagle had stopped talking for a moment. When Nicole looked at the alien again, his mesmerizing eyes seemed to be expressing an emotion. "Besides, you are special to us. You have played a key role in this endeavor."

Is it possible, Nicole thought suddenly, still staring at the Eagle's fascinating eyes, *that this electronic creature actually has feelings? Could Richard have been right when he insisted that there are no aspects of our humanity that could not be eventually duplicated by engineering?*

"We waited as long as we could to wake you," the Eagle continued, "to minimize the length of time that you would have to spend in less than ideal conditions. Now, however, we are preparing to enter another phase of our operations. As you can see, this room was emptied, except for you, long ago. In another eight to ten days we will begin dismantling the walls. By then you should have recuperated enough."

Nicole asked again about her family and friends. "As I told you before," the Eagle said, "everyone survived the long sleep. However, the adjustment to living in what your friend Max calls the Grand Hotel has not been easy for anybody. All of those who were with you in the Emerald City, plus the girl Maria and Ellie's husband, Robert, were originally assigned to two large rooms, side by side, in one section of the starfish. Everyone was told that the living arrangements were only temporary, and that eventually they would be transferred to better quarters. Nevertheless, Robert and Galileo were not able to adapt successfully to the unusual conditions in the Grand Hotel."

"What happened to them?" Nicole asked with alarm.

"They were both transferred, for sociological reasons, to another, more highly regulated area of the spacecraft. Robert was moved first. He went into a severe depression shortly after he awakened from the long sleep and was never able to break out of it. Unfortunately, he died about four months ago. Galileo is all right physically, although his antisocial behavior has continued."

Nicole felt a deep sorrow upon hearing the news of Robert's death. She was sad for Nikki, who had never really had a chance to know her father, and for her daughter Ellie. Nicole had hoped that the marriage . . . She shook her head. Nicole admitted to herself that she had never really understood Robert. *He was so complex,* she thought. *Talented, dedicated, yet surprisingly dysfunctional on a personal level.*

"I guess," she commented to the Eagle, "that the energy I expended to save Katie and Robert from the octospider agents was wasted effort."

"Not really," the Eagle replied simply. "It was important to you at the time."

Nicole smiled and thought how wise the Eagle was in his understanding of humans. She stifled a yawn.

"Let me help you back to bed," he said. "You've been up long enough for the first time."

Nicole was very pleased with herself. She had finally managed a full lap around the perimeter of the room without stopping.

"Bravo," the Eagle said, coming up beside her. "You are making fabulous progress. We never thought that you would walk so well in such a short period of time."

"I definitely need some water now," she said, smiling. "This old body is sweating furiously."

The Eagle retrieved a glass of water from the table. When she was finished drinking, Nicole turned to her alien friend. "Now are you going to keep your part of the bargain?" she said. "Do you have a mirror and a change of clothes in that suitcase over there?"

"Yes, I do," the Eagle answered. "And I even brought the cosmetics you requested. But first I want to examine you to see how your heart responded to the exercise." He held a small black device in front of her and watched some markings appear on the tiny screen. "That's good," he said. "No, that's excellent. . . . No irregularities at all. Just an indication that your heart is working very hard, which would be expected in a human your age."

"May I see that?" Nicole asked, pointing at the monitoring device. The Eagle handed it to her. "I suppose," she said, "that this thing is receiving signals from inside my body . . . but what exactly are all those squiggles and strange symbols on the screen?"

"You have over a thousand tiny probes inside your body, more than half in the cardiac region. They not only measure the critical performance of your heart and other organs, but also regulate such important parameters as blood flow and oxygen allocation. Some of the probes even supplement the normal biological functions. What you are seeing on the screen is summary data from the time interval when you were exercising. It has been compressed and telemetered by the processor inside you."

Nicole frowned. "Maybe I shouldn't have asked. Somehow the idea of all that electronic junk inside me is not very comforting."

"The probes are not really electronic," the Eagle said, "at least not in the way you humans use the word. And they are entirely necessary at this point in your life. If they weren't there, you wouldn't survive even one day."

Nicole stared at the Eagle. "Why didn't you just let me die?" she asked. "Do you have some purpose for me yet that justifies all this effort? Some function I must still perform?"

"Perhaps," the Eagle said. "But perhaps we thought you might like to see your family and friends one more time."

"I find it difficult to believe," Nicole said, "that my desires play any significant role in your hierarchy of values."

The Eagle did not respond. He walked over to the suitcase, which was sitting on the floor beside the table, and returned with a mirror, a damp cloth, a simple blue dress, and a cosmetics bag. Nicole slipped out of the white nightgown she had been wearing, wiped herself all over with the cloth, and put on the dress. She took a deep breath as the Eagle handed her the mirror. "I'm not certain I'm ready for this," she said with a wan smile.

Nicole would not have recognized the face in the mirror if she had not mentally prepared herself first. Her face looked to her like a crazy quilt of bags and wrinkles. All her hair, including her eyebrows and eyelashes, was now either white or gray. Nicole's first impulse was to cry, but she gamely fought back the tears.

She searched the features in the mirror, guided by her memory, for vestiges of the lovely young woman she had been. Here and there she could see the outlines of what was once considered to be a beautiful face, but the eye had to know where to look. Her heart ached as Nicole suddenly remembered a simple incident years earlier, when she was a teenager walking along a country road with her father near her home in Beauvois. An old woman using a cane had been coming toward them and Nicole had asked her father if they could cross over the road to avoid her.

"Why?" her father had asked.

"Because I don't want to see her up close," Nicole had said. "She is old and ugly. She makes me shiver."

"You too will be old someday," her father had answered, refusing to cross the road.

I am old and ugly, Nicole thought. *I even make myself shiver.* She handed the mirror back to the Eagle. "You warned me," she said wistfully. "Maybe I should have listened."

"Of course you're shocked," the Eagle said. "You have not seen yourself for sixteen years. Most humans have a difficult time with the aging process even if they follow it day by day." He extended the cosmetics bag in her direction.

"No, thank you," Nicole said despondently, refusing the bag. "It's a hopeless situation. Not even Michelangelo could do anything with this face."

"Suit yourself," the Eagle said. "But I thought you might want to use the cosmetics before your visitor arrives."

"A visitor!" Nicole said, with both alarm and excitement. "I'm going to have a visitor? Who is it?" She reached out for the mirror and the cosmetics.

"I think I'll leave it as a surprise," the Eagle said. "Your visitor will be here in a few minutes."

Nicole put on lipstick and powder, brushed her gray hair, and straightened out and plucked her eyebrows. When she was finished, she cast a disapproving look in the mirror. "That's about all I can do," she said, as much to herself as to the Eagle.

A few minutes later the Eagle opened the door on the other side of the room and went outside. When he returned there was an octospider with him.

From across the room Nicole saw the royal blue color spill out of its boundaries. "Hello, Nicole. How are you feeling?" the octospider said.

"*Dr. Blue!*" Nicole yelled excitedly.

* * *

Dr. Blue held the monitoring device in front of Nicole. "I will be staying here with you until you are ready to be transferred," the octospider physician said. "The Eagle has other duties at present."

Bands of color raced across the tiny screen. "I don't understand," Nicole said, looking at the device upside down. "When the Eagle used that thing, the readout was all in squiggles and other funny symbols."

"That's their special-purpose technological language," Dr. Blue said. "It's incredibly efficient, much better than our colors. But of course I can't read any of it. This device actually is polylingual. There's even an English mode."

"So what do you speak when you communicate with the Eagle and I'm not around?" Nicole asked.

"We both use colors," Dr. Blue responded. "They run across his forehead from left to right."

"You're kidding," Nicole said, trying to picture the Eagle with colors on his forehead.

"Not at all," the octospider answered. "The Eagle is amazing. He jabbers and shrieks with the avians, squeals and whistles with the myrmicats."

Nicole had never seen the word "myrmicat" in the language of color before. When she asked about the word, Dr. Blue explained that six of the strange creatures were now living in the Grand Hotel and that another four were about to burst forth from germinating manna melons. "Although all the octospiders and humans slept during the long voyage," Dr. Blue said, "the manna melons were allowed to develop into myrmicats and then sessile material. They are already into their next generation."

Dr. Blue replaced the device on the table. "So what's the verdict for today, Doctor?" Nicole asked.

"You're gaining strength," Dr. Blue replied. "But you're only alive because of all the supplemental probes that have been inserted. At some time you should consider—"

"—replacing my heart. I know," said Nicole. "It may seem peculiar, but the idea does not appeal to me very much. I don't know exactly why I'm against it. Maybe I haven't yet seen what remains to live for. I know that if Richard were still alive . . ."

She stopped herself. For an instant Nicole imagined she was back in the viewing room, watching the slow-motion frames of the last seconds of Richard's life. She had not thought about that moment since she awakened.

"Do you mind if I ask you something very personal?" Nicole said to Dr. Blue.

"Not at all," the octospider said.

"We watched the deaths of Richard and Archie together," Nicole said, "and I was so distraught that I could not function. Archie was murdered at the same time, and he was your lifelong partner. Yet you sat beside me and gave me comfort. Did you not feel any sense of loss or sadness at Archie's death?"

Dr. Blue did not respond immediately. "All octospiders are trained from birth to control what you humans call emotions. The alternates, of course, are quite susceptible to feelings. But those of us who—"

"With all due respect," Nicole interrupted softly, touching her octospider colleague, "I wasn't asking you a clinical question, doctor to doctor. It was a question from one friend to another."

A short burst of crimson, then another of blue, unrelated, slowly flowed around Dr. Blue's head. "Yes, I felt a sense of loss," Dr. Blue said. "But I knew it was coming. Either then or later. When Archie joined the war effort, his termination became certain. And besides, my duty at that moment was to help you."

The door to the room opened and the Eagle entered. The alien was carrying a large box full of food, clothing, and miscellaneous equipment. He informed Nicole that he had brought her space suit and that she was going to venture out of her controlled environment in the very near future.

"Dr. Blue says that you can speak in color," Nicole said playfully. "I want you to show me."

"What do you want me to say?" the Eagle replied in orderly narrow color bands that started on the left side of his forehead and scrolled to the right.

"That's enough," Nicole said with a laugh. "You are truly amazing."

Nicole stood on the floor of the gigantic factory and stared at the pyramid in front of her. Off to her right, less than a kilometer away, a group of special-purpose biots, including a pair of mammoth bulldozers, were building a tall mountain. "Why are you doing all this?" Nicole said into the tiny microphone inside her helmet.

"It's part of the next cycle," the Eagle replied. "We have determined that these particular constructions enhance the likelihood of obtaining what we want from the experiment."

"So you already know something about the new spacefarers?"

"I don't know the answer to that," the Eagle said. "I have no assignment associated with the future of Rama."

"But you told us before," Nicole said, not satisfied, "that no changes were made unless they were necessary."

"I can't help you," the Eagle said. "Come, get in the rover. Dr. Blue wants to have a closer look at the mountain."

The octospider looked peculiar in her space suit. In fact, Nicole had laughed out loud when she had first seen Dr. Blue with the glove-fitting white fabric covering her charcoal body and her eight tentacles. Dr. Blue also had a transparent helmet around her head, through which it was easy to read her colors.

"I was astonished," Nicole said to Dr. Blue, who was sitting beside her as the open rover moved across the flat terrain toward the mountain, "when we first came outside. . . . No, that's not a strong enough word. You and the Eagle had both told me that we were in the factory and that Rama was being prepared for another voyage, but I never expected all this."

"The pyramid was built around you," the Eagle interjected from the driver's seat in front of them, "while you were sleeping. If we had not been able to build without disturbing your environment, it would have been necessary to awaken you much earlier."

"Doesn't this entire business just amaze you?" Nicole continued to face Dr. Blue. "Don't you wonder what kind of beings conceived of this grand project in the first place? And also created artificial intelligence like the Eagle? It is almost impossible to imagine."

"It's not as difficult for us," the octospider said. "Remember, we have known about superior beings from the beginning. We only exist as intelligent creatures because the Precursors altered our genes. We have never had a period in our history when we thought we were at the apex of life."

"Nor will we, ever again," mused Nicole. "Human history, whatever it turns out to be, has now been profoundly and irrevocably altered."

"Maybe not," the Eagle said from the front seat. "Our data base indicates that some species are not significantly impacted by contact with us. Our experiments are designed to allow for that possibility. Our contact occurs during a finite interval, with only a small percentage of the population. There is no continuous interaction unless the species under study takes overt action to create it. I doubt if life on Earth at this very moment is much different than it would have been if no Rama spacecraft had ever visited your solar system."

Nicole leaned forward in her seat. "Do you know that for a fact?" she said. "Or are you just guessing?"

The Eagle's answer was vague. "Certainly your history was changed by Rama's appearance," he said. "Many major events would not have occurred if there had not been any contact. But a hundred more years from now, or five hundred. . . . How different will Earth be then from what it would have been?"

"But the human point of view *must* have changed," Nicole argued. "Surely the knowledge that there exists in the universe, or at least existed in some earlier epoch, an intelligence advanced enough to build an interstellar robotic spacecraft larger than our greatest city cannot be cast aside as insignificant information. It creates a different perspective for the entire human experience. Religion, philosophy, even the fundamentals of biology must be revised in the presence—"

"I am glad to see," the Eagle interrupted, "that at least some small measure of your optimism and idealism has survived all these years. Recall, however, that in New Eden the humans *knew* that they were living inside a domain especially constructed for them by extraterrestrials. And they were told, by you and others, that they were being continually observed. Even so, when it became apparent that the aliens, whoever they were, did not intend to interfere in the daily activities of the humans, the existence of those advanced beings became irrelevant."

The rover arrived at the base of the mountain. "I wanted to come over here," Dr. Blue said, "out of curiosity. We did not have any mountains, as you know, in our realm on Rama. And not many in my region of our home planet when I was a juvenile. I thought it would be nice to stand on the top."

"I have commandeered one of the large bulldozers," the Eagle said. "Our journey to the summit will only take ten minutes. You may be frightened in spots because of the steepness of the climb, but it is perfectly safe, as long as you wear your seat belts."

Nicole was not too old to enjoy the spectacular climb. The bulldozer, as large as an office building, did not have very comfortable seats for passengers and some of the bumps were quite violent, but the vistas that opened up as the trio ascended were definitely worth the trouble.

The mountain was over a kilometer high and about ten kilometers around its approximately round circumference. Nicole could clearly see the pyramid in which she had been staying when the bulldozer was only a quarter of the way up the mountain. Farther away, in all directions, the horizon was dotted with isolated construction projects of unknown purpose.

So now it all begins again, Nicole thought. *This rebuilt Rama will soon enter another set of star systems. And what will it find? Who are the spacefarers who will next walk across this ground? Or climb this mountain?*

The bulldozer halted on a plateau very near the summit and the three passengers disembarked. The view was breathtaking. As Nicole surveyed the scene, she recalled her wonder on that very first trip into Rama, when she had been riding down the chairlift and the vast alien world had stretched out in front of her. *Thank you,* she thought, addressing the Eagle in her mind, *for keeping me alive. You were right. This experience alone and the memories it triggers are more than enough reason to continue.*

Nicole turned around to face the rest of the mountain. She saw something small flying in and out of some bushy-looking growths, red in color, that were no more than twenty meters away. She walked over and captured one of the flying objects in her hand. It was the size and shape of a butterfly. Its wings were decorated with a variegated pattern without symmetry or any other design principle that Nicole could discern. She let one go and then captured another. The pattern on the second Raman butterfly was altogether different, but still rich in both color and decoration.

The Eagle and Dr. Blue walked up beside her. Nicole showed them what she was holding in her hand. "Flying biots," the Eagle said without additional comment.

Nicole marveled again at the tiny creature. *Something astonishing happens every day*, she remembered Richard saying. *And we are then always reminded of what a joy it is to be alive.*

2

Nicole had barely finished her bath when the two biots entered the room. One was a crab and the other looked like a small truck. The crab used a combination of its powerful pincers and its formidable array of ancillary gadgetry to cut Nicole's sleeping container into manageable pieces. The pieces were then stacked in the bed of the truck. On its way out of the room less than a minute later, the crab grabbed the white bathtub and all the remaining chairs and piled them on top of the stacks in the truck bed. It then put the table on its own back and disappeared from the empty room behind the truck biot.

Nicole straightened her dress. "I'll never forget the first time I saw a crab biot," she commented to her two companions. "It was on the huge screen in the Newton control center, years and years ago. We were all terrified."

"So today's the day," Dr. Blue said in color several seconds later. "Are you ready to check into the Grand Hotel?"

"Probably not," Nicole said with a smile. "From what you and the Eagle have said, I guess I have enjoyed my last moment of solitude."

"Your family and friends are very excited about seeing you," the Eagle said. "I visited them yesterday and told them you would be coming. You'll stay with Max, Eponine, Ellie, Marius, and Nikki. Patrick, Nai, Benjy, Kepler, and Maria are next door. As I explained to you last week, Patrick and Nai have been treating Maria as their own daughter since shortly after everyone awakened. They know the whole story of how you rescued Maria during the bombing."

"I don't know if 'rescued' is exactly the correct word," Nicole said, remembering clearly her last hours in the old Rama spacecraft. "I picked her up because there was no one to look after her. Anybody would have done the same thing."

"You saved her life," the Eagle said. "Not more than an hour after you left the zoo with the girl, three large bombs devastated her compound and the two adjacent sections. Maria certainly would have been killed if you hadn't found her."

"She is now a beautiful and intelligent young woman," Dr. Blue said. "I met her once briefly several weeks ago. Ellie says Maria is incredibly energetic. According to Ellie, the girl is the first one awake in the morning and the last one in bed at night."

Like Katie, Nicole couldn't help but think. *Who are you, Maria?* she wondered. *And why were you sent into my life at just that moment?*

"Ellie also told me that Maria and Nikki are inseparable," Dr. Blue continued. "They study together, eat together, and talk incessantly about everything. Nikki has told Maria all about you."

"How is that possible?" Nicole said with a smile. "Nikki was not yet four years old the last time that I saw her. Human children don't retain memories from that early."

"They definitely do if they sleep through the next fifteen years," the Eagle said. "Kepler and Galileo also have very clear recollections of their early days. . . . But we can talk while we travel. It's time for us to leave now."

The Eagle helped Nicole and Dr. Blue put on their space suits. Then he picked up the suitcase of Nicole's belongings. "I've put your medical bag in here with your clothes, as well as the cosmetics you've been using these last several days," he said.

"My medical bag?" Nicole said. She laughed. "Goodness, I had almost forgotten. I had it with me, didn't I, when I found Maria? Thank you."

The trio walked out of the room, which was on the bottom floor of the large pyramid. A few minutes later they moved through the great arched entrance to the building. Outside, in the bright light of the factory, the rover was waiting for them. "It will take us about half an hour to reach the high-speed elevators," the Eagle said. "Our shuttle is parked at the Dock, on the uppermost level."

As the rover moved away, Nicole turned around and looked behind her. Beyond the pyramid was the tall mountain they had climbed three days before. "So you really have no idea why the butterfly biots are there?" Nicole said into the microphone in her space helmet.

"No," said the Eagle. "My assignment covers only your cycle."

Nicole continued to stare behind her. The rover passed a set of tall poles, ten or twelve altogether, connected by wires at the top, middle, and bottom. *All this will be part of the new Rama,* Nicole thought. Suddenly it occurred to her that she was about to leave the world of Rama for the very last time. A powerful feeling of sadness swept over her. *This has been my home,* she said to herself, *and I am going away forever.*

"Would it be possible," Nicole said to the Eagle without turning around, "for me to see any of the other parts of Rama before we leave for good?"

"What for?" the Eagle asked.

"I'm not exactly certain," Nicole answered. "Maybe just so I can linger for an extra hour in my memories."

"The two bowls and the Southern Hemicylinder have already been completely remodeled. You would not recognize them. The Cylindrical Sea has been drained and removed. Even New York is in the process of being dismantled."

"But it's not completely destroyed yet, is it?" Nicole asked.

"No, not yet," replied the Eagle.

"Then can we go there, please, just for a short while?"

Please indulge an old woman, Nicole thought. *Even though she doesn't understand why herself.*

"All right," the Eagle said, "but we'll be delayed. New York is in another part of the factory."

They were standing on a parapet near the top of one of the tall skyscrapers. Most of New York was gone, the buildings bulldozed into heaps by the awesome power of the large biots. What was left was twenty or thirty buildings around one plaza.

"There were three lairs underneath the city," Nicole was explaining to Dr. Blue. "One for us, one for the avians, and a third occupied by your cousins. I was down inside the avian lair when Richard came to rescue me—" She stopped. Nicole realized that she had told Dr. Blue the story before and that octospiders never forgot anything. "Do you mind?" she asked.

"Please continue," the octospider said.

"During the whole time that we were here, none of us on this island knew that there were entrances to some of these buildings. Isn't that amazing? Oh, how I wish that Richard were still alive and I could have seen his face when the Eagle opened the door to the octahedron. He would have been so shocked.

"Anyway," Nicole said, "Richard came back inside Rama to find me. And then we fell in love and figured out how to escape from the island using the avians. It was such a glorious time, so many years ago. . . ."

Nicole stepped forward, grabbed the rail with both hands, and gazed around her. In her mind's eye she could see New York as it had been. *Over there were the ramparts. Out beyond was the Cylindrical Sea. And somewhere in the middle of those ugly heaps of metal was the barn and the pit in which I nearly died.*

The tears came suddenly, surprising her. They poured out of Nicole's eyes and ran down her cheeks. She did not turn around. *Five of my six children were born over there,* Nicole thought, *underneath that ground. Just outside our lair we found Richard after he had been gone for two years. He was comatose.*

The memories came tumbling into her mind, one after another, each bringing a vague heartache and a new flow of tears. Nicole could not stop them. At one moment she was again descending into the octospider lair to save her daughter Katie, at another she was feeling the excitement and exhilaration of soaring over the Cylindrical Sea, attached by a harness to three avians. *We must eventually die,* Nicole thought, wiping her eyes with the back of her hand, *because there is not any room left in our brains for more memories.*

As Nicole gazed out across the broken landscape of New York, transforming it in her mind's eye into what it had been years before, she had a sharp recollection of an even earlier epoch in her life. She remembered a cold late autumn evening at Beauvois during her last days on Earth, just before Genevieve and she had gone skiing at Davos. Nicole was sitting with her father and her daughter in front of the fireplace in their villa. Pierre had been very reflective that evening. He had shared with Nicole and Genevieve many special moments from his courtship with Nicole's mother.

Later, at bedtime, Genevieve had asked her mother a question. "Why does Grampa talk so much about what happened long ago?" the teenager had said.

"Because that is what is important to him," Nicole had answered.

Forgive me, Nicole thought, still staring out at the skyscrapers in front of her. *Forgive me, all you elderly people whose stories I ignored. I did not mean to be rude or condescending. I just did not understand what it meant to be old.*

Nicole sighed, took a deep breath, and turned around.

"Are you all right?" Dr. Blue asked.

She nodded. "Thank you for this," Nicole said to the Eagle, her voice breaking. "I'm ready to go now."

She saw the lights as soon as their small shuttle cleared the hangar. Even though the lights were still over a hundred kilometers away, they were already a magnificent sight against the background of blackness and distant stars.

"This Node has an extra vertex," the Eagle said, "forming a perfect tetrahedron. The Node you visited near Sirius did not have a Knowledge Module."

Nicole stared out the window of their shuttle, holding her breath. It looked unreal, like a figment of her imagination, this illuminated construction turning slowly in the distance. There were four large spheres at the vertices, connected to each other by six linear transportation corridors. Each of the spheres was exactly the same size. Each of the six long thin lines connecting them was exactly the same length. At this distance the individual lights inside the transparent Node blurred together, so the entire facility appeared to be a great tetrahedral torch in the darkness of space.

"It's beautiful," Nicole said, unable to find any other words to express the awe she was feeling.

"You should see it from the observation deck of our living quarters," Dr. Blue said from beside her. "It is dazzling. We are close enough that we can see the different lights inside the spheres and even follow the vehicles zooming back and forth along the transportation corridors. Many of the residents at the Grand Hotel stay on deck for hours at a time, amusing themselves by making guesses about the activities represented by the movement of the lights inside."

Nicole felt goose bumps rising on her arm as she stared silently at the Node. She heard a faraway voice, Francesca Sabatini's voice, and a poem that Nicole had first memorized as a schoolgirl.

> *"Tyger! Tyger! burning bright,*
> *In the forests of the night,*
> *What immortal hand or eye*
> *Could frame thy fearful symmetry?"*

"Did he who made the Lamb make thee?" Nicole thought as the tetrahedron of light continued to turn. She remembered a late-night conversation with Michael O'Toole while they were staying at the Node near Sirius. "We must unfetter God after this experience," he had said. "And remove our homocentric limitations on Him. The God who created the architects of the Node must surely be amused by our pathetic attempts to define Him in terms we humans can readily understand."

Nicole was fascinated by the Node. Even from this distance, as it turned slowly around, the different aspects presented by the tetrahedron were hypnotizing. As she watched, the facility moved into a position where one of the four equilateral triangles forming its empty faces was in a plane perpendicular to the flight path of the shuttle. The Node looked entirely different, as if it had no depth. The fourth vertex, which was in reality some thirty kilometers beyond the plane on the other side from Nicole, appeared to be a nexus of light in the center of the facing triangle.

When the shuttle abruptly changed direction, the Node was no longer visible. Instead, off in the distance, Nicole could see a solitary light yellow star. "That's Tau Ceti," the Eagle said to her, "a star very much like your sun."

"And why, if I may ask," Nicole said, "is this Node here, in the neighborhood of Tau Ceti?"

"It is an optimum temporary placement," the Eagle answered, "to support our data-acquisition activities in this part of the galaxy."

Nicole nudged Dr. Blue. "Do your engineers sometimes speak meaningless gobbledygook in color?" she said with a smile. "Our host just gave us a nonanswer."

"We are more humble as a species than you are," the octospider replied. "Again, it's probably because of our relationship with the Precursors. We don't pretend that we should be able to understand everything."

"We have spoken very little about your species during the time since I awakened," Nicole said to Dr. Blue, suddenly feeling self-centered and apologetic, "although I do remember your telling me that your former Chief Optimizer, her staff, and all those who prosecuted the war had all been terminated in an orderly manner. Is the new leadership working out all right?"

"More or less," Dr. Blue answered, "considering the difficulty of our living situation. Jamie works at the lower echelon of the new staff, and he is busy almost every waking hour. We have not really been able to reach anything like an equilibrium in our colony because there is constant outside friction."

"Most of which is caused by the humans on board," the Eagle added. "We haven't discussed this subject before, Nicole," he continued, "but now is probably a good time. We have been surprised by the failure of your fellow beings to adapt to interspecies living. Only a very few of them are comfortable with the idea that other species may be as important and capable as they are."

"I told you that soon after we met years ago," Nicole said. "I pointed out to you that for a variety of historical and sociological reasons, there is a vast range in the way that humans respond to new ideas and concepts."

"I know you did," the Eagle replied, "but our experience with you and your family misled us. Until we woke up all the survivors, we had reached the tentative conclusion that what happened in New Eden, with the aggressive and territorial humans seizing control, was an anomaly, to be explained by the particular composition of the colonists. Now, after watching a year of interactions at the Grand Hotel, we have concluded that we did indeed have a typical collection of humans inside Rama."

"It sounds as if I may be entering an unpleasant situation," Nicole said. "Are there other things that I need to know before we arrive?"

"Not really," the Eagle said. "We now have everything under control. I'm certain your colleagues will share with you the most important details from their experiences. Besides, the current situation is only temporary, and this phase is almost over."

"At first," Dr. Blue said, "all the survivors from Rama were scattered throughout the starfish. In each ray there were some humans, some octospiders, and a few of our support animals that were permitted to survive because of their critical role in our social structure. That was all changed a few months later, primarily because of the continued aggressive hostility of the humans. Now the living quarters for each species are concentrated in a single region."

"Segregation," Nicole said ruefully. "It is one of the defining characteristics of my species."

"Interspecies interaction occurs now only in the cafeteria and other common rooms in the center of the starfish," said the Eagle. "More than half the humans, however, never leave their ray except to eat, and they studiously avoid interaction even then. From our point of view, human beings are astonishingly xenophobic. There are not many examples in our data base of spacefarers who are as sociologically backward as your species."

The shuttle turned in a new direction and again the magnificent tetrahedron filled their view. They were much closer now. Many individual light sources could be resolved, both inside the spheres and in the long, slender transportation lines that connected them. Nicole gazed at the beauty in front of her and sighed heavily. The conversation with Dr. Blue and the Eagle had depressed her. *Maybe Richard was right*, Nicole thought to herself. *Maybe humanity cannot be changed unless its entire memory is wiped clean and we begin anew, in a fresh environment, with an upgraded operating system.*

Nicole's stomach was churning as the shuttle approached the starfish. She told herself not to worry about silly things, but she nevertheless felt uncomfortable about her appearance. Nicole looked in the mirror as she touched up her makeup. She was not able to mitigate her anxiety. *I am old*, she thought. *The children will think I'm ugly.*

The starfish was not nearly as large as Rama had been. It was easy for Nicole to understand why it was so crowded inside. The Eagle had explained to her that the intercession had been a contingency plan and that Rama had arrived at the Node, as a result, several years earlier than originally scheduled. This particular starfish, an obsolete spacecraft that had somehow been spared the recycling process, had been remodeled into a temporary hotel to house the occupants of Rama until they could be moved elsewhere.

"We have given strict orders," the Eagle said, "that your entry should be as smooth as possible. We don't want your system taxed any more than necessary. Big Block and his army have cleared the halls and common areas leading from the shuttle station to your room."

"So you will not be going with me?" Nicole asked the Eagle.

"No," he replied. "I have work to do over at the Node."

"I will accompany you through the observation deck, as far as the entrance to the human ray," Dr. Blue said. "Then you will be on your own. Luckily your quarters are not far from the ray entrance."

The Eagle remained in the shuttle while Nicole and Dr. Blue disembarked. The alien birdman waved good-bye to them as they entered the air lock. When, a few minutes later, they moved into a large dressing room on the other side of the air lock, Nicole and Dr. Blue were greeted by the robot known as Big Block.

"Welcome, Nicole des Jardins Wakefield," the giant robot said. "We are glad that you have finally arrived. Please put your space suit on the bench to your right."

Big Block, who was just under three meters tall, almost two meters wide, and constructed of rectangular blocks similar to those played with by human children, looked exactly like the robot that had supervised the engineering tests Nicole and her family had undergone at the Node near Sirius years earlier, before their return to the solar system. The robot hovered over Nicole and the smaller octospider.

"Although I am certain," Big Block said in his mechanical voice, "that you will not cause any problems, I want to remind you that all commands given by me or one of the similar, smaller robots are to be followed without hesitation. It is our purpose to keep order in this spaceship. Now follow me, please."

Big Block turned around, pivoting on the joints in its midsection, and rolled forward on its single cylindrical foot. "This large room is called the observation deck," the robot said. "Ordinarily it is the most popular of our common rooms. We have emptied it temporarily tonight to make it easier for you to reach your living quarters."

Dr. Blue and Nicole stopped for a minute in front of the huge window facing the Node. The view was indeed spectacular, but Nicole could not focus her attention on the beauty and order of the superb extraterrestrial architecture. She was anxious to see her family and friends.

Big Block remained on the observation deck while Nicole and her octospider companion walked along the wide hallway that encircled the spacecraft. Dr. Blue explained to Nicole how to locate and identify the places where the small trams stopped. The octospider also informed Nicole that the humans were in the third ray, moving in either direction from the shuttle station, with the octospiders in the two rays immediately clockwise from the station. "The fourth and fifth rays," Dr. Blue said in color, "are designed differently. All the other creatures live there, as well as those humans and octospiders who have been placed under guard."

"Is Galileo, then, in some kind of prison?" Nicole asked.

"Not exactly," Dr. Blue replied. "There are just many more of the smaller block robots in that part of the starfish."

They stepped off the tram together after traveling halfway around the starfish. When they reached the entrance to the human ray, Dr. Blue held the monitoring device in front of Nicole and read the output colors on the screen. Based on the initial data that she saw, the octospider used the cilia underneath one of her tentacles to request more information.

"Is something wrong?" Nicole asked.

"Your heart has undergone a few palpitations in the last hour," Dr. Blue said. "I just wanted to check the amplitude and frequency of the irregularities."

"I'm very excited," Nicole said. "It's normal in humans for excitement to cause—"

"I know," Dr. Blue said, "but the Eagle instructed me to be very careful." There were no colors on the octospider's head for several seconds while Dr. Blue studied the data on her screen. "I guess it's all right," she said finally, "but if you experience the slightest chest pain or surprising shortness of breath, do not hesitate to push the emergency button in your room."

Nicole gave Dr. Blue a hug. "Thank you very much," she said. "You have been wonderful."

"It has been my pleasure," Dr. Blue said. "I hope everything goes all right. Your room is number forty-one, down that hallway, about the twentieth door on the left. The tram stops every five rooms."

Nicole took a deep breath and turned around. The smaller tram was waiting for her. She shuffled toward it, sliding her feet on the floor, and boarded after a farewell wave to Dr. Blue. A minute or two later Nicole was standing in front of an ordinary door with the number forty-one painted on it.

She knocked. The door opened immediately and five smiling faces greeted her. "Welcome to the Grand Hotel," said Max, with a wide grin and his arms open wide. "Come in and give an Arkansas farm boy a hug."

Nicole felt a hand on hers as soon as she stepped into the room. "Hello, Mother," Ellie said. Nicole turned and looked at her youngest daughter. Ellie was graying at the temples, but her eyes were as clear and sparkling as ever.

"Hello, Ellie," Nicole said, breaking into tears. They would not be the last tears she would shed during the several hours of the reunion.

3

Their room was a square, approximately seven meters on a side. Along the back wall was an enclosed bathroom, with a washbasin, a shower, and a toilet. Next to the bathroom was a large open closet that contained all their clothes and other belongings. At bedtime the sleeping mats, which were rolled up each day, were removed from the closet and placed upon the floor.

The first night Nicole slept between Ellie and Nikki, with Max, Eponine, and Marius on the other side of the room beside the table and six chairs that were the only furniture in their living quarters. Nicole had been so exhausted that she had fallen asleep even before the lights had been switched off and everyone else had finished preparing for bed. After sleeping for about five hours, Nicole had awakened abruptly, temporarily uncertain where she was.

As she lay in the dark and the silence, Nicole thought about the events of the previous evening. During the reunion she had been so overwhelmed by her emotions that she had not really had time to sort out her reactions to what she was seeing and hearing. Immediately after Nicole had entered the room, Nikki had gone next door for the others. For the next two hours there had been eleven people in the crowded room, at least three or four of them talking all the time. Nicole had had brief conversations with each person individually during those two hours, but it had been impossible for her to discuss anything in depth.

The four young people—Kepler, Marius, Nikki, and Maria—had all been very shy. Maria, whose stunning blue eyes stood out in contrast to her copper skin and long black hair, had dutifully thanked Nicole for rescuing her. She had also politely acknowledged that she had no memories of any kind from the time period before she went to sleep. Nikki had been nervous and diffident in her brief tête-à-tête with her grandmother. Nicole thought she had detected some fear in Nikki's eyes; however, Ellie told Nicole later that what she had seen had probably been awe, that so many stories had been told about Nicole that Nikki felt she was meeting a legend.

The two young men had been polite, but not forthcoming. Once during the evening Nicole had seen Kepler staring at her from across the room with great intensity. Nicole reminded herself that she was the first really old human the boys had ever seen. *Young men in particular,* Nicole thought, *have difficulty with women who are old and phthisic. It shatters their fantasies about members of the opposite sex.*

Benjy had welcomed Nicole with an uninhibited embrace. He had lifted her off the floor with his strong arms and yelled with joy. "Mama, Mama," he had said, turning around in circles with Nicole's head above his. Benjy had seemed quite well. Nicole had been startled to discover that his hairline had receded and that he now looked decidedly avuncular. Later she had told herself that Benjy's appearance was really not that surprising, since he was about forty years old.

Her greetings from Patrick and Ellie had been very warm. Ellie had looked tired, but she had said it was because she had had a full day. Ellie had explained to Nicole that she had taken it upon herself to stimulate interspecies social activity at the Grand Hotel. "It's the least I can do," Ellie had said, "since I speak the octospider language. I'm hoping that you'll give me a hand as soon as you have your strength."

Patrick had spoken quietly to Nicole about his concern for Nai. "This Galileo situation is tearing her apart, Mother," her son had said. "She is furious because the blockheads, as we call them, removed Galileo from the normal living areas without much explanation and without anything that we would call 'due process.' She is also angry because she is not allowed to spend more than two hours a day with him. I'm certain she is going to ask you for assistance."

Nai had changed. The spark and softness were gone from her eyes and she was uncharacteristically negative, even in her first remarks. "We are living in the worst kind of police state here, Nicole," Nai had said. "Far worse than under Nakamura. After you are settled, I have many things to tell you."

Max Puckett and his adorable French wife, Eponine, had both aged, like everyone else, but it was clear that their love for each other and for their son, Marius, sustained them on a day-to-day basis. Eponine had shrugged when Nicole asked her if the crowded living conditions bothered her. "Not really," she had replied. "Remember, I lived in the orphanage in

Limoges as a child. Besides, I'm just delighted to be alive and have Max and Marius. For years I never thought I would live long enough to have any gray hair."

As for Max, he had remained his ornery, irrepressible self. His hair too was mostly gray, and he had lost a little of the bounce in his step. But Nicole could tell from his eyes that he was enjoying his life. "There's this fellow I see regularly in the smoking lounge," Max had told Nicole during the evening, "who is a big admirer of yours. He somehow escaped the plague, although his wife didn't. Anyway"—Max had then grinned—"I thought I'd fix you two up as soon as you have some free time. He's a little younger than you are, but I doubt if that will be a problem."

Nicole had asked Max about the problems between the humans and the octospiders. "You know," Max had said, "the war may have taken place fifteen or sixteen years ago, but none of the humans has any intervening memories to soften his anger. Everyone here lost somebody, a friend or a relative or a neighbor, in that horrible plague. And they can't quickly forget that it was the octospiders who caused it."

"In response to the aggression of the human armies," Nicole had said.

"But most of the humans don't see it that way. Maybe they believe the propaganda Nakamura told them and not the 'official' war history, presented by your friend the Eagle soon after we were moved here. The truth is that most of the humans hate and fear the octospiders. Only about twenty percent of the people have made any attempt to mix socially, despite Ellie's courageous efforts, or to learn anything about the octos. Most of the humans stay in our ray. Unfortunately, the cramped living quarters do not help to alleviate the problem."

Nicole now rolled over on her side. Her daughter Ellie was sleeping facing her. Ellie's eyes were twitching. *She's dreaming,* Nicole thought. *I hope not about Robert.* She thought again about her reunion with her family and friends. *I guess the Eagle knew what he was doing in keeping me alive. Even if he doesn't have anything specific for me to do. As long as I don't become an invalid or a burden, I can be helpful here.*

"This will be your first major Grand Hotel experience," Max said to Nicole. "Every time I go to the cafeteria during open hours, I am reminded of Bounty Day in the Emerald City. Those weird creatures that came along with the octospiders may be fascinating, but I'm a damn sight more comfortable when they're not around."

"Can't we wait until it's our period, Dad?" Marius asked. "The iguanas frighten Nikki. They gawk at us with their yellow eyes and make such repulsive clucking noises while they are eating."

"Son," Max said, "you and Nikki can wait with the others until our segregated lunchtime, if you want. Nicole wants to eat with *all* the residents. It's a matter of principle to her. Your mother and I are going to accompany her to ensure that she learns the cafeteria routine."

"Don't worry about me," Nicole said. "I'm sure that Ellie or Patrick—"

"Nonsense," Max interrupted. "Eponine and I are delighted to join you. Besides, Patrick has gone with Nai to see Galileo, Ellie is over in the recreation room, and Benjy is reading with Kepler and Maria."

"I appreciate your understanding, Max," Nicole said. "It is important for me to make the right kind of statement, especially at the beginning. The Eagle and Dr. Blue didn't tell me much about the details of the trouble . . ."

"You don't need to explain," Max replied. "In fact, last night after you fell asleep, I told Frenchie I was certain that you would want to mix." He laughed. "Don't forget, we know you very well."

After Eponine joined them, they walked out in the hallway. It was mostly empty. A few people were walking in the corridor on their left, away from the center of the starfish, and a man and a woman were standing together at the entrance to the ray.

The trio waited two or three minutes for the tram to arrive. As they drew near to the final stop, Max leaned over to Nicole. "Those two people standing at the ray entrance," he said, "are not just passing time. They're both big activists on the Council. Very opinionated and very pushy."

Nicole took the arm that Max offered her as they disembarked. "What do they want?" she whispered as the pair started walking toward them.

"I don't know," Max mumbled quickly, "but we'll find out soon enough."

"Good day, Max. Hello, Eponine," the man said. He was a portly man in his early forties. He looked at Nicole and broke into a wide politician's smile. "You must be Nicole Wakefield," he said, reaching out to shake hands. "We've all heard so very much about you. . . . Welcome . . . welcome. I'm Stephen Kowalski."

"And I'm Renee du Pont," the woman said, advancing and also extending her hand in Nicole's direction.

After exchanging a few pleasantries, Mr. Kowalski asked Max what the three of them were doing. "We're taking Mrs. Wakefield to lunch," Max replied simply.

"It's still common time," the man said with another big smile. He checked his watch. "Why don't you wait forty-five minutes more and Renee and I will join you? We're on the Council, you know, and we would like very much to speak to Mrs. Wakefield about our activities. Certainly the Council will want to hear from her in the very near future."

"Thanks for the offer, Stephen," Max said. "But we're all hungry. We want to eat now."

Mr. Kowalski's brow furrowed. "I wouldn't do that if I were you, Max," he said. "There's a lot of tension at the moment. After that incident yesterday in the swimming pool, the Council voted unanimously to boycott all collective activities for the next two days. Emily was especially incensed that Big Block put Garland on probation and took no disciplinary action of any kind against the offending octospider. That's the fourth consecutive time that the blockheads have ruled against us."

"Come on, Stephen," Max said. "I heard the story at dinner last night. Garland was still in the pool fifteen minutes *after* our special time had expired. He grabbed the octo first."

"It was a deliberate provocation," Renee du Pont said. "There were only three octospiders in the pool. There was no reason for one of them to be in the lane where Garland was swimming laps."

"Besides," Stephen said, "as we discussed in the Council last night, the specifics of this particular incident are not our primary concern. It is essential that we send a message to both the blockheads and the octospiders, so that they know we are united as a species. The Council is going to meet in special session again tonight to draw up a list of grievances."

Max was becoming angry. "Thank you for keeping us informed, Stephen," he said brusquely. "Now if you'll just step aside, we would like to go to lunch."

"You're making a mistake," Mr. Kowalski said. "You will be the only humans in the cafeteria. We will, of course, report this conversation at the meeting of the Council tonight."

"Go ahead," said Max.

Max, Eponine, and Nicole walked out into the main corridor that formed an annulus around the central core of the starfish. "What's the Council?" Nicole asked.

"A group—self-appointed, I might add—that pretends to represent all the humans," Max replied. "At first they were just a nuisance, but in the last few months they have actually begun to wield some power. They've even recruited poor Nai into their ranks by offering to help solve the Galileo problem."

The big tram stopped about twenty meters to their right and a pair of the iguanas disembarked. Two of the block robots, who had been standing unobtrusively off to the side, walked out into the corridor between the humans and the strange animals with the fearsome teeth. As the iguanas passed around them back along the wall, Nicole recalled the attack on Nikki at the Bounty Day ceremony.

"Why are they here?" Nicole asked Max. "I would have thought that they were too disruptive."

"Big Block and the Eagle have both explained to full human assemblies, on two separate occasions, that the iguanas are essential for the production of that barrican plant, without which the octo society would be all screwed up. I didn't follow all the details of the biological explanation, but I do remember that fresh iguana eggs were a vital link in the process. The Eagle stressed repeatedly that only the bare minimum number of iguanas were being maintained here in the Grand Hotel."

The trio was near the entrance to the cafeteria. "Have the iguanas caused much trouble?" Nicole asked.

"Not really," Max said. "They can be dangerous, as you know, but if you cut through all the crap put out by the Council, you conclude that there have only been a few incidents in which the iguanas launched an unprovoked attack. Most of the altercations have been started by humans. Our boy Galileo killed two of them one night in the cafeteria during one of his violent outbursts."

Max noticed Nicole's strong reaction to his last comment. "I don't want to be telling tales out of school," he said, shaking his head, "but this Galileo business has really torn our little family apart. I promised Eponine I would let you talk to Nai about it first."

The smaller block robots were constructed in the same general pattern as Big Block. A dozen of them were serving food in the cafeteria, and six or eight others were standing around the eating area. When Nicole and her friends entered, four or five hundred octospiders, including two giant repletes and eighty or so midget morphs eating on the floor in the corner, were sitting in the cafeteria. Many of them turned to watch as Max, Eponine, and Nicole passed through the line. A dozen iguanas, seated not far from the serving line, stopped eating and eyed the humans warily.

Nicole was surprised at the large variety of things to eat. She chose some fish and potatoes, as well as some octospider fruit and their orange-tasting honey for her bread.

"Where does all this fresh food come from?" she asked Max as they sat at a long empty table.

Max pointed up. "There's a second level to this starfish. All the food for everybody is raised up there. We eat very well, although the Council has complained about the lack of meat."

Nicole took a couple of bites of her food. "I think I ought to tell you," Max said quietly, leaning across the table, "that a pair of octospiders is headed in your direction."

She turned around. Two octospiders were indeed approaching. Out of the corner of her eye Nicole also saw Big Block hurrying toward their table. "Hello, Nicole," the first octospider said in color. "I was one of Dr. Blue's assistants in the Emerald City Hospital. I just wanted to welcome you and thank you again for helping us out."

Nicole searched vainly for a distinguishing mark on the octospider. "I'm sorry," she said in a friendly tone, "I can't place you exactly."

"You called me Milky," the octospider said, "because at the time I was recovering from a lens operation and I had excess white fluid . . ."

"Ah, yes," Nicole said with a smile. "I remember you now, Milky.

Didn't we have a long discussion at lunch one day about old age? As I recall, you had a hard time believing that we humans remained alive, whether we were useful or not, until we died of natural causes."

"That's right," Milky answered. "Well, I don't want to disturb your dinner, but my friend very much wanted to meet you."

"And to thank you also," said Milky's companion, "for being so fair about everything. Dr. Blue says that you have been an example for all of us."

Other octospiders began to rise from where they were sitting in the cafeteria and to line up behind the first two octos. The colors for "thank you" were visible on most of their heads. Nicole was deeply moved. At Max's suggestion, she stood up and spoke to the line of octospiders. "Thank you all," she said, "for your warm welcome. I really do appreciate it. I hope I have a chance to visit with each of you while we are living here together."

Nicole's eyes drifted to the right of the line of octos and she saw her daughter Ellie with Nikki standing beside her. "I came as soon as I could," Ellie said, coming over and kissing her mother on the cheek. "I should have known," she added with a slight smile. She gave Nicole a vigorous hug. "I love you, Mother," Ellie said. "And I have missed you so very much."

"I explained to the Council," Nai said, "that you had just arrived and did not fully understand the significance of the boycott. I believe they were satisfied."

Nai opened the door and Nicole followed her into the laundry area. Using the washers and dryers they had seen in New Eden as a basis, the aliens who had outfitted the Grand Hotel in a hurry had built the free laundry room not far from the cafeteria. Two other women were in the large room. Nai purposely chose to use the machines at the far opposite side, so that she could have a private conversation with Nicole.

"I asked you to come with me today," Nai said as she began to sort the clothing, "because I wanted to talk to you about Galileo." She paused, struggling. "Forgive me, Nicole, my feelings on this subject are so strong. I'm not certain—"

"It's all right, Nai," Nicole said softly. "I understand. Remember, I'm a mother too."

"I'm desperate, Nicole," Nai continued. "I need your help. Nothing that has ever happened in my life, not even Kenji's murder, has affected me like this situation. I am consumed by anxiety for my son. Even meditation does not give me any peace."

Nai had divided the clothes into three piles. She put them into three washing machines and returned to Nicole's side.

"Look," she said, "I'll be the first to admit that Galileo's behavior has not been perfect. After the long sleep, when we were moved over here, he was very slow to become involved with the others. He would not participate in the classes Patrick, Ellie, Eponine, and I set up for the children, and when he did, he would not do any homework. Galileo was surly, difficult, and unpleasant to everyone except Maria.

"He never would talk to me about what he was feeling. The only thing he seemed to enjoy was going over to the recreation room for muscle-building exercises. He has, incidentally, become very proud of his physical strength."

Nai paused for a moment. "Galileo is not a *bad* person, Nicole," she said apologetically. "He is just confused. He went to sleep as a six-year-old and woke up at the age of twenty-one, with the body and desires of a young man."

She stopped. Tears had formed in her eyes. "How could he have been *expected* to know how to act?" Nai said with difficulty. Nicole reached out with her arms, but Nai did not accept her offer. "I have tried, but I haven't been able to help him," Nai continued. "I don't know *what* to do. And I'm afraid now it's too late."

Nicole recalled her own sleepless nights in New Eden when she had often wept out of frustration about Katie. "I understand, Nai," she said softly. "I really do."

"One time, only one time," Nai said after a pause, "did I ever have a glimpse beneath that cold exterior Galileo wears so proudly. It was in the middle of the night after the business with Maria, when he returned from his session with Big Block. We were out in the corridor together, only the two of us, and he was wailing and beating on the wall. 'I wasn't going to hurt her, Mom, you must believe me,' he yelled. 'I love Maria. I just couldn't stop myself.'"

"What happened with Galileo and Maria?" Nicole asked when Nai stopped again for a few seconds. "I haven't heard the story."

"Oh," Nai said, surprised, "I was certain that someone would have told you about it by now." She hesitated for a moment. "Max said at the time that Galileo had tried to rape Maria and that he might have succeeded if Benjy had not come back to the room and dragged him off the girl. Later Max admitted to me that he might have overreacted when he used the word 'rape,' but that Galileo had definitely been 'out of line.'

"My son told me that Maria had encouraged him, at least initially, and that they had dropped to the floor while kissing. She was still enthusiastically participating, according to Galileo, until he started pulling down her pants. That was when the struggle began."

Nai tried to calm herself. "The rest of the story, no matter who tells it, is not very pleasant. . . . Galileo admits that he hit Maria several times after she started screaming and that he held her down and continued to pull off her pants. He had locked the door. Benjy broke it down with his shoulder and threw himself at Galileo with all his force. Because of the noise and the property damage, Big Block was there, as well as many onlookers."

There were more tears in Nai's eyes. "It must have been horrible," Nicole said.

"That night my life was shattered," Nai said. "Everyone condemned Galileo. When Big Block put him on probation and returned Galileo to the family unit, Max, Patrick, and even Kepler, his own brother, thought the punishment was too light. And if I ever hinted that maybe, just maybe, beautiful little Maria *might* have been partially responsible for what occurred, I was told by everybody that I was 'unbalanced' and 'blind to the facts.'

"Maria played her part perfectly," Nai continued, with undisguised acrimony in her voice. "She admitted later that she had willingly kissed Galileo—they had kissed twice before, she said—but insisted that she had started saying no *before* he pulled her down on the floor. Maria wept for an hour immediately after the incident. She could barely talk. All the men tried to comfort her, including Patrick. They were all convinced before she even said anything that Maria was blameless."

Soft bells sounded, indicating that the washing cycle was complete. Nai rose slowly, walked over to the machines, and put the clothes in a pair of dryers.

"We all agreed that Maria should move next door with Max, Eponine, and Ellie," Nai began again. "I thought that time would heal the wounds. I was wrong. Galileo was ostracized by everyone in the family, except for me. Kepler would not even speak to his brother. Patrick was civil, but distant. Galileo withdrew deeper into his shell, stopped attending classes altogether, and spent most of his waking hours by himself in the weight room.

"About five months ago I approached Maria and basically begged her to help Galileo. It was humiliating, Nicole," Nai said, tears entering her eyes again. "There I was, an adult woman, pleading for favors from a teenage girl. I had first asked Patrick, Eponine, and then Ellie, each in turn, if they would talk to Maria for me. Only Ellie had made an effort to intercede, and she informed me, after her attempt, that the appeal would have to come directly from me.

"Maria finally agreed to talk to Galileo," Nai said bitterly, "but only after forcing me to listen to a harangue about how she still felt 'violated' by Galileo's attack. She also stipulated both that a sincere, written apology from Galileo should precede the meeting and that I should be personally present during their discussion to preclude any unpleasantness."

Nai shook her head. "Now, I ask you, Nicole," she said, "how in the world could a sixteen-year-old girl who has been awake for only two years in her entire life have *possibly* become so sophisticated? Somebody—and my guess is Max and Eponine—had been counseling her on how to behave. Maria *wanted* to humiliate me and to make Galileo suffer as much as possible. She certainly succeeded."

"I know it seems unlikely," Nicole said, "but I have met people with incredible natural gifts who know intuitively at a very early age how to deal with any possible situation. Maria may be one of them."

Nai ignored her comment. "The meeting went very well. Galileo cooperated. Maria accepted the apology that he wrote for her. For the next few weeks she seemed to go out of her way to include Galileo in whatever the young people were doing. But he was still a stranger in their group, an outsider. I could see it. And I suspect that he could too.

"Then one day in the cafeteria, while the five of them were sitting together—the rest of us had eaten early and had already returned to our rooms—a pair of iguanas sat down at the other end of their table. According to Kepler, the iguanas were purposely repulsive. They lowered their heads into their bowls, noisily sucking up those wriggling worms they love so much, and then stared at the girls, especially Maria, with their beady yellow eyes. Nikki made some comment about not being hungry anymore and Maria agreed with her.

"At that point Galileo rose from his seat, took a couple of steps toward the iguanas, and said 'Shoo, go away,' or something similar. When they didn't move, he took another step in their direction. One of the iguanas jumped at him. Galileo grabbed that first iguana by the neck and shook it ferociously. It died of a broken neck. The second iguana also attacked, seizing Galileo's forearm with its powerful teeth. Before the blockheads arrived to break up the fracas, Galileo had beaten the iguana to death against the top of the table."

Nai seemed surprisingly calm as she finished the story. "They took Galileo away. Three hours later Big Block came to our rooms and informed us that Galileo would be permanently detained in another part of the spacecraft. When I asked why, the super blockhead told me the same thing that he has told me every time since when I have asked the question: 'We have determined that your son's behavior is not acceptable.'"

Another sequence of short bells announced that the drying cycle was complete. Nicole helped Nai fold the clothes on the long table. "I'm allowed to see him only two hours each day," Nai said. "Although Galileo is too proud to complain, I can tell that he is suffering. The Council has listed Galileo as one of the five human beings being 'retained' without proper justification, but I do not know if their grievances are being seriously heard by the blockheads."

Nai stopped folding clothes and put her hand on Nicole's forearm. "That's why I'm asking you for help," she said. "In the alien hierarchy, the Eagle ranks even higher than Big Block. It's obvious that the Eagle pays careful attention to what you say. Would you, please, for my sake, talk to him about Galileo?"

*   *   *

"It's the right thing," Nicole said to Ellie, taking her belongings from the closet. "I should have been in the other room from the beginning."

"We talked about it before you came," Ellie said. "But both Nai and Maria said it was all right for the girl to move back next door so that you could be here with Nikki and me."

"Nevertheless . . ." Nicole said. She put her clothes on the table and looked at her daughter. "You know, Ellie, I've only been here a few days, but it strikes me as terribly peculiar how absorbed everyone is in the day-to-day trivia of life. And I'm not talking only about Nai and her concerns. The people with whom I have chatted in the cafeteria, or in the other common rooms, spend an astonishingly small percentage of their time discussing what's *really* going on here. Only two people have asked me questions about the Eagle. And up at the observation deck last night, while a dozen of us were staring out at that staggering tetrahedron, nobody wanted to discuss *who* might have built it, and for what purpose."

Ellie laughed. "Everyone else has been here for a year already, Mother. They asked all those questions long ago, for many weeks, but they did not receive any satisfactory answers. It's human nature, when we cannot answer an infinite question, to dismiss it until we have some new information."

She picked up all her mother's things. "Now, we have told everyone to leave you alone and let you take a nap today. Nobody should be coming in the room for the next two hours. *Please,* Mother, use this opportunity to rest. When Dr. Blue left last night, she told me that your heart was showing signs of fatigue, despite all the supplemental probes."

"Mr. Kowalski was certainly not happy," Nicole commented, "about having an octospider in our ray."

"I explained it to him. So did Big Block. Don't worry about it."

"Thank you, Ellie," Nicole said. She kissed her daughter on the cheek.

4

"Are you ready, Mother?" Ellie asked, coming in the door.

"I guess so," Nicole answered. "Although I certainly feel foolish. Except for the game yesterday with you, Max, and Eponine, I haven't played bridge for years."

Ellie smiled. "It doesn't matter how well you play, Mother. We talked about that last night."

Max and Eponine were waiting in the hallway at the tram stop. "Today will be very interesting," Max said after greeting Nicole. "I wonder how many others will show up."

The Council had voted the night before to extend the boycott again for three additional days. Although Big Block had responded to the list of grievances and even persuaded the octospiders, who outnumbered the humans eight to one, to yield more time in the common areas for the exclusive use of the humans, the Council had felt that many of the responses were still not adequate.

There had also been a discussion at the Council meeting about how to enforce the boycott. Some of the more vocal attendees at the meeting had wanted to establish punishments for those who ignored the boycott resolution. The meeting had concluded with an agreement that Council officers would "actively engage" those humans who continued to disregard the Council's recommendations to avoid interactions with all other species.

The tram in the main corridor was nearly empty. A half dozen octospiders were in the first car, and three or four more octos plus a pair of iguanas were sitting in the second. Nicole and her friends were the only humans on board.

"Three weeks ago, before this latest round of tension began," Ellie said, "we had twenty-three tables for our weekly bridge tournament. I thought we were making a lot of progress. We were averaging five or six new human attendees each week."

"How in the world, Ellie," Nicole asked as the tram stopped and another pair of octospiders boarded their car, "did you ever think up the idea for these bridge tournaments? When you first mentioned playing cards with the octospiders to me, I thought you were out of your mind."

Ellie laughed. "In the beginning, soon after we had all settled here, I knew that it would take some kind of organized activity to encourage interaction. People were just not going to walk up to an octospider and begin a conversation, not even with a blockhead or me along as an interpreter. Games seemed like a pretty good way to stimulate mixing. That worked for a little while, but it quickly became obvious that there was no game at which the most proficient human could match any of the octospiders. Even with handicaps."

"Late in the first month," Max broke in, "I played chess with your buddy Dr. Blue. She gave me a rook and two pawn advantage to start the game, and still cleaned my plow. It was very demoralizing."

"The final blow was our first Scrabble tournament," Ellie continued. "All of the prizes went to the octospiders, even though all the words used were in English! That was when I realized that I had to come up with a game in which humans and octospiders did not play *against* each other.

"Bridge turned out to be perfect. Each pair consists of one human and one octospider. It is not necessary for the partners to talk to each other. I have prepared convention cards in both languages, and even the dullest human can learn in one session the octo numbers from one to seven and their symbols for the four suits. It has worked fabulously well."

Nicole shook her head. "I still think you are crazy," she said with a smile. "Although I will acknowledge a touch of brilliance as well."

There were only fourteen other people in the card room of the recreation complex at the time the bridge tournament was scheduled to start. Ellie adapted well, deciding to have two separate games, one for the "mixed pairs," as she called them, and another contest solely for the octospiders.

Dr. Blue was Nicole's partner. They agreed on a five-card major bidding approach, one of six codified by Ellie, and sat down at a table near the door. Because the seats for the octospiders were higher than those for the humans, Nicole and her partner were sitting eye to eye—or, more appropriately, eye to lens.

Nicole had never been an exceptional bridge player. She had learned to play originally as a student at the University of Tours, when her father, concerned that she did not have enough friends, had encouraged her to become involved in extracurricular activities. Nicole had also played some bridge in New Eden, where the game was the social rage during the first year after settlement. However, despite some natural flair for the game, Nicole had always thought that bridge consumed too much time and that there were too many other, more important things to do.

It was apparent to Nicole from the outset that Dr. Blue, as well as the other octospiders who came to the table with their human partners to play in the duplicate tournament, was a superb card player. On the second hand Dr. Blue played a "three no trump" contract that was exceedingly difficult, using finesses and a terminal squeeze like a human bridge professional.

"Well done," Nicole said to her octospider partner after Dr. Blue made the contract plus one overtrick.

"It's very simple once you know where all the cards are," Dr. Blue answered in color.

It was fascinating to watch the octospiders handle the mechanics of the game. They removed the cards from the traveling boards with the two last joints of a solitary tentacle, aided by the cilia, of course, and then held their hands in front of their lenses with three tentacles, one on either side and a third one in the middle. To place a card on the table, an octospider used whichever tentacle was closest to the card in question, balancing it among the cilia during its descent.

Nicole and Dr. Blue engaged in their usual lively conversation between hands. Dr. Blue had just told Nicole that the new Chief Optimizer had been puzzled by the latest action from the Council, when the door to the card room opened and in walked three humans, followed by Big Block and one of the smaller blockheads.

The woman in the lead, whom Nicole recognized as Emily Bronson, the president of the Council, glanced around the room and then headed for Nicole's table. A move had just been called, and Ellie and Dr. Blue had been joined by the octospider Milky and her partner, a pleasant-looking middle-aged woman named Margaret.

"Why, Margaret Young, I'm astonished to see you here," Emily Bronson said. "You must not have *heard* that the Council extended the boycott last night."

The two men who had entered the room with Ms. Bronson, one of whom was Garland of the swimming pool incident, had followed her over to Nicole's table. All three of them were standing over Margaret.

"Emily . . . I'm sorry," Margaret replied with her eyes downcast. "But you know how I love bridge."

"There's a lot more than games at stake here," Ms. Bronson said.

Ellie had risen from a nearby table and now made an appeal to Big Block to stop the disruption. But Emily Bronson was too quick. "All of you," she said in a loud voice, "are showing your disloyalty by being here.

If you leave now, the Council will not hold it against you. If you stay, however, after having been warned—"

Big Block now intervened and informed Ms. Bronson that she and her friends were indeed disrupting the game. As the trio turned to leave, more than half of the humans rose from their chairs to follow.

"This is preposterous," a voice with astonishing clarity and power said. Nicole was standing in her place, leaning on the table with one hand. "Sit back down," she said in the same tone. "Do not allow yourself to be bullied by a hatemonger."

All the bridge players returned to their seats. "Shut up, old woman," Emily Bronson said in anger from across the room. "This is none of your concern." Big Block escorted her and her companions out the door.

"You don't have any idea, do you, Mrs. Wakefield, what any of the objects are?"

"Your guess is as good as mine, Maria," Nicole answered. "They probably had special meaning, in some way, for your mother. I thought at the time that the silver cylinder implanted under your mother's skin was some kind of zoo identifier, but since none of the zookeeping staff survived the bombing and very few of the records remain, it's unlikely that we will ever be able to verify my hypothesis."

"What's a 'hypothesis'?" the girl asked.

"It's a tentative assumption or explanation for what's happened, when there's really not sufficient evidence to come to any definite answers," Nicole said. "By the way, I must say that your English is quite impressive."

"Thank you, Mrs. Wakefield."

They were sitting together in the communal lounge just off the observation deck. Nicole and Maria were both drinking fruit juice. Although Nicole had been in the Grand Hotel for a week already, this was the first time she had had a private moment with the girl she had found amid the octospider zoo ruins sixteen years earlier.

"Was my mother really pretty?" Maria asked.

"She was striking, I remember that," Nicole said, "even though I couldn't see her very well in the dim light. She appeared to have your same coloring, maybe a little lighter, and was of medium build. I would have guessed she was thirty-five years old or maybe slightly less."

"And there were no signs of my father?" Maria asked.

"None that I saw," Nicole said. "Of course, under the circumstances I did not make a very thorough search. It's possible that he might have been wandering somewhere in the Alternate Domain looking for help. The fence that enclosed your compound had been flattened in the bombing. I worried, when we woke up the next morning, that your father might have been looking for you, but I later convinced myself, based on what I had seen in your shelter, that you and your mother lived alone."

"So is it your hypothesis that my father had already died?" Maria said.

"Very good," Nicole replied. "No, not necessarily. I wouldn't be that specific. It just did not look as if anyone else had lived there in your enclosure for some time."

Maria took a drink of her juice and there was a momentary silence at the table. "You told me the other night, Mrs. Wakefield," the girl said, "when we were talking with Max and Eponine, that you presumed my mother, or maybe both my parents, had been kidnapped much earlier by the octospiders, from a place called Avalon. I didn't understand completely what you were saying."

Nicole smiled at Maria. "I appreciate your politeness, Maria," she said. "But you're certainly part of the family—you can call me Nicole." Her mind drifted back to New Eden—it seemed so long ago—and then Nicole realized that the girl was waiting for an answer to her comment.

"Avalon was a settlement outside of New Eden," Nicole said, "in the dark and cold of the Central Plain. It was originally created by the government of the colony to quarantine those people who had a deadly virus called RV-41. After Avalon was built, the dictator of New Eden, a man named Nakamura, convinced the Senate that Avalon was also a perfect place for other 'abnormal' humans, including those who protested against the government and those who were mentally ill or retarded."

"It doesn't sound like a very nice place," Maria commented.

Benjy was there for over a year, Nicole was thinking. *He never talks about it.* She began feeling guilty about not having spent enough private time with Benjy since she had awakened. *But he has never once complained.*

Again Nicole had to force herself to pay attention to her conversation with Maria. *We old people have drifting thoughts,* she said to herself. *Because so many things we see and hear remind us of memories.*

"I have done some checking already," Nicole said. "Unfortunately, all the administrative personnel from Avalon died in the war. I have described your mother to a few of the people who spent considerable time in Avalon, but none of them remember her."

"Do you think she was a mental patient?" Maria asked.

"That's possible," Nicole replied. "We may never know for certain. Your necklace, incidentally, is our best clue to your mother's identity. She was clearly a devotee of the order of the Catholic church started by Saint Michael of Siena. There are some other Michaelites on board, Ellie says. I intend to talk with them when I have the time."

Nicole stopped and turned toward the observation deck, where a commotion had started. A few humans and a large group of octospiders were pointing out the window and gesticulating wildly. A couple of people raced off toward the main corridor, presumably to bring back others to observe whatever it was they were seeing.

Nicole and Maria left their table, walked up the steps to the deck, and looked out the large window. In the distance, beyond the tetrahedron of lights, a huge, flat-topped spacecraft that resembled an aircraft carrier was approaching the Node. Nicole and Maria watched for several minutes without speaking as the new spacecraft loomed larger and larger.

"What is it?" Maria asked.

"I have no idea," Nicole answered.

The observation deck filled rapidly. The doors were constantly opening as more humans, octospiders, iguanas, and even a pair of avians came into the room. The crowd began to press against Nicole and Maria.

The flat-topped vehicle was extremely long, longer even than the transportation corridors connecting the spheres of the Node. Several dozen big transparent "bubbles" were scattered around its surface. The carrier stopped near one of the spherical vertices of the Node and extended a long transparent tube that fit neatly into the side of the sphere.

The deck was in turmoil. All kinds of creatures were pushing, pressing to move closer to the window. A pair of iguanas leaped upward against the window in the weightlessness and were quickly joined by ten to twenty humans. Nicole began to feel claustrophobic and tried to move out of the way. There was no room through the mob. Nicole was pushed in all directions. She lost contact with Maria. A strong wave caught Nicole from the side and smacked her against the wall. Nicole felt a sharp pain in her left hip upon impact. In the ensuing melee, she might have been trampled and injured even more except that Big Block and the blockheads swept into the mob and restored order.

Nicole was badly shaken when Big Block reached her. The pain in her hip was unbearable. She could not walk.

"It's just part of being old," the Eagle said. "You must be more careful." He and Nicole were alone in her apartment. The others were eating breakfast.

"I do not like being fragile," Nicole said. "Nor do I like not doing things because I'm afraid of injuring myself."

"Your hip will heal," the Eagle said. "But it will take a while. You're lucky it's only badly bruised and not broken. At your age a broken hip can make a human a permanent invalid."

"Thanks for the words of reassurance," Nicole said. She took a small sip of her coffee. She was lying on her mat with her head lifted up slightly by several pillows. "But enough about me. Let's move on to more important things. What is that flat spacecraft all about?"

"The other humans have already started calling it the Carrier," the Eagle said. "That's a very appropriate name."

There was a short silence. "Come on, come on," Nicole said in a cranky voice, "don't play coy with me. I'm lying here doped up and still in pain. It shouldn't be necessary for me to drag the information out of you."

"This phase of the operation will soon be over," the alien said. "Some of you will be transferred to the Carrier, and the rest of you will move over to the Node."

"And what happens then?" Nicole asked. "And how is it decided who goes where?"

"I can't tell you that yet," the Eagle said. "But I will tell you that you will be going to the Node—although if you tell anyone else what I have just shared with you, I will not in the future give you any more advance information. We want the transition to be orderly."

"You always want things to be orderly . . . Ouch," Nicole said as she changed positions slightly. "And I must say you have not given me very significant information."

"You know more than anyone else."

"Big deal," Nicole grumped, taking another sip of coffee. "By the way, do you have any fancy doctors over there in the Node who can wave a magic wand over this bruise and make it go away?"

"No," said the Eagle, "but we can give you a new hip if you like. Or a pseudo-hip, as I guess you would call it."

Nicole shook her head. She winced as she jostled her hip while putting her coffee cup on the floor. "Being old is shit," she said.

"I'm sorry," the Eagle said. He started to leave. "I'll look in on you whenever I can."

"Before you go," Nicole said, "I have one other item of business. Nai wanted me to ask you to intercede on Galileo's behalf. She would like him returned to the family."

"It's irrelevant now," the Eagle said as he was leaving. "You'll all be out of here in four or five days. Good-bye, Nicole. Don't try to walk—use the wheelchair I brought you. Your hip won't heal unless you keep your weight off of it."

5

It was early in the morning, before most of the humans had awakened. Nicole had been out in the long hallway for half an hour experimenting with the controls on the arm of her wheelchair. She had been surprised that the chair could move so swiftly and quietly. As she raced past the series of conference rooms halfway down the kilometer-long corridor, Nicole wondered what kind of advanced technology was contained inside the sealed metal box beneath her chair. *Richard would have loved this wheelchair,* she thought. *He probably would have tried to take it apart.*

She passed a few humans out in the hallway, most shuffling along in an attempt at a morning exercise walk. Nicole laughed to herself as a pair of shufflers moved quickly out of her way. *I must look very strange,* she thought, *a gray-haired old woman zooming down the hall in a wheelchair.*

She turned around just after she drove by the small tram, which was carrying a handful of passengers toward the common areas for an early breakfast. Nicole continued to press the acceleration button on her chair until she was going faster than the tram. The people in the tram stared at her with astonishment as she passed them. Nicole waved and grinned. A few moments later, however, when a door a hundred meters in front of her opened abruptly and two women walked out into the corridor, Nicole realized that it was not safe for her to be driving so fast. She slowed down, still chuckling to herself at the thrill the speed had given her.

As she drew near to her own apartment, Nicole saw the Eagle standing at the end of the ray where it merged with the annulus encircling the starfish. She drove over beside him.

"You look like you're having fun," the Eagle said.

"I am," Nicole said with a laugh. "This chair is a fantastic toy. It has almost made me forget about the pain in my hip."

The Eagle waved toward a lounge on the other side of the annulus. "Let's go over there, please," the alien said. "I would like to talk to you in private."

Nicole drove her chair across the main annulus until she reached the ramp leading to the lounge. The Eagle, who was walking behind her, motioned for her to continue. A dozen octospiders were sitting around the room. The Eagle and Nicole chose a spot off to the right, where they could be alone.

"The Carrier has almost finished its tasks over at the Node," the Eagle said. "Twelve hours from now it will make a short stop near this vehicle to pick up some more passengers. I will announce after lunch who will be moving to the Carrier."

The alien turned and looked directly at Nicole with his intense blue eyes. "Some of the humans may not be pleased with my announcement. After the decision was made to split your species into two separate groups, it was immediately apparent to me that it would be impossible to achieve a division that would not make some people unhappy. I would like some help from you in making this process as smooth as possible."

Nicole studied the remarkable face and eyes of her alien companion. She thought she remembered seeing, once before, a similar look from the Eagle. *Back at the Node,* she recalled, *when I was asked to do the video.*

"What is it that you want me to do?" Nicole asked.

"We have decided to allow a degree of flexibility in this process. Although all the individuals on the list for transfer to the Carrier *must* accept their assignments, we will permit some of those who are assigned to the Node to request reconsideration. Since there will be no interaction between the two vehicles, in the case of strong emotional attachments, for example, we would not want to force—"

"Are you telling me," Nicole interrupted, "that this split may permanently break up families?"

"Yes, it may," the Eagle replied. "In a few instances, a husband or a wife has been assigned to the Carrier, while the spouse is on the list for the Node. Similarly, there are some cases where parents and their children will be separated."

"Jesus," exclaimed Nicole. "How in the world can you, or anyone, arbitrarily decide to separate a husband and a wife who have chosen to live together, and expect them to be happy? You'll be lucky if there is not a widespread revolt after you make your announcement."

The Eagle hesitated for a few seconds. "There was nothing arbitrary in our process," the alien said at length. "For months now we have been carefully studying voluminous data on every single creature currently living in the starfish. The records include complete information from all the years in Rama as well. Those who have been assigned to the Carrier do not, in one way or another, meet our necessary criteria for transfer to the Node."

"And what exactly are those criteria?" Nicole asked quickly.

"All I can tell you now is that the Node will feature an interspecies living environment. Those individuals who have limited adaptability have been assigned to the Carrier," the Eagle replied.

"It sounds to me," Nicole said after a few seconds, "as if some subset of the humans in the Grand Hotel has been rejected, for some reason, and not found 'acceptable'—"

"If I understand your choice of words," the Eagle now interrupted, "you are inferring that this split divides the two groups on the basis of merit. That is not exactly the case. It is our belief that most of those in either group will, in the long run, be happier in the environment to which they have been assigned."

"Even without their spouses or children?" Nicole said. She frowned. "Sometimes I wonder if you have really observed what motivates the human species. 'Emotional attachments,' to use your words, are usually the most essential component in any human's happiness."

"We know that," the Eagle said. "We had a special review of every single case where families will be broken apart by the split, and we made some accommodations as a result. In our judgment, the remaining family divisions, which are not as numerous as this discussion might suggest, are all supported by the observational data."

Nicole stared at the Eagle and shook her head vigorously. "Why was this split never mentioned before? Never once in all the discussions of the impending transfer did you ever even suggest that we were going to be divided into two groups."

"We hadn't decided ourselves until fairly recently. Recall that our intercession with the affairs on Rama took us into a contingency regime in our planning matrix. Once it became clear that some kind of split would be necessary, we didn't want to upset the status quo."

"Bullshit," Nicole said suddenly. "I don't believe that for a moment. You *knew* what you were going to do long ago. You just didn't want to listen to any objections."

Using the controls on the arm of her chair, Nicole turned around and faced away from her alien companion. "No," she said firmly, "I will not be your accomplice in this matter. And I am angry that you have compromised my integrity by not telling me the truth before now."

She pushed the acceleration button and started toward the main corridor.

"Is there nothing I can do to change your mind?" the Eagle said, following her.

Nicole stopped. "I can only imagine one scenario in which I would help you. Why don't you explain the differences between the two living environments and let each individual from each species decide for himself or herself?"

"I'm afraid we can't do that," the Eagle said.

"Then count me out," Nicole said, activating her wheelchair again.

Nicole was in a foul mood by the time she reached the door to her apartment. She leaned forward in her chair and entered the combination sequence on the panel in the middle of the door.

"Hello, Mrs. Wakefield," Kepler said as Nicole entered the room. "Patrick and Mother are out looking for you. They were worried when they didn't find you in the hallway."

Nicole drove past the young man and into the room. Benjy came out of the bathroom with only a towel wrapped around him. "Hello, Mama," he said with a big smile. He noticed the look of displeasure on Nicole's face and hurried over beside her. "What's wrong?" he asked. "You haven't hurt yourself again . . . ?"

"No, Benjy," Nicole said. "I'm fine. I just had a disturbing conversation with the Eagle."

"What about?" Benjy said, taking her hand.

"I'll tell you later," Nicole said after a brief hesitation. "After you dry off and get dressed."

Benjy smiled and kissed his mother on the forehead before returning to the bathroom. The sinking feeling in her stomach that Nicole had experienced during her conversation with the Eagle now returned. *Oh, my God*, she thought suddenly. *Not Benjy. Surely the Eagle was not trying to tell me that we are going to be separated from Benjy.* She remembered the Eagle's comment about "limited capabilities" and started to panic. *Not now. Please not now. Not after all this time.*

Nicole thought about a special moment from years earlier, when the family had been at the Node for the first time. She had been alone in her bedroom. Benjy had entered tentatively to find out if he was welcome to join the family on its trip back to the solar system. He had been immensely relieved to discover that he was not going to be separated from his mother. *He has suffered enough already*, Nicole said to herself, recalling Benjy's assignment to Avalon while she was in prison in New Eden. *The Eagle must know that, if he has really studied all the data.*

Despite her conscious attempts to remain calm, Nicole could not stifle the combination of fear and frustration that was rising inside her. *I would have preferred to die in my sleep*, she thought bitterly, fearing the worst. *I cannot say good-bye to Benjy now. It will break his heart. And mine too.*

The door to the apartment opened. Patrick and Nai entered, followed by the Eagle. "We found this friend of yours in the hallway, Mother," Patrick said, greeting her with a kiss. "He told us that the two of you had been having a conference. Nai and I were worried."

The Eagle walked over beside Nicole. "There was another subject I wanted to talk to you about as well," the Eagle said. "Could you please join me outside for another couple of minutes?"

"I guess I have no choice," Nicole answered. "But I am not going to change my mind."

A full tram passed the Eagle and Nicole just as they exited from the apartment. "What is it?" Nicole asked impatiently.

"I wanted to inform you that all the different manifestations of the sessile species, as well as the remaining avians, will be in the group that is transferred to the Carrier this evening. If you still have any desire, as you indicated to me once during a conversation shortly after you first awakened here, to interact with the sessile and to experience what Richard described—"

"Tell me something else first," Nicole interrupted, grabbing the Eagle by the forearm with surprising strength. "Will Benjy and I be separated by this split you're going to announce this afternoon?"

The Eagle hesitated for several seconds. "No, you will not," he said eventually. "But I shouldn't be telling you any of the details."

Nicole heaved a sigh of relief. "Thank you," she said simply, managing a smile.

There was a protracted silence. "The sessiles," the Eagle started again, "will not be available to you after—"

"Yes, yes," Nicole said. "That's a great idea. Thank you very much. I would like to pay my respects to a sessile. After I eat breakfast, of course."

The smaller block robots were very much in evidence in the ray that housed the avians and the sessiles. The ray was divided into several separate regions by walls that ran from the floor to the ceiling. The blockheads policed the entrances and exits from these regions and were also stationed at each of the tram stops.

The avians and sessiles lived at the back of the ray, in the last of the separate compounds. Both a blockhead and an avian were guarding the entrance when the Eagle and Nicole arrived. The Eagle jabbered and shrieked in response to a series of questions from the avian. After they entered the compound, a myrmicat approached them. It began to communicate with the Eagle in bursts of high-frequency sound that originated from the small circular orifice below its dark brown, milky oval eyes. Nicole marveled at the fidelity of the Eagle's whistling response. She also watched in fascination as the second pair of myrmicat eyes, attached to stalks raised ten to twelve centimeters above its forehead, continued to pivot and survey the surroundings. When the Eagle had finished his conversation with the myrmicat, the six-legged creature, who resembled a giant ant when standing still, raced down the hall with the speed and grace of a cat.

"They know who you are," the Eagle said. "They are delighted that you have come for a visit."

Nicole glanced up at her companion. "*How* do they know me?" she said. "I have only occasionally seen a few of them in the common areas, and I have never actually interacted."

"Your husband is a god to this species. None of them would be here if it were not for him. They know you from your images that were inside his memory."

"How is that possible?" Nicole asked. "Richard died sixteen years ago."

"But the record of his stay with them is carefully preserved in their collective memory," the Eagle said. "Every myrmicat emerges from its manna melon with significant knowledge of the key components of its own culture and history. The embryonic process that occurs inside the melon not only provides physical nourishment for the growing and developing being, but also passes critical information directly into the brain—or its equivalent, anyway—of the fledgling myrmicat."

"Are you telling me," Nicole said, "that these creatures begin their education before they are *born*? And that there is stored knowledge inside those manna melons I used to eat that is somehow implanted in the minds of the unborn myrmicats?"

"Exactly," the Eagle replied. "I don't see why you should be so astounded. Physically, these creatures are nowhere near as complex as your species. The embryonic development process for a human is vastly more subtle and complicated than theirs. Your newborns arrive in the world with a staggering array of physical attributes and capabilities. Your infants, however, are still dependent on other members of the species for both their survival and their education. The myrmicats are born 'smarter' and therefore more independent, but they have much less potential for total intellectual development."

They both heard a shrill sound coming from a myrmicat fifty meters or so down the corridor. "It is calling us," the Eagle said.

Nicole moved her wheelchair slowly forward and settled at a speed consistent with the Eagle's walking pace. "Richard never told me that these creatures preserve information from generation to generation."

"He didn't know," the Eagle said. "He *did* figure out their metamorphic cycle, and that the myrmicats passed information to the neural net or web or whatever the final manifestation should be called. But he didn't even suspect that the most important elements of that collective information were also stored in the manna melons and passed to the next generation. Needless to say, it's a very strong survival mechanism."

Nicole was intrigued by what the Eagle was telling her. *Imagine*, she was thinking, *if somehow human children could be born already knowing the essentials of our culture and history. Suppose something like the placenta contained, in compressed form, enough information. It sounds impossible, but it must not be. If at least one creature can do it, then eventually . . .*

"How much data are passed through the manna melons to the newborns of the species?" Nicole asked as they drew near to the beckoning myrmicat.

"About one-thousandth of one percent of the information present in a fully mature specimen like the one in which Richard resided. The primary function of the final manifestation of the species is to manipulate, process, and compress the data into a package for inclusion in the manna melons. Just how this data management process works is something we have been studying.

"The neural net you will encounter in the next few minutes, incidentally," the Eagle continued, "was originally just a small sliver of material, containing critical data compressed using what must be a brilliant algorithm. We have estimated that in that small cylinder Richard carried to New York years ago was an information content equivalent to the memory capacity of a hundred adult human brains."

"Amazing," Nicole said, shaking her head.

"That's only the beginning," the Eagle said. "Each of the four manna melons carried by Richard had its own special set of compressed data. They all germinated into myrmicats in the octospider zoo. The neural net now contains all those experiences as well. I expect that you're in for quite an adventure."

Nicole stopped her wheelchair. "Why didn't you tell me all this earlier? I might have spent more time—"

"I doubt it," the Eagle interrupted. "Your first priority was to reestablish your connections to your own species. I don't think you were ready for this until now."

"You have been manipulating me by controlling what I see and experience," Nicole said without rancor.

"Perhaps," the Eagle answered.

Nicole was surprisingly fearful when she finally encountered the neural net up close. The Eagle and she were together in a room not unlike the apartment Nicole shared in the human ray. A pair of myrmicats was sitting behind them, against the wall. The sessile net or web occupied about fifteen percent of the room, back in the right corner. There was a gap in the center of the dense, soft white material that was just large enough for Nicole and her wheelchair. Nicole complied with the Eagle's request to roll up her shirtsleeves and lift her dress above her knees.

"I suppose," she then said with some trepidation, "that it expects me to drive into that space and that it will wrap its filaments around my body."

"Yes," said the Eagle. "And it has been told by one of the myrmicats to release you at your request. I will stay here the entire time, if that's any comfort to you."

"Richard," Nicole said, still delaying her entrance, "told me that it took a long time for any real communication to develop."

"That will not be a problem now," responded the Eagle. "Certainly part of the information stored in the original sliver was data about methods that could be used to communicate efficiently with human beings."

"All right, then," Nicole said, passing her hand nervously through her hair, "here I go. Wish me luck."

She drove into the gap in the cottony network and turned off the power in her wheelchair. In less than a minute the creature had surrounded her and Nicole could not even see the outline of the Eagle across the room. Nicole tried to reassure herself as she felt first hundreds and then thousands of tiny threads attaching themselves to her arms, legs, neck, and head. As she expected, the density of threads was highest around her head. She recalled Richard's description: *The individual filaments were incredibly thin, but they must have had very sharp parts underneath. I didn't even realize that they were inserted well inside the outer layers of my skin until I tried to pull one off.*

Nicole stared at a particular clump of threads about a meter away from her face. As this ganglion eased slowly toward her, the other elements in the delicate mesh shifted position. A shiver ran down her spine. Her mind accepted, finally, that the net surrounding her was a living creature. It was only moments later that the images began.

She realized immediately that the sessile was reading from her memory. Pictures from earlier in her life flashed through Nicole's mind at a fantastic rate, none lingering long enough even to provoke an emotion. There was no order to the images—a childhood memory from the woods behind her home in the Parisian suburb of Chilly-Mazarin would be followed by a picture of Maria laughing heartily at one of Max's stories.

This is the data transfer stage, Nicole thought, remembering Richard's analysis of the time he had spent inside the neural net. *The creature is copying my memory into its own. At a very high rate.* She wondered briefly what in the world the sessile would do with all the images from her memory. Then suddenly in her mind's eye Nicole vividly saw Richard himself in a large chamber that had a vast, incomplete mural on its walls. The image became a full motion picture set in the chamber. The clarity of the individual frames was overwhelming. Nicole felt as if she were watching a color television set located somewhere inside her brain. She could even see the details of the mural. As Nicole watched, a myrmicat directed Richard's attention to specific items in the wall paintings. Around the room a dozen other myrmicats were sketching or painting the unfinished sections of the mural.

The artwork was superb. It had all been created to give Richard information about what he could do to help the alien species survive. Part of the mural was a textbook about their biology, which explained in pictures the three manifestations of their species (manna melon, myrmicat, and sessile or neural net) and the relationships between them. The images Nicole saw were so sharp that she felt she had been transported to the room where Richard had been. She was therefore startled when the internal film she was watching suddenly underwent a jump discontinuity and presented a picture of the last good-bye between Richard and his guide myrmicat.

Richard and the myrmicat were in a tunnel at the bottom of the brown cylinder. The motion picture lingered lovingly on every detail of this final farewell. The bearded Richard looked overburdened carrying the four heavy manna melons, two leathery avian eggs, and the cylinder of web material in the pack on his back. But even Nicole, seeing the determination in Richard's eyes as he departed from the doomed myrmicat habitat, could understand why he was such a hero to their species. *He risked his life*, she reminded herself, *to save them from extinction*.

More images flooded her mind, pictures from the octospider zoo recording events after the germination of the manna melons Richard had originally carried to New York. Despite their clarity, Nicole couldn't bring herself to concentrate on the images very closely. She was still thinking about Richard. *Not since I awakened have I allowed myself to miss your company*, Nicole said to herself, *because I thought such behavior showed weakness. Now, seeing your face again so clearly and remembering how much we shared, I realize how ridiculous it is to force myself not to think about you.*

A fleeting image of three human beings—a man, a woman, and a tiny baby—raced through Nicole's mind, catching her attention. *Wait*, Nicole almost screamed out loud. *Back up. There was something that I wanted to see.* The neural net did not read her message. It continued with the progression of pictures. Nicole suspended her thoughts about Richard and focused intently on the images appearing on the television inside her brain.

Less than a minute later she saw the trio again, walking with the octospider zookeeper past the front of the area housing the myrmicats. Maria was in her mother's arms. Her father, a dark and handsome man with gray at his temples, was dragging one of his legs as if it were broken. *I have never seen that man before*, Nicole thought. *I would have remembered him.*

There were no more images of Maria or her parents. The stream of pictures racing through Nicole's mind showed the transfer of the myrmicats to another venue, away from the zoo and the Emerald City, sometime before the bombing began. Nicole presumed that the last sequence of images she was shown took place during the time that all the humans and octospiders in Rama were asleep. *Not long thereafter*, Nicole thought, *if I understand their life cycle correctly, the four myrmicats resulting from Richard's melons became net material. With all these memories intact.*

The pictures in her mind became altogether different. Now Nicole was seeing some images of scenes that she believed were from the home planet of the sessiles, ones that Richard had once excitedly described to her.

Nicole had purposely positioned her right hand next to the control panel of her wheelchair when she had entered the web. When she now pressed the power button and then reverse, the slight motion of the chair immediately registered with the sessile. The images stopped instantly, and the threads of the creature were subsequently withdrawn.

6

The next day, an hour before the beginning of the lunch period, a part of one wall in each starfish apartment transformed into a large television screen. The residents were then informed that an important announcement was forthcoming in thirty minutes.

"This is only the third time," Max told Nicole as they waited, "that we have had any kind of general transmission. The first was immediately after we arrived here and the second was when it was decided to segregate our living quarters."

"What's going to happen now?" Marius asked.

"I suspect we're going to find out the details of our move," Max answered. "At least that's the leading rumor."

At the appointed time, the Eagle's face appeared on the monitor. "Last year, when you were all awakened and moved from Rama," the Eagle said, simultaneously giving the same message in colored strips moving across his forehead, "we told you that this vehicle would not be your permanent home. We are now ready to transfer you to other locations, where your living conditions will be markedly better."

The Eagle paused a few seconds before continuing. "All of you will not be transferred to the same place. About one-third of the current starfish residents will move to the Carrier, that huge, flat spacecraft that has been stationed near the Node for most of the last week. During the next few hours, the Carrier will finish its business over at the Node and move in this direction. Those of you who are transferring to the Carrier will do so after dinner tonight.

"The rest of you will be moved to the Node in another three or four days. Nobody will be left here on the starfish. I would like to stress again that the accommodations in both places will be excellent and far superior to those in this vehicle."

The Eagle stopped for almost half a minute, as if he were allowing time for his audience to react to what he had already said. "When this meeting is over," the Eagle then said, "each of the apartment television screens will repeatedly cycle through the list of all creatures on board, ordered by apartment number, and display the transfer assignments. Reading the displays is very simple. If your name and/or identification code appears on the monitor in black letters against a white background, you will be transferred to the Carrier. If your name is written in white letters against a black background, you will remain here for the next few days and will eventually be moved over to the Node.

"For your information, on the Carrier each species will have its own self-contained living area. There will be no interspecies mixing, except of course for the required symbiotic arrangements. By contrast—"

"That ought to please the leaders of the Council," Max commented quickly. "They have been agitating for complete separation for months."

"—the living situation at the Node will involve regular interspecies communication and activity. We have attempted, in assigning individuals to the two locations, to place each of you in the environment best suited for his personality. Our selections were done carefully, based upon our observations both here at the starfish and during the years on Rama.

"It is important that all of you realize that there will be *no* interaction between the two groups after the transfers take place. Let me say that in another way, to make certain there is no misunderstanding. Those moving to the Carrier tonight will *never* again see any of the residents who are going to be transferred to the Node.

"If you have been assigned to the Carrier," the Eagle continued, "you should begin packing immediately and should be completely ready to move before you come to dinner. If you are among those who have been designated to move to the Node and do not believe that your assignment is appropriate, you may request that your assignment be reconsidered. Tonight, after all residents currently assigned to the Carrier have completed their transfers, I will meet in the cafeteria with those who think they want to switch from the Node to the Carrier.

"If any of you have questions, I will be at the big desk in the lounge for the next hour."

"What did the Eagle say to you?" Max asked Nicole.

"The same thing he said to the twenty other people in the lounge who were asking the same question," Nicole replied. "No changes are possible for those who have been assigned to the Carrier. Reconsideration will only be given to those scheduled for transfer to the Node."

"Was that when Nai . . . uh, broke down?" Eponine asked.

"Yes," Nicole said. "Until then she had held herself together fairly well. When she initially came over to our apartment, after the lists had been shown for the first time, I thought she was remarkably calm. She obviously must have convinced herself initially that Galileo's assignment was some kind of clerical mistake."

"I can understand how she must feel," Eponine said. "I'll admit that my heart skipped a few beats until I saw that all the rest of us were together on the list to be transferred to the Node."

"I bet that Nai is not the only one upset by the assignments," Max said. He stood up and started to walk around the room. "This is really a mess," he said, shaking his head. "What in the world would *we* have done if Marius had been assigned to the Carrier?"

"That's easy," Eponine answered quickly. "You and I would both have applied to go with our son."

"Yep," said Max after a momentary pause. "I suspect you're right."

"That's what Patrick and Nai are now discussing next door," Nicole said. "They asked the young people to leave so they could talk in private."

"Do you think Nai can handle all this additional stress so soon after the . . . incident?" Eponine asked.

"She really has no choice," Max said. "They only have a couple more hours to make a decision."

"She seemed much better to me twenty minutes ago," Nicole said. "The light sedative had definitely taken effect. Both Patrick and Kepler were being very gentle with her. I think Nai frightened herself most of all with her outburst."

"Did she actually attack the Eagle?" Eponine asked.

"No. One of the blockheads restrained her immediately when she screamed," Nicole said. "But she was out of control—she might have done anything."

"Shit," said Max, "if you had told me while we were living in the Emerald City that Nai even had the capacity for violence, I would have told you—"

"Only someone who has been a parent," Nicole interrupted, "can possibly understand the powerful feelings that a mother has where her children are concerned. Nai has been frustrated for months. I can't condone her reaction, but I can certainly understand—"

Nicole stopped. The knock on the door repeated. Patrick entered the room a few seconds later. His face betrayed his anxiety. "Mother," he said, "I need to talk to you."

"Eponine and I can go out in the hallway," Max said. "If that would help."

"Thanks, Max. Yes, I would appreciate it," Patrick said with difficulty. Nicole had never seen him so upset.

"I don't know what to do," Patrick said as soon as he was alone with Nicole. "Everything is happening so fast. I don't think Nai is being rational, but I don't seem to be able . . ." His voice trailed off. "Mother, she wants us *all* to apply for reconsideration. Everyone. You, me, Kepler, Maria, Max . . . all of us. She says otherwise Galileo will feel abandoned."

Nicole looked at her son. He was close to tears. *He hasn't had enough life to deal with a crisis like this,* she thought quickly. *He's only been awake for a little more than ten years.*

"What is Nai doing now?" Nicole said softly.

"She's meditating," Patrick answered. "She said it would calm and heal her spirit . . . and give her strength."

"And are you supposed to convince the rest of us?"

"Yes, I guess. But Mother, Nai has not even considered that anyone might not agree with what she is proposing. She believes that what we should all do is absolutely clear."

Patrick's pain was obvious. Nicole wished that she could reach out, touch him, and make his agony go away. "What do you think we should do?" Nicole asked after a period of silence.

"I don't know," Patrick said, starting to pace around the room. "Like everyone else, I noticed as soon as the list was posted that all the active Council members were being transferred to the Carrier, as well as most of the humans who had been removed from the normal living quarters. The people we like and respect, as well as almost all the octospiders except some of the alternates, are going to the Node. But I sympathize with Nai. She can't bear the thought that Galileo will be isolated, permanently cut off from the only support system he has ever known."

What would you do, a voice inside Nicole's head asked her, *if you were Nai? Didn't you panic earlier today when you were afraid that you might be separated from Benjy?*

"Will you talk to her, Mother," Patrick entreated, "as soon as she has finished meditating? She will listen to you. Nai has always said how much she respects your wisdom."

"And is there anything particular that you want me to say to her?" Nicole asked.

"Tell her . . ." Patrick said, wringing his hands, "tell her it's not her place to decide what would be best for everyone in our group. She should focus on her own decision."

"That's good advice," Nicole said. She gazed at her son. "Tell me, Patrick," she said several seconds later, "have you decided what you are going to do if Nai switches to the Carrier and none of the rest of us do?"

"Yes, I have, Mother," Patrick said quietly. "I will go with Nai and Galileo."

Nicole parked her wheelchair in a corner in front of the observation window. She was alone, as she had requested. The afternoon had been so emotional that she felt completely drained. Nicole had thought initially that her meeting with Nai had gone quite well. Nai had listened carefully to Nicole's advice, without much comment. Nicole had therefore been quite astonished an hour later when Nai, seething with anger, had confronted her along with Max, Eponine, and Ellie.

"Patrick tells me that *none* of you are going to come with us," Nai had said. "Now I see what rewards I have earned for my steadfast devotion all these years. I dragged my twin boys away from their own home out of loyalty to you, my friends. I deprived Galileo and Kepler of ever knowing a normal childhood because of my respect and admiration for you, Nicole, my role model. And now, when for once I ask a favor . . ."

"You're being unfair, Nai," Ellie had said softly. "We all love you and are appalled at the thought of being separated permanently from you and Galileo. Believe me, if it weren't so clear that the Node is preferable for all of us—"

"Ellie, Ellie," Nai had said, dropping on her knees beside her friend and bursting into tears. "Have you forgotten all the hours I spent with Benjy out in Avalon? Yes, I admit that I did it of my own volition, but would I have given so much of myself to Benjy if he was not your brother and you were not my best friend? I *love* you, Ellie. I need your support. Please, please come with us. You and Nikki, at least."

Ellie had also wept. Before the confrontation was over, there was not a dry eye in the room. In the end Nai had apologized profusely to everyone.

Nicole took a deep breath and stared out the window. She knew that she needed a break from all the emotional turmoil. Twice during the afternoon she had felt twinges of pain in her chest. *Even all those magical probes*, she thought, *cannot protect me if I do not take care of myself.*

The huge Carrier was now stationed only several hundred meters away. It was an awesome engineering construction, far larger even than it had seemed when it was over by the Node. The spacecraft was parked sideways, so only a part of it could be seen from the window. The top of the Carrier was a long flat plane broken only by small, scattered equipment complexes and the transparent domes—or bubbles, as they had originally been called—that were located in an orderly pattern throughout the length and breadth of the plane. Some of the domes were quite large. One, directly in front of the window, rose over two hundred meters above the flat plane. Other domes were very small. Parts of eleven of the transparent bubbles were visible from the observation window. During the approach of the Carrier earlier in the afternoon, when the entire spacecraft could be seen, a total of seventy-eight domes had been counted.

The underbelly of the Carrier had an external surface of metallic gray. It extended below the plane about a kilometer, with gently sloping sides and a rounded bottom. From a distance the underbelly looked insignificant compared to the vast flat surface which was at least forty kilometers long and fifteen kilometers wide. However, up close it was clear that an enormous volume was contained inside that drab structure.

As Nicole watched in fascination, a small indentation in the side of the gray exterior, just below the surface, expanded and grew into a round tube moving outward from the Carrier. The tube drew near to the starfish and then, after some minor vernier corrections, was affixed to the main air lock.

She felt a touch on her arm and turned to the side. It was Dr. Blue. "How are you feeling?" the octospider said in color.

"Better now," Nicole replied. "But I had some bad moments earlier this afternoon."

Dr. Blue scanned Nicole with the monitoring device. "There were at least two major irregularities," Nicole told her doctor. "I remember both of them quite clearly."

The octospider doctor studied the colors flashing on the small monitor. "Why didn't you call me?" she said.

"I thought about it," Nicole answered. "But so much was going on. And I figured you were busy with your own—"

Dr. Blue handed Nicole a small flask containing a light blue liquid. "Drink this," the octospider said. "It will limit your cardiac response to emotional stress over the next twelve hours."

"And will we still be together, you and I," Nicole asked, "after the Carrier departs? I didn't study your part of the list very carefully."

"Yes," Dr. Blue answered. "Eighty-five percent of our species will be transferred to the Node. More than half the octospiders moving to the Carrier are alternates."

"So, my friend," Nicole said after drinking the liquid, "what do you make of all this transfer business?"

"Our best guess," Dr. Blue said, "is that this entire experiment has reached a significant branch point and that the two groups will be involved in radically different activities."

Nicole laughed. "That's not very specific," she said.

"No, it's not," the octospider calmly agreed.

There were eighty-two humans and nine octospiders present in the cafeteria when the Eagle convened the reconsideration meeting five minutes after the last starfish resident originally scheduled for transfer to the Carrier had departed through the air lock. Only those who had officially requested reconsideration were permitted to attend the meeting. Many other members of all species were still lingering on the observation deck and in the common areas, talking about the departure procession and/or waiting to learn the outcome of the Eagle's meeting.

Nicole had returned to her post at the observation window. She was sitting in her wheelchair, staring out at the Carrier and reflecting on the scenes she had witnessed during the last hour. Most of the departing humans had been in a festive mood, openly delighted that they would no longer be living among aliens. There had been some sad farewells at the door to the air lock, but actually surprisingly few.

Galileo had been allowed to spend ten minutes with his family and friends in the common area. Patrick and Nai had assured the young man, who had demonstrated very little emotion of any kind, that they and his brother, Kepler, who was still packing, would be joining him in the Carrier before the evening was over.

Galileo had been one of the last humans to leave the starfish. He had been followed by the small contingent of avians and myrmicats. The neural net material and the remaining manna melons had been packed in large crates and had been carried by a contingent of the block robots. *I'll probably never see any of your kind again*, Nicole had thought as the trailing avian had turned and issued a shriek of good-bye to the onlookers.

"Each of you," the Eagle said as he began the meeting in the cafeteria, "has requested that your assignment be reconsidered and that you be allowed to switch your future home from the Node to the Carrier. At this time I want to explain two additional differences between the living environments in the Carrier and the Node. If, after weighing this new information, you still wish to have your assignment changed, then we will accommodate you.

"As I told you this afternoon, there will be no interspecies mixing in the Carrier. Not only will each species be isolated in its own habitat, but also there will be *no* interference of any kind by *any other* intelligence, including the one I represent, in the affairs of each species. Not now, not *ever*. Each species in the Carrier will be on its own. By contrast, life in the interspecies world at the Node will be supervised. Not as heavily as it has been here on the starfish, but supervised nevertheless. We believe that oversight and monitoring are essential when different species are living together.

"The second additional factor may be the most important of all. There will be no reproduction in the Carrier. All of the individuals who inhabit the Carrier, of *every* species, will be rendered forever sterile. Every element necessary for a long and happy life will be provided for those living in the Carrier, but nobody will be allowed to reproduce. By contrast, there will be no reproduction constraints imposed at the Node.

"Please let me finish," the Eagle said as several members of the audience tried to interrupt with questions. "You each have two more hours to decide. If you still want to transfer to the Carrier, simply bring the bags you have already packed and request Big Block to open the air lock."

Nicole was not surprised that Kepler no longer wanted to switch to the Carrier. The young man had clearly had a difficult time making up his mind in the first place and had only requested reconsideration out of loyalty to his mother. Since that time, he had spent most of the afternoon with Maria, whom he obviously adored.

Kepler enlisted everyone in the extended family in case there was an argument with his mother, but no dispute developed. Nai agreed that Kepler should not be deprived of the pleasure of being a father. Nai even magnanimously suggested that Patrick might want to reevaluate his own decision, but her husband was quick to point out that she was past her childbearing years and, besides, he had already been a father, in many ways, to Galileo and Kepler.

Nicole, Patrick, Nai, and Kepler were left alone in one of the apartments for the very final good-byes. It had been a day of tears and raging emotions. All four of them were emotionally exhausted. Two mothers said good-bye, forever, to two sons. There was a touching symmetry in the final comments. Nai requested that Nicole guide Kepler with her wisdom; Nicole asked Nai to continue to give Patrick her unselfish, unconditional love.

Patrick then lifted both the heavy bags and threw them over his shoulders. As Nai and he walked out the door, Kepler stood beside Nicole's wheelchair, holding her phthisic hand. Only after the door closed did the river of tears run from Nicole's eyes. *Good-bye, Patrick*, she thought with a heartache. *Good-bye, Genevieve, Simone, and Katie. Good-bye, Richard.*

7

The dreams came one after another, sometimes without any break. Henry laughed at her for being black, then a supercilious colleague from medical school stopped her from making a bad mistake during a routine tonsillectomy. Later Nicole walked on a sandy beach with dark clouds hovering overhead. A silent caped figure beckoned in the distance. *That's death*, Nicole said to herself in the dream. But it was a cruel joke. When she reached the figure and touched its outstretched hand, Max Puckett removed his cape and laughed.

She was crawling on her bare knees in a dark underground cement pipe. Her knees had begun to bleed. *I'm over here*, Katie's voice said. *Where are you?* Nicole asked, frustrated. *I'm behind you, Mama*, Benjy said. Water began to fill up the pipe. *I cannot find them. I cannot help them.*

Nicole was swimming, with difficulty. There was a strong current in the pipe. It swept her away, carried her outside, became a creek in a forest. Nicole's clothes caught on a bush that overhung the creek. She stood up and brushed herself off. She began walking on a path.

It was night. Nicole could hear a few birds and see the moon above her through the occasional breaks in the tall trees. The path wound back and forth. She came to a junction. *Which way should I go?* Nicole asked herself in the dream. *Come with me*, Genevieve said, emerging from the forest and taking her hand.

What are you doing here? Nicole said. Genevieve laughed. *I could ask you the same thing.*

A young Katie was coming toward them on the path. *Hello, Mother,* she said, reaching out for Nicole's other hand. *Do you mind if I walk with you? Not at all,* answered Nicole.

The forest thickened around them. Nicole heard footsteps behind her and turned around while she was still walking. Patrick and Simone returned her smiles. *We're almost there,* Simone said. *Where are we going?* Nicole asked. *You must know, Mrs. Wakefield,* Maria answered. *You told us to come.* The girl was now walking beside Patrick and Simone.

Nicole and the five young people entered a small clearing. In the middle was a burning campfire. Omeh walked around from the other side of the fire and greeted them. After they formed a new circle around the fire, the shaman threw his head back and began to chant in Senoufo. As Nicole watched, Omeh's face began to peel away, revealing his frightening skull. Still the chant continued. *No, no,* said Nicole. *No. No.*

"Mama," Benjy said. "Wake up, Mama. You're having a bad dream."

Nicole rubbed her eyes. She could see a light on the other side of the room. "What time is it, Benjy?" she said.

"It's late, Mama," he answered with a smile. "Kepler has gone to breakfast with the others. We wanted to let you sleep."

"Thank you, Benjy," Nicole said, moving slightly on her mat. She felt the pain in her hip. She glanced around the room and remembered that Patrick and Nai were gone. *Forever,* Nicole thought briefly, fighting the return of her sorrow.

"Would you like to take a shower?" Benjy asked. "I could help you undress and carry you over to the stall."

Nicole looked up at her balding son. *I was wrong to worry about you,* she thought. *You would do fine without me.* "Why, thank you, Benjy," she said. "That would be very nice."

"I'll try to be gentle," he said, unbuttoning his mother's gown. "But please tell me if I hurt you."

When Nicole was completely naked, Benjy picked her up in his arms and started to walk toward the shower. He stopped after he had taken two steps. "What's wrong, Benjy?" Nicole asked.

Benjy grinned sheepishly. "I didn't think the plan through very well, Mama," he said. "I should have adjusted the water first."

He turned around, set Nicole back down on her mat, and crossed the room to the shower. Nicole heard the water running.

"You like it medium hot, don't you?" he called out.

"That's right," Nicole answered.

Benjy returned and picked her up a few seconds later. "I put two towels down on the floor," he said, "so it wouldn't be too hard or too cold for you."

"Thank you, son," Nicole said.

Benjy talked to her while Nicole sat on the towels on the floor of the shower and let the refreshing water pour over her body. He brought her soap and shampoo when she requested them. When she was finished, Benjy helped his mother dry off and dress. Then he carried her over to her wheelchair.

"Bend down here, please," Nicole said as she settled into her chair. She kissed him on the cheek and squeezed his hand. "Thank you for everything, Benjy," she said, unable to stop the tears that were forming in her eyes. "You have been a marvelous help."

Benjy stood beside his mother, beaming. "I love you, Mama," he said. "It makes me happy to help you."

"And I love you too, son," Nicole said, squeezing his hand again. "Now, are you going to join me for breakfast?"

"That was my plan," said Benjy, still smiling.

Before they were finished eating, the Eagle walked up to Nicole and Benjy in the cafeteria. "Dr. Blue and I will be waiting for you in your room," the Eagle said. "We want to give you a thorough physical examination."

Sophisticated medical equipment had already been set up in the apartment when Nicole and Benjy returned. Dr. Blue injected additional microprobes directly into Nicole's chest and later sent another set of probes into her kidney region. The Eagle and Dr. Blue conversed in the octospider's native color language throughout the half-hour examination. Benjy assisted his mother when she was asked to stand or move around. He was completely fascinated by the Eagle's ability to speak in color.

"How did you learn to do that?" Benjy asked the Eagle at one point in the examination.

"Technically speaking," the Eagle replied, "I didn't learn anything. My designers added a pair of specialized subsystems to my structure, one that would allow me to interpret the octospider colors and the other to make the color patterns on my forehead."

"Didn't you have to go to school or anything?" Benjy persisted.

"No," the Eagle said simply.

"Could your designers do that for *me*?" Benjy asked several seconds later, when the Eagle and Dr. Blue had resumed their discussion of Nicole's condition.

The Eagle turned around and looked at Benjy. "I'm a very slow learner," Benjy said. "It would be wonderful if someone could just put everything into my brain."

"We don't quite know how to do that yet," the Eagle said.

When the examination was over, the Eagle asked Benjy to pack all of Nicole's things. "Where are we going?" Nicole asked.

"We're going for a ride in the shuttle," the Eagle said. "I want to discuss your physical condition with you in some detail and take you where any emergency could be quickly handled."

"I thought the blue liquid and all those probes inside me were enough—"

"We'll talk about it later," the Eagle said, interrupting her. He took Nicole's bag from Benjy. "Thank you for all your help," the alien said.

"Let me make certain that I have understood this last half hour of discussion," Nicole said into the microphone of her helmet as the shuttle neared the halfway point between the starfish and the Node. "My heart will not last more than ten days at most, despite all your medical magic; my kidneys are currently undergoing terminal failure; and my liver is showing signs of severe degradation. Is that a fair summary?"

"It is indeed," said the Eagle.

Nicole forced a smile. "Is there any good news?"

"Your mind is still functioning admirably, and the bruise on your hip will eventually heal, provided the other ailments don't kill you first."

"And what you are suggesting," Nicole said, "is that I should check into your equivalent of a hospital today over at the Node and have my heart, kidneys, and liver all replaced by advanced machines that can perform the same functions?"

"There may be some other organs that need to be replaced as well," the Eagle said, "as long as we are performing a major operation. Your pancreas has been malfunctioning intermittently, and your entire sexual system is out of spec. A complete hysterectomy should be considered."

Nicole was shaking her head. "At what point does all of this become senseless? No matter what you do now, it's only a matter of time until some other organ fails. What would be next? My lungs? Or maybe my eyes? Would you even give me a brain transplant if I could no longer think?"

"We could," the Eagle replied.

Nicole was quiet for almost a minute. "It may not make much sense to you," she said, "because it certainly isn't what I would call logical . . . but I am not very comfortable with the idea of becoming a hybrid being."

"What do you mean?" the Eagle asked.

"At what point do I stop being Nicole des Jardins Wakefield?" she said. "If my heart, brain, eyes, and ears are replaced by machines, am I still Nicole? Or am I someone, or something, else?"

"The question has no relevance," the Eagle said. "You're a doctor, Nicole. Consider the case of a schizophrenic who must take drugs regularly to alter the functions of the brain. Is that person still who he or she was? It's the same philosophical question, just a different degree of change."

"I can see your point," Nicole said after another brief silence. "But it doesn't change my feelings. I'm sorry. If I have a choice, and you have led me to believe that I do, then I will decline. At least for today anyway."

The Eagle stared at Nicole for several seconds. Then he entered a different set of parameters into the control system of the shuttle. The vehicle changed its heading.

"So are we going back to the starfish?" Nicole asked.

"Not immediately," the Eagle said. "I want to show you something else first." The alien reached into the pouch around his waist and pulled out a small tube containing a blue liquid and an unknown device. "Please give me your arm. I don't want you to die before this afternoon is over."

As they approached the Habitation Module of the Node, Nicole complained to the Eagle about the "less than forthright" way the dividing of the starfish residents into two groups had been handled. "As usual," Nicole said, "you cannot be accused of telling a lie—just of withholding critical information."

"Sometimes," the Eagle said, "there are no good ways for us to complete a task. In those cases we choose the least unsatisfactory course of action. What did you expect us to do? Tell the residents in the beginning that we couldn't take care of everyone forever, generation after generation? There would have been chaos. Besides, I don't think you give us enough credit. We rescued thousands of beings from Rama, most of whom probably would have died in an interspecies conflict without our intervention. Remember that everyone, including those assigned to the Carrier, will be allowed to complete his or her life."

Nicole was silent. She was trying to imagine what life on the Carrier would be like without any reproduction. Her mind carried the scenario into its likely distant future, when there would be only a few individuals left. "I wouldn't want to be the last human left alive in the Carrier," she said.

"There was a species in this part of the galaxy about three million years ago," the Eagle said, "that flourished as a spacefarer for almost a million years. They were brilliant engineers and built some of the most amazing buildings ever seen. Their sphere of influence spread rapidly until they dominated a region covering more than twenty star systems. This species was learned, compassionate, and wise. But they made one fatal error."

"What was that?" Nicole asked on cue.

"Their equivalent to your genome contained an order of magnitude more information than yours. It had been the result of four billion years of natural evolution and was extremely complicated. Their initial experiments with genetic engineering, both on other species and on themselves, were an unqualified success. They *thought* they understood what they were doing. However, without their knowledge, slowly but surely the robustness of the genes that were being transferred from generation to generation was deteriorating. When they finally understood what they had done to themselves, it was too late. They had preserved no pristine specimens from the early days, before they had begun to modify their own genes. They could not go back. There was nothing they could do.

"Imagine," the Eagle said, "not just being the last member of your group on an isolated spaceship like the Carrier, but being one of the terminal survivors of a species rich in history, art, and knowledge. Our encyclopedia contains many such stories, each containing at least one object lesson."

The shuttle moved through an open port in the side of the spherical module and came to a gentle stop against a wall. Automatic gantries on each side were deployed to keep the vehicle from drifting. There was a ramp from the passenger side of the shuttle to a walkway, which in turn led toward the hub of the transportation complex.

Nicole laughed. "I was so engrossed in our conversation," she said, "that I didn't even look at this module from the outside."

"You wouldn't have seen much that was new," the Eagle said.

The alien then turned to Nicole and did something very unusual. He reached across the shuttle and took both of her gloved hands. "In less than an hour," he said, "you are going to experience something that will astound you and also arouse your emotions. Originally, we had planned that this excursion would be a complete surprise. But with your weakened condition, we can't risk the possibility that your system might be overpowered by emotional input. Therefore, we have decided to tell you first what we're about to do."

Nicole felt her heart rate increase. *What is he talking about?* she thought. *What could be so unusual?*

"We will board a small car that will travel several kilometers into this module. At the end of this short journey you will be reunited with your daughter Simone and Michael O'Toole."

"*What?*" Nicole shouted, tearing her hands away from the Eagle and placing them on the side of her helmet. "Did I hear you correctly? Did you say that I was going to see Simone and Michael?"

"Yes," the Eagle replied. "Nicole, please try to relax."

"My God!" Nicole exclaimed, ignoring his comment. "I cannot believe it. I just cannot believe it. . . . I hope that this is not some kind of cruel trick."

"I assure you that it is not."

"But how can Michael still be alive?" Nicole asked. "He must be at least a hundred and twenty years old."

"We have helped him with our medical magic, as you call it."

"Oh, Simone, *Si-mone!*" Nicole cried. "Can it be? Can it really be?"

Despite the pain in her hip and the unwieldy space helmet, Nicole almost jumped across the seat to give the Eagle a hug. "Thank you, oh, thank you," she said. "I cannot tell you how much this means to me."

*   *   *

The Eagle steadied Nicole's wheelchair on the escalator as they descended into the center of the main transportation complex. She looked around briefly. The station was identical to the one she remembered from the Node near Sirius. It was about twenty meters tall and laid out in a circle. Half a dozen moving sidewalks surrounded the central display, each running into a different arched tunnel leading away from the complex. Above the tunnels, to the right, were a pair of multilevel structures.

"Do the intermodule trains depart from up there?" Nicole asked, remembering a ride with Katie and Simone when the girls were both young.

The Eagle nodded. He pushed her wheelchair onto one of the moving sidewalks and they left the center of the station. They traveled several hundred meters in a tunnel before the moving sidewalk stopped. "Our car should be just to the right, in the first corridor," the Eagle said.

The small car, which opened from the top, had two seats. The Eagle lifted Nicole into the passenger seat and then folded the wheelchair into a compressed configuration no larger than a briefcase, which he stored in a pocket area inside the vehicle. Shortly thereafter, the car moved forward through the maze of light cream windowless passageways. Nicole was extraordinarily quiet. She was trying to convince herself that she was indeed about to see the daughter whom she had left in another star system years and years ago.

The ride through the Habitation Module seemed interminable. At one point they stopped and the Eagle told Nicole she could remove her helmet. "Are we close?" she asked.

"Not yet," he answered, "but we are already in their atmospheric zone."

Twice they encountered fascinating aliens in vehicles moving in the opposite direction, but Nicole was too excited to pay attention to anything except what was going on inside her head. She was barely even listening to the Eagle. *Calm down,* one of Nicole's inner voices said. *Don't be absurd,* another voice replied, *I'm about to see a daughter I haven't seen for forty years. There's no way I could remain calm.*

"In its own way," the Eagle was saying, "their life has been as extraordinary as yours. Different, of course, altogether different. When we took Patrick over to see them very early this morning—"

"What did you say?" Nicole asked abruptly. "Did you say that Patrick saw them this morning? You took Patrick to see his father?"

"Yes," said the Eagle. "We had always planned for this reunion, as long as everything went according to schedule. Ideally neither you nor Patrick would have seen Simone and Michael and their children—"

"*Children!*" Nicole exclaimed. "I have more grandchildren!"

"—until after you were settled at the Node, but when Patrick requested reconsideration . . . well, it would have been heartless to let him leave forever without ever seeing his natural father."

Nicole could no longer contain herself. She reached over and kissed the Eagle on his feathered cheek. "And Max said you were nothing but a cold machine. How wrong he was! Thank you. . . . For Patrick's sake, I thank you."

She was trembling from excitement. A moment later Nicole could not breathe. The Eagle quickly stopped the small car.

"Where am I?" Nicole said, emerging from a deep fog.

"We are parked just inside the enclosed area where Michael, Simone, and their family live," the Eagle said. "We have been here for about four hours. You have been sleeping."

"Did I have a heart attack?" Nicole asked.

"Not exactly. . . . Just a significant malfunction. I considered taking you immediately back to the hospital, but I decided to wait until you awakened. Besides, I have most of the same medications here with me."

The Eagle looked at her with his intense blue eyes. "What do you want to do, Nicole?" he said. "Visit with Simone and Michael as planned, or go back to the hospital? It's your choice, but understand—"

"I know," Nicole interrupted him with a sigh, "I must be careful not to become too excited." She glanced at the Eagle. "I want to see Simone, even if it's the last act of my life. Can you give me something that will calm me but will not make me goofy or put me to sleep?"

"A mild tranquilizer will only help," the Eagle said, "if you consciously work to contain your excitement."

"All right," Nicole said. "I'll do my best."

The Eagle eased the car onto a paved road lined with tall trees. As they drove, Nicole was reminded of the autumn in New England she spent with her father when she was a teenager. The leaves on the trees were red, gold, and brown.

"It's beautiful," Nicole said.

The car rounded a curve and drove past a white fence enclosing a grassy area. There were four horses in the enclosure. A pair of human teenagers were walking among them. "The children are real," the Eagle said. "The horses are simulations."

At the top of a gentle hill was a large two-story white house with a sloped black roof. The Eagle pulled into the circular drive and stopped the car. The front door of the house opened an instant later and a tall, beautiful, jet-black woman with graying hair came outside.

"Mother!" Simone yelled as she raced for the car.

Nicole barely had time to open her door before Simone flung herself into her mother's arms. The two women hugged and kissed, weeping profusely. Neither of them could speak.

8

"It was a bittersweet visit with Patrick," Simone said, putting down her coffee cup. "He was here for over two hours, but it seemed like only a few minutes."

The three of them were sitting at a table that looked out on the rolling farmland that surrounded the house. Nicole was temporarily staring out the window at the bucolic scene. "It's mostly an illusion, of course," Michael said. "But a very good one. Unless you knew better, you would think you were in Massachusetts or southern Vermont."

"This whole dinner has seemed like a dream," Nicole said. "I have not yet accepted that any of this is really happening."

"We felt that way last night," Simone said, "when we were told that we were going to see Patrick this morning. Neither Michael nor I slept a wink." She laughed. "At one point during the night we had convinced ourselves that we were going to meet a 'fake' Patrick, and we thought of questions we could ask that nobody except the real Patrick could answer."

"Their technological skills are awesome," Michael said. "If they wanted to create a robot Patrick and pass him off as the genuine article, it would be very difficult for us to ascertain the truth."

"But they didn't," Simone said. "I knew within minutes that it was really Patrick."

"How did he seem to you?" Nicole asked. "In all the confusion of the last day, I didn't have a chance to talk to him very much."

"Resigned, mostly," Simone said, "but certain that he had made the correct decision. He said it would probably be weeks before he had sorted through all the emotions he had experienced in the last twenty-four hours."

"That must be true for all of us," Nicole said.

There was a brief silence at the table. "Are you tired, Mother?" Simone asked. "Patrick told us about your health problems, and when we received the message this afternoon that you had been delayed . . ."

"Yes, I'm a little tired," Nicole said. "But I certainly couldn't sleep. At least not immediately." She backed her wheelchair away from the table and lowered her seat. "I would, however, like to use the powder room."

"Certainly," Simone said, jumping up. "I'll come with you."

Simone accompanied her mother down a long hall with a simulated wooden floor. "So you have six children living with you here," Nicole said, "including three that you carried?"

"That's right," Simone said. "Michael and I had two boys and two girls by the 'natural method,' as you called it. The first of the boys, Darren, died when he was seven. It's a long story. If we have time, I'll tell it to you tomorrow. All the rest of the children were developed from embryos in the laboratories."

They had reached the door to the powder room. "Do you know how many children the Eagle and his colleagues have developed from your eggs?" Nicole asked.

"No," Simone answered. "But they did tell me that they took more than a thousand healthy eggs from my ovaries."

On the way back to the dining room, Simone explained that all the children who had been born by the "natural method" had lived their whole lives with Michael and her. Their spouses, who were of course also the product of Michael's sperm and her eggs, had been selected as the result of a comprehensive genetic matching technique developed by the aliens.

"So these were arranged marriages?" Nicole asked.

"Not exactly," Simone said. She laughed. "Each natural child was introduced to several possible mates, all of whom had passed the genetic screening."

"And you've had no problems with your grandchildren?"

"Nothing that is 'statistically significant,' to use Michael's term," Simone replied.

When they reached the dining room, the table was empty. Michael told them that he had moved the coffeepot and cups into the study. Nicole activated her wheelchair controls and followed them into a large, masculine study with dark wood bookshelves, and a fire burning in the fireplace.

"Is the fire real?" Nicole asked.

"Indeed it is," Michael said. He leaned forward in his soft chair. "You have been asking about the children," he said, "and we certainly want you to meet them, but we didn't want to overwhelm you."

"I understand," Nicole said, taking a sip from a fresh cup of coffee, "and I agree with you. You certainly could not have had such a leisurely, informative dinner if there had been six more people."

"And don't forget the fourteen grandchildren," Simone said.

Nicole looked at Michael and smiled. "I'm sorry, Michael," she said, "but *you* are the part of this evening that is the most unreal. Whenever I look at you, my mind balks. You must be forty years older than I am, but you look not a day over sixty, and definitely younger than when we left you at the Node. How is this possible?"

"Their technology is absolute magic," he said. "They have reworked virtually every part of me. My heart, lungs, liver, entire digestive and excretory systems, and most of my endocrine glands have all been replaced, some several times, by smaller, more efficient functional equivalents. My bones, muscles, nerves, and blood vessels are all buttressed by millions of microscopic implants that not only ensure the critical functions are accomplished, but also, in many cases, biochemically rejuvenate the aged cells. My skin is a special material they only recently perfected, which has all the good properties of real human skin but never ages or develops warts or moles. Once a year I go over to their hospital. I'm unconscious for two days, and when I emerge I am literally a new man."

"Would you mind coming over here," Nicole said, "and letting me touch you?" She laughed. "I don't need to put my fingers through the holes in your hands, or anything like that, but you can certainly understand that what you are telling me is difficult to believe."

Michael O'Toole crossed the room and knelt beside the wheelchair. Nicole reached out and touched the skin on his face. It was smooth and supple, like a young man's. His eyes were fresh and clear. "And your brain, Michael," Nicole asked softly. "What have they done to your brain?"

He smiled. Nicole noticed that there were no wrinkles in his forehead. "Many things," he said. "When my memory started to slip, they reconditioned my hippocampus. They even supplemented it with a small structure of their own—to give me more capacity, they said. About twenty years ago they also installed what they described as a 'better operating system,' to sharpen my thinking processes."

Michael was less than a meter away from her. The light from the fire reflected off his face. Nicole was suddenly swept away by a flood of memories. She recalled what close friends they had been in Rama, as well as their moments of intimacy when Richard had been gone and presumed lost. She touched his face again.

"And are you still Michael O'Toole?" she asked. "Or have you become something else, part human and part alien?"

He stood up without saying anything and walked back to his chair. He moved like an athlete, not like a man who was more than one hundred and twenty years old. "I don't know how to answer your question," he said. "I can remember clearly all the details of my childhood in Boston, and every other important phase of my life. As far as I know, I am still more or less the same."

"Michael is still extremely interested in religion and creation as well," Simone added. "But he has changed some—all of us are altered by our experiences in life."

"I have remained a devout Roman Catholic," Michael said, "and I still say my daily prayers. But naturally my view of God, and of humanity too, has been drastically changed by what Simone and I have seen. If anything, my faith has strengthened . . . primarily because of my enlightening conversations with . . ."

He stopped and glanced across the room at Simone. "In the early years, Mother," she said, "when Michael and I were alone at the Node, near Sirius, there were many difficulties. We had only each other to talk with. I was still just a girl, and Michael was a mature man. I could not discuss physics or religion or many of his other favorite topics."

"There were no major problems, you understand," Michael said. "Still, we were both lonely, in a peculiar sort of way. What we had together was remarkable and enriching. . . . But we both needed something else, something additional.

"The Nodal Intelligence, or whatever we should call the power that was taking care of us, sensed our difficulty. It also recognized that the Eagle could not fulfill our individual needs. So a companion—like the Eagle, in a sense—was created for each of us."

"It was a stroke of genius," Simone said, "that removed the emotional tension that was threatening our perfect marriage. When Saint Michael—"

"Let me tell it, please," Michael interrupted. "One night, almost two years after you and the others had left, Simone was in the bedroom of the apartment nursing Katya when there was a knock on our door. I assumed that it was the Eagle. When I opened the door, however, a young man with dark, curly hair and blue eyes, a perfect reconstruction of Saint Michael of Siena, was standing there. He informed me that the Eagle would no longer be interacting with us and that he would be my new intermediary with the intelligence governing the Node."

"Saint Michael," Simone said, "came equipped with a vast set of knowledge of Earth history, and Catholicism, and physics, and all the other subjects about which I was totally ignorant."

"*Plus*," Michael said, rising from his chair, "he was willing to answer questions about what was going on around us at the Node. Not that the Eagle wasn't, but Saint Michael was much warmer, more personal. It was as if he had been sent by them, or by God, to be a companion for my mind."

Nicole glanced back and forth from Michael to Simone. Michael's face was positively radiant. *His religious fervor has not waned,* she thought. *It has only been redirected.*

"And is this Saint Michael character still around?" Nicole asked, swallowing the last sip of her coffee.

"Absolutely," Michael said. "We did not introduce Patrick to him—the time was too short, as Simone said—but we definitely want you to meet him." Michael walked across the room, suddenly bubbling with energy. "Do you remember all those infinite questions Richard used to ask, about who built the Node and Rama, and what was the purpose of this and that? Saint Michael knows all the answers. And he explains everything so eloquently!"

"Goodness," said Nicole, with just a slight trace of sarcasm in her voice, "he sounds fantastic. Much too good to be true. When will I have the privilege of meeting Saint Michael?"

"Right now, if you would like," Michael O'Toole said expectantly.

"All right," Nicole said, stifling a yawn. "But remember I'm a tired, ailing, crotchety old woman. I can't stay up forever."

Michael walked briskly to the far door of the study. "Saint Michael," he called, "would you come in please and meet Simone's mother, Nicole?"

A few seconds later what looked like a young human priest in his early twenties, dressed in a dark blue robe, entered the room and crossed to Nicole's wheelchair. "I am delighted," Saint Michael said, with a beatific smile. "I have heard about you for years."

Nicole extended her hand and studied the alien intently. There was absolutely nothing she could see that would identify this individual as anything other than a human being. *My God*, Nicole thought quickly, *not only is their technology fantastic, but also their rate of learning is staggering.*

"Now let's get one thing straight at the outset," she said to Saint Michael with a wry smile, "there are too many Michaels here. I do *not* intend to address you regularly as Saint Michael. It's not my style. Do I just call you Saint, or Mike, or even Mikey—what do you prefer?"

"When they're both around I call my husband Big Michael," Simone said. "That seems to work fine."

"All right," Nicole said. "As Richard always said, 'When in Rome . . .' Sit down, Michael, here close to my wheelchair. Big Michael has praised you so highly I don't want my bad hearing to cause me to miss any of your pearls of wisdom."

"Thank you, Nicole," Saint Michael said with a smile of his own. "Michael and Simone have extolled your virtues as well, but they clearly understated the cleverness of your wit."

He has a personality too, Nicole thought. *Will wonders never cease?*

An hour later, after Simone had helped her to bed in the guest room at the end of the hall, Nicole was lying on her side staring toward the windows. Although she was very tired, she could not sleep. Her mind was too active, going over and over the events of the day.

Maybe I should ring for something to help me sleep, Nicole thought, her hand automatically feeling for the button on the table beside her bed. *Simone said Saint Michael would come if I called. And that he could do anything the Eagle could.* Having assured herself that she could indeed summon help if her insomnia persisted, Nicole turned back to her most comfortable sleeping position and allowed her mind to float freely.

Her thoughts focused on what she had seen and heard since she had arrived at this isolated enclave in which Michael, Simone, and their family lived. Saint Michael had explained that this pseudo–New England was a small section inside the Habitation Module of the Node and that there were several hundred other species who were semipermanent residents in the near vicinity. Why, Nicole had asked, had Big Michael and Simone chosen an everyday existence separate from all the others?

"For years," Nicole remembered Michael O'Toole responding, "we lived in a multispecies environment. In fact, both during and after our four natural children were born, we were whisked, or so it seemed, from place to place, testing both our adaptability and compatibility with a wide range of other plant and animal species. Saint Michael confirmed at the time what we suspected, namely that our hosts were purposely exposing us to a variety of environments to gather more information about us. Each new venue was another challenge."

Big Michael paused for a moment, as if he were struggling emotionally. "The psychological hardships were immense in those early days. As soon as we adapted to a given set of living conditions, they were abruptly changed. I still believe that Darren's death would not have occurred if everything hadn't been so strange in that underground world. And we nearly lost Katya when she was only two or so and her curiosity was mistaken by a squidlike sea creature as an act of aggression."

"After we were put to sleep the second time," Simone said, "and transported to this Node, both Michael and I were exhausted from the years of tests. The children were grown by then and starting to have families of their own. We requested, and were granted, some privacy."

"We still go out into the other world," Michael added, "but we interact with the exotic beings from distant star systems because we want to, not because it is a necessity. Saint Michael briefs us regularly on the comings and goings of the basketball creatures, the sky-hoppers, and the flying turtles. He is our information window to the rest of the Node."

Saint Michael is extraordinary, Nicole thought, *and much more advanced even than the Eagle. He answers all questions with such certitude. But there's something about him that makes me wonder. Are all those crisp answers about God and the origin and destiny of the universe really correct? Or has Saint Michael somehow been programmed, based on Michael's love of catechismic processes, to be his perfect alien companion?*

Nicole rolled over in bed and considered her own relationship with the

Eagle. *Maybe I'm just jealous*, she thought, *because Michael seems to have learned so much . . . and the Eagle has been unwilling or unable to answer my questions. But who is better off, the child with a mentor who knows and tells everything or the one whose teacher helps the child find her own answers? I don't know . . . I don't know. But that was one hell of an impressive performance by Saint Michael at the easel.*

"Don't you see, Nicole?" Big Michael had jumped up from his chair for the umpteenth time. "We're all participating in God's great experiment. This *entire* universe, not just our own galaxy, but all the galaxies that stretch to the end of the heavens, will provide one single data point for God. He, She, or It is searching for perfection, for that small range of initial parameters which, once the universe is set into motion by the transformation of energy into matter, will evolve, over billions of years, into one perfect harmony, a testimony to the Creator's consummate skill."

Nicole had had some difficulty following the higher mathematics, but she had certainly understood the gist of the diagrams that Saint Michael had drawn on the easel in the study. "So at this moment," Nicole had said to the alien with the curly hair and the blue eyes, "there are countless other universes evolving, each having been started by God with different initial conditions, and God has somehow slipped you, the Eagle, the Node, and Rama *inside* this particular evolution process to acquire information? And the purpose of all this is so that God can define some mathematical construct associated with creation that will always produce a harmonious result?"

"Exactly," Saint Michael had responded. Again he had pointed at the diagram on the easel. "Imagine that this coordinate system I have drawn is a symbolic, two-dimensional representation of the available hypersurface of parameters defining the creation instant, the moment that energy is first transformed into matter. Any arrangement or vector representing a specific set of initial conditions for the universe may be depicted as a single point in my diagram. What God is, and has been, searching for is a very special closed dense set located on this mathematical hypersurface. This special set He is seeking has the property that *any* of its elements—that is, any arrangement of conditions for the instant of creation chosen from *within* this set—will produce a universe that will eventually end in harmony."

"It's a nearly impossible problem," Big Michael said, "to create a universe that will end up with all living beings proclaiming the glory of God. If there is not enough matter, the explosion and inflation of the creation instant results in a universe that expands forever, without sufficient interaction of the individual components during evolution to produce and sustain life. If there is too much matter, then there is insufficient time for life and intelligence to develop fully before gravity causes the Great Crunch that ends the universe."

"Chaos confounds God as well," Saint Michael explained. "Chaos is an outgrowth of all the physical laws governing the evolution of any created universe. It prevents the accurate prediction of the outcomes of large-scale processes, so God cannot, a priori, simply calculate what is going to happen in the future and therefore, by analytical techniques, isolate the zones of harmony. Experimentation is the only possible way for Him to discover what He is seeking."

"The structure opposing God's design is overwhelming," Big Michael added. "In order for God to succeed, not only must life and intelligence evolve from raw subatomic particles made into atoms by stellar cataclysms, but also this life must reach such a level of both spiritual self-awareness and technological capability that it can actively transform everything around it."

So God, Nicole thought in her room, remembering the discussion, *is the ultimate designer, the ultimate engineer. He or She or It shapes the moment of creation in such a way that, billions of years later, living beings attest to the wonder of creation.*

"There's a part of this I still don't understand," Nicole had said to the two Michaels and Simone near the end of the evening. "Why must God create so many universes to conduct this experiment? Once the existence of a harmonious outcome has been verified, doesn't the task become easy? Can't the initial conditions for that universe simply be replicated?"

"That's not a difficult enough problem for God," Saint Michael had responded. "God wants to know the extent of the zone of harmony in the hypersurface of creation parameters, plus all the mathematical characteristics of the zone. Besides, I don't think you yet appreciate the scope of God's problem. Only a minuscule fraction of all possible universes can end up harmonious. The natural outcome of the transformation of energy into matter is a universe with no life at all, or, at best, aggressive, temporary living creatures who are more destructive than constructive. Even a small region of harmony inside an evolving universe is a miracle. That's why the whole enterprise is such a challenge for God."

Big Michael had then jumped up again. "What God is looking for is a universe which, before it dies in the Big Crunch, has achieved *total* harmony. That's not just every living species from every world working together for the mutual good, but every subatomic particle of His creation actively participating in that harmony. For a while, I myself couldn't comprehend the full grandeur of this concept. Then Saint Michael told me about a species that makes living beings out of rock and dirt, as our biblical God did, by transmuting and rearranging the elements. *Total* harmony requires that advanced species like us use our technological tools to transform inanimate and nonliving things into creatures that contribute to the harmony."

Nicole remembered that she had announced, at about this point in the conversation, that her mind was overloaded and she wanted to go to bed. Saint Michael had asked her to wait just a few more minutes so that he could summarize what he felt had been a slightly disorganized discussion. Nicole had agreed.

"Going back to your original question," Saint Michael had said, "each of the Nodes is part of a hierarchical intelligence gathering information throughout this particular galaxy. Most galaxies, including the Milky Way, have a single superstation, which we call the Prime Monitor, located somewhere near its center. The set of Prime Monitors was created by God at the same moment the universe began and then was deployed to learn as much as possible about the evolutionary process. The Nodes, the Carriers, and all the other engineering constructs you have seen were in turn designed by the Prime Monitor. The entire activity, including what has been going on since the first Rama spacecraft entered your solar system years ago, has as its objective the development of quantitative criteria, for use by the Creator, that will enable subsequent universes to conclude in glorious harmony, despite the chaotic tendencies of the natural laws."

Nicole had not been able to say anything for over a minute. "This conversation has been absolutely mind-boggling," she had finally said, activating her wheelchair. "And now I am completely exhausted."

But not so exhausted that I can sleep, she thought. *How could anybody sleep after having had the purpose of the universe explained?* Nicole laughed to herself in bed. *I can't imagine what Richard would have said after that discussion. A good theory, perhaps, but how does it explain the African dominance in the World Cup between 2140 and 2160? Or is the meaning of life no longer 42?* She laughed again. *Richard would have appreciated Saint Michael, no doubt, but he would have had hundreds of questions. We would have made love as soon as we returned to the room and then talked all night. . . .*

Nicole turned over on her side. The ramifications of what she had heard that night were overwhelming. But was any of it really true? Nicole understood that she would never know for certain. *It is a beautiful, stirring concept*, she thought. As Nicole drifted off to sleep, visions of universes exploding into being danced in her mind's eye.

9

Nicole woke up refreshed and with a surprising amount of energy. She started to push the button beside her bed, but decided against it. Instead she struggled into her wheelchair. She rolled over to the windows and pulled the curtains.

It was a beautiful morning outside. There was a little creek off to her left, and three children, probably between eight and ten years of age, were skipping stones across a small pool in the creek. As Nicole gazed out the windows at the perfectly simulated fields and trees and rolling hills, she felt temporarily young and full of life.

Maybe I should let them repair me after all, Nicole thought. *Replace all my damaged and worn-out parts. I could live here, with Simone and Michael. Maybe I could even teach my great-grandchildren a thing or two.*

The three children left the creek and raced across a green field to where the horses were enclosed. The boy ran the fastest, but he barely beat the smaller of the two girls. The trio laughed together and called the horses over to the fence.

"The boy is Zachary," Big Michael said from behind her. "The two girls are Colleen and Simone. Zachary and Colleen are Katya's children, Simone is Timothy's oldest."

Nicole had not heard him enter the room. She turned around in her wheelchair. "Good morning, Michael," she said. Nicole glanced back at the window. "The children are all gorgeous."

"Thank you," Michael said, walking over to the window. "I am a very lucky man," he said. "God has granted me a fascinating life with unbeliev-able riches."

They watched in silence as the children played. Zachary mounted a white horse and began to show off. "I was sorry to hear about Richard's death," Michael said. "Patrick told us the story yesterday. It must have been horrible for you."

"It was," Nicole replied. "Richard and I had developed such a wonderful friendship." They faced each other. "You would have been so proud of him, Michael. He was a different man in his last years."

"I suspected as much," Michael said. "The Richard I knew would never have volunteered to place himself in jeopardy, especially to save the lives of others."

"You should have seen him with his granddaughter Nikki, Ellie's little girl. They were inseparable. He was her 'Boobah.' . . . He found tenderness so late in life."

Nicole could not continue. A sudden heartache overwhelmed her. She drove over to the bedside table and took a drink from the bottle of blue liquid.

She returned to the window. Outside, the girls were now on horseback also and some kind of game was under way.

"Patrick told us that Benjy had grown into a fine adult," Michael said, "limited in some ways, of course, but quite remarkable considering his basic ability and the long periods of sleep. He said that Benjy was a living tribute to your talents, all of them, and that you had worked with him tirelessly, never letting him use his handicap as an excuse."

It was Michael's turn to choke up. He turned to Nicole with tears easing out of both of his eyes and placed his hands in hers. "There's no way I can ever thank you enough for raising those two boys with such care. Especially Benjy."

Nicole looked up at him from her wheelchair. "They are our sons, Michael," she said. "I love them very much."

Michael wiped his nose and eyes with a pocket handkerchief. "Simone and I want you to meet our children and grandchildren, of course," he said, "but we both agreed that there was something we should tell you first. . . . We didn't know exactly how you would respond. However, it would not be fair not to tell you, because otherwise you might not understand why the children are reacting—"

"What is it, Michael?" Nicole interrupted. She smiled. "You're certainly having a hard time coming to the point."

"I am indeed," he said, crossing the room and pushing the button beside Nicole's bed twice in rapid succession. "Nicole, what I am about to say is a bit delicate. . . . Remember last night, when we told you that both Simone and I had alien companions?"

"Yes, Michael," Nicole said.

"Look outside," he said after a moment's hesitation. "There's someone I want you to see."

Michael came over beside Nicole and took her hand. She stared out the window. A woman in her late forties, athletic, with dark copper skin, had left the house and was walking quickly toward the horse compound. Both the woman's figure and her gait seemed familiar to Nicole. The children saw the woman, waved, and came toward her on their horses.

Nicole watched Zachary yell the woman's name and suddenly she understood. Nicole was thunderstruck. The woman turned around briefly and Nicole saw herself, exactly as she had been when she had left the Node forty years earlier. It was difficult for her to keep her emotions under control.

"It was you that Simone missed the most," Michael said, acknowledging the look of astonished recognition on Nicole's face. "So it was only natural that the aliens fashioned a companion for her from your image. She is a remarkable simulation. Not just her physical appearance, which you can see for yourself, but also her personality. Simone and I were amazed, especially in the beginning, at what a perfect duplication job they had done. The alien talked like you, walked like you, even thought like you. Within a week Simone was calling her 'Mother' and I was calling her 'Nicole.' She has been with us ever since."

Nicole gazed at the simulation of herself without saying a word. *The facial expressions and even the gestures are correct*, she thought. She continued to stare fixedly as the woman approached the house with the three children.

"Simone thought you might be a little upset, or maybe feel displaced, when you discovered that this simulation of you had been living with the family for all these years. But I assured her that you would be fine, that it would simply take a little while for you to adjust to the idea. . . . After all, as far as I know, no human being has ever been replaced by a robot copy of herself before."

The alien Nicole picked up one of the girls and twirled her around in the air. Then all four of them bounded up the steps and across the threshold of the house.

They call her Granny, Nicole thought. *She can run, and ride horses, and toss them in the air. She is not phthisic and confined to a wheelchair.* An emotion that Nicole did not like, self-pity, began to grow inside her. *Maybe Simone has not even missed me that much*, she said to herself. *Her 'mother' has been here all these years, at her beck and call, never aging, never asking for anything.*

Nicole sensed that she was going to cry. She pulled herself together. "Michael," she said, forcing a smile, "why don't you give me a minute to prepare myself for breakfast?"

"Are you sure you don't need any help?" he asked.

"No, no . . . I'll be fine. I just want to wash my face and put on a little makeup."

The tears came a few seconds after the door closed. *There is no place for me here either,* Nicole said to herself. *There is already a granny, a better one than I could ever be, even if she is only a machine.*

Nicole said almost nothing on the ride back to the transportation center. She was still quiet as the shuttle left the Habitation Module and pulled out into space.

"You don't want to talk about it, do you?" the Eagle said.

"Not really," Nicole said into the microphone in her helmet.

"Are you glad you went?" the Eagle inquired several seconds later.

"Oh, yes . . . absolutely," she replied. "It was one of the most out-standing experiences of my life. Thank you very much."

The Eagle adjusted the flight of the shuttle so that they were moving slowly backward. The huge illuminated tetrahedron dominated the view out their window.

"The replacement procedure could be performed this afternoon," the Eagle said. "By early next week you would look younger than Big Michael."

"No, thanks," said Nicole.

There was another long period of silence. "You don't seem very happy," the Eagle then said.

Nicole turned to look at her alien companion. "I am," she said. "And I am especially happy for Simone and Michael. It's wonderful that their life has been so fulfilling." Nicole took a deep breath. "Maybe I'm just tired," she said. "So much has occurred in such a short period of time."

"That's probably it," the Eagle said.

Nicole was deep in thought, methodically reviewing everything that had happened to her since she had awakened. The faces of Simone and Michael's six children and fourteen grandchildren swept through her mind. *A handsome lot,* she said to herself, *but without much variation.*

It was another face, one she remembered clearly from her own mirror, that returned to her mind's eye most often. She had agreed with Simone and Michael that the other Nicole was an unbelievable likeness, an absolute triumph of advanced technology. What Nicole had not even been able to discuss with them was how strange it was meeting and carrying on a conversation with herself as a younger person. Or how peculiar she felt knowing that a machine had replaced her in the hearts and minds of her own family.

Nicole had watched silently while the other Nicole and Simone had laughed about an argument that Simone had had with her little sister Katie years before at the Node. As the alien had recalled the details of the story, Nicole's memory too had been refreshed. *Even her memory is better than mine. What a perfect solution to the whole problem of aging and dying. Capture a person in the prime of her life, with all her powers intact, and preserve her forever as a legend, at least in the eyes of her loved ones.*

"How do I know for certain that the Michael and Simone that I talked with yesterday and this morning are the real humans and not just an even higher-fidelity simulation than the other Nicole?" Nicole asked the Eagle.

"Saint Michael said you asked several pointed questions about Big Michael's early life," the Eagle said. "Weren't you satisfied with the answers?"

"But I realized while we were in the car an hour ago that some of that information may have been in Michael's biographical file from the Newton, and I know that you had access to that data."

"For what purpose would we possibly have gone to such lengths to mislead you?" the Eagle said. "And have we ever behaved in a similar fashion before?"

"How many more of Simone and Michael's children are still alive?" Nicole asked a few minutes later, changing the subject.

"Thirty-two more are here at this Node," the Eagle answered. "And more than a hundred in other places."

Nicole shook her head. She remembered the Senoufo chronicles. *And her progeny shall be spread among the stars. . . . Omeh would be pleased*, she thought.

"Have you perfected, then, your ex-utero development of humans from fertilized eggs?" Nicole said.

"More or less," the Eagle replied.

Again they flew in silence for a long time. "Why didn't you ever tell me about the Prime Monitors?" Nicole asked next.

"It wasn't permitted, at least not until you awakened. And since then the subject hasn't come up."

"And is everything Saint Michael said true? About God and chaos and the many universes?"

"As far as we know," the Eagle said. "At least that's what is programmed in our systems. None of us here has ever actually seen a Prime Monitor."

"And is it possible," Nicole asked, "that the whole story is a myth of some kind, created by an intelligence above you in the hierarchy, as the official explanation to give out to human beings?"

The Eagle hesitated. "That possibility exists. I would have no way of knowing."

"Would you know if something different, some other explanation, had ever been programmed in your systems before?"

"Not necessarily," the Eagle said. "I am solely responsible for what is retained in my memory."

Nicole's behavior remained unusual. She interrupted her protracted periods of silence with bursts of apparently unrelated questions. At one point she asked why some Nodes had four modules and others three. The Eagle explained that the Knowledge Module created a tetrahedron out of the Nodal triangle in about every tenth or twelfth Node. Nicole wanted to know what was so special about the Knowledge Module. The Eagle told her that it was the repository of all the acquired information about this part of the galaxy.

"It's part library and part museum, containing a colossal amount of information in a variety of forms," he said.

"Have you ever been inside this Knowledge Module?" Nicole asked.

"No," the Eagle answered, "but my current systems contain a complete description of it."

"Can I go there?" Nicole said.

"A living being must have special permission to enter the Knowledge Module," the Eagle said.

When Nicole spoke again, she asked about what was going to happen to the humans who would be transferred to the Node in another day or two. The Eagle explained patiently, in response to one short question after another, that the people would live in the Habitation Module in a test environment with several other species, that they would be closely monitored, and that Simone, Michael, and their family might or might not be integrated with the humans who were moving to the Node.

Nicole made her decision several minutes before they reached the starfish. "I want to stay here only for tonight," she said slowly. "So that I can say good-bye to everybody."

The Eagle looked at her with a curious expression. "Then tomorrow," Nicole continued, "if you can obtain permission, I want you to take me to the Knowledge Module. . . . Once I leave the starfish, I want all medication suspended. And I want no heroic efforts if my heart goes into distress."

Nicole looked straight ahead, through the front of her space helmet and out the window of the shuttle. *It is definitely the right time,* she said to herself. *If only I have the courage not to waver.*

"Yes, Mother," Ellie said, wiping her tears again. "I *do* understand, I really do. But I'm your daughter. I love you. No matter how much logical sense it might make to you, there's just no way I can be happy about never seeing you again."

"So what am I supposed to do?" Nicole said. "Let them change me into some kind of bionic woman so I can hang around forever? And be the grande dame of the community, sententious and puffed up with self-importance? That is certainly not very appealing to me."

"But everyone admires you, Mother," Ellie said. "Your family here loves you, and you could spend years getting to know all of Simone and Michael's family. You would never be a problem to any of us."

"That's not really the issue," Nicole said. She turned her wheelchair around and faced one of the bare walls. "The universe is in constant renewal," she said, as much to herself as to Ellie. "Everything—

individuals, planets, stars, even galaxies—has a life cycle, a death as well as a birth. Nothing lasts forever. Not even the universe itself. Change and renewal are an essential part of the overall process. The octospiders know this well. That's why planned terminations are an integral part of their overall replenishment concept."

"But Mother," Ellie said from behind her, "unless there is a war, the octospiders only put individuals on the termination list who are no longer making enough of a contribution to their society to justify the resources being expended. There is no cost to us for keeping you alive. And your wisdom and experience are still valuable."

Nicole turned around and smiled. "You are a very bright woman, Ellie," she said. "And I will acknowledge that there is truth in what you are saying. But you are conveniently ignoring the two key elements in my decision, both of which I have already explained at great length. . . . For reasons neither you nor anybody else may be able to understand, it is important to me that I be able to choose my own time of death. I want to make that decision *before* I am either a burden or out of the mainstream of activity, and while I still have the respect of my family and friends. Second, it is my feeling that I do not have any defined niche in the post-transfer world. Therefore I cannot justify, in my own mind, the massive physiological intervention that will be necessary before I can function without being a problem for others. From so many different points of view, now seems to be an excellent time for me to make my exit."

"As I told you at the very beginning," Ellie said, "your cold, rational analysis, whether correct or not, should not be the only consideration. What about the feeling of loss that Benjy, Nikki, I, and the others will experience? And our sorrow will be increased by the knowledge that your death at this time could have been avoided."

"Ellie," Nicole said, "one of the reasons I came back to say good-bye to you and the others was to try to assuage any feeling of loss that you might have after my death. Again, look at the octospiders. They do not grieve."

"Mother," Ellie interrupted, fighting the return of the tears, "we are *not* octospiders, we are human beings. We *grieve*. We feel desolate when someone we love dies. We know, in our minds, that death is inevitable and that it is all part of the universal scheme, but nevertheless we weep and feel an acute sense of loss."

Ellie paused for a moment. "Have you forgotten how you felt when Richard and Katie died? You were devastated."

Nicole swallowed slowly and looked at her daughter. *I knew this would not be easy,* she thought. *Maybe I shouldn't have come back. Maybe it really would have been better if I had asked the Eagle to tell everyone I had died of a heart attack.*

"I know you were upset," Ellie said softly, "to find out that an alien robot had replaced you in Michael and Simone's family. But you shouldn't overreact. Sooner or later all of their children and grandchildren will learn that there can be no substitute for the real Nicole des Jardins Wakefield."

Nicole sighed. She felt she was losing the battle. "I did acknowledge to you, Ellie, that I felt there was no place for me in Michael and Simone's family. But it is unfair for you to imply that my reaction to the other Nicole is the sole, or even the main reason for my decision."

Nicole was becoming exhausted. She had planned to talk first to Ellie, then to Benjy, and finally to the rest of the group before she went to sleep. Ellie had been much more difficult than she had expected. *But were you being realistic?* Nicole asked herself. *Did you really think Ellie would say, "Great, Mother, it makes sense. I'm sorry to see you go, but I understand completely"?*

There was a knock on the door of the apartment. The Eagle looked at the two women after the door was opened. "Am I intruding?" the alien asked.

Nicole smiled. "I think we are ready for a short break," she said.

Ellie excused herself to go to the bathroom and the Eagle walked over to Nicole. "How's it going?" he said, bending down to the level of the wheelchair.

"Not so well," Nicole answered.

"I thought I'd drop by," the Eagle said, "to tell you that your request to visit the Knowledge Module has been approved. Assuming the basic situation you described to me in the shuttle is still valid."

Nicole brightened. "Good, " she said. "Now if I can just summon the courage to finish what I have started."

The Eagle patted her on the back. "You can do it," he said. "You are the most extraordinary human we have ever encountered."

Benjy's head was resting on her chest. Nicole was on her back with her arm wrapped around her son. *So this may be the last night of my life,* she thought as she drifted toward sleep. A small tremor of fear rushed through her and she forced it aside. *I am not afraid of death,* Nicole said to herself, *not after what I have already experienced.*

The visit from the Eagle had refortified her. When her conversation with Ellie had resumed, Nicole admitted that there was merit in all of Ellie's points and that she didn't mean to cause distress for her friends and family, but that she was determined to proceed with her decision. Nicole had then pointed out to Ellie that Benjy and she, and to some extent the others, would have an opportunity for additional individual growth in her absence, because there would no longer be an authority figure around to whom they could appeal.

Ellie had told Nicole that she was a "stubborn old woman," but that, because of her love and respect, Ellie would try to be supportive in the few remaining hours. Ellie had also asked Nicole if she intended to do anything specific to hasten her death. Nicole had laughed and told her daughter that no unusual steps would be necessary, for the Eagle had assured her that without supplementary medication her heart would fail in a matter of hours.

The conversation with Benjy had not been that difficult. Ellie had volunteered to help explain everything and Nicole had accepted her offer. Benjy knew that his mother was suffering and in poor health, and he had no knowledge that the aliens possessed the medical ability to fix her problems. Ellie had assured Benjy that Max, Eponine, Nikki, Kepler, Marius, and Maria would all still be part of his everyday world.

Of the larger group, only Eponine had had tearful eyes when Nicole had informed them of her decision. Max had said that he wasn't completely surprised. Maria had expressed sadness that she hadn't spent more time with the woman who had "saved my life." Kepler, Marius, and even Nikki had all been unsure of themselves and hadn't known what to say.

While she was preparing for bed, Nicole had promised herself that she would locate Dr. Blue first thing in the morning and say a proper good-bye to her octospider friend. Just before she had switched out the lights, Benjy had approached his mother and asked, since this would be their last night together, if he could cuddle with her "like I did when I was a little boy." Nicole had agreed, and after Benjy had snuggled up against her on the mat, tears had run across her cheeks and moistened her ears.

10

Nicole awakened early. Benjy was already up and dressed, but Kepler was still asleep on the far side of the room. Benjy patiently helped Nicole shower and dress, as he had before.

Max came into the apartment a few minutes later. After waking up Kepler, he walked over to Nicole's wheelchair and took her hand. "I didn't say much last night, my friend," Max said, "because I couldn't find the right words. . . . Even now, they seem so inadequate. . . ."

Max turned his head away. "Shit, Nicole," he said in a breaking voice, without facing her. "You know how I feel about you. You are a beautiful, beautiful person."

He stopped. The only sound in the room was the water running for Kepler's shower. Nicole squeezed his hand. "Thank you, Max," she said softly, "it means a lot to me."

"When I was eighteen," Max said hesitantly, turning back to look at Nicole, "my father died of a rare kind of cancer. We all knew it was coming. Clyde and Mom and I had watched him wither away for several months. But I still didn't believe it, even after he was lying in the coffin. We had a small service at the cemetery, just our friends from the neighboring farms plus an auto mechanic from De Queen, a man named Willie Townsend who got drunk with Dad every other Saturday night."

Max smiled and relaxed. He loved telling stories. "Willie was a good ole son of a bitch, a bachelor, hard as nails on the outside, and soft as putty underneath. He was jilted by the De Queen High School homecoming queen when he was a young man and never again had a girlfriend. Anyway, Mom asked me if I would say a few words over my dad at the graveside service, and I agreed. I wrote them myself, memorized them carefully, and even practiced once out loud in front of Clyde.

"Come the service, I was ready with my speech. 'My father, Henry Allan Puckett, was a fine man,' I began. I then paused, as I had planned, and looked around. Willie was already sniffling and was looking down at the ground. Suddenly I couldn't remember what I was supposed to say next. We all stood there in the hot Arkansas sun for what seemed like forever but was probably only thirty seconds or so. I never did remember the rest of my speech. Finally, out of both desperation and embarrassment, I said 'Aw, fuck,' and Willie chimed in immediately with a loud 'Amen.'"

Nicole was laughing. "Max Puckett," she said, "there cannot be anyone like you anywhere in this universe."

Max grinned. "Last night, when Frenchie and I were in bed, we were talking about that other Nicole the aliens had created for Simone and Michael, and Ep wondered if they could make a robot Max Puckett for her. She liked the idea of having a perfect husband who always did exactly what she asked—even at night. We laughed until our sides hurt trying to imagine, well, you know, what the robot might or might not be able to do in bed."

"Shame on you, Max," Nicole said.

"Actually it was Frenchie who really got imaginative. Anyway," Max said, "I was sent over here with a specific purpose, to inform you that we are having a catered breakfast next door, courtesy of the blockheads, as part of our attempt to say good-bye, or wish you 'bon voyage,' or whatever is appropriate. And that it will start in exactly eight more minutes."

Nicole was delighted to discover that the mood at breakfast was light and pleasant. She had stressed several times the night before that her departure should not be a time for sorrow, that it should be celebrated as the end of a wonderful life. Apparently her family and friends had taken her remarks to heart, for she saw only an occasional somber face.

Ellie and Benjy sat on either side of Nicole at the long table set up by the block robots. Next to Ellie was Nikki, then Maria, and Dr. Blue. On the other side Max and Eponine were beside Benjy, then Marius, Kepler, and the Eagle. During the meal Nicole noticed with surprise that Maria was actually conversing with Dr. Blue. "I didn't know you could read colors, Maria," Nicole said, a clearly complimentary tone in her voice.

"Only a little," the girl said, slightly embarrassed by the attention. "Ellie has been teaching me."

"That's great," Nicole commented.

"Of course the real linguist in this group," Max said, "is that strange birdman at the end of the table. We even saw him yesterday talking to the iguanas in bizarre clicks and screeches."

"Yuch," said Nikki, "I wouldn't want to talk to one of those nasty creatures."

"They have an altogether different way of looking at the world," the Eagle said. "Very simple, very primitive."

"What I want to know," Eponine said, leaning forward and directly addressing the Eagle, "is what I have to do to get an alien robot companion of my own. I'll take one that looks like Max here, except is not ornery and has certain other improved attributes."

Everyone laughed. Nicole smiled to herself as she looked around the table. *This is perfect*, she thought. *I couldn't have asked for a better farewell.*

Dr. Blue and the Eagle gave her one last dose of the blue liquid while Nicole was arranging her bag. She was glad to have a private moment to tell Dr. Blue good-bye. "Thank you for everything," Nicole said simply, hugging her octospider colleague.

"We will all miss you," Dr. Blue said in color. "The new Chief Optimizer wanted to organize a grand send-off, but I told her I did not think it would be appropriate. She asked me to tell you good-bye on behalf of our entire species."

They all accompanied her to the air lock. There was one final round of smiling hugs, at wheelchair level, and then the Eagle and Nicole passed through the air lock.

Nicole sighed as the Eagle lifted her into her seat in the shuttle and folded the wheelchair.

"They were great, weren't they?" Nicole said.

"They love and respect you very much," the Eagle replied.

Once they left the starfish, the great tetrahedron of light was again turning slowly in their view. "How do you feel?" the Eagle asked.

"Relieved," Nicole said, "and a little frightened."

"That's to be expected," the Eagle said.

"How long do you think I have?" Nicole asked several seconds later. "Before my heart gives out?"

"That's hard to say exactly."

"I know, I know," Nicole said impatiently. "But you guys are scientists. You must have done some computations."

"Between six and ten hours," the Eagle said.

In six to ten hours I will be dead, Nicole thought. The fear was more palpable now. She could not push it completely aside.

"What's it like to be dead?" Nicole asked.

"We thought you'd ask that question," the Eagle answered. "We are told that it's similar to being unpowered."

"Nothingness, forever?" Nicole said.

"I guess so."

"And the act of dying itself?" she said. "Is there anything special about that?"

"We don't know," the Eagle said. "We were hoping that you would share with us as much as you can."

They flew in silence for quite a while. Ahead of them, the Node grew quickly in size. At one point the spacecraft changed its orientation slightly and the Knowledge Module moved to the center of their window. During the final approach, the other three vertices of the Node were below them.

"Why do you want to spend your final moments in the Knowledge Module?" the Eagle asked as they drew nearer to the magnificent tetrahedron.

Nicole laughed. "Now, that's a preprogrammed question if ever I heard one," she said. "I can already see my answer stored in some almost endless file, under *Death: Human Beings,* and other related categories."

The Eagle did not say anything.

"When Richard and I were marooned in New York years ago," Nicole said, "and did not think we had much of a chance to escape, we talked about what we would like to be doing during the last moments before our deaths. We agreed that our first choice would be making love together. Our second choice was to be learning something new, to be experiencing the thrill of discovery one last time."

"That's a very advanced concept," the Eagle said.

"And a practical one too," Nicole said. "Unless I miss my guess, this Knowledge Module of yours will be intriguing enough that I will not even be aware that the last seconds of my life are ticking down. If I am completely involved in something right up until the end, maybe the fear of death won't overpower me."

The Knowledge Module now filled their entire window. "Before we enter," the Eagle said, "I want to give you some information about this place. The spherical module is actually three separate concentric domains, each with a specific purpose. The outermost and smallest region is focused on knowledge associated with the present, or near present. The next inner region is where all the historical information about this part of the galaxy has been stored. The large inner sphere contains all the models for predicting the future, as well as stochastic scenarios for the next eons."

"I thought you had never been inside," Nicole said.

"I haven't," the Eagle replied. "But my Knowledge Module data base was updated and expanded last night."

A door in the outer surface of the sphere opened and the shuttle started to enter. "Just a minute," Nicole said. "Do I understand that I will almost certainly never leave this module alive?"

"Yes," said the Eagle.

"Then will you please turn this vehicle around slowly and let me take one last look at the outside world?"

The shuttle executed a slow yaw maneuver and Nicole, sitting forward in her seat, gazed fixedly out the window. She saw the other spherical modules of the Node, the transportation corridors, and, in the distance, the starfish, where her family and friends were packing their bags for their transfer. In one orientation the yellow star Tau Ceti, so much like the Sun, was the only large object in the window, and despite its radiance and the scattered light from the Node, Nicole could still discern a few other stars against the blackness of space.

Nothing in this scene will be changed by my death, Nicole thought. *There will just be one less pair of eyes to observe its splendor. And one less collection of chemicals risen to consciousness to wonder what it all means.*

"Thank you," Nicole said after the full turn was completed. "We may now proceed."

11

Vehicles entering the Knowledge Module from space, as well as the tubes arriving from the other three modules, all ended up at a long slender station located on one side of the midlevel annulus that completely encircled the huge sphere.

"There are only two entrances, a hundred and eighty degrees apart, into each of the three concentric domains of the Knowledge Module," the Eagle said as Nicole and he were carried swiftly along the annulus by a moving sidewalk. To their right was the transparent outer surface of the module. On their left was a cream-colored, windowless wall.

"Will I be able to take off my suit and helmet soon?" Nicole asked from her wheelchair.

"Yes, after we enter the exhibits," the Eagle said. "I had to specify some kind of tour—they couldn't change the atmosphere of the entire module overnight—and in those places you will not need your space suit."

"So you have already selected what we are going to see?"

"It was unavoidable," the Eagle said. "This place is immense, much larger than one of the hemicylinders of Rama, and absolutely crammed full of information. I tried to design our tour based on my knowledge of your interests and our allocated time. If it turns out that there are other things—"

"No, no," Nicole said. "I wouldn't have any idea what to request. I'm certain that what you did was fine."

They were approaching a place where the moving sidewalk stopped and a broad corridor went off to the left. "By the way," the Eagle said, "I didn't explain to you that our tour is restricted to the outer two regions. The Predictions Domain is off limits for us."

"Why is that?" Nicole asked, activating her wheelchair and moving along the corridor beside the Eagle.

"I don't know for certain," he said. "But it doesn't really matter, if I understand your purpose here. There will be more than enough to occupy you in the two available domains."

In front of them was a high blank wall. As the Eagle and Nicole approached, a wide door in the wall opened inward, revealing a tall circular room with a ten-meter-diameter sphere in its center. The wall and ceiling of the room were both cluttered with small fixtures or equipment and many strange markings. The Eagle told Nicole that he had no idea what any of it meant.

"What I *have* been told," the alien said, "is that the orientation for your visit to this domain is supposed to take place inside that sphere in front of us."

The gleaming sphere divided in half at the midsection. The upper half of the hollow ball lifted up just enough that the Eagle and Nicole could pass underneath into the interior of the sphere. Once they were inside, the top half of the sphere returned to its original position and they were completely enclosed.

It was only dark for a second or two. Then small scattered lights illuminated some of the side of the sphere that was facing them. "It's decorated with a lot of detail," Nicole commented.

"What we're looking at," the Eagle said, "is a model of this entire domain. Our point of view is from the inside, as if we were at the very center of the Knowledge Module and neither of the two inner domains existed. You'll notice that the way the objects are placed along and against the surface, not only in front of and behind us, but also above and below us, nothing intrudes into the empty central space more than a fixed distance. The outer wall of the next concentric domain is located at that spot in the *real* module. Now the lights will show you, on the model, where we will be going in the next few hours."

A large sector of the inner sphere surface facing them, about thirty percent of the area altogether, was suddenly visible in a soft light.

"Everything in the lit region," the Eagle said, making a circular gesture with his hand, "is associated with spacefaring. We will confine our tour to this portion of the domain. The blinking red light on the surface in front of us is where we are presently."

As Nicole watched, a red line of lights moved quickly up the surface, stopping at a point above her head where there was a picture of the Milky Way Galaxy. "We will go first to the geography section," the Eagle said, pointing at the place where the line of lights had stopped, "then to engineering, and finally to biology. After a short break, we will continue into the second domain. Any more questions before we start?"

They drove up what appeared to be an ascending ramp in a small car similar to the one they had used in the Habitation Module during Nicole's visit with Michael and Simone. Although the path in front and behind them was illuminated, whatever was beside the car was always in the dark.

"What's around us?" Nicole asked after they had been driving for almost ten minutes.

"Data storage mostly, plus a few exhibits," the Eagle said. "It is dark so that you are not unnecessarily distracted."

Eventually they stopped beside another tall door. "The room you are about to enter," the Eagle said, setting up Nicole's wheelchair, "is the largest single room in this domain. It is half a kilometer across at its widest point. Inside currently is a model of the Milky Way Galaxy. Once we enter, we will be standing on a mobile platform that we can command to take us to any point in the room. It will be mostly dark inside, and there will be displays and structures both above us and below us. You might feel as if you are going to fall, but remember that you are weightless."

The view from the platform was spectacular. Even before they began to move toward the center of the vast room, Nicole was overwhelmed. Lights representing stars were everywhere in the blackness that surrounded them. Single stars, binaries, combination triples. Small, stable yellow stars, red giants, white dwarfs—they even passed directly over an exploding supernova. In every location, in every direction, there was something different and fascinating to see.

After a few minutes the Eagle stopped the platform. "I thought we'd start here, where you are familiar with the territory," he said.

Using a pointer with multiple light beams, he indicated a nearby yellow star. "Do you recognize this place?"

Nicole was still staring at the endless lights in all directions. "Are all hundred billion stars in the galaxy actually modeled in this room?" she asked.

"No," the Eagle replied. "What you are seeing here is only a large section of the galaxy. I'll explain more to you in a few minutes when we go to the top of the room and can look down on the central galactic plane. I brought you to this particular spot for another purpose."

Nicole recognized the Sun, and the Centauri triple, its closest neighbor, and even Barnard's star and Sirius. She could not remember the names of most of the other stars in the local neighborhood of the Sun. She did, however, manage to locate another solitary yellow star not too far away.

"Is that Tau Ceti?" she asked.

"Yes, indeed," said the Eagle.

Tau Ceti seems so close to the Sun, Nicole thought, *but in reality it is so very far away. That means the galaxy is larger than any of us could possibly comprehend.*

"The distance from the Sun to Tau Ceti," the Eagle said, as if he were reading her mind, "is one ten-thousandth of the distance across the galaxy."

Nicole shook her head as the platform began to move away from the Sun and Tau Ceti. *There is so much more than I had ever imagined,* she thought. *Even my journeys have taken place in an insignificantly small region of space.*

Off the moving platform to Nicole's right, the Eagle projected a three-dimensional line drawing in the shape of a rectangular solid. By manipulating the black device that he was holding in his hand, he made the volume of the solid alternately larger and smaller.

"We have many different ways to control what is projected in this room," the Eagle said. "With this device we can change the scale and zoom in on any particular region of the galaxy. Let me show you. Suppose I put the red light here, in the middle of the Orion Nebula. That marks the desired initial position of the platform. Then let me expand this geometrical shape to enclose about a thousand stars. . . . Now, presto."

It was pitch-black in the room for about a second. Then suddenly Nicole was again dazzled, but this time by a different set of lights. The clusters and individual stars were much more clearly defined. The Eagle explained that the entire room was now contained inside the Orion Nebula and that the longest room dimension was now the equivalent of a few hundred light-years, instead of sixty thousand light-years as before.

"This particular area is a stellar nursery," the Eagle said, "where stars and planets are just being born." He moved the platform toward the right. "Over here, for example, is an infant star system, in the early stages of formation, with many of the characteristics that your solar system had four and a half billion years ago."

He inscribed a small solid figure around one of the stars, and a few seconds later the room was filled with the light of a young sun. Nicole watched a gigantic solar storm move across the moiling surface. A coronal burst arced high above her head, shooting a finger of orange and red into the blackness of space.

The Eagle steered the platform toward a much smaller, distant body, one of about a dozen accumulations of mass that could be identified in the region closely surrounding the young star. This particular planet had a slightly reddish molten surface. As they watched, a large projectile crashed into the hot fluid, ejecting material from the surface and setting up vigorous wave motion in all directions.

"According to our statistical data," the Eagle said, "this planet has a nontrivial probability of producing life after a few billion years of evolution, once this period of bombardment and formation is concluded. It will have a solitary, stable host star, an atmosphere with sufficient climatic variation, plus all the chemical ingredients. Here, see for yourself. Keep your eyes on that planet. I am going to activate a special routine that scans quickly through the bottom half of the periodic chart and displays quantitative data about the comparative number of atoms of each kind that exist in that boiling stew."

A magnificent visual display appeared in the blackness above the infant planet. Each separate atom contained in the planet's mass was indicated both by a specific color and by its number of neutrons and protons. The size of the atom showed its comparative frequency in the mix. "Note that there are significant densities of carbon, nitrogen, the halogens, and iron," the Eagle said. "These are the critical atoms. They were all created by nearby supernova in the not too distant past and have enriched the organizational possibilities of this forming body. Without complex chemistry, there cannot be efficient life. If iron were not available to be the central atom of hemoglobin, for example, on your planet, the oxygen distribution system of the many advanced life-forms would be much more inefficient."

So the process continues, Nicole thought, *eon after eon. Stars and planets form out of the cosmic dust. A few of the planets contain the right chemical stuff that might eventually lead to life and intelligence. But what organizes this process? What unseen hand causes these chemicals to become more and more complex and structured in time, until they reach even the state of self-awareness? Is there some yet-to-be-formulated natural law about matter organizing itself according to specified rules?*

The Eagle was now explaining how unlikely it was that life would evolve in star systems that contained only simple atoms like hydrogen and helium, and none of the more complex, higher-order atoms forged by dying stars in supernova explosions. Nicole began to feel an overpowering insignificance. She longed for something on a human scale.

"How small can you shrink this room?" Nicole said suddenly. She laughed at her own awkward phraseology. "To be more precise," she continued, "what is the ultimate resolution of this system?"

"The finest level of detail possible," the Eagle said, "is at a scale of four thousand ninety-six to one. At the other extreme, we can display an intergalactic scene with a greatest dimension of fifty million light-years. Remember, our interest in activities outside the galaxy is limited."

Nicole was doing some mental calculations of her own. "Since the longest dimension of this room is half a kilometer, at the highest level of detail this room would be filled by a piece of real estate roughly two thousand kilometers long?"

"That's right," the Eagle said. "But why are you asking?"

Nicole was becoming more excited. "Could we zoom in on the Earth?" she asked. "And let me fly over France?"

"Yes, I guess so," the Eagle answered after a short hesitation. "Although that is not what I had planned."

"It would mean a lot to me."

"All right," the Eagle said. "It will take a couple of seconds to set up, but we can do it."

*   *   *

The flight began over the English Channel. The Eagle and Nicole had been sitting on the platform at the top of the dark room for approximately three seconds when there was an explosion of light beneath them. After Nicole's eyes finally adjusted, she recognized the blue water underneath them and the shape of the Normandy coastline. Off in the distance the Seine emptied into the Channel.

She asked the Eagle to station the platform over the mouth of the Seine and then to move slowly toward Paris. The sight of the familiar geography evoked a strong emotional response in Nicole. She remembered clearly the days of her youth, when she had wandered carefree throughout this region with her beloved father.

The model below them was superb. It was even three-dimensional when the sizes of the geographical features and buildings below them were above the limits of resolution of the alien system. In Rouen, the famous church where Joan of Arc had temporarily recanted was half a centimeter tall and two centimeters long. Off in the direction of Paris, Nicole could see the familiar shape of the Arc de Triomphe rising from the surface of the model.

When they reached Paris, the platform hovered for a few seconds over the sixteenth arrondissement. Nicole's eyes fell briefly upon a particular building below her. The sight of that building, a modern convention center, brought back an especially poignant moment from her adolescence. *To my precious daughter, Nicole, and all the young people of the world, I offer one simple insight*, she heard her father's voice say again. He was near the end of his speech accepting the Mary Renault Prize. *In my life I have found two things of priceless worth: learning and loving. Nothing else—not fame, not power, not achievement for its own sake—can possibly have the same lasting value.*

An image of her father filled Nicole's mind. *Thank you, Papa*, she thought. *Thank you for taking such good care of me after Mother died. Thank you for everything you taught me.*

A powerful, painful yearning brought a rush of tears to Nicole's eyes. For an instant she was again a child, and she wanted desperately to talk to her father about her coming death. Slowly, deliberately, Nicole fought against the emotions that were threatening to overwhelm her. *This is not what I wanted to feel right now*, she said to herself with difficulty. *I wanted to leave all this behind.*

She turned her face away from the model of France below her.

"What is it?" the Eagle asked.

Nicole forced a smile. "I want to see something else," she said. "Something spectacular . . . and new. How about an octospider city?"

"Are you certain?" the Eagle said.

Nicole nodded.

The room became dark immediately. Two seconds later, when Nicole turned around to face the light, the platform was flying over a vast ocean of deep green.

"Where are we?" she asked. "And where are we going?"

"We're presently about thirty light-years away from your Sun," the Eagle replied, "on the first oceanic planet colonized by the octospiders after the disappearance of the Precursors. We're over the sea, obviously, about two hundred kilometers away from the most famous of the octospider cities."

Nicole felt a surge of excitement as the platform zoomed across the sea. In the distance she could already see the vague outline of some buildings. For a moment she imagined that she was an adventurous space traveler arriving at this planet for the first time, eager to see the wonders of the fabulous cities that other interstellar travelers had described.

Nicole momentarily turned her attention to the ocean below her. "Why is this water so green?" she asked the Eagle.

"The top meter of this part of the ocean is a rich ecosystem of its own, dominated by a special genus of photosynthesizing plant whose varied species, all green in color, provide housing and food for as many as ten million separate creatures. Some of the individual plants cover more than a square kilometer of territory. The Precursors created this domain originally. The octospiders found it and improved upon it."

When Nicole glanced up, the speeding platform had nearly reached the city. Hundreds of buildings of various shapes and sizes were spread out below them. Most of the octospider city's buildings were built on the land, but some appeared to be floating on the water. The densest collection of these structures was along a narrow peninsula that extended slightly into the sea. At the end of that peninsula stood three huge green domes, very close together, that dominated the city skyline.

At the periphery of the city was a wide outer circle of eight smaller domes, each of which was connected by linear transportation features to the central domes. Each of these outer domes was a distinct and different color. Almost all of the buildings in the section of the city surrounding an outer dome had been painted with the same color. Out in the ocean, for example, the brilliant red dome had eight long, slender red spokes, representing other buildings, extending outward from it in a balanced geometrical pattern.

All the buildings of the city lay inside the circle defined by the eight colored domes. Nicole's immediate favorite was a strange brown-colored structure floating on the water. It appeared to be almost as large as the huge central domes. From above, the rectangular building looked like twenty layers of a densely packed lattice, with material from birds' nests filling the open areas inside each of the hundreds of cells.

"What is that?" Nicole asked, pointing from the platform.

"These particular octospiders are very advanced in microbiology," the

Below Nicole the Milky Way was confined to a small space in the center of the room. "The universe is an ever-expanding sequence of neighborhoods and voids," the Eagle was saying. "Look how empty it is around the Milky Way. Except for the two Magellanic Clouds, which really don't qualify as galaxies, Andromeda is our nearest galactic neighbor. But it is very far away. The distance across the greatest dimension of the Milky Way is only one-twentieth of the distance to Andromeda."

Nicole was not thinking about Andromeda. She was absorbed in delightful philosophical musings about life on different worlds, about cities, and about the likely range of creatures made from simple atoms who had evolved, with or without help from superior beings, into consciousness. She savored the moment, knowing that very soon there would be no more of the flights of imagination that had enriched her life so much.

Eagle replied. "That structure, which extends incidentally another te
meters deep into the ocean, contains over a thousand different habitats f
species in the micrometer size range. What you're looking at is essential
a supply station, containing the excess population for each of these tir
beings. Octospiders needing any of these creatures come to this building
requisition them."

Nicole's eyes feasted on the unusual architecture below her. In h
mind's eye she could see herself walking on the streets, looking around
amazement at a variety of creatures far greater even than the menagerie sh
had encountered in the Emerald City. *I want to go there*, she said to hersel
I want to see.

She asked the Eagle to move the platform directly over one of th
large green domes. "Is the inside of this dome," Nicole asked, "similar
what was in the Emerald City?"

"Not really," the Eagle replied. "The scale is altogether different. Th
octospider realm in Rama was a compressed microcosm. Functions whic
are normally separated on their planets by hundreds of kilometers
distance were forced, because of space limitations, to be located in more
less the same area. In the advanced colonies of the octospider genus, f
example, the alternates do not have a community just outside the cit
gates—they live on an entirely different planet."

Nicole smiled. *A planet full of alternates*, she thought. *Now*, that *woul
be quite a sight.*

"This particular city is the home for more than eighteen millio
octospiders, if we count all the different morphological variations," th
Eagle said. "It is also the administrative capital for this planet. Within th
gates of the city live close to ten billion individual creatures, representin
fifty thousand species. The extent of the city is roughly equivalent to Lo
Angeles or any of the great urban areas on your Earth."

The Eagle continued to tell her facts and statistics about th
octospider city beneath their platform. Nicole, however, was thinking abou
something else. "Did Archie live here?" she said, interrupting her alie
companion's encyclopedic monologue. "Or Dr. Blue, or any of the octospi
ders that we met?"

"No," the Eagle replied. "In fact, they did not even come from thi
planet or star system. The octospiders in Rama came from what is know
as a 'frontier colony,' one especially designed genetically for interactio
with other intelligent life-forms."

Nicole shook her head and smiled. *Of course*, she said to herself,
should have suspected that they were special.

She was growing tired. After another few minutes Nicole thanked the
Eagle and said that she had seen enough of the octospider city. In an instant
the domes, the brown lattice structure, and the deep green sea vanished.
The Eagle returned the platform to the top of the large chamber.

12

"We spent so much time in that exhibit," the Eagle said after he finished the scan, "that I think maybe we should revise our tour."

They were sitting side by side in the car. "Is that your diplomatic way of telling me that my heart is failing more rapidly than you expected?" Nicole asked, forcing a smile.

"No, not really," the Eagle said. "We really *did* spend almost twice as much time as I had planned. I hadn't even considered the overflight of France, for example, or the visit to the octospider city."

"That part was wonderful," Nicole said. "I wish I could go there again, with Dr. Blue as my guide, and find out more about the way they live."

"So you liked the octospider city better than the spectacular views of the stars?"

"I wouldn't say that," Nicole replied. "It was all fantastic. What I have seen already has reconfirmed that I chose the right place to . . ." She did not finish the sentence. "I realized while I was on the platform that death is not just the end of thinking and being aware," she said, "it is also the end of feeling. I don't know why that wasn't obvious to me before."

There was a short silence. "So, my friend," Nicole said brightly, "where do we go from here?"

"I thought we'd go next to engineering, where you can see models of Nodes, Carriers, and other spacecraft, after which, if we still have enough time, I plan to take you to the biology section. Some of your ex-utero grandchildren are living in that region, in one of our better Earthlike habitats. Nearby is another compound housing a community of those intriguing aquatic eels or snakes that we encountered once together at the Node. And there is a taxonomic display that compares and contrasts, physically, all the spacefarers that have been studied in this region."

"It all sounds great," Nicole said. She laughed suddenly. "The human brain is amazing. Guess what just popped into my mind? The first line of Andrew Marvell's poem 'To His Coy Mistress': 'Had we but world enough, and time, This coyness, lady, were no crime . . .' Anyway, I was going to say that since we do not have forever, let's go first to the Carrier display. I would like to see the spacecraft in which Patrick, Nai, Galileo, and the others will be living. After that, we'll see how much time is left."

The car began to move. Nicole noted to herself that the Eagle had not said anything about the results of his scan. The fear came back, stronger now. *"The grave's a fine and private place,"* she recalled. *"But none, I think, do there embrace."*

They were together on the flat surface of the Carrier model. "This is a one sixty-fourth scale model," the Eagle said, "so you have some sense of how large the Carrier really is."

Nicole stared off into the distance from her wheelchair. "Goodness," she said, "this plane must be almost one kilometer long."

"That's a decent guess," the Eagle said. "The top of the actual Carrier is roughly forty kilometers long and fifteen kilometers wide."

"And each of these bubbles encloses a different environment?"

"Yes," the Eagle said. "The atmosphere and other conditions are controlled by the equipment that is here on the surface, as well as the additional engineering systems down below in the main volume of the spacecraft. Each of the habitats has its own spin rate to create the proper gravity. Partitions are available to separate species, if necessary, inside one of the bubbles. The residents from the starfish have been placed in the same domain because they are comfortable in more or less the same ambient conditions. However, they do not have any access to each other."

They were moving down a path among the equipment emplacements and the bubbles. "Some of these habitats," Nicole said, examining a small oval protrusion rising above the plane no more than five meters, "seem too small and confining to hold more than just a few individuals."

"There are some very small spacefarers," the Eagle said. "One species, from a star system not too far from yours, is only about a millimeter in length. Their largest spacecraft are not even as big as this car."

Nicole tried to imagine an intelligent group of ants, or aphids, working together to build a spacecraft. She smiled at her mental picture.

"And all these Carriers just travel from Node to Node?" she asked, changing the subject.

"Primarily," the Eagle said. "When there are no longer any living creatures in a particular bubble, that habitat is reconditioned at one of the Nodes."

"Like Rama," Nicole said.

"In a way," the Eagle said, "but with many significant differences. We are always intently studying whatever species are inside a Rama-class spacecraft. We try to place them in as realistic an environment as possible, so that we can observe them under 'natural conditions.' By contrast, we do not *need* any more data about the creatures assigned to the Carrier fleet. That's why we don't intercede in their affairs."

"Except to preclude reproduction. By the way, in the structure of your ethics, is preventing reproduction somehow more humane, or whatever your equivalent word is, than terminating the creatures directly?"

"We think so," the Eagle replied.

They had reached a location on the top of the Carrier model where a pathway branched off to the left back to the ramps and hallways of the Knowledge Module. "I think I've accomplished what I wanted here," Nicole said. She hesitated for a moment. "But I do have a couple of other questions."

"Go ahead," the Eagle said.

"Assuming Saint Michael's description of the purpose of Rama and the Node and everything else is correct, aren't you yourself disturbing and changing the very process you're observing? It seems to me that just by being here and interacting—"

"You're right, of course," the Eagle said. "Our presence here *does* slightly impact the course of evolution. It's a situation analogous to the Heisenberg Uncertainty Principle from physics. We cannot observe without influencing. Nevertheless, our interactions can be considered by the Prime Monitor and taken into account in the overall modeling of the process. And we do have rules that minimize the ways in which we perturb the natural evolution."

"I wish that Richard could have been with me to hear Saint Michael's explanation of everything," Nicole said. "He would have been fascinated, and, I am sure, would have had some excellent questions."

The Eagle did not reply. Nicole sighed. "So what's next, Monsieur le Tour Director?" she said.

"Lunch," said the Eagle. "There are a couple of sandwiches, some water, and a delicious piece of your favorite octospider fruit in the car."

Nicole laughed and turned her wheelchair onto the pathway. "You think of everything," she said.

"Richard didn't believe in heaven," Nicole said as the Eagle completed another scan. "But if he could have constructed his own perfect afterlife, it would definitely have included a place like this."

The Eagle was studying the weird squiggles on the monitor in his hand. "I think it would be a good idea," he said, looking up at Nicole, "to skip some of the tour . . . and go directly to the most important exhibits in the next domain."

"That bad, huh?" Nicole said. She was not surprised. The occasional pain she had been feeling in her chest before the visits to France and the octospider city had now become continuous.

The fear was constant now as well. In between every word, every thought, she was acutely aware that her death was not very far away. *So what are you afraid of?* Nicole asked herself. *How can nothingness be that bad?* Still the fear persisted.

The Eagle explained that there was not enough time for an orientation to the second domain. They passed through the gates into the second of the concentric spheres and drove for about ten minutes. "The emphasis in this domain," the Eagle said while driving, "is on the way everything changes in time. There is a separate section for every conceivable element in the galaxy that is affected by, or affects, the galaxy's overall evolution. I thought you'd be especially interested in this first exhibit."

The room was similar to the one where the Eagle and Nicole had first seen the Milky Way, except that it was considerably smaller. Again they boarded a moving platform that allowed them to move around in the dark room.

"What you are going to watch," the Eagle said, "requires some explanation. It is essentially a time-lapse summary of the evolution of spacefaring civilizations in a galactic region containing your Sun and about ten million other star systems. This is approximately one ten-thousandth of the entire galaxy, but what you will see is representative of the galaxy as a whole.

"You will not see any stars or planets or other physical structures in this display, although their locations are assumed in developing the model. What you will see, once we begin, are lights, each representing a star system in which a biological species has become a spacefarer by at least putting a spacecraft in orbit around its own planet. As long as the star system remains a living center for active spacefarers, the light in that particular location will stay illuminated.

"I am going to start the display about ten billion years ago, soon after what has evolved into the current Milky Way Galaxy was initially formed. Since there was so much instability and rapid change at the beginning, no spacefarers emerged for a long time. Therefore, for the first five billion years or so, up until the formation of your solar system, I will run the display rapidly, at a rate of twenty million years per second. For reference purposes, the Earth will begin to accrete roughly four minutes into this process. I will stop the display at that time."

They were together on the platform in the large chamber. The Eagle was standing and Nicole was sitting beside him in her wheelchair. The only light was a small one on the platform that allowed the two of them to see each other. After staring around her at the total darkness for more than thirty seconds, Nicole broke the silence. "Did you start the process?" she asked. "Nothing's happening."

"Exactly," the Eagle replied. "What we have observed, from watching other galaxies, some much older than the Milky Way, is that no life emerges until the galaxy settles down and develops stable zones. Life requires both a few steady stars in a relatively benign environment *and* stellar evolution, resulting in the creation of the critical elements on the periodic chart that are so important in all biochemical processes. If all the matter is subatomic particles and the simplest atoms, the likelihood of the origin of life of any kind, much less spacefaring life, is very very small. Not until large stars go through their complete life cycles and manufacture the more complex elements like nitrogen, carbon, iron, and magnesium do the probabilities for the emergence of life become reasonable."

Below them an occasional light flickered, but in the entire first four minutes, no more than a few hundred scattered lights appeared, and only one endured for longer than three seconds. "Now we have reached the time of the formation of the Earth and the solar system," the Eagle said, preparing to activate the display again.

"Wait a moment, please," Nicole said. "I want to make certain I understand. Did you just show me that for the first half of galactic history, when there was no Earth and no Sun, comparatively few spacefarers evolved in the region around where the Sun would eventually form? . . . And that of those spacefarers, almost all of them had a species life span of less than twenty million years, and only one managed to survive for as long as sixty million years?"

"Very good," the Eagle said. "Now I am going to add another parameter to the display. If a spacefarer has succeeded in traveling outside his own star system and has established a permanent presence in another— which you humans have of course not yet done—then the display acknowledges that expansion by illuminating the other star system as well, with the same color light. Therefore we can follow the spread of a specific spacefaring species. I am also now going to change the rate of the display by a factor of two, to ten million years per second."

Only half a minute into the next period, a red light came on over in one corner of the room. Six to eight seconds later, it was surrounded by hundreds of other red lights. Together they shone with such intensity that the rest of the room, with its occasional solitary or pair of lights, seemed dark and uninteresting by comparison. The field of red lights then abruptly vanished in a fraction of a second. First the inner core of the red pattern went dark, leaving small groups of lights scattered at the edges of what had once been a gigantic region. A blink of the eye later and all the red lights were gone.

Nicole's mind was operating at peak speed as she watched the lights flashing around her. *That must be an interesting story,* she thought, reflecting on the red lights. *Imagine a civilization spread out over a region containing hundreds of stars. Then suddenly, pfft, that species is gone. The lesson is inescapable. For everything there is a beginning and an end. Immortality exists only as a concept, not as a reality.*

She glanced around the room. A general recurring pattern was developing as more and more regions hosted an occasional passing light, indicating the emergence and disappearance of another spacefaring civilization. Because even those beings that spread out and colonized adjoining star systems lived for such a brief time, only rarely did they come into proximity with a companion spacefaring civilization.

There has been intelligence, and spacefaring, in our part of the galaxy since before there was an Earth, Nicole thought, *but very few of these advanced creatures have ever had the thrill of sustained contact with their peers. . . . So loneliness too is one of the underlying principles of the universe—at least of this universe.*

Eight minutes later the Eagle again froze the display. "We have now reached a point in time ten million years before the present," he said. "On the Earth, the dinosaurs have long since disappeared, destroyed by their inability to adapt to the climate changes caused by the impact of a great asteroid. Their disappearance, however, has allowed the mammals to flourish, and one of those mammalian evolutionary lines is starting to show the rudiments of intelligence."

The Eagle stopped. Nicole was looking up at him with an intense, almost pained expression on her face. "What's the matter?" the alien asked.

"Will *our* particular universe end in harmony?" Nicole asked. "Or will we be one of those data points that helps God define the region He is seeking by being *outside* the desired set?"

"What prompts you to ask that question right now?" the Eagle said.

"This whole display," Nicole answered, waving with her hand, "is an amazing catalyst. My mind has dozens of questions." She smiled. "But since I don't have time to ask them all, I thought I would ask the most important one first.

"Just look at what has happened here," she continued, "even now, after ten billion years of evolution, the lights are widely scattered. And none of the groupings that exist have become permanent or widespread, even in this relatively small portion of the galaxy. Surely if our universe is going to end in harmony, sooner or later lights indicating spacefarers and intelligence should be illuminated at almost every star system in every galaxy. Or have I misinterpreted what Saint Michael meant by harmony?"

"I don't think so," the Eagle said.

"Where is our solar system in this current display?" Nicole now asked.

"Right there," the Eagle said, using his light beam pointer.

Nicole glanced first at the area around the Earth and then quickly surveyed the rest of the room. "So ten million years ago, there were about sixty spacefaring species living among our closest ten thousand stellar neighborhoods. And one of those species, if I understand that cluster of dark green lights, originated not too far from us and had spread to include twenty or thirty star systems altogether."

"That's correct," said the Eagle. "Should I run the display forward again, at a slower rate?"

"In a little while," Nicole said. "I want to appreciate this particular configuration first. Up until now everything has been happening in this display faster than I could possibly absorb it."

She stared at the group of green lights. Its outer edge was no more than fifteen light-years from where the Eagle had marked the solar system. Nicole motioned for the Eagle to start the display again and he told her the rate would now be only two hundred thousand years a second.

The green lights moved closer and closer to the Earth and then they suddenly disappeared. "Stop," yelled Nicole.

The Eagle halted the display. He looked at Nicole with a quizzical expression.

"What happened to those guys?" Nicole said.

"I told you about them a couple of days ago," the Eagle said. "They genetically engineered themselves out of existence."

They almost reached the Earth, Nicole thought. *And how different all history would have been if they had. They would have recognized immediately the intellectual potential of the protohumans in Africa and would doubtless have done to them what the Precursors did to the octospiders. Then we . . .*

In her mind's eye, Nicole suddenly had an image of Saint Michael, calmly explaining the purpose of the universe in front of the fireplace in Michael and Simone's study.

"Could I see the beginning?" Nicole asked the Eagle.

"The beginning of what?" he replied.

"The beginning of everything," Nicole said eagerly. "The instant when this universe began and the entire process of evolution was set in motion." She waved her hand toward the model below them.

"We can do that," the Eagle said after a brief pause.

"We have no knowledge about anything *before* this universe was created," the Eagle said a moment later as Nicole and he stood together on the platform in total darkness. "We do assume, however, that some kind of energy existed before the instant of creation, for we have been told that the matter of this universe resulted from a transformation of energy."

Nicole looked around her. "Darkness everywhere," she said, almost to herself. "And somewhere in that darkness—if the word 'somewhere' even has any meaning—there was energy. And a Creator. Or might the energy have been *part* of the Creator?"

"We don't know," the Eagle said after another short pause. "What we *do* know is that the fate of every single element in the universe was determined in that initial instant. The way in which that energy was transformed into matter defined eighty billion years of history."

As the Eagle spoke, a blinding light filled the room. Nicole turned away from the source and covered her eyes. "Here," said the Eagle, reaching into his pouch. He handed Nicole a special pair of glasses.

"Why did you make the simulation so bright?" Nicole asked after adjusting her glasses.

"To indicate, at least in some measure, what those initial moments were like. Look," he said, pointing below them, "I have stopped the model at 10^{-40} seconds after the creation instant. The universe has existed for only an infinitesimal length of time, yet already it is rich in physical structure. This incredible amount of light is all coming from that tiny chunk of cosmic broth below us. All that 'stuff' forming the early universe is completely alien to anything we could recognize or understand. There are no atoms, no molecules. The density of the quarks, leptons, and their friends is so great that a pinch of the 'stuff' no larger than a hydrogen atom would weigh more than a large cluster of galaxies in our era."

"Just out of curiosity," Nicole said, "where are you and I at this moment?"

The Eagle hesitated. "Nowhere would be the best answer," he said eventually. "For illustrative purposes we are outside the model of the universe. But we could be in another dimension. The mathematics of the early universe do not work unless there were initially more than four dimensions. Of course everything in space-time that will later become our universe is contained in that small volume producing the awesome light. The temperature over there, incidentally, if the model were a true representation, would be ten trillion times hotter than the hottest star that will eventually evolve.

"Our model here has also distorted the concepts of size and distance," the Eagle continued after a brief pause. "In a moment I will start the simulation of the early universe again, and we will be overpowered as that compact blob of radiation explodes outward at an astonishing rate. While the simulation of what the cosmologists call the Inflation Era is occurring, the assumed size of this room will also be increasing rapidly. If we did not change the scale, you would be unable now to see the structure of the universe at 10^{-40} seconds without a fantastic microscope."

Nicole stared below her at the source of light. "So that minuscule warped globule of hot, heavy stuff was the seed of everything? From that tiny stew of subatomic particles came the great galaxies you showed me in the other domain? It doesn't seem possible."

"Not just those galaxies," the Eagle said. "The potential for *everything* in the cosmos is stored in that peculiar superheated soup."

The small globule suddenly began to expand at an enormous rate. Nicole had the feeling that the outside of the globule was going to touch her face at any moment. Millions of bizarre structures formed and disappeared in front of her eyes. Nicole watched in fascination as the material seemed to change its nature several times, moving through transitional states as peculiar and foreign as the earlier superheated globule.

"I have run time forward in the model," the Eagle said several seconds later. "What you see out there now, approximately one million years after creation, would be recognizable to any dedicated student of physics. Some simple atoms have formed—three kinds of hydrogen, two of helium, for example. Lithium is the heaviest known atom that is plentiful. The density of the universe is now roughly equivalent to the air on Earth, and the temperature has fallen to a comparatively comfortable one hundred million degrees, or twenty orders of magnitude *less* than it was at the time of the hot globule."

He activated the platform and guided it among the lights and clumps and filaments. "If we were really smart," the Eagle said, "we would be able to look at all this early matter and predict which 'lumps' would eventually become galactic clusters. It was at about this time that the first Prime Monitor appeared, the only intruder into this otherwise natural evolution process. No monitoring could have been done earlier, because the process is so sensitive. Any kind of observation during the first second of creation, for example, would have completely distorted the resultant evolution."

The Eagle pointed at a tiny metallic sphere in the center of several huge agglomerations of matter. "That first Prime Monitor," he said, "was sent by the Creator, from another dimension of the early universe, into our evolving space-time system. Its purpose was to observe what was occurring and to create, as necessary, with its own intelligence, the other observing systems that would together gather all the pertinent information on the overall process."

"So the Sun, the Earth, and every human being," Nicole said slowly, "resulted from the unpredictable natural evolution of this cosmos. The Node, Rama, and even you and Saint Michael were produced from a directed development designed originally by that first Prime Monitor."

She paused, glancing around her, and then turned to the Eagle. "*You* could have been predicted shortly after the moment of creation. I, and even the existence of humanity, came from a process so mathematically perverse that we could not even have been predicted a hundred million years ago, which is only *one* percent of the time since the beginning of the universe."

Nicole shook her head and then waved her hand. "All right," she said, "that's enough. I'm overloaded with the infinite."

The great room became dark again except for the small lights on the floor of the platform. "What is it?" the Eagle said, seeing a look of distress on Nicole's face.

"I'm not certain," she said. "I feel a kind of sadness, as if I had experienced a deep personal loss. If I have understood all this, then humans are far more special than you, or even Rama. The odds are very much against any creatures even nearly like us ever arising again, either in this universe or any other. We are one of the fluke products of chaos. You, or at least something like you, probably existed in all those other universes the Creator is supposedly observing."

There was a momentary silence. "I guess I had imagined," Nicole continued, "after listening to Saint Michael, that there would be human voices in that harmony God was seeking. Now I realize that it is only on the planet Earth, in this particular universe, that our songs—"

Nicole felt a sharp burst of pain in her chest. It remained intense. She struggled to breathe, convinced for several moments that the end was coming immediately.

The Eagle said nothing, but watched her carefully. When Nicole finally caught her breath, she spoke in short, broken clauses. "You told me . . . at lunch . . . a personal place . . . where I could see family and friends . . ."

They talked briefly in the car while the pain was momentarily bearable. Both the Eagle and Nicole knew, without either of them saying anything, that the next attack would be the last.

They entered another of the exhibit areas in the Knowledge Module. This room was a perfect circle, with a space in a small floor section in the middle where the Eagle could stand next to Nicole's wheelchair. They crossed to their central location and watched as humanlike figures began to replay events from Nicole's adult life in each of the six separate theater settings that closely surrounded them.

The verisimilitude of the replays was astonishing. Not only did all Nicole's family and friends look exactly as they had at the time that the events had taken place, but all the sets were perfect reconstructions as well. In one of the scenes Katie was water-skiing boldly near the shore of Lake Shakespeare, laughing and waving with the reckless abandon that was her trademark. In another Nicole watched a re-creation of the party the little troupe on Rama II had held to celebrate the one thousandth anniversary of the death of Eleanor of Aquitaine. Seeing Simone at age four and Katie at two, and both Richard and herself when they were still young and vigorous, brought tears to Nicole's eyes.

It has been an astonishing life, Nicole thought. She rolled her wheelchair into the scene from Rama II and the action stopped. Nicole leaned over and picked up the robot TB that Richard had created to amuse the little girls. It felt properly weighted in her hands.

"How in the world did you do this?" Nicole asked.

"Advanced technology," the Eagle replied. "I couldn't explain it to you."

"And if I went over there, where Katie is skiing, would the water feel wet to my touch?"

"Absolutely."

Nicole rolled out of the scene holding the pseudo-robot in her hands. When she was gone, another TB materialized and the scene continued. *I had forgotten, Richard,* Nicole said to herself, *all your brilliant little creations.*

Her heart granted her a few more minutes to enjoy the vignettes taken from her life. Nicole thrilled again to the moment of Simone's birth, relived her first night of love with Richard not long after he found her in New York, and experienced for a second time the fantastic array of sights and creatures that had greeted Richard and her when the gates of the Emerald City had first opened to them.

"Can you replay any event from my life that I might want?" Nicole asked, feeling a sudden constriction in her chest.

"As long as it happened after you arrived at Rama and I can find it in the archives," the Eagle replied.

Nicole gasped. The final heart attack was under way. "Please," she said, "may I see my last conversation with Richard before he left?"

It won't be long, a voice inside Nicole said. She clenched her teeth and tried to concentrate on the scene that had suddenly appeared in front of her. Richard was explaining to pseudo-Nicole why he was the one who should accompany Archie back to New Eden.

"I understand," pseudo-Nicole said in the scene.

I understand, the real Nicole said to herself. *That is the most important statement anyone can ever make. The whole key to life is understanding. And now I understand that I am a mortal creature whose time of death has come.*

Another surge of intense pain was accompanied by a fleeting memory of a Latin line from an old poem: *Timor Mortis conturbat me. But I will not be afraid because I understand.*

The Eagle was watching her closely. "I would like to see Richard and Archie," she said, laboring, "their final moments . . . in the cell . . . just before the biots came."

I will not be afraid because I understand.

"And my children, if they can somehow be here. And Dr. Blue."

The room became dark. Seconds ticked by. The pain was terrible. *I will not be afraid . . .*

The lights came on again. Richard and Archie were in their cell immediately in front of Nicole's wheelchair. She heard the biots open the cellblock door down the hall.

"Freeze it there, please," Nicole said with difficulty. Just to the left of the scene with Richard and Archie, her children and Dr. Blue were lined up in a tableau. Nicole struggled to her feet and walked the few meters to be among them. Tears poured from her eyes as she touched one final time the faces that she loved.

The walls of her heart began to collapse. Nicole stumbled into the scene in Richard's cell and embraced the representation of her husband. "I understand, Richard," she said.

Nicole dropped to her knees slowly. She turned to face the Eagle. "I understand," she said with a smile.

And understanding is happiness, she thought.